Lynne Heitman ~~~~~ for 14 years, latterly as their General Manager at Logan Airport, Boston. Born in Dallas in 1957 she mistakenly became a cheerleader for a year before graduating as an MBA.

Also by Lynne Heitman

First Class Killing
The Hostage Room

LYNNE HEITMAN OMNIBUS

Hard Landing

Parts Unknown

Lynne Heitman

sphere

SPHERE

This omnibus edition first published in Great Britain in 2007 by Sphere
Copyright © Lynne Heitman 2007

Previously published separately:
Hard Landing first published in the United States in 2001 by Onyx,
a division of Penguin Putnam Inc.
First published in Great Britain in 2001
by Little, Brown and Company
Paperback edition published by Warner Books in 2002
Copyright © Lynne Heitman 2001
Parts Unknown first published in the United States in 2002 by
Random House, Inc.
First published in Great Britain in 2002 under the title *Tarmac*
by Little, Brown and Company
Paperback edition published by Time Warner Paperbacks in 2004
Copyright © Lynne Heitman 2002

A CIP catalogue record for this book is available from the British Library.

ISBN: 978-0-7515-4011-6

Papers used by Sphere are natural, recyclable products made from
wood grown in sustainable forests and certified in accordance with
the rules of the Forest Stewardship Council.

Printed and bound in Great Britain by Mackays of Chatham Ltd.
Paper supplied by Hellefoss AS, Norway

Sphere
An imprint of
Little, Brown Book Group
Brettenham House
Lancaster Place
London WC2E 7EN

A Member of the Hachette Livre Group of Companies

www.littlebrown.co.uk

Hard Landing

Prologue

Angelo rolled over, reached across his wife, and tried to catch the phone before it rang again. He grabbed the receiver and held it before answering, listening for the sound of her rhythmic breathing that told him she was still asleep.

"Yeah?"

"Angie, get your ass out of bed. You gotta do something for me."

He recognized the voice immediately, but didn't like the tone. "Who's this?"

"Stop screwing around, Angie."

He switched the phone to his other ear and lowered his voice. "What the hell you doin' calling over here this time of the night? You're gonna wake up Theresa."

"I need you to find Petey."

"You gotta be kiddin' me." He twisted around to see the clock radio on his side of the bed. Without his glasses, it took a serious squint to turn the blurry red glow into individual digits. Twelve-twenty, for God's sake, twelve-twenty in the friggin' morning. "I got an early shift and it's raining like a sonofabitch out there. Find him yourself."

"I'm working here, Angie. I can't leave the airport."

"Never stopped you before. Call me tomorrow."

"Don't hang up on me, damn you."

The receiver was halfway to the cradle and Angelo could still hear the yelling. *"Don't you fucking hang up on me!"* But that wasn't what kept him hanging on. *"You owe me. Do you hear me? More than this, you owe me."* It was the desperation—panic even. In the thirty years he'd known him, Big Pete Dwyer had never even come close to losing control.

Angelo pulled the receiver back. With his hand cupped over the mouthpiece, he could smell the strong scent of his wife on it—the thick, sweet fragrance of her night cream mixed with the faintly medicinal smell that seemed to be everywhere in their home these days. "What the hell's the matter with you?"

"If you never do nothing else for me, Angie, you gotta do this thing for me tonight."

The old bedsprings groaned as Theresa turned. When he felt her hand on his knee, he reached down and held it between both of his, trying to warm fingers that were always so cold lately. She was awake now anyhow. "I'm listening."

"He's probably in one of those joints in Chelsea or Revere. There's gonna be some guys out looking for him. I want you to find him first."

"Are you talkin' about cops? Because I ain't gonna—"

"No. Not cops. I can't talk right now."

Big Pete had to raise his voice to be heard, and for the first time Angelo noticed the background noise. Men were shouting, work boots were scraping the gritty linoleum floor, and doors were opening and slamming shut. "What's going on over there?"

"Just do what I tell you."

"What do you want I should do with him? Bring him over to you?"

"Fuck, no. Angie, you're not getting this. Find Petey and stash him somewhere until I finish my shift. Keep him away from the airport, and don't let no one get to him before I do. No one. Do you hear?"

The line went dead. Angelo held the receiver against his chest until Theresa took it from his hand and hung it up. "What time is it?" she murmured.

"It's twelve-thirty, baby. I gotta go out for a little while."

"Who was that?"

"Big Pete needs me to find his kid."

"Again?"

"Yeah, but this time there's something hinky about it. Something's going on."

"Mmmmm . . ."

He leaned down and kissed his wife on the cheek. "Go back to sleep, babe. I'm gonna take the phone off the hook so nobody bothers you."

The big V-8 engine in Angelo's old Cadillac made the bench seat rumble. He sat with his boot on the brake, shaking the rain out of his hair and waiting for the defroster to kick in. With fingers as cold and stiff as his wife's had been, he tapped the finicky dome light, trying to make it come on. Where the hell were his gloves, anyway, and what was that garbage on the radio? Damn kids with their rap music, if you could even call it music. He punched a button and let the tuner scan for his big band station while he searched his pockets for gloves.

"*. . . with friends and family on that flight are advised to* *go to the Nor'easter Airlines terminal at Logan Airport, where representatives—"*

Angelo froze. What the hell . . .? He wanted to turn up the volume, but couldn't get his hand out of his pocket. His heart started to pound as he tried to shake loose and listen at the same time.

"Again, if you've just joined us, we're receiving word—"

The scanner kicked in and the rage-filled rant of a midnight radio call-in host poured out. Angelo yanked his hand free, leaned down and, god*damm*it, cracked his forehead on the steering wheel. Still squeezing the glove in his fist, he jabbed at the tuner buttons until the solemn tones of the newscaster emerged again from the static.

". . . we know so far is that Nor'easter Airlines Flight 1704, a commuter aircraft carrying nineteen passengers and two crew members, has crashed tonight just outside of Baltimore."

Angelo put both hands on the steering wheel to keep them from shaking.

"That flight did depart Logan Airport earlier this evening. The information we have at this hour is that there are no survivors, but again, that report is unconfirmed."

The bulletin repeated as Angelo reached up and used the sleeve of his jacket to wipe the condensation from the windshield. He peered through the streaked glass and up into the black sky. There was nothing to see but a cold, spiteful rain still coming down. But he felt it. He felt the dying aircraft falling to the earth, falling through the roof of the old Cadillac. He felt it falling straight down on him.

Goddamn you, Big Pete. Goddamn you.

Chapter One

When the seat belt sign went out, I was the first one down the jetbridge. My legs wobbled, my muscles ached, and my feet felt like sausages stuffed into leather pumps that had been the right size when we'd boarded six hours earlier. All I wanted to do was get off the airplane, check into my hotel, sink into a hot bath, and forget the five hours in the air, the half hour in a holding pattern, and the interminable twenty-five minutes we'd spent delayed on the ground because, the captain had assured us, our gate was occupied.

The captain had told an airline fib.

When I'd looked out my window and down at the ramp, I'd seen no wingman on my side of the plane, which meant we hadn't been waiting for a gate, we'd been waiting for a ground crew to marshal us in. Hard to imagine. It's not as if we'd shown up unexpectedly. The crew that finally did saunter out was one man short and out of uniform. I made a mental note.

At the bottom of the bridge, the door to the departure lounge was closed. I grabbed the knob and could have sworn it was vibrating. I turned the knob, pushed against the door—

and it slammed back in my face. Odd. Behind me, fellow passengers from the flight stomped down the jetbridge and stood, cell phones and carry-ons in hand, blinking at me. I gave it another shot, this time putting my shoulder into it, and pushed through the obstruction, which, to my embarrassment, turned out to be a family of four—mother, father, and two small children. They'd been pinned there by a teeming mob, the size and scope of which became clear when the door swung wide, and the rumble I'd heard became a full-fledged roar.

There must have been a thousand people smashed into the departure lounge, at least twice the number that would be comfortable in that space. Judging by their faces and the combustible atmosphere, they were all supposed to be somewhere besides Logan Airport in Boston. It was Ellis Island in reverse—people trying to get out, not in.

The gate agent who had met our flight was past me before I knew it.

"Excuse me," I said, but my voice evaporated into the crowd noise. I tried again.

"Baggage claim is that way, ma'am." Without bothering to look at me, the agent pointed down the concourse, turned, and vanished into a wall of winter coats.

I stood and watched the current of deplaning passengers flow through the crowd and out to baggage claim, quiet hotel rooms, and hot baths. Technically, I could have joined them. I was anonymous in Boston, and my assignment didn't officially begin until the next day. But in the end, I did as I always did. I worked my way over to one of the check-in podiums, stowed my coat and bag in a closet, clipped on my Majestic Airlines ID, and went to work.

I spotted a senior ticket agent shuttling through the crowd from gate to gate, moving with as much authority as circumstances would allow. When I caught up with her, she was conferring with a young blonde agent at one of the podiums.

"You'll have to wait your turn," she snapped before I even opened my mouth. "There's a line."

If there was a line at this podium, it was cleverly disguised as an angry throng. I slipped around the counter and stood next to her. "I'm not a passenger. I'm the new general manager."

She checked my badge, eyes dark with suspicion, thinking perhaps I was an imposter volunteering to be in charge of this mess.

"I'm Alex Shanahan. I came in on the Denver flight."

"The *new* GM? That didn't take long."

"What's the problem here?"

"You name it, we've got it, but basically we're off schedule. Nothing's left on time for the past two hours. In fact, nothing's left at all."

I read her name tag. "JoAnn, maybe I can help. If I could—"

"Are you *deaf*? Or are you *stupid*?"

We both turned to look across the podium at a man who was wearing an Italian suit with a silk tie that probably cost more than my entire outfit. As he berated the younger agent, she stared down at her keyboard, eyes in the locked position.

"Do you *know* how many miles I fly on this airline every year?" He pointed his phone at her and her chin started to quiver. "I *will* not sit in coach, I *will* sit in first class, and you *will* find me a seat if you have to buy someone else off this *goddamn airplane*."

Even in a lounge filled with angry people, this guy was

drawing attention. I leaned across the podium so he could hear me. "Can I help you, sir?"

"Who the hell are you?"

I took him aside and listened to his patronizing rant, maintaining eye contact and nodding sympathetically so that he could see my deep concern. When he was finally out of steam, I explained that the situation was extreme and that we might not get him up front this time. I asked him to please be patient and work with us. Then I promised to send him two complimentary upgrades. Frequent fliers respond to free upgrades the way trained seals respond to raw fish. It took a promise of five upgrades, but eventually, with one more parting shot about our "towering display of incompetence," he took my card and my apology and faded away.

I found JoAnn heading for another podium. "At least give me the number to Operations," I said, tagging after her. "I can call the agent there."

She scribbled the number on the back of a ticket envelope and handed it to me. I used my own cell phone and dialed.

"Operations-this-is-Kevin-hold-please." Kevin's Irish accent seemed far too gentle for the situation. When he came back, I told him what I needed.

"Have you talked to Danny about this?"

I plugged a finger in my non-phone ear and turned my back to the crowd. "If he's not standing there with you, Danny's too far away to be in charge right now. I need help now, Kevin. If you can't help me, someone's going to get killed up here."

There was a brief pause, then, "Go ahead."

I spoke to Kevin for five minutes, taking notes, asking questions, and getting advice. When I hung up, the noise, much like the frustration level, was on the rise and JoAnn was contemplating a call to the state troopers. I couldn't see how a couple of big guys with guns and jackboots would calm the waters, so I asked her to wait. I found a functioning microphone, pressed the button, and took a deep breath.

"I'm Alex Shanahan, the general manager for Majestic here at Logan."

The buzz grew louder.

I kicked off my shoes, climbed on top of the podium, and repeated my introduction. When people could see *and* hear me, it made all the difference.

"Ladies and gentlemen, I apologize for the inconvenience of this evening's operation. I know you're uncomfortable and you've had a hard time getting information, so that's where we're going to start. Is anyone out there booked on Flight 497 to Washington, D.C.?" A few hands shot up hopefully. Others followed more hesitantly.

"Your flight was scheduled to depart at 5:15. The aircraft just came in, and the passengers from Chicago are deplaning as I speak at Gate"—I checked my notes—"Forty-four." Heads popped up here and there as people stretched to see the gate. "We can either clean the cabin, or we can get you on board and out of town. How many of you want to leave now?" I had to smile as every hand in the place went up.

"I'm with you, people, but right now I'm asking the passengers booked to D.C. Be prepared, ladies and gentlemen, that the cabin will not be as clean as you're accustomed to on Majestic, but you'll be gone and we'll still be here." As I continued, flight by flight, the noise began to recede, the agents worked the queues, and some semblance of order began to emerge.

Four hours later, at almost ten o'clock, the last passenger

boarded. I closed the door and pulled the jetbridge. The agents had either gone to punch out or to other parts of the operation, leaving the boarding lounge as littered and deserted as Times Square on New Year's Day. I was hungry, I was exhausted, I was wired, and I hadn't felt this good in almost eighteen months, not since I'd left the field. There is nothing like an epic operating crisis to get the adrenaline surging.

I went to the closet to retrieve my coat and bag, and in my hyped-up state nearly missed what was tacked to the inside of the closet door. It had been crazy when I'd first opened this door, but even so I would have noticed a sheet of notebook-size paper at eye level—especially this one. I took it down and stared at it. It was a crude drawing of a house with a sharply pitched roof. At the apex of the roof was a wind vane resembling a rooster. Inside the house in the attic, a woman hung from a rope, her head twisted to a grotesque angle by the coil around her throat. Limp arms dangled at her sides, her tongue hung out of a gaping mouth, and her eyes, dead eyes, had rolled back in her head. My adrenaline surge receded and I felt a thickening in my chest as I read the caption. The name Shepard, scrawled below, had been crossed out and replaced with my name—Shanahan.

"It's a message."

I jumped, startled by the sound of the voice, loud and abrupt in the now-deserted terminal. JoAnn stood behind me, arms crossed, dark eyes fixed on the drawing in my hand. "That's part of the message, and tonight's operation was the rest of it."

"What are you talking about?"

"I didn't get it until you showed up," she said, "but now it makes sense. They must have found out you were coming in tonight."

"Who?"

"The union. The boys downstairs are telling you that you may think you're in charge of this place, but you're not. And if you try to be"—she pointed to the drawing in my hand—"You're going to end up just like the last one."

"Ellen Shepard killed herself," I said.

"Yeah, right." She gave me a sour smile as she turned to walk away. "Welcome to Boston."

Chapter Two

"I can see the fucking aircraft from my office, Roger. It's sitting on the apron waiting for a gate. Send someone out there, they can hand the goddamned thing through the cockpit window."

The voice emanated from behind one of two closed doors. It was lean, tough, and rapid-fire, with a boxer's rhythm of quick cuts and clean jabs. I couldn't place the accent exactly, but Brooklyn was a good guess. Whoever it was, he was in early. I'd wanted to be the first one to the office on my first day.

"Roger, listen to me. *Would you listen to me?* We can't wait one more minute. The hospital's been on call for this thing for hours. For all I know, they already got the guy cut open."

The second office, I assumed, had belonged to my predecessor and would now be mine. I tried the knob. Locked. With nothing else to do, I checked out my new reception area. It was a typical back office operation for an airline, a neglected pocket of past history filled with forty-year-old furniture built to last twenty. This one had the extra-added features of being small and cramped. There was a gunmetal gray desk—unoc-cupied—that held a phone, a ten-key adding machine, a well-used ashtray, and an answering machine, of all things. Behind the desk on the floor was a computer. I could have written WASH ME in the dust on the monitor. The copy machine was ancient, the file cabinets were unlabeled, and the burnt orange chairs and low table that made up the seating area cried out for shag carpet. The whole office was light-years away from the smooth teakwood desks, sleek leather chairs, and turbo-charged computers at headquarters in Denver.

I was so glad to be back in the field.

"I'm trying to tell you," thundered The Voice, "you don't *need* a gate for this. There's gotta be somebody around. *Jesus Christ*, Roger, I gotta do *everything* myself?"

The phone slammed, the door flew open, and he was past me, his voice trailing him down the corridor along with echoes of his hurried footsteps. "I'll be with you in a minute. I just gotta go . . . do . . ." And he was gone. I looked into the office he'd just vacated. Sitting quietly in a side chair was an uncom-monly spindly young man, probably early twenties, with wavy blond hair, a pale complexion, and long legs covered with white cotton long johns. He wore a tight lime green bicycle shirt that emphasized his narrowness, and a pair of baggy shorts over the long underwear. A praying mantis in Birkenstocks. "Oh, hey," he said when he saw me.

"How are you?" is what I said, when "Who are you" would have worked much better.

"Kidney."

"What?"

"I'm waiting for the kidney," he said. "It was supposed to come in early this morning, but someone at the airlines screwed up. It just got here. I think the dude's going to get it himself."

Something clicked and the alternative dress made sense. "You're a courier."

He nodded. "Working for the hospital."

"Was that Dan Fallacaro?"

"That's what he told me." Something out on the ramp drew his attention. "There he is, man. Cool."

He unfolded himself from the chair and stepped over to the side wall of the office, which was a floor-to-ceiling window onto our ramp operation. Sure enough, the figure that had just about plowed me under was now sprinting across the concrete through the rain toward a B737 idling on the tarmac. He had on a company-issued heavy winter coat, but no hood or hat, and he carried a lightweight ladder. The courier and I stood side by side in the window watching as Dan Fallacaro climbed the ladder, banged on the cockpit window with his fist, then waited, soaked to the bone, to receive a small cooler about the size of a six-pack. He cradled it under his arm as he stepped down and collected his ladder. When he turned to jog, gently, back to the terminal, I saw that he hadn't even taken time to zip his jacket.

"Awesome," said the courier. "I didn't know you could do that."

"Some people wouldn't do that."

The courier checked his watch. Thinking about that fragile cargo, I had to ask, "Are you a bicycle courier?"

"In Boston? You think I'm crazy? I've got a Ford Explorer. See ya."

While I waited for Dan to reappear, I went back to the reception area. When the phone on the reception desk rang, I grabbed it. "Majestic Airlines."

"Hey, Molly . . ." It was a man's voice, strained, barely audible over the muffled whine of jet engines and the sound of other men's voices. "Molly, give Danny a message for me, wouldya?"

"This is not—"

"I can't hear you, Molly. It's crazy down here. Just tell him I got his package on board. I handed it to the captain myself. Make sure you tell him that part, that nobody else saw it."

"Who is this?"

"Who the hell do you think? This is Norm. And tell him I put her name on the manifest, but not the Form 12A, like he said. He'll know."

Norm signed off, assuming to the end that he'd been speaking to Molly.

The heavy door on the concourse opened and shut, those same hurried footsteps approached, and he was there. Dan Fallacaro in the flesh, out of breath, and *sans* cooler.

"Nice save," I said. "I'd hate to be responsible for the loss of a vital organ on my first day."

"Thanks." He peeled off the wet winter coat. Underneath, his sleeves were rolled up, his tie was at half-mast, and the front of his shirt was damp. It clung to his body, accentuating a chassis that was wiry, built for speed. From what I'd seen, his metabolism was too fast to sustain any spare fat.

"I'm Alex Shanahan," I said, extending my hand.

"I know who you are. I work for you." He wiped a wet palm on his suit pants and gave me a damp, perfunctory handshake. "Dan Fallacaro. How you doing?" Even though he looked past me, not at me, I could still see that he had interesting eyes, the kind that gray-eyed people like me always coveted. They were green, a mossy green that ran to dark brown around the edges of the irises. His phone rang and he shot past me into his office.

I waited at a polite distance until the call ended, then waited a while longer until it was clear he wasn't coming back and he wasn't going to invite me in. I moved just inside his doorway and found him sitting at his desk, drying his face and hands with a paper towel. If he felt any excitement about my arrival, he managed to keep it in check.

"What's the story with the kidney?" I asked.

"It got here late."

"How'd that happen?"

"Somebody in Chicago put it on the wrong flight. Had to be rerouted."

"You didn't have enough gates?"

"Nope."

"Because you're off schedule?"

"Yep."

"How come?"

"Winter."

"Uh-huh. Why'd you have to go get it yourself?"

He unfurled another towel from the roll on his desk and snapped it off. "Because Roger Shit-for-Brains is on in Operations this morning, I can't find my shift supervisor, and even if I could, no one would do what he says." He bent down to wipe off his shoes.

"By any chance, is Norm your shift supervisor?"

He popped up. "Did he call?"

"Just now," I said. "He gave—"

Dan grabbed the phone . . .

"He gave me a message for you."

. . . slammed the receiver to his ear . . .

"Do you want the message?"

. . . started to dial . . .

"The package you asked him to take care of is onboard."

. . . and stopped. "He told you that?"

"He said he put the name on the manifest but left it off the 12A. He handled it personally and no one else saw it."

He hung up the phone slowly, as if relinquishing the receiver would be a sign that he believed me, a sign of good faith he wasn't ready to offer. With one hand he tossed the wet paper towel into the metal trash can, where it landed with a thud. With the other he pulled a comb from his drawer and dragged it haphazardly through his thick, damp hair. "Molly can get you settled in." He raised his voice, *"Mol, you out there?"*

If Molly was within a hundred yards, she would have heard him, but there was no response.

"For chrissakes, Molly, I saw you come in."

A woman's voice floated in. "I told you before, Danny, I wasn't going to answer when you bellowed."

Satisfied, he stood up and began gathering himself to leave. "She can get you set up," he said, grabbing a clipboard and keys from his desk. I could have been the droopy potted plant in the corner for all that I was registering with him.

"We need to talk about last night," I said as he walked out the door.

"What about last night?" he snapped, executing a crisp about-face.

"Since you weren't around and I was, maybe I can brief you."

He folded his arms across the clipboard and held it flat against his chest. "The shift supervisor wasn't answering his radio," he began, accepting the unspoken challenge, "and the cabin service crew chief was AWOL along with everyone else

on his crew. No one was cleaning the cabins. The flight attendants wouldn't take the airplanes because they were dirty, and
they wouldn't clean 'em themselves because it's not in their
contract. The agents were trying to do quick pickups onboard
just to get them turned when they should have been working
the queues." His words came so fast he sounded like a machine
gun. "Chicago was socked in. Miami took a mechanical, and
there was only one functioning microphone which you used to
make announcements while standing on top of the podium at
Gate Forty-two."

"You didn't mention that I was barefoot."

"It's not because I didn't know." He had enough self-control
not to actually sneer, but he couldn't do much about his brittle
tone.

"And you didn't mention the hundreds of inconvenienced
passengers, all of whom were jammed into the departure
lounge screaming for blood. I thought we were going to have
to offer up one of the agents as a human sacrifice."

His grip on the clipboard tightened. "What's your point?"

"My point is that the operation last night was a complete
disaster, and there was some indication that it was all orches-
trated for my benefit—some kind of 'Welcome to Boston'
message from the union."

"Who told you that?"

"It doesn't matter. I'm now in charge of this place, you are
my second in command, and I think we should talk about this.
I want to understand what's going on."

"Last night is handled."

"What's handled?"

"I spoke to the shift supervisor about not answering his
radio. As far as the crew chief on cabins, I've got a disciplinary

hearing scheduled for Thursday. He was off the field. I know he was, everybody knows he was, but no one's going to speak up, much less give a statement, so I'll put another reprimand in his file, the union will grieve it, and you'll take it out. End of story."

"Is that how things work around here, or are you making a prediction about me?"

"I need to get to work," he said. "Is there anything else?"

"Could we . . . do you mind if we sit down for a minute? I'm having a hard time talking to the back of your head."

His jaw worked back and forth, his green eyes clouded over, and his deep sigh would have been a loud groan if he'd given it voice. But he moved back behind his desk, immediately found a pencil, and proceeded to drum it against the arm of his chair.

I closed the door and settled into the seat across from him. "Dan, are you this rude, abrupt, and patronizing with everyone? Or is this behavior a reaction to me specifically? Or maybe you're unhappy with someone else, Roger-Shit-for-Brains, for example, and taking it out on me." I thought of another option. "Or maybe you're just an asshole."

His reaction was so typically male it was hard not to smile. He looked stunned, flabbergasted, as if my annoyance was totally unprovoked. Who, me?

"Why would I be mad at you? I don't even know you."

"Exactly my point. Most people have to get to know me before they truly dislike me."

He stared for a few seconds, then laid the pencil on his desk, and rubbed his eyes with the heels of his hands. When he was done, I noticed for the first time how thoroughly exhausted he looked. His eyeballs seemed to have sunk deeper into their

sockets, his face was drawn, and his cheeks were hollowed out
as if he hadn't had a hot meal or a good night's sleep in a
week.

That's when I got it.

"You're upset about the ashes, aren't you?" He fixed those
dark green eyes on me in a tired but riveting gaze. "The ones
Norm handled for you."

"Goddamn him—" He was up on his feet and ready to go
after Norm, and I knew I was right.

"Norm didn't tell me."

"Then who did?"

"I figured it out myself. Form 12A is a notification of human
remains onboard. He said he put the box in the cockpit and
not in the belly, so I have to assume the remains weren't in a
coffin. And since your boss hung herself last week—"

"Last Monday. She died last Monday night."

"So another reason you might be this angry and upset is
that you and Ellen Shepard were friends and I've walked in
on a particularly difficult time because today is the day you're
shipping her ashes home."

He sank back into his chair, dropped his head back, and
closed his eyes. He looked as if he never wanted to get up
again.

"Why all the mystery? Why not put her name on the manifest?"

"Because I didn't want the scumbags downstairs stubbing
out cigarettes in her ashes."

"Tell me you're exaggerating."

"We're talking about the same guys who screwed over
almost a thousand passengers last night just to send a 'fuck
you' message."

I sat back in my chair, and felt my excitement about the new job and being back in the field drain away.

"I should have been here," he said, his head still back, eyes glued to the ceiling. "But I had to—I just should have been here."

He didn't actually say it, but that sounded as close to an apology as I was going to get. "I'm sorry about Ellen, Dan."

"Did you know her?"

"No."

His head popped up. "Then why would you be sorry?"

"Because you knew her."

This time when he bolted up, I couldn't have stopped him if I'd tackled him.

"Debrief is at 0900 sharp," he said, throwing the door open. "It's your meeting if you want it."

I sat and listened one more time to the sound of his footsteps fading down the long corridor. The door to the concourse opened and closed, and I knew he was gone. Eventually, I pulled myself up and went out to meet my new assistant.

"Don't take it personally," she said when she saw me. "He's that way with everyone."

Molly had a flop of dark curls on her head, big brown eyes, and full red lips that occupied half her face. Her olive complexion suggested Hispanic blood, or maybe Portuguese, this being Massachusetts. She was probably in her late fifties, but her dainty stature made her seem younger. She was thin, almost bird-like, but judging from the hard lines around her eyes and the way she'd spoken to Dan, she was more of a crow than a sparrow. At least she had a voice like one.

She squinted at me. "You're the new GM."

"And you're Molly."

"Danny's been a little upset these past few days."

"Judging from my first"—I checked my watch—"fifteen hours in this operation, he's got good reason."

She leaned back in her chair, crossed her legs, and took a long, deep, sideways drag on a skinny cigarette, all the time looking me up and down like girls do in junior high when they're trying to decide who to be seen with in the school cafeteria. She might not have been inside a junior high school for over thirty years, but she still had the attitude.

"So they sent us another woman," she said, eyebrows raised.

"Apparently."

With a swish of nylon on nylon she rose from the chair and sidled around to my side of her desk. It's possible I'd passed muster, but more likely she couldn't resist a golden opportunity to dish.

"He found her, you know."

"Who?"

"Ellen."

"Dan found Ellen's body?"

"When she didn't come in that morning, he's the one who drove up to her house. She was in the attic." Molly reached around to the ashtray on the desk behind her and did a quick flick. "When he found her, she'd been hanging there all night."

I reached up instinctively and put a hand on my own throat, which was tightening at the thought of what a body looks like after hanging by the neck for that long. With my thumb, I could feel my own blood pumping through a thick vein. "It must have been horrible for him. Were they friends?"

She nodded as she exhaled. "He won't talk about it, but, yeah, he hasn't been the same since. Like I said, we don't take it personally." She reached behind the desk again and opened a drawer, this time coming back with a big, heavy ring chock-full of keys. "I'll let you into your office."

She went to the door, and I stood back and watched her struggle with the lock.

"How's everyone else around here taking it?" I asked. "What's the mood?"

"Mixed. People who liked her are upset. People who didn't are glad she's gone. It's that simple. More people liked her than didn't, but the ones that didn't hated her so much, it made up for all the rest."

"Mostly guys down on the ramp, I hear. Not the agents."

She nodded. "You showing up the way you did last night and doing what you did, that's given them all something else to talk about. Everyone's waiting to see what you're like, what you're going to do about Little Pete." The lock was not releasing and she was getting frustrated.

"Who's Little Pete and why is he 'Little'?"

"Pete Dwyer Jr. He's the missing crew chief, the one who caused all that trouble last night. Most of it, anyway. Everyone calls him Little Pete because his pop works here, too. Big Pete runs the union."

"I thought Victor Venora was president of the local."

"Titles don't mean much here. And they have nothing to do with who's got the real power."

"And who would that—"

With a final, forceful twist, the door popped open. *"Cripes!"* Molly jerked her hand away as if it had been caught in a mouse-trap. "I broke a nail. Damn that lock." She took the mound of keys, marched back to her desk, presumably for emergency repairs, and called back over her shoulder, "Go in. I'll be with you in a minute."

The door swung open easily at my touch. The office was slightly larger than Dan's. Instead of one floor-to-ceiling window on the ramp-side wall, it had two that came together at the corner. Unlike Dan's office, the blinds were closed, filtering out all but a few slats of daylight that fell across the floor like bright ribbons. The air smelled closed-in, faintly musty. In the middle of the space, dominating in every way, was a massive, ornate wooden desk. Its vast work surface was covered with a thick slice of glass. Underneath was a large, carved logo for . . . *Nor'easter* Airlines?

"Some desk, huh?" Molly leaned against the doorjamb with a new cigarette.

"It looks out of place," I said, walking over to open the blinds.

"It belonged to the president of our airline."

"Our airline" was how former Nor'easter employees always referred to their old company, which had teetered at the precipice of bankruptcy until Bill Scanlon, the chairman and CEO of Majestic, *our* airline, had sailed in and saved the day. As a result, Scanlon was revered by most Nor'easterners. It was the rest of us Majestic plebeians they resented.

I didn't tell her that no one at Majestic headquarters would have been caught dead with a desk like that. It didn't match the corporate ambiance, which was simple, spare, and, above all, featureless.

When I pulled the blinds, the sun splashed in on a linoleum floor that was wax-yellow and dirty. The corner where I was standing was covered with a strange white residue, almost like chalk dust. It reminded me of rat poison. The morning light brought grandeur to the old desk, showing polish and detail I hadn't noticed. I also hadn't noticed the single palm print now clearly visible in the dust that coated the glass top.

"Has anyone been in here since Ellen died?"

"Danny and I were both in here looking through her Rolodex for someone to contact. Turns out an aunt in California was her closest living kin. If you need anything, it's probably in there"—she pointed with her cigarette at the desk—"Supplies and all. Ellen was pretty organized that way." She turned to go and caught herself. "Oh, I should warn you, don't keep anything important in there. It doesn't lock anymore."

"Is it broken?"

"You could say that." She moved into the office and perched on the arm of one of the side chairs.

I walked around to the working side of the desk. The handsome wood facings of the drawers were scarred and scratched around the small locks, and the top edges were splintered and broken where someone had pried them open. I put my finger into a sad, gaping hole where one of the locks was missing altogether. "What happened here?"

"The union."

"The union broke into this desk? Why?"

"Just to prove they could."

That was a comforting thought. I stood up and looked at her. "What did Ellen do that had them so upset?"

"Well, let's see. She was a woman, she was from Majestic, and she wanted them to work for their wages instead of sitting around on their butts all day. That's three strikes."

I slipped the hangman's drawing out of my briefcase. I felt a tingling in my neck when I looked at it. I handed her the page. "Have you ever seen this before?"

"Not that version. Where did you get it?"

"Someone left it for me last night as some kind of a message."

She shook her head. "That didn't take long. I guess they figure they'll start early with you, keep you on the defensive from the beginning."

"It means they knew I was coming in on that flight."

"No doubt."

"And they saw where I'd put my bags, which wouldn't have been easy in all that chaos. Someone was watching me."

She shot a stream of smoke straight up, and handed the drawing back. "They're always watching."

I followed the smoke as it drifted up to the ceiling. This was apparently old hat to Molly, but I found it hard not to feel just a little shaken up by a drawing of a woman hanged by the neck with my name on it.

Molly stood to go.

"Did someone steal her pictures, too?" I asked.

She looked where I was looking, at the bare walls. "This office is exactly the way she left it," she said. "She never hung any pictures."

"How long was she here?"

"Almost thirteen months."

The walls were painted an uncertain beige, and had scars left over from previous administrations, where nails and picture hangers had been torn out. I walked over and touched a big gouge in the Sheetrock where the chalky center was pushing through.

"She didn't leave much behind, did she?"

Chapter Three

Molly was putting the call on hold just as I walked through the door.

"How was your first debrief?"

"Long."

"You've got a call on line one," she said, "and it must be important because he never waits on hold and he never calls this early."

I checked my watch. It was ten o'clock in the morning. "Who is it?"

"Your boss."

"Uh-oh." The quick flash of nerves was like a caffeine rush. "Where's he calling from?"

"He's in his office in D.C."

She said something else, but I didn't hear what because I was already at my desk, bent over the notes I'd made from debrief, cramming for whatever question Lenny might think to ask about last night's operation. Someone I admired and deeply respected once told me that the best opportunities to make a good impression come from disaster—from how well you handle it. Last night certainly qualified as a disaster, and I was about to test that theory on my new boss.

After a quick moment to gather my thoughts, I made myself sit down, then picked up the receiver. "Good morning, Lenny. How are you?" Jeez, I sounded like such a stiff.

"Very well, Alex. And how you doin' this morning?" His deliberate Louisiana drawl sounded as if it were floating up from the bottom of a trash can, and I knew he had me on the speaker phone. I hated speaker phones. You could be talking to a crowd the size of Yankee Stadium and never know it.

"I'm well, Lenny, thank you."

"Can we talk about a few things this morning?"

"Of course." I heard the whisper of pages turning and imagined him leafing through his tour reports, zeroing in on Boston's, and reading with widening eyes about the debacle from last night. But I was ready, poised to jump on whatever he chose to ask.

"So . . ."

I waited, muscles tensed.

" . . . when did you get in?"

"Last night."

"Good trip out?"

"Uh, yes. The trip was fine."

"Glad to hear it."

The pages continued to turn. I inched a little farther out on the edge of my seat, straining to hear, waiting for the real questions to start. And waiting. And . . . and . . . I couldn't wait. "Lenny, we had a few problems in the operation last night. I don't know if you saw the tour report, but—"

"Was it anything you couldn't handle?"

"No, we handled it. It was—"

"Good. Listen, I need to ask you to do something for me."

Not exactly the grilling I'd anticipated. The paper rustled again and this time the sound was more distinct, a slow, lazy arc that I recognized. Lenny wasn't leafing through tour reports. He was reading a newspaper. I eased back in my chair and relaxed. No pop quiz today. Disappointing, in a way. "What can I do to help?"

After a short pause I heard a click, and I knew he'd taken me off the speaker phone. "You've got a ramper up there, an Angelo DiBiasi. Have you heard this story?" Without the squawk box his voice had an instantly intimate quality. The rest of the world was shut out. Only I could hear what he was saying.

"No, I haven't heard the story."

A group of ticket agents, talking and laughing, burst into the reception area and greeted Molly. I rolled my chair backward across the floor until I could reach the door and launch it shut.

Lenny was still talking. "He's one of the night crawlers, works midnights. I knew him when I was there. You knew I used to work in Boston, right? Before I came to D.C.?"

"I did." He'd mentioned it no less than six times during my interview.

"Anyway, old Angie's gotten himself into a little trouble."

"What did he do?"

"Damned if I can tell. He may have been in the wrong place at the wrong time regarding a cargo shipment"—which meant he was stealing—"but I feel bad about terminating a guy with over forty years in, I don't care what he did."

Forty years? I was used to stations out West, where twenty years was a lot of seniority. "What's his status?"

"Fallacaro fired him, he filed for arbitration, and now he's waiting for his hearing. But Angie's not a bad guy. You have far worse up there, and the thing is, his wife is sick. He's sixty-three years old. It could take up to a year to get his case heard, and I'd prefer not to put the two of them through it."

The group outside was getting louder, and I had to pay close attention. I could hear what he was saying, but what I needed to know was what he wasn't saying, and I had the sense that there was a lot. "If Angelo's on to arbitration, that means Ellen denied his grievance."

"Yes. Yes, she did and I can understand why. Ellen needed to establish herself as the authority there. But you don't have that situation. You've got much more field experience than she did, and now that you're sitting in the general manager's chair, it's perfectly legitimate for you to overturn the firing. As you know, I can't get involved until after arbitration."

When I didn't respond, I felt Lenny trying to read my silence. He wanted me to simply agree to do what he'd asked, but it was hard when I didn't know the players. Overturning a firing was a big deal. It would send a strong message about me to all of the people who worked in the station. I wanted to make sure it was a message I wanted to send.

"You still there, Alex?"

"Sorry, Lenny. I'm still here."

"Have you had a chance to hook up with Victor Venora?"

"He's on my list, but I haven't gotten to him yet."

"Here's an idea for you," he offered, his tone brightening considerably. He was taking a new tack. "You set a meeting with Victor, a president-of-the-local-GM-get-acquainted sit-down, and the first thing you do before he even opens his big mouth is tell him you're bringing Angie back. Start right in with a gesture of goodwill to the union. You'll knock his socks off."

I swiveled in my chair so that I could see out the window, looking for breathing room. Lenny was closing me in. I tried to decide if I was being crafty and shrewd or obstinate and stubborn. Sometimes they felt the same to me. What I knew was that he wanted me to commit to a deal without even knowing what this guy Angelo did and he wanted me to do it without making him ask explicitly, in which case it would forever be my idea. It didn't sound that risky and I had no reason to distrust Lenny, but I'd also been burned by bosses in the past for agreeing to far less.

I had to go with crafty and shrewd.

"Lenny, stealing is automatic grounds for termination, and—"

"I never said he was stealing."

No, he hadn't. But he'd just given me the way out. "You're absolutely right. You didn't say that, and it's clear that I need to gather some facts so that I'm more prepared to discuss this with you. I hope you don't mind if I take a day or so to do a little research. I'd like to talk to Dan, since he's the one who fired him."

We either had a pregnant pause or he was still reading the newspaper and checking out the sale at Barney's. I waited through his long exhale, and I could feel the test of wills making the phone line stiffen. I started to worry. This was my new boss, after all.

"I apologize, Alex."

"Excuse me?"

"I really do. Now that I think about it, I see that I'm putting you in a tough spot. I know you have to get your feet on the

ground, and I know what a tough bunch you've got up there.
I'm just trying to give you some ideas because I want you to
do well, that's all. Take your time, gather some facts, and see
if you don't agree with me on this Angelo situation. But whatever you decide, it's your call."

I was feeling less crafty by the second. How hard would it
be to do what I was asked for once in my life? "I'll look into
it right away," I said, and I meant it.

He hung up, leaving me squarely on the side of obstinate
and stubborn.

The crowd of agents was gone when I opened the door. I
signaled to Molly, who was just finishing a phone call, then
went back to my desk and waited. When she came in, she was
reattaching an enormous clip earring to her phone ear.

"What's up?" she asked.

"What did Angelo DiBiasi do?"

"He stole a thirty-six-inch color TV set. Tried to, anyway."

My heart began to sink. "There's no chance of a mix-up or
misunderstanding? No question about what happened?" *No
possible grounds for overturning his termination?*

"The only question is how Angie could be so stupid. Danny
caught him loading it into his car. He fired him on the spot
because it was theft and theft—"

"—is automatic grounds for dismissal. I know. What's wrong
with his wife?"

"Breast cancer. She had it once, and now she's got it again."
Molly turned glum. "Poor Theresa," she sighed. "Seems like
she's been sick forever."

My heart went right ahead and sank.

Chapter Four

The afternoon shift had already begun by the time I finally made my way downstairs to meet Kevin, the operations agent who had been so helpful the night before. Compared to the bright, soaring spaces reserved for paying customers, little attention is paid to employee-only areas at an airport. For the most part, the spaces down below were rabbit warrens, and this one was no exception. Graffiti covered the walls, trash overflowed the bins, and flattened cigarette butts littered the concrete floor. A door left open somewhere let in a cold draft that carried the smell of jet fumes in to mingle with the bitter aroma of burned coffee.

Kevin was on the other side of a door with a window labeled OPERATIONS. He stared at his monitor, with a phone balanced on one shoulder and a radio clutched in his other hand. He looked as capable and businesslike as he had sounded. When I saw that he probably had a few years in, I wasn't surprised. The Operations function is Darwinian—survival of the calmest.

When he heard me come in, he nodded in my direction and kept talking into the radio. "We need to hold that gate open for the DC-10. It's on final."

I couldn't make out the response, but whoever was talking sounded confused. Kevin wasn't. "Because it's the only gate I've got left that will take a 'ten. Everything else is narrow-body only."

While I waited, I reacquainted myself with an Ops office. This one, rectangular and about ten paces long, had what they all had—weather machines, printers of every kind, monitors, radios, phones, and file cabinets. It also had a bank of seven closed-circuit TV monitors. According to the labels, there was one camera for each of the six gates, Forty through Forty-five, and one for Forty-six—a slab of bare concrete used for the commuter operation, which was ground-loaded, no jetbridge. On the wall was a picture of our leader, the Chairman and CEO of Majestic Airlines. It was a black-and-white head shot that wouldn't have been out of place if this were 1961 and it was hanging next to an eight-by-ten glossy of John F. Kennedy. He stared out at me, and I stared back, knowing how insulted the great Bill Scanlon would be to hang in such a cheap plastic frame. I tried not to linger over the photo, to look away, to move on. But I hadn't been able to move on for the better part of the last year.

Normally, the only thing that makes the end of a relationship bearable is that many of the painful reminders of the person you are trying to stop loving can be removed from your life. You can throw away pictures, burn letters, and give all those books he gave you to the used bookstore. But as long as I worked for this airline, Bill Scanlon would always be gazing down from the wall in some office, reminding me of the way he used to look at me. Or I would come across his signature on a memo and remember the way his hand used to feel resting lightly on my hip. His imprint on this company—indeed, on the entire industry—was so broad and deep, I would never really get away from him. After all, he was, according to *BusinessWeek*, "The Man Who Saved the Airlines." Looking at the image of his face, I felt what I had felt almost from the first day without him in my life. I missed him.

Kevin finished his call and stood to greet me, bending slightly at the waist and extending his hand in a gesture that seemed oddly formal given the setting. "Welcome to Boston, Miss Shanahan. Kevin Corrigan, at your service."

I shook his hand. "Call me Alex."

"Thank you, I shall with pleasure." The glint in his clear blue eyes suggested a wry intelligence, and the Irish accent I'd heard over the radio was even more charming in person.

"You saved the operation last night, Kevin. But don't tell anyone because I'm getting all the credit."

"As well you should." He sat back in his chair and swung around to face his computer, raising his voice to accommodate for having his back to me. "It's good of you to come down. Usually I toil in complete obscurity, unless someone wants to yell or complain. In that case," he chuckled, "I'm far too accessible. How are you settling in?"

"Good. I'm over at the Harborside Hyatt until I get a chance to look for a place."

"Doesn't sound too homey."

"Based on what I saw last night, I need to be close to the airport for a while. I'm hoping that was the worst of it, that it can only get better."

"Not necessarily, but that's why you're here, isn't it?" He swung around and grinned at me, eyebrows dancing. "After all, you did ask for this assignment."

"How did you know that?"

"Everyone knows. In fact"—he reached over to rip something off the printer—"everyone knows everything about you."

My neck stiffened as I thought about the hangman's drawing in the closet last night. I didn't think I wanted everyone to know everything about me, particularly where I was at all times, but I was hoping that's not what Kevin meant. "I'd be really embarrassed if everyone knew my shoe size."

"Shall I give you the rundown?"

I rested my hips against the long work counter that served as his desk. "Give it to me straight."

"You've been with the company fourteen years, all on the Majestic side. You started out as an airport agent and worked your way up from there. You've lived and worked in a dozen different cities. Somewhere along the way you managed an MBA by going to night school. You've spent the past eighteen months at headquarters getting staff experience. That done, you're on a fast track to VP, maybe even to be the first woman vice president in the field."

I secretly loved hearing that last part. "You should write my résumés. Who's the detective?"

"There are no secrets here. One day someone knows. Before long everyone knows, and then it's as if we've always known."

"So I'm finding out." I pulled down a clipboard hanging on a nail and checked out the tour report. I hadn't seen a tour report in the entire eighteen months I'd been in headquarters, so now I was taking every chance to look at one, to remind myself that I was back in the field, and every time I did, it gave me a little boost. It was like hearing a favorite old song that comes on the radio after a long absence and being reminded of how much you liked it. This evening looked more promising than last—skies were clear, at least for now, all equipment was in service, and no crew chiefs were on the sick list. I hung the clipboard back on its nail and drifted back over to the window, a chest-high rectangle that ran the length of the office.

Directly outside, two rampers were loading bags onto a belt loader and up into the belly of the aircraft. Their movements were slow, disinterested. Not far away was a cluster of carts and tractors painted in Majestic's deep purple colors. Paint was peeling, windows were cracked, and parking was confused and disorderly. In the distance, Delta's operation gleamed. Even from where I stood, their safety markings and guidelines in reflective white and yellow paint were bright and visible. Every piece of equipment was in its proper place, and everyone was in uniform. I turned back into the office. "What's going on around here, Kevin?"

"I beg your pardon?"

"Crew chiefs are walking off their shifts, Dan Fallacaro looks as if he's just stepped out of his own grave—"

"Don't blame Danny. He's a good man and it's not his fault. He's the best operating man around."

"I'd like to think so, but to put it kindly, he's been a little hard to pin down. Everyone is whispering, no one is doing any work, this place is a mess, and no one here seems to notice."

"No one does notice. We're all accustomed to it."

"Are you saying this is normal?" I walked around so that I could see his face because it looked as if . . . he *was*. He was smiling. "Did I say something funny?"

He glanced up from his screen. "Oh, no, I'm sorry. It's just that you sound like all the rest when they first get here. People who come into this operation from the outside are always shocked and amazed. Don't worry, it will wear off."

"I don't want it to wear off. I'd rather fix the problems."
Jeez, was I really that pompous and self-important? "All I'm
saying is—"

"I know what you're saying. What Ellen found out and
what you will, too, is that nobody wants this place fixed or
else it would have been done a long time ago. The game is
rigged."

"I don't believe that."

"You will."

"Maybe it was true during the Nor'easter years, but the
merger makes it a new game with new rules."

"That's what Ellen thought, too," he said.

"Maybe Ellen Shepard wasn't the right person for the job.
The field is a whole different story than staff, and she had no
operating experience. Everyone in the field wondered how she
even got this job. And we all resented her for getting it, at least
until she killed herself."

"It would be nice to think that, wouldn't it? That she
succumbed to the pressures of the job?"

"I've heard that the pressures were pretty intense."

"No doubt about that. I came to work one day and the
freight house was on fire. A week later, all of the computer
monitors in the supply room were smashed to smithereens.
One night a full twenty-five percent of the entire midnight shift
called in sick. And you couldn't keep track of all the stuff that
was stolen off this field. Worse than that, she was getting phone
calls at home, threats and warnings of a personal nature." He
shook his head. "Terrible stuff. Very sad if you liked the woman,
which I did." The phone rang and he paused before picking it
up. "Ellen Shepard wasn't under pressure, she was under siege."

I'd stared out the window long enough, so this time I

checked out the bulletin board. Most of what was up there was old enough to have turned yellow and curled at the edges. Kevin finished his call.

"All this harassment," I said, "was because she was trying to change around a few shifts and cut overtime?"

"Ellen Shepard is not dead because she tried to cut overtime, and it's not because of any personal problems she may have been having. That's just the convenient party line. Her problems were all right down here on the ramp. One of them in particular just got the better of her that night, that's all."

"Which one?"

"Can't say."

"Why not?"

"I keep my beliefs to myself," he said. "That's the secret to my longevity."

"Don't tell me you're one of the conspiracy theorists."

His expression didn't change.

"That is an absurd rumor," I said, with a little more passion than necessary. "The police ruled Ellen's death a suicide. And besides, if Ellen was murdered by one of her employees, what possible motive would the company have to cover it up?"

"I've been at Logan a long time," he said, "long enough to know that every rumor has some seed of truth, no matter how small."

There was just enough calm rationalism in his tone to unnerve me. If I believed he knew how to optimize gates and which aircraft to dispatch and when, why wouldn't I believe him about this? "You're really starting to disturb me, Kevin."

"You should be disturbed." He stood up, walked over to the closed door, and mashed his cheek against the glass window, peering first to the left and then to the right. He came back

Lynne Heitman

to me and whispered in a tone that was urgent and serious. "This is not a safe place, especially for a woman, and if no one told you that, they should have." The twinkle had gone out of his eye. "Don't try to take on the union. Don't try to be a hero, and don't expect to make your career in this place. Just put in your time and get out in one piece. That's the best advice I can give you."

Then he turned around and went back to work as if the conversation had never happened.

I went to the window and watched the rampers working their flight. The sky, still clear, was already darkening in the early winter afternoon. I saw more winter gear on the ramp. Heavier coats. Gloves. It was getting colder, and I wrapped my arms tightly around me to keep from shivering. Low clouds were gathering in the western sky and I wondered, if I were outside, could I smell snow coming?

Chapter Five

Dan was already working when I arrived the next morning. I stood in the back of the ticketing lobby and watched through the crowd of passengers as he checked bags and issued boarding passes. He was doing it just right, moving them through like cattle at auction, but somehow making each cow feel special, as if they were the only one in the chute.

When I moved behind the counter, I spotted Dan's briefcase on the floor along with a pile that turned out to be his overcoat and suit jacket. He hadn't made it to his office yet.

"Anything I can do to help here?" I asked.

"I think we've got it covered," he said, poking at his keyboard with two fingers.

"I'm on my way to the office. Do you want me to take your coat and jacket?"

"They've been in worse places." He beckoned to the woman who was next in line.

"Okay." All I could do was try. "When you're finished here, I'd like to talk to you about a few things. How much longer do you think you'll be?"

He stepped up into the bag well and gauged the length of his line. "Fifteen minutes."

I checked his line, too, and it looked like a good thirty minutes to me. "When you're finished, meet me down on the concourse for coffee," I said. "I'll buy."

Dan greeted his next passenger while I walked down the length of the counter, greeting the morning shift as I went, trying to tie names to faces and get to know my new employees.

Forty-five minutes later, Dan was sitting across the table from me at the Dunkin' Donuts, turning a black cup of coffee blond with five packets of sugar and two plastic tubs of cream.

"You should take up smoking," I said. "It would be better for you."

"We're all going to die sometime." As he took a sip, his eyes scanned the concourse like radar for any problem that might need his immediate attention. His plan seemed to be to give everyone and everything except me his close attention.

"I want to know what's going on around here."

"Say again?"

"I think you heard me."

"I heard you, but I have no idea what you're referring to."

"You do know, and this thing you're doing right now, this deflecting, it's annoying as hell. It'd be easier if you would just answer the question."

He chewed on the plastic stirrer and, in his own good time, turned slightly in his chair, enough that I could claim a small measure of progress.

"I spent time yesterday talking to some of my new employees," I said, leaning closer so that I wouldn't have to raise my voice. "Half of them believe that Ellen Shepard was murdered by someone who works downstairs on the ramp. Almost all of them think that you've gone off the deep end since her suicide."

"What's that supposed to mean?"

"That you're out of touch, disappearing, not answering your beeper. They can't find you when they need you. Last night's a good example."

He started to get agitated, but then clamped down as if he didn't want me to see his reaction. As far as I could tell, he didn't want me to know anything about him. "People are going to think what they're going to think," he said coolly, "and no one needs to worry about me."

"All right. Let's not worry about you. Let's talk about the operation. This whole place is paralyzed by rumors about Ellen Shepard, and almost no one believes she killed herself."

His eyes narrowed. "And why do you think that is?"

"Because no one is talking to them. No one is giving them the facts and answering their questions. In the absence of the truth, they're going to think the worst."

"And you know what the truth is?"

"I know the police investigated, ruled the death a suicide, and closed their investigation. I know she was found hanging in her home, and I know that you're the one who found her after she'd been there all night. I also know that she was your friend."

He was angled back, still chewing on the stirrer. He was wearing an enigmatic little smile and shaking his head, the message being that I would never get it.

"If there's more to it, why don't you tell me?"

"You want to know the rest of it?" The smile faded. "Ellen died a week ago. Since then not one representative of Majestic Airlines outside of this station has done a single thing to pay their respects. No flowers, no phone calls, no letters or cards. Not from Lenny or goddamned Bill Scanlon. Just a whole bunch of cover-their-ass questions." He almost knocked over his coffee and made a great save before slumping back in his chair. "The first thing we heard from outside the station was you showing up from headquarters to take her place."

"I'm not from headquarters. I've spent eighteen months there out of fourteen years. I've got as much field experience as you do."

"Whatever."

"Is that what's going on here? Do you resent me because you think you should have gotten this job?"

"I wouldn't take the job if they begged me."

"Is it because I came from staff?" That was my last guess. I wasn't going to play twenty questions trying to figure out what his problem was.

"All I know is you're on the fast track," he said, "and I'm going to be in Boston forever. So it doesn't matter to me. You understand?"

"No."

"You can take all the credit when things go well, you can blame me when they go wrong. I don't care about my career. I don't care about getting promoted. What I do care about is being left alone to do my job the way I need to. Just because I'm not out where people can see me all the time doesn't mean I'm not doing my job. And the next time you want to know something about me, ask me and not my employees."

Dan's name boomed from the loudspeakers. Before they could even finish paging him, he was on his feet gathering up all the dead sugar packets and heading for the trash.

"Dan, if you walk away from me like you did yesterday, it's

going to make me angry, which might not make any difference to you, but it will ruin my entire day because I'm going to have to spend it trying to figure out how to deal with you." He stood with the trash in one hand, his cup in the other, staring down the concourse toward the gates. "I don't want to *deal* with you." I said, backing off a little, "I want to *work* with you."

He tapped his chair a few times with his free hand. He didn't sit down, but neither did he walk away.

"Losing a friend in the way that you did has got to be tough. If there is anything I can do to make it easier for you, I will do it."

"I'll deal with it."

"Fine. While you're dealing with it, think about this. Do you want to work with me? If you don't, we'll discuss alternatives."

His hand grew still on the back of the chair. "I'm not leaving here."

"That's not what I asked you to think about. Do you want to work next to me? That's the question and I want a definitive answer."

"I'm not leaving Boston," he said flatly, then stalked over to toss his garbage. He came back and said it again, just in case it wasn't clear. "There's no way I'm leaving Boston. And if you and this fucking company try to get rid of me the way you did Ellen, I'm going to blow the whistle on what's going on around here, so help me God."

He turned quickly and he was gone. He must have spotted the confused elderly woman as we were talking because he went straight for her. He read her boarding pass, offered his arm, and helped her to her gate. Then without looking back, he melted into the river of passengers, gliding smoothly through the crowd, weaving in and out until I couldn't see him anymore.

He'd disappeared on me again, leaving me to sort through a whole bunch of responses I never had a chance to give, and one big question. What exactly *was* going on around here?

Chapter Six

Molly was long gone by the time I made it back to my office, and Dan had been cagey enough to get through the rest of the day yesterday and all day today without bumping into me once. There had been Dan-sightings all over the airport, but I never managed to catch up with him. I sat down at my desk to try to find the bottom of my in-box.

I dispensed with the mail from headquarters—the usual warnings, threats, and recriminations disguised as reports, memos, and statistics—putting it aside to ignore later. I reviewed the station performance report from Dan, which said we were over budget and underperforming. No kidding. And I drafted a perfunctory response to a perfunctory question from Lenny asking why that was. Most of what was left was from the suspense file, things that Ellen Shepard had reviewed and filed for later handling. Many of the documents had her handwritten notes in the margins. Her handwriting was careful, neat, and very controlled. You could have used it to teach cursive writing to schoolchildren. Halfway through the stack, I began

to get a sense of her, to hear her voice. She spoke a language
we shared, the language of work.

You could tell by her questions that she was new to an
operation. She had lots of them—questions about the equipment, manning, about why we do things the way we do, about
people who worked for her and how much things cost and why.
Her inexperience showed, but so did her doggedness. When
she hadn't gotten a thorough answer, she'd simply asked again.
And judging from her correspondence with the union, she didn't
back down. She may have been a staff person and she may
have taken a good field assignment away from someone more
qualified—say, for instance, me. But I had to admit that she
had worked hard. She had tried.

When I finally hit the bottom of the stack, I had one item
left that I didn't know what to do with. It was an invoice from
a company called Crescent Security. It had no notes, no questions, nothing to indicate why it was there and what I should
do with it. So I did what I usually did in those situations—
suspense it for a few days and deal with it later. With that taken
care of, I sat back in my chair and stared straight ahead. It had
already been dark for several hours, and the windows had
turned into imperfect mirrors, reflecting back to me a picture
of institutional emptiness—and there I was in the middle of it.
As I sat and stared at my reflection, which was particularly
chalky in the hard-edged, artificial glare of the fluorescent
lights, I wondered, vaguely, what other people like me were
doing tonight. I wondered if Ellen had ever looked at herself
like this and wondered the same thing.

It occurred to me that if I couldn't see out because of the
light, then anyone on the ramp could look up and see in. From
down there my office must have looked like a display case in

the Museum of Natural History. I went over to close the blinds and took a quick peek outside. I was relieved to see the operation humming along. Tugs were rumbling back and forth, tractors were pushing airplanes off the gates, and crews were loading boxes and bags and trays of mail into the bellies of large aircraft. A line of snow showers had passed us by to the south, bringing in its wake slightly warmer air that hung in a dense, wet fog that diffused the light on the ground and softened the scene. If Monet had painted our ramp, it would have looked like this.

It was time to go home—or at least back to my hotel. I did a quick search of the desk, thinking maybe I would find the file on Angelo DiBiasi so I could keep my promise to Lenny. I hadn't had a chance to ask Disappearing Dan about the case, and at the rate I was going, it would be another week before I was ready to make a decision. I found a drawer filled with hanging files, each with a color-coded tab labeled in Ellen's handwriting. I riffled through the neat rows and found nothing on Angelo. I tried the middle drawer. Nothing there except company phone books, a bound copy of the union contract, a few office supplies, and a pocket version of the OAG. The Official Airline Guide was a typical airline employee accouterment, a schedule for all airlines to all cities. Ellen's was more current than mine, so I threw mine out and tossed hers into my briefcase. When I did, something slipped out from between the pulpy pages. It was a United Airlines frequent flier card—and it was issued in Ellen's name.

What was she doing with this? Only real passengers had these. The only point in having one was to earn free air travel, and we already had that. And to earn miles you had to, God forbid, pay for your ticket. Airline employees would do almost

anything before they did that. I thumbed through the guide
to see if Ellen had been gracious enough to highlight a
destination or turn any corners down. I should have known
better. I was willing to bet that Ellen had been a bookmark
kind of a girl—no turned-down pages allowed. The guide had
neither, but on the back of the card was the phone number
for customer services. If United was like our airline, I could
call their electronic system and get the last five segments she'd
flown, a very helpful feature if you've forgotten where you've
been.

I dialed the number and connected. The electronic gate-
keeper asked for the account number, which I punched in
straight from the card. The second request was a stumper. I
needed Ellen's zip code. The airport zip code didn't work,
which meant she must have used her home address on the
account.

I hung up and went to look for it in Molly's Rolodex. I
hadn't realized how quiet it was in the office until the phone
rang in the deep silence and nearly launched me out of my
shoes. As I answered the phone, I felt guilty, as if I'd tripped
an alarm with my snooping. "Majestic Airlines."

"The Marblehead police are trying to get in touch with you."
It was Kevin on the other end and he didn't bother to say hello.

"Why?"

"They're holding Danny."

"For what?"

"I'm not sure, but they want you to go and pick him up. Do
you want the cop's name and number?"

I took down the information as well as directions on how
to get to Marblehead. It was about thirty-five minutes up the
coast from the airport.

"I've got another call," he said. "Do you need anything else?"

"No. *Wait* . . . What's in Marblehead?"

"Ellen Shepard's house."

The buzzer was loud in the quiet lobby. When it stopped, the door to the back offices opened, and Detective Pohan leaned out to greet me, keeping one foot back to prop open the door. He was in his late forties with a slight build, baleful brown eyes, and a droopy mustache that was as thick as the hair on his head was thin. "You got here quick. I appreciate that. You want to come on back?"

I followed him down a long, narrow aisle that ran between a row of offices to the right and a cluster of odd-sized cubicles to the left. I noticed there wasn't a whole lot of activity. Maybe the Marblehead detective squad didn't have much call for a night shift.

The last office in the row was a conference room. The door was closed, but I could see Dan through the window, sitting alone at a table. All eight fingers and both thumbs were drumming the tabletop. I couldn't see it, but I would have bet that his knees were bouncing like a couple of pistons.

Pohan reached for a file from his desk. "Ellen Shepard's landlord says Majestic Airlines is handling the affairs of the deceased."

"We are?"

"We've been instructed to call this fellow in Washington if we have any problems." He held the file open, inviting me to read the name he was pointing out. "Here, I don't have my glasses on. What is that? Castle? Castner?"

"Caseaux," I said, emphasizing the last syllable the way

Lenny did. "Leonard Caseaux. I work for him."

Pohan nodded in Dan's direction. "This one asked us to call you first."

"He did?" I checked again to see if this was the right guy. What was bad enough that Dan had felt a need to call me, of all people? "Why is he here, Detective?"

"He was caught breaking into Ellen Shepard's house."

"Breaking in?"

"It's the second time. The first time the landlord saw him trying to climb through a window. This time he got all the way through, but he set off the burglar alarm."

I looked at Dan through the window. He'd grown still and was staring down at the table like a wind-up toy that had wound down. He looked sad. "Do you mind if I talk to him?"

"Go ahead. He's not in custody or anything."

Pohan opened the door and followed me through. Dan popped up immediately and stood with his hands in his pockets. "I'm sorry about this," he said, trying to look at me as he spoke, but mostly maintaining eye contact with the floor. His cockiness was all gone. It was hard to be angry with him when he looked like a guilty puppy about to be smacked with a rolled-up newspaper.

"Why were you crawling through Ellen's window?"

"To get into the house."

"For what possible reason?"

His eyes cut over to Pohan. From the way they looked at each other, I knew Dan and the detective had covered this ground before. Pohan checked his watch, dropped the file on the table, and sighed deeply. "Why don't we sit down?"

When we were all settled, Pohan took charge. Nodding in Dan's direction, he said, "You can ask him, but my guess is he's looking for whatever we missed that will prove that Ellen Shephard was murdered."

The hair on the back of my neck stood up. Rumors were one thing, but hearing the word "murdered" uttered by an official detective in these official circumstances gave it more weight than I would have liked. "Is there reason to believe she was?"

"None."

I turned to Dan. "What makes you believe Ellen was murdered?"

"Because I know she didn't kill herself."

Pohan leaned forward, elbows on the table, hands clasped together. "Mr. Fallacaro, I know Miss Shepard was a friend of yours, and I know you think we didn't do all we could, but we can't change the facts of this case."

I could almost see Dan's blood pressure rising, so I went for a diversion. "For my benefit, Detective, could you outline the facts of the case?"

Pohan leaned back in his chair and reached up to stroke his mustache in what seemed to be an old habit. He let his attention linger on Dan for another moment, then opened the file.

"There was no evidence of forced entry. According to you, Mr. Fallacaro, the dead bolt was locked when you got there. You used the landlord's key to get in."

He paused for confirmation, got none.

"All windows and doors were secured. No evidence of a struggle. According to the autopsy, the only signs of trauma were in the neck area around the rope. No blows to the head. Landlord identified the rope. Said it had been in the attic of the house for several years, so no one brought it in with them.

She was on prescribed medication for chronic depression—"

"She was taking antidepressants?" I asked.

"Yes."

I looked at Dan, but it was impossible to tell if he had known that already. If he hadn't, he was hiding it well.

"We found an empty bottle of wine in the house. From her blood alcohol, it looks like she drank the whole thing herself that night. Drugs, alcohol, depression . . ." His voice trailed off as he closed the file and spread his hands over it. "This thing was ruled a suicide from the get-go, and we have found nothing to indicate that she was murdered."

Dan's chair squealed lightly as he sat back from the table. "She never would have killed herself," he said, "but if she did, she would have left a note."

"That's not always the case. You might be surprised to know that most suicide victims don't leave notes."

Pohan's patience impressed me. Dealing with angry and grieving survivors must be part of his job, the same as dealing with irate passengers was part of mine. I'd rather have mine.

Dan was shaking his head, looking as if he'd never, ever be convinced. Pohan was the more rational of the two men, but Dan was the one I had to work with.

"Detective, I didn't know Ellen, but from what I've seen, she was meticulous. If she took the time and effort to hang herself, which is not an impulsive act, wouldn't you think she would have included a note in her planning?"

He leaned back in his chair. "She was thirty-five years old and unmarried. She had no family. By all accounts, she wasn't seeing anyone. Who would she leave a note for?"

Dan's response was volcanic. "She had friends. People cared about her."

Pohan raised his hands as if to still the waters. "I'm sure she did. It's clear that you cared about her. All I'm saying is maybe she didn't know that. Maybe that's all part of the explanation for why she did it."

It was hard to argue a point like that. I watched Dan as he rocked back and forth in his squeaky chair. Pohan watched us both. "This isn't the cleanest way to close this thing out," he said. "Lots of unanswered questions, I know, but that's what happens in suicides. Unfortunately, I've seen it over and over. I'm sorry."

No one said anything and Pohan discreetly checked his watch, probably thinking there wasn't much else to say. When we didn't make any move to leave, he smiled sheepishly. "Listen, I'd offer you some coffee or something, but I've got to pick up my kid. Hockey practice."

"Of course," I said. Then I looked at Dan, slouched down in his chair, defeated. "Detective, I know you have instructions to call Mr. Caseaux, but do you think this time you'd be comfortable letting me handle things?"

His face scrunched up under the big mustache, and I knew I was asking him to do something he didn't want to do. "I said I'd call you first, but I never said I wouldn't call Caseaux. We have pretty specific instructions."

"I know you do. How about if I promise this won't happen again? I'll give you my personal guarantee."

I don't know if it was my sincere request or the fact that he was late for hockey practice, but he agreed.

"Thank you," I said. "Just one more thing. Is Ellen's house still considered a crime scene? Is that part of the problem with Dan being there?"

"No. We've finished our investigation, but Mr. Fallacaro has no authorization to be in the house, and if he doesn't stay out, he's going to get shot. The landlord lives across the street, and the old guy watches his property like a hawk. He usually takes his shotgun when he goes over to check on the place."

"All right."

When I stood up, they did, too. Dan was out the door in a flash. Pohan paused to give me a business card.

"Detective, thanks so much for your help. I—we really . . ."

When I turned to find Dan, he was already down the corridor getting himself buzzed out the door.

Pohan watched him go, shaking his head in a way that seemed almost mournful. "There's one thing you learn pretty quick in this line of work," he said. "Things aren't always as they seem. But then, sometimes they're exactly as they seem."

Chapter Seven

Even though it was almost nine o'clock at night, Sal's Diner was filled with the aroma of a greasy griddle, and I knew my nice wool coat was going to carry the scent of frying bacon right out the door with me and into next week.

Dan was hunched forward with his fingers woven around his cup, staring into his coffee. "Why'd you'd come?" he asked.

"Because of our close personal relationship."

He dipped his head even more, almost hiding the brief flush of embarrassment that colored his face. "I know, I know. I haven't been much help—"

"You've been a complete asshole."

He accepted the rebuke without comment. It felt so good, I threw in another one for good measure. "I understand that you lost a friend, and I can even understand why you might resent me, but you never even gave me a chance."

"What was I supposed to think? Here you are, this big-time fast-track superstar hand-picked by Scanlon to come in and *handle* things for the company. I figured it was your job to shut me down or report back on what I was doing."

"You thought I was brought in here by no less than the chairman of the company to keep an eye on *you*?" I wasn't mad at him anymore because he'd called me a superstar. "You must be pretty important. Either that, or I'm not."

"That's not . . . I didn't mean . . ." When he finally raised his eyes, I smiled to let him know I was teasing him. He sat back, exhaled deeply, and seemed to relax for the first time all evening. He draped his arm across the back of the booth and pulled one leg up next to him on the bench seat. The waitress took the move as a cue to come over, top off his coffee, and leave the check. When he reached over and pulled it to his side of the table, I figured we'd turned a corner.

"Why don't you just tell me what's going on with you, Dan?"

"I know what everyone thinks," he said. "I know what the police are saying, and I know you believe them. But there is no way Ellen Shepard killed herself. No fucking way. She was murdered."

His tone was even, he held steady eye contact, and he was completely calm for the first time since I'd met him. There was no question in my mind that he believed what he was saying. "Who do you think killed her?"

"Little Pete Dwyer."

"The missing crew chief from Sunday night?"

"Right."

"Why him?"

He shrugged vaguely and stared up at the ceiling. "I hear things."

"You're going to have to do better than that, Dan. Don't treat me like a fool."

He knocked back the rest of his coffee, and the knee started going again as he regarded me. I waited.

"Okay," he said finally. "I've got nothing hard. Just a lot of suspicious stuff, people talking, things Ellen was doing lately that I didn't get."

"Like what?"

"In the last few weeks before she died, she was doing a heavy duty research job on Little Pete Dwyer. She was asking a bunch of questions, reading his personnel file, looking at all his performance reviews."

"She could have been looking for a way to deal with the guy. I've done that, especially with a hard case, trying to figure out why they are the way they are."

"You don't need to do research to know why this guy's a shithead. It's because of the old man, Shithead Sr. They're two of a kind. And anyway, it doesn't explain why she had me staking him out."

"Staking him out? You mean, sitting in a car in the shadows, drinking bad coffee, and waiting for him to show up so you can, what . . . *tail* him?"

"Yeah."

I looked for the ironic smile, a sign that he was kidding, exaggerating at least. He was perfectly serious. "You guys were in your own B-movie. What did you find out?"

"We found out Angelo DiBiasi's got balls bigger than his brains. Poor bastard. Talk about being in the wrong place at the wrong time. I'm sitting in the truck down by the freight house waiting for Little Pete to show up, and Angie rolls by in a tug dragging a TV set on a dolly. I caught up with him just as he was loading it into his car."

"What happened with Little Pete?"

"Busting Angie basically blew my cover."

"And you never found out why Ellen was after him?"

He shook his head. "I assumed she got a tip from her snitch."

"Snitch?"

"She had a snitch down on the ramp, a guy who used to tip her off."

Of course she did. "Why don't you just ask the snitch what it was about?"

"I don't know who the guy is. She kept it a secret to protect him." He must have noticed a hint of skepticism in my expression. "I know this doesn't make much sense," he said, "but it will. Ellen always made sense. I just don't have all the pieces yet."

"What reason would Little Pete have to kill Ellen?"

"I think it must have been for the package."

I stared at him.

"Oh, yeah. I didn't tell you this. One night I was at the airport later than usual, and Ellen comes into her office. She picks up the phone and starts talking to someone about something that's in this package. Then my phone rings, I answer it, and that's it. She knows I'm there. She gets up and closes the door, so that's all I got."

"How could you fail to mention that little detail?"

"Because so much stuff has been happening around here that I sometimes can't keep it all straight. And you're the first person I've been able to talk to about it. I figure he killed her for the package."

"You don't know that." We were jumping to some very large conclusions here with very few facts, something that was against my religion. "What could have been in this package?"

"I don't know. Could be she found out about one of Little Pete's scams, or the old man's. She could have had enough to fire their asses."

"He would have killed her to keep his job?" I tried not to sound as alarmed as I felt, but between this discussion and the one with Kevin, I felt my management prerogatives becoming more and more limited.

"She may have uncovered something that would put them both in jail. That would be enough to send Little Pete over the edge. He's not exactly the most stable guy to begin with."

"Is that where you've been disappearing to at night? To stake out Little Pete?"

"I've been trying to keep an eye on him, but it's impossible with just me. Near as I can figure, he's been AWOL four times since she died."

"Four times in nine days. When does he work?"

"He doesn't. That's what you saw on Sunday night. But his pop always covers for him, and none of his union brothers are going to rat him out." Dan was concentrating hard on one of the sugar packets left over from his coffee. He was folding it smaller and smaller until it was the size of a toothpick. "Where do you think he goes when he disappears like that?"

"To a bar," I guessed, "or home to sleep. Maybe to a girlfriend's house."

"He comes up here to Marblehead."

"Do you know that for sure?"

"One night I followed him halfway up here, but he must have spotted me because he turned around and went to a bar in Chelsea. Then tonight I find out the old guy, the landlord, he's been complaining to the police about someone coming in and out of Ellen's house in the middle of the night."

"That would be you, wouldn't it?"

"No. The cops assumed it was me but it wasn't, because if

I could walk in the front door, why would I be climbing through the friggin' window?"

I had to think about that. Dan used a logic that was uniquely his own. "That would say that Little Pete has the security code and a key to the house. Why would that be?"

"The guy who killed her had the code—the code and the key. You heard what Pohan said. No forced entry."

I was beginning to understand his logic. It was circular. "Dan, that's not the only thing he said. What about the antidepressants and the alcohol? Did you know about any of that?"

"Yeah. No. I mean, antidepressants keep you *from* being depressed, right? *Anti*depressants. So if she was taking them, she wasn't depressed. And she wasn't a boozer. A drink of wine every now and then, but I never saw her drunk." He knew he was stretching, and he knew I knew. But he was so certain and he was trying so hard to convince me—it didn't hurt to listen and besides, I had no place else to be but my hotel room by myself.

"If he killed her," I said, "I wouldn't expect him to come back to the house, the proverbial scene of the crime."

"He's looking for the package. That's why I've been trying to get in the house, to find it."

"So your theory is that he killed her for this package, but he's still looking for it."

"Right. She probably hid it somewhere."

I thought about the splintered desk in my office. "Are you sure it's in the house?"

"Without a doubt. She never left anything important at the airport."

Thinking of the desk reminded me of Ellen's frequent flier card. "Do you know why Ellen would be flying full-fare on United?"

He shook his head. "Ellen never traveled anywhere. And even if she did, there's no way she'd pay for a ticket. Nobody in the business does that."

The card was stiff in the pocket of my skirt. I could feel it. And I could feel myself getting sucked right off that slick, vinyl banquette and into the Ellen Shepard affair. I knew if I showed that card to Dan, that was exactly what would happen. But I couldn't very well sit on it when he was struggling so hard to make sense of her death. Besides, I had to admit to at least a little curiosity. I dug it out and laid it on the table in front of him.

"What is this?" He had a hard time picking the flat card off the table. Finally, he slipped it off the edge and into the palm of his hand.

"Ellen had a frequent-flier account at United."

"That doesn't make any sense." He looked up at me. "You know what I think this is?" He put the card back on the table and then picked it right up again. "She was probably earning miles with her credit card or phone calls or some shit like that. I even saw on TV the other day where you can earn miles for buying hair plugs."

"I doubt she was doing *that*."

"What I'm saying is this by itself doesn't mean she was buying airline tickets."

"If you know Ellen's home zip code, we can figure that out right now." I reached over the table and turned the card in his hand so he was looking at the back. "There's a customer service phone number."

"I don't know what it is up here. Oh-two-something ... *wait*." He dropped the card and pulled something that looked like tissue paper from his breast pocket. "Have you got a cell phone?"

I pulled my phone from the pocket of my bacon-scented coat.

"The cops wrote me a ticket for being at the house. It's got the address and the zip. Ready?"

He read me the number and I dialed in again. When I got to the request for the zip code, I punched in the number he gave me, and I was in. Dan watched closely as I went through the menu. The first option gave me her total miles. Eighteen thousand. She had definitely used this account. I punched the selection for the last five segments traveled and signaled Dan for a pen, which he produced immediately. As the computer reeled off the destinations, I jotted the city codes down on my napkin. Dan's eyes grew wider with each one—DEN, SFO, ORD, IAD, and MIA. Next to each city code I wrote the date of travel.

As I punched off and tucked the cell phone away, he grabbed the napkin. "We have service to San Francisco and Chicago and Washington Dulles. We fly nonstop to Miami and, for God's sake, the company's headquartered in Denver. What the hell was she thinking, paying for travel?"

"Given that you never even knew she was gone, I'd say she was doing it to hide her trips. If she'd flown on Majestic, people at the station could have tracked her through the system, right? They'd have known where she was going."

"Hell, they'd know what seat she was sitting in and what drink she ordered. People in this station are worse than the CIA that way." He picked up the card again and tapped it on his index finger. "Can I keep this? I want to call my buddy over at United. He can get me all the activity on the account. Maybe we can figure out what she was doing."

The waitress came around for the third time, and for the

third time we told her we didn't need anything else. This time she loitered long enough that Dan pulled out a few bills and paid the check. I noticed he'd left her a generous tip. We in the service business appreciate each other.

Dan sat in the passenger seat as we cruised down mainstreet Marblehead in my rented Camry. Every once in a while he'd let out a big sigh and shift around, as if the seatbelt was just too constraining. We were on our way to Ellen's house, where he could pick up his car.

I tapped the steering wheel with my two gloved index fingers, trying to find the best way to ask the question. "Dan, why do you think Ellen was being so secretive?"

"What do you mean?"

What I meant and didn't know how to ask was why *she* didn't clue him in if they were such great friends. Why the secret travel? Why not include him on the snitch, or whatever was going on with Little Pete? "Don't take this the wrong way, but you seem so determined, obsessed even, with finding out what happened to her. You're obviously very loyal to her, to her memory." I was trying to watch the road and check his reaction at the same time, but he was staring out the window and I couldn't see his face. "If she was involved in something that pertained to the station and its employees, why didn't she include you more than she did?"

He continued to stare out the window, leaving me to wonder if I'd overstepped the bounds of our tenuous new friendship. I rolled up to a stop sign and sat with my foot on the brake.

"Dan?"

The bright neon tubing in the window of a corner yogurt shop cast an eerie pink glow into the car, illuminating his profile when he turned to look straight ahead. "Did you ever hear of a guy named Ron Zanetakis?"

"Ramp supervisor at Kennedy?"

"Newark. I worked for him when I was a ramper down there. When I was getting ready to leave to come up here for my first management job, he gave me this little speech, like he was my old man or something. He told me how to be a good manager."

A honk from behind reminded me that I was still standing at the stop sign. I moved ahead. "Which is how?"

"Never walk past the closed door."

"What does that mean?"

"Manager's walking through the operation and comes across a door that's supposed to be open, but it's closed. He puts his ear to the door and hears something going on in there. Nobody knows he's at the door, and the easiest thing in the world would be to walk away. But the good ones, they will always go through the door. If it's locked, they'll bust it down. They're not afraid to know what's going on. Ellen never walked past. She was never afraid here, which is why I can't believe she'd kill herself over a few threatening phone calls. And she always backed me. Maybe she didn't always tell me what she was doing, but one thing I knew is when I went through the door, she'd be right behind me. Turn here," he said, almost after it was too late, "go five streets and hang a left. Her house is down at the end on the right."

When I made the first turn, I stole a glance. Dan was staring straight ahead through the windshield, but didn't appear to be looking at anything. He didn't even seem to be in the car with me. "That meant a lot to you, Ellen backing you up?"

"It may not sound like much, but in a place like Logan, it's important. To me, anyway." His voice drifted off and he went back to whatever place he'd been in.

I began to count streets. Ellen's street was a blacktop road. The only sound in the car was the wheels popping as we rolled over random bits of gravel, and I wondered if it had sounded this way the morning he had come to find her.

A low-slung black coupe parked under a single street lamp was the only car on the dead-end street. I assumed it was Dan's and pulled in behind. The clock on the dashboard showed eleven minutes after ten. The house was up on a slope and I was too low down to see it, so I stared straight ahead, just as Dan did. But I was looking at a thick stand of great old trees, winter bare in the intermittent moonlight.

"I was thinking, Dan, if you wanted to get into the house, why wouldn't we get permission and use the front door?"

"Can't. Lenny got himself put in charge by the aunt in California, and he's keeping the place locked up tight. No one gets in unless he says so."

It was hard to tell if he was exaggerating. Dan had his own way of presenting the facts. If it was true, it seemed pretty odd to me. "He's probably trying to be nice and help her out. Maybe this aunt is old. Maybe she doesn't travel. Have you asked him? You could even offer to help."

"I'm not one of Lenny's favorite people. In fact, I'm on his permanent shit list."

I looked at him and I knew, just knew, that every question was going to raise ten more.

"It's a long story," he said, reading my mind. Then he turned in his seat to face me, and I could have sworn I saw a light-bulb over his head. "But I bet he'd let *you* in."

"Dan—"

"You could offer to help get things organized up here. He'd probably tell the landlord it's okay and—"

"*Dan.*"

"What?"

"I'm not sure how involved in this I want to get. I'm already enough of an outsider around here, and the job itself is going to be as much as I can handle. And if Lenny finds out what happened tonight, I won't be one of his favorite people either."

He slumped back in his seat, the lightbulb clearly extinguished. "What you're saying is it would be a bad career move to find out that someone in the company murdered Ellen."

"That's not what I said, and it's not fair." Although he did make a good point. Not that I had to protect my career at all costs. But I also didn't want to throw it away trying to prove that a woman was murdered by an employee of Majestic Airlines if she really did kill herself.

"You're right." He popped open the car door. "That was a cheap shot. But maybe you could just think about it." He stepped out, then leaned over and poked his head back in. "Thanks for coming up tonight. I really didn't think you'd do it."

"Call me impulsive."

"Impulsive, my ass," he laughed. "You may have surprised me, but I don't get the feeling you surprise yourself much."

I smiled because he had me and we both knew it. "I don't know why I came up. I don't know why I'm interested in this whole thing. I'm still working that out. But the thing with Lenny, I will think about it."

"See you tomorrow, boss."

After he'd turned his car around and was moving down the street toward the highway, I did a U-turn, intending to follow.

But with the car facing the opposite direction, I had a full view of Ellen's house. It was built on a rise, gray clapboard with black shutters bracketing its many windows. I wondered if Ellen's walls inside were bare. As I thought about it, I started to understand why the ones in her office might have been. Photos, posters, and paintings. Prizes, awards, and certificates. Each would have revealed a piece of her—where she'd been, who she'd loved, what she'd accomplished. Even what she'd dreamed about. I was beginning to understand what Kevin meant when he'd said there were no secrets at Logan. In such a place, it was no longer a mystery to me why Ellen Shepard would want to keep some part of herself to herself.

I took one last look, leaning into the dashboard so I could follow the line of the pitched roof all the way up to the point. My stomach did a little shimmy when I saw what was up there and realized why I recognized it. It was the rooster wind vane, the same one that was on the mystery drawing. Whoever had drawn that sickening picture had been to Ellen's house.

Chapter Eight

The last cherry tomato in my salad was rolling around in the bottom of the bowl, slick with salad dressing and eluding the dull prongs of my little plastic fork. No one was watching, so I plucked it out, dropped my head back, and plopped it into my mouth. At least I thought no one had been watching. I looked up to find my office filling up with men in deep purple Majestic ramp uniforms.

"Can I help you gentlemen?" I asked, dumping the plastic salad bowl into the garbage. It had felt like more, but it turned out to be only four guys. Even so, as I watched them mill about my office, I began to appreciate for the first time the value of having a desk the size of an aircraft carrier. It gave me the opportunity to peer steely-eyed across its vast, cherry-stained horizon at people who barged in unannounced, uninvited, and apparently unencumbered by any respect for my authority.

"We're here for the meetin'."

The man who'd spoken was fifty-ish with a pinkie ring and hair too young for his face. It was jet black and worn in a minor pompadour.

"I don't remember calling a meeting," I said, "and I don't know who you are."

"I'm president of Local 412 of the International Brotherhood of Groundworkers. This here's my Business Council, and we come for Little Pete's hearing."

The youngest of the four men was posed against the wall, staring vacantly out the window and looking like an underwear model. No one had mentioned that Little Pete was not little at all, and not just because he was well over six feet tall. He had a thickly sculpted, lovingly maintained bodybuilder's physique, which was shown to good effect by the shrink-wrap fit of his uniform shirt. He was an intimidating presence, more so when I thought about Dan's belief, Dan's *fervent* belief, that this man had killed Ellen. When he glanced over at me and we locked eyes, my mouth went dry.

The other three men were smaller, older, and resoundingly ordinary by comparison. I addressed myself to The Pompadour. "You're Victor Venora."

He neither confirmed nor denied, simply gestured to his right, "George Tutun, secretary," and to his left, "Peter Dwyer Sr. He's the vice president. Like I said, we're here for the meetin'."

I stole a quick look at the senior Dwyer, the man Dan had referred to as "Shithead Sr." Just as Little Pete wasn't little, Big Pete wasn't big. "If I'm not mistaken, Victor, Dan's the one who's chairing the hearing for Pete Jr."

"He ain't around."

I checked the clock on my desk, a more discreet gesture than looking at my wristwatch, although why I cared about being polite, I couldn't say. "Perhaps because you're three hours early. That meeting is set for four o'clock."

"This time worked out better for us."

"I see." Ambush. Instead of sending one steward with Little Pete, which would have been routine for a disciplinary discussion, all the elected officials of the Boston local of the IBG had shown up. To up the ante, one of the council members was Little Pete's father. Either they'd had success in the past with such brute-force tactics, or they took me for a spineless moron.

"Well, I'm delighted to meet you, all of you. If you'll excuse me . . ." I moved out from behind my desk, stepped between Victor and Big Pete, and poked my head out to find Molly, who was just coming back from lunch. "Molly, would you beep Dan and ask him to come to my office?"

"He's with the Port Authority," she said, peeking around me to see who was there. "You want me to interrupt?"

"Please. When he gets here, ask him to come in, but first tell him his four o'clock meeting arrived early."

"So that's what's going on," she said, shaking her headful of heavy brown curls. "Don't let them rattle you. They do this all the time." Which meant they didn't necessarily believe I was a spineless moron, but they were there to find out.

The humidity level in the small office was on the rise as I closed the door and settled back in. All the warm bodies were throwing off heat. They'd also brought with them the earthy smell of men standing around indoors while dressed to work outdoors. I didn't mind. It reminded me they were on my turf.

Victor was droning on as if we were still in mid-conversation ". . . unless you want we should wait for Danny . . ."

"Why would I want that?"

"Maybe you'd want to let him handle things from here on out."

My audience was watching, even Little Pete, waiting to see

if I would scurry to safety through the escape hatch Victor had just opened. Somewhere in the back of my brain, Kevin's warning was rattling around. "Don't take on the union," he'd said. I looked at the elected officials of the IBG standing in front of me and considered his advice. For about half a second.

"Dan will be joining us shortly, and if you'd like to wait for him, I'd certainly respect that. Otherwise, I'm ready to proceed. Pete Jr."—I gestured to the chair across the desk from me— "would you mind sitting here?" He began to stir himself as I surveyed the others. "Which one of you is his steward?"

"Big Pete." Victor apparently spoke for everyone today.

"Okay. Not to be rude, but why are the rest of you here? I only ask because I'd like to know if things work differently in Boston than everywhere else in the system."

"We just thought this being your first disciplinary hearing and all—"

"This is not my first disciplinary hearing, but if you want to stay, you're welcome."

They looked at each other, but no one left, so I began. Pete Jr. was now sitting in front of me, making his chair look small and picking at a scab on his forearm. The expression on his face was lazy and dull, and I almost wondered if there was anyone home in there.

"Where were you between five and nine p.m. on Sunday?"

"Working my shift," he mumbled.

"Why couldn't anyone raise you on the radio?"

"I don't know."

"He didn't have a radio," said Victor helpfully. "That's on account of you people not buyin' enough."

I ignored Victor and concentrated on Little Pete. He somehow managed to look hard and coddled at the same time. He wore his dark hair in what I think they call a fade—longer on top and buzzed short on the sides. Something like you might see on a quasi-skinhead. But he also had curving lips that seemed frozen into a pampered sneer. When Victor spoke for him, he'd look down and pick at the crease in his pants or the arm of the chair. But when I spoke to him, he'd look straight at me, and behind that bored, dullard expression his eyes would be on fire, as if the very sight of me set him off. There was creepiness behind those eyes, residue from some long-smoldering resentment that couldn't have anything to do with me, but felt as if it had everything to do with me. It was unsettling.

"Even without a radio," I said, "if you were working your shift, then you can explain to me what happened that night and why your crew was not around to clean the cabins."

"He don't know nothing about that," Victor said, louder this time.

"You'd have to be comatose not to have noticed those problems. Either that or absent altogether, and I'm not talking to you, Victor."

I looked up at him and knew immediately that I had made a mistake. Victor was breathing faster, his cheeks puffed out, and his voice rumbled up from someplace way down low. "We *ain't* got enough manpower. We *ain't* got enough equipment. We *can't* spend no overtime. *How do you people expect us to do our jobs?*"

Manpower shortage. Jeez. The oldest, most tired argument in the industrialized world. "First of all, stop yelling at me. Second, the afternoon shift may or may not be understaffed," I said evenly, "I don't know. It has nothing to do with the fact that Pete Jr. as crew chief did not answer his radio all night. He wasn't in his assigned work area, nor was any member of his crew." It was an attempt to bring the discussion back to where it belonged, but the guy who was supposed to be the subject of the meeting had found another blemish to inspect, this one on his elbow. I stared at him, feeling frustrated and trying not to show it.

"Petey"—the elder Dwyer smacked his son on the back of his head with his glove—"sit up, boy. Show some respect."

I was regarding Pete Sr. in a whole new light when Victor erupted again. "You got guys running *all* over the ramp *trying* to keep up. Someone's gonna get *hurt* out there, and it'll be on *management's head.*" He took a quick breath, "On top of that, you got Danny Fallacaro sneaking around all hours of the night spying on your own workers. Spying on good men trying to do an honest day's work. George, what do they call that . . . that thing they did to Angelo?"

"Entrapment."

Holy cow. George could speak after all. "What's wrong with a manager visiting one of his shifts?" I asked. "That's his prerogative."

"That's not what he's doing. He's—"

Victor stopped. Pete Sr. had laid a discreet hand on his arm. "You're absolutely correct, miss. Danny's got a right to go anywhere in the operation at any time. Just as you would. The thing is," he paused for a pained smile, "an unexpected visit kinda sets the guys off. Makes everybody nervous. Makes 'em feel like they're doing something wrong even when they're not."

"That ain't the thing, Pete."

"Shut up, Victor." Big Pete's voice was low and calm and raspy, and it cut through Victor's blustering like a scythe through tall grass. "Do you mind if I sit?" he asked me, making it clear that the real meeting was about to begin.

"Not at all."

Without having to be told, Little Pete sprang up like a jack-in-the-box, leaving the chair vacant for his father. I was now staring across the desk at Big Pete. He had his son's square face and hair the color of my mother's silver when it hadn't been polished for a while. Between gray and brown, the color of tarnish, and it looked as if he cut it himself. Maybe without a mirror. His skin was weathered but reasonably unlined for a man who had spent much of his life on the ramp. Being out in the elements worked on people differently. Usually it aged them, but with this man it seemed to have worked in the opposite way, wearing away all but the hardest bedrock of bone, muscle, and gristle.

"The problem I see," he began, "is the men are starting to feel nervous. And when the men get nervous, there's no telling what they'll do. The whole situation becomes"—he tilted his head one way, then the other as if the right word would shake out—"unpredictable."

There were lots of people in the office, but Pete's manner, his tone of voice, the way he looked at me, excluded everyone but the two of us.

"Unpredictable?"

"Look at it this way." He tapped my desk lightly with his index finger. "Boston's a high-profile city, high visibility—especially after what's just happened. You got a lot of people watching you. What I'm sayin', if things go good, all credit to you. If things go wrong, well . . ." He sat back, resting his hands lightly on the arms of the chair. "There's been some sat in your chair who didn't deal so good with that kind of pressure. But then, they didn't have your experience, neither."

Pete Sr.'s eyes were an interesting shade of gray, an anti-color. They were cunning and observant and, I was sure, conveying a message only I was meant to receive. Little Pete was all heat, but I understood now that I had far more to worry about from his father, who was ice cold. And at that moment, delivering a big fat threat.

"It's like this thing with Angelo," he said. "You know about Angelo, right?"

"I know what I need to know about Angelo."

"The thing of it is, Angie's got forty-two years in—"

"Forty-one."

He smiled graciously. "I stand corrected, but can you imagine that? One night he's working his shift, doing his job, and he gets scooped up in some kind of a sting operation and fired over what amounts to some misunderstanding."

"Which part was the misunderstanding? The part where he took a TV out of the freight house or the part where he was loading it into his car?"

Pete was unfazed. "If he's left alone, you don't know but that misunderstanding coulda been cleared up to everyone's satisfaction without no one losing his job. That's what the union's for. But that's not my point. What the men out there are thinking is what kind of a place we got here when management sneaks around in the middle of the night laying traps for us? I don't think that's how you want to handle things."

"How would I want to handle things?"

"First off, we can forget about this manpower problem for now. We'll work with what we got. Then maybe, as a goodwill gesture to the men on the ramp, you could see your way clear to bringin' Angie back to finish out his forty-second—excuse me, forty-first year. And one more thing . . . Danny Fallacaro starts going home to bed at night."

I leaned back in my chair and tried to figure out how that deal was good for me. Then I tried to figure out how we'd arrived at the point of talking about a deal for Angelo instead of reviewing Little Pete's lousy performance. It had happened when Big Pete had taken over the negotiation, and when had this become a negotiation, anyway? I scanned their faces. They were all watching me, but Big Pete was the only one who gave me the feeling he could read my thoughts.

"Let me see if I can understand what's going on here," I said. "You show up in my office uninvited at a time when you know Dan is somewhere else." I nodded toward Victor. "Bad Cop here sets the table by making a demand for additional manning, something you know you're not going to get. Then you, Good Cop, graciously withdraw the request if I agree, as a 'goodwill gesture,' to bring back Angelo the thief, and by the way, keep Dan off the midnight shift. And nowhere in there is any acknowledgement of the fact that Pete Jr. spent most of his shift Sunday night somewhere else besides the airport."

He smiled, letting me know that I had nailed the situation, and he didn't much care.

"The problem I'm having is, I don't see your leverage," I said, "unless you're implying that a certain element of disruption will occur in the operation if you don't get what you want."

By the time I was finished, the room had fallen completely silent. No coughing or shuffling or sniffing. I could smell the pungent vinegar dressing floating up from the salad plate in the bottom of the garbage. Big Pete was squinting out the window. "I didn't say nothing like that."

"Good, because I'm not prepared to simply bring Angelo DiBiasi back on payroll because you threatened me." Given what had just transpired, I was inclined to never bring him back, no matter what Lenny wanted.

Big Pete was wistful. "If that's what you gotta do . . ."

"As for Dan, I've been here three days, he's been here three years. You can see how it would be difficult for me to question his judgment. That being said, there is something I want."

Big Pete turned away from the window suddenly very interested.

"I want the jokes about Ellen Shepard's death to stop. I want every cartoon, every drawing, and every sick reference to disappear from the field. Forever. If that could happen, then maybe Dan and I would both sleep better at night."

"And he'd be sleeping at home?"

"Yes."

"That can be arranged. But I really think you should reconsider on Angelo. It would mean a lot to me personally."

"And I think you should consider that leaving the field in the middle of a shift is as much grounds for termination as stealing a television." I glanced over at Little Pete, who was studying his thumbnail, and I was almost relieved when he didn't look up. I turned back to his father. "Let's call that friendly reminder my goodwill gesture."

Big Pete heaved a great, doleful sigh. When he stood, I noticed he was less than six feet tall, much less physically imposing than his son, but still a man who commanded all the attention in the room when he wanted to. When he started to move, so did everyone else. Before he walked out, he leaned across my desk, offering one hand and putting the other palm down on the glass. It made me think of the palm print I'd seen there on my first day. When I took his hand, it felt cold. "Welcome to Boston, miss. Working with you is going to be a real pleasure."

After they'd left, I stood for a long time with my arms wrapped around me. I couldn't tell which had given me the chill, Big Pete's cold hand or his gray eyes, which seemed even colder. I looked down at the palm print he'd left on my desk. Then I leaned over and, using the sleeve of my blouse, wiped every last trace of it away.

Chapter Nine

"I can't believe the balls on those scumbags, showing up like that." Dan slid down into the chair where first Little and then Big Pete had sat earlier in the day and started drumming the armrests with his fingertips. He'd called in just as the hearing had broken up. Once he'd heard that he'd missed all the fun, he'd spent most of the afternoon in the operation. "What else did they want?"

"Two things. For me to bring Angelo back and for you to stop your nightly surveillance."

"What did you tell them?"

"That I wouldn't bring Angelo back—not yet, anyway—and that you would stick to the day shift from now on."

"Why'd you make that deal?"

"Because I wanted to show the union I'd work with them, which I'm willing to do up to a point. Besides, I don't think we gave up much. It's dangerous for you to be lurking around the airport in the middle of the night, and you weren't finding anything anyway."

He was wounded—his finger tapping ceased—but it passed

quickly. He started again almost immediately.

"Why is everyone so hot for me to bring Angelo back? He seems pretty small-time to me."

"Who's everyone?"

"Lenny wants me to deal him back. Now these guys are trying to turn the screws. The more people try to make me do it, the less I want to, and I don't even know the guy."

"Lenny's just a lazy bastard trying to make nice with his buddies in the union. Big Pete's trying to show you and everyone else that he's in charge. As far as anybody else, Angie's been around forever. Everybody knows him and his wife, knows she's been real sick. He's got these baby grandsons. They're twins and they're so cute, these kids. A lot of us went to their christening last year."

"You sound sympathetic."

He shifted his weight and started bouncing one knee in rhythm with the tapping. "I got no problem with what happened to Angelo. To me, stealing is stealing. By the same token, the thing you've got to understand is the guy's been doing it for years, ever since he's been on midnights, anyway. Dickie Flynn and Lenny before him, they knew what he was up to, but they couldn't be bothered."

The sharp vinegar flavor from the garbage still hung in the air. I joined Dan on the other side of the desk, taking the second guest chair and getting some distance from the smell. "Dickie Flynn was the guy Ellen replaced?"

"Yeah. He was the last Nor'easter GM."

"Did you work for him?"

"He had my job when I first got here from Newark, and I worked for him as a ramp supervisor. Dickie worked for Lenny, who was still the GM. Once the Majestic deal closed, Lenny moved up to vice president and down to D.C. Dickie and I both got bumped up."

"What was he like?"

"Dickie? A walking disaster. The guy was in the bag ninety-eight percent of the time. It's a miracle the place was still standing after he left."

"And Lenny put up with that?"

"Molly and I covered for him. She ran the admin stuff and I ran the operation. Besides, Lenny never saw the worst of it. It wasn't until after he left for D.C. that the hard boozing started."

"He had to have known."

Dan shrugged. "I never try to figure out what Lenny knows."

"What happened to Dickie?"

"His wife left him, took the kids, he lost all his money. Same things that happen to a lot of people in life, only he couldn't handle it. Started hitting the bottle."

"No, I meant why did he leave the company."

"Poor bastard got stomach cancer and died about six months ago."

"That's sad."

"A goddamned waste is what it was. I never met a better operations man than Dickie Flynn when he was sober. What I know about the operations function I learned from Dickie."

"Was he as good as Kevin?"

"Better. Dickie started out as an operations agent, then he went to the ramp and then freight. I think he also did a stint on the passenger side." He shook his head. "What a waste. The guy was a mess right up until the day he died."

"What about Lenny? Did you ever work for him?"

"Not directly."

"Why did you say the other night that he doesn't like you?"

"Because he doesn't. What do you want to do about Angelo?"

I laughed. "If you don't want to tell me, why don't you just say so?"

"It's not that. It's a long and boring story and not all that important and I'm tired."

"All right, let's talk about Angelo. He's sixty-three years old with a sick wife and forty-one years of service to the company. With a story like that, no arbitration panel is going to let a termination stand. Lenny wants me to bring him back, so I should do it before the panel does it and takes the credit. I score points with my boss and the union."

"You're probably right."

"Then why don't I want to do it?"

"Because you're stubborn."

"Are you sure he's harmless?" I asked.

"He's harmless."

"And you don't have a problem with it?"

"Not me, boss."

"All right."

"So you want me to bring him back?"

"All right means I'll think about it some more."

Dan laughed at me, then segued into a big yawn, which made me yawn and reminded me of just how long this day had been. I stood up to stretch. "Let me ask you something else. If Ellen did find something out about Little Pete, does it stand to reason Big Pete would be involved?"

"Little Pete wouldn't know what shirt to put on in the morning if it wasn't for his old man."

"That's what I thought. I was speculating on how things

might be different around here if we could blow both Petes out the door. Victor is incredibly annoying, but I'd still prefer dealing with him over Big Pete. And I can't think of one good reason to have Little Pete around. He's scary."

"I told you."

I went over to the window and shifted the angle of the blinds so that it would be harder to see inside the office, if anyone had been so inclined. It was already dark again. I hadn't left the airport once in daylight. Come to think of it, it was dark in the morning when I came in. I was beginning to feel like a vampire. "Do you have any idea what Ellen may have had on father and son?"

"Drugs."

"Really?"

"I was thinking last night after I got home how out of the blue one day, for no reason, she starts asking me a bunch of questions about the Beeches."

"The Beechcraft? The commuter?"

"Yeah. Those little mosquitoes we fly down to D.C. three times a day. Our last flight of the day connects to the Caribbean."

"Southbound is the wrong way for drug trafficking."

"It connects on the inbound, too. Her questions were all about the cargo compartments, capacity, loading procedures. I think she was trying to figure out how much extra weight they could take. Maybe where you could hide a package. She also asked me for a copy of the operating procedures for the ramp."

"Wait a second . . ." I went to the overhead cabinet of my credenza and opened it. "She had her own procedures manual. It's right here. Why would she want yours?"

Dan came around the desk and pointed at the logo emblazoned across the manual. "Those are Majestic's procedures."

"Not surprising, considering we are Majestic Airlines."

"We weren't always, not here in Boston, anyway. She wanted
my old Nor'easter manual. I gave it to her and now it's gone."

"That's very odd." I slid the manual back onto the shelf.
"You haven't been Nor'easter for over two years."

He went back to his seat while I turned around, opened the
file drawer in my desk, and thumbed through the plastic tabs.
"Something was in here the other night having to do with
Nor'easter . . . here it is." When I reached down and pulled it
up, all I had was an empty hanging file with a label. The
Nor'easter/Majestic Merger file was missing. It was the only
one that was. I showed Dan the empty file.

"Could mean nothing," I said.

"Nothing around here means nothing."

I left the file on my desk as a reminder to ask Molly about
it. "I don't know about the merger or the Beechcraft or the
procedures manual. What I do know is that you could go to
jail for running drugs, to say nothing of losing your job."

I smiled at Dan and he smiled back. "I like the way you
think, Shanahan."

"Are you free tomorrow night?"

"Friday night? Are you asking me out on a date, boss?"

"I got a call this afternoon from Human Resources in
Denver. Ellen's Aunt Jo in California was named as beneficiary
in Ellen's life insurance policy, and they were missing some
information. Lenny wasn't around, so they called me and I in
turn offered to contact Aunt Jo for them. Jo Shepard is her
name. She's the older sister of Ellen's late father. Did you ever
talk to her?"

"No."

"How did you know where to send the ashes?"

"Lenny left me a message. He's been dealing with her from the start."

"Yeah, from what I gather, Aunt Jo is older and doesn't travel much. When Lenny called to inform her about Ellen, he offered the company's assistance in handling her affairs. Selling her car, getting rid of the furniture, paying final bills. She took him up on his offer, had a power of attorney prepared and sent to him."

He slumped back in his chair and groaned. "We'll never get into that house."

"Not so. She's overnighting a copy to me. It should be here tomorrow."

The spark came back into his eyes. You could even have called it a gleam. "Are you shitting me?"

"I explained to her who I was. I told her who you were and that we were here in Boston and we wanted to help, too. I figured it was worth a shot. She was more than happy to have all the help she could get, and since the power of attorney designates 'authorized representatives of Majestic Airlines' as her proxy, it will work for us, too."

Dan was shaking his head, taking it all in. "Jesus Christ, Shanahan, I can't believe you did that. You're all right, I don't care what anyone says."

"I hope Lenny feels the same way when he finds out."

"Who cares what Lenny thinks? Better to ask forgiveness than permission. That's what I always say."

"I care what Lenny thinks, and look how well it's worked for you."

He bounced out of the chair and headed for the door,

looking as if he had things to do and places to go.

"I've already talked to Pohan," I said, calling after him. He stopped just outside the door. "You call the landlord. We'll need to get a key. And see if he knows how to change the code on the burglar alarm. If he doesn't, call the security company. If you can get that done tomorrow, we can go tomorrow night—that is, if you're free."

I could have seen his ear-to-ear grin in the dark. "I'll clear my calendar."

Chapter Ten

The sound of the car doors slamming cracked so sharply in the sleepy neighborhood, I halfway expected the neighbors to come out on their porches to see about the disturbance. While Dan went to get the key from the landlord, I stood by his car and stared up at the house. No one had closed the curtains in Ellen's house or drawn the blinds, leaving the windows black, unblinking, the interior exposed to anyone who dared to approach. I had agreed to this search—I had made this search possible—but now that I was here, it seemed like a better idea in concept than in practice.

Dan arrived and handed me the key. There was no ring, no rabbit's foot, nothing but a slim, bright sliver that disappeared into the palm of my gloved hand.

"Let's go, boss. I'm freezin' my ass off out here."

"Aren't you . . ." I couldn't find the right word because I knew he wasn't afraid. A feeble gust of wind came up, sending long-dead leaves scuttling over the blacktop. "Aren't you even a little uneasy about going in there?"

"No. Why?"

I looked up again at the forbidding structure. "I don't know. I just think—"

"Shanahan, you're thinking too much. Follow me." And he was off. When I caught up, he was waiting for me on the porch. While he held open the aluminum screen door, I used the light from the street to find the dead bolt. It was dim, but I could still see that the cylinder was as shiny as a new quarter.

"New locks?"

He nodded. "She's the one who put in the security system, too. The landlord wouldn't pay for it."

I took off my glove and touched the lock face. It felt cold. "Something must have scared her."

The dead bolt slid back easily, and the same key worked in the knob. A piercing tone from the security system greeted us. I knew that it was just a reminder to disengage the alarm. Even so, it felt like one last warning from the house, one last chance to turn back. Dan slipped past me and, reading from a minuscule scrap of paper, punched a six-digit code into the keypad on the wall. The buzzer fell silent, leaving the house so still I almost wanted the noise back.

"I'm going to start in the basement," Dan said, already halfway to the back of the house.

"We need to reset this alarm," I called, making sure he could hear me. "Wasn't that the whole point of getting a new code?"

"Oh, yeah." He came back, referred again to his cheat sheet, and punched in a different string of numbers. "There you go, all safe and sound."

He was gone before I could respond. The air in the house was frigid. It felt dense and tasted stale, as if a damp breeze had drifted in from the ocean some time ago and never found a way out. And there was an odor. Faint. Sweet. From the body? How would I know? I didn't know what a dead body smelled like.

I shot the dead bolt, turning the interior knob on the shiny new lock Ellen had installed. She'd felt the presence of danger, taken reasonable precautions to keep it outside her door. But she had not been safe. If she had killed herself, then the real threat had been inside the house, inside with her. On the other hand, if she hadn't killed herself—I wrapped my coat a little tighter—then it was really dumb for us to be in here.

The rooms were slightly dilapidated, showing the house's age, but the residue of grander times lingered. Chandeliers hung from high ceilings, although some of the bulbs were out. The decor, at least the part Ellen had contributed, was impeccable—simple, spare pieces placed in sometimes surprising but always perfect relation to one another. And unlike those of her office, the walls were not bare. They were hung with paintings and prints that were contemporary and seemed to be carefully selected. Edward Hopper had been a favorite, with his haunting images of urban isolation and people staring into the middle distance, into their own desolation.

As I moved from room to room, I looked for evidence that intruders had been there. I saw no drawers open, no seat cushions askance. Still, I had an odd feeling that Dan was right, that the soul of the house had been disturbed, that Ellen's sanctuary had been violated in some way.

I had the same feeling upstairs, standing at the foot of her bed, staring at the brocade comforter and the elegant pile of matching pillows. I hadn't made my bed once since I'd moved out of my mother's house. I didn't see the point. Ellen had made her bed either the morning of the day she'd died, or— this was a really strange notion—would she have taken time to make it before she'd gone upstairs to kill herself?

The rest of the bedroom was predictably uncluttered, as was her bathroom, but when I opened her bedroom closet, I was stunned—and then I laughed out loud. I had finally found something about this woman that was authentic and unguarded and completely, delightfully out of control. Her walk-in closet was a riot. It wasn't messy as much as . . . relaxed. Especially compared to the rest of the house. It was as if her compulsion to shop had fought a battle with her obsession for order. Order never had a chance. Hanging racks to the left and right were crammed with silk blouses and little sweaters and wool suits and linen slacks and one linen blazer that I found particularly swanky. Her shoes had completely overwhelmed the handy shoe shelf and escaped to the floor.

It took a long time to search the closet—she'd owned a lot of handbags that I had to go through—and when I was finished, I didn't want to leave. For one thing, it was warmer in there. But mostly, standing in that closet I recognized Ellen as a real person, a person who had an obvious weakness for natural fibers and good leather pumps. I could have gone shopping with this woman, and we would have had a good time.

I was turning to leave when a single sheet of lined paper tacked to the inside of the closet door caught my attention. It had dates and distances and entries penciled in Ellen's hand, and when I looked around on the floor, I had to smile. There were two pairs of well-worn, mud-covered running shoes, the expensive kind, lined up right next to her trendy little flats. Ellen had been a runner, too. I did what all runners do—immediately checked her distances against mine. I might not have had her discipline—she ran more often than I did and on a schedule as rigid as everything else about her life—but I had endurance. I ran farther.

Something creaked in the ceiling directly above my head, something loud. Dan was supposed to be in the basement, but . . . there it was again. Loud, groaning footsteps. Definitely footsteps. I was on the second floor and the noise was coming from overhead, so either Dan wasn't in the basement anymore, or—I flinched at the sound of a muffled thud—someone was in the attic.

I stepped quietly into the hallway. A door was ajar, framed by a light from behind. Through the opening I could see the wooden steps inside that climbed, I assumed, to the attic.

More footsteps and then another loud crash. I held very still and listened, feeling every footstep in my chest as if it were my own ribs creaking under the weight rather than the dry hardwood planks overhead.

"Is that you, Dan?"

The second thud had a different quality, more like a deliberate kick, followed by "JesusChristsonova*bitch*. Yes, it's me."

I let out the deep breath I hadn't even known I'd been holding, climbed the steep stairs, and emerged through a planked floor into the attic. It smelled of mothballs and lumber, and my eyes were drawn immediately to the apex of that familiar pitched roof where I knew Ellen had hung from a rope until Dan had come to find her.

He was sitting on a trunk rubbing his shin. He must have left his coat and tie somewhere. His collar was unbuttoned and I could see the band of his cotton T-shirt. It was warmer in the attic than any other part of the house, except for Ellen's closet maybe, but still cold. I picked my way over to where he was sitting, careful not to step off the planks.

He looked up at me. "What do you think 'fish' means?"

"Is this a trick question?"

"Look at this." He handed me a page from a desk calendar for Monday, December 22, 1997, with the handwritten notation that said FISH 1016.96A.

"Fish? I have no idea. Was this in her office?"

"On the floor behind the desk."

"On the floor? Where's the rest of the calendar?"

"Gone. So's the tape from her answering machine."

"Which one? Inbound or outbound?"

"They're both gone."

"Wow," I said, "that sounds kind of . . . not random. As if whoever took them knew her and had talked to her on the phone. That wouldn't be Little Pete, would it?"

"It could have been if he was calling in threats to her."

"I guess you're right. The rest of the house doesn't look as if it's been searched. If someone's been in here, they were hunting for something specific and they knew where to look." I tapped the calendar page with a fingernail as I tried to think about what we hadn't found. "Did you find any computer diskettes? Or maybe an organizer? Did she carry a briefcase?"

"There's no organizer or disks. Her briefcase is downstairs, but there's nothing in it but work stuff."

"What about her car?"

"It's in the garage. I checked it a few days ago. There's nothing in it."

I looked at the note again. Fish. What could that possibly have to do with anything? He waved me off when I tried to give it back to him. "You keep it. I'll just lose it."

I stuck the calendar page into the pocket of my coat and sat next to him on the trunk. "You have no idea what they might be looking for?"

"Not a clue."

The space was large for an attic. Several matching foot-lockers were randomly scattered around the floor, as was some old furniture, too tacky to have been Ellen's. For an attic the place was clean, but still not the image I would want to take to my grave. Several cardboard boxes were stacked neatly to one side. "Have you checked these boxes?"

"No. That's why I came up here. Want to take a look?"

We went through the boxes and lockers. Each one had a colored tag, the kind the movers use for inventory, and it made me think about my own moving boxes, which had tags on top of tags. We found nothing that you wouldn't expect to find in the attic—Christmas ornaments and old tax records and boxes of books and clothes. The most intriguing box was labeled PERSONAL MEMENTOS. I wanted to sit in the attic, take some time, and go through it piece by piece, but for reasons other than what we'd come for. I wanted to find out about Ellen.

When we were finished, Dan and I sat on a couple of the lockers and looked at each other. Illuminated by the bare bulb from the ceiling, his face was all pale angles and deep hollows.

"She didn't have any shoes on."

"What?"

"The rope was over that high beam there." He pointed up into the apex of the roof. "One end of it, anyway. The other end was knotted around that stud. The cops think she climbed up on this and kicked it over." He went over to one of the lock-ers and nudged it with his toe. "She was wearing some kind of a jogging suit thing, but nothing on her feet. They were white. That's what I saw first when I came up the stairs. Her feet were totally white and . . . I don't know . . . like wax or some-thing. It's funny because it was pretty dark up here, but there was light coming from somewhere." He checked around the attic, finding a window at the far end covered with wooden slats, like blinds closed halfway. "Through there, I guess. She was facing me. Hanging, but perfectly still, which was weird. And her eyes . . . I thought your eyes closed when you died." He bowed his head, and when he raised it again, the light over his head showed every line in his face. "When I think about that day, I still think about her feet. I'd never seen her bare feet."

He found the trunk again, sat down, and put his face in his hands. "I'm so tired tonight."

I didn't know what to say, so I said nothing. I thought about what it must have been like for him standing by himself in the attic, looking at her that way. I wondered how something like that changes you. As I watched him rubbing his eyes, I found myself wishing I had known him before he had seen her like that.

"Did you see any mail when you were downstairs?" He'd summoned the energy to stand up.

"No, come to think of it. But I wasn't looking."

"I'm going down to see if I can find it."

"I'll be right down. I'm going to turn off the lights first." And I wanted something from her closet. I didn't know why, but I wanted her running log. As Dan clopped loudly down the wooden stairs, I took one last look around the attic and the personal mementos box caught my eye again. It had neat handles cut into the sides, and when I picked it up, it wasn't heavy. I decided to take it also because it didn't belong in the place where she'd died.

I carried the box and the running log to the bottom of the staircase and went back up to get the lights. Dan had not only left every light burning in every room he'd searched, he'd also left a couple of drawers open in Ellen's desk along with the cassette door on the answering machine. Dan was right. Both of the tapes were missing. I had closed everything up and reached over to turn off the desk lamp when I noticed the red light on the fax machine. It was out of paper. According to the message window, there was a fax stored in memory. I knew Ellen would have paper nearby, and it didn't take long to find it. I dropped it in the tray and waited. After a few beeps, the machine sprang to life, sucked one of the pages into the feeder, and started to turn it around, spitting it out, bit by tiny bit. With a surge of nervous anticipation I plucked it out. A second one started right behind it.

It was written in cutout letters like a ransom note. It wasn't addressed to me. It wasn't meant for me, but it still made me shaky enough that I had to sit down. It said, "Ellen Shepard is proof that dogs fuck monkeys." I sat in her chair and stared at it. It had to be from someone at the airport, from one of her employees, and how sick was that? Having to show up at work every day knowing that you might be glancing at or talking to or brushing past the person who wrote this? Thinking about harassment in the abstract was one thing. Holding it in your hands was another.

Probably because I knew what was coming, the second one seemed to take even longer. This one was handwritten, the message scrawled diagonally. "Mind your own business, cunt."

And they kept coming, one after another, each more crude and disgusting than the last. As they rolled off, I checked the time and date stamps and the return fax number. They'd all been sent in the middle of the night from the fax machine in the admin office—my office. But at least they were old. At

least there wasn't someone at the other end right this minute
feeding the stuff in as fast as I could pull it off. Real-time
torment—that was a thought that made my stomach lurch, and
it occurred to me that maybe she had left the paper tray empty
for a reason.

The last one to roll off was another one-liner, this one typed.
"Regular place, regular time on Tuesday" was all it said. There
was no name and no signature. According to the time stamp it
had been sent at 2307 hours on Saturday, January 3—two days
before she died—from a Sir Speedy in someplace called Nahant.
It was from the snitch. Had to be. I put it in the pile, turned
off the light, and was into the hallway when I heard it. It was
so sudden and unexpected in the mostly dark, empty house that
it was like an electric shock to my heart. It took a moment for
me to calm down and realize that it was only the sound of the
phone ringing. Ellen's phone. It was a perfectly ordinary, every-
day sound and it scared me stiff. That it rang only once and
stopped was even more chilling. Right behind it came the sound
of the fax machine powering up again in the dark office. It was
a sound that was so common, so mundane, and it was one of
the most frightening things I'd ever heard.

I called for Dan. No answer. He could have been anywhere
in the huge old house. The fax began to print and my pulse
rate began to climb. I called again and then realized that even
if he came, he wasn't going to do anything for me that I
couldn't do for myself, right? It was just a fax machine, for
God's sake.

I turned on the light and went back into the office, creeping up to the machine as if it was a rattlesnake. The page
scrolled out slowly, leaving me to read it one word at a time.
"We're" . . . the machine seemed louder than before . . .

"watch" . . . and slower . . . "ing" . . . and it took everything
I had not to just rip it out before it was finished . . . "We're
watching you" is what it said and below that the number 1018.

At first I couldn't move, then I couldn't move fast enough. I
was out of there, banging off the hallway walls and down that
grand staircase. I'm not sure my feet even touched the ground.
I tried the front door. Locked. Trapped. Then I remembered the
dead bolt . . .

Dan, just coming up from the basement, took one look at
my face. "What happened?"

"I just got . . . there's this message." I started to show him,
but there wasn't time. "We have to go. Right *now*."

"All right. Just let me reset the alarm."

I had a hard time threading the key into the lock, and then
again on the other side. When we were in the car, I showed
him the last fax that had rolled off. He held it up to the light
of the street lamp. "What's this number, this 1018?"

I cringed to even think about it. "It's my hotel room."

"Those bastards," he said. "I swear I'm gonna kill someone
before this is over."

"*Who* exactly? What *bastards*? Who would know we were
here unless they followed us? They could be watching right now."

"Let them watch." He started the engine, but paused to turn
on the dome light and look at the fax more closely. "It came
from the airport. Fucking Big Pete. It's starting all over again."

I reached up and turned off the light.

"Calm down, Shanahan."

"Why?"

"They're just trying to scare you."

"Mission accomplished. Let's get out of here, Dan. Right
now."

As he pulled away from the curb and drove down the quiet street, I peered into every parked car, checked for movement behind every swaying tree. I wasn't sure I'd ever feel safe again.

"You might want to do one thing," he said, after we'd gone a few blocks in silence.

"What?"

"Change hotel rooms."

"Hotel rooms? I might want to change cities."

Chapter Eleven

When I arrived at the airport Monday morning, Molly was already bent over her desk in the quiet office, lost in deep concentration.

"You're in early," I said.

Her head snapped up as she swung around in her squealing chair. I flinched and, trying not to spill my tea, dropped my keys.

"Ohmygod . . . don't sneak up on me like that."

"I'm sorry. I wasn't aware I was sneaking." I reached down for the keys. "What are you doing here? It's not even seven o'clock."

Hand to her chest, she drew a couple of theatrical breaths. "It's time for invoices. I save them up and do them once a month. And I'm going to need signatures, so don't go too far. Here"—she handed me my morning mail—"this should keep you busy."

"Yes, ma'am. Come in when you're ready." As she turned back to her work, I unlocked the door and fled to the sanctity of my own office, where I could continue to unravel in private.

I was still unhinged from Friday night. I was supposed to
have spent the weekend apartment hunting. Instead, I'd holed
up in my hotel room eating room-service food and watching
pay-per-view movies. The only times I'd gone out were to run,
and every time I had, I'd looked over my shoulder at least once
and resented it.

With my coat off, my tea in hand, and the mail in front of
me, I tried to go through my morning routine. But the normal
routine did not include standing up to adjust the blinds three
times, or rearranging the chairs in front of my desk, or straightening all the pencils in my drawer. It seemed that Ellen had
already done that, anyway.

After not having looked all weekend, I finally gave in and
pulled the faxes out of my briefcase. Nothing about them had
changed since Friday, and they were just as offensive in the
light of day. I still felt that scraping in the pit of my stomach
when I looked at them, but I couldn't stop looking at them.
Molly arrived, giving me a good reason to put them aside.
Face down.

She pushed through the door with a heavy ledger, an accor-
dion file, and a large-key calculator, all of which she arranged
methodically on her side of my desk.

"All you need is a green eyeshade," I said.

"Never mind what I need. I've got a system, and it's worked
fine for some twenty-two years. The bills get paid on time, we
don't pay them twice, and the auditors are happy."

"Before we start, I have a question for you," I said. "Do
you know where I can rent a VCR for my hotel room?"

"Are we boring you already?"

"I've watched every pay-per-view movie offered this month,
some twice. I need something fresh."

"I'll see what I can do. One of the agents' husbands repairs TVs. I'll bet I can get you a deal."

"I'll bet you can."

She handed me a ticket envelope. "Sign this first."

I opened it and looked inside, trying to decipher her loopy handwriting. "What's this?"

"It's a pass."

"I know it's a pass," I said, signing. "But who is Our Lady of the Airwaves? Patron saint of radio broadcasts? Sister Mary Megahertz?"

"Air*ways*," she said, snatching it back, "not waves. It's the chapel here at the airport. They have an auction every year and we always donate a pass."

"Ah." Ellen's frequent-flier travel popped into my mind. "Did you ever request any passes for Ellen on United?"

"I never requested any passes for her, period. She spent all her time here at the airport. Weekends, too."

"So you didn't know she was buying tickets on United."

"She was most certainly not doing that. I would have known."

She gave me the first invoice. One hundred and fifty thousand dollars for three hundred barrels of deicing fluid, a reminder that I was in a true cold-weather station for the first time in my career. "How many of these will I sign this winter?"

"Could be two, could be ten. Depends on the weather."

"That narrows it down." I signed and passed it back. "I found a frequent-flier card in the desk. Ellen flew at least five times on United that we know about. Dan's finding out if there were more."

She handed me the next invoice without a word. It was to reimburse a passenger whose coat had caught in the conveyor belt at the security checkpoint, and it was almost a hundred bucks.

"This is pretty expensive dry cleaning," I said.

"It was a suede coat."

"Was the belt malfunctioning?"

"No. In fact, the checkpoint supervisor thinks the passenger might have done it on purpose trying to get a new coat."

I signed it and handed it back. "Wouldn't be the first time. What about Ellen's travel?"

"I'll believe it when I see it. You'll have to prove it to me."

"All right. Dan's got the card. He can prove it to you."

The next invoice was for ticket stock, and the one after that for snow plowing in the employee parking lot. I signed them all. "Molly?"

"Ummmm . . ." She was busy shuffling papers.

"I found something in Ellen's suspense file the other night, and I don't know what to do with it. It was a copy of an old invoice from 1992. It had no notes or instructions. Any idea why she may have had it?"

"Let me see it."

The mystery invoice from Crescent had popped out of suspense and was in my in-box again. I dug it out and gave it to her. "Did she ask you to pull it for her?"

"No. Means nothing to me."

"Do you know the company?"

"Sure. Crescent Security. They've done some work for us, nickel-and-dime stuff like background checks, but I haven't heard anything about them for a few years. Do you want me to do anything with it?"

"Stick it back in follow-up for next week. If nothing comes up by then, toss it."

"One more." The last invoice she gave me covered the cost of a new windshield for one of the tugs on the ramp. It was attached to a requisition, which had been approved by Ellen.

I read the explanation. "Wear and tear?"

"With a baseball bat. The boys on the ramp were upset about the last bid." She started to collect her files, then glanced over matter-of-factly. "So, what did you two find up in Marblehead? Anything?"

"What?"

"You and Danny were up there on Friday, weren't you?"

"How did you know that?"

"Everyone in the station knew."

Catching my reaction, she stopped sorting the files. "Oh, please. It's not like you can sneak around. You have four hundred people working for you, and every single one feels entitled to know what you're up to at all times, especially if it has to do with Ellen."

I turned the faxes over and slid them across the desk to her, keeping the one from the snitch and the one to me aside. "I found these."

She paged through the stack, no more affected than if she had been flipping through wallpaper samples.

"These are nothing," she said with a dry chuckle. "You should see what they wrote about her in the bellies of airplanes."

"Is this amusing?"

She shifted all the way back in her chair, looking more surprised than angry. But then her neck stiffened, and so did her backbone. "What do you want me to say? Yes, it's horrible. And yes, it offends me. But it doesn't surprise me. You work around here long enough and you get used to it. That's the way it is."

"This is *not* nothing." I snatched the faxes from the desk and held them up, surprised at my own angry reaction. But I couldn't help it. It was all starting to get to me. "How can anyone ever get used to this?"

Her trademark red lips seemed to grow more vibrant. Then I realized it was really her face growing more pale. "I don't believe I like your tone."

She stood up and huffed out, leaving all her files on my desk and me staring at the spot in the chair where she had just been. The lemon had been floating in my tea too long, and it tasted bitter when I drew one last sip. I slammed the cup into the trash, then sat by myself and tried to figure out whom exactly I was mad at.

"Molly?"

She must not have gone far because she was back instantly, standing in the doorway, hands on her hips.

"I'm sorry, Molly, that was uncalled for."

"Why are you yelling at me?" she demanded. "Why are you yelling at all?"

"Come back in and I'll show you."

"Can I bring my cigarettes?"

"Yes."

When she was good and ready, she strolled back in and sat down, closing the door behind her. In my entire career with Majestic, I'd never spent so much time with the door closed. I pulled the "We're watching you" fax out and showed it to her. "This came to me Friday night at Ellen's house. I was standing right there and the thing just rolled off." I pointed at the number. "That's my hotel room." Remembering the sound of the machine in that silent house set off a shiver. "It scared the shit out of me."

She shook her head and resumed her seen-it-all attitude, sticking a cigarette between her lips and talking around it. "I've got to admit, that would be upsetting, but it doesn't mean someone followed you. I told you, all the agents at the counter were chattering like magpies about how you and Danny were going up to Marblehead to find Ellen's 'murderer.'" She rolled her eyes as she fired up.

"How do people know these things?"

"As far as the hotel room, that's easy. Someone probably knows someone who knows someone at the Hyatt. Otherwise, they eavesdrop. They read the mail when it comes in. They listen in on phone conversations. They have friends and cousins and brothers and sisters who work around town. They compare notes and put two and two together. That's why we always close the door."

I thought back to last week. The door had indeed been open when Dan and I talked about getting the power of attorney and going up to Marblehead.

Molly was perched on the edge of her chair watching me, her small, manicured hands dangling off the ends of the armrests. "Molly, do you believe Ellen was murdered?"

She shook her head. "It makes for good gossip, but it just doesn't fit with the facts. I'm sorry."

I wasn't, and for the first time since I'd gone to Ellen's house, my shoulders came down from around my ears. "Help me understand what's going on around here."

She nodded as she drew deeply on the cigarette, letting her eyes close and leaving a bright red ring around the white filter. "About three months ago, Ellen changed the manning on the ramp. There's nothing wrong with what she did. In fact, it was probably overdue. But bottom line, it made for fewer full-time union jobs and a lot of favorite shifts being moved or going away. She also cut the overtime, which to some was worth as much as their salary. And, she cracked down on sick-time abuse, vandalism, theft and pilferage."

"In other words, she was doing her job."

"If this were anyplace but Boston, I'd agree with you." She spoke with great patience and tolerance, making the most of her role as station historian. "But here you have to take history into consideration, and management has a history of looking at these problems with a wink. Either that or a blind eye. When Lenny ran the place, he winked a lot. Dickie Flynn was blind. Blind drunk."

"And Ellen was neither one."

"That is a true statement."

"Dan told me about Dickie."

"What did he tell you?"

"That his wife and kids left him and he went into the tank."

"He would say that." She took a drag and stared out the window for a long time, lost in her own thoughts. "Like oil and water, those two. Danny always resented covering for Dickie, and Dickie was usually threatening to fire Danny for one reason or another. As if he could. The place would have run into the ground without Danny."

"Dickie wasn't an alcoholic?"

"He was, but Dickie was a sweet man who got lost somewhere along the way. Something happened to him, I don't know what, but it wasn't because his wife left him. Twyla and the girls adored him. She never would have left him if not for the drinking."

"What about Lenny? What kind of manager was he?"

"A deal maker. Lenny's a very charming guy when he wants

to be, but truth be told, he only cares about making the numbers and getting promoted. You'll get along fine with him if you just make the numbers. That's where Ellen got into trouble."

"How?"

"Coming over from Majestic and being young and a woman and from staff, she was trying to prove herself. I think she tried too hard, went at it too fast, and tried to change everything at once. You have to work slowly around here, especially with the union."

"Is that when the abuse started?"

"At first the union did like they always do when they get threatened. Slowed down the operation, delayed flights, set fire to the place. Equipment started disappearing or going out of service, and they wouldn't come to Ellen's meetings. The usual stuff."

"*That's* the usual stuff?"

She shrugged. Smoke drifted through her lips as she nodded toward the slightly crumpled faxes on my desk. "But then these type messages started showing up, and I felt like something changed. They were, like you say, more personal. And she started getting them at home. As far as I know, the union has never taken their grievances into a manager's home. On the other hand, they never had to work for a woman before, either. Maybe that's what really set them off."

"When did things start to get personal?"

"Two, maybe three weeks ago. Around the time she found the dead rat in her mailbox.

"A dead rat?"

"Yeah, it was disgusting. Head was crushed, all stiff and dried out."

"How do you know?"

"She took a picture."

"That's certainly presence of mind."

"She wanted to have proof. I think that's when she changed her locks and, if you ask me, that was the beginning of the end. Ellen was always so put together. You know what I mean? The hair, the nails, the clothes. But after that it was almost like she didn't care. She put in more and more hours at the airport, most of the time in her office with the door shut. I think she was afraid to go home. I'm pretty sure she was losing weight."

"Tell me about her last day."

"She was here in her office by herself all morning with the door shut. She took a few calls, but mostly I think she was calling out. About one o'clock I saw the light on her line go off, the door opened, and she came out. She was trying to hide it, but her nose was all red and she had sunglasses on. She told me she wasn't feeling well, packed up, and went home. I never saw her again."

"You have no idea what happened?"

"No. And usually I know everything. Whatever it was, she kept the secret well."

"I wonder if she confided in anyone. You don't know who she was talking to right before she left that day?"

"No. She was answering her own phone. I do have a log of all her phone messages, if you think that would help." She went out to her desk, this time taking her invoices with her. When she came back, she had yet another of her ledgers, which she opened on my desk in front of me. It was a single-spaced listing of callers, dates, and times of messages Molly had taken for Ellen.

"Are you keeping tabs on me, too?"

She turned to a page with my name across the top. Listed

were all the messages I'd received since I'd been there.

"Dickie used to accuse me of not giving him messages," she said, "like he could even remember anything that happened from one day to the next. That's when I started keeping track. It really comes in handy sometimes."

I studied the pages, several pages with Molly looking over my shoulder. "These non-Majestic people, do you know who they were to Ellen?"

"When someone calls, I ask what's it about. If they say, I write it down on the message. I don't log that part, but I can remember most of them. Like this one"—her bracelets rattled in my ear as she reached across to point out an entry—"this was the woman who used to cut her hair. Here's a call from her aunt on Ellen's birthday. It was the only message I ever took from her. This woman here, I remember she wouldn't say what she wanted and she never left her phone number. Said it was personal."

"Julia Milholland. Sounds very old Boston. She called three times in one week?"

"She was trying to set up some kind of an appointment with Ellen."

I pulled out a pad, copied down Julia Milholland's name, and checked out the rest of the list. "Matt Levesque. I know him. He's a manager in the Finance department. We've done work together."

"He was usually returning Ellen's calls. I think she worked with him on the merger. And he's a director now, not a manager."

"Ellen worked on the merger?"

"She came here from that assignment, some kind of a task force."

I opened the drawer and pulled out the empty hanging file labeled NOR'EASTER/MAJESTIC MERGER. "Do you happen to know where this file is?"

"I don't know where it is now, but she had it on her desk a couple of weeks ago."

I copied down Matt's number. "I think it's time I called my old pal Matt and congratulated him on his promotion."

Chapter Twelve

"I've got Lenny on line one," Molly called from her desk, "and Matt Levesque on line two. Matt says he's only going to be in for a few more minutes."

I checked the time. It wasn't even six o'clock in Boston, which meant it was still early in Denver. "Tell Matt I have to talk to my boss and it'll be maybe ten minutes. Ask him to please wait."

I took a moment to review my list. I'd been keeping track of things to tell Lenny, or things he might ask me. There was the freight forwarder who'd had his shipment of live lobsters stolen out of our freight house for the third time in a month. There was the ever escalating incidence of sick time and corresponding overtime on the ramp. There was the FAA inspector who we'd caught trying to sneak a handgun through our checkpoint—a surprise inspection we'd passed. And there was Angelo. His was the first name on the list and the only one I'd done nothing about. I knew I'd end up bringing him back, but so far I hadn't been able to pull the trigger. Dan was probably right, I was just being stubborn. I picked up. "I know why you're calling, Lenny."

"You do?" He had me on the box again.

"I've been a little slow in following up on Angelo, but I'm going to get to it this week and I'll make a decision. You have my commitment."

"That's good, Alex. It's not why I was calling, but it's good to know you haven't forgotten my request. Hold on for me, would you?"

I slumped down in my chair and eavesdropped as he signed something for his secretary and asked her to send it out right away. I should have known better than to open with a mea culpa. It set exactly the wrong tone and who knows? He may have gone through the entire phone call and never raised the issue. Damn.

"I see we think alike, Alex." Lenny was back.

"In what way?"

"I just got off the phone with Jo Shepard out in California." Uh-oh.

"She tells me you two had a nice chat."

I slumped down in the chair even more. I was close to horizontal, and the Angelo issue was starting to look more and more workable. At least with Angelo, my sin was in having done nothing. I couldn't make the same claim with Aunt Jo. I almost blurted out my second mea culpa, but decided to wait for his reaction first. "I spoke to her last week." I said. "Human Resources called from Denver and needed some information."

"Why didn't you tell me that you and Ellen knew each other?"

"We didn't. Did Jo Shepard tell you that we did?"

"No. But I surmised that the two of you must have been friends. Otherwise, why would you be interested in gaining access to her house?"

"Well, it wasn't that so much as I thought I could help her

with Ellen's personal effects. There doesn't seem to be anyone else."

"Is that why you went up there on Friday? To help with her effects?"

I squeezed my eyes shut. Did everyone know everything that I did? I might as well post a daily schedule. This was getting out of hand. I didn't want to be lying to my boss. "No. No, that's not why I went up there, Lenny. The truth is that Dan has a theory—"

"That Ellen was murdered by the union in Boston. And he wants to get into her house to find the proof. Am I close?"

"You're right on target." I should have guessed that he would have known.

"Alex, listen to me. You should have called me before doing something like that . . . and I suppose I should have warned you about Fallacaro."

"What about him?"

"He's bad news, Alex. He's already ruined a couple of careers, including his own. And he didn't do Ellen any favors. He's always got his own agenda working, and I'm sure he does here, too."

I sat up straight. "What do you mean by that?"

"He's the one who encouraged Ellen to take such a hard line with the union. She got caught in the cross fire. Now he blames himself, and his way of dealing with it is to deny the obvious, to insist that she was murdered." Lenny's Southern accent grew deeper and richer as his frustration grew. I'd promised myself when I'd called Aunt Jo not to regret it later, not to do that to myself. Fat chance. As I listened to Lenny, I felt the guilt like a clinging vine growing around that defiant resolve and squeezing the life out of it.

Lenny was still going. "And I'll tell you something else. He's destructive. This ridiculous story is destructive for the airline, and as the Majestic Airlines representative in Boston, Alex, it's your job to make sure that a damaging and false story like that doesn't get out of hand. I don't want to see myself on *Sixty Minutes.* Do you?"

"Of course not, but this doesn't seem like Mike Wallace territory to me."

"No? Think about it. Five years ago you had the female ramp supervisor at Northwest who was murdered at Logan. Now here's another young woman dead at Logan, this time with Majestic. She was young, single, not that experienced, working in a tough place with a tough union. Majestic is high-profile, Bill Scanlon is high-profile, and she picked a strange way to die. You could spin an interesting tale."

That was true, but ... "You make it sound as if the company is trying to hide something."

"No. No matter what Dan Fallacaro says, Ellen killed herself. If we did anything wrong, it was in not getting her out of there before it was too late." He paused for a long time, and when he spoke again, his voice was softer, with more rounded corners than sharp edges. "That was my fault. I should have seen how overwhelmed she was." He picked up the receiver. "Alex, I'm not going to make the same mistakes again. It's my job to keep you focused on the right things, and that's all I'm trying to do. Pay attention to the airport and what needs to get done there. Get the numbers up and don't get distracted. I'll hold Scanlon off until you can get things under control there."

"*Scan*lon?" My heart did a double clutch.

"Boston has been receiving what you might call unusual

interest from the chairman." He stretched out the middle 'u'—
un-yooo-su-al. "I've had calls from him almost every day since
you've arrived."

"About what?"

"About the problems in your station. I know you've only
been there a week, but he's not interested in excuses. I can
only do so much before he loses patience with the both of us."

Lenny had no idea how hollow his threat was. I wasn't afraid
of Bill. But I also didn't want him interested in my operation.
I stood up, paced over to the window, turned around, paced
back, sat down, and stood up again. I didn't want to see him;
I didn't want to talk to him on the phone; even talking about
him touched on a nerve that was still painfully exposed. Moving
to Boston had been a way to put distance between us, and he
had promised to honor that decision. I could only hope that
in spite of any problems I was having here or what Lenny might
say, he would keep his promise.

"Do you understand?" Lenny asked me.

"I understand."

"I appreciate your commitment on Angelo," he said, "and
I'd like to ask for another. My plan is to send someone up there
from my Human Resources staff here in D.C. to handle Ellen's
personal effects, someone who has some training in this area.
For my peace of mind, can you promise me that you will work
on the problems at the airport until I can free someone up?"

"Yes, I can do that."

"That means you will stay out of Ellen's house?"

I really had no good reason not to make him that promise.
"I'll stay out."

"Do I have your word?"

"You have my word."

"Good. Now, all you have to do is ask and I'll take care of Fallacaro for you. You can bring in your own guy—or gal."

I didn't think I knew any "gals." "Take care of him how?"

"I'll make him a ramp supervisor in the farthest place I can find from New Jersey."

"Do you mean Boston?"

"I mean New Jersey. Newark. If he gives you any more trouble, tell him that. And call me when you've come to a decision about Angelo."

"I will."

When I hung up, Molly was in the doorway with her coat on. "Matt's calling back. He got tired of waiting and hung up."

I checked my second line, unaware that it had even rung.

"And I'm going home. Don't forget that tomorrow is Tuesday and you've got your staff meeting."

"Thanks, Molly. Have a good evening."

I punched up Matt's call. He'd been promoted since the last time I'd seen him, so instead of a manager's cubicle in the midst of the hoi polloi, he'd be in a big window office sitting in a high-backed swivel chair behind his turbo desk.

"Have you got your feet up on the desk, Matt?"

"That's what it's for, isn't it?"

"And I'll bet you haven't looked at the mountains for a week." Matt had a magnificent view from his side of the building. I'd spent most of my time in headquarters gazing out the window at the canvas peaks of Denver International Airport and in the background, the real thing—the majestic peaks of the great Rocky Mountains.

"We're much too busy to appreciate the natural beauty of our surroundings. I hear it's more exciting where you are. What's it like out there?"

"It's like an airport, Matt." I checked the view out my window, where I could see a line of purple tails with Majestic logos, one on every gate. "We have airplanes here and passengers and cargo. You should come out sometime and see what kind of business you're in."

"No time for that." I heard the clacking of his computer keys, and I knew he was checking e-mail. "I'm talking about all the rumors. Word here is everyone in Boston thinks someone murdered Ellen Shepard. Don't you feel weird? I feel weird, but you're sitting in her chair."

"What happened to her is not contagious, Matt, and I like to think of it as my chair now." I touched the armrest, felt the rough, nubby weave that wore like iron. This chair was probably going to survive the next twelve general managers. "I feel sad about what happened to Ellen, not weird. She was more than a rumor. You know that. You worked with her."

"That was two years ago," he said. "She wasn't suicidal when I knew her."

"I'm not sure she would have announced it, particularly to a sensitive guy like you. How did she sound when you talked to her last week?"

"How'd you know I talked to her?"

"You left a trail of phone messages. What did she want?"

"She had some questions about an old Finance project. I don't think it would pertain to anything you're doing now."

His voice was taking on that arch, staffy quality that really got under my skin. It was a good thing I'd known him since he was a baby analyst. "Matt, if you don't want to tell me what she wanted, say so, but don't give me that secret Finance handshake bullshit."

The clacking keys went silent. "Why do you need to know? Are you thinking she was murdered?"

"I've got some problem employees here, and I think Ellen was building a case to get rid of at least one of them. If she was, I'd like to finish what she was doing."

"Hold on." I heard him get up and close his office door. "That's not why she called," he said when he was back, "but I'll tell you anyway. She was looking for an old schedule, something from our task force days."

"The Nor'easter Acquisition Task Force?"

"Yeah. We worked on it together. She wanted the schedule of purchase price adjustments."

I opened a drawer, found a pad of paper, and started taking notes. "What's a purchase price adjustment?"

"Adjustments to the price Majestic paid to buy Nor'easter."

"What's special about them?"

"Nothing. They're just expenses that are incurred as part of the deal, so they get charged against the purchase price instead of normal operations. That's why you keep them separate."

"What are some examples?"

"Lawyers. You have to have lawyers to negotiate and draft documents for the transaction, and they charge a fee for that. Accountants, consultants, anyone we hire for due diligence. We wouldn't purchase their services if we weren't doing the deal, so their fee gets charged to the deal."

"That doesn't sound particularly relevant to the ramp in Boston."

"I told you."

"There's a schedule of these charges?"

"Yeah. Ellen maintained it when she was on the task force. She didn't have a copy of it anymore, so she called me."

"What does it look like?"

"It's nothing but a spreadsheet. Down one side you've got the payee and the nature of the expense if it's not obvious. Down the other you've got the dollar amount."

"Why would she be interested in something like that two years after the fact?"

"I haven't got a clue."

"You don't know, or you're not telling me?"

"She wouldn't say. I told her where to find it and that was it."

"Which is where?

"Archives. All the merger files have been archived for about a year now."

"Can you send a copy of that schedule to me?"

"I'd have to sign it out, and I don't think I want my name on anything having to do with Ellen Shepard. That whole subject is taboo around here right now. We're not even supposed to be thinking about it, much less talking about it. I could get into trouble."

"Come on, Matt. How many times did I bail you out in the past? Don't you remember that time when you were working on that appropriations request for San Francisco and you needed that information right away and I was the one who went back out to the airport that night to get it—"

He groaned. "Look, I don't know what you're doing up there, but if I get you this thing, you have to keep my name out of it."

"Your sterling reputation is safe with me."

My second line lit up and flashed several times before I remembered Molly wasn't out there to pick it up. Then my beeper went off. I checked the number.

"There's something going on here, Matt. Operations is beeping me. Would you just send a copy of everything Ellen asked for?"

"Yep. But we never had this conversation."

"If you say so, Matt."

Kevin was talking the instant I punched the second line. "You'd better get down here," he said. "We've got a problem."

Chapter Thirteen

I walked down the corridor past the door labeled MEN'S
LOCKER ROOM. The second door had no designation, just
two flat globs of hardened putty where the ready room sign
might have been at one time. I could hear masculine voices
inside.

For as many years as I'd worked in the field, it still wasn't
easy for me to walk into a ready room. Some airports were
better than others, but for the most part, the ramp was domi-
nated by men and the ready room was where they congregated
to do what men in packs do. I took a moment to gather myself,
then pushed through the door.

There were eight guys in there, all in various stages of readi-
ness—eating, reading the newspaper, playing cards. One was
sleeping. All conversation ceased abruptly with my arrival, leaving an old color TV set to provide the soundtrack. I felt as if
I was trespassing in the boys' secret clubhouse.

"Gentlemen," I said, concentrating on keeping my voice
strong and steady, which wasn't easy, the way they were staring. "I haven't had a chance to meet most of you. I'm Alex

Shanahan, the new general manager, and I'm looking for the assignment crew chief."

Most of them went back to what they'd been doing. A few stared with a bored expression that was probably reserved just for management. Since it was an evening shift, most of the men were on the younger side, some just out of high school. They had that pale, hardened look of kids who had grown up in the dark spaces of big cities. I had no friends in this room.

I was really wishing I'd worn a skirt with pockets because I couldn't decide what to do with my hands. That I was even aware of my hands was a bad sign. "Let me ask you again—"

"He ain't here." The voice floated up from the other side of a La-Z-Boy recliner.

I walked around and found a man with a dark, curly beard, a bald head, and a prodigious belly. He seemed right at home reclining in front of a TV.

"Do you know where he is?"

"Could be anywhere."

"I guess that means he could be in here."

"He's not in here."

He tapped his fingers on the cracked Naugahyde armrest. I searched the concrete walls. "Why isn't the assignment sheet for this shift posted?"

The response came from behind me, and it was a voice I recognized. "Because everybody on my shift knows their job." Big Pete leaned against the wall next to what appeared to be an inside entrance to the men's locker room. He must have just come in, because if he'd been back there the whole time, I would have felt his presence.

"Someone *doesn't* know their job," I said. "We have a Majestic Express flight that's been in for twenty minutes. No one met the trip, the bags are still onboard, and the passengers are down in claim waiting."

"There's no one in here who's on the clock," he said without even so much as a perfunctory check around the room. "One of us goes out there, you're going to pay double-time. Your shift supervisor would know that. Or Danny."

Dan was at a meeting off the field, and my shift supervisor was stuck with a customer down at the freight house—probably the forwarder with the lobsters, or without the lobsters, as the case may be—but I saw no reason to explain all that. "I think you and I can resolve this."

"We could," he said, "but as you can see, I'm not on the clock yet." He was dressed in street clothes and completely relaxed, a man in full command of his environment. We were on his turf now.

"If the contract says double-time, then I'll pay double-time. And I will also take the name of the ramper who didn't cover the flight."

Out of the corner of my eye, I saw a man at the far end of the room stand and pull on his jacket. "I'm on the clock," he said. "I'll work it."

I turned to look at him. He was probably in his early forties, with the sturdy legs and all-over thickness that develop naturally from a lifetime of hard physical labor. His manner was brusque—rough even—but there was gentleness in his face that had somehow managed to survive even in this unforgiving place.

"Johnny, you're not on the clock." Pete stared at him, firing a couple of poison darts intended to shut him down. It probably worked on everyone else.

"I am on the clock." Johnny's manner toward Big Pete was

polite and entirely dismissive. "You don't have to pay double-time," he said to me. "I'll work it myself."

"That's against procedures, Johnny. The union ain't responsible if you get hurt."

The big man turned and faced Big Pete, his massive arms stacked like firewood across his chest. "The union ain't responsible for my safety," he said, "and thank God for that."

Pete turned and crossed his arms also. Now the two men were face-to-face. "You pay dues like everyone else here, John."

"That don't make you my representative, Peter."

Someone had killed the volume on the TV, so the only sound came from a guy sitting at a wooden table munching potato chips. Another had stopped in the middle of tying his shoe and was still bent over his knee, watching the drama unfold. John wasn't moving a muscle, and Big Pete was no longer leaning against the wall. The way they looked at each other made it clear that whatever was between these two had not started that day, and wasn't going to end there.

Big Pete, as calculating as a cockroach, must have figured the same thing because with a slight nod of his head and a fleeting smile he defused the tension. The moment passed and everyone resumed normal activities. Without another word, John was out the door, pulling his hood over his head. I watched through the window as he lumbered across the ramp, climbed into a tug, and drove away.

There was a swinging door where Big Pete had been standing. I made a management decision not to follow him into the men's locker room. Instead, I walked out of the boys' clubhouse and went to see Kevin, as much to see his friendly face as anything else.

* * *

"Who is this guy John or Johnny?" I asked when the Operations office had cleared out and Kevin and I were the only ones left in the room.

"Mr. John McTavish, one of your better employees." He turned his chair around and stretched his legs straight out. "He and his brother both. Between the two of them they do the work of six men."

"I don't know about his brother, but John doesn't seem to be afraid of Big Pete."

"Johnny's not afraid of much. Did they go at it, those two?"

"There was some testosterone present."

"Not surprising. There's bad blood there. They were on opposite sides of a contract vote a few years back. Johnny Mac for, and the Dwyers against. It was bitter."

"What contract vote?"

"The IBG vote. It was on the last Nor'easter contract proposal, the one just before the merger. And a seminal moment it was in the long and lively history of this grand operation. For the IBG, too, you could say. It split the Brotherhood right down the middle."

I smiled. I did enjoy Kevin's hyperbole. "A labor contract that was a seminal moment? Do tell."

"Three years ago when the IBG contract came up for negotiation, Nor'easter was in dire straits, as I'm sure you're aware. The company made a proposal to the union asking for what amounted to a laundry list of concessions and give-backs. When the proposal came up for a vote, some of the brothers took one side, the rest took the other."

"I'm guessing Big Pete Dwyer would be a hard-liner."

"Right you are. No concessions to management, ever, no matter what. Johnny McTavish was on the other side. His feeling was, if they didn't help bail the company out, there would be no more company. And he was right. The contract lost by the slimmest of margins, and that's the reason Nor'easter is gone today, may she rest in peace."

"At least you guys didn't go bankrupt."

"Tell that to the four thousand people Majestic laid off. That was over two years ago, and most of us still haven't gotten over the shock."

"It doesn't appear that John and Big Pete have buried the hatchet, either."

"No. I don't think they ever will. Dwyers and McTavishes, they are cut from different cloth."

From my vantage point at the window, I could see John unloading the bags from the stranded Majestic Express. "How is it no one showed up to work this flight?"

"The kid who usually works it called in sick. That's what I was told."

"Okay, but any one of forty or fifty rampers on shift could have covered."

"Sure, they could have, the problem being, in this station most rampers won't work the Express."

"What does that mean? We have seven Expresses every day. You're saying they refuse to work them at all?"

"It's not the Express so much as they won't work prop jets. Won't go near 'em, especially the senior men. Usually the junior guy on shift gets stuck with the trip."

"Okay, I give up. Why won't they work the props?"

"It's because of the crash."

"What cra—" I stopped for a moment. "The Baltimore crash?"

He nodded. "Nor'easter Express flight 1704. Went down on

approach just outside of Baltimore, which is why most people remember it that way. What they don't remember is that the flight originated in Boston."

"Which means it was loaded here."

"Precisely. Rampers are a superstitious lot. And it's not just them. You won't find many in this station that will talk about The Incident. Bad luck. That's how we refer to it, 'The Incident,' just so you'll know."

"When was that? Ninety-four? Ninety-five?"

"Twenty-two hundred hours on the evening of March 15, 1995. Easy to remember."

"The Ides of March," I said. "Not to be indelicate or disrespectful in any way because I know it must have been extremely difficult for everyone here, but that was years ago. You're not even the same airline, and furthermore, if I remember right, the cause of that crash was pilot error. It had nothing to do with the ground operation."

"Ah, but that's the nature of superstition, isn't it? It's neither rational nor reasonable."

"Is it possible this superstition can be explained by the fact that rampers simply don't like to work these little airplanes because they're a pain in the ass to load?"

His coy smile said it all.

I reached up to rub my temples because my head was throbbing, and as soon as I realized that, it occurred to me my legs were aching, and when I noticed that, I couldn't help but feel the stiffness in my neck. I'd been in this station nine days, and every day had been longer than the one before.

"Kevin, I came into this job under the impression that I was supposed to be in charge of this operation at Logan. How come I can't find anything that I'm in charge of?"

He laughed. "We do have a unique way of doing things here. It takes a little getting used to."

"Has anyone ever tried to take action with the union on this issue?" Just contemplating the idea made me want to go to the hotel, get in bed, and pull the covers over my head. But that was probably just what they wanted.

"It's so ingrained now, most of the boys would rather lose their job than work a prop. You'd have to fire them all."

Big Pete was making his way across the ramp, in uniform now and apparently on the clock.

"I don't think so," I said. "You'd just have to fire the right one."

Chapter Fourteen

According to Ellen's running log, the Esplanade along the Charles River had been one of her favorite haunts. It was in the heart of the city, nowhere near Marblehead, yet she'd gone back to it over and over. I understood why when I tried it myself. With the skyline of Boston to the south, Cambridge to the north, and the Charles in between, there was something dazzling to gaze at from every angle, especially on a night like this when the clear winter air brought the lights of the city so close.

It felt good to run, to be outside and not cooped up in my hotel room watching videos. I'd made a decision not to feel threatened every minute of every day, to take charge of my life again, and it felt good.

I'd left my cell phone in the car, which didn't help much when my beeper went off somewhere around the Harvard Bridge. I had to run around Cambridge until I found a pay phone. The number on the beeper wasn't one I recognized, and when I dialed, it didn't even ring once.

"Shanahan?"

"Dan?"

"I've been beeping you for twenty minutes."

"Twenty minutes, huh?" It was ten minutes, at most.

"What's that noise?" he asked. "Where are you?"

"I'm out running. Is this your car phone number?"

"Yeah. I'm on my way to the airport. If we get cut off, it's because I'm in the tunnel."

"Why don't you tell me why you called *before* you go into the tunnel?"

"There was a fight tonight at the airport. Two rampers got into it. They called me about a half hour ago from the hospital."

"Who's hurt and how bad?"

"It was Little Pete Dwyer and Terry McTavish. Little Pete's at the hospital. Cuts and lacerations. I don't know about Terry."

"Is Terry McTavish John's brother?"

"Yep."

"That's a coincidence."

"That two guys with the same name are brothers?"

"No, no. We had a stare-down last night between John McTavish and Big Pete. It was when you were at that sales meeting."

"Shocked the shit out of me," he said. "Terry's not a guy who causes trouble."

"Do you know what the fight was about?"

"No idea. I'm on my way in to do the investigation."

"Do you want help? I can be there in an hour."

"No. I want you to hear the grievance, so you need to stay out of the action. That way it never has to go out of the station."

"You don't want it to go to Lenny."

"When Lenny hears our grievances, he always finds for the

union. Or he makes some deal. There's nothing they can do bad enough that Lenny won't cut a deal and bring 'em back to work."

"That sounds like an exaggeration."

"You can check the record."

"All right. What time is it? I don't have a watch on."

"It's just after nine." The connection was starting to break up. "What are you doing out so late?"

"Call me when you're finished and give me the details," I said, ignoring the question. He sounded like my mother.

"You gonna be at the hotel?"

Before I could answer, the line went dead. He must have gone into the tunnel.

A United B767 under tow crept along the outer taxiway toward the maintenance hangar. I could see it from my hotel window. Except for anti-collision lights, the aircraft was dark, all engines off. Moving like that through the night, it looked like a submarine running in deep water.

It had been almost three hours since Dan had called about the fight. I imagined him down there, interviewing closed-mouth rampers, trying to conduct an investigation, trying to figure out who had done what to whom. It was hard waiting. I could have beeped him, but I knew he'd call when he had something.

The Celtics were on TV keeping me company. Listening with one ear, I knew it was late in the campaign and the Celts were out on the West Coast getting clobbered by Golden State, of all teams. I came away from the window, stood in the light of the TV, and stared blankly. Someone in the hometown team's shamrock green uniform had just been called for goaltending.

I started to turn it off, but then sat on the bed instead and watched.

My father had loved basketball. And football. And baseball most of all. His hometown Cubs were his favorite, but he'd watch any team. He'd sit by the hour in front of the TV, which is what he used to do instead of engaging with the rest of the world, including my brothers, my sister, and me. I started sitting and watching with him, and pretty soon he started teaching me all the rules, all the teams, and all the players. I was a good student. He'd quiz me, and when I knew one he didn't expect, his face would light up and he'd be so proud. And when he'd fall asleep, I'd still be watching, trying to learn more names, to memorize more stats so that when he woke up, I could make his face light up again. I began to love the thing he loved, which was as close as I ever got to him.

The Warriors were on a 12–0 run, and there didn't seem to be much hope. Besides, I'd lost the thread. I didn't know any of these players. I reached up with the remote and clicked it off.

For a while I sat on the bed and stared at the phone. Eventually, I was staring not at the phone but into the corner of my room where I'd left Ellen's box of personal momentos. I hadn't touched it since the night we'd bolted from her house. I'd started to a couple of times—Dan asked about it almost once a day—but over the weekend I hadn't wanted to be reminded. After Lenny's call on Monday, I wasn't sure I wanted to open it up at all. I knew that if I did, I'd find out all kinds of details about Ellen, the odd and unique ones that would turn her into a person to me. If I opened that box, Ellen would come out and sit in the room next to me and talk to me and I'd get to know her and pretty soon I wouldn't be able to put her back.

I stared at the phone a little longer. Stood up. Paced around. Wished I had brought work home with me. The second time I looked at the box, it was already too late. I went to the corner, picked it up, and hoisted it onto the bed. Before opening it, I laid my hand over it, palm flat, pausing for a moment before disturbing the contents. Then I lifted the lid and began.

Dan had tossed in the mail he'd found at the house, and it was right on top. It was a large stack until I took out all the coupon flyers and catalogues. What was left was a couple of bills and a plain postcard. Not much different from my own mail. According to her bills, Ellen had paid a fortune to heat that big house, and she was a frequent purchaser of cable pay-per-view movies, the single woman's best friend. At the Marblehead Athletic Club she'd charged the same bagel and cream cheese at the juice bar three days a week, every week, in December. Four times in the month, once a week on Mondays, she'd been charged fifty dollars for something coded PT, which I took to mean personal trainer. I started to put it back into the envelope when I noticed the date of her last session—January 5. It was the day she died. Seemed strange to work out, then go home and hang yourself. A phone number was provided on the invoice. I put it aside to call sometime when it wasn't the middle of the night.

The last item, the postcard, had looked like junk mail because of the computer-generated address label, but the single line of type across the back identified it as something far more interesting. "Have been unable to contact you by phone," it read. "Please call me." And it was signed by none other than Julia Milholland, the mystery woman with the old-Boston name. Whoever she was, she was persistent. And discreet. Not only had she never left a clue in her multiple phone messages, the front of the card was blank. No title, affiliation, or company name, but there was a return address on Charles Street. I put it with the health club invoice.

The rest of the box was filled with Ellen's ubiquitous hanging files with colored labels, which is not how I stored anything personal. I thought the one labeled LETTERS was promising, but I didn't get too far into the newsy notes from Aunt Jo and chatty letters from high school and college chums before realizing that what I needed was a box of letters *from* Ellen.

She'd kept a stack of photo ID's, mostly from school, work, and health clubs. I remembered seeing Ellen at a few company functions and meetings. I knew what she had looked like, but this was the first time I'd seen a picture of her. She had chin-length red hair and hazel eyes. She had high cheekbones that came down to a rather square jaw. She wasn't pretty in the classic fashion model sense, but she was attractive in an unusual way. She didn't smile much, it seemed, at least not in the photos. I lined them up in chronological order and watched her age all the way up to the last one taken in Boston. The first was a Florida State driver's license issued on her sixteenth birthday. I stared at it for a long time before I was satisfied there was nothing in her smile, nothing in her eyes to portend a life already almost half over.

If people can be defined by the things they keep and the things they let drift away, for Ellen, so specific in everything she did, it would be particularly true. Nothing was in that box that hadn't meant something to her. What surprised me was that they meant something to me, too. Mass cards for the deceased, some with the last name Shepard, reminded me of a worn leather box my mother had kept in the basement, filled with old family photos, black-and-white, stiff with age. It reminded me of a picture I'd found in that box of my mother on her graduation day from a Catholic grade school in St. Louis. She was squinting into the camera, wearing a shy smile. It was the first time I'd ever seen my mother as a girl. I stared at that picture forever. She'd looked hopeful, something I'd never seen in her in real life. It was the first time I'd understood that she had been young once, that she had lived a life before me, one that didn't include me.

Ellen's rosary was in a velvet pouch with a First Holy Communion label stitched in gold. I hadn't thrown mine away, but I hadn't kept it, either. I didn't know what had happened to it. This one was tiny and delicate, made for eight-year-old hands with mother of pearl beads and a simple gold crucifix. I hadn't held a rosary in so long, I'd forgotten what it felt like.

Her birth certificate was there from a hospital in Dade County, Florida. When I pulled out an unlabeled file in the back, a news clip fell onto the cotton sheets. When I turned it over, I was confused for a moment because the woman staring back from the brittle, yellowed newsprint could have been a seamless addition to the chronology of Ellen's ID photos. It could have been Ellen in middle age. But it was a photo of her mother, and this was her obituary.

Anna Bache Shepard had died when she was forty-eight years old. She'd been survived by Joseph T. Shepard, her husband of nineteen years, and her fourteen-year-old daughter, Ellen. Services were held at Christ the King Catholic Church in Miami Shores. I read the clipping a second time, wondering why she'd died so young, but there was no cause given. I understood why after I'd read the only other document in the file, her death certificate. Ellen's mother had committed suicide. She'd hanged herself.

Chapter Fifteen

The phone finally rang—at 5:14 A.M. At some point during the night, very late, I'd leaned against the headboard, put my head back to rest, and fallen into a dreamless sleep. When I opened my eyes, the lights were still on, the contents of Ellen's box were spread across my bed, and Anna Bache Shepard's death certificate was still in my hand.

"You weren't sleeping, were you, Shanahan?" Dan used his louder-than-normal car phone voice, and the line crackled.

"Are you on your way home?" I swung my feet to the floor and stood up to stretch, my spine popping in three places. My left arm was asleep, dead weight hanging from my shoulder. It began to tingle as I shook it.

"I'm just pulling into the parking lot of your hotel. I'll meet you downstairs in two minutes."

We made a good pair, the two of us, waiting in the lobby for the coffee shop to open. Dan sat forward on a low couch, knees bumping the faux-marble table that held his notes. His soft, faded jeans somehow stayed up without the benefit of a belt. His white cotton dress shirt was open at the collar and filled with those tiny wrinkles you get from wearing your clothes around the clock. He had the same wrinkles under his eyes.

"Like I told you last night," he said, "it was Little Pete Dwyer and Terry McTavish beating the crap out of each other. Both of them got hurt, and neither one will say what happened." He glanced up and caught me stifling a yawn. "Shanahan, if I'm the one who was up all night, how come you look like shit?"

"I was with you in spirit," I said, remembering the puffy-eyed, slack-haired visage in my bathroom mirror this morning. I'd been tempted to wear my sweatshirt with the hood up, drawstring pulled tight. Instead, I'd put my hair in a ponytail, washed my face, and declared myself presentable. "How bad were the injuries?"

"Terry's got a big bruise on the side of his head and a broken hand. From what I hear, Little Pete's got stitches over one eye, but I never saw him. My dumbfuck shift supervisor took his statement, drove him to the hospital, and let him go home from there. Lazy bastard. He didn't even do a substance test."

"Fighting isn't necessarily enough for probable cause."

"He could have used aggression for probable cause. That's what I did for Terry. I had him pee in the bottle when I took him to the hospital to get his hand set. I can tell you right now, though, it's going to come back clean. Terry McTavish is a Boy Scout."

"What do their statements say?"

"Little Pete claims self-defense all the way." He leafed through his file, found the page he wanted, and pulled it out. "Says he was walking across the ramp when Terry jumped him from behind and threw him to the ground. That's it. Except for the fact that he's a lying sack of shit."

"What's Terry's story?"

"He doesn't have a story. I spent all night trying to crack him. All I could get him to say was he had a good reason to do what he did, and he shouldn't lose his job over it."

"No witnesses?"

"None that are talking."

"Do you think—" I stopped and glanced around the lobby. The desk clerk was in the back, and the lone bellman was across the floor out of earshot. Still, I lowered my voice. "Maybe this has something to do with your drug-smuggling theory. Terry could have stumbled into something, and now he's afraid to say what."

"I don't think so. I've been asking around, some of my off-the-record sources. The ones who will say anything swear there's nothing like that going on at Logan at the moment. I don't know if that's the truth, or if it's because Little Pete is involved, but I'm getting nothing on drugs. Dead battery."

"What does your gut tell you about last night?" I was learning that Dan was always in close communication with his gut.

"I think Little Pete was drunk last night, and whatever happened came out of that."

"Drunk during his shift?"

"It wouldn't be the first time."

"Little Pete's a drunk?"

"I thought you knew," he said.

"How would I know that?"

"It's common knowledge."

"Not to someone who's been here two weeks."

He shrugged. "Sorry, boss."

I had a bad feeling, the shaking, rolling, want-to-throw-up seasick feeling I always got when I heard about airport employees drinking on the job. I could just see Little Pete Dwyer careening around the ramp devoid of motor skills, around *airplanes*, in a forklift or a loader. God forbid he should smack into an engine or punch through a fuselage. God help us all if he did it and never told anyone. "How big is his problem?"

"More like everyone else has a problem, because when Little Pete's drunk, he's mean as hell. He hit a guy in the head with a hand-held radio once because the guy changed the channel on the TV."

"Why is he still working here?"

"That particular time, Lenny made a deal and brought him back. The guy he hit went on permanent disability."

"Why would Lenny bring him back? If he's as truly self-serving as everyone says, I wouldn't expect him to take that kind of a risk."

"I told you about the deals, and Lenny's made a lot of 'em to protect this kid. Every time he gets into trouble, they send him to rehab. He's been twice." Dan was drumming his pencil, eraser end, on the table, making a noise that seemed loud in the quiet lobby. "I can't see Terry jumping anyone," he said, "but I can see it the other way around, with Terry the one who was defending himself."

"I don't suppose there's a chance in hell he'll tell us what happened."

"No. The Dwyers and the McTavishes hate each other. But still, Terry's not going to rat out a union brother and get him fired."

"Would he give up his own job to protect a drunk? Because

if I have to get rid of them both to get Little Pete off the ramp, I will."

"With what I've got now, you'd have a hard time busting Little Pete. With no test and no witnesses, I can't prove he was under the influence, and without a statement from Terry, I never will."

"How about this? We keep them both out of service while we conduct our investigation and do some interviews. If we can prove Little Pete was drinking on the job, we get rid of him for good. At a minimum, we can force him back into rehab. In the meantime, maybe Terry reconsiders his story."

"If he doesn't?"

"Then screw him. I don't care about the union and the brotherhood and all that crap. If he's comfortable letting a drunk work next to him on the ramp, he deserves to be gone, too."

"If it comes down to him losing his job, we might see one or two of the decent guys come forward. The McTavishes have a lot of support around here, which we're going to need. I have to tell you, if you terminate Little Pete, you're going to start a war."

"Are you suggesting we leave him out there?"

"I'm just telling you the facts, boss. That's my job."

I sat back in the cushy, crushed velvet love seat and considered my limited options. That seemed to be the drill here—separate the bad options from the worse options and pick one. "Can you handle a backlash on the ramp if we end up terminating?"

"Like I said, the guys like Terry and his brother's got some influence. I think we can ride it out. But it won't be much fun."

"I'll bring Angelo back. That might take some of the

pressure off. It'll certainly get Lenny off my back. What do you think?"

"It's about goddamned time. You've been talking about doing it since you got here."

We both turned as we heard the sound of the doors sliding apart. The coffee shop was open for business. I reached for the file I'd brought down from my room, stood up, and stretched again. I couldn't seem to get all the kinks out. "Come on," I said. "I'll buy you breakfast. I've got something else I need to talk to you about."

Dan was staring out the window. If it had been summer, he would have been gazing at a lush, terraced courtyard, a carpet of flowering plants, and a swimming pool. But it was darkest January, the floodlights were on, and instead of a shimmering, turquoise blue surface, he was staring at a heavy brown tarp covered with winter's debris. In his hand was the death certificate for Ellen's mother. When he finally spoke, his voice was as blank as his face. "She never said anything about this to me."

"I don't think she told anyone," I said. "Not anyone at work, anyway. You'd have to think if someone knew about it, they would have spoken up. It wasn't in her personnel file." I scanned the obituary again. "Ellen was fourteen when this happened. It had to be painful for her to talk about."

When he didn't respond, I didn't know what else to say, so I drank my orange juice. It was canned, but tart enough to wash away the taste of going to bed too late and getting up too early. The only other patron in the coffee shop, a blonde woman, sharply professional in a sleek suit and sleeker haircut, sat across the floor at a table by herself. We both looked at her when she sneezed.

"Someone knew," he said, turning back to the conversation, his eyes bright with the energy of a new theory.

"Someone knew what?"

"Whoever killed her knew about the mother's suicide. That's why he hung her, to make it look like she killed herself, too. Don't you see that?"

I was about to answer when the waiter arrived. As he served us, I sat back and marveled at Dan. He was either so deep in denial he couldn't see straight, or the most resilient man I'd ever met. Maybe both. The other possibility was that Lenny had been telling the truth, that this unnatural obsession of his was driven by the deepest guilt. "Dan, you have the ability to take any set of facts and form them to support your own theory. Don't you *see* that? I don't understand why you're being so obstinate about this."

"I told you—"

"I know," I said, "she was a good boss and your friend and you're loyal, but this is getting a little absurd. Look at that death certificate and think about what it means."

He picked up his fork and poked at his four runny eggs, a side of pancakes, three strips of soggy bacon, and a stack of toast. The spread looked like something he'd usually enjoy, but not today. He put the fork down. "Okay, what's your theory?"

"Dan, I didn't know Ellen, so all I can do is draw my conclusions from the facts. She came to Boston from staff with a sterling reputation and lots of enthusiasm. She took on a job here for which she wasn't qualified. After thirteen months of trying as hard as she could to turn the station around, she wasn't any further along than the day she arrived. She might have even lost ground. And she was being harassed in the most contemptible way for trying."

He was staring at his eggs.

"It seems to me that something went really wrong for her, Dan. The police have no evidence of murder. Ellen was being treated for chronic depression. She didn't have much in her life besides her job. She was used to being successful, and when it looked as if she might fail in Boston, maybe she felt that her whole life was a failure. It can feel that way sometimes, believe me. And now we find out that her mother killed herself."

I picked at my breakfast, too. The oatmeal with brown sugar had sounded better than it tasted, and I was getting depressed just watching the way Dan was hurting and thinking about Ellen's situation. I abandoned the gummy substance in my bowl and went to the all-liquid breakfast of orange juice and milk. I waited a few uncomfortable moments for a response. When nothing was forthcoming, I went right to the bottom line. "Lenny called me yesterday and asked us to back off this thing, Dan. Maybe it's time."

"Sleazy bastard," he muttered.

"He didn't seem sleazy about it. He seemed to be covering the company's ass and maybe his own. What is it between the two of you?"

"Why? What did he say?"

"He said . . . he said that you were the one who pushed Ellen into taking a hard line with the union and that the reason you're so adamant about how she died was because you feel guilty. You can't accept the fact that she might have killed herself."

Dan's face started to flush. "And you believed him?"

"I don't know what to believe. I know that there's something going on between you and Lenny that you won't talk about. And I feel that there has to be more to your relationship with Ellen that you're not telling me about. Did you two have a thing, because if you did, it doesn't make any difference to me—"

"Don't ever say that, Shanahan. Don't ever say that again. Everything I told you was the truth."

"But are there things you haven't told me?"

We stared at each other, and it became clear that he wasn't going to dignify my question with a response. He countered with his own question. "Did Lenny offer you a promotion if you could make me stop asking questions?"

"What?"

"A promotion. That's what you care about, right? Your career?"

I slipped back in my seat and took a deep breath. I tried to keep in mind that he'd been up all night dealing with recalcitrant employees. But I wasn't one of them. "You're right," I said evenly. "I do care about my career, and I don't want to be made to feel that the things I want are any less important, or in some way less noble, than what you want. I don't believe the issues are that simple."

He sat back, clasped his hands across his stomach, and stared up at the ceiling. His eyes were red and tired, and when he looked back at me, something in them had changed. "I'm sorry," he said quietly. "It's easy for me to say I don't care about my career because I don't have one. And it's been that way for so long, I forget sometimes what it might feel like if I did have something to lose. You're right. This is not your fight."

He had an amazing ability to make me feel validated and guilty at the same time. "This isn't my fight, but I do have a stake in how things turn out. If we can find a way to get rid of the Dwyers, I'd be most pleased. And you do have something to lose—at least Lenny thinks so."

"What else did he say?"

"He said that if I wanted, he'd bust you down to ramp supervisor and move you out of Boston to a station as far away from New Jersey as he can find."

Dan's face turned ashen, then, almost immediately, heart-attack red. "He *said* that?"

"That's exactly what he said."

"Son of a *bitch*." He flung his napkin onto his plate. "Mother*fucker*." When he shot out of his chair, he nearly tipped it backward, bumped the table with his thigh, and rattled all the silverware.

The sleek one glanced up, but only long enough to turn the page of her newspaper.

Dan paced an intense loop around a row of empty tables, came back to ours, then made the loop again. All I could do was hope he stayed in the coffee shop long enough to tell me what I'd said.

"He couldn't even say it to me directly," he mumbled, making another loop. "Yellow ratfuck scumbag."

"Do you want to sit down and tell me what's going on?"

I could see a vein pulsing in the side of his throat as he settled back in and shoved the remains of his breakfast out of the way. "My kid lives in New Jersey. He's threatening to send me away from my kid. That's what's going on."

I wasn't sure I'd heard right. "Did you just say you have a child?"

"She lives with her mother and grandparents down in Newark. I can't fucking believe he would even say that." He banged the table with the heel of his hand and got jelly on his cuff. I gave him my napkin and he wiped it off, carelessly at first, then more deliberately. Even after it was clear the spot wasn't going away, with his mouth set in a grim line and his eyes losing focus, he kept working it.

I reached across the table and took the napkin away. "What's her name?"

"What?"

"Your daughter, what's her name?"

"Michelle. Michelle Marie. She's six."

"She lives in Newark, you said?"

"Belleville. Just outside." He checked his watch.

"What are you thinking?"

"I'm gonna call him. As soon as he drags his ass to work, I'm gonna tell him—"

"I don't think that's a good idea. Tell me what is going on between you."

He sat unusually still, avoiding eye contact. No fingers drumming, no knees bouncing up and down. "I need the key to the house."

"You need to go home and get some sleep."

"Just give me the goddamned key."

This time he got the sleek woman's attention. And the waiter's. And mine. I stared at him, more confused than angry and hoping to chalk the outburst up to too much frustration and too little sleep.

He let out a long, deflating sigh and appeared to regroup. "All I want is to put an end to this. I can't take much more. I'm too tired and I'm afraid of what I'm going to do if Lenny threatens me like that again. If there's a package in that house, I'm going to find it. So can I please have the key?"

* * *

The waiter brought the check for me to sign. While Dan waited in the lobby, I went upstairs for the key to Ellen's house. As I watched him walk out the front door with it, I couldn't help but think that he'd never answered my question. Were there things he wasn't telling me?

Chapter Sixteen

Pete Dwyer Sr. was waiting for me that morning, staked out in the reception area with a newspaper, a couple of bear claws from Dunkin' Donuts, and a big cup of coffee. I knew he'd heard me coming down the corridor, but he didn't bother to look up until I spoke.

"Why is it so hot in here?" I asked, sliding out of my coat. It must have been ninety degrees in the office suite. Pete had peeled off most of his outer layers, and still he looked steamy and flushed, maybe because he was sipping hot coffee.

"Damn heating system," he said, almost spitting the words out. "One more thing around here that don't work."

"Are we responsible or is the airport authority?"

"It's the airport. At least once every winter the heating system in the whole building goes wacky. Usually takes them a week to fix it."

"A *week*?" A withering prospect.

He folded his paper, collected his breakfast, and stood right behind me as I unlocked my office door. Once inside, he settled into one of the desk chairs, looking more at home in my office than I did, and watched me with those cool gray eyes, cool despite the ambient temperature and the hot beverage.

"I can't believe you're drinking hot coffee."

"I was outside working all night. It ain't this hot out there."

"Then let's go out there." I didn't wait for an answer, just grabbed my coat and walked out. After a stop for hot tea, we went to the outbound bag room, where it was noisy but forty-five degrees cooler than my office. It was also the heart of the downstairs operation at this time of the morning. Bags and boxes came down in a steady stream from the ticket counter and from skycaps on the curb into the cavernous concrete bag room to be sorted, loaded into carts, and driven to the airplanes—hopefully the right ones.

I leaned in toward Pete and raised my voice to be heard over the grinding of the bag belts and the rumbling of the tugs streaming by with their bag-laden carts. "What can I do for you?"

He stuffed the last of his bear claw into his mouth and licked the sugar off his thumb. "Let's go to the office," he said.

I followed him to the far corner where a couple of flimsy Sheetrock walls with glass windows came together to form an office for the bag room crew chief. He took the desk chair for himself, leaving a rolling secretary's chair with a cracked leather seat and one armrest for me. We could still see the action in the bag room through the windows, but the rumbling of the system was muted, the closed door offering some relief from the constant grinding of the belts. It was quiet enough that I could hear the sound of Big Pete's palms polishing the skin of a grapefruit that had suddenly appeared in his hands. It must have been in the office. He took out a letter opener and began to peel it.

"Is that grapefruit yours?"

"You're holding an innocent man out of service," he announced, completely ignoring my question. "Petey was just an innocent bystander in this thing last night."

"I'm learning that no one is innocent here, and Victor's the union president, so why are you talking to me about this?"

"I don't trust Victor to handle the important stuff"—his eyes cut to my face—"and neither do you."

"Why do you say that?"

"It's true, ain't it?"

It was, of course, and though I didn't want to believe I'd been that transparent, I appreciated the respect he showed by telling me that I had been. It meant I could be equally blunt in return. "If Little Pete was a bystander, why would he have twelve stitches in his head? And I don't think Terry McTavish broke his own hand."

"Man jumps you from behind out of the clear blue and throws you down on the ramp, you're entitled to protect yourself."

"I haven't met Terry, but I'd like to meet the man who could sneak up on your son and throw him to the ground."

He suppressed a smile. "Must have been the element of surprise."

"Must have been. Look, I think I already know what happened last night." He drew back and looked at me all stiff-necked and squinty-eyed. "So instead of you trying to convince me it didn't, just tell me what you want."

He threw part of the peel in the trash, then leaned back and propped his feet up on the desk, his heels resting on the old, stained blotter. "All right. I know you're in a position here. You got appearances to think about, and you got to take some kind of action." As the peel fell away and the fresh citrus smell filled the office, I noticed that he had a hard time stripping the fruit because his fingernails were so short—painfully short— and ragged. They were not much more than nubs, and I knew that he was a nail biter because I had been, too. Big Pete Dwyer struck me as a lot of things, but a nail biter wasn't one. I wondered what it was that made him nervous.

He noticed me staring at his nails and dug his fingers into the fruit, pulling the sections apart. "To my way of thinking," he continued, "Terry threw the first punch. You want to can his ass, we won't fight you. I can guarantee he won't even file a grievance."

"And what happens to Little Pete?"

"He didn't do nothing, so he should come back to work." The grapefruit peel went into the garbage, and a slice of the fruit disappeared into his mouth.

"It's funny how that worked out." I shifted to find a comfortable spot on the cracked leather seat. There wasn't one, so I stood. "You and John McTavish get into a pissing contest the other night. The next thing I know, his brother Terry is in trouble under questionable circumstances. Is Terry aware that his union representative is offering up his job? More to the point, is John?"

"You don't need to worry about what goes on inside the union. You just need to worry about yourself." For a moment he actually made eye contact and held it. "I'm trying to help you out here."

It might have been my imagination, but he seemed oddly sincere even though he was trying hard not to be. There was no question he was trying to help himself and his son, but it was also possible that he truly believed he was helping me, too.

"I appreciate the gesture," I said, "but it sounds as if your son is the one who needs help. I understand he has a problem with alcohol."

Pete didn't even stop chewing. "Yeah? Who says so?"

"He's worked under the influence in the past, I think he's doing it now, and I suspect he's the one who instigated the trouble last night, not Terry McTavish."

"My son ain't got no problem like that. If he did, nobody down here would tell you."

His face had betrayed nothing as he sucked another slice into his mouth and spat out a seed, but it wasn't without effort. I heard it in his voice. It was in the measured way he spoke and the precise way he formed his words. The strain was there. It sounded old, scabbed over, and I thought maybe I understood what made him chew his nails. Big Pete was no different than any other father with a screw-up for a son. I almost felt sorry for him.

"How much longer do you think you can cover for him? You can't watch him all the time."

"You don't have no case against my son." He finished off the last wedge and wiped his fingers on a piece of paper from the trash can. "You never will."

"I don't want him working around airplanes," I said.

"If he's working the ramp, he's working around airplanes."

"Then I'm going to have to find a way to make sure he's not working the ramp. What if he causes an accident? Could you live with yourself?"

"You shouldn't even say something like that."

"It scares you, too, doesn't it?"

He stood up slowly, more like uncoiled, and brushed a few wayward flakes of glazed sugar from his uniform shirt. He started

toward me and didn't stop until I could smell the grapefruit on
his breath. The muscles in my back tensed, and for the first time
I felt uncomfortable with him. "My son is my responsibility," he
said. "You leave him to me and you won't have no problems.
But you push this thing, and you're going to regret the day you
ever asked for this job."

I started to breathe a little faster. "Are you threatening me?"

He stepped around me, opened the door, and let the bag
room noise come in. Then he leaned down and whispered in
my ear. "Think about what happened to the girl who was here
before you." I stared straight ahead, fixing my gaze on the letter
opener he'd left on top of the desk. "You're all alone out here,
just like she was, more alone than you think. I wouldn't want
you to get depressed and kill yourself."

I turned to look at his face, but he was already through the
door and gone. I would never smell grapefruit again without that
awful feeling of my heart dropping into the pit of my stomach.

Molly was at her desk fanning herself and looking as if she
might pass out.

"Is someone working on fixing the heat?"

"This happens every year," she said breathlessly.

"So I hear. Why don't you go out and get some fans? Charge
it to the company."

"It's the middle of winter in Boston. Where am I going to
find fans?"

"How should I know, Molly? *Just do something.*"

I went into my office and slammed the door. I went back
to my desk and straight to my briefcase, where I found the fax
from Ellen's house, the one asking for a meeting at the same
time, same place. I smoothed it flat on the desk and wrote

directly on the page, "Saturday, 7:00 PM, Ciao Bella on Newbury Street." It was the only restaurant in town that I knew. I signed my name, went out to the machine, and punched in the number to Sir Speedy in Nahant. My finger froze over the Enter button, giving me one last chance to appreciate what I was doing. I had no idea who had sent this message, and it was just my own instinct saying that it was friend, not foe. But I needed more people on my side, and if this was someone Ellen had trusted, maybe I could trust him or her, too.

I punched the button, the machine whirred to life, and the message was gone.

Chapter Seventeen

Friday afternoon was the worst possible day to cancel a flight. We'd taken two mechanicals back-to-back and cancelled them both. I'd spent the past several hours at the ticket counter helping to rebook a couple hundred inconvenienced passengers. Rebooking is a technical term. It means presenting hostile travelers with a list of terrible alternatives and asking them to choose one. It usually takes a while.

I was almost past Dan's office door before I realized he was in there sitting at his desk, tie loosened and sleeves rolled up. He'd changed his shirt since breakfast yesterday morning, but his eyes were still bleary. He was using one hand to prop up his head and the other to turn the pages of something that had his complete attention.

"If I'd known you were here, I would have invited you up to the ticket counter to take part in our latest disaster."

He responded without looking up. "I just got in. I've been up at Ellen's house all day."

"Which means you've been up for two straight days."

"Here, before I forget . . ." He dug into his pocket and came out with Ellen's house key. "I also went to the post office and got her mail forwarded to the airport."

"Good plan." I sat down and peeled off my shoes. "Did you find anything? Answering machine tapes, perhaps? Or a fish?"

He gave his head a weary shake. "I've searched every square inch of that place. Whatever she was hiding, I don't think it's in the house, unless it's behind a secret panel or something. With that old place, who knows? But I did find out one thing." He lowered his voice to the point that it was almost just a rumble. "I talked to the old guy, the landlord, and he said the alarm went off again the other night. The police came, but no one was there. You know what that means." He didn't need a response from me. "Someone tried to go in who didn't have the new security code."

"Didn't that make you nervous, being up there by yourself and knowing that?"

He looked at me, and I knew there was no point in pursuing the subject.

The item he'd been studying so intently was a wall calendar. "Are you planning your next vacation?"

"This is Molly's calendar from last year. My buddy over at United got me the list of Ellen's destinations from their frequent flyer desk. Altogether she took fifteen trips, and thirteen of them she could have flown on us. The two we don't fly are to Pittsburgh and Charleston. She got miles for every trip, so you were right. She bought tickets like a real passenger."

I turned the calendar so that I could see the dates. "Did you tell Molly? Because she didn't believe me."

"Yeah. Neither one of us can."

The calendar was from an insurance company, the kind they

give out free every year. It had pictures of Massachusetts tourist
attractions through the seasons. We were looking at November
and Bunker Hill in the snow. Dan had penciled in the three-
digit city codes for Ellen's destinations throughout the year.
Most corresponded with an ELS, Molly's designation for Ellen,
and an explanation of a dentist appointment or an off-site meeting or a personal day off. For some, she must have flown out
that night and come back the next morning, because there was
nothing on the calendar. No time lost.

"Any pattern or interesting sequence?" I asked.

"Nothing jumps out at me, but I'm working on it. My next
step is to call the GMs in those stations."

"If she was sneaking around, flying under cover of another
airline, it's not likely she'd check in with colleagues while she
was there."

"I know, but I don't know what else to do."

"Is there any connection to the Beechcraft angle?"

"I thought of that," he said. "If there is, I can't figure what
it is, other than the fact that we fly them out of here. Big deal."

"You said she had questions about the Beeches. What
kind?"

"Like I said, a lot of questions about the cargo compartments, how much weight they can take, position of the fuel
tanks, that kind of stuff. That's why I made the connection to
drugs."

"But we don't think it was drugs, right? So what was it?"

He shrugged.

"Why don't you try to find another copy of that Nor'easter
procedures manual?" I said. "If we looked through it ourselves,
maybe we can figure out what she was doing with it."

We stared at each other. We were glum. Stumped and glum.

Finally, I reached for the calendar and pulled it into my lap. "When was her first secret trip?"

He checked his list. "A little over a year ago. Not too long after she got here."

I leafed backward through the months, reading the various notations Molly had made and charting the station's recent history in reverse. Besides Ellen's travel days, there were employee birthdays and company anniversaries, retirement luncheons, and the annual Christmas party. September of last year had an entry in red with big arrows pointing to it. It was always an event when Bill Scanlon passed through your station.

"You believe Ellen started her investigation a few weeks ago, right?"

"A little longer, sometime before Christmas."

"If her first trip was over a year ago, then it's hard to relate the travel to the investigation. In fact . . ." I flipped a few pages as the idea settled into my brain. I flipped a few more and I knew I was right. "What these look like to me are secret rendezvous, especially those overnighters."

"What, like she was meeting someone?"

"Someone she didn't want anyone to know she was meeting."

"Why?"

"What do you mean, why? Why does a woman usually have a secret rendezvous?"

"You mean like she was having an affair? No way."

I knew I was right. It felt right, but I had to figure out a way to convince Dan without telling him that my conjecture was based on my own personal experience traveling through the shadowland of whispered conversations, furtive plans, and hidden destinations. "Dan, we've already established this woman's ability to keep secrets. I think it's very possible that she was hooking up with someone in these cities."

His pained expression, lips pursed and eyebrows drawn together, was one I was coming to recognize, because he displayed it every time we found out something about Ellen he didn't know or like. He began to roll down his sleeves and button his cuffs. Something under his desk rattled when he bumped it with his foot. He kicked it impatiently and then again before he looked under the desk.

"Oh, *shit*." He checked his watch, then reached under and came up with an overnight bag. "I gotta get out of here."

"Where are you going?" As far as I knew, Dan didn't travel anywhere except back and forth to Logan Airport.

"Jersey. I'm going down to see my kid."

"Michelle."

"Yeah, I called her last night and told her I was coming. She'll be waiting for me." As he put on his jacket, he couldn't stop grinning. It was an unabashed, I'm-crazy-about-this-kid-and-don't-care-who-knows-it smile. "She's a pisser. I can't believe some of the stuff she comes up with."

I smiled, too, picturing a miniature female Dan racing around at Mach speeds, spewing invectives. "Does she talk like you?"

It took him a moment to get my drift, but when he did, he was horrified. "No fucking way. I don't swear around my kid." He put his hand over his heart. "On my mother's grave, she has never heard me cuss. Not once. Not my kid."

"If you say so." He unzipped the bag and started loading in files and printouts. I snatched them all back, including the calendar. "I'll take care of this."

"You sure?"

"If you're going to be with your daughter, *be* with her. And by the way, why did I have to hear about her from Lenny?"

"I don't know. It never came up." He closed the bag and looked at me. "You got any?"

"Kids? No."

"Ever been married?"

"No."

"See that? I didn't know that about you. It never came up."

I squeezed back into my shoes and followed him to the reception area. "Hold on, I'll walk you to your gate." I grabbed my coat and briefcase, closed up my office, and we started walking. It was hard to talk as we pushed through the crowded concourse, so I waited until we'd arrived at his gate. The agents on his flight were boarding stragglers, so I had a chance to tell him about my tête-à-tête with Big Pete. I kept my voice low so no one could eavesdrop.

"Am I doing the right thing not bringing back Little Pete?" I asked.

The bag thudded to the floor as he leaned back against one of the windows. "I think you're doing the right thing—" He caught himself and started again. "I *know* you're doing the right thing. The question is, can we deal with the consequences? And I'm not just talking about here in Boston. Have you talked this over with your boss?"

"Not exactly."

"I'll tell you what's going to happen. Assuming we could even get Terry McTavish to talk and we can nail Little Pete in the first place, Lenny is going to find some way to make a deal with the union and bring him in through the back door. Lenny will be a hero and we'll look like idiots."

"If we can prove that the guy was drunk on the job and physically attacked another employee, I can't see how Lenny could bring him back, if for no other reason than self-preservation. Setting aside all the issues of moral responsibility and self-righteous breast-beating, in terms of pure self-interest, knowing what we know—"

"Suspect. What we suspect. Right now we can't prove anything."

"You're right, but if we get to the point where we can prove it, we would have no choice but to pursue his termination. And if Lenny was aware of the same facts, he'd be on the hook, too."

"You're going to threaten him?"

"I'm simply going to make him aware of all the facts. Maybe in writing."

"Sneaky, but be careful. Lenny has no problem looking out for his self-interest. It's your interest I'd be worried about. He'll find a way to get what he wants and blame all the bad stuff on you. He did it to Ellen over and over." He checked the activity at the boarding door. "By the way, is next week soon enough on Angelo? I thought I'd call him when I get in on Monday."

"Monday's fine," I said. "I can't wait to meet the famous Angelo. In my mind, he's almost achieved mythic stature."

"What are you doing this weekend, boss? Looking for apartments?"

"No. And I won't be having as much fun as you will. I'm going to keep an eye on the operation, and if I have time, I might also go back to Marblehead."

"You're going back up?" He hoisted the bag onto his shoulder. "I thought you gave your word to Lenny."

"I only said I wouldn't go into the house. I'm going to check out Ellen's athletic club, talk to her trainer. If I'm reading her invoice correctly, she did a training session a few hours before she died, which seems odd to me. I've also got this mystery woman, Julia Milholland. If she ever calls me back, there might be something to do there."

He was grinning. "I knew you'd come around."

"I haven't come around. I'm simply getting a few questions answered to my own satisfaction."

"Whatever you say." The gate agent motioned to Dan. I walked with him through the boarding lounge.

"One more thing," I said. "Remember I showed you that fax I found on Ellen's machine at her house? The one setting up a meeting? I faxed it back with a request for a meeting of my own."

"For when?"

"Tomorrow night."

"Shanahan, you sure you want to do that alone? We don't know who this is."

"If it was someone who was working with Ellen, giving her information, he could be helpful."

"What if it's not that person? What if it's the person who swiped the answering machine tapes? Ever think of that?"

Actually, I hadn't. "I set it up at a restaurant, so it'll be crowded, lots of people around. Besides, he probably won't even get the message. I thought it was worth a shot."

"We've got to go, Danny." The gate agent was getting nervous.

Dan went to the podium and jotted a phone number on an empty ticket jacket. "This is where I'll be in Jersey. It's my cousin's place. I'll be back no later than Sunday morning, but you call me if you need me. I'll come back."

"Nothing's going to happen, and I don't want to take you away from your weekend with your daughter."

"Just take it, Shanahan."

I took the envelope. Then I followed him as far as the boarding door and watched him stroll down the jetbridge, chatting with the agent.

"Dan . . ."

He stopped and turned, while the agent kept going. "Yeah, boss?"

"Have a great weekend with Michelle."

He was wearing that high-beam grin again as he turned to board the aircraft. He went off to see his little girl, and I went back to my hotel.

Chapter Eighteen

Marblehead was different in daylight. Twenty miles north of Boston, it was one of those classic New England seaside communities. It had the dense, layered feel of a European village, with narrow, winding streets nestled among the hills and tall trees. The houses were immaculate, three-hundred-year-old clapboard boxes painted the perfect shade of peach or gray or blue or yellow with shutters to match, wreaths on the doors, and brick driveways with flowerpots. All of them. They looked more like museums than houses, and I had the impression that the people who occupied them lived among us but not of us, which, come to think of it, was not inconsistent with how Ellen had lived.

A brunette, milky-skinned twenty-something named Heather was behind the counter at the Marblehead Athletic Club. When she saw me approaching, she laid two big, fluffy towels on the counter. This must be a good club. You could always tell by the quality of the towels. And since they had to be doled out by the staff and not left lying around for anyone to use, it must be a very good club.

"What locker can I get for you?"

"I'm here to see Tommy Kerwin. I have an appointment."

"Oh." She whipped those towels back and secured them in a safe place behind the counter. "I'll page him for you."

"Thank you."

Ellen's personal trainer was in his twenties, a solid block of muscle in a forest green Marblehead Athletic Club T-shirt and black shorts. His build reminded me of those Rock'em Sock'em Robots, the kind where the head pops up when you hit them just right.

"You have her same job," he said, studying my card.

"I have Ellen's job, yes."

"Do you know why she killed herself?" I was glad to see genuine interest in his eyes and not morbid curiosity.

"We're trying to figure out why. That's why I wanted to talk to you."

"Me?" His eyes widened as he handed the card back.

"I think you may have been one of the last people who saw her that last day."

He shook his head emphatically. "I didn't see her."

The invoice I'd found in Ellen's mail was in my organizer. I pulled it out and pointed to the PT entry. "Doesn't this mean she had a session with you that day? I took it to mean Personal Trainer."

He squinted as he studied the statement. "She was scheduled, but she canceled that afternoon. She just missed the cut-off by like a half hour and I had to charge her. It's club policy. She understood."

"When was her appointment?"

"Regular time, seven o'clock on Monday night."

"And what's the cutoff?"

"You have to cancel at least six hours in advance not to get charged."

Which meant she'd probably called from the airport sometime after one o'clock. "Did she say why she was canceling?"

"No. I asked her if anything was wrong, because she hardly ever missed, and if she did, she always gave me a reason. Not that I needed one. She was paying me. Anyway, she said something had come up and she didn't want to reschedule, but she'd call me later. That was it."

"How'd she sound?"

"What do you mean?"

"Well, she did what she did only a few hours after you spoke to her. I wondered if she might have sounded depressed or sad or, I don't know, anything out of the ordinary."

His face tightened as he seemed to consider for the first time his place in the sequence of events leading up to Ellen's death.

"She was maybe, I don't know, distracted. It was hard to tell."

A sharp outburst ricocheted out of the racquetball court and bounced around the small lobby where we were seated. Tommy, a man of few words, was staring at me waiting for the next question, and I wished I was better at this sleuthing stuff. I didn't know what to ask, or even what I was looking for. "What kind of a workout did she do?"

"It was a killer," he said, warming quickly to the new subject. "It would all be on her workout card in here."

I followed Tommy into the weight room, where two men and a woman were working through the Nautilus circuit and enduring the loud, pounding disco music that seems to be the required soundtrack at health clubs everywhere. While he searched a two-drawer file cabinet, I stood around feeling over-dressed in jeans and a sweater.

"Here it is."

I looked down at the stiff pink card he'd handed me. Tommy was right. Ellen's workout had been a killer, with three reps of squats, leg presses, preacher curls, back extensions, lat raises, and lots more. She even did pull-ups. Twelve of them. On my best day I could maybe do three, and that was only with lots of grunting and cheating. "She worked hard," I said.

"No matter how hard I made it for her, she wanted more. And she did everything I gave her." He pushed the drawer closed and leaned against the cabinet with his arms crossed. "When I read about her in the paper, that's the part I couldn't believe. Why would she work so hard to stay in shape, to stay healthy, then . . . do that?"

I tapped the card with my fingernail. "I don't know," I said. But what I thought was that it was the same compulsion that drove her to work like a dog, to organize and label everything in her life, to try to be perfect in all things. Working out was just another way to try to achieve perfection.

Tommy's name came over the loudspeaker for a call on line one. He looked relieved to have an excuse to end the conversation.

I held up the card. "Can I keep this?"

"I guess. I'd just throw it away."

I thanked him, and while he found a phone, I headed out through the lobby and toward my car.

"Excuse me, miss?" It was Heather calling from behind the front desk, catching me just as I hit the door. "Is someone going to clean out her locker?"

* * *

The trainer was trying without luck to remove Ellen's combination lock with a set of jumbo wire cutters. They'd sent a female trainer into the locker room with me, and she was not familiar with the tool. The longer she struggled, the more I wilted in the eucalyptus-scented humidity from the sauna. When the cutters slipped for the third time, I reached up and held the lock steady, albeit with the very tips of my fingers. Using both hands, she found the right leverage and, with a mighty squeeze, sliced through the thick metal hook. The lock fell away, I opened the door, and we both looked inside.

"I'll see if I can find you some sort of a bag," she said.

I started at the top and worked down. On the top shelf was a tray well-stocked with tubes, squeeze bottles, Q-tips, cotton balls, combs. Her brush still had strands of her red hair. Hanging on hooks on the walls were sweat pants, T-shirts, and a couple of baseball caps. An old, faded sweatshirt turned out to be from Wharton, Ellen's business school alma mater. In a strange way, I liked that it felt stiff when I pulled it out, and it smelled of dried sweat. Almost every other aspect of Ellen's life for me was past tense, but the fragrance of running was so familiar that I could imagine the living Ellen in that sweatshirt, just in from a long, exhilarating run through a bright New England winter morning. Or an evening jog along the Esplanade.

At the bottom of the locker was a pile of clean socks, a few running bras, and two pairs of neatly folded tights. When I reached down to pull the clothes out, my fingers scraped something hard, something that was definitely not wearable. I pulled it out. It was a video. A *video?* In her gym locker? And not just any old video. If the cover was any indication, it was pornographic—really pornographic. What in the world was she doing with this? And where was the actual video? When I picked it up, all I had in my hand was an empty box. I hoped to hell we weren't going to find some dark and twisted corner of Ellen's soul because I didn't want to. I had started to like Ellen, at least the parts of her that I could see, and the parts that I could see were helping me understand the parts I couldn't.

Somewhere out of the steam I heard the voice of a woman, then the response of her little girl. I stuffed the box underneath the stiff sweatshirt and dropped the whole thing in the pile on the floor.

There was more in the bottom of the locker, and as I shoved aside the rest of the socks, I felt a tingle, an all-over buzz, because right there in the locker was a binder with the Nor'easter logo. It was Dan's missing procedures manual, and when I saw what was underneath that, the tingle turned electric. Bulging, well used, and fuzzy at the corners, it was Ellen's Majestic/Nor'easter merger file, the one that had been missing from her desk. I trolled around in the gym clothes, thinking the answering machine tapes might be in there. I was looking inside the socks when the trainer returned.

"This is all I could find," she said, holding open one of two brown paper bags.

"That'll work." I quickly stuffed the clothes and toiletries into the first bag, the files, the video box, and the procedures manual into the second. "Thanks for your help."

A bag under each arm, I backed through the swinging locker room door, walked past Heather at the front desk, and out into the morning air, cool against the eucalyptus dampness on my skin and in my hair. The bag of clothes went into the trunk, the files up front with me.

* * *

I didn't even wait to get back to Boston. I pulled into the first coffee shop I could find—they're called crumpet shops in Marblehead—ordered my morning tea, and started with the procedures manual. It was thick and dense and filled with pretty basic stuff, like how to load airplanes. I learned a lot about Nor'easter's ramp procedures, which hadn't been much different from everyone else's, and nothing about why Ellen had found the manual so interesting that she'd taken it with her to the gym. It wasn't exactly a book you'd prop up in front of you on the stair climber. Occasionally, I'd come across notes in the margins, but not in Ellen's handwriting. They always pertained to information on that page, and I assumed they were Dan's. But the first page of the Beechcraft section was marked with a paper clip. So was a diagram of the aircraft, which showed top and side elevations, positions of seats and the cargo compartments, forward and aft. But that was it. There was no indication of why it would be of interest to her.

Almost an hour later, I was drowning in Irish breakfast tea. I'd finally broken down and bought a scone. I don't like scones—to me they taste like warm rocks, sometimes not even warm—but it was all they had. What would have been wrong with serving a bagel or a piece of wheat toast? I was turning pages in the merger file, reading tedious notes, memos, legal documents, and remembering exactly what I had so disliked about my assignment in headquarters. Then I found it. Nestled in among the other papers was a check stub. It was dated April 1995. There was no name, but it was in the nice round amount of ten thousand dollars, and it had been issued by none other than Crescent Security, same as the name on the invoice I'd re-suspended twice. Molly had described Crescent Security as a nickel-and-dime firm that did background checks, which couldn't have been more than a couple of hundred bucks apiece. I tried to remember the amount on the invoice. I didn't think it was more than a few hundred dollars. I knew it wasn't anywhere near ten thousand.

The shop had filled up since I'd been there, and several heads turned my way when my beeper went off. They looked at me as if my cell phone had gone off in church. I checked the display and was surprised not to see the number from Operations. It was a number that was vaguely familiar, but I couldn't place it, so I ignored it. With only a few pages left in the file, I wanted to get to the back. When I got there, I was glad I did.

Stuck in the back of the file as if it didn't belong there was a single sheet of paper folded in half. Handwritten in black ink on the white page was one paragraph.

I think of how my life would be without him, and the thought of letting go scares me to death. I can't think about it directly, so I creep up close to the thought, walk around the feeling, touch it, pull back. When I get too close, I have trouble breathing. My lungs fill up with something cold and heavy, and I feel myself going under. And then I think about my life before him, about the work that filled my days and the ghosts that walked the nights with me, and I feel myself going under again and the only thing that keeps my head above water is the motion of reaching up for him. And I can't let go. Because when I'm with him, I exist. Without him, I'm afraid I'll disappear, disappear to a place where God can't save me and I can't save myself.

The air suddenly felt thicker, harder to breathe. Even if it hadn't been in her handwriting, I would have known that Ellen had written those words. I recognized her voice—the *longing* in her voice. I read it again. Who was she writing about? Had he left her? Is that why she'd 'disappeared'? Because she hadn't known how to save herself? I put the page down, pushed back from the table, and leaned over. I took a few deep breaths, releasing each one in a long exhale. In my mind I saw Ellen writing those words. I saw her reaching out, reaching up for him and trying not to drown. What I couldn't see was his face, the face of the man she was reaching for. And I couldn't see him reaching back for her. She was reaching into emptiness, and I knew what that felt like.

A large woman pushed behind my chair, trying to get by. She brushed against my shoulder, and her touch made me shrink away, pull into myself. It was time to go.

Out in the car, I sat with the door open and the note in my hand, feeling the fresh ocean air on my face and listening to the calls of the seagulls. Up until then Ellen had been elusive to me, hiding amidst the color-coded labels and the calligraphic handwriting and the bare walls of her office. But on this page, in these words, she didn't hide, and it was almost painful to see her so clearly, like looking into the sun after a long walk in the dark. I flipped the page over hoping for a signature or a date, some clue as to who inspired it. Nothing. It could have been written a month ago. It could have been written five years ago. I had a strong feeling based on nothing more than instinct that it was more like last month.

I read it again, this time more slowly. There were no cross-outs, no corrections. The thoughts and words seemed to have flowed out onto the page fully formed, as if she couldn't hold them back. Toward the end the handwriting loosened, almost a tangible representation of the author coming unraveled.

Maybe Ellen had left a suicide note after all.

"Harborside Hyatt, how may I direct your call?"

No wonder the number on the beeper had been familiar. It was my own hotel.

"This is Alex Shanahan. I'm a guest and someone from the hotel beeped me."

"Hold on." I used the Muzak moment as an opportunity to turn up the volume on the cell phone so I could hear over the road noise. Traffic on Route 1A was beginning to build.

"This is the front desk. May I help you?"

I repeated my story to the clerk and waited after he, too, put me on hold.

"Miss Shanahan, this is the concierge." Yet a third hotel employee, this one female, and yet another opportunity to repeat my explanation.

"We received an urgent fax for you this morning," she told me, "with instructions to contact you immediately."

An urgent fax. How dramatic. Probably from Lenny. "Do you have it there?"

"Yes. May I read it to you?"

"Go ahead."

"It says, 'Meet tonight, seven o'clock at Ciao Bella.' "

My scalp began to tingle and my eyeballs went dry. Ciao Bella. The secret code word. "That's it?"

"Yes, it seems to be. There's no signature or cover page."

"Could you look at the time stamp across the top and tell me where it came from?"

"It was sent at nine-forty this morning from Sir Speedy in Nahant."

The meeting was on. "Thank you. Leave it there for me, and I'll pick it up when I get in. Oh . . ."

"Yes?"

"One more thing. Where did you get my beeper number?"

"It was on the fax with the instructions to contact you."

"Okay, thanks again."

The steering wheel had become hard to manage because my hands were sweating so much. I couldn't get the temperature right in the car, and the eucalyptus smell from my hair was too strong in the enclosed space. I should have taken my coat off for the ride back. I had no idea who Mr. Nahant was or even if he was a he, for that matter. Whoever it was, he knew my beeper number, which was a whole lot more than I knew about him.

Chapter Nineteen

The hinges squealed, the door to the restaurant opened, and yet another party arrived at Ciao Bella not to have dinner with me. Fifteen minutes had stretched to thirty, thirty to forty-five. I had eaten too much bread with garlic-infused olive oil and watched a silent hockey game on the set over the bar. Anticipation had given way to frustration, frustration to starvation, and finally to ravioli. Twenty minutes after I'd finished eating, I was still there and still alone. I gave the waitress a big tip for holding her table so long and went out to Newbury Street.

I'd wasted an entire afternoon clenched in nervous anticipation, pacing around my hotel room, speculating as to who the mystery man was and what he could tell me. I'd worked up a good head of anxiety, and now I had no place to put it. The bright New England Saturday had disappeared, turning first to gray, then to a cold, steady rain that had lasted all afternoon. It wasn't exactly ideal weather for strolling, but it had stopped raining, so I decided to anyway.

Most of the shops on Newbury were closed, but their elegant

bay windows up and down both sides of the street were dazzling, especially dramatic on a moonless night. Filled with four-button Armani suits, Cole-Haan shoes, and soft leather Coach bags, the bright lights of commerce lit up the red brick sidewalk as the quaint iron street lamps never could.

I lingered at a few of the windows and stopped at one to look at a pair of pleated slacks. I was trying to remember the last time I'd bought something for myself when I saw—felt, really—a quick, cutting movement out of the corner of my eye. The street was alive with foot traffic, but this was too quick for that leisurely pace, and more furtive, like a rat dashing for its hole. I searched the passing faces, but these were no more familiar to me than the ones at the restaurant had been. Too much pasta, maybe. Definitely too much tension.

I forgot about the slacks and kept moving, bundling up against the gusting wind as I crossed Arlington and headed into the Public Garden. I'd been there a couple of times since I'd come to town. On the one occasion that I'd actually kept an appointment to look for an apartment, the realtor had made a point of walking me through twice, and for good reason. It was enchanting in daylight, even in winter. But at night, when you're already edgy and sluggish and overstuffed, it's a different story.

Inside the wrought iron fence, sheltered by the old trees, the wind died down and it was much quieter. Quiet enough that I heard the twig snap behind me. Or did I? It was hard to hear anything over the rising tide of panic pounding in my ears. Yes, someone was there, I was sure of it, and if I couldn't hear him or see him, I could feel his presence the way you could feel a shadow moving across the sun.

A tendril of a cold breeze found some exposed skin on the

back of my neck and sent a wicked shiver underneath my jacket. He could be anywhere, behind a tree or a statue. The park was closing in on me, and at the same time I felt completely exposed.

I put my head down and walked faster. I was listening and concentrating so hard that I almost rammed headfirst into a couple coming toward me. I had to pull up short and stop abruptly to let them pass. I turned to watch them. They were arm in arm, laughing and pushing close for warmth. Seeing the two of them together made me feel even colder and more alone.

As I turned to go, a voice came out of nowhere: "You picked a bad place to meet," he said—and he was talking to me. For a moment I couldn't move at all. That's the moment I considered running away as fast as I could. I probably should have. Instead, I turned back to find him.

I scanned the area behind me and couldn't see anything. My hands were stuffed into my pockets, and I could feel my shoulders squeezing together, could feel my body almost on its own trying to get narrow so I could hide in plain sight. I tried to swallow, but the cold air had long since stolen the moisture from the back of my throat.

"That restaurant was too crowded."

"Do I know you?"

"I work for you." When he spoke again I spotted him, at least his silhouette, about twenty feet away next to a large tree and well back in the shadows. He was bulky and solid, built like a ramper and dressed in dark clothing. I couldn't see his face, but I knew I'd heard the voice. I just wished I knew if that was good or bad.

He stepped out of the dark. I strained to see as he walked

out of the shadows. He came closer and closer, but I still couldn't see. I was reconsidering the running-away alternative when he finally stepped into the light and I could see his face. It was a face I recognized. "John McTavish, right?"

"Yeah. I didn't mean to scare you. I'm sorry."

I started breathing again; then I took off my glove and offered my hand. He quickly averted his eyes, as if this naked appendage, pale and vulnerable in the dim light, was a part of my body he wasn't supposed to see. He made no move to return the gesture, so I stuck my hand back in my pocket.

"How'd you know it was me?" he whispered.

"I didn't know it was you," I said, matching his whisper, "but I know who you are. I would remember anyone who stood up to Big Pete."

He was perfectly still, as I'd seen him in the ready room, the only movement coming from his eyes, quick and alert, locking onto the faces of occasional strangers who happened by, making sure, I presumed, they were strangers. It was disconcerting to see him this nervous.

"Then why'd you send the fax?"

"On a hunch. I found your note to Ellen on the fax machine at her house."

He thought that over. "You took a big chance."

I didn't even want to think about all the chances I'd been taking. "Could we go someplace where it's warm and talk about this? My ears are so cold they're burning. I think that's a bad sign." I took a hopeful step in the direction of Charles Street, but he didn't budge. He didn't even turn in my direction.

"Why'd you want to meet?" he asked.

"I want to know why Ellen Shepard killed herself."

"Is that what you think? That she did that to herself?"

I walked back and stood right in front of him, sniffling. My nose was starting to run from the cold, and I didn't have any tissues. "Do you know otherwise?"

He still wasn't moving, and I knew what he was thinking. If he knew or he didn't, why tell me? I reached back for what I'd been feeling the moment I'd sent that fax. "I'm having a hard time with the union, with Big Pete, and maybe even with my own boss. I'm feeling overmatched and I'm looking for help. That's why I sent it. I need help, and I thought that if you were willing to help Ellen, you might help me, too."

He stood for a moment longer in his zippered jacket, T-shirt, and jeans, an ensemble that struck me as lightweight for the conditions. Then he offered his hand, big and callused, and I grabbed it. He wasn't wearing gloves, but his skin was warm anyway. For the first time he looked me in the eye. "Let's go," he said. "You shouldn't be out here by yourself."

"Too many windows," he explained, referring to Ciao Bella. "We would have been sitting right out on the street in one of the busiest parts of town."

"Would it be that bad to be seen with me?"

"By the wrong people, yeah, it would."

No one was going to see us here. We'd tried two other places before he'd approved of this one, a basement space off Charles Street with exposed brick, a big fireplace, but no windows and only two patrons besides us. I noticed how tiny the coffee mug looked in John's hands. I remembered his quiet confidence as he'd stood in the middle of the ready room and stared down Big Pete. And now he was telling me there was something at the airport that scared *him*. We were sitting in front of the fire, but I couldn't seem to feel its warmth.

"I told you why I sent the message," I said. "Why did you respond?"

He set the mug aside and rested his arms on the table, making a solid piece of furniture feel rickety. "My brother, Terry . . . I heard Big Pete offered him up in a deal for Little Pete."

"He did."

"I also heard you didn't take him up on it, so I figured you would maybe listen to the whole story before you made a decision."

"I'm more than willing to hear your brother's story, but he's not talking. I'm beginning to wonder if he was even at his own fight."

"He was there, and it's a good thing."

I sat back and studied John's face. It was a big face with a slightly crooked nose, a wide forehead, and a look of disgust that he was trying unsuccessfully to hide. "Little Pete was drunk, wasn't he?"

"They didn't do the test. How'd you know that?" He looked at me hard. "Is someone else talking to you?"

"No. I hear things. And next time, if there is a next time, there will be a test. The supervisor is being disciplined."

"For all the good that will do."

"Tell me what happened. If you want help for your brother, I need to know."

He let loose a long, dispirited sigh, then began, reluctantly, to tell me the story. "Little Pete was tanked up when he got to work that night. He sat in the bag room for a few hours drinking, from what I hear, about a dozen minis straight up. Myers's Rum—dark, that's what he likes. Then he got in a tractor, and while he was driving across the ramp, he fell out."

"He *fell out* of a tractor?"

"That's how he cut his head."

My chest started to tighten as if something were squeezing the breath out of me. Sometimes I threw my anger right out like a fishing net, catching what and whoever happened to be in range. But I couldn't be angry with this man. How could I? This time the rage seemed to settle in my chest and stay there like asthma. "Did Terry tell you this?"

"Yeah. But I also checked with enough guys I know it's true."

"So there were witnesses."

His back stiffened and he stared into his coffee cup. "I'm not giving any names. I'm only speaking for my brother here."

"I understand."

"So Little Pete's down on the ramp bleeding, but the tractor is still going. It misses the aircraft on Forty by about a foot and rams a bag cart instead. Also runs over a B727 tow bar. Terry sees all this and tells him to get somebody to drive him home. Little Pete says go to hell and starts staggering for the tractor. Terry tries to stop him and that's when Little Pete jumps him. You can check it out. The maintenance log will show a tow bar out of service that night."

I didn't need to check. He was telling the truth.

"And that's not even the worst of it."

"It's not?" I was almost afraid to hear the rest.

"Little Pete was running a crew that night, and one of his guys figured out while they were loading the airplane that he'd reversed the load."

I sat back in my chair. I couldn't even find the words to comment.

"Fortunately," John said, "they caught it before it ever left the gate. His crew sent him inside while they fixed it."

I felt numb just thinking about what could have happened. It's one thing to lose a bag or delay a flight and ruin someone's day. It's quite another to put them on an airplane that won't stay in the air because the load's not properly balanced and the load is not properly balanced because the crew chief was so drunk he couldn't tell the front of the aircraft from the rear. That would be hard to explain.

"Terry has to give a statement, John."

"He's waiting to see what you'll do to him if he won't."

"I'll fire him."

He nodded. "That's what I told him. If he says what happened, will he keep his job?"

"It's the only way he'll keep his job."

"And Little Pete gets canned?"

"If it's the last thing I do."

He angled toward the fireplace, turning his entire upper body, moving the way heavily muscled men have to move. His eyes were fixed on the dying flames, and he looked tired. More than tired, bone-weary. It was the same look I'd seen on Dan a few times. I waited. I knew he'd talk again when he was ready.

"When I first started at the airport," he said, still staring into the fire, "I was working down on the mail dock. My second or third day on the job, the union sent down a steward to tell me to slow down. He told me I was showing everybody up and if I wanted to keep working there, I should ease off. I told him to go pound sand."

"How'd they take it?"

"They gave me one more warning. Then one night in the parking lot, these two guys come up from behind and jump me. The one tried to grab me, I broke his arm. The other one ran away when he heard the bone snap."

The fire popped and I winced. "You broke his arm?"

"He had a baseball bat. They didn't bother me much after that."

I checked out the bulging biceps underneath his T-shirt and wondered what had possessed anyone to come at him in the first place. "Is this job that important to you?"

His chair creaked ominously as he leaned back. "I worked on my pop's fishing boat when I was growing up, me and my brother both. Out in the morning when it was still dark, home after dark. Miserable, cold, and wet, and you worked all day long. Pop didn't pay us much, but he taught us one thing—someone pays you to do a job and you agree to do it, then you do it. That's it." He turned back to the fire. "We get good money and benefits for throwing bags a few hours a day and sitting around in the ready room watching TV the rest of the shift. On top of that, you and your whole family get to fly around basically for free. It's not like we're skilled labor. This is a good job for someone like me. It's how I'm going to put my kids through college, and nobody's going to run me off."

"You have a family?"

"I got a wife and two kids, three and seven."

"It sounds as if they tried to run you off and failed."

"I can take care of myself. But it's different when it's your family, and I'll tell you something else, Little Pete scares the shit out of me. There's something wrong in the head with that kid. He's okay when he's around Big Pete, but when he's not, it's like he goes crazy or something. And when he's drunk, forget about it. When he's sober you never know what he's going to do, and when he's tight it's getting so it's tough even for his pop to deal with him."

"Do you believe he could kill someone?"

The lines in his forehead deepened. "If Petey'd been one of the guys who jumped me that night in the parking lot, he wouldn't have run off. I can't watch Terry all the time and no offense to you, but I'm sure as hell not going to count on the company to protect him. The company's just as likely to cut a deal and bring Petey back to work."

I wanted to say that that would never happen. I wanted to assure him that once Lenny had all the details, as I had now, there would be no way we'd bring Little Pete back to work and no way Terry would be fired. I couldn't tell him that because I didn't know it. Lenny was still a mystery to me. "Tell your brother to sit tight while I figure out what to do. I'll find a way to work all this out."

"How?"

"I have no idea. And tell him thanks."

"I will."

I sat quietly while he found a poker and tried without success to get the fire going again. When he'd settled back in, I asked him if he wanted more coffee.

"I'm working a shift starts at four in the morning. I gotta get some sleep tonight."

That may have been a clue that he wanted to go home, but I liked sitting with him. In spite of how I felt about everything else, I felt safe with him, and that was something I hadn't felt for a while. "John, you said something outside about Ellen's death not being a suicide. Do you believe she was murdered?"

"I don't know." He said it in a way that made it clear we

weren't going to talk about it that night, or maybe ever, and I had to respect that. I tried something easier.

"How did you hook up with Ellen?"

"I was trying to get my brother a job at the airport."

"That doesn't seem so hard."

"The union didn't want another one like me around, so they poisoned him with the supervisors. They said if Terry got hired, they'd slow down the operation, set something on fire. I told her about it, and she interviewed him personally and made them put him on. After that, I told her if she ever needed help to call me."

"And she did."

"Yeah."

"What about?"

He did yet another visual sweep of the restaurant, but no one we knew was there, including our waiter. "There was something she needed . . . this package."

I sat bolt upright, nearly tipping the table into his lap. "What kind of a package?"

"I don't know, about this big"—letter-sized—"a plain brown envelope with tape and dust all over it."

"What was in it?"

"She didn't say I should look in it, and she didn't open it in front of me, so I don't know what it was."

In this one case, I wished he'd been a tad less principled. I couldn't ask the questions fast enough. "Why did she need you to get it?"

"It was in the ceiling tiles in the men's locker room. Dickie must have tossed it up there sometime when he was working here."

"Dickie Flynn?"

"He's the one told her where it was."

"Why was it in the ceiling?"

"Guys use the ceiling for a hiding spot when they're in a hurry."

"Doesn't seem all that convenient."

"Say they're helping themselves to the catering cart, stealing minis. After cocktails, they don't want to walk around with empty bottles knocking around in their pockets, and they don't want to leave 'em lying around in trash cans, so they toss them up there. The ceiling has rattled around here for years, decades even."

"But no one ever came upon this package?"

"It was way off in the corner. You wouldn't find it unless you knew what you were looking for."

"That means it could have been up there for a while. And you can't even hazard a guess as to what this was about? She never said?"

"No, I don't know. But I think Angie might."

"Angie as in 'Angelo'?"

"Yeah. He had something she needed, and she wanted to put the squeeze on him."

"DiBiasi?" I had to pause for a moment and regroup. I had clearly hit the mother lode, and I was having a hard time assimilating all the new data. "I thought Angelo was small-time. An afterthought. Wrong place, wrong time, that whole story."

John shook his head. "Angelo was the target all along. That whole stakeout thing was just to make it look like they grabbed him up by accident. I gave her some help on the thing."

"Ellen set him up?"

"As far as I know, the whole thing was her idea."

"I'll be damned." I sat back and let this new information settle over everything else that we knew. It added whole dimensions to what I had learned about Ellen. And it forced a new appreciation for how deep the swamp was getting. Packages, setups, stakeouts. Missing files, missing tapes, missing videos. Maybe a mystery lover. I didn't know if we'd ever find the bottom or what we'd find if we got there. What I did know was that I was following Ellen's tracks right into the depths.

"This Angelo thing," I asked, "was it before or after the package?"

"After."

"So he might be connected somehow to that envelope. Maybe that's why the union's pushing so hard to get him back," I said. "And Lenny, too, I suppose. They're trying to take away my leverage. I didn't even know I had leverage. John, I know you don't know what was in the package, but did Ellen ever say anything about the Beechcraft?"

He looked puzzled. "No. Not to me."

"How about fish?"

"Fish?" More puzzled still. "Like scrod?"

"I don't think so, but I don't know. Crescent Security?"

He shook his head.

"Ellen seemed to be working on something, collecting information. It may have something to do with the Majestic-Nor'easter merger or the Beechcraft. We were even thinking Little Pete might have been involved in drug running."

"No. That I would have heard about. Besides, Big Pete would kill Petey with his bare hands if he found out he was into drugs. He's already close to killing him over the booze."

"Does he really care about him as much as it seems?"

"Yeah, he cares about him, but part of it is he feels guilty, too, like he passed on the disease. Big Pete was a boozer himself until just a few years ago—the whole time Petey was growing up, anyway. He's always trying to get him to go to A.A. meetings with him. The kid won't go."

Big Pete's chewed-up fingernails started to make some sense. We sat for another few minutes in silence before he started fidgeting, making it clear he wanted to leave.

"John, would it be all right if I contacted you again?"

"Do you have something to write with?"

I found a stubby pencil in my jacket, down with the pocket lint and old movie ticket stubs.

"You can leave a message at this number," he said, writing on a cocktail napkin, "and I'll get in touch with you."

The number was familiar. "Where is this?"

"Sir Speedy up in Nahant. My sister works there."

One mystery solved.

Charles Street, still damp from the rain, was threatening to freeze over, and the brick sidewalk was slick and precarious. John offered to drive me back to the hotel, but I knew he didn't want to be seen with me and I wasn't keen on lying in the backseat under a blanket.

"John, did anyone know you were talking to Ellen?"

"Not even my brother. And you can't tell anyone. Even Fallacaro."

"You don't trust Dan?"

He didn't answer, so I put my hand on his arm and made him stop walking. "Are you saying you don't trust Dan?"

He looked away for a long time as if trying to find the words. "Here's the way I see it," he said. "If she had trusted him, she would have had him get her the package, right?"

He didn't wait for an answer, which was good because I

didn't have one. I watched him disappear down a side street and into the shadows; then I turned and started for a cab stand. I was still trying to digest that last thought when it occurred to me that the address on Julia Milholland's postcard was somewhere on Charles. One-forty-two . . . 146, maybe. I went from door to door reading labels on buzzers and peering through plate-glass windows into dry cleaners, drugstores, and gift shops. I came to 152 Charles Street and found it occupied by something called Boston-in-Common. An article written by Ms. Milholland herself was posted right in the window. It was advice on how to find your perfect mate. Boston-in-Common was a dating service.

The cab dropped me off in front of my hotel. I reached through the window to pay, and when I turned around, I felt him out there, felt him before I saw him standing off to the side in a leather jacket with the collar turned up in front of his face. I didn't need to see his face to recognize Little Pete.

"What are you doing here?" I asked, trying not to show surprise. Or anything else.

"I came to see you."

It had stopped raining, but it hadn't stopped being cold, so the perspiration dripping down his face was disturbingly out of place. Rivulets tracked around the ugly, swollen row of stitches that snaked through his right eyebrow. The thought of how he had gotten them made me even more nervous, and I wondered if he was drunk again.

"If you want to talk to me, do it at work." I hoped I was sounding annoyed and in command.

His fist shot into the air. I flinched and stepped back, almost stumbled backward, certain that his arm, like a tree limb, was about to crash down on my head.

"I can't come to work," he whined.

The blow never came; it was only a gesture of his frustration. No matter. My pulse was racing. I wasn't nervous, I was scared. He wasn't staggering and I didn't notice any slurring, but he was wasted. I could see it now that I could see his eyes.

"That's what union reps are for," I said, inching backward and plotting my path to the front door of the hotel.

"I don't *need* my *fucking pisshead union rep mouthpiece* talking for me." A man coming out through the door of the hotel reacted to Little Pete's harsh tone—or maybe the harsh language—with a grim scowl. I reacted by moving closer to the door.

"What happened," he said, his voice elevating with each of my steps back, "wasn't my fault. It's that fucking McTavish."

It was there, that flash of rage, the one I'd seen in his eyes when he'd looked at me during his hearing. I still had no idea where it came from or why it had anything to do with me. All I knew was that seeing it in those dull, drunken eyes sent a cold shiver right through my soul.

"Don't ever approach me like this again."

I turned and headed for the door. Thankfully, he didn't follow, just yelled after me. "I'm not losin' my fucking job over this. *You're not takin' my fucking job.*"

Inside the elevator I reached out and pushed the Door Close button. When it didn't close fast enough, I pressed again and again and again. I don't think I took a breath until I got into my room and locked the door. I know that my heart rate didn't come down until hours later when I finally fell asleep.

Chapter Twenty

D an's sneakers squealed on the varnished floor as he looped under the basket and in one fluid motion rolled in a left-hand runner.

"High school ball?" I asked.

"Yeah, but that's not where I really learned to play." His perimeter shot was equally good. He knocked it down, grabbed the ball, and stood in front of me, sweating in an old hooded sweatshirt and what appeared to have been sweat pants at one time. They were cut off at the knees. "Playgrounds in Newark. Me and my cousins played for money."

"Hustler, huh? In Newark, no less. You're probably lucky to be alive."

When I dropped my backpack and pushed up the sleeves of my sweater, he handed me the ball and cut to the basket. I passed it back and he sank a twelve-footer.

"How was your trip?"

"Good."

"Why did you come back last night?"

"I thought the weather might get bad here. Besides, Sunday

is family day down there. They all go to Mass and come home and put on a big spread, and everybody wants the kid around for that." He shrugged. "I'm not part of the family anymore." He bounced the ball to me. "You didn't have to come over here," he said. "I would have met you somewhere."

I dribbled a few times and hoisted a shot that banged off the rim. I used to do it better in seventh grade, but at least I didn't heave it underhanded. "My hotel room was closing in on me. I'm just glad you take your beeper to the gym. Or whatever this is."

"This is my neighborhood rec center."

"How come there aren't more people recreating?"

"This place will be jammed this afternoon with a thousand screaming kids, which is why I come in the morning. But when I get more time, I'm going to coach a kid's basketball team."

"Teach them how to hustle?"

"Sure," he grinned, "why not?" He looped up one last shot from under the basket, missed, and followed the ball as it bounced over to a row of wooden bleachers. I followed him, and we sat on the bleachers in a wedge of sunlight that came through a row of high windows. With the mint green cinderblock walls, the heavy double doors, and light mildew odor, I could have been back in gym class.

"I've got to ask you something before I forget," I said. "You haven't talked to Angelo yet, have you?"

"I was going to call him tonight, tell him to get ready to get his ass back to work. He's got Sunday-Monday off, so he wouldn't be in until Tuesday. That's what you wanted, right?"

"I changed my mind. I don't want to bring him back yet."

"Why not?"

I really wanted to tell him the whole story about how Ellen

set up Angelo. I wanted to tell him about the package and ask him what he thought Angelo might know. But I couldn't. "I want to wait another day or two and see what happens." I watched for a reaction, wondering if that reply sounded as tepid as it felt. But if he was any more curious than that, he didn't say.

"We've got no problem with Angie because he's already terminated, but we have to do something about Little Pete and Terry McTavish. Wednesday night will be a week, so I have to either start termination proceedings or bring them back."

"I don't suppose Vic might agree to an extension."

"I can talk to him, but if I do they're going to be pissed. They know that Terry hasn't said a word. They know we haven't got jackshit and they're going to want him back. Not Terry, but Little Pete."

"Ask him anyway."

"All right."

"He came to see me last night."

"Victor?"

"Little Pete. He was waiting at my hotel when I got back from dinner."

"I'm going to kill him," he fumed, squeezing the ball until I thought it would burst. "I'm going to go over to his fucking house—"

"Good, Dan, that's all I need, to be working on this by myself." I unbuckled the pack and started unpacking. "At least wait until you see what I found in Marblehead. I was very busy up there yesterday." Exhibit one was his Nor'easter procedures manual, and exhibit two was the merger file. "These were in Ellen's locker at the health club."

"No shit." He threw the towel around his neck and grabbed

the manual. "You're pretty good at this, Shanahan."

It was nothing but a throwaway comment, but it still gave me a lift, the kind I seemed to get from any pat on the head for any reason. "Guess what else was in there?"

I whipped out the porno video box and he grabbed it, eyes wide. "Jesus Christ, Shanahan. What are you doing with this?"

"It was in Ellen's locker with all this other stuff."

"She had this? No way. Ellen was a Catholic, and a good one, too. Not like me. I never even heard her swear." He popped it open. "Where's the tape?"

"I found it that way."

He turned the box over a few more times, reading everything that was written on it, which wasn't much, then set it aside with a look of complete bewilderment. Still shaking his head, he reached for the merger file. "Anything in here?" The check stub from Crescent was right on top. He glanced at it and went on. "Anything in this file about fish?"

"No fish. And no answering machine tapes, either." I reached across, pulled out the stub, and showed it to him. "Have you ever heard of this company?"

"Means nothing to me."

"When did you say you came to Boston?"

"May 23, 1995."

"Just a month after this check was issued. But it doesn't ring any bells?"

"Nope. Why?"

"Ellen had a copy of an invoice from Crescent Security in her follow-up file. Here it is again popping up in the merger file. A couple of things are starting to feel significant to me, even if it's just because they keep coming up, and the Majestic-Nor'easter merger is one of them." I slowed down and reminded myself not to reveal things I'd learned from John, things I wasn't supposed to know. "First, Ellen came to work in Boston fresh off her assignment on the Nor'easter acquisition task force, which might not mean anything except that a few weeks ago she pulled this file," I tapped the manila folder on his knee, "and ended up hiding it under her gym socks. At the same time she developed a keen interest in your Nor'easter procedures manual—specifically the Beechcraft— and also stashed it away with the socks. She contacted a colleague from the merger project and asked him where to find documents that had to do with the deal."

"What kind of documents?"

I explained what I had learned from Matt. "She was explicit about what she wanted. These were schedules having to do with a certain kind of pre-merger expense, something called purchase price adjustments, which is a fancy way of describing a list of vendors and how much we paid them for services related to the deal."

"What would the merger have to do with Little Pete?"

"I have no idea."

The last thing I pulled out was the handwritten paragraph. After he took it from me, he read it so fast you would have thought it made his eyes burn. Then he flipped it over to check the back. Finding nothing more than I had, he folded it up and thrust it back without a word.

I took it back and unfolded it. "That's Ellen's handwriting, isn't it?"

"So? You don't know how old it is. It could be ten years old."

"Why so defensive?"

"I told you she wasn't seeing anyone."

"Let's just postulate that it's current, shall we? I think Ellen was seeing someone in secret, Dan. I believe that's what the travel on United was all about. She could have been flying around to meet him and didn't want everyone to know." The postcard from Boston-in-Common was in one of the side pockets from my backpack. I pulled it out and handed it to him. Thank goodness I'd brought visual aids, because he was turning into a tough audience. "Ellen belonged to a dating service."

"C'mon, Shanahan," he said, stuffing the card back into my pack. "That's not what that card says. It doesn't say anything."

"The address from that card matches the address of a place called Boston-in-Common on Charles Street. I saw it, and it's a dating service. Maybe she met someone there. Maybe she fell in love. Is that so hard for you to believe? It's possible she got dumped and having cared so deeply for this person—"

"Are you saying she killed herself over some guy?"

"Listen to what she wrote, Dan." I read him the last line. " *'Without him I'm afraid I'll disappear, disappear to a place where God can't save me and I can't save myself.'* She sounds as if she's afraid to live without him."

"Why would she keep it a secret?"

"I don't know, Dan. Ellen had lots of secrets. I'm going to Boston-in-Common tomorrow when they're open to see if they'll give me any information, although I doubt that they will. They strike me as discreet beyond belief, these people."

Dan jumped down to the floor and began pacing back and forth along the front of the bleachers, dribbling the ball as he went. "She didn't kill herself over some guy." He punctuated the thought with one hard bounce of the ball.

"You already said that."

"But you don't agree."

"I don't think we need to agree on that point. I'm curious enough to keep digging, no matter how she died, and I'll share everything I find with you, just as I have so far."

"But you do think that, don't you? That she climbed up on that locker and put a rope around her neck and jumped off."

I finished buckling the backpack, set it aside, and tried to figure out exactly what I did think about this woman.

"I believe there were two Ellens, Dan—the one she showed to the world, and the one she kept to herself. That's why we continue to find things that surprise you. Since I didn't know her at all, it's possible I can see things you can't, or at least see them differently. That paragraph she wrote, it's the truest, most authentic thing I've found so far about her. The dating service, her mother's suicide, these feel like the real Ellen to me, and the real Ellen feels very sad. And I don't know why she kept that from you."

The bleachers rattled as he climbed back up, dropped down to the bench beside me, and wedged the ball between his old-fashioned high-tops. "Do you know when she joined this dating service?" He spat out the word "dating" as if it were an anchovy.

"Hopefully I can find out tomorrow."

He leaned back on his elbows and squinted up into the windows. "The reason I can't believe she had any kind of relationship going on is because of something she said to me once. She was always talking about how great it was that I had a kid and how I should never take it for granted. So one day I said something stupid like, 'It's not rocket science. You can do it, too.' She said it was too late. Here she is thirty-five years old and she's talking like she's eighty-five. She just laughed and said, 'What am I going to do? Quit my job, get married, and raise a family with someone I haven't even met?' I said, 'Why not? People do it all the time.' She said she'd made her choice a long time ago without even knowing it. And she said I wouldn't understand because I'm a guy."

"Did you understand?"

"No."

"She was saying she chose work."

"But that's not a choice she made without knowing it."

"I would say it differently. To me, it's not the choice that's unknown, it's the consequences. Like choosing a path you think is going to . . . I don't know, Paris. But you end up in Tulsa, Oklahoma, and you can't figure out where you made the wrong turn. The truth is, you've been on the road to Tulsa all along, and the day you wake up and figure it out is probably a day too late."

"It's never too late for anything."

"You begin to feel that it is, and that's all that matters. It becomes a self-fulfilling prophecy."

"She could have quit her job."

"That's easy to say, but I love what I do, and I believe Ellen did, too. When I dispatch an airplane every night that's going to be in London the next morning, or reach up and put my hand on the side of an aircraft engine, I still get the same charge I got the first time I ever did it. I love this business. I love the moving parts and every different way things can get screwed up. I love how hard it is to put it all back together, or to just keep it together on any given day. I love Majestic Airlines, and being part of a great company, even with all the demands that come with it. It's my home. It's more of a home than I ever had. I don't know who I'd be if I wasn't the person who did this job."

I took the ball from between his feet, stood up, tried another shot, and missed again. "Maybe that's why Ellen joined the dating service."

"Why?"

"To find out who she was outside of this job. Could be you talked her into believing it wasn't too late."

I walked across the court to retrieve the ball. My arms felt heavy as I leaned down to pick it up. It was the same heaviness I always felt when I allowed myself to think about my life, my choices, and the things I wished I'd done differently.

"You gonna tell me you feel that way, too?"

"I'll be thirty-two in a few months. I have no husband, no kids, and no prospects. I don't even have a dog. My apartment in Denver is filled with boxes I never unpack. Boston is supposed to be my new home, but I've been here two weeks and I've spent about five minutes thinking of finding a place to live. If it were up to me, I'd probably stay in temporary housing until it's time to move again. It makes it easier to leave that way."

I squared to the basket, dribbled twice, and really focused. If Ellen had believed that it wasn't too late, I envied her. When I let the shot go, it arced perfectly, angled off the glass, and swished through the net. The bank was open, as my dad always used to say. I looked over at Dan. He was watching me with his chin in his hands, elbows on his knees.

"No," I said, turning back to face the basket, "I don't think I'll be seeing Paris. But maybe Tulsa's not such a bad place. At least that's what I tell myself."

The ball rolled into a corner and died.

Chapter Twenty-one

Boston-in-Common looked more like an art gallery than a dating service. It had polished hardwood floors, subtle indirect lighting, and small photographs with large mats punctuating smooth bare walls. It felt expensive and minimalist, and I felt out of place. I'd never been near a dating service before, and as far as I was concerned I could have gone my entire life without visiting one. Not that I'd ever had much luck on my own, but there was something about the *arranged* aspect of the whole affair, the forced conviviality that seemed so artificial. The very idea gave me the willies.

"Welcome to Boston-in-Common. May I take your coat?"

A young Asian woman with perfect, pale skin, red lipstick, and a helmet of precisely trimmed, gleaming black hair came out from behind her chrome desk and waited for me to slough off my coat.

"Sure, but it's pretty wet." I pushed a clump of matted hair out of my face. My newspaper-umbrella hadn't provided much cover, and it was not a good day for suede pumps, Scotchguarded though they might be. I felt as if I was standing on two wet sponges. "I have an appointment with Julia Milholland."

"Yes, we've been expecting you, Ms. Shanahan. Would you like to freshen up?" I took that to mean, "You look like hell and you ought to at least comb your hair," but I smiled and she pointed the way to the ladies' room.

When I looked in the mirror, I had to admit she was right. I hadn't been sleeping well, my running schedule was screwed up, and I wasn't eating right, all of which made me grumpy. I was spending my time either at the airport or digging around in Ellen's life, and my complexion was beginning to take on that Dan Fallacaro pallor. I felt even more disheveled thinking about what kind of place this was and why people came here. There wasn't much I could do except pass a comb through my damp hair and pretend I was supposed to look this way. I'd never been much good at primping.

The sound of heels on hardwood preceded the arrival of Julia Milholland. She was what people called a handsome woman, impeccably dressed with unusually good posture. Though she was probably closer to sixty, she looked fifty, and when she introduced herself she asked me to call her Julia. How convivial of her. Perhaps it was my own state of mind, but as I followed her back to her office, she appeared exceedingly well rested to me.

After she settled in behind her desk, she clasped her hands together and smiled at me across her desk as a pediatrician would smile at her patient. "Now then, Alex, let's get you started."

"I apologize if I misled you, Ms. Mil—Julia, but I'm not here to sign up for the service. I'm here to ask you about one of your members." I handed her my business card. "Ellen Shepard."

She didn't even glance at the card, much less take it. I laid it on the desk.

"I'm sorry," she said stiffly. "If I had known, I would have told you over the phone and saved you the trip. We are very protective of our clients' privacy, and I can't tell you anything unless you have Ellen's permission."

My shoulders sagged. I'd assumed she knew about Ellen. I don't know why. It's not as if someone had sent out announcements. Now I was going to have to tell her. I sat up straight in my chair and pushed that stubborn hair out of my eyes. "I have some bad news, Julia. About Ellen."

She turned her head slightly. "Oh?"

"She died. Two weeks ago."

An elegant gasp escaped from her lips as she touched her chin lightly with her fingertips. "Oh, my. I just talked to her last . . . oh, dear. What happened?"

"It appears that she took her own life."

Her hand moved to her throat, her fingers searching for an amulet hanging from a gold chain around her neck, some kind of a Chinese character. She found it and held on tight. "That poor, poor woman."

"Did you say you just spoke to her? Because I saw in her mail that you were trying to contact her. I had the impression you were having a hard time."

Julia, still holding the amulet, was considering my business card again and not listening. At least she wasn't answering.

"Ellen didn't leave a note," I said, "and when I found your name in her mail, I thought you might be able to help. I assumed that she was a client."

"Yes and no."

"I beg your pardon?"

"Let me tell you how our process works, and I think you'll understand." She let go of the necklace long enough to peel a form off a stack at her elbow and pass it across the desk. "When a client signs up at Boston-in-Common, we ask them to fill out this questionnaire, and then sit for a seven- to ten-minute video."

I looked at the form. A background check for a cabinet post couldn't have been more thorough. The questions were what I considered to be personal, some deeply, and I felt exposed just reading it.

"Information from the questionnaire goes into our database. We run comparisons until we find a match. The two clients, the matches, read each other's questionnaires and view each other's videos. If they both like what they see, we get them together."

"Did Ellen do the questionnaire and the video?"

"She sat for the video over a month ago, I think." Julia paged back in her desk calendar. "Yes, it was Tuesday, December 2. She brought her questionnaire with her when she came in. I made a match for her almost immediately. It wasn't hard. She was shy, but I found her to be very attractive and quite charming with a wonderful sense of humor."

"Would you be willing to give me the match's name?"

"Of course not. It wouldn't help you anyway because she never met him. I couldn't reach her to give her his contact information, which is why I sent the card. When she finally did call back, it was to cancel the service."

"Cancel the service?"

"Yes. She said something had come up. She didn't want her money back, but she knew it was not going to work out for her. She resigned her membership before she ever met one

man. I was astounded because she had been so . . . so . . ." I
waited, but she became transfixed by a spot on the desk, and
it seemed as if her batteries had just run down.

"Excited?"

"No. I think determined is possibly more accurate."

"How much money did she forfeit?"

"Eighteen hundred dollars."

"Eighteen *hundred?* What do you get for *that?*"

Julia lifted her chin just enough so that she could look down
her nose at me. "We are a very exclusive service, Ms. Shanahan.
The fee is for an annual membership, and it includes one match
each month."

I wanted to ask about guarantees and warranties and liqui-
dated damages, but that would have been pushing it, especially
since I wasn't here to plop down eighteen hundred clams.
"Okay. So if you sign up and pay the fee, you're probably serious about meeting someone."

"We only accept candidates who are serious and"—she fixed
me with a meaningful, clear-eyed, all-seeing look—"emotionally available."

I felt exposed again. Worse than exposed. X-rayed. The radiator in the corner, painted off white to match the walls, had
kicked in and the office was filling with that dry radiator heat
that I always found so uncomfortable. Finally she continued.

"I told Ellen I would keep her account active for a few
months in case she changed her mind. She thanked me and
told me to close the account."

"She was that sure?"

"Yes. She said she knew she would never be back . . ."

Her voice died and I watched Julia's face transform as
Ellen's statement came back to her with new meaning. The

lines grew deeper and she was now looking all of her sixty years.

"If you're agreeable, Julia, it would help me to get copies of Ellen's materials." I pulled out Aunt Jo's power of attorney and handed it to her. "As I said, I have authorization from the family."

She put on a pair of glasses, perused the document, and then looked at me over the tops of the lenses. "May I make a copy of this? I'd like to check with my attorney before I release anything, if that's all right." Julia was not a spur-of-the-moment kind of person.

"Would it be possible for me to wait while you did that? Maybe I could use the time to watch Ellen's video."

She took off her glasses, turned and watched the steady rain outside, and I thought she was considering my request. "You meet all kinds of people doing this work," she said, still staring, "and they all come in saying they're ready to change their lives. But it takes courage and so many of them don't have it. I thought Ellen did, which is why I was so surprised when she quit. I thought it had been a long, hard struggle for her, but that she was ready, and though I didn't know her well, I believed that good things were about to happen for her." She set her glasses softly on the desk and looked at me, her face still strong, but her eyes glistening like the wet windowpane. "I find this all very sad, Miss Shanahan, very sad, indeed."

I didn't know what to say and my voice was stuck in my throat anyway, so I just nodded.

A still photograph is perfectly suited to the memory of the dead. An image frozen forever, it captures the very essence of death to the living, the infinite stillness, the end of aging. I'd seen the pictures of Ellen, but when her video image came up on the bright blue screen and when I heard her voice for the first time, she came alive, alive in a way that made me feel the void where she used to be.

The first thing I noticed was her hair. I'd known it had been red, but the color was richer and deeper than I'd imagined, and under the lights it shone like polished mahogany. She wore it in a chin-length blunt cut that softened her square jaw. Her hazel eyes were riveted to a point just off camera, and she wore the same expression that we all do when we're at the wrong end of a camera lens—horrified. But even as uncomfortable as she appeared, I felt her presence. It was strength or determination or perhaps the sheer force of will it took for her to sit there and subject herself to something I knew I couldn't do. I was impressed.

"We'll start with an easy one, Ellen." It was Julia from off-camera, her blue-blooded Beacon Hill voice easily recognizable. "Why don't you tell us about yourself?"

"I'm originally from Fort Lauderdale. I went to college at the University of Florida, then graduate school at Wharton in Pennsylvania." I was surprised at Ellen's voice. It was almost husky with a tinge of a Southern accent.

"What did you study?"

"Finance."

"Your graduate degree is an MBA?"

"Yes."

The pause was long enough to be awkward, and I imagined Julia hadn't expected such spare, to-the-point answers. But she was a pro and she recovered. "I must say, I'm not very good with numbers, and I always admire people who are. I think you have such an interesting job, Ellen. Will you tell us about it?"

"I work at the airport. I'm the general manager for Majestic Airlines here in Boston."

"That sounds like a big job, and a tough one, especially for a woman." Julia was definitely not of our generation. "What exactly does a general manager do?"

"That's the first thing I had to learn when I arrived. I came to the field straight from a staff job, which means I didn't have the experience to do this work, and it's been challenging."

She gave an articulate, detailed description of her job—our job. As she talked about her work, her face relaxed and grew more animated. Her voice grew stronger, and she spoke with such pride about her position, I felt bad for ever having questioned her right to be in it.

"I have the ultimate responsibility for getting our passengers where they want to go on time with all their belongings. But it's my employees who determine how well we do that. My most important job is giving them a reason to want to make it work."

I couldn't have said it better myself.

"Do you get to fly for free?" Julia asked the question with the sense of awe and wonder that always made me smile. For people not in the business, flight benefits are absolutely irresistible.

"Yes," Ellen said, smiling as well, "that's a great benefit. I don't travel as much as I'd like, but I'm hoping for some changes."

Julia jumped on the opening. "Can you elaborate on that? It sounds as if you're making lots of changes in your life."

The quick shift seemed to catch Ellen off guard. She tried another smile, but it was tight and tentative, and it came out more like a grimace. We weren't talking about work anymore.

She began slowly, reaching for every word. "I started working when I was in high school. I worked through college, worked through business school, and started my job with Majestic two weeks after I graduated. I would have started sooner, but I needed two weeks to move. I've been working ever since."

I sat in my curtained cubbyhole at Boston-in-Common with my earphones, listening to Ellen talk and nodding my head. Except for the fact that I went to graduate school at night after I'd started working, she could have been describing my life.

"I love my work," she added hastily, "and I have no regrets. I love the airline. But there are long hours and you move every couple of years. It's hard to . . . there are sacrifices . . . you can get fooled into thinking that you're happy and sometimes you make choices that aren't right for you."

She seemed torn between wanting to sell herself and needing to unburden herself. For someone with no regrets, she looked very sad as she stared down into her lap.

"I've always picked people, situations that were never going to work out. I'm here because I want to stop doing that." She reached up with a manicured finger and gently brushed away a strand of hair that had fallen into her eyes. She wasn't even trying to smile anymore. "I hope it's not too late."

"It's never too late, Ellen." Julia's response was automatic, but then there was a pause and I imagined that she was a little stunned by Ellen's frankness. Some of the perkiness had gone out of her voice. "One final question, dear. Describe for me a picture of your life if all your dreams came true."

Ellen turned slightly and for the first time gazed completely off-camera, the way she might if she was looking for her response through a window. But I knew she wasn't. I knew she was looking inside and she was struggling, trying to suppress her natural inclination to close herself off, to deny herself even the simple pleasure of saying her dream out loud. Because if you never say it out loud, you can still pretend the reason you don't have it is because you never wanted it to begin with. Anything else hurts too much.

"I believe it's a gift to know your dreams." Ellen had gathered herself and leveled her gaze directly at me—at the camera. "If I'd known before what my dreams were going to turn out to be, I'd have made different choices. That's not to say that I wouldn't have worked, but my priorities would have been different. I want . . ." She paused, started to speak, stopped, and tried again. "I want to learn to let people know me. I want to meet a man who wants to know me better than anyone else does. I want to be a mother so that I can leave something behind. If there's a place for me in this world, I want to find it. That's my dream."

She smiled into the camera, a radiant, hopeful, almost triumphant smile. That was the last image of her as the tape ran out and the screen went blank.

I stood in Boston-in-Common's sheltered entryway and stared out at the cold rain. It was one of those gloomy days where indoors you have to keep the lights on and outside there's no way to stay dry because of the wind. It was the kind of winter day that seeps through to your bone marrow and makes you feel that you're never going to get warm again.

Ellen's video was under my coat where I could protect it. I'd watched it twice waiting for Julia, thinking both times that she'd been wrong; it can be too late. It had been too late for Ellen, and I had the feeling that when she'd sat for that video, Ellen had somehow known that.

I turned on my cell phone and dialed the airport.

"Molly?" The rain started to pound the bricks harder, and I had to step back not to get splashed.

"I've been calling you for an hour," she said. "Where have you been?"

"I had to run an errand. I told you I was going out."

"You didn't say you'd be unreachable."

"Can't I have an hour to myself?"

"No skin off my nose." I heard her taking a drag on her cigarette. "I just thought you'd like to know that your bag room blew up."

Chapter Twenty-two

When I saw the news trucks parked in front of the terminal, I knew it was going to be one of the days where I wished somebody—anybody—had my job instead of me. Bombs at the airport always made for good press, but reporters scared me almost as much as anything that could happen in the operation, including bombs.

I went the back way, where I could enter from the ramp. I followed the flashing lights, the official uniformed personnel, and the acrid, sinus-searing odor. I pushed my way through the crowd of employees at the door, wondered vaguely who was working the trips, and flashed my ID at the trooper standing guard. He lifted the yellow tape and let me in, where I joined what must have been twenty-five firemen, state troopers, inspectors, Port Authority employees, mechanics, and various others crowded into the concrete, bunker-like space. The way they were milling and talking, it almost looked like some absurd cocktail party, except that one wall and part of the ceiling was totally black, fire hoses were lined up on the wet cement, and right in the middle of everything was a blackened bag cart, misshapen and still smoldering, its singed contents splayed around the floor. There were lots of skis—actually, pieces of skis.

I felt the same way I do at cocktail parties, as if the action swirling around me had nothing to do with me, but not for the same reason. I looked around at the destruction, and I knew that of all the people in this room, I was the one, the only one, responsible for what had happened here.

I spotted my rotund supervisor talking to someone who looked important. Norm introduced me to George Carver, the fire chief. The chief was a large man, late fifties, with stern hazel eyes.

"It could have been a lot worse, Miss Shanahan," he said.

"Was anyone hurt?"

"No. As luck would have it, there was no one at all in the bag room when the device went off."

I wasn't feeling that lucky. "Can you tell me what happened? I was off-site and just got back to the field."

We stepped over a fire hose as he led me to the bag cart, basically a metal box on wheels with two open sides covered by plastic curtains and a bisecting shelf. This one was slightly cockeyed, and the curtains were shredded and melted. I could smell the burned plastic.

"You had some kind of a small homemade explosive device that was probably about here." He pointed with his pen to a spot on the floor of the cart. "You see how this is bowed up?" He was referring to the shelf, which now looked like one of the golden arches. "And it was on this side. You see how the blast went out this way?" The concrete wall on the ramp side was covered in black soot. A computer that had been sitting on a rickety table lay shattered on the ground. He took me around to the other side. "Virtually no damage over here to your bag belt. This side of the cart was packed to absorb the shock and force the damage the other way."

Damned considerate. "You said there was no one in here at the time?"

"Right."

"And it was a single bag cart in the middle of the floor? Not a train?"

He nodded. "You people will have to do your own investigation to rule out whether or not the thing came in on an aircraft. I don't think it came in in a checked bag. My eyeball opinion is that someone rolled this cart in here, packed it, stuck in a device, and ran like hell."

"Jesus." I stared at a B727 parked on the gate less than two hundred yards away. Through the porthole windows I could see passengers moving down the aisle to their seats. My knees felt weak as I began to absorb the enormity of what could have happened.

Chief Carver followed my gaze. "Like I said, it could have been worse. We'll be conducting our own investigation and giving you a complete report. I should be able to tell you what kind of a device it was. We'll put it with all the rest of our reports on Majestic Airlines incidents at Logan."

"You've seen this before?"

"Bombs, bomb threats, fires. You name it. Your guys are real flamethrowers. I keep warning you people that someone's going to get hurt."

"Have you ever identified any of these flamethrowers?"

"No, and unless someone who saw something or heard something steps up, we won't catch this guy, either."

"If anyone knows about this, we'll find them." I tried to

look and sound confident, but I knew full well how the union closed ranks. So did he. He responded with a look that was the equivalent of a pat on the head.

We had to step out of the line of sight of a trooper taking photographs. Someone from the Port was motioning to me. "Chief Carver, I'm glad to have met you, although I'm sorry about the circumstances. I'd like to come over and talk about some preventive measures we could take to avoid this sort of thing in the future."

"That would be refreshing. You know where to find me."

I grabbed Norm, who seemed to be standing around observing. "Where's Dan?"

"He heard you were on your way, so he decided someone had to keep the operation going."

"Good." I turned him toward the faces peering in at us through one of the open garage doors. "You see all those people? Get the ones in Majestic uniforms to work and tell the rest of them to go back to their own operations." I pointed out a train of carts on the ramp filled with inbound bags. "Then figure out how we're going to get all those bags back to the pissed-off people on the other side of that door. See if we can use USAir's claim area for the evening."

"They're going to want to get paid."

"We'll pay them. Let me know what you find out. And get as many agents as can be spared down to baggage claim. It's going to be a nightmare out there."

I took one quick look to see if Big Pete was among the gawkers, but I didn't see him. It wasn't his shift, and that wouldn't have been his style anyway. But I felt his presence. He might as well have written his initials in the black soot on the wall.

I stood in front of the damaged cart with my hands in my pockets so that no one could see how they were trembling. Things were getting out of hand, and I had to start asking just how far they would go. Norm was herding people back to work, but some remained in the doorways staring at me. I was in charge. I was supposed to know what to do, but nothing in my experience had prepared me for anything like this.

I kicked at the remains of a suitcase at my feet. The Samsonite logo was still intact, and the handle had a tag with a business card inside. I did the only thing I was sure I could do. I picked it up, walked through the door to the passenger side, and started looking for its owner.

Chapter Twenty-three

I was hoping my phone would stop ringing by the time I'd found my key and opened the door to my hotel room. No such luck.

"Hello?"

"God, what's the matter with you? You sound like you're on your last legs."

It was Matt. I dropped down on the bed and just kept going until I was horizontal. My left hamstring—a constant reminder of an old running injury—was throbbing, my neck was stiff, and the rest of my muscles were tightening so rapidly I'd be lucky if I didn't fossilize right there, staring up at the spackled ceiling. "My bag room blew up today. The union planted a bomb to send me a message."

"Back here we use e-mail for that."

Usually Matt could make me laugh, but not tonight. There wasn't much that could make me happy tonight. I found the remote and turned on the TV, leaving the sound off, so I could see if I'd made the late news. Then I dropped my shoes on the floor and shimmied on my back closer to the middle of the bed so I could elevate my feet. "Obviously, you've already heard."

"It would be hard not to. That's all anyone's been talking about around here. Your name is on everyone's lips."

I knew Matt was right, and that was not a good thing. You never wanted to be a topic of conversation around headquarters, especially after the story had time to marinate into a juicy rumor. For the first time since I'd been in Boston, I wondered what Bill thought about my situation. I worried about what he was being told, and I really, really wanted his advice. Or maybe I just wanted someone to talk to, someone to be there for me the way he used to. That was one of the things I missed most of all.

"Tell me you're calling because you have my files, Matt."

"The archivist can't find them. He's still looking."

"That seems odd."

"You wouldn't say that if you'd seen the archives. It's a big warehouse filled with thousands of boxes and one poor guy who's supposed to keep track of everything. I'm surprised he ever finds anything. Which brings me to my next question. Do you want the other thing she asked for, the invoices? Because if you do, I have to go to a separate—"

"Ellen asked for invoices?"

"She wanted copies of the actual invoices to go along with the purchase price adjustment schedule. I suppose you want hard copies, too."

"As opposed to what?"

"Fish."

I sat up so abruptly I had to wait for the blood to rush back into my head. "Did you say fish?"

"Fish, feesh—whatever you want to call it—the microfiche is here in the building."

Microfiche? How was I supposed to have figured that one out?

"But she didn't want the fish. She said she needed the hard copies, which are over in Accounting. If you want those, too, I have to put in a separate request."

"Hang on, Matt."

Ellen's stuff was starting to get mixed up with my own. I stood in the middle of the room in my stocking feet and tried to divine the location of that page from her calendar, the one Dan had given me at the house for safekeeping. Where exactly had I put it to keep it safe? Briefcase? No. Table stacked high with things I didn't know where else to put? No. The box on the floor . . .? *Yes.*

The page with the fish reference was mixed in with the mail. "1016.96A. Is that the reference on the microfiche?"

"I don't know. I told her to call Accounting, but that doesn't sound like their filing system. Usually they have a date embedded in there somewhere, and besides, I just told you she wanted hard copies, not fiche."

"Oh, yeah. You did say that."

"Thank you."

The moment of enthusiasm passed. I sank back down on the bed and took off my pantyhose, which wasn't easy with one hand holding the phone. "What would hard copies have that microfiche wouldn't?"

"Signatures. I assumed she wanted to see who approved payment of the invoices. That's all that pre-purchase schedule is—a list of invoices."

"Invoices." I said it almost to myself. "Like Crescent Security."

"What is that?"

"A local vendor. It keeps turning up in Ellen's things. I found a copy of an old invoice, and she had a check stub from Crescent stuck in her merger file. What would a local vendor in Boston have to do with the merger?"

"If it was a Nor'easter vendor, nothing. Majestic and Nor'easter were two separate entities before the merger. Separate management, separate accounting, separate operations."

Without my pantyhose on, I could think better and I remembered the conversation with Kevin. "But there is something that linked Boston to the merger. It's the IBG contract, the last one before the deal. From what I understand, the failure of that contract triggered the sale of Nor'easter."

"That wasn't just Boston. That was a company-wide IBG vote, and I'm going to have to go soon or I'm going to be late for my condo association meeting."

"But it's true, isn't it? If the contract had passed, there wouldn't have been a deal."

"Very true. In essence, the Nor'easter board rolled the dice and put the future of the company into the hands of the IBG."

"And they lost."

"No, they won. At the time Nor'easter's largest shareholder was a group of venture capitalists. They'd already sucked all the cash out of the business and were looking to bail out. They figured the union would vote down the contract proposal, which meant the VC's could cash out and blame it on them. Of course it was good for us, too. The night we found out it was dead, the entire task force went out to a bar and celebrated. Even Scanlon came." He was talking faster and I knew he wanted to hang up.

"So the venture capitalists would have had incentive to make sure the contract failed. But wouldn't that have lowered the value of their investment?"

"Nor'easter would have been worth more with a signed agreement with their largest union, but these guys bought into the company originally on the cheap, so even at a reduced price they all made out. I really do have to go, but if I find this stuff for you, you're not going to ask for anything else, are you?"

"I don't know." Matt was shifting into serious self-protection mode, and his tone had taken on an every-man-for-himself quality. I reached for the remote control and started surfing the dial. "Is someone giving you a problem?"

"I don't want to get on Lenny's shit list. You've heard what he's been saying about you, right?"

My finger froze mid-surf, and my hamstring started throbbing again. "What has he been saying?"

"That you can't handle the union and he's probably going to have to come up there himself. And if he does that, then he's going to have to bring someone else in, and he's all concerned about the management turnover in the station and what it's doing to 'those poor employees because they've been through so much already.' You see why I don't want him mad at me?"

"He said he's going to replace me?" I dropped the remote behind me. It fell off the edge of the bed and clattered to the floor. "Who's he been talking to?"

"The only guy who counts."

"He said that to Bill Scanlon?" That was one question answered. I now knew what Bill was being told. What I didn't know was what he believed. "How do you know?"

"He told Scanlon's entire staff. He brought it up at the monthly planning session. If you ask me, he's covering his ass in advance in case anything else goes wrong."

"Goddamn him. He is such a liar. I just got off the phone

with him at the airport. He was unbelievably supportive. 'These things happen,' he said, 'don't worry about it, it's not a reflection on you.' He's flying up here tomorrow."

"We don't call him the Big Sleazy for nothing."

"The what?"

"He's from New Orleans. That's what we call him."

In spite of everything, I had to smile. The Big Sleazy. I'd never heard that one before.

"You still want all this stuff," he asked, "if I can find it, right?"

"Yes, and call me when you have something."

He hung up and so did I. My channel surfing had stopped on the Animal Planet station. The mute was still on. In the silence I watched a baby turtle on his back in the sand on a beach. He was fighting to roll over, to right himself so that his shell was on top. His tiny turtle flippers flapped desperately as he rolled from side to side. I knew how he felt. I was starting to understand how Ellen must have felt. Lenny was my boss. He was supposed to be on my side, to provide cover while I was fighting it out on the front lines. Everything I found out about Lenny made him more contemptible to me. But in the end, I knew I could deal with Lenny. What I couldn't deal with was the thought that Bill Scanlon might start to question my abilities, to believe that I was failing out here. I went to my briefcase and found my address book. The phone number was right where I'd put it, unlabeled and written lightly in pencil inside the back cover. I hadn't used it in over a year, had even made myself forget the number that I had known by heart. But I'd never erased it and I never forgot it was there.

I sat on the bed staring at the phone until I could make myself pick up the receiver. Even after I'd dialed, the pattern on the keypad so familiar, it was an effort not to hang up. The call rolled to voice mail and I thought I was saved, but then I heard his voice. It was a recorded message, but it was *his* voice and my entire being responded as it always had to the timbre, the cadence, the rhythm of it. It was the perfect pitch to reach something inside of me, and the sound of him reminded me of the feel of him, the taste of him. All I had to do was speak, to leave a simple message, to say what I needed, but all I could do was sit on the edge of the bed, the room blurring around me, listening as the electronic operator demanded that I put up or hang up.

I hung up.

The baby turtle was gone when I checked the screen. I found the remote under the bed and waited a few seconds before turning off the TV, but he was nowhere in sight. I would never know if he had walked away or been carried away.

Chapter Twenty-four

D an turned from the window and paced the length of my office. He'd rearranged the chairs to give himself a lane in front of my desk. As he paced, he continued his report, ticking off the points one by one. "We're using USAir's inbound claim until we can get ours up and running again, which might take up to two weeks. They're charging us an arm and a leg for it, but we don't have a choice. We're closing off all access to ours while we put it back together. No damage to any of the aircraft, but Maintenance had to check out everything that had been parked at that end of the building when the thing went off. We delayed three flights, canceled the last, and rebooked everyone on United and American."

"We lost the revenue?"

"We didn't have any choice, boss. Nothing of ours was going that way that would have gotten them to Denver last night. A few people were so spooked they didn't go at all."

"I guess we ruined a few vacations. How many bags were lost?"

"Thirty-seven items for twenty-two passengers. Everything

in the cart was blown up or burned beyond recognition, mostly skis."

"I know about the skis. I spent several hours in baggage service last night letting people scream at me. It's amazing how attached people can get to their skis. A couple of guys even wanted the pieces back. It was painful."

"We've got inspectors all over the place," he said, "Port Authority security, investigators, state troopers. I'm dodging the media and trying not to trip all over the headquarters people who've come out to 'help' us."

"As far as the media," I said, "I called Public Relations again this morning. Refer all inquiries to them." I stood up and leaned back against my credenza, resting my hips against the edge of the work surface. Somehow, it didn't feel right to be sitting down through all of this. "This is because of Little Pete, isn't it? About not bringing him back to work?"

"If it's not, it's an incredible fucking coincidence. I talked to Vic yesterday morning about delaying the decision, yesterday afternoon the bag room blows up. I'd say the two could be related."

I didn't know whether to be nervous or angry. I settled for being generally uncomfortable and continuously on edge. "What do you think we ought to do, Dan?"

"We've got the employee meetings set up. You had your say with the Business Council last night."

"Sure, that was effective. 'We'll do everything we can to help you through this,'" I said, mimicking Victor's insipid tone, "'but we need to know exactly how you're going to protect our men.'"

Dan stopped pacing. The second he slipped down into one of my side chairs, I took his place. The distance from wall to window was exactly seven paces. On one of my laps, I closed

the door. "There has to be something we can do that will get
their attention."

"I think you've already gotten their attention, boss. As far
as doing something about it, here's what's going to happen.
We'll do our investigation, the fire department will do theirs.
No one will talk, which means nothing concrete will come out
of it, which means you can't blame the union because you can't
prove they did it, which means you can't take formal measures
against them."

"I don't want to back down on this, Dan."

"You might not have much choice. If Terry McTavish was
not talking before, he sure as hell is not going to be talking
now. Besides . . ." He gazed out the window at an empty expanse
where an aircraft should have been. The gate closest to my
window was out of service while the jetbridge was being
repaired. "I'm not sure it's the best thing for you to hold out
against Big Pete."

I turned and stared at him. "How can you say that? Should
we give them what they want because they blew something up?
Or set something on fire? Or slowed down the operation?
That's why we're in this spot to begin with."

"No, it's not. It's not because of something you did, or I
did, or Ellen did. It's Lenny. This station went to hell while he
ran it, it got nothing but worse when Dickie was in charge, and
as long as Lenny's your boss, nothing is going to change. You
can't take on this union without the company's support, and
as far as it goes out here, Lenny is the company. Makes no
difference to me. I'm not going anywhere. But you were right
the other day. You've got something to lose."

The mention of Lenny reminded me of the upended turtle.
I'd been so tired after yesterday, but after Matt had told me

about how my own boss had been trashing me behind my back, I'd spent most of the night stewing instead of sleeping. I'd gotten out of bed this morning exhausted, but clear on one point—if I was going, I wasn't going out on my back. I stood in the window and stared down at the empty ramp. "Do you think Scanlon knew what was going on in Boston while Ellen was here?"

"No."

"Do you know that for sure?"

"Think about it. You know Lenny's not going to let on to his boss, and I know Ellen wouldn't have filled him in."

"No?"

"She always thought that she could handle Lenny, that he would help her if he understood what was really going on, and if she couldn't make him understand, then it was her fault. She felt like she owed him for giving her the job. She said he was the only guy in the field operation who would have taken a chance on her."

I turned back to the window, thinking that Ellen was the one who had taken the chance, not Lenny. Taken a chance and lost.

Dan came and stood next to me. "Speaking of the asshole, when's Lenny due in?"

"Not until two o'clock. Why? Do you want to meet his flight?"

"After what he said about my kid, I might kill him if I see him. Besides, that's your job. That's why GMs get the big bucks. Do you need anything else before he shows up?"

"Maybe some oxygen. Do we have extra coverage while he's here?"

"I called in a couple of supervisors from their day off, and

I had a talk with some of the better crew chiefs. As soon as I can find him, I'm going to have another long chat with Victor just to let him know that I'm watching. Things are going to smooth out if I have to break balls personally."

"Listen"—I turned to check the door, forgetting that I had already closed it—"I talked to my Finance guy again last night, and I found out what fish means. It's microfiche."

"No shit?"

"He also told me that Ellen asked for invoices related to those pre-purchase adjustments, but she asked specifically for hard copies because she wanted to see the signatures. We're thinking she wanted to see who had approved payment of those invoices."

"Do you think those invoices are somehow related to the one you found from . . . what was it called?"

"Crescent Security. I think there's a link between the deal and the Nor'easter operation in Boston. I think it has something to do with the IBG contract that failed, and I think Crescent Security is part of it. Molly's going to pull all the information she can find on them in the local files. If Matt ever sends me the documents, we might find the connection."

As we watched, a driver pulling a train of three carts came out of the outbound bag room too fast, made a sharp turn, and sent two boxes and a suit bag flying across the ramp. He never looked back.

"Fucking moron." Dan moved toward the door. "Tell Finance Guy to hurry up. If Lenny's coming up here, we may be running out of time. By the way," he said, pausing in the open doorway, "you looked good on TV last night, really in control. Even I was reassured."

He dashed out laughing at my expense, as Molly strolled in

with the morning mail. "You should have worn some lipstick if you were going to be on TV."

"Believe it or not, I didn't get dressed yesterday morning with the idea that I would end the day on WBZ."

"You should never leave the house without a tube of lipstick."

"Thank you, Miss Manners."

I took the pile of mail and went back to my desk. Molly was in no hurry to get to work. She stood in front of my desk, perusing the office like an interior decorator. "When are you going to hang something on these walls?"

"I don't know. I think all that stuff is in storage right now."

I sifted through the mail quickly, threw half of it away, and tossed the rest into my in-box. Molly hadn't budged.

"Danny showed me Ellen's frequent flier card," she said, "and that list of trips she took."

"Are you convinced now?"

"I have a theory," she said, sounding more provocative than usual. "I think she was having an affair, a secret affair."

I leaned back in my chair. "Why do you think that?"

That's all she'd been waiting for. She closed the door and dragged one of the chairs in front of the desk and settled in. "I'll grant you, I didn't know anything about this travel business, but I thought something had been going on even before that. She used to get these phone calls. Usually she'd close the door, but sometimes I overheard and whoever she was talking to"—she raised her eyebrows—"she had the tone. You know the one I mean?"

I thought about Ellen's note, I thought about the voice I'd heard on the phone last night, and I knew exactly what she was talking about. "It's the way you talk to someone you love."

"Exactly. It's the tone. Kind of low and sexy and quiet. After one of those calls her whole mood would change. She'd be happy for the rest of the day. And sometimes she'd come in all dressed up for nothing in particular. If you ask me, those were the days she was going to meet him and wanted to look her best. That's what the travel was all about. She didn't want anyone to know."

"Did she ever talk to you about it?"

She dismissed the idea with a quick shake of her head. "Ellen was way too private for that. But sometimes a girl just knows, and I knew something was going on."

"Did you know about the dating service?"

"Dating service? When was this?"

"Recently. She joined and quit all within the past two months."

Again with the abrupt head shake. "Whatever was going on with her started right after she got here and went right up until the end. In fact, remember I told you about that last day, when she came out of her office crying? Maybe she got dumped. Women have killed themselves for less."

Even with all the intrigue and threats, the questions, the mystery package, it was still hard to argue with depression, alcoholism, Detective Pohan, and genetics. Ellen's mother had killed herself. And when you added a possible broken heart . . . Molly and I were definitely on the same track, but did that make it so?

"Dan doesn't believe she was having an affair," I said. "In fact, he emphatically disagrees."

She ran one of her perfectly lacquered nails along the edge of her gold bracelet. "Danny doesn't want to believe anything bad about Ellen."

"If having a boyfriend makes you bad, we'd all be in trouble."

"Oh, it's not the *what* that bothers him, it's the *who*." She raised her dark eyes, and I realized this was the point she'd been building to all along.

"Do you know who it is?"

"It was Lenny."

I think my jaw might have actually dropped. I leaned forward until my chin was almost on the desk. *"Lenny?"*

"I think she always had a little thing for him ever since he gave her this job, and he's not hard to persuade in that area. I've lost track of his extracurricular activities since he left the station, but more than a few of the girls around here got to know Lenny when he was the boss, if you get my drift."

"Lenny *Caseaux?*"

"Sure. He's a good-looking guy, and that Southern accent of his can be charming in a deep-fried sort of way. Besides, he's the boss. Power is always sexy."

"I guess so. I just never thought of him as anything *but* my boss. Isn't he married?"

"Why do you think they kept it a secret?"

I could see why Dan would be upset by the idea. "Do you really believe she would have killed herself over Lenny?"

"Here's what I think. Ellen worked too hard, she had no life, and she felt like she was getting old. If he showed the slightest interest in her, she might have decided that it was better than being alone."

I thought about Ellen's dating video. By her own admission, she'd picked situations that were never going to work out. This one certainly would have qualified. I reached up to rub my eyes and it felt good until I remembered, too late, that I was wearing mascara.

Molly just shook her head. "I can find out for sure," she said as she handed me a tissue from her skirt pocket. "I can check the list of her destinations against his travel schedule. The executive secretaries post the officers' travel calendars in the computer. We can see if they were together in the same cities."

"You need a password to get into the site."

Her full red lips curved into a feline smile. "Give me a few days."

The phone rang and she answered it in my office as I used a small mirror from my desk—Ellen's mirror—and tried to repair my raccoon eyes.

"Speak of the devil," she said, hanging up.

"Make my day and tell me Lenny's not coming."

"He's not coming." She walked around to the front of the desk. "He's here."

"He's here. *Now?*" I bolted from the chair and threw on my suit jacket. "He's not supposed to be in for three hours." I opened the door and ran out, trying to smooth my collar on the way. I was halfway out to the concourse when I had to double back.

"Where is he, anyway?"

Chapter Twenty-five

Lenny was on the phone when I arrived at the USAir terminal, which was good because I needed time to catch my breath. He was talking on the last in a long bank of pay phones, the only voice in an otherwise deserted departure lounge. When I moved into his line of sight, he turned away and I was left staring at his back. Hard to give that a positive interpretation, but then I wasn't too pleased with him, either.

Few people were in evidence this early afternoon, mostly stragglers moving on sore feet toward baggage claim.

I felt him approaching behind me before I heard him. I turned and looked, and for a fraction of a second he was just staring down at me. Then a broad smile spread across his face and his eyes crinkled at the corners. "I apologize for being early," he said, sounding like a colonel from the Confederate army. "I hope I have not disrupted things too much for you."

Molly was right. He could be charming when he wanted to. "I'm happy to accommodate your schedule," I said, trying not to sound like a Southern belle.

"It's understandable you weren't here to meet my trip. I

should have called you. Just remember when the chairman comes through your city, you have to keep better track because he is always on time, no matter when he arrives." He gave me that smile again, only this time it was less charming than condescending. "I make it a point never to let him wander around one of my stations without me. You never know what he might turn up."

He started walking, and I had to move briskly to keep up with his long-legged stride. My two-inch heels made me five foot ten, and I still only came up to Lenny's chin. He was tall and quite narrow and wore only custom-tailored European suits. There was a story floating around about how he used to expedite his shirts to Paris on one of our overnight flights to have them dry-cleaned there. I didn't know if it was true, but judging by the way he wore his clothes, the way he carried himself, and especially the way he lightly touched his collar when he smiled, I could believe it.

"Anything blow up today?"

"Nothing today," I said, ignoring the sarcastic tone. I was determined not to let him get to me.

"Well, that *is* a positive sign. I'd like you to fill me in on the situation with Petey Dwyer. How is it he was attacked by another employee and you're holding him out of service?"

"That's not what happened." And since when did Little Pete become Petey to Lenny?

"It is what happened according to the statements of the two people involved." He looked across his shoulder and down at me. "I wish I had heard that from you."

"I'm sorry I didn't brief you. I should have." I really should have. That was a tactical error that gave him an excuse to be self-righteous. "No one has the full story yet on what happened that night, but the situation is more serious than it might look on the surface. Little Pete caused the fight, he was drunk when it happened, and he consistently works his shift under the influence. We're trying to find—"

"Do you have any proof of what you're saying?"

"Not yet, but we're working on building a case."

"But you're not going to be able to do it, are you? You and I both know that. Therefore, I find it puzzling that we are going through all this upset. Can you enlighten me?"

More passengers were beginning to fill the concourse as we walked. A woman dragging a rolling bag was coming straight at me, reading her ticket and not paying attention. I had to step around her to avoid a head-on collision. Lenny kept going.

I was prepared to enlighten him, to try anyway, but when I caught up he was still talking. "You were supposed to come up here and calm things down," he was saying. "So far the operation has deteriorated, you've completely alienated the union over some meaningless shoving incident, and now you've reneged on your deal with Vic to bring back Angelo. Oh, and the bag room blew up. Is it any wonder the place is in an uproar? I thought you could handle this operation, Alex, but I'm losing my confidence in you. Your performance has been staggeringly disappointing."

I was losing patience, in no small part because I couldn't even keep up to talk to him.

"With all due respect, Lenny, even if all of that were true, I can't see how it justifies setting off a bomb in the bag room. I think we have to deal with that situation separately. If you want, I can address your other concerns individually."

Now he was getting frustrated, and it gave me a warm glow inside. He glanced at me and I smiled sweetly.

"What's going on with Angelo?" he asked.

"In light of recent events, I've decided to freeze all negotiations with the union. Angelo's status is on hold."

"I see. Well, I'm here to help you get it off hold, and here's how we're going to do that. We're meeting with the union, you and I, and we're going to find a way to work things out. What I mean by that is at the end of the meeting, we will have a plan for returning Angie to service and for Petey coming back to work. I'm afraid we'll have to fire the McTavish kid since he instigated the fight. He will surely grieve the action, and when he does I'll be happy to hear his grievance. That should help you remain focused on what it is you have to do here."

"I am focused, Lenny. I'm focused like a laser beam on the problem we have with Pete Dwyer Jr."

"What problem?"

"Little Pete is drinking on shift. He's a danger to himself, his fellow employees, and the operation. The other night before the fight, he was so drunk he reversed the load on one of his trips. We're very fortunate his crew caught it before it left the gate. If I can prove what he's doing, I won't bring him back to work under any circumstances." I didn't look at Lenny, but his pace slowed and I could feel him tensing. He seemed to be growing taller. I wet my dry lips and went on, trying to stay calm but getting more and more wound up. "If you force me to bring him back or make that decision yourself, it's going to be on you because I'm going to go on record and document my concerns in writing."

He stopped so abruptly that I shot ahead and had to backtrack.

"I understand your concerns, I do," he said. "And I wouldn't want you to do anything that makes you uncomfortable, so I'm

going to find a way to allay those concerns. But let me give
you a word of advice." He was smiling, his tone was sickly
sweet, and I was concentrating on breathing, having lost the
natural rhythm of respiration. "Unless and until you can prove
any of what you're saying, it would be unwise to generate even
one word of documentation. Because if you did, I would have
to consider you to be reckless, unnecessarily hostile to the
union, and lacking in the judgment it takes to run this station,
in which case I would be forced to terminate your employment
with this company. Understood?" He turned to go, then
stopped again. "And that's not even taking into account the
insubordinate and deceitful manner in which you've engaged
yourself in the matter of Ellen Shepard's death. Shall we discuss
how you came into possession of that power of attorney and
what you've been doing with it?"

We were standing in the middle of the vast ticketing lobby,
where we were surrounded by a swirl of people and bags and
skycaps and carts and animal carriers. But all I could hear was
the edge under the drawl, and it was sharp enough to cut
diamonds. I knew I'd crossed the line, and I knew I had been
stupid to threaten him. I could have anticipated the consequences. But having him articulate them with such cool confidence made my knees weak.

When it came down to it, I figured Bill would intervene if
Lenny tried to fire me. But I didn't want to put him in that position, and besides, it would be tricky with Lenny involved. Lenny
wasn't stupid. No matter what happened, my career at Majestic
would be forever compromised. I felt my self-confidence
crumple. I felt my anger deflate. "I understand."

He moved in close enough that I could smell his tangy aftershave. Then he actually put his hand on my shoulder. It felt

like a rat had perched on my suit jacket, and it was all I could do not to smack it off. "Let me give you some advice," he whispered. "Don't ever threaten me again. If you do, you'd better have what it takes to follow through, or it will be the last thing you do in this company. Now," he said with a jaunty smile, "let's go see your operation."

Chapter Twenty-six

I'd spent the entire excruciating day with Lenny, crawling through every inch of the operation, including the bomb damage. It had taken a monumental effort just to be civil around him, partly because I couldn't stand him, mostly because I couldn't stand myself with him. The last thing I wanted to do when I got back to my hotel was go out again. I'd collapsed face down across the bed, fully clothed. If the carpet had been on fire, I'm not sure I could have roused myself to run for safety. But the phone rang and it turned out to be the one guy who could change my plans.

"I been trying to reach you most of the day."

John didn't say hello, but I recognized his voice. Boarding announcements blared in the background over the constant hum of milling crowds, so I knew he was at the airport, probably at a pay phone upstairs. I always pictured him on a pay phone when he called, huddled over with one hand cupped around the receiver and the other hiding his face.

"Are you on break?"

"Yeah, but I'm off in an hour. I got your message. What's up?"

If I had told him over the phone that his brother was about to be fired, I could have saved the trip. I could have stayed on the bed, ordered room service, and spent the evening feeling sorry for myself. But I was talking to a man who had gone out on one long limb for me. I changed my clothes and dragged myself out to meet him.

He came around the bend at Tremont, and I immediately picked him out of the crowd by his stevedore's build and his lightweight dress. What was it with this guy? Everyone on the street, including me, had every inch of flesh covered, and he looked as if he was going to a sailing regatta. Topsiders, jeans, a sweater, and a windbreaker. His one concession to the cold was a knit cap pulled down over his ears.

"Don't you ever get sick dressing like that?"

"Never. I love this weather. Great for working. What I can't stand is the heat in the summer. It makes you slow."

He took a deep, sustained breath and indeed seemed to draw energy from the cold. Just watching him made my lungs frost. "Can we at least get out of the wind?"

"Sure."

We weren't far from the Park Street T stop, so I suggested we get on a subway to nowhere.

"There's lots of guys on the ramp take the T to work," he said, shaking his head. "But that gives me another idea."

I followed him past a knot of sidewalk vendors clustered around steaming carts filled with roasted chestnuts and hot pretzels. We went through the swinging doors, down the wide concrete stairs to the underground station, and for the cost of two eighty-five-cent tokens, into the bowels of Boston mass transit. As we moved down the crowded platform, I noticed that most of the rush-hour commuters were dressed too warmly for the underground air, but seemed too tired to do anything but sweat. I could feel their collective exhaustion. It felt like my own.

John disappeared down another set of concrete stairs, into a narrow subtunnel. When I caught up, he was leaning against one of the tiled walls.

"Here?"

"You said you wanted to get out of the wind."

The sound of the trains grinding and creaking above rolled down into the tunnel, but didn't seem to disturb the man curled into a drunken fetal stupor to my right. He was breathing—I checked—and by the smell of him, other bodily functions were also in good working order. I wrinkled my nose and tried to shut out the fetid air. "You're comfortable down here?"

He laughed. "I told you I used to work on a fishing boat. What's the news on Terry?" he asked as I peeled off my hat, gloves, and scarf.

"Lenny Caseaux's in town."

"We heard."

Of course they had. "He's not enthusiastic about the way I've been handling things. He's going to bring Little Pete and Angelo back to work, and he's going to hear Terry's grievance himself."

"That's it then for Terry."

It would have been easier if I had seen some anger in him, or even cynicism. But there was nothing like that, just the hopelessness, and the bleak acceptance that showed on his face and made me ashamed to be in the same chain of command with Lenny. John deserved better. So did his brother. So did I, for that matter, and I was feeling like a total loser for not standing up to Lenny on behalf of all of us. "I can keep pushing him," I said, "but he's already trying to take me out of my job."

"He said that?"

"Pretty much."

"I know you did what you could," he said, showing at least as much concern for me as for his brother, "and it's not worth giving up your job. Besides, I'd rather have you as GM than some of the others he could bring in."

We were quiet, both staring at the floor. The ground was covered with discarded handbills, some wet and soaked through, promising all manner of lewd exhibition at a gentlemen's club down the street. I pushed a few of them around with the toe of my boot, trying to find a way to ask what I wanted to know. I decided on the direct approach. "John, do you know who planted the bomb?"

He shook his head. "No."

"Would you tell me if you did?"

He pushed his knit cap higher, then whipped it off altogether and wiped the sweat off his forehead with the back of his sleeve. "I wouldn't tell you everything that goes on down there, but I would tell you that. Settin' off a bomb on the ramp so close to the fuel tanks, an aircraft sittin' right there on the gate—that's just stupid. People coulda been killed."

"I'm thinking it was Big Pete's idea."

"Nothing that big would happen without Big Pete knowing about it. But he didn't plant the thing, and you'd never find a way to prove it was him told someone to do it."

"What's the message?"

"They're trying to scare you, to let you know you're not in charge. You pissed 'em off when you took out Little Pete.

They're not used to being challenged like that. The only other one ever did it was Ellen."

"And look what happened to her."

"What? I didn't hear you."

"Nothing." I hadn't even been aware that I'd said it out loud. "John, tell me what you know about the IBG contract vote, the one that triggered the merger."

"Why? You think it has something to do with all this?"

"Maybe. I keep running into references to the Majestic-Nor'easter deal, and the only link I can find to Boston is that IBG contract."

"Maybe it has to do with Big Pete tanking that contract."

I stared at John and not because I didn't believe him, because I did. It was just so amazing what came out of his mouth when I figured out the right questions to ask. And it all seemed to be common knowledge floating around downstairs that never made it upstairs. "How did he do that? I thought it was a company-wide vote. Would he have had that much influence?"

"He had as much as he needed. Back then at Nor'easter, Boston was the biggest local of the IBG by far. However the vote went here, that was how the vote was going to go for the company, and Big Pete wanted it killed."

"You wanted the proposal to pass?"

"The way I saw it, the union shouldna had to give nothing back, but I knew if we merged we'd lose jobs. It happens every time. A lot of guys agreed with me till their tires started getting slashed, or their windows got broken, or they got acid poured on their car. One guy's Rottweiler turned up dead. Broken back."

"Someone broke a Rottweiler's back?" My own vertebrae stiffened at the thought.

"I told you about Little Pete, how he acts when he gets drunk."

"It was him?"

"He couldn't keep his mouth shut about it. Wanted everyone to know how he used a baseball bat. The way I look at it, it was a lucky thing it was just the dog."

"Jesus Christ. What would be in it for Big Pete to kill the contract? What would he care? He was senior enough not to lose his job. So was the kid, right?"

"He was paid off, pure and simple. He tried to make it look like he was taking a hard line for labor, but that guy doesn't believe in anything, doesn't stand for anything."

"Who paid him?"

"I don't know. There were so many deals and payoffs back then, it was hard to keep them all straight."

I began sorting through the list of loose ends, hoping to find one that he could shed light on in his matter-of-fact way. I'd already asked him about the Beechcraft. I'd found out what "fish" meant. Still unexplained was the porno video and Ellen's secret liaisons.

"John, this is awkward . . . I'm not sure how well you knew Ellen, but I've found a couple of things I'm wondering about. We—I think that Ellen may have been seeing someone, taking secret trips to meet him. Given the amount of scrutiny she received, I was wondering if anyone downstairs—"

"You think she was going with someone on the ramp?"

He began shifting his considerable weight from side to side, foot to foot, and I had the momentary thought that it might have been him. Nah. "I was actually thinking that someone from the ramp might have seen or heard something. It seems like a subject that would draw interest among your colleagues." He was shifting faster and faster, and I knew I was on to something. "Is it true, John? Has someone said something to you?"

He turned and leaned one shoulder against the wall and looked straight down so I couldn't see his face. "I don't think I should talk about this. What good would it do now?"

A surge of excitement pushed through my tired muscles and exhausted brain. He *knew.* "It might help us figure out what happened to her."

He considered that for a moment as he let out a long sigh. "One of my guys was in Miami last year for a wedding. He had to fly back on United on an overnight to get back for his shift, and he saw the two of them at the airport that night. He was on Majestic and she was on my guy's flight on United. When she saw my guy, she started acting really antsy, trying to hide."

"Who, John? Who was the man on Majestic?"

"Lenny Caseaux."

I leaned against the wall next to him. "Your guy saw Ellen and Lenny together in Miami?"

"Yeah, but they were acting funny, like ignoring each other."

"Like two people act," I said, "when they don't want to be seen together." What a dispiriting thought. "So it's true after all."

"I made my guy promise not to tell anyone, and I don't think he ever did. I never heard anyone else talking about this."

"Ellen was good at keeping secrets"—I looked at him—"and you were a good friend to her." My second wind had blown out, and I was ready to go. "I think I'm going to get on one of those trains and head back to the airport. I'm out of gas."

"Before you do, there's something else I gotta tell that I wish I didn't have to."

I could tell by the catch in his voice that it was something I wasn't going to like. In fact, he was so uncomfortable that he couldn't even look at me. It was alarming. "What? What is it?"

"There's been some talk downstairs . . ."

"About what?"

"About you. About Little Pete. He's got nothing better to do these days but sit around and get plastered, and he's worked up a pretty good hard-on about you—" He caught himself and blushed. "I'm sorry, I—"

"Go on, what is he saying?"

"The word is that he's talking about how something could happen to you like it did the last one, to Ellen."

He was staring straight down, talking slower and slower with every new revelation. I wanted to grab him by those broad shoulders and shake him. "What *else*?"

"He's saying that suicide's no good. Who would believe two in a row, right? But an accident, maybe . . ." He didn't have to finish. He had finally made eye contact and was looking at me as if I was in real trouble.

"Oh, my God." I started pacing the narrow tunnel, back and forth, the soles of my boots slick on the damp floor. "This is . . . how can he . . . *what kind of a place is this?*"

"I know," was all he could come up with.

We stared at each other for a moment, the dank air pressing in, feeling like more of a presence in the tunnel than the live human being curled up on the ground.

"Does he mean it? Should I be worried, or is it just talk?"

Before he could respond, a train rumbled overhead. He waited for the train to pass before answering. But I saw the answer in his eyes, and even standing in that stuffy passage-way wearing too many clothes, I felt a chill, one that came from someplace deep and refused to pass. When it was quiet again, I asked him, "John, do you believe that Ellen was murdered?"

He checked the tunnel both ways and moved closer. "When you're downstairs, you worry most when it's quiet. A thing happens, something's going on, you can't go nowhere without you hearing all about it, the stuff that's true and especially the stuff that isn't. GM dies. Kills herself. You'd expect nothing but talk about it, all day, every day."

"Nobody's talking?"

"Everybody's looking over their shoulder, but no one's talk-ing."

"But you haven't heard anything definitive, right? You don't know anything for sure."

"That's the thing I'm saying. Nobody ever says it for sure, but that don't mean they don't know."

I started piling the rest of my layers back on—coat, hat, scarf. I felt claustrophobic in the tunnel. I wanted to be out in the open, around people. "I don't want to do this alone, John. I can't."

"I'll help you best I can."

"I know you will, but I'm talking about Dan. I want to tell him all this stuff."

He sucked in his upper lip and raised his eyes to the ceil-ing, and I knew I'd put him on the spot. Frankly, I didn't care. "I have to tell him I have a source, John. I won't tell him it's you, but I need his help, and if I don't tell him I'll never be able to explain where all this information is coming from. And I want to tell him about these threats. Please, John."

He switched to staring at the knit cap, which he was work-ing with both hands. "You trust him?"

"I do trust him, and if you don't, I wish you'd tell me why.".

His answer was a shrug. "All right. If you think you have to. But it's under the condition that you never use my name."

"Thank you. I'm leaving and I know you don't want to walk with me, but will you keep an eye on me from a distance until I get onto the train? Better yet, I think I'll take a cab."

"Sure, and I'll tell Terry what you tried to do for him."

I started to walk, then remembered something else I'd meant to ask before I'd become terrorized. "Was Angelo involved in this vote fixing? Is that why Ellen would have wanted to talk to him?"

"Whatever Big Pete's into, Angelo knows about it."

"They're friends?"

"For years."

"Do you have any influence with Angelo?"

"Nobody influences him except his wife, Theresa."

"Okay." I wasn't sure how that helped me. "Thanks."

I turned one way in the tunnel, and he went the other over to the inbound platform. As I reached the top of the stairs, I turned and looked for him. He'd been watching me from behind a post, and as I headed out of the station and to the street, he stepped onto a train and didn't look back.

I had once felt safe with John. Now I didn't feel safe with anyone.

By the time I slid the plastic card key into the slit in my hotel room door, it was almost ten o'clock. My clothes felt damp and heavy, and I couldn't wait to peel them off.

The orange message light on my phone was on, its reflection

blinking in the dark room like some kind of a coastal beacon signaling a warning in the night.

I flicked on the light, took one step in, stopped short. I took another halting half step and my mind went blank, short-circuited by the scene right in front of me. All the dresser drawers were open. My clothes were on the floor. My brief-case was on its side, its guts spilled out on the table. I stood in the silent room with both hands pressed against my heart, trying not to panic. Only, it wasn't silent. A noise—a sweeping sound, back and forth. It was ... Jesus, it was coming from behind me and it sounded like ... I made myself turn around, and when I saw it, my heart turned to ice and all the blood pumping through it turned cold.

It was a *noose,* a big, stiff noose with a big knot, and some-one had looped it over the thing—that metal door thing, the pneumatic arm. I'd set it in motion when I'd walked in, and it was still swinging like a pendulum, scratching lightly against the paint. I tried to make my brain work, but it wouldn't. I tried to make my body respond, but it wouldn't. I couldn't take my eyes from the noose. It felt like a living thing, like a bird that could fly off the hook where it was perched and ensnare me, wrap itself around my neck, and squeeze the eyeballs out of my head. The sick drawing of Ellen emerged from some feverish corner of my memory. I stumbled back, then a thought, a horrible thought as my gaze flew around the room—he could still be *in* here. I blew straight out the door and down to the lobby, where I had the front desk call security.

An hour later, I was checked into the Airport Ramada, the seedier of the two airport hotels. I walked into my new room, went straight to the phone, and dialed the number from my address book, the one I had never really forgotten no matter how hard I'd tried. This time when his voice came on I closed my eyes and counted to myself and after the beep I left my number and my message, "I need to talk to you. Please call."

Chapter Twenty-seven

"So the only thing missing was this tape?" Dan was trying to be somber and concerned as we stood in the window at Gate Forty-two, but he couldn't completely hide his excitement. A hotel room invasion was exactly the kind of thing that got his blood flowing. Too bad it had happened to me and not him.

"A tape is missing, but it's definitely not the one he was looking for. The East Boston Video Vault is not going to be pleased with me. It was their only copy of *The Wild Bunch*, the anniversary edition."

"What's that?"

"It's an old western. A classic."

He stared.

"Sam Peckinpah? William Holden? Ernest Borgnine?"

"I never would have pegged you for westerns, Shanahan."

"I love westerns, but this is not just a western. It's a—"

A crashing noise rattled through the silent concourse. I flinched, then realized it was the wire-mesh gate at the throat of the concourse. Someone at the security checkpoint had rolled it up into its nest in the ceiling, probably Facilities Maintenance doing their daily calibration of the metal detectors. It was four-thirty in the morning, and the Logan operation of Majestic Airlines was open for business.

"Take it easy, boss."

"I'm edgy."

"Do you think it was Little Pete who was in your room?"

"Yes, I do. He touched all my things. My clothes were all out of the drawers. In the bathroom my toothbrush and my razor, my makeup, it was all there but moved, everything moved so that I would know that it had been touched. It felt personal. I felt him there. It made my skin crawl."

Dan leaned back against the window, hands in his pockets, and crossed one foot over the other at the ankle. He looked as if he'd gotten dressed in the dark this morning. His shirt-tail was out, his tie was draped around his neck, and one button was missing from his shirt. I probably didn't look much better, although I had fewer parts to deal with. I had on a simple dark brown and slate blue turtleneck sweater, a long, heavy one that came down almost to my thighs. I wore it over a brown suede, shin-length skirt and leather boots, and is it any wonder I had every inch of my body covered up this morning? Our coats were in a pile on one of the chairs in the row behind us.

"We know he knows where you were staying," Dan said. "He's got plenty of free time on his hands since he's not working, and he hates your guts." He threw me a sideways glance and grinned.

"This is not funny to me."

"I'm sorry, boss. I'm teasing you. I'm getting you back for not telling me that you found Ellen's snitch."

"I did what I thought was right. He's paranoid about someone finding out what he's doing, and I can't blame him. Everyone knows everything that goes on in this place."

He tapped his knuckles and then his St. Christopher's ring on the vertical metal strut that separated the large windowpanes. It was the only noise in a quiet concourse that felt cavernous at that time of the morning. "Well, fuck him," he said finally, almost to himself.

"Excuse me?"

"Fuck him if he doesn't trust me."

"It's good that you're not taking this personally. Let's focus on his information and not him."

"Okay. Why would Little Pete take your copy of—what the hell is it? *The Wild Bunch?*"

"Obviously, he thought it might be something else. Now I have a box with no video. Sound familiar?"

"The porno box in Ellen's gym locker."

"Exactly. I had plenty of time to think about this when I was lying awake all last night staring at the ceiling. I think that Dickie Flynn sent Ellen a videocassette. That's what was in the mystery package."

"Why would they think you have it, especially when you don't?"

"All I can figure is that someone found out I rented a VCR, jumped to the conclusion that I had found the tape, and came looking. But *only* for the tape. All the stuff from Ellen's box, her files and mail, it was dumped on the floor but it was all still there."

"What does the snitch say?"

"I haven't had a chance to ask him, but the package he described would have been about the right size. It could have been a videocassette, but he never looked inside the envelope, so he wouldn't know for sure." When I leaned against the window next to Dan, the glass felt cold on my arm all the way through my thick sweater. "I think we're looking for Dickie Flynn's videocassette, I think it's the key to whatever happened to Ellen, and the Dwyers think we already have it."

Dan tilted his head from side to side, trying out the idea. "What's on the tape?"

"I don't know. Let's start with why Dickie Flynn would send his package to Ellen in the first place. Did he even know her?"

"He knew her. She went to visit him when she heard he was sick. Between Nor'easter and Majestic the guy had given thirty-five years to the company, and she figured someone should pay their respects. Lenny couldn't be bothered."

"Did you go?"

"No. Dickie was an asshole. Just because he was dying didn't make him any less of an asshole. Don't get me wrong. I didn't wish stomach cancer on the guy. God forbid anyone should have to go that way, but he always treated me like dirt, and I didn't want to be a hypocrite."

Out of the corner of my eye, I caught sight of an agent hurrying through the concourse on her way to start an early shift. She waved as she went by, and we waved back. If she was surprised to see us there at that hour she didn't show it.

"When did Ellen make this visit?"

"When we first heard he was dying, maybe six months ago. Sometime late last summer." He laughed. "Ellen came back and she said he was an asshole, too."

"Last summer's too early. When did he die?"

"Around the holidays. Thanksgiving, I think. Molly went to the funeral. She'd know."

That timing worked better. I took a few steps toward the podium at the gate, unmanned and locked up at this hour. When I had it straight in my mind, I came back. "Right before he died, sometime around Thanksgiving, Dickie Flynn sent Ellen a secret tape, something he'd hidden away years before when he still worked here. She watched it and whatever she saw caused her to start an investigation. We don't know what it was about, but the next thing she did was call Matt Levesque wanting to know where she could find her old merger files. We found her own personal merger folder hidden in her gym locker. She was on the task force and knowledgeable on details of the transaction."

"So she found out something hinky about the merger."

"I think so, and it has to be the IBG contract, the one that was voted down because that happened right here in Boston. And it was significant. That contract failing as much as guaranteed that the deal would go forward. My source tells me that Big Pete was paid to tank it."

"That's a rumor. It's always been the rumor, but no one knows for sure."

"I'll bet Dickie Flynn knew for sure. Maybe he sent Ellen some kind of proof of the contract fraud or tampering or whatever you'd call it, and she was trying to put together a case. The package is evidence, and that's why Big Pete wants it."

"You think this proof is on a tape?"

"That's part of what we don't know. I also don't understand why Ellen wanted your Nor'easter procedures manual. What the heck was her interest in the Beechcraft, anyway? And Crescent Security. We don't know the significance of that."

I felt my shoulders sag with the weight of all we didn't know, but Dan was looking at things from a different angle. "We know a lot more than we did this time last week," he said brightly.

A passenger settled in not far from us, a businessman with two newspapers and a cup of coffee. We moved a couple of windows farther down the concourse.

"We know something else, too, Dan. Ellen was spending time with Lenny. They were seen together in the same airport ignoring each other. Molly's going to check Lenny's travel schedule against Ellen's list of destinations. That will tell us for sure."

He had turned toward the window and was looking down on the ramp, where a three-inch blanket of snow had fallen during the night. He was either wearing down or he'd decided to stop wasting his breath, because even though he was shaking his head, he didn't argue. All he said was, "What next?"

"Angelo."

"What about him?"

"That stakeout Ellen sent you on, the target all along was Angelo, not Little Pete. Ellen set him up. It sounds as if she wanted to fire him and trade his job back for information."

"I guess there's a good reason Ellen didn't tell me anything about what she was doing."

"I don't know, Dan."

He rubbed the side of his face with the palm of his hand. "So Angie knows something, which is why you didn't want me to bring him back."

"I'm sorry I couldn't explain that, but now we have to figure out how to get him to talk and we have to hurry. Lenny's trying to get his arbitration hearing scheduled within the next couple of weeks."

"If he does, we're screwed. The arbitrators will probably

bring him back, and even if they don't, after arbitration Lenny can do whatever he wants."

"Yes, but until then it's still my call. This is the station where he was fired, and I'm now the chief operating officer here. Lenny can't do anything, not formally anyway, without an exception from the international, and he needs Scanlon's permission to do that."

Things were beginning to move outside. The pristine white expanses between the gates were beginning to look like abstract paintings, clean canvases brushed with black tire tracks in wide arcs and tight loops.

"I'm going down to check on the deicing operation," he said. "I'll let you know when I get in touch with Angie."

"Good. Thanks for coming in so early. Hey . . ." I had to call after him because he'd shifted into airport speed and was almost to the stairwell. "You left your coat."

After he was gone, it was just the passenger and me. I turned to the window for one last look at the peaceful scene before it was completely obliterated. There was an aircraft on every gate, and the snow on their long, smooth spines and broad, flat wings looked like soft down comforters. Later, when the sky was brighter and the aircraft were preparing for departure, all trace of it would have to be cleared off under the high-pressure blast of the deicing hose. But for now the dry white crystals softened the rough edges and brought grace and gentleness to a hard place. If I stared long enough, I could almost believe the illusion. Maybe that was Dan's problem with Ellen. He was having a hard time letting go of the illusion.

I stayed out in the concourse until the first departures had gone, greeting passengers, lifting tickets, and assisting the agents. By the time I made it to my office, Molly was in.

"What are you doing here?" she asked, eyes wide.

"I work here."

"Did you forget about your meeting?"

Chapter Twenty-eight

They were staring at me. People gaping from the window of a passing city bus couldn't have looked more vacant. Except for feet shuffling and throat clearing, a random cough here and there, I could get no reaction out of the twenty-five or thirty rampers gathered in front of me. They were slumped on benches and in chairs, clustered in the doorways, and arrayed around the walls of the ready room among raincoats hung from hooks. The rain gear showed more animation.

I'd already done my short presentation, giving them the facts on the bag room bombing, passing around pictures of the twisted cart and ruptured skis. We—rather, I—had already discussed the costs of reconstruction, interim use of USAir's bag claim, and passengers' belongings blown to smithereens.

"Does anyone have any questions?"

Silence.

The apathy was so impenetrable, it felt like an act of aggression, and one that had been coordinated in advance. I didn't need to be liked by these people, but I could not walk out of there without some acknowledgment, no matter how tiny, that bombing the bag room—or anything else—was not okay.

Big Pete, coming off the end of his shift, was leaning against a wall in the opposite corner. Still in uniform, he was, as always, outwardly nondescript with several layers of shirttails out and uncombed hair.

"Pete, as the union representative, do you have anything to say?"

For the longest time he didn't move or respond. Finally, he shifted slightly so that he was more angled toward the room, gave me one of those languid, crocodile-in-the-sun blinks, and began to hold forth. "First off, I want to say that the union don't condone this sort of activity."

At the sound of his raspy voice, some of the congregation turned their eyes in his direction. The ones that didn't looked out the window.

"Second, I want you to know I don't think none of you was any part of this. To me, it was someone from off the field who breached security, come onto our ramp, and did this thing. Maybe some kind of a terrorist like we're always hearing about."

Even some of the rampers were having a hard time keeping straight faces.

"I want everyone to be alert. The fact is, we ain't as safe here as we'd like to think. Anyone not wearing his badge, don't be afraid to challenge him. And if you got something on who might have done this thing, the union wants you to come forward and give it to management." He nodded graciously, and when he turned the floor back over to me, it was with a smug expression that seemed to ask, "Great performance, eh?"

I went back to my flip chart and found a great big red marker, the perfect symbol for how I was feeling. "I want to say one more thing just to add to Pete's point. No matter who perpetrated this act, this number"—I underlined the total cost of the bombing, twice—"translates into seven or eight full-time *union* jobs a year that could go away because someone was trying to send a message"—I looked at Pete—"no matter who that was." I capped the felt-tipped pen and checked my hands for leaking ink. "We can't even calculate the revenue we'll lose because passengers generally try to avoid airlines that have been bombed. You junior employees should pay particular attention. You're at the bottom of the seniority list, and you're the ones who will be out on the street. Given the sliding salary scale, it's going to take about ten to twelve of you to get to this number. Pete's right. It's in all of our best interests to make sure this never happens again."

I was encouraged by a stirring in the hallway, a murmuring that seemed to move into the room and run through the group like a lit fuse. I was getting through to them.

"That may be," Pete said with a polite sneer, "but we're all in the same union, and it ain't gonna work to try and set us against each other. Besides, management is responsible for the security of the operation. If you can't keep the ramp safe for us to work, you might want to start worrying about your own job."

The room fell quiet. Blood rushed to my head. I could feel my face heating up. An appropriately clever response would deflect attention from me and put him in his place, but with thirty pairs of eyes trained on me, I couldn't quite grasp it.

"Friend"—the voice exploded through the doorway and into the room—"her job is none of your concern."

My head snapped around so I could see if my ears were deceiving me. The crowd at the door parted as if they were being unzipped, and in walked Bill Scanlon—chairman, CEO, airline legend.

I was stunned—suddenly and completely struck dumb in front of a room full of my employees. I should have stepped forward, extended my hand in the usual professional greeting, and welcomed him into the room. Not that he ever needed any welcome, but it would have given me something to do besides stand rooted to the painted cement floor. But I couldn't. I couldn't even summon the will to take my eyes off him.

The dull murmur grew to an excited buzz as he strode on long legs into the center of the room, right where he was most comfortable.

"Sorry to drop in on you like this." His smile was crisp and, I felt, coldly impersonal.

I was swamped by a flood of emotions, none of which I could show, and for what seemed like the longest time, my mouth was open but I was afraid to speak, afraid of what might come out and when something finally did—'That's all right' is what I think I said—it sounded once removed, as if I were speaking in the voice of a passing stranger who had found my empty vessel of a body and moved in. But I knew it wasn't a stranger in there because the one emotion that kept crashing forward like the biggest wave in a pounding storm was fear. I was afraid that he was angry, that he had come all the way to Boston to fix what I couldn't fix. I was profoundly worried that I had let him down and that he was here to tell me.

But when he turned to slip out of his long cashmere coat—midnight blue—his eyes locked on mine for just a second longer than necessary, and for that one second it was as if he'd taken all the excitement he'd brought into the room, pulled it into a bouquet, and offered it to me as a secret gift. His eyes said what he couldn't say out loud: I am so excited to see you.

While he handed his coat and then his suit jacket to Norm, who had sprung from his seat to take them, the storm inside me ceased, the churning stopped, and the sun came out.

Bill smiled graciously at Norm, thanked him without the slightest trace of condescension, and turned to me. He was ready to go to work. "With your permission—"

"The floor is yours."

"You might want to get someone to take notes."

"Of course." As if I wouldn't remember every word that was about to be spoken. I was noticing how warm it was in the room, at least ten degrees hotter since he'd walked in. But maybe that was just me.

The group did not accommodate me as it had the chairman, and I had to elbow my way to a spot near the door where I could be available yet unobtrusive. The room was getting more crowded as ticket agents filtered down from upstairs. Majestic employees never missed a chance to see up close "the man who'd saved the airline," and to see him in a surprise visit was a double bonus.

I asked one of the agents to call Molly and have her track down Lenny, and then settled in to watch the show.

He stood in the center of the room in his pressed cotton shirt, exquisite but understated tie, and suit pants that were perfectly tailored to his lanky build. Some men might have felt out of place in that dingy room, just as I almost always did. But he was a man with the unwavering conviction that where he was was where he belonged and that the surroundings—whether it was a maintenance hangar or a Senate chamber—would conform to him.

"Ladies and gentlemen," he said quietly, letting his voice

draw them in, "we have picked a tough business in which to make our livings, you and I. Don't you agree?"

No one moved. Everyone agreed.

"I look at some of these other hotshots who run businesses, and I think to myself every day, they've got it made compared to us. Think about the software business. Those guys in Silicon Valley, they've got a high-margin business, markets that are growing exponentially, new markets opening up every day, and they get to come to work in shorts and sandals." His smile let us all in on the gentle teasing. "Who couldn't make money doing that? Or take the money guys on Wall Street, investment bankers and fund managers. In a market as robust as the one we have today, they don't even have to come to work to turn a profit." He was gliding around the small space, making it look bigger than it was, stopping now and then to pick someone out of the crowd and focus his entire being on them. "But you and me, we don't have it that easy. We have this massive, complicated machine"—he opened his arms wide, as if holding the entire contraption in his own two hands—"with more moving parts than any human and most computers can comprehend. We've got weather issues, we've got scheduling issues— airplanes, pilots, and flight attendants who all have to be scheduled according to their specific labor contracts. We've got regulatory requirements, environmental requirements, and constraints of air-traffic control. And we deal with machines, so we have the ever unpredictable maintenance variable."

Heads around the room bobbed in solemn agreement.

"You're on the front lines here," he said. "You know better than anyone how every day we have to mesh it all together in a way that works best for the customers, the employees, and the shareholders. We go home every night, and every morning we have to get up and do it all over again from scratch, because we have no inventory. Am I right?"

Of course he was right. He was tapping into the mother lode of truth for these people—for any people—telling them how difficult their jobs were, how hard they worked, and how no one understood them better than he did. He could communicate with anyone on any level about anything. And he could make you agree with him. He could make you want to agree with him. That was his gift. He had the ability to find a way to lead you wherever he wanted you to go. I tried to remember that there were good reasons why we weren't together anymore. Watching him work, it was hard to think of exactly what they were.

"We don't make money in this business unless we grind it out every day, seven days a week, twenty-four hours a day. We do this at Majestic with more success than our competitors. How is that?"

"We're better than they are," someone yelled from the back, one of the rampers who had been unconscious for my segment.

"Are we?" Bill picked him out with his eyes and challenged him for giving the easy answer, but obviously the one he had expected. "Our planes look just like their planes, our cabins are just as crowded, and our leg room equally deficient. We don't fly any faster than they do. Why are we better?"

No one dared risk another response that didn't work. A brief pause stretched to a long one, and still no one spoke up, and still he didn't say anything. He waited until the moment when the silence was unbearable, then answered his own question.

"The way we make money, the only way anyone makes money running an airline, is by running it better," he waited a beat, ". . . and faster," another beat, ". . . and cheaper than the next guy, by demonstrating a deeper commitment to our customers, and by being nothing less than relentless when it comes to keeping our costs down. *Relent*less, ladies and gentlemen."

He had ended up next to the flip chart and stood there now, scanning the audience, seeing everyone and everything, letting no one off the hook. When he stopped, he was staring at me. "I'm not going to speculate on the identity of the person or persons who set off a bomb in my operation the other night," he said. "That would be a waste of time—yours and mine."

It was as if he had set off his own bomb in the crowded room. No one was moving; they might have all stopped breathing. He swept the room again with eyes that seemed darker. "And I would never accuse anyone of doing something like that deliberately. You have a fine management staff here in Boston and capable union representation, and I'm confident they will work this situation out. When I came in, your manager was talking to you about how incidents like this can affect people's jobs, people who had nothing to do with what happened. That doesn't seem right, does it?"

Every muscle in my body stiffened, down to the arches in my feet. I'd seen him too many times not to know that something was coming. I watched him walk the perimeter of his stage, moving slowly enough that everyone could see him as he passed. "I'm going to go one better." When he stopped, he was staring at Big Pete, holding eye contact as if he had his hand on the back of his scruffy neck. "If I ever find out that someone who works for me planted that bomb, that they put themselves, their fellow employees, our passengers, and our equipment at risk, I'll shut this operation down."

People turned to look at each other, to see if they'd heard what they thought they'd heard. As they began to absorb what he was saying, Bill waited, milking the moment for every bit of drama. "I'll take every last job out of this city and move them to Philadelphia or Providence or Wilmington, Delaware. I don't care."

He spotted the spring water dispenser, and we all watched as he went over, plucked off a paper cup, and filled it. "And if you don't think I'll do it, my friends, try it again." He knocked back the water, turned, and searched the crowd.

"Any questions?"

"Nice of you to show up for work, Leonard." Bill eyed Lenny as the three of us stood around the table in a small conference room in the Peak Club, our haven for first-class passengers and very frequent fliers. Lenny looked as if he'd been dragged out of bed early, which is apparently what had happened.

"Bill, we had no idea you were coming"—he shot me a suspicious look—"did we?"

"No one knew," Bill snapped, "which is exactly what I wanted. My meeting in New York canceled this morning, so I decided to come up here and shake these people up. How was that?" he asked me. "Will that help you out?"

"Tremendously," I said evenly, playing my role in the charade. "Thank you. Do you want to meet with anyone else, maybe the next—"

"You won't need any more meetings. The message has been delivered."

I nodded. Here was a man keenly aware of his own impact.

He reached into his briefcase for a single, wrinkled piece of paper and put it on the table in front of us. It was a copy of the awful drawing that had been delivered to me on my first evening in the station, the one of the hangman's noose with Ellen at the end of it. "I want to know about this."

"Bill, you know what that is. It's just the guys downstairs blowing off steam—"

"No, it's not, Lenny. What this is, Lenny, is bad for business. People who have time to draw pictures and send them to me have too much time on their hands. People who are spreading rumors are not working."

Lenny stuck his hands in his pockets and decided not to pursue the point.

Bill turned back to me. "Now, what about this bomb? What have you learned?"

"The fire department is investigating," I said, feeling more confident. This was a subject I knew something about. "They don't expect to find anything. We have Corporate Security and Aircraft Safety on site. We're almost certain a ramper planted the bomb—"

"There's no evidence of that, Bill. We have to be careful about making accusations."

Bill glared at him. I expected burn marks to appear on Lenny's ecru cotton shirt. "What we have to be careful about is that the thieves, thugs, and criminals that you hired in your day do not get it into their heads that they can threaten or intimidate any member of my management staff and get away with it. You just lost one general manager in a most unpleasant manner." He held up the page again. "Do you really think it's a good idea to have this stuff floating around?"

I didn't look at Lenny because if I had, I surely would not have been able to hide the warm satisfaction that was welling up inside me.

"I just want to know one thing from you." Bill had turned to me. "Do you feel safe?"

Lenny looked at me. I looked at Bill. "Excuse me?"

"You're the one who has to live and work here every day. I want to know if you feel comfortable in this station, and I want you to tell me if you don't."

Well now, here was a loaded question if there ever was one. Lenny was still watching me closely. If I admitted I was sometimes afraid, would I be taken out of the job? And never offered another good one again? If I didn't, was I giving up all future rights to being scared? For the first time I noticed the music that was being piped into the room through an undersized overhead speaker—a tin can version of *I Honestly Love You*. It seemed as if the entire song had played through twice before I came up with my answer. "I'm fine here."

Bill's eyes narrowed slightly, and I had the feeling he was trying to decide if that was my real answer or my for-show answer. The real answer was that I wasn't always comfortable there, and I didn't want to leave Boston. Lenny had no reaction.

"Okay," Bill said, plowing on to the next subject, "here's what you do. You get that bonehead in here who runs the local. What's his name?"

"Victor Venora."

"Get him in your office and tell him exactly what I just said in the meeting. One more incident that even looks suspicious, and I will shut this operation down so fast, it will make his empty head spin."

"Would you really do it?" I asked.

The expression on his face left me feeling stupid for asking.

"You run this station, Alex, not the union. Don't let them

push you around, and don't be afraid to be an asshole."
Simultaneously, I was nodding, looking serious, and berating
myself for being so thrilled at the sound of him saying my name
again. "And you, Leonard, I expect you to give her whatever
support she needs to get that done."

As he closed his briefcase, he addressed us both. "I want to
see this place turn around, and fast. If it doesn't, I will hold
both of you responsible. Do you understand?" He waited until
we acknowledged what he had said. "Good. I'm going downtown to meet with some portfolio analysts. Lenny, you come
with me and let her do her job."

He blew out the door with Lenny in tow and left me standing there. When I checked my watch, I realized how completely
disoriented and out of sync I was. The whole encounter had
taken a little over an hour. It wasn't even ten o'clock in the
morning.

Chapter Twenty-nine

It was one of those yawns that brought tears to my eyes, the kind so wide and deep, it threatens to turn your face inside out. The black-and-white pictures on the closed-circuit TV monitors blended into one big, blurry gray image. Sort of how my day had gone.

"I hear I missed all the excitement this morning," said Kevin, coming through the door and sounding uncommonly bright. Either that or I was uncommonly dull.

It was the beginning of his day while mine was thankfully coming to an end. "That's what you get for bidding nights."

"Indeed, but had I known, seeing Himself in person would have been worth bounding out of bed early."

"No one knew. He just materialized in the ready room like a bolt of lightning. It was vintage Scanlon."

"So I heard. The whole place is a-twitter." He chuckled as he hung up his coat, walked over, and stood next to me. "Did he really say he was going to shut us down?"

"Unequivocally."

"I hope the message got through. I don't want to be unemployed." He surveyed the wall of electronic windows to the ramp, then reached up and wiped a smudge off one of the screens. "What are we looking at here?"

"Are these cameras set up to record?"

"No."

"Were they ever?"

"They were never intended for that." His rolling chair squealed as he settled in and immediately started cracking his knuckles, one by one. "You're not thinking of surveilling the ramp, are you?"

"No, but why not? Other stations do it."

"Obviously, you haven't heard about Dickie Flynn's fiasco."

I walked over and leaned against his work counter as he began his ritual, the kind we all go through to get ourselves prepared for another day of work. "Dickie Flynn surveilled the ramp?"

Kevin's motions were efficient and practiced, and he talked to me without once ever interrupting his flow. "Dickie used to go through his phases, his different kind of management phases. He tried management by intimidation, but no one was ever scared of him. He tried management by consensus, but no one ever agreed with him, much less each other. At one time he got frustrated and tried management by spying."

"Spying?" I tried to sound only casually interested. "With video cameras?" It wasn't easy.

"Cameras everywhere. The bag room, the ready room, the lunchroom. What he never quite accepted was the fact that you can't have secret surveillance in a twenty-four-hour-a-day operation, which was the fatal flaw in his scheme."

"People knew about the cameras."

"Of course they did. He even tried moving them every few

days, but within hours the union would have the locations posted on bulletin boards all over the field. He finally gave up the ghost after one night when someone swapped all of the tapes with several—how shall I put this delicately—adult entertainment features."

"Porno tapes?" I straightened up so abruptly, I drew a quizzical look from him.

"From what I understand, the full range. Something for everyone—heterosexual, homosexual, bestiality . . ."

As he talked, I stared down at the toes of my boots, glassy-eyed, and let the outside world drift away as the pieces began to coalesce in my head. The monitors drew me back, and I studied each one closely as figures moved across the black-and-white screens setting up gates and working the flights. The pictures were clear and the cameras high-quality, but far enough away that I couldn't distinguish faces.

". . . yes, indeed, shocking stuff," he was saying, "but not so shocking they didn't all gather in the ready room for a matinee, mind you—"

"Kevin, are you saying someone brought a bunch of porno videos to the airport one night and swapped them out for surveillance videos?"

"It would appear so."

"Which means it's likely that Dickie's surveillance videos came right out of the machines . . . and straight into the porno boxes." I was talking more for my own benefit now and feeling less and less fatigued.

"I can't say, but I would imagine so."

The sound of my beeper was usually an intrusion, but particularly so when it erupted at that moment. I didn't recognize the number.

"Kevin, did they ever find out who stole the tapes?"

"Surely you jest?"

"Were these good-quality cameras he used? Like these?"

"Dickie never spared any expense when it came to spending the company's money."

I checked my watch. Four o'clock. "Can I borrow your ramp coat?"

"I would be honored."

"Thanks." The phone rang, and when he picked up I grabbed the coat and a set of truck keys from a hook on the wall and made for the door. Dickie Flynn had sent Ellen a surveillance video. A *surveillance* video. I couldn't wait to tell Dan. If I was lucky, I could still catch him at his meeting across the ramp at the post office. As I rushed down the corridor, my beeper went off again.

Whoever it was didn't want to wait.

Chapter Thirty

The maître d' at Locke-Ober was a small-boned man with a black suit and a face as stiff as his starched white cuffs. The gold name tag on his jacket read Philip.

"Good evening," I said.

He glanced past me into the empty foyer. Locke-Ober had not even admitted women until 1970, so he was no doubt searching for my husband. Finding no escort, he defaulted to me. "May I help you?"

"Yes, thank you. I'm meeting someone for dinner." Although the way my stomach was flipping around, it was going to be hard to eat.

He hovered over his reservation book. "What is the gentleman's name, please?"

"The *party's* name is William Scanlon." Jeez.

Philip's demeanor transformed instantly as I grew in social stature right before his very eyes. Twit.

"Indeed, Mr. Scanlon is here. He's in the bar. I'll let him know his guest has arrived."

"I'll find him, if you'll point me in the right direction."

"Certainly. The bar is right this way." He tugged on one cuff and motioned toward the bar. "Tell Mr. Scanlon we'll hold his table as long as he'd like."

That's what I'm here for, Philip, to deliver messages for you.

The prevailing theme in the bar was dark, dense, and heavy. Polished paneling covered the walls, thick and ponderous furniture filled the floor space, and reams of suffocating fabric absorbed all light from the windows. The air was filled with the blended odor of a dozen different cigars.

I peered through the mahogany haze and found him at the bar, holding court. He was wearing the same gray suit from this morning with a different but equally spiffy silk tie and that electric air of self-confidence the rest of us mere mortals found so mesmerizing. Take the people in this bar. Nobody here worked for him; I doubt anyone even knew him. Yet when he laughed, they smiled. When he spoke, they leaned in to hear what he had to say. He effortlessly commanded all the attention in the room through the sheer force of his personality.

"Alex Shanahan." His voice cut through the dampened acoustics, calling everyone's attention to—me. The stares were discreet, but intense enough to raise the humidity level inside my suit a few damp degrees, and he knew it. He smiled serenely as he reached for his wallet and turned toward the bar.

Rather than stand in the doorway on display, I worked my way through the room and ended up standing right behind him. Too close, it turned out, because when he turned to leave, he almost knocked me flat.

"Ah," he said, reaching out to steady me, "and here you are."

I thought he let his hands linger. I thought he did, but

couldn't be sure. What I was sure of was the jolt that moved from his hands through my arms and all the way down my spine, almost lifting me off the floor, the stunning reminder of the powerful physical connection that had always been between us—and how little it would take to reignite the flame. He felt it, too. I saw it on his face. I saw it in his eyes, and I knew that if I'd had any true desire to keep my distance from him, I wouldn't have come here tonight.

"Thank you for coming," he said, adjusting his volume down for just the two of us. "Hungry?"

"Yes." Not really. "They're holding your table."

"Then let us go and claim it." He gave my arm one last squeeze.

Philip, with his maître d' sixth sense, was waiting for us with two menus. He personally escorted us upstairs to our table, draped a napkin across my lap, and addressed himself to Bill. "Sir, it's nice to have you back with us."

"It's always nice to be back. Ask Henry if he has any more of that cabernet I had last time. That was quite nice." He looked at me. "And a white burgundy, also. Tell him to bring the best that he's got."

"Yes sir, I'll send him right over. Enjoy your dinner."

Philip melted back into the dining room while Bill leaned back, stretching his long legs out and making the table seem even smaller and more intimate. I kept my hands buried in my lap, my feet tucked under my chair.

He touched the silver on each side of his plate, tracing the thick base of his knife and the flat end of his spoon. "It is white burgundy, isn't it?"

He looked at me in the dim glow of the table candle flickering between us, and a slow smile started—an open, ingenuous smile that was not for the entertainment of the masses but just for me. When he smiled that way, it changed him. When he smiled that way, it changed me.

"You know I like burgundy," I said. "You never forget anything."

He pushed his plate forward and leaned on his elbows as far toward me as the table would allow. "I haven't forgotten anything about you. Until I picked up your message, I thought you'd forgotten about me."

I studied his face: the long plane of his cheeks, the curve of his forehead, the shape of his eyes, the way they sloped down slightly on the sides and kept him looking almost boyish. No, I hadn't forgotten anything. That was the problem. No matter how hard I tried and no matter how much distance I put between us, I couldn't forget him.

"That was quite an entrance you made this morning."

"Dramatic, wasn't it?" He brightened at the memory, like a little kid on Christmas day. He did love being Bill Scanlon. We both leaned back, making way for the wine steward, who had arrived with a silver ice bucket, two bottles, and other assorted sommelier paraphernalia.

"You surprised me," I said.

He shook his head and grinned. "I don't think so. If you hadn't wanted to see me, you never would have called. You opened the door. All I did was walk through it."

"More like blew it up."

He laughed and so did I. It felt good to laugh with him again.

Henry poured our wine and, after more gratuitous bowing and scraping, receded into the background.

Bill offered a toast. "Here's to blowing up the door . . .

and any other barriers left between us."

We touched glasses. This morning when he had stared down Big Pete, his eyes had seemed almost black. But in this light they were clear amber, almost sparkling. It was like looking into a flowing stream and seeing the sun reflected off the sandy bottom. I had missed seeing myself reflected there.

I put my glass down, searching for and finding the precise depression in the tablecloth where it had been. "Where did you get that hangman's drawing?"

"Someone sent it anonymously. I usually throw things like that away, but since it was your station—"

"I know, and I'm sorry about that. I can explain—"

"Are you seeing anyone?"

I blinked at him. He waited, eyebrows raised. I took another drink of the chilled wine, letting it roll over my tongue. "No."

"Why not?"

Because I haven't gotten over you. "Do you know what that drawing means? Has Lenny told you—has anyone told you what's been going on around here?"

"Lenny makes a point of not telling me anything, which is one of the reasons why I'm here."

"Are you saying you don't know anything about the rumors and why they set that bomb off?"

"I didn't say that. I said that Lenny didn't tell me. And I don't want to talk about him. Were you seeing anyone in Denver?"

I inched back. He didn't move, and yet he felt so much closer. In our good times I'd always felt better with him—safer, surer of my footing. He had confidence to burn, and sometimes when I'd touched him, I'd known what that felt like, not to be afraid of anything.

"Why do you want to know if I was seeing someone?"

"Because I heard that you were."

"And why would that matter to you?"

I didn't feel the pointed end of that question until he straightened up as if he'd been poked in the stomach. He reached for the bottle of red and poured another glass. When he drank the wine, I could almost track its warming flow through his system, and it seemed to me that he was trying to relax, trying to get the words just right. That he didn't have the right words and exactly the right way to say them was disarming.

"I used to see you around headquarters," he said, "across the cafeteria, turning a corner at the end of a corridor. Or sometimes I'd be sitting in a meeting and I'd see you walk past the open door." He shook his head and smiled, as if the memory gave him pleasure. "You know how my office looks out over the parking lot? I'd watch for you in the evenings going out to your car. I'd stay at my desk waiting, finding something to do. I never wanted to go home until I saw you."

I stared down at my hands in my lap and remembered all of the times I'd stood at my car and glanced up for him— quickly and furtively so that no one, especially Bill, would catch me—just to know that he was there. And I remembered the emptiness I'd felt when the light was off and he was gone. I'd never seen him looking back. But then, that had been the story all along. I'd always reached for him and never felt him reaching back.

"Alex, I couldn't stand the thought that you were with someone else. It made me crazy. A hundred times over the past year, I almost called you."

"Why? To find out if I was seeing anyone else? Because in

the end, Bill, when I wanted you to call me, when I needed to hear from you, you weren't there."

"As I recall, you dumped me." He said it with a little smile, trying but not succeeding to sound light. "You didn't want to see me anymore."

I caved back into my chair, instantly weary from the notion that as hard as I'd tried to help him understand, he hadn't gotten it then, and he still didn't get it. "It was not you, Bill. It was never you. It was the circumstances. For me, they began to overwhelm everything, and you wouldn't change them."

"Alex, I couldn't go public about us."

"I wasn't asking you to call a press conference. All I wanted was to stop sneaking around like a couple of fugitives. I wanted to be able to go out to dinner without worrying that someone might see us together. I wanted to stop feeling as if I wasn't worthy of being with you. The longer that went on, the more I started to feel that you . . . you were ashamed of me."

"You know that wasn't it. I was about to be named chairman, and I could not be involved with a woman who worked for me. The company has rules about that. And it wouldn't have been good for you, either."

I resisted snapping back. I had always hated it when he'd made a decision that clearly benefited him, then turned it around to make it sound as if he were really doing it for me.

He reached for the bread, which I hadn't even noticed had arrived, and tore off a piece that was dark and dense. "All I'm saying is you could have given it a little more time. You could have waited."

"The minute I raised the issue, Bill, the very second I spoke up and finally asked for what I wanted, you backed off. You were suddenly unavailable. You were in meetings. You were traveling. You stopped calling." I took a breath and tried to steady my voice, which was starting to inch up the decibel scale. I wanted to tell him how deeply painful that had been, how thoroughly destabilizing, how it had removed from me any sense of security and self-confidence I'd managed to nurture in the shelter of our relationship. But I thought if I did, I would start crying. "It wasn't about timing, Bill. It was you not wanting to be with me as much as I wanted to be with you."

There. I'd said it. I'd ripped off the scab, and it hurt as much now as it had then. Maybe more.

"And the worst part, the worst thing you ever did to me, was to not tell me. You disappeared. First, you didn't want to be seen with me—"

"That is not true, and you know it."

"—then you vanished from my life. And I had to keep going to meetings with you and sit across the table from you and watch you give presentations. And you, all the while ignoring me, or pretending I wasn't there. I couldn't stand it anymore. That's why I left." I reached out and touched the base of my wineglass. "At least I told you I was leaving. You were gone long before we ever said goodbye."

The words were old, the feelings familiar, the hurt still there. This was well-trod territory for us, and I was disappointed to realize that there was nothing new here.

Henry reappeared to top off our glasses. As he served, I looked out at the other tables, because I couldn't look at Bill. What do you know? We weren't the only two people in the world tonight. A sprinkling of women dotted the dining room, but I could hear only men's voices. It was as if the years of exclusivity in this place had filtered out the sound of a female voice. I tried to tell from their faces what they were saying. Were they happy? Sad? Hurt?

The cubes rattled as Henry slipped the bottle of burgundy back into the ice bucket. I looked at Bill. "Why would you come here like this? Why would you want to dredge all this up again?"

"You called me."

"I called for professional support."

His gentle smile acknowledged my stubborn self-deceit and, at the same time, let me get away with it. "You're so smart about these things, Alex—smarter than I am. I thought you would have figured it out by now."

"I haven't figured anything out, Bill."

It was his turn to look around the room and gather his thoughts. "You scared me."

"I what?"

He leaned forward and lowered his voice. He was speaking quietly, but with so much urgency, I couldn't look away. "You're right. I did back off. At the time I thought . . . I don't know what I thought, that it was best for you, that with two careers, both of us in the same company, it was never going to work out. But the truth was, I was thinking about you all the time. When I was with you, when I wasn't with you. I couldn't get you out of my head."

"That's how people feel when they're in love. It's how I felt about you."

"I never felt that way about my ex-wife—or anyone else, for that matter. I thought that because I couldn't control this thing, it was a weakness, some kind of a failure of will. I've never lost control like that. I thought the best thing was to take a break, to let things cool off a little."

"If you had just told me that's what you were doing—"

"I wasn't thinking about what that might do to you. It was a mistake and I came here to apologize to you. I'm sorry, Alex. I'm sorry."

I sat back in my chair and felt the resentment I'd been carrying around, the intractable knot of bitterness, begin to melt like the butter softening on the plate in front of me. I looked at his face. He'd shaved since this morning, shaved for me. I remembered how it felt to touch his hair. It was thick and dark and rich, the kind of hair Italian and Greek men take to their graves.

"All I can tell you is that I miss you. I miss talking to you and holding you and laughing with you. There's no one else in my life that I feel that way about. And I miss being with you, making love to you. When I got your message, I can't tell you how that made me feel after so long. And when I saw you today in that meeting, being that close without being able to touch you, I thought I was going to grab you right there in front of all those people. I took it out on poor old what's his name with the funny hair."

"Big Pete."

"Even now . . . just seeing you again . . ."

I could feel his eyes on me, on my hair, on my eyes, my lips, my throat, and I began to feel a flush rising under that big sweater.

"I need you," he said. It was a statement so elegant in its simplicity and so powerful, I felt the distance he had come to say it to me, and not geographical distance.

His hand, when he offered it to me, palm up, looked like a cradle. The candle in the center of the table threw an odd light on it, making it seem to glow in the dim corner where we sat.

Leaving him had been painful beyond belief, like cutting off one of my arms at the shoulder with a dull knife. The wound still throbbed, especially at night. Or early in the morning before dawn when my room was silent and my bed was empty and I was thinking about starting another day alone. I always told myself that it had been the best thing for me, that there had been good reasons. But time and distance had made it harder to remember what they were. And even if I could, this close to him, it wouldn't have mattered. It might not have mattered even if he hadn't said he was sorry. What mattered at that moment was his hand reaching out to me. What mattered were the things my body still remembered when I closed my eyes. I felt him in my skin, my muscles, my bones— every part of me, the deepest part of me remembered how I'd felt with him and wanted to feel again.

I woke up in the dark and he was breathing next to me, the long, measured breathing of deep sleep. When my eyes adjusted, I could see his face, half buried in the pillow, lips parted like a boy's. His hair had fallen down over his eyes, and I resisted the urge to push it away, to put my lips softly on his. I didn't want to wake him.

As I turned to the other side, he put one arm around me and pulled me close until my skin was next to his. I put my arm over his and it felt exactly right, as if we were two pieces of broken ceramic fit back together, fit together so tightly that the wound disappears.

I went to sleep thinking I could feel his heartbeat, thinking that I never wanted to wake up alone again.

Chapter Thirty-one

The air felt steamy when I opened my eyes, and warm, like a tropical rain forest. I expected Bill to appear from the bathroom, an apparition in the moist vapor, but his voice came from across the room. He was at the desk talking on the phone. I smiled at the sight. He was obviously discussing weighty issues because he had his professional voice on. But he was sitting, legs crossed, wearing nothing but a thick white towel across his lap. He caught me watching and signaled that he'd be off soon. I stretched lavishly in the big Four Seasons bed—I couldn't reach the bottom with my toes or the sides with my fingertips—then curled up into a twist of cool, extremely high-thread-count hotel sheets.

"Call me back when you figure it out." His tone suggested it should have already been figured out. "I've got a conference call in an hour. Don't make me late."

He hung up and sat at the desk, staring at me, forehead wrinkled, looking concerned.

"Who . . ." I cleared the sleep out of my voice. "Who was that?"

"Tony Swerdlow."

"In Denver?" I checked the bedside clock-radio.

"I'm about to negotiate one of the biggest aircraft deals in the company's history, and this guy's home in bed sleeping."

"Bill, that's what people do at three-thirty in the morning."

"Not if they haven't done their work. He's a week late with my performance data, I'm talking to Aerospatiale in an hour, and I can't wait any longer."

"No one sleeps until the Big Cheese is satisfied."

The teasing brought a smile. He wrapped himself in the towel and came over to the bed, leaned down and kissed me. "Especially you."

The feel of his smooth chest against the palm of my hand, the smell of him, the taste of him—after going without him for so long, one night was not enough. "Come back to bed."

"I have to shave."

"For a conference call?"

"I don't want to be late. They're already going to be ticked off."

"Why?"

"Because I'm supposed to be there in person." He smiled, waiting for me to catch on.

"And instead you're here with me."

I had to let that sink in. In all our time together, I'd been the one to arrange my life around him. I couldn't remember a single time when he'd done it for me. The fact that he had this time was surprising. More than surprising. It was shocking—and really sexy.

He straightened to go, but I reached out and barely caught the corner of his towel. It came off easily with a quick flick of the wrist. When he tried to grab it, I drew it under the covers with me.

He stood for a moment looking at the clock, but I pulled back the sheets to invite him in, and he slipped into my arms and stretched out beside me.

"You make me stupid," he murmured softly in my ear.

His skin was warm, his hair still damp from the shower. Last night in the dark, I had rediscovered his body—the way his back curved under my hand, the feel of the rough scar on his knee when it brushed against my leg, the way his long eyelashes felt soft on my face when he closed his eyes.

I found the line of his backbone and traced it up and down, going a little farther each time until I heard the catch in his breath and felt his hands on my back.

"How am I ever going to work around you? I can't keep my hands off you." And he couldn't. "You made me crazy yesterday in that meeting. I was imagining you under that sweater, thinking about what it would be like to take it off you."

"Show me."

I felt his hand on my hip. "This is where it started, right? About here?"

"More like here." I pushed his hand down until I felt it on my thigh.

"Mmmm, I think you're right." Then slowly, very slowly, he pushed the imaginary sweater up—a millimeter at a time, his fingertips like feathers tracing the shape of my hipbone, the curve of my waist, stopping to linger on all those good places he still remembered.

"Don't stop doing that," I whispered.

He lifted my hands over my head and ran a fingertip up the

underside of each arm. I closed my eyes and as he moved over me, I wrapped myself around him and felt the letting go. Boston, the ramp, Lenny and the Petes, Ellen Shepard and Dan Fallacaro—none of it was important. Nothing mattered except the feel of him inside me and this moment.

"I have to get dressed." He was lying on his back with his eyes closed. Untangling his legs from mine, he rolled off the bed and found his towel, which had somehow ended up on the floor. Before he went into the bathroom, he pulled the sheet and then the blanket all the way up and tucked them under my chin. "Don't distract me anymore."

By the time he came back out, I had gathered in all the pillows on the bed and propped myself up so that I could watch him. I'd always loved watching him dress.

"I need to ask you something," I said.

"What?"

"Why do you have Lenny working for you?"

"Because he's got valuable contacts in Washington, which has proved very helpful on some of these big route-authority cases. He's not my best operating guy, he's definitely high-maintenance, but I can get what I need from him." He chose two ties and held them against his suit for me to see.

"I like the darker print," I said, "and Lenny doesn't get the job done. He hires fools like me or like Ellen who will go to any lengths not to fail, which means he won't fail."

"Which means I won't fail. What's wrong with that?"

"Don't you care about his methods?"

He put the rejected tie back, then sat on the edge of the bed with his back to me, pulling on his socks. "Is that why you called? Because you're having problems with Lenny?"

"Do you think I would call you to intervene in a dispute with my boss?" When he didn't answer, I poked him through the covers with my big toe. "Do you?"

"No. So what is going on? And tell me fast because I've only got twenty minutes." He went into the bathroom, then came out searching. "Have you seen my watch?"

"It's right here." I plucked it off the nightstand and tossed it to him. "I get twenty minutes?"

"We would have had more time if we hadn't—"

"All right, I'll give you the Cliff Notes version." I adjusted the pillows so that I could sit up straight. "I'm not sure that Ellen Shepard killed herself."

He paused while buckling the watch and looked up. "That's a provocative statement."

"It's possible someone killed her and made it look like a suicide."

"I had a feeling that's what this was all about."

"Why?"

"Because it's a perfect setup for you. It appeals to all of your instincts as defender of the weak, pursuer of justice, she who rights all past wrongs—"

"I take it you don't believe the rumors about Ellen's death."

"All this talk, those dreadful drawings, that's the kind of mean-spirited gossip traded in by people with small minds who live in small worlds and have nothing better to do but chatter on about this sad woman. It's a tragic, tragic situation, and no one should be using it for their entertainment."

"I don't have a small mind, I don't find this entertaining, and this is *my* twenty minutes."

"It makes me angry."

"So you said. You also said you'd listen to me."

"I'm sorry. Go ahead."

"Ellen got involved in something right before she died. It had to do with Big Pete Dwyer and his son and some guy who works on the ramp named Angelo who might be the key to everything. I think what it all may have to do with is someone paying off Big Pete Dwyer to tank the IBG contract vote that made the merger happen. I suspect Lenny's involved, too, but I don't know how yet."

"First of all, Lenny didn't make the merger happen and neither did this Big Pete asshole. I made that deal happen. Second"—he was making one last check in the mirror, straightening his tie, smoothing his hair—"I hate to tell you this, but none of this is news."

"It's not?"

"That business about the contract has been rumored for years. And I can tell you exactly how Lenny would have been involved."

"You can?"

"He's the one who was supposed to have made the payoffs, and the reason is, when Nor'easter sold, he cashed in all his stock options. Don't ask me how he got them, but he had a pile of them with really low strike prices."

"He did?"

"The guy made a fortune."

"So Lenny is part of this after all."

"I didn't say that. I said it's been rumored. No one has ever proved anything."

"The proof is in the package," I said, connecting the dots.

"What package?"

"Do you know who Dickie Flynn was?"

"The drunk who used to run your station."

"He died last year, but before he did, he sent Ellen a packet of material that he'd hidden in the ceiling of the men's locker room at the airport. I think it was a surveillance tape from the ramp, but whatever it was, I'm beginning to think she was killed for it."

"Why didn't the police find any of this?"

"No one in this Boston operation ever has or ever will talk to the police. But I've got a source, a guy I've been talking to down on the ramp."

"How do you know he's not twisting you around for fun?"

"He's not. I know he's not. He's the one who went and got the package for Ellen."

"Does he have it?"

"Nobody has it. We think Ellen may have stashed it—"

"Who's 'we'?"

"Dan and I, Dan Fallacaro. We haven't been able to find it yet. One thing I know is, we're not the only ones looking. Someone ransacked my hotel room, and it's pretty clear they were looking for Dickie's package."

"What?"

"That was the night I called and left you the message. I think it was Little Pete."

"You're just telling me about this? Did you tell Corporate Security? I can call Ted Gutekunst right now—"

"I told them, I told the police, I changed hotels, and I've calmed down a lot."

He walked over to the bed, hands in his pockets, looking as if he was ready to handle the situation right then and there. "I'm not sure you should be calm about this."

"I think I can find the package," I said, "this surveillance video. It would help you get rid of Lenny, wouldn't it?"

"Maybe, but—"

"Even if Lenny had nothing to do with any of this, he was guilty of not backing Ellen up. This is a hard job, and when she needed help he wasn't there. I suspect he may have even been working against her, which I can't understand because they were sleeping together. Maybe they had some kind of a falling-out."

"How did you know they were sleeping together?"

I looked at him. "How did *you*?"

"I asked Lenny."

"And he confirmed it?"

"He denied it, which is all I needed to hear. He has a reputation for that sort of thing."

"Then I'll ask you again, why is he still here?"

"Look," he said, "I'm beginning to think we put Ellen in a job she couldn't handle to begin with, and that Lenny put too much pressure on her and made a tough situation worse by getting personally involved with her. He created an environment where she couldn't succeed. He's going to answer for it, don't worry. But in the end when she couldn't handle it, she made the final choice, not Lenny. And if she was involved with him, she made that choice, too. If I tried to police all the affairs in this company, illicit and otherwise, I'd never get anything else done."

"That's a cop-out, Bill."

"Did you know Ellen Shepard?"

"No, but—"

"I did. She was on my merger task force, and I can tell you this—she was more fragile than people think. And high-strung."

"That doesn't mean—"

"I *knew* her, Alex. And I know you. You can't save Ellen

Shepard. It's too late. Don't let this thing be more about you
than it is about her. You do that sometimes and you know it.
I have whole squads of people who are trained for work like
this. There's no reason for you to be involved. I don't want you
to be. It's not good for you and it worries me." His attention
wandered to the clock on the nightstand. "Alex, I have to get
ready for this call. I'm sorry. We can talk more later. We should
talk more about this." He disappeared into the next room.

I found one of the hotel's thick white robes hanging on the
back of the bathroom door. It wrapped around me one and a
half times, but it did what I needed. He was out in the sitting
area sorting through his briefcase.

"I need just a couple more minutes," I pleaded. "I promise."

He checked his watch again. "Well, they won't start without me, that's for sure. It might even be a good negotiating
strategy to be a little late. Go ahead."

"I need your help on one thing, Bill." I told him the tale of
Little Pete and Terry McTavish.

"You say you have a source?" he asked.

"It's the same one I told you about before. He's a ramper
and he's as close to Terry as you can get. He's not intimidated
by the powers that be in the union. He's a good man. I trust
him."

"What about this Little Pete person? What are we doing
about him?"

"I heard on my way out tonight that Lenny's already brought
him back to work."

He didn't say it, but Lenny was in for a bad day. "Can you
nail him again?"

"We plan to make it a priority. Guys like him always give
you another chance."

"So you want this McTavish kid to have his job back?"

"He doesn't deserve to be fired."

"Done."

"Thank you," I said, "and I'm not finished talking to you about Ellen."

"You can talk all you want," he said, picking up the phone. "Just don't do anything that might get you hurt. Please."

After a night at the Four Seasons, my own hotel seemed alarmingly inadequate when I went back to change. As I passed the front desk, I picked up my messages. The first one said, "Where are you?" Dan had wanted to know at eight-thirty and again at nine-fifteen last night. But the message from Molly was the one that made me sorry to be running so late. "Re: Crescent Security," it said, "You're not going to believe this."

Chapter Thirty-two

Dan savored the last of his fried potato skins. Stuffed to overflowing with sour cream and bacon, the skins made up one-third of the deceptively named Fisherman's Platter. The other two-thirds were fried onions and nachos. The cholesterol extravaganza was his typical order at The Lobster Pot, a cheesy, overpriced airport restaurant and our usual luncheon venue at the Majestic terminal.

He noticed me staring. "What?"

"Does the word angioplasty mean anything to you?"

"Don't start with me, Shanahan." He licked the sour cream off his finger. "This is one of the few pleasures I have left in my life."

The waitress slapped the check on our table while she was yelling something to the bartender. They knew us at The Lobster Pot, knew they didn't have to waste any service on a captive audience.

"What did you want to talk about, boss?"

I looked again around the restaurant, checking the bar and all the corners. "You haven't seen Lenny, have you?"

"Lenny wouldn't be caught dead in a place like this. Besides, I think Scanlon has him running around on something. He hasn't been here much."

I gave silent thanks to Bill. I hadn't even thought to ask him for a Lenny distraction. I scooted my chair around until I was right next to Dan. "Crescent Security," I said, "I know what it is."

"And you waited all the way through lunch to tell me?"

"I waited until Victor and his cronies left. They were sitting two tables over."

He checked the tables across the room, now empty. "What did you find out?"

I pulled the computer printout off the chair next to me, cleared a space on the table, and set it in front of him. He began thumbing through it. "What is this?"

"Molly researched the station files for anything on Crescent Security. She looked as far back as the local files go, which is like—"

"Seven years."

"Right. She found nothing. So she called HDQ and had them run a summary of all payments to Crescent Security by either Boston Nor'easter or Boston Majestic. This is what she got."

He turned the pages, running his index finger down the dollar column. "It looks like . . . what, fifty, sixty thousand a year?"

"It averages out to forty grand a year for five years," I said. "Over two hundred thousand bucks in total."

"What's it for?"

"No one knows."

"What do you mean by that?"

"Molly has no recollection of processing a single payment to this company, there are no local records, and yet Crescent received a couple of hundred thousand dollars in payments which were approved out of this station."

"What about Molly's ledger books? Have you ever seen those goddamned things? Even if the files were lost, she would have had it all in there, chapter and verse. That's why she does it that way, so nothing gets paid that's not supposed to."

"I'm telling you, there are no local records. But Accounts Payable in Denver had copies of the invoices." I showed him the faxes Molly had given me, slick paper faxes that wouldn't stay flat. We had to be the last office operation in the world without a plain paper fax machine. "Check these out."

He pinned the pages to the table and searched them one at a time. "Looks like they're coded right. These are the accounts Nor'easter used for security background checks, I think. They should have written that in the comments box. Signed by Lenny, but he would have signed if he was general manager. If Molly didn't code them, who did?"

"Lenny."

He let go of the faxes and they immediately curled. "Give me a break. Lenny would rather break his own arm than code an invoice. I don't think he's ever once cracked a chart of accounts since I've known him."

"Molly recognized his handwriting in the coding box."

Dan unfurled one page and looked again, concentrating on the handwritten account codes. He got the connection; I could see it on his face when he looked up at me. "The sevens."

"Exactly. She says Lenny crossed his sevens like that, European style."

"She's right. Fuckin' Lenny. Wants the world to think he

was born in France. In the meantime, he's from some back-water hick town down in Louisiana."

"He's from New Orleans."

"That's what I said. What did Crescent do for us? Forty grand is a lot of background checks."

"I don't think they did anything. Here's what I think. Lenny had Crescent send these invoices to him directly. He'd code them, sign them, and forward them to Accounts Payable. Molly never saw them, and he kept no copies around for her to stumble over. Accounts Payable would cut the check and send it directly to Crescent."

"But Crescent never did anything for the money and Lenny knew it."

"Right."

"Jesus Christ, you're saying he was stealing?"

"Embezzling."

He sat back and shook his head. "That makes no sense, Shanahan. Two hundred grand is tip money to Lenny. The guy is loaded."

"From the deal."

"Right. He hit the jackpot."

"Why didn't anyone bother to tell me this?"

"I figured you knew."

"I didn't. And besides, this scam was going on before the deal."

"True." He leaned over his plate and rummaged for an onion ring. "You don't know who these Crescent people are?"

"The address on the payments was Elizabeth, New Jersey."

"I know Elizabeth. That's not too far from where I grew up."

"Wherever they were, they're gone now, but I figured out

something else, too. Do you know what they call New Orleans?"

"You mean like the French Quarter and Mardi Gras?"

"When you fly into New Orleans at night from the south, you come in over the Gulf of Mexico and you can see the lights of the city. It's beautiful, and it's shaped like the moon—a crescent moon."

He stared at me, onion ring poised over the cocktail sauce.

"New Orleans is known as the Crescent City, Dan. Crescent Security was Lenny. It had to be."

He dropped the onion ring, took the napkin from his lap, and slowly wiped the grease from his fingers. "I'll be damned."

"Lenny was stealing from Nor'easter to pay himself. And I think he was using the money to make payoffs. That's what the stub was doing in Ellen's merger file. Remember the stub for ten thousand dollars?"

"Yeah."

"I'll bet it was a payoff and Crescent was some kind of a clearinghouse for him—a way to make his illegal payoffs look legitimate."

Dan sat staring at the printout. His face was blank. I'd expected more of a reaction than that. Molly had given me the Crescent payments, but the rest I'd figured out, and it all fell into place. I loved it when that happened, but he was unmoved. "What's the matter?"

"Do you think this had anything to do with Ellen?"

"Yeah, I do. The way we knew about Crescent was because of the reference in her files. My first thought was that this was the money used to buy the IBG contract. She found out about it, and that's what got her into trouble. That might be the connection."

"But now you don't think so?"

"I'm not sure. The payments started a long time before there was ever any thought of selling Nor'easter. And look at the last page of that printout."

He flipped to the back and almost knocked over the light-house peppermill in the process. He was oblivious, but I caught it in time. I pointed at the last entry. "See how the payments stopped in August 1994. Molly told me that the contract vote wasn't until November. She said it screwed up everyone's Thanksgiving, so the timing doesn't work, but even if it did, there's less than thirty grand here for 1994. At first I thought it didn't seem like enough to buy a contract. But then I thought, How would I know? I heard about a guy on the news once who paid a professional hit man five thousand dollars to have his wife murdered. That seemed low to me, too."

Dan was rubbing his forehead, looking worried.

"What's the matter with you?"

"Nothing. It's just . . . the thing is . . . I don't think that's what this money was for. I think that money had to come from somewhere else."

"That's what I'm saying, too, that this was the everyday fraud fund. There was a bigger one somewhere else for special occasions."

"So, Ellen knew about this?"

"She must have."

"What else did you find out?"

"That's it. I've got Molly doing more research. She's into it now. She's taking it personally that Lenny corrupted her system."

"Yeah, she would."

I paid the check. Lunch was on me to celebrate finding the

dirt on Lenny. Dan still wasn't excited enough for me, and he was actually walking slower than I was as we headed down the concourse to the office. "Are you all right?"

"What? No, I'm fine. But I got a call this morning from my ex. Michelle's got the flu. I thought I might fly down and surprise her this afternoon. Take her a milkshake or something. Is it all right with you? You can beep me if you need me."

"Don't be silly. Take as much time as you need. In fact, why don't you stay down there for the weekend? The only thing I have on the schedule is this meeting with the third shift tonight about the bomb."

"Are you going to be okay for that?"

"Sure." He stood there, hands in his pockets, shifting from one foot to the other. He was obviously anxious to take off. "Give me a call and let me know how she's doing."

"I will," he said, pulling away at Mach speed. "Thanks."

Chapter Thirty-three

It was a few minutes before one in the morning when I left Operations and headed to the ready room. My version of the bag room bomb speech was going to be a pale imitation of the chairman's, but I still owed the midnight shift a face-to-face meeting. I touched the face of my watch. Bill had left on the last flight to Denver. He should be getting in about now. It had taken months for me to stop thinking about him this way, wondering in any random moment where he was and what he was doing. It was funny—maybe scary—how quickly and how vividly it had all come back. It was almost as if he had never gone from my life.

Thinking of him made me feel good, good enough to bypass my usual moment of insecurity and push through the ready room door without hesitation. I was thinking that I was where I belonged. Too bad all that self-confidence was wasted.

The spicy aroma of a microwaved burrito lingered in the air. The door behind me squealed as it swung back and forth on squeaky hinges, and the room where I was supposed to be holding a meeting was completely empty. And in case that message was too subtle, the one written on my flip chart with a thick black marker was more direct. It said, "Fuck you, Shanahan." Anonymous, of course. I could almost feel my skin thickening as I stood there. This kind of stuff was losing impact with me. I was more upset about having stayed up this late for nothing.

I went through the swinging door and straight back to Operations.

"Pete Dwyer, midnight crew chief, Pete Dwyer, please respond with your location. Over." I released the button on the radio and waited. Kevin had gone home and the Ops office was quiet. I called again, and waited again. The third time, I called for anyone knowing the location of Pete Dwyer. Lo and behold, someone responded. Whoever it was suggested the bag room.

"Outbound or inbound?"

No response.

I'd check the outbound first, but the inbound bag room was still under construction and off limits to employees, reason enough to believe that that's exactly where Pete would be.

Kevin's Majestic ramp coat was hanging where he always kept it, on a hook by the door. It was about a foot shorter than my shin-length skirt and bulky as a fireman's gear, but it kept me warm on the long, gusty walk across the open ramp.

As I suspected, the door to the inbound bag room was open, pinned against the wall by a heavy brick. From outside the doorway, I could hear the quiet shuffling of what I knew were heavy construction tarpaulins hanging from the ceiling inside, but the lights were off and I couldn't see a thing. It was unsettling and I probably should have turned around right then, but more unsettling was the fact that the light switch was not in the obvious place by the door and dammit, I had no clue to where it was. I hated being in a new job.

I called into the bag room for Pete. The only answer was the swishing of the tarps as a rogue gust of wind kicked up, scattering old bag tags and finding all the parts of me that weren't covered by Kevin's coat. He still wasn't responding on the radio, and the longer I stood out in the mostly deserted operation calling Pete's name, the more duped and idiotic I felt. Best to go back to my hotel and deal with Big Pete Dwyer and his recalcitrant shift mates in the light of a new day. Or evening.

When I turned to go, my heel stubbed against something hard, and I tripped into something—no, some*one* who was standing behind me. Jesus, *right* behind me. I bounced off, stumbled back, and almost bolted.

"I hear you been lookin' for me." His face was hidden under the hood of a cotton sweatshirt that came up from under his coat and engulfed his entire head. But the raspy voice was unmistakable.

"God*dammi*t, Pete, what the hell are you doing?" I was tingling from a delayed surge of adrenaline, and my stomach felt as if he'd stomped on it with that heavy boot I'd tripped over.

"Lookin' for you."

"Why didn't you answer my radio call?"

"I was answering nature's call."

"You didn't have your radio with you?"

"I said, I was taking a leak. I had my hands full. Besides, I'm here now, ain't I?"

"And as respectful as ever."

It was eerie the way his voice floated out of the black hole where his face was supposed to be. He was like a sweatsuit version of the grim reaper. It bothered me, bothered me a lot, that he'd sneaked up on me and I'd been oblivious enough to let him.

"Let's go to Operations," I said, "I want to talk."

"We can talk in here."

He was past me, through the door, and behind the tarp before I had a chance to react. I heard a heavy snap and the lights came on. Pete knew where the light switch was located. When he emerged, his hood was down, revealing a face that was unshaven and a head full of thinning gray hair that stood up in uneven tufts. Hood hair. Looking at his face, I couldn't understand why he covered it at all. His leathery, lined skin struck me as adequate winter protection.

"This is a hard-hat area, Pete."

"I won't tell if you don't."

The ramp behind me was empty, and I could feel the isolation. We were in a godforsaken spot in the middle of a cold night, and no one knew I was out here. I hesitated.

"I ain't gonna bite you," he said, recognizing his advantage. "I just want you to see something, that's all."

He stood waiting with the tarp pulled to one side. Eventually, my curiosity trumped my cautiousness, and besides, Big Pete wasn't going to bite me. From what I'd heard, he might tell someone else to bite me, but he would never do it himself.

"After you," I said, stepping through the plastic portal, "and show me where the light switch is, if you don't mind."

"Sure." He led me to an open fuse box in the corner. "The switch on the wall ain't been fixed yet, so you got to use these." One breaker was thrown. He flipped another as we stood there. Nothing happened.

"What was that for?"

"You'll see."

We continued through the maze of hanging blue walls, moving circuitously toward the north bag belt. The inbound bag room was smaller than the outbound and served a much simpler purpose. Two oval carousels—racetracks we called them—wrapped around the wall that separated the concrete from the carpet. The moving belts carried bags from the rampers in the bag room to the passengers in claim. The belts were controlled by a panel of buttons on the wall, which is where I found Pete when I caught up with him.

"Ready?" he asked.

"For what?"

He pushed a button. Three warning blasts sounded, the gears began to grind, and the ancient conveyor mechanism sputtered to life, complaining against the cold. This would explain the second circuit breaker he'd thrown.

"Watch the security door." He pointed with one of his stubby fingers to the opening in the wall where the bags fed through to the passenger side. The heavy security door had lifted automatically when the belt had started to move, leaving nothing but a curtain of rubber strips that swayed with the motion of the belt.

"Are you watching?"

"I'm watching."

He hit the emergency shutdown switch. The alarm blasted again, the belt lurched to a halt, and the security door dropped in a free-fall from its housing, crashing onto the belt with a force, both thunderous and abrupt, that made me jump about a foot off the ground. "Jesus *Christ*."

"It's defective."

"I hope so."

He was right next to me, once again standing too close for my comfort. I took a step away as he propped his foot up on the belt and took out a pack of Camels—unfiltered. The belt was off, the bag room was quiet, and the sound of his lighter snapping shut was loud in the strange stillness that followed the resounding crash.

"One of my guys got his foot almost took off by that thing about six months back. He was trying to kick a jammed bag through when some idiot over there hit the emergency stop." He nodded toward the wall, indicating that "the idiot" had been a passenger in the claim area.

"Is he all right?"

"He's on long-term disability and his foot don't look much like a foot no more. But thank God he didn't lose it."

I stood, hands down in the gritty pockets of Kevin's coat, shifting from foot to foot, trying to keep the feeling in my toes. The cold from the concrete was seeping up through the thin leather soles of my pumps and I shivered, but not from the cold. I was imagining what a bone-crushing force like that could do to a man's foot. It was exactly the reaction he was hoping for and we both knew it.

He was leaning forward on his knee and looking at me pleasantly, as if we'd met in a bar to talk over old times.

"Why are you showing me this?"

He stared at the burning end of his cigarette. "I hear the McTavish kid is coming back."

"So what?" Not a snappy comeback, to be sure, but no one had told me, officially anyway, that Terry was coming back and it ticked me off that Big Pete was continually better informed than I was. "Besides, Little Pete's coming back, and the only thing Terry did was save him from an even bigger screw-up than the one he actually caused."

"I don't know what screw-up you'd be referring to."

"The one where he reversed the load on one of his trips because he was drunk."

The fact that I knew one of his secrets didn't seem to bother him. He offered a nod in my direction that was almost deferential. "That was a ballsy move, going around Lenny the way you did. I gotta give you credit for that. Lenny's a piece of shit, but he ain't easy to push around, neither." He took another deep drag, his cheeks hollowing out as he inhaled, then exhaled slowly, directing the stream up toward the ceiling.

"I also gotta ask myself, how is it you seem to know so much about what's going on down here with us."

"I'm well connected."

"Either that or you got a snitch . . ."

Something in the back of my neck began to tighten.

". . . Which means we got a rat."

The smoke from his cigarette drifted up toward the ceiling, a ceiling still black with soot from the bombing this man had most certainly engineered. I was starting to get the idea. That tightening in my neck twisted a little more. "Say what you mean to say."

"All right. I know about Johnny McTavish. I know he's been feeding you information. I know that's part of why his kid brother got his job back."

I held perfectly still, which was just as well since all sensation had long since abandoned my feet.

"Is that what this demonstration is all about? Is this a threat to make me stop looking for whatever it is you and I aren't looking for?"

"This ain't nothing more than a friendly reminder that the ramp is a dangerous place. Accidents happen all the time, and even though you ain't out here that much, other people are." He looked at me with those chameleon eyes. "We don't like rats down here. That guy who got his foot flattened, he was a rat, and he was lucky it wasn't his head got caught in that bag door. Johnny Mac's a pretty tough guy, but his bones break just like everybody else's. Just like yours." He stepped a little closer. "Just like hers."

My heart thumped against my rib cage. "What are you talking about?"

"I hear that's how she died—broken neck." He snapped his fingers. "Just like that. That's how quick it can happen." He pressed his lips into a thin smile that to me was the equivalent of fingernails on a blackboard. "Can you imagine that?"

"You sick, sleazy bastard."

"What happened to that woman should never have happened," he said, "but it did. It's done and nothing you can do will change that. Nothing. This ain't your fight, and what you're looking for, nobody wants you to find it. Nobody."

For the first time I felt real panic, as if I was in over my head, as if something I'd started was about to spin dangerously out of my control. I wanted to run to a phone to call John, to call Dan, to call everyone I knew and make sure they were safe tonight. And I wanted to get out of there. "I'm leaving."

He dropped the cigarette on the cement floor and crushed it out under his boot. Then he stood in front of me, this time at a polite distance, with his hands in the pockets of his coat. "Listen to me. There's nothing happening around here that ain't been happening for a long time, and by the time you figure that out, that it ain't worth it, it's going to be too late. I hate to be the one to tell you, but you got no friends here, including that asshole Fallacaro."

The numb feeling in my toes began to creep ever so slowly into my calves, my knees . . . "What about him?"

"He's been lying to you right from the beginning."

. . . my thighs, my hips, and my stomach . . .

"Who do you think told me about Johnny Mac being a rat?"

"What you're saying about John McTavish is not true. But even if it was . . ." My words couldn't keep up with my brain. "What would be in it for Dan to tell you something like that?"

"He didn't tell me. He told your boss."

"Why would he tell Lenny something . . ." The cold, dry air was sticking in my throat, and it was getting painful to breathe, almost impossible to talk, and now I was completely numb. I didn't feel cold. I didn't feel anything. "Dan hates Lenny. He wasn't even in Boston most of the time that Lenny was here."

"You know about Crescent Security, I know you do. But do you know where it was located?"

I opened my mouth to answer and closed it.

Pete was watching me closely, nodding. "Crescent Security was run by Lenny's brother-in-law in Elizabeth, New Jersey, which is just down the road from Newark. He used it for payoffs. He needed to pay someone off, he made them a Crescent contractor. He needed to collect, he'd send a bill from Crescent. But sometimes he needed to move large amounts of cash in secret, and that's where your buddy came in. It was the Danny Fallacaro delivery service—Jersey to Boston, hand-delivered. Better than FedEx. That's how he got into management. He was just another bag slinger before that . . . one of us."

I tried to find some equilibrium, because the concrete floor was falling out from under me. I wanted to say I didn't believe him, but I couldn't find my voice.

"If you don't believe me, ask him." Pete lifted his hood over his head, and when he turned to go, I could no longer see his face, could only hear his voice. "Ask him about locker thirty-nine. He'll know."

Chapter Thirty-four

The track at the East Boston Memorial Stadium is right in Logan's front yard, encircled by a noisy four-lane road that loops into and out of the terminals. But as I came down the back stretch, the only sounds I heard were my feet pounding the track and my own labored breathing as I sprinted the last quarter mile at a pace I could barely sustain, pushing toward the finish, arms pumping, chest heaving, tapping into my last reserves of energy. When I was finished running this morning, I didn't want to have anything left.

Coming out of the last curve, a sharp, familiar pain flashed like a hot poker from behind my left knee straight up the back of my thigh, and I knew I'd pushed too hard. Again. My hamstring had been aggravated for two years, but I'd never stopped running long enough to let it completely heal. I shifted down to a trot and then a walk, hands on my hips and favoring the left side.

"Shanahan . . ."

I shielded my eyes so I could peer down the track, but I didn't need to see. The tenor and cadence of Dan's voice had

become as familiar to me as my own. He was standing in the
middle of my lane, completely out of place in his gray worsted
suit, pant legs flapping around his Florsheim shoes. He had his
hands stuck down in the pockets of his camel-hair coat, which
was about an inch too long for his frame. Behind him, the traffic flowed over the access road nonstop, moving like sludge out
of the airport. The sky over his head was bright and clean and
blue.

"You pick the strangest places to have meetings, boss."

The jaunty tone was jarring. I'd been in a black pit in the
hours since I'd talked to Big Pete, unable to sleep, too upset
to eat. I was doing the only thing I knew would make me feel
better. But there are only so many miles you can run before
your body breaks down and you have to face the hard things
in life, and there wasn't much that was harder than what I was
about to face with Dan.

"How was the meeting last night?" he asked when I was
closer.

"The meeting didn't happen," I said, wiping the sweat out
of my eyes, "but I had a long talk with Big Pete."

My bag was over on the bleachers. The pain in my leg was
getting worse. It felt sharp, serious, as if something important
had ripped. Every step hurt worse than the last as I limped
across the track and toward the bag. Dan was close on my
heels. "What'd that piece of shit have to say?"

The last few words were drowned in the roar of an aircraft
leaving the runway on the other side of the terminal. I glanced
up, then he did, and we both stood and watched it climb out.
The sun glinted off the clean lines and graceful curves of a
B767, one of my favorite fleet types. As it banked over the
harbor, the royal purple tail with the mountain-peak logo

made it easily identifiable as one of ours. I watched until I couldn't see it anymore, then pulled a thin hotel towel from my bag and started wiping down, first my face, then my neck. I was breathing normally again, but the ache in my leg had migrated to my heart, which felt as if it was throbbing, not beating.

"Doesn't look much like there's a blizzard coming, does it? But that's what they're saying." He was still staring at the sky, but toward the west. "Tomorrow night at the latest."

The words came up and caught in my throat, but I finally spat them out. "What's locker thirty-nine, Dan?"

At first he didn't move, just kept staring at the sky, looking for that storm coming. Then he slowly rolled his head back and closed his eyes. His breath condensed in a thin stream as a long exhale left his lips. He looked as if the air was literally flowing out of him, like a balloon that would end up crumpled and shriveled at my feet.

"Fucking Pete Dwyer," he said quietly. It was not the reaction of an innocent man.

I leaned over and tried to stretch, telling myself I needed to ease some of the stiffness out of that hamstring, but really finding a reason to turn away. When I bent over and flattened my back, a rush of cold air sneaked under my jacket, found the moisture between my shoulder blades, and sent a sick shiver through my bones. Once I started shaking, I couldn't stop.

"What did he say about me?"

"That you were one of Lenny's guys. That you were the one who delivered the cash from Crescent Security in New Jersey to Lenny in Boston."

"That little pisshead." He smacked one of the metal benches

hard with his fist, sending a loud, vibrating *bong* through the entire section of bleachers and, apparently, his arm. *"Goddammit."* He grabbed his wrist, whirled around, took a few steps away and came right back. "You've got to let me explain this, Shanahan." It was more a plea than a statement.

I looped the towel around my neck, packed my gear, and zipped the bag.

"You can't just walk away without—I can't believe this." The words spilled out as he paced in a crazy loop, stopping and starting, shaking out his wounded wrist. *"Fucking asshole* Dwyer. Ask me anything, just stay here and let me explain."

"I can't." My voice cracked. I could barely talk and I could feel myself shutting down, sector by sector.

"When, then? When can I explain this to you? Shanahan—" He grabbed my arm, panicked fingers digging through a jacket, a sweatshirt, and a layer of long underwear. He was probably holding tighter than he realized. I looked down at his shoes, black loafers covered with a light dusting of orange track sand. Athletic fairy dust. If only it could make this go away.

"What's locker thirty-nine?"

He loosened his grip, and when I looked into his eyes, I knew that he was going to break my heart. His hands fell to his sides as he turned to watch another liftoff. I watched him.

"Thirty-nine is Lenny's lucky number. He hit in Vegas one time, or maybe it was Atlantic City. I can't remember. Roulette or something. I guess he won big." His voice was steady, but he looked as if it hurt to keep his eyes open. My own eyes were burning as I watched him turn even farther away. "It's the airport locker where I made the drops. We had two keys so I'd put the envelope in there and he'd have someone pick it up."

A heaviness, a dreariness settled like a dull pain into my chest. I hadn't realized until that moment how much I had wanted this not to be true, how much hope I'd been holding out. I didn't want to let it go. I blamed him for making me let it go.

"Goddamn you. God*damn* you, Dan. All of this talk about honesty and integrity and honoring Ellen's memory. Going through the closed door. It's all bullshit. You're one of those guys behind the closed door."

He stood with his head down, taking whatever I had to dish out. If I'd wanted to shoot him, I don't think he would have objected. "Did Ellen know?" I asked.

"I—I never told her."

"Is that why she didn't tell you what she was doing? She thought you might tell Lenny?" My body had cooled down, but I was hot and getting hotter, fueled by a growing rage, the kind I hadn't felt in a long time. "Like you told him about the snitch."

His eyes grew wide. "I didn't tell him about Johnny. I swear I didn't."

I gaped at him as he chattered on, not believing that he didn't realize what he'd just said.

". . . And I never betrayed Ellen. I told her the truth. And everything I've told you has been the truth."

"How did you know it was John?"

"What?" As I stared at him, his confusion slowly gave way to panic as he figured it out, too. "Somebody from the ramp told me. I don't even remember who it was."

"I don't believe you, Dan." I picked up my gym bag and

slung it over my shoulder. "You're one of them ... and I never saw it coming. Shame on me."

"What he's talking about, that stuff happened a long time ago. It had nothing to do with Ellen. It has nothing to do with you."

"How can you say that? I believed you. I trusted you and you lied to me."

"How? How did I lie?"

"By letting me believe you were someone you're not."

"I'm not even smart enough to be someone I'm not. Jesus *Christ*. I was gonna tell you—would you *stop*, please."

He reached for my arm, but this time I pulled away. We stood at the gate of the airport track facing each other, both breathing hard. The cars were blasting by just a few yards from where we were standing, and the noxious fumes were starting to make me sick. Something was making me sick, and I thought if I didn't get away from him, I was going to pass out. I stepped closer so I didn't have to yell over the road noise.

"The person I thought you were, Dan, I really liked that guy. Now I wish I'd never met you."

He stepped back, and we stared at each other for another trembling moment. The expression on his face moved with stunning speed from guilt to anger to sadness and finally to something that I could only describe as pure pain, like a big open wound. I could see that I had hurt him. It didn't make me feel any better.

Instead of walking up to the traffic light, I waited for an opening and made a limping dash across the four-lane road. I could still hear the blaring horns when I got to my room and slammed the door behind me. I took off my sweaty clothes layer by layer and left them in a damp pile on the floor. After

my shower—history's longest hot shower—I went to the
window to close the curtains, looked down, and saw him still
there, sitting alone in the bleachers, hunched against the wind
like an old man. I don't know how long he stayed there. I closed
the curtains and never looked again.

Chapter Thirty-five

I answered the phone without taking the cool, wet washcloth
from my eyes.

"Lenny's going ballistic." Molly's voice broke through the
dreamy haze between awake and asleep. "He says he hasn't
seen you in two days and wants me to find out if you're ever
coming back to work again."

"What did you tell him?"

"That you had an appointment downtown."

"Who am I meeting with?"

"One of our big freight forwarders. Are you going to come
in at all today, or should I make up something else?"

"Make up something else."

"He's not going to like it. You've already got him muttering to himself."

"What time is it?"

"They don't have clocks in that hotel?"

"Molly . . ."

"It's almost noon. You want to tell me what's going on?"

"Not really. Any messages?"

She was quiet, deciding if she was going to be put off that easily. She must have calculated her odds of success from the sound of my voice and found them to be not in her favor.

"Matt Levesque called. He wants you to call him back. And Johnny McTavish called."

"What did he say?"

"That he was returning your call."

"Did he leave a number?"

"Are you kidding? He wouldn't even leave his name, but I knew it was him."

"All right. Call me here if anything else comes up."

"Are you sure you're—"

"I'm fine, Molly."

"Suit yourself."

She hung up in a huff. I flipped the cloth to the cool side and drifted back into my half sleep.

I thought about letting the phone ring this time, but the hotel had no voice mail, just one overburdened desk clerk that might never get around to taking a message.

"Hello."

"Someone knows."

It was Matt. I'd been dozing long enough that the washcloth was dry and stiff. I pushed it off and covered my aching eyes with my hand. "Who knows what?"

"I got nailed. My boss called me in this morning. She wanted to know why I requested that pre-purchase agreement file from archives, and I couldn't exactly say it was for any project I'm working on now."

"How'd she know?"

"She didn't share that with me."

Dan was the only person who knew I had been talking to Matt and why. I tried not to think about that. "What did you tell her?"

"I told her the truth, that you called and asked me as a personal favor to pull the files. You didn't think I was going to throw myself in front of that train for you, did you?"

"I didn't ask you to lie for me. Did you say anything about Ellen?"

"She didn't ask and I didn't tell. But she did rip me a new asshole for not keeping her informed of a request from outside the department. I think that satisfied her for the time being."

"I'm sorry, Matt. I didn't intend for you to get into trouble. It's not worth it." I swung my feet to the floor, but couldn't find the energy to move from the edge of the bed. So that's where I sat, my head in my free hand. "None of this was worth it."

"I detect a note of despair, of profound disappointment, perhaps a hint of cynicism . . . definitely bitterness—"

"I'm not bitter," I snapped rather bitterly. "I'm just done. This was never my fight to begin with. And now it's over."

According to the clock-radio, it was 1:27 in the afternoon, but the room was still dark, almost all natural light blacked out by those mausoleum hotel draperies. Very disorienting. I went to the bathroom to check the damages in the mirror. My eyes were bloodshot from crying, the bags underneath disturbingly pronounced, and my hair, which had been wet from the shower when I'd gone to bed, had dried into a free-form fright wig.

"Am I talking to myself here?"

"I'm sorry, Matt. Did you say something?"

He let out an exasperated sigh. "I said, when the files never

showed up from archives, I started thinking about who else
might have kept a copy of the pre-purchase adjustment schedule. And then it hit me—our outside accounting firm keeps
copies of everything. So I called a guy who worked with us on
the deal, one of the baby bean-counters they had in here and
he had it on disk. Pulled it right up. He was so proud of himself.
Probably figures there's a promotion in it. What would that
make him? A senior bean-counter?"

"This is the schedule Ellen created? The one she was looking for?"

" 'Majestic Airlines Proposed Acquisition of Nor'easter
Airlines. Pre-purchase Adjustments for the Twelve-Month
Period August 1994 through July 1995.' I've got it right here
in front of me. There's a list of vendors with the date and
amounts paid. But if you don't want to hear about it, that's
fine. It just seemed important to you at the time, which is why
I went out on a limb for you, but don't let that influence your
decision in any way. Don't worry about any possible damage
to my career, and just forget the fact that I was sneaky enough
to find—"

"Matt."

"What?"

"Be quiet."

"Okay."

I was trying to decide whether the soft pounding in my head
was a headache or the faint heartbeat of a curiosity that refused
to die. Across the room, a sliver of bright light shone through
where the curtains almost met. The telephone cord was just
long enough for me to walk over there. The drapes felt nubby
when I ran my finger along the edges, and I wondered if I
would see Dan if I opened them. The thought of him still sitting

in the bleachers with his head down made me sad. Angry. No, sad.

"You're still there, right, because I don't have all day to work on this."

"I'm thinking," I said.

I could hang up. I could refuse to learn whatever it was he was dying to tell me. I could skate through the rest of my time in Boston, letting Big Pete run the place, doing what Lenny wanted, never questioning his motives, never knowing what really happened to Ellen, or what was in that package. I'd probably even get promoted. I'd become the first female vice president for Majestic Airlines in the field—my dream come true.

And it would never feel right. Never.

I pulled the curtains back and let the afternoon light come in. "Read me the list."

"Now you're talking." Matt began to read, ticking vendors off the list so quickly at first, I had to slow him down. We'd gone through about twenty names, and he was getting bored and speeding up again, when I heard it.

"Stop. Back up and read me that last one."

"Cavenaugh Leasing?"

"That one just after that."

"Crescent Consulting."

"Crescent Consulting? Not Security?"

"Believe it or not, I can read."

"Majestic made payments to Crescent Consulting? Is that what that means?"

"Yep."

"*Before* the merger?"

"That's what this says."

"How much?"

Pages shuffled at his end while I looked around for my brief-case. Where the hell had I dropped it? The room wasn't that big.

"Roughly three quarters of a million bucks over eight months."

"Three quarters of a *million*?" My heart thumped an excla-mation point. "That's it. That's got to be it."

"Got to be what?"

The corner of my briefcase peeked out from under the bedspread. I dropped to my knees, opened the case, and found the file on Crescent inside. With the phone wedged between my shoulder and ear, I began digging, looking for Molly's computer printout. "What was the timing of the payments, Matt?"

"Three installments—two hundred thousand in October '94, two hundred more in December of that year, and three hundred in July of '95."

I sat on the floor, leaned back against the bed, and flipped through the printout until I found what I needed. Molly had said that the IBG contract vote had ruined everyone's Thanksgiving. I'd made a note of the specific date—November 20, 1994. So, a payment in October, the contract vote in November, and a payment in December. Merry Christmas, Lenny.

"When did the Majestic-Nor'easter deal close?"

"July 21, 1995."

And one big incentive bonus the next year when the deal closed.

"Are you going to tell me what this Crescent Consulting is?"

"I told you before. It's that local vendor used by Nor'easter in Boston in the early nineties, allegedly for background checks and other odd jobs. It turns out that Crescent Security is also Lenny Caseaux. I suspect Crescent Consulting is, too."

"Can't be. It's a conflict of interest to be the vendor providing services to the company you work for."

"He didn't provide any services."

It took him a nanosecond to work through the logic. "No way."

"Way."

"That's embezzling."

"Yes, indeed." I flipped the printout closed and got to my feet so I could pace. "When Lenny Caseaux was the GM in Boston, he stole over two hundred grand from Nor'easter by paying fake invoices to this Crescent Security company. It was nickel-and-dime stuff—it took him five years—and it didn't seem like enough to buy a union contract. But seven hundred thousand in ten months would be plenty."

"Buy a contract? You lost me."

"Lenny paid Big Pete to make sure Nor'easter's IBG contract proposal failed."

"Who's Big—"

"Pete Dwyer," I said. "He runs the union up here."

"Lenny bought the contract—"

"—to make the merger happen." I paced around the bed and back again. "That's exactly what I'm saying."

"And then got Majestic to pay for it." Matt was getting into it now. "Brilliant. The guy's a genius."

"A genius? I think you're missing the bigger picture here."

"Okay, so he's an evil genius. I never would have guessed that Lenny Caseaux had the brains to pull off something like this and not get caught. Contract fraud, election tampering—you're talking federales here. The FBI. Probably the Securities and Exchange Commission since it impacted the value of the company. Definitely fertile ground for shareholder lawsuits. No wonder everyone wants to keep this buried. And he got away with it."

"That's the part I don't get. I can understand how he could approve payments to himself at Nor'easter, although why the auditors didn't catch it, I'll never know."

"From a financial controls standpoint, Nor'easter was a nightmare. That part would have been easy. The genius of the plan was getting Majestic to fund the payoffs."

"How could he have done that? He didn't work for Majestic at the time, and he couldn't approve those payments himself."

"You said that Crescent was a security company." I could hear Matt sucking on his pen as he talked, something he always did when he was into heavy thinking.

"A fake security company."

"Lenny could have set up Crescent as a provider of consulting services to the deal. As part of due diligence, they could have been hired to review training programs, check compliance, test checkpoints, stuff like that. With a deal like this, you can do just about anything. You've got consulting fees all over the place, and it just becomes part of the negotiation as to who's going to pay for what. He probably got an agreement that Crescent could bill Majestic instead of Nor'easter. It even makes sense because Nor'easter was short on cash at the time. And the fact that it was a pre-purchase adjustment makes it that much easier to hide. There's no budget, and two hundred grand a pop wouldn't really stick out compared to the other charges on this list." He snorted. "You should see the attorneys' fees."

"So Lenny and the other Nor'easter investors who wanted to cash out of the airline business anyway figured out a way to get Majestic to pay the kickbacks which ultimately insured that Majestic would buy their company—at a profit. And Lenny apparently set it up."

"I told you, pure genius," he said.

"I still don't get how he could even get Crescent considered as a vendor. As you said, someone would have to negotiate that."

"That's easy. Lenny Caseaux sat on the negotiating team for Nor'easter."

"He did?"

"Yeah, I thought you knew that. That's where I met him."

"Did Ellen know him back then?"

"We all knew him. He's not exactly shy. And he was always hanging around Ellen."

I thought about what Molly had said about how Ellen might have responded to Lenny, to someone who showed interest in her. "Did they seem . . . did they know each other well?"

"Who?"

"Lenny and Ellen."

"They spent a lot of time together, which is why it makes sense that she's the inside person."

"Ellen?" The spiral phone cord caught on the frame at the foot of the bed and nearly sent the phone flying.

"As you pointed out, Lenny needed someone on the team to approve his invoices and not ask questions. Lenny Caseaux and Ellen Shepard spent so much time together people started thinking they had a thing going on. So it works like this: Lenny-who-is-Crescent sends her the invoices and she approves them. Majestic cuts a check to Crescent and the paperwork goes to file. Lenny buys the contract, the deal goes through, and he and his pals cash in. Ellen gets her promotion to a job for which she has not a single qualification. And there you have it. Makes perfect sense."

"Do you have any proof at all for what you're saying, or is it all just conjecture?"

"What do you think happened to the original of Ellen's pre-purchase agreement schedule, the one that was in archives?"

"I have a feeling you're going to tell me."

"Ellen swiped it."

"What are you talking about?"

"After she called me and I told her where she could find the files, she flew to Denver, went out to the archives warehouse, and took it."

"How do you know this?"

"When the archivist couldn't find the file, I took a ride out there just to make sure he knew what to look for. When my secretary made the request, all she'd given him was a reference number. When I described to him the schedule that I wanted and told him that it was in the merger files, he told me that Ellen had been there in person. In the flesh."

"Does he know her?"

"He doesn't get that many visitors, and he remembered her red hair. It reminded him of his sister. She asked him to show her where the merger files were. Who else could it have been? Something must have happened to make her think that it was going to come out and she needed to hide the evidence."

"Something like what?"

"I don't know. You found out about it, didn't you? Maybe someone else up there knew about it."

"Lots of people up here seem to know about this," I said,

"but no one talks. It's like the Irish Mafia."

"Maybe someone threatened to talk. Whatever . . ."

I thought about the mysterious Angelo and whatever he knew and the fact that Ellen had fired him. I thought about Dickie Flynn and his deathbed confession. I slid down to the floor, where I could reach into my briefcase. "When was this trip to archives?" If Ellen had been in Denver, it would likely be on her list of secret travel destinations.

"He said it was the first day he was back at work after the holidays."

The last trip she'd taken had been to Denver—United on December 29. It was right there on the calendar. She went out and back in the same day. Eight hours of flying and only three hours on the ground in Denver. You'd have to have a singular purpose in mind to do that. I felt so disappointed. Betrayed, even. "You didn't even know her," is what Bill had said to me, and he'd been right. And the package, maybe we couldn't find the package because she'd destroyed it. "What about the hard copies of the invoices, the signatures?"

"Gone, too, although no one in Accounting remembers seeing her there."

"I just can't believe this about her. Can you, Matt? You knew her. Can you really see Ellen doing something like that?"

"I think I have a way to find out for sure. What if I can find out who signed the Crescent invoices?"

"Then you would be very clever, indeed. I thought there were no copies around."

"We had this admin support person on the task force, Hazel. She was viciously organized. It was scary. And she worked with Ellen a lot."

"Did you know her?"

"She loved me. I used to bring her lattes in the morning just to stay in her good graces. I figure I'll buy her another double-tall for old time's sake and find out what she's got. I doubt if she'd have copies of the invoices, though. The best she might have is some kind of record of who signed. That sounds like something she'd do. If Ellen signed them, then we'd know for sure."

I pulled myself up and wandered back to the window. "When do you think you might know something?"

"I've already got a call in to Hazel. As soon as I get something one way or the other, I'll call you." There was a slight pause. I'd run out of things to say and was just waiting for him to run out of steam. "You haven't commented on my theory, Alex. It's pretty amazing, don't you think, how all the pieces fit, and especially how I figured it all out?"

"Very elegant, Matt. It's a very elegant theory."

After I hung up, I stared down at the empty bleachers. Dan was long gone, and so was the blue sky. The overcast sky was so intense in its bland whiteness, it hurt my eyes. I was tempted to close the curtains, but I didn't. If I was going to work, I needed light.

Most of Ellen's things were in and on top of her personal mementos box, which was back in the corner of the room. All in one motion I hoisted it onto the bed. Several items slipped off the top and fanned out over the sheets like a deck of cards. Pick a card, any card. I slipped a file from the middle of the stack, one that I'd already read twice. Armed with a bottle of water from the mini bar, I settled in on the bed and began to read it again. The next time I looked up, it was after five o'clock.

I picked up the phone and dialed the office. There was no reason to think Molly would still be at work, but as the phone rang and rang, I was hoping. Please, please, please, please, please pick up. Finally she did.

"Molly, did you ever get that password for the officers' calendars?"

Chapter Thirty-six

When my eyes adjusted to the low light, I saw two people kneeling in prayer—a Delta flight attendant in the last pew to the left, and Dan in the first pew on the right. With his head bowed, he was on his knees below a statue of the Virgin Mary.

I stood in the back and surveyed the windowless chapel. A single spotlight shone on a heavy wooden cross over the raised altar. The only other light came from rows of offertory candles along the walls. The design of the church was slick and modern, but the smell was ancient—of old incense and burning candles, oil and ashes. I hadn't been inside a Catholic church for over fifteen years, not since my father's funeral, but I still recognized that smell. This was a place where people brought their sins.

When I arrived at Dan's pew, I genuflected and made the sign of the cross. He saw me, crossed himself, and slid back in the seat, propping both feet up on the kneeler. Instead of his usual bouncing and fidgeting, he was still. "You're Catholic?" he asked, his voice barely above a whisper.

"Not anymore."

"Why not?"

I looked at the gleaming white marble altar, hard and unforgiving. "The whole deal is presided over by aging, celibate white men whose job it is to tell you how to live a clean and pure life in a dirty and complicated world. It doesn't make any sense to me, and I don't need help feeling guilty. What about you?"

"My kid's always asking me if I go, so I do. Besides, it's the only place on the field where it's quiet enough for me to think." His voice was so low that only the two of us could hear.

"What are you thinking about?"

"My grandmother. She raised me." He tipped his head back and stared up at the ceiling. "She used to tell me that men were put on the earth to take care of women."

"That's quaint."

"She was a tiny Italian woman, but she was a pistol. Nobody messed with her. 'Husbands are supposed to take care of their wives, and fathers are supposed to take care of their children,' she'd say, 'and that's the only way it works.'"

"Do you believe that?"

"I believed it all my life. And now my wife has left me, my little girl sees me twice a month if I'm lucky, Ellen is dead, and you hate my guts." He rubbed his eyes and focused on the offertory candles burning at the bare ceramic feet of the Virgin Mary. Most of the candles were lit, evidence that there were still people who believed. "I don't think my grandmother would be proud of me." His voice trailed off, and all I could hear was the sound of the flight attendant in the back saying her rosary, the beads tapping lightly against the wooden pew. "Ellen knew," he said.

"What?"

"Vic Venora told her about me, about locker thirty-nine. That was the last conversation I had with her. She did the same thing you did, she stormed off. Only that was the last time I ever saw her. Alive anyway." He stared into the flames of the offertory candles and for a moment seemed transfixed by them, by the light of other people's prayers. "I can't stop thinking that if she hadn't found out or if I'd told her myself, she could have trusted me. She wouldn't have tried to do this thing on her own. I could have helped her. But I never got a chance to explain it to her."

And just like that, it all fell into place. His obsessive pursuit, his endless rationalizing, his reckless disregard for himself: it was all driven by the most powerful and relentless of all impulses—guilt. "Explain it to me, Dan. I'd like to understand."

He stared down at his shoes, his face heavy and his eyes unseeing. He began slowly. "I was twenty-eight years old, still working as a ramper in Newark. I'd been married five years and was still living in my father-in-law's house. I was working my ass off every day, and every night I was taking classes, trying to get into management. One day Stanley calls. Stanley Taub. You know him?"

"He used to be the GM in Newark for Nor'easter."

"Right. He didn't know me from a hole in the wall, but he calls me to his office and tells me he's got a shift supervisor job open on the ramp. Asks me, do I want it? I couldn't fu— I mean, I couldn't believe it. I thought he was kidding. Then he says there might be a few things I'd have to do that I might not like. I tell him I'll clean toilets if I have to. I'll wash his car. I was going to make some decent money for the first time in my life, so I said, fine, sign me up."

Even now he couldn't hide a hint of the excitement he must

have felt. "Stanley wasn't talking about cleaning toilets, was he?"

He shook his head. "At first he'd ask me to do stupid shit, like drive him into the city and drop him off so he wouldn't have to park. Then he started telling me without really telling me to stay out of certain areas on certain shifts. 'I don't think you need to be down in cargo tonight,' he'd say, 'I've got it covered.'"

"And you stayed away?"

"I didn't know I had a choice. I thought the deal was to do what he said or go back to slinging bags, and there was no way I was gonna do that. The baby was already two years old, and if I had to kill myself, I was getting us our own apartment. I did what I was told."

"Where did Lenny come in?"

His head hung so low, he was almost talking into his shirt. "Lenny needed someone to run these envelopes up to Boston from Jersey, and Stanley recommended me."

I stared down at my hands in my lap. "Envelopes full of cash?"

"Swear to God, Shanahan, I never looked. My instructions were to fly to Boston and leave the envelope in locker thirty-nine at the Nor'easter terminal, so that's what I would do, then turn around and go back home. I never knew who picked it up. I never heard of Crescent Security. I never even knew what the envelope was for. Didn't want to."

I believed him. Not knowing or wanting to know would have been inconceivable to me, but it was as much a part of his character as loyalty to his boss. "How much money did you make for all this?"

He put his hands beside him on the pew, rocked forward,

and stared down at his shoes so that I couldn't see his face. "I got paid extra overtime without working it. It came in my paycheck."

That couldn't have been much, and it was so much like him to sell out at a price that was far too low. "Why did you stop?"

"Michelle." He tilted his head, looked at me, and couldn't suppress the smile. "She was so beautiful, so perfect. One day she looked up at me with those big innocent eyes, and I saw myself the way she might see me and I got scared. I started feeling like I didn't deserve her and that God was going to punish me, take her away from me. I decided I would never again do anything that wouldn't make my kid proud, and I never took another dime."

"Lenny couldn't have been too pleased."

"He told me I'd never get promoted as long as he was drawing breath, but what else was he gonna do? Fire me for not stealing anymore?"

"You were in Boston by then?"

"Yeah. You know, the whole time I was in the union working the ramp, everyone down there was sticking it to the company in every way they could. Every day I had a chance to do it, too, and I never did. I put on a shift supervisor's uniform and I find out management's stealing more than anyone and I'm thinking, If everyone's sticking it to the company, who is the company?"

He sat back with his shoulders slumped and his hands folded in his lap, looking as if he'd taken a pretty good beating from the world, and I realized that in his mind he had never lied to me. He never could have. Everything he was, everything he wanted to be, was right there on his face. If I had known him when he was scamming, I would have known he was scamming, the same way I knew now that he was telling the truth.

"Did you tell Big Pete about John McTavish?"

"On my grandmother's eyes, I did not tell him."

"Do you know how he found out?"

"No, but I've been thinking about it, and I remember now how I found out. Victor Venora. He made a point of tracking me down to tell me."

"That could have been Big Pete making sure that you knew. The real question is, How did those guys find out?"

He looked all around the chapel and then back at me. "Why did you call me?"

"Because I calmed down. I got a little perspective, and I decided I was a jerk for believing Big Pete and not giving you a chance to explain."

"Thank you." he said, his voice hoarse, ragged.

"My pleasure . . . and there's more. I've spent the past five hours going through every piece of mail, every document, everything I have that belonged to Ellen, and I think I've figured some things out. I need to tell you about it."

"I'm on my way to meet Angelo. Come with me and we'll talk on the way."

Chapter Thirty-seven

"Can you believe this shit?" Dan guided the car into the bumper-to-bumper flow of Route 1A. "We're never going to make it. Angelo's gonna bolt before we get up there."

The exit to the Sumner Tunnel, the short way into town, was closed to all but taxi cabs and buses. It was a traffic-control measure that usually happened at the airport this time of night on Fridays. A trooper stood in the road with the lights of his blue-on-blue State of Massachusetts patrol car flashing and rain dripping from the bill of his cap. Using a flashlight, he'd funnel reluctant drivers onto the dreaded detour route. And there was no more reluctant driver than Dan at that moment.

"God*dammit*." He banged the steering wheel, then banged it again for good measure.

"Calm down. There's nothing we can do about this. Where are we going?"

"Angie's worried about being seen with us. He's got us going way the hell out to some dive in Medford or Medfield or some goddamned place." He leaned forward and wiped the fog off the window with the sleeve of his jacket. When he had cleared a hole big enough, he craned his neck and peered up into the sky. "I don't like the way it looks out there."

I made my own porthole. All I could see were sheets of rain falling on us from out of a pitch-black sky. "This is supposed to turn to snow later."

"I know. What's the big discovery?"

This wasn't exactly the venue I had in mind for breaking the news, but it would have to do. I turned in my seat so that I could face him. "My friend Matt called earlier today."

"Finance guy Matt?"

"He found a copy of the schedule of pre-purchase adjustments, the one Ellen was looking for."

As I explained about the seven hundred thousand dollars and the three payments and Crescent and everything but the part about Ellen being involved, he was riding the brakes, inching into the traffic, and I was mainly talking to the back of his head. "You're not listening to me."

"I am listening," he insisted. "There were three big payments from Nor'easter to Crescent, which is really Lenny, and he used the money to buy the contract. That's your big news?"

"The payments to buy the contract came from Majestic, not Nor'easter. *That's* the big news, Dan. Lenny—or someone—figured out a way to get Majestic to pay for the whole thing. But to make it work, he needed a partner on the inside at Majestic, someone on the task force to approve his fake invoices to Crescent." I took a deep breath. "It could have been Ellen."

He hit the brakes abruptly, and we both slammed against the seat belts.

"Son of a *bitch*." For a split second I thought he was yelling at me, but his anger was directed at the driver of a panel truck who was maneuvering to merge from behind us. Dan deftly cut him off. "Who's saying that about her?"

"Matt." I shifted around in my seat. My jeans were starting to feel tight. "And me, Dan. I think it's possible that she was involved."

"This is a joke, right?" He glared at the driver of the truck in the rearview mirror. "I can understand that fucking pisshead finance guy thinking something that stupid. What is he, like twelve years old? But you, Shanahan, what is that? You're mad at me so Ellen's dirty, too?"

"Ellen and Lenny worked on the merger together. They were on different sides of the negotiation, but apparently they became close. That project lasted eight months."

He was stiff-necked, gripping the steering wheel and staring straight ahead. "That doesn't prove anything, for chrissakes."

"I've been working on this all afternoon, going over and over every detail. I went through it all again—the box we brought down from her house, her letters, her files, her documents. I watched that dating video about a dozen times, and I went through a whole pile of her mail that had been forwarded to the airport—"

"What did you expect to find?"

"Some kind of a clue as to her motives. Why she was involved in all this."

"She was involved because that cocksucker Dickie Flynn got her involved when he sent her that package."

"I think she was involved before she got that package. Think about it. She could have turned that package over to the feds, or Corporate Security. She didn't tell anyone what she was doing. She was sneaking around on other airlines. And I found something in her files. She requested and received extraordinary signature authority while she was on the task force."

"So what?"

"Under her normal authority, she couldn't have signed those Crescent invoices. They were too big. She made special arrangements so that she could."

"Can't you just believe that she wouldn't have done something like that?"

"But she did. I found the request and the approval in her files."

"I'm talking about the whole scam. I'm telling you she wasn't that kind of person."

I leaned back against the passenger door. "Dan—"

"I say she was clean, that she was trying to do the right thing, and you won't take my word on that. So what it comes down to is, you don't believe me. You don't trust me." He ran a nervous hand through his hair and stared through the wet windshield into the red blur of tail-lights. The combativeness in his voice had gone. He sounded almost plaintive. "You don't trust me."

The only sounds in the car were the blasting heater and the sluicing of the wet windshield wipers, steady as a metronome. I turned around to face front and wished like hell that we weren't stuck in traffic, that we could put some distance between us and this place we were in.

"Listen to what I've found, then you can decide for yourself. Six days before she died, Ellen made a trip to Denver. I don't know if you remember her list of secret trips, but it was on there. It was the last destination."

He didn't respond, but I knew he remembered.

"She flew out and back the same day, and it looks as if it

was a special trip to visit the archives. The archivist remembers her. She asked to see the pre-purchase adjustment schedule. When Matt went looking for the same documents a few days ago, they were gone. The original invoices with the signatures are also missing."

"That doesn't mean she took them."

"Come on, Dan—"

"Or *if* she took them, and I'm not saying she did, she took them to build the case against Lenny. That's what we've been saying all along. She took them to keep them safe."

"Then where are they? Where is the evidence?"

"We'll find it."

"Think about this. If she was on the inside working the scam with Lenny, then her signature would be on those invoices. Destroying them would be one way to cover up her own involvement."

"Give me one good reason why she would be involved in something like this."

"She was sleeping with Lenny."

He swung his entire upper body around to face me. If we'd been going any faster than four miles an hour, we might have swerved off the road into a ditch. "Bullshit, Shanahan, bullshit. I told you before that's crap."

"Molly pulled up Lenny's travel schedule from the past eighteen months. When we checked it against Ellen's list, ten of the fifteen cities matched. Ten. And one of the five that didn't was the last trip to Denver. She was in the same city with him ten different times. In secret."

His head canted to one side, slowly, almost like a door opening. The traffic was picking up and spreading out, and he had to pay more attention to the road. Maybe that explained why he didn't say another word for almost three miles—a long, slow three miles.

He finally broke his silence. "Was Lenny in Boston the night she died?"

"There's no record that he flew into Boston," I said, "but I think he was here. He could have driven."

"Why do you think that?"

I reached into my back pocket, pulled out an envelope, and opened it up. "I found this letter in her mail. It just came this week."

"What is it?"

I pulled it from the envelope. It was too dark to read, but I didn't have to. "This is a letter from a place called Maitre d' Express. It's a dinner-delivery service."

"Like Domino's Pizza?"

"No. They only do the delivery part. You can order from lots of different restaurants around town, and they bring it to your house. Inside is a credit card receipt and a letter saying that Ellen still has to pay for her last order even though she never took delivery."

"What does that have to do with anything?"

"It was for the night she died."

He looked over at me but didn't say a word.

"The receipt was for one hundred fifteen dollars. Twenty-five was for the delivery from Boston to Marblehead. That leaves ninety dollars, which even by Boston standards is a lot for one meal. So I called Maitre d' Express and they had a record of the order in their computer. One appetizer, two salads, and two entrees from Hamersley's. At eight o'clock she called and cancelled, but it was too late. The order had already been made up, so she was charged anyway."

Shadows moved in and out of the car with the steady flow
of headlights streaming toward us. I watched his face. He was
working his jaw, but I saw no other sign that he was listening.

"Here's what I think happened that day. Ellen spoke to
Lenny on the phone sometime during the morning. I don't
know what was going on between them, but he must have
talked her into seeing him that night at her house. Before she
left work, she cancelled her trainer's appointment for that night
at the gym, but according to her running log, she went running
that afternoon along the Charles, so she wanted to get a workout in, but didn't want to keep the appointment that night. She
got home around four and called this place to order dinner for
the evening."

"And when Lenny showed up he killed her."

"One thing's for sure. Whoever killed her knew her. He had
access to the house, probably a key, and the code for the security system. Or she let him in. No forced entry. He knew about
her mother, knew enough about her and her life to make the
murder look like a plausible suicide."

"Why would he kill her?"

"Could be that Dickie's package triggered something.
Maybe there was some kind of blow-up between the two of
them and they stopped trusting each other. Maybe she was
accumulating the evidence to use against him. It's clear that
Ellen had the evidence, not Lenny, and he's still looking for it,
he and his pals the Dwyers."

At the end of our exit ramp, he took a right turn that put
us on a poorly lit spur. I looked out the window at an industrial area of aluminum-sided warehouses and vast parking lots
filled with eighteen-wheelers backed up to raised concrete
loading docks. It was lonely and cold and desolate.

"The thing I don't get," I said, "is why she cancelled the dinner. What happened to her between four in the afternoon when she ordered and eight o'clock when she cancelled?"

He had nothing to say to that. Neither one of us said another word for the rest of the drive out.

Angelo DiBiasi's white stubble crept down the soft roll of flab at his throat. His worn cotton T-shirt covered a narrow chest, which ballooned into a big, hanging gut that kept him from pushing in close to the table. With one eye almost shut, he cocked the other at me as he spoke to Dan. "Why'd you go and bring her for?"

"Don't start with me, Angie. I told you I might bring her."

"And I told you not to—"

"Which just goes to show you're not in charge here. You're the one who's sitting at home on your butt with no job, and she's the one who can bring you back, so be nice."

Dan's tone had an urgent edge, as though he was running out of time and patience, even though we'd just arrived. We were at a fluorescent island of a truck stop by the side of the highway. It had stools at a long counter and ashtrays on every wobbly table.

When Angelo looked at me again, it was with eyes that were puffy and red-ringed, the kind you get from lying awake at night. Or crying. Or both. I offered him my hand across our sticky Formica table and introduced myself. "I'm sorry about your wife, and I hope we can work something out."

He switched his cigarette to his other hand and returned the gesture. His fingers were long and thin in my hand, the only part of him that seemed delicate.

"Let's get this over with." He let go and turned back to

Dan. "I don't want to be seen with the two of youse." He took a quick tobacco hit, then moistened his lips with the tip of his tongue. "You bring something in writing describes this deal?"

"We don't have a deal yet," Dan said, "which is why we're talking."

"That's not what you told my wife. Why'd you have to go and call her anyway? You got no right calling and bothering her with my business." His chest puffed out and his back stiffened, and he looked like an old rooster as he shook his head full of white hair. "What you did, a man should never do to another man."

Dan stirred his coffee. "I'm sorry I had to bother Theresa, but since she's the one who's sick, I thought she had the right to know there was a way for you to get your job back. You didn't tell her." He lifted the cup to his lips, had another thought, and put it back down without drinking. "And besides, you've got a strange idea of what's right. She starts chemo in two weeks and you're out boosting TV sets, getting yourself fired and losing your medical benefits."

"I was taking that TV home for her," he sputtered, "so she'd have it to watch when—" He stopped abruptly and turned toward the window. It was a big picture window that looked out over the parking lot, where snowflakes were beginning to drift down into the rain puddles. His cigarette was wedged tightly between his thumb and index finger. We sat in silence and watched as he smoked it all the way down to the filter. As soon as he stubbed out the butt, he started a new one. "Tell me again," he said wearily. "what you want and what you got."

Dan put both elbows on the table. "I don't know what it is you know, Angie, but my boss went to a lot of trouble to try to talk to you before she died, so I've got to think it's big. You give me what she was looking for, and we'll bring you back to work. No termination, no hearings or arbitration, none of that shit. You just come back tomorrow like you never left."

"You're talking about the boss killed herself, right. Not this one." He nodded in my direction without looking at me, and I couldn't tell if he was genuinely confused or yanking Dan's chain.

"I'm talking about Ellen Shepard."

"How am I supposed to know what she wanted? I never even met her."

"Don't waste my fucking time, Angie. I'm not in the mood."

Angelo sat back and kicked one leg out, stretching as if he had a sore knee. "Why should I tell you anything? I can get the same deal from Big Pete without being no snitch."

"If Big Pete's going to bring you back, it means he's doing it through Lenny, and if Lenny wants to bring you back, he has to wait until after arbitration. Those are the rules, Angie, and who knows how long a hearing might take? Yours probably won't take much longer than what?" Dan checked with me. "Six months?"

"I once had a guy who waited a whole year," I offered helpfully.

"I'll take a little time off." Angelo glanced nervously from Dan to me and back. "Now's a good time anyway."

"Right," said Dan, "and at the end of your 'vacation,' maybe you're at work with full back pay. Then again, maybe you wait six months and never come back. Hard to say what happens with an arbitration panel. But let's say you do get back. Do you know what's waiting for you here?"

Angelo stared, his breathing growing shallow between drags.

"Me."

He'd been close to the edge from the beginning, and now I saw perspiration forming on his upper lip.

"If you come back off Lenny's deal, Angie, I'm going to make you my own personal rehabilitation project. I'm going to see to it that you never have time to think about stealing again because you'll be working your ass off."

Dan edged closer, pushing the ashtray out of the way. Angelo's eyes shifted back and forth, trying not to focus on Dan but unable to look anywhere else.

"I'll sit guys down to make sure you've got work to do, Angie. You won't have a second to yourself, and if you try to steal from me again, I'm gonna catch you and that's going to be it. You'll be out on your ass for good."

"That's harassment."

"Nothing in the contract says I can't make you do your job."

"Jesus fucking Christ, Danny." He stubbed out his butt, jamming so hard, stale ashes spilled onto the table. "I don't got enough problems without you threatening me all over the place?" He lowered his head, squeezed his eyes shut, and massaged his temples with the heels of his hands, turning his entire face crimson in the process. Between the cigarettes, the sick wife, pending unemployment, and Dan's pressure, I feared for the guy's vascular health.

"Angelo," I said, "here's another way to look at it. Your wife starts chemotherapy in two weeks."

He nodded, eyes still shut.

"Take our deal and your benefits will be restored tomorrow. Take Lenny's deal and you're going to have to sit out for six months, maybe longer, with no benefits and no guarantees. How are you going to pay the bills in the meantime?" His hands slipped around to cover his eyes. "Do you want your wife worrying about that when she's trying to get well? Your wife's peace of mind means a lot to you, I can tell. Tell us what you know, come back to work, and give her that peace of mind. It would be worth more to her than a TV."

He looked at me through bloodshot eyes. "Full back pay?"

"Yes."

"All my benefits, including flight bennies?"

"Of course."

He slumped back in his chair and studied the ceiling as he wiped his nose with the back of his hand. When he finally sat forward, Dan and I leaned in, too. In that moment before he began, as we all stared at each other, I knew that this was as close as we'd been to the truth—any truth—about Ellen Shepard's death, and I could barely hold still. I watched Angelo's face and everything seemed to slip into slow motion as he opened his mouth and said, "I want a better deal."

"A better *deal*?" I couldn't believe I'd heard right.

"I want to retire today, but I want the last two years of my salary and full benefits, including my pension."

"Are you out of your fucking mind?" Dan spoke for both of us.

"You got me in a position where I got no choices, Danny. I got forty-one years in, and I ain't walking away with nothing."

"You got yourself in this trick bag and you got some balls trying to use it to jack us up."

"Listen to what I'm saying to you." He looked around the diner and lowered his voice. "That lady boss of yours, the other one, she was right. I do know something. And if she knew it, too, that's why she's dead. So I'm askin' you, if they killed her, how long do you think I'd last down there on the ramp?"

Dan and I exchanged a glance. No one else was in the diner with us except the kid who was working the counter and doing his homework. I could hear the squeaking of his highlight pen as he marked his textbook. A prickly wave danced up the back of my neck and crawled underneath my hair. "Angelo." My heart was pounding in my throat, and I was surprised that my voice didn't waver. "Do you know that Ellen was murdered, that she didn't kill herself? Do you *know* this?"

He nodded. "I know too much for my own good."

"You *miserable motherfucker*. All this time you didn't say any—"

I laid my hand on Dan's arm. "Tell us what you know, Angelo, and I'll get you whatever you want." I looked into his eyes and I knew, no matter what Big Pete had promised him, that he was scared, that he loved his wife, and he wanted to get this over with. Even so, he held out as long as he could, until the corner of his mouth began to quiver. "There's two parts to this story," he said finally. "There's who killed her, and there's why. I'll give you the who tonight. You get me my deal and I'll give you the rest."

Dan pulled away from me and sat back, arms crossed tightly across his chest. I nodded to Angelo and he began.

"Big Pete, Little Pete, and Lenny—used to be Dickie, too, before he kicked the bucket—they was all involved in this thing happened here a few years back, and it turned out that she somehow knew this secret and was gonna blow the whistle."

"What secret?" I asked. "Was it the IBG vote?"

"I ain't sayin' what it had to do with until I get my deal, but it wasn't that. That was nothing. What I will tell you, certain people weren't where they said they were the night when she got killed."

The prickly feeling came back, only this time I felt it across my whole body.

"It so happens that night I was down at the employee parking lot taking care of some personal business. While I was there, Little Pete comes flying up in that big truck his pop bought for him. He's coming back to work in the middle of his shift, which was stranger than hell because once he's gone he never comes back."

"What time?" I asked.

"Around midnight."

"Was he drunk?" asked Dan.

"He'd had a few, but I've seen him a lot worse. I gave him a ride up to the line so he could find Big Pete. On the way up, he was jumpy, like he needed a drink. He couldn't stop yapping about how big changes was coming because of him and everything was going to get back to normal."

"What did you take that to mean?" My throat was tightening.

"Nothing. The kid's always spoutin' off about something. But he kept pushing, so I asked him, does he know this on account of his pop telling him? Because everybody knows that's the only way the kid ever knows anything is it comes from his pop, right? I tell him this and it pisses him off. He says his pop didn't know nothing about it, that he and Lenny had a scam going." Angelo lowered his eyes and blew out a long stream of smoke that scattered the wisps of ashes off the table. "Finally, he couldn't keep it in no more and he just comes right out and says it. The dumbfuck bastard sits right in my tug and tells me he just killed the lady boss."

Dan's fist slammed down on the table, dumping over Angelo's coffee cup. Angelo bounced back and out of the chair. I shot straight up. My chair flew back and tipped over as the hot liquid spread across the tabletop. Dan was the only one who didn't react. He sat there frozen, his arm still flat against the table, his fist squeezed so tight it was shaking. Hot coffee soaked the sleeve of his cotton shirt. I looked at him and he looked back. "Son of a bitch," he said. "That fucking son of a bitch killed her. I knew it."

I pulled a wad of napkins from the chrome napkin holder and dropped them into the spilled liquid. I lifted Dan's arm out of the mess and handed him a wad. Eventually, we settled back into our seats and I asked Angelo, "What else did he say?"

"I told him he was full of shit. To prove it." He glanced nervously at Dan. "He showed me the key to her house."

"Where did he get the key?" I asked.

"Lenny gave it to him."

The table was covered with wet, sepia-colored mounds that looked like sand dunes and smelled like stale French roast. The smell of cold coffee was making me sick, and I could barely put two thoughts together, but I tried. Ellen must have set up the date to meet Lenny at the house. Lenny gave the key and the security code to Little Pete and sent him in his place. So they both killed her. "Does anyone else know what happened that night?"

"No. Big Pete made sure of that after he found out. He was so mad, I thought he was going to kill that kid. He had me drive Little Pete home."

"So Big Pete knows everything."

"Absolutely."

"What about the package?" I asked.

"What package?"

"Dickie Flynn's package in the ceiling."

"I don't know nothing about no package."

"Tell us, Angelo," I asked, "why they had to kill her."

He shook his head.

"Will you tell the police?"

"I ain't saying dick to no cops, and I ain't telling you no more." He stood up and slipped his jacket on. Then he leaned over the table and lowered his voice. "Get me my deal and I'll give you what you need. It's time it all come out, anyway."

The windshield wipers in Dan's car were fighting a losing battle with the blowing snow. The car shuddered against another strong blast of wind. We were idling in the parking lot of the diner, waiting for the heat to kick in. Both of us were staring straight ahead. After a while I noticed that the window was fogged and we couldn't see anything. I tried to block out everything but the facts, because everything but the facts scared me to death.

"It's pretty strange," I said, blowing on my fingers, "that Angelo was willing to tell us that Ellen was murdered, that Lenny set it up, and that Little Pete did it. But he won't tell us why."

"He thinks he's got more leverage on the why. It's how he thinks he's going to get his deal."

"That's what I'm saying. He's telling us without telling us that the motive for Ellen's murder is bigger than the murder itself. What do you think it is?"

"I don't know and I don't give a fuck." Dan wasn't wearing his gloves, and his hands looked like bones wrapped around the steering wheel. "I'm going to kill Little Pete. And when I'm done with him, I'm going after that other prick Lenny. I'm going to wrap my hands around his fucking pencil neck just like—"

"We have to go to the police, Dan."

"Are you deaf? Angie just said he wouldn't talk to the police."

"They'll make him talk. That's what they do. I don't want the two of us to be the only ones who know what he said."

"The police already gave up on this, remember?" He put the car in reverse, wedged his arm behind my seat, and twisted to look behind him. He screeched backward, stopped quickly, and slid on the quickly icing concrete.

"Where do you want me to drop you off?" he asked, glowering at me through the dark.

"Drop me *off*?"

"You can do what you want. I'm going to the airport."

"Wait." I grabbed his arm, trying to think fast as he was about to put the car in gear and set in motion something that could only end badly. "I'll make a deal with you. I won't call the police until we find Dickie's package if you promise to stay clear of Little Pete."

"You don't think there is a package anymore, remember?"

"I don't know if there is or not, but let's keep looking."

He stared straight ahead, grinding his teeth and tapping one finger on the wheel. "I already looked everywhere I could think of for that package."

"We haven't really looked at the airport."

"It's not there."

"We haven't looked. You want to make sure that Lenny gets nailed for this, don't you? If there's evidence against Lenny, it's in the package."

He tapped a few more times, started to nod slowly, then put the car in gear and swung out onto the highway.

"Deal," he said, just before he hit the gas.

Chapter Thirty-eight

Dan was sitting with his legs crossed on the top of my desk, fidgeting with a ruler. He looked as if he were in a life raft on a sea of papers. In a final spasm of manic frustration, we'd taken Ellen's neatly labeled files and binders and dumped them all onto the floor—and found nothing. With no place else to look, we'd gone over every inch of that massive desk, thinking the package might be concealed in some secret compartment. That idea had turned out to be as flaky as it sounded.

"I still don't know why you thought it would be here," he said for the fifth time. "She never kept anything important at the airport. I keep trying to tell you that."

"It was worth a shot," I replied for the fifth time, "before we schlepped all the way up to Marblehead again."

I was sitting on the floor in the corner in a zombie-like trance. I was so tired, my brain was beginning to seize up like an engine running without oil. I couldn't remember the last time I'd eaten, and worst of all, the heat had kicked into high gear again and the temperature in the office was approaching critical. But I knew that if I let myself feel any of that, I'd never move from that spot, and I had to get Dan away from the airport. I had no idea if either of the Dwyers was on shift, but I didn't want to take any chances.

I checked my watch. Almost nine o'clock. "If we're going up to the house tonight, we'd better get moving."

A cell phone twittered and we locked eyes.

"Don't look at me," he said. "I don't carry one of those damn things." He jumped down from the desk, and I crawled over to the mound of papers, the apparent source of the ringing.

"Here it is." He pulled my backpack from under one of the piles and handed it over. I dug out my phone and punched up the call.

"I found you."

The sound of Bill's voice was like a rush of cool air in that arid desert of an office. The minute I heard it, I felt the muscles in my shoulders release and the tension flow out. In so many ways, he was exactly what I needed right then. "Can you hold on?"

"Is this a bad time?"

"No. Just give me a second." I covered the phone with my hand. "Dan, I'm sorry, I need to take this call."

He was scratching the top of his head with the ruler. It took him a moment, but he caught on. "Which means get the hell out of here." The ruler clattered onto the desk as he headed out the door and closed it behind him.

From the sound of the background noise, Bill was in his car. "I am so glad you called. Where are you?"

"I'm back in Colorado. What are you doing up there? Lenny's hysterical."

I started to move in a tight figure eight around the piles on the floor. "Did he call you?"

"Yes, he did, which means he's truly desperate because he never calls, even when he should. And who is this guy Angelo?"

I froze. "He mentioned Angelo?"

"He said you were trying to do an end-around and offer Angelo a deal without telling him. Lenny wants to approach the IBG International and make his own deal to bring him back to work. Should I let him?"

"*No.* Absolutely not. Jesus." I paced a little faster and my shoulder muscles started to bunch again. Angelo must have told Lenny that he'd talked with us, but why on earth—maybe to play both ends against the middle. "Bill, whatever you do, don't let Lenny make that deal. If anything, Angelo needs to be protected from Lenny. Protected from himself, too, it sounds like."

"Tell me who he is and why any of this is significant."

"I told you about Angelo. He's the ramper that Ellen fired before she died. Dan and I met with him tonight, and he told us that Lenny had Ellen killed."

"He told you *what*?"

"Little Pete killed her, but Lenny gave him the key to her house. Angelo actually saw it."

"Saw the murder?"

"No, the *key.*" I was talking too fast, frustrated that he wasn't keeping up. "The night of the murder, Little Pete came back to the airport and showed Angelo the key he used to get into Ellen's house, to get in the house and kill her."

"Where are you right now?"

"At the airport. *Are you listening to me?*"

"Alex, you have to get out of there. If any of this is true—"

"I need one more day, and I need you to approve *my* deal for Angelo. He told us who killed her, but he wouldn't tell us why. I need to know why—"

"*You* need to know?"

"Yes, I need to know." I kicked one of the piles of paper on the floor. "It has something to do with that package from Dickie Flynn and I think we can find the package if we have a little more time. And if we find the package, we get Lenny." Assuming there still was a package.

When I slowed down enough to notice, all I could hear was the sound of his breathing. And then I couldn't even hear that. "Bill, are you there?"

"Listen to me carefully," he said, his voice calm and steady. "Don't think about what you're going to say next. Just shut up and listen."

I stared up at the old yellow tiles in the ceiling. I couldn't believe how wound up I was—and how annoyed. I wanted him to be in a frenzy, too, to support my frenzied-ness. But he was so rational he was making me feel like a raving madwoman. I was losing perspective, which is exactly what he was about to tell me and exactly what I didn't want to hear. "I'm listening."

"If what you're saying is true—"

"It's all true, I know it—"

"I asked you to listen to me."

"I'm sorry. It's just . . . you sound as if you don't believe me."

"It doesn't matter what I believe. That's what I'm trying to make you see. If Lenny knows that Angelo talked to you, then it's not up to me how much time you have." He paused to let that sink in. "Do you understand now?"

I wiped the perspiration out of my eyes with the short sleeve of my T-shirt. He was right. If Lenny knew that Angelo had talked to us, then the Petes knew and that could not be a good thing for any of us—especially Angelo.

"I'm bringing in the FBI," he said, "and I'm sending Corporate Security out. Tom Gutekunst will be on the red-eye tonight. He can be in Boston first thing tomorrow morning."

"Angelo's not going to talk to Corporate Security or anyone else. Don't you . . ." I paused for a moment to get the shrillness under control. He was right; I was wrong. He was being reasonable, and I was being stubborn to the point of petulance. But I couldn't let it go. "Don't you want to know what Angelo knows, which is why Ellen was killed?"

Big sigh. "What about Fallacaro? What if he goes with Gutekunst tomorrow?"

"If it's too dangerous for me, it is for Dan, too."

"Maybe so. But I'm not in love with Dan Fallacaro."

"I'm not going to bail out and leave Dan to finish this—" What did he just say? I switched the phone to the other ear. Maybe I wasn't hearing right. "What did you say?"

"I said that I'm in love with you, Alex."

My knees almost gave way.

"I am hopelessly . . ."

My hands trembled.

". . . desperately . . ."

Tears welled up in my eyes.

". . . pathetically in love with you."

I had to reach around, find the edge of the desk and lean back. He'd never even said that he loved me—needed me, wanted me, but never that he loved me, much less desperately loved me, and even though I'd been aching to hear it,

I'd never asked him to say it because I was afraid of what I might hear.

"I don't want to lose you again. I don't want a life without you in it."

I tried to keep my thoughts from racing. I dropped my head all the way back and let his words roll over me. He was in love with me. And I couldn't stop smiling.

"I'm out here in Denver," he went on, "completely helpless while you're running around in Boston with some people who are apparently quite dangerous. All I want is for you to exercise some good judgment. Is that so much to ask?" The background noise was gone, and I knew that his car had stopped. Without the interference he sounded closer, as if he were there with me, whispering in my ear. "If you're worried about Fallacaro, then tell him to leave, too. But whether he goes or not, I want you out, Alex. I want you safe." He let out another long sigh. "Now I have to go. I'm late for a dinner, and I've been sitting outside the restaurant for twenty minutes."

"There's so much more to this that I have to tell you." But at the moment my head happened to be in the clouds and I couldn't remember what it was.

"Tell me tonight. I'll call you. Right now I have people waiting for me inside. But I'm not going to hang up until you give me your word. Will you go home tonight and wait for help?"

I would jump off a cliff for him right now. "Yes, I'll go home."

"Good."

"But how about this? When Tom shows up tomorrow, I'll give him everything we've found out, but I'm going with him to talk to Angelo. And we have to go back up to Marblehead to look for that package."

"What about tonight?"

"I'll take Dan and we'll go home. Just don't let Lenny bring Angelo back."

The line began to pop and crackle, then grew into a steady stream of static, and I lost him for a moment. "Bill?"

"I heard you," he said, cutting in and out, "and I'm losing my battery. I'll call you later tonight, on the *hotel* phone."

"I'll be there. Bill . . ." He didn't answer. "Are you there?" Nothing. "I love you, too," I said softly, but the connection was gone.

Dan was in his office with his feet up on the desk. He had the computer keyboard in his lap, and he was scanning the monitor.

"What are you doing?"

"Checking the work schedule for tonight."

"You're looking for Little Pete."

"I just think it's a good idea to know where he is."

"And is he working?"

"Not according to the schedule posted yesterday."

I breathed a silent sigh of relief. "I'm sorry about kicking you out."

"I understand. You women all have your secrets."

"You should talk."

He allowed a little touché smile. "Can we get the hell out of here," he moaned, "before I melt? It's a long way up to Marblehead."

"I'm ready, but we're not going to Marblehead. I've got some things to tell you."

"Hey," he yelled as I headed back to my office. "what's all over your butt?"

"Excuse me?"

"You've been sitting in something. Your ass is all white."

I twisted one way and then the other, trying to see behind me. Sure enough, there was something that looked like chalk dust all over my jeans. "I don't know." I tried to dust it off and got it all over my sweaty hands. "I think it's from that corner over by the window where I was sitting. There's been a pile of this stuff on the floor since the day I got here. It doesn't say much for our cleaning crews."

"I can't take you anywhere, Shanahan. You're a mess."

I went back to my office and loaded up my backpack. While I waited for Dan, I went to the corner to investigate the strange white residue on the floor, the stuff that had reminded me of rat poison on my first day in the station. I crouched down and rubbed a bit of it between my fingers. It felt grainier and heavier than chalk dust. There was no obvious source at the base of the wall or around the window. I stood up, wiped my hands on my jeans, and was starting to go when I saw more of it on top of my two-drawer file cabinet. My backpack hit the ground with a thud as I stood and stared straight up at the ceiling. It wasn't chalk dust.

"Dan." He didn't answer. *"Dan,"* I yelled, climbing up on the cabinet, "Come in here."

"What?" he yelled back. "I'm coming."

He walked in just as I was pulling a brown envelope out through the space where the corner tile had been. More of the white stuff had fallen when I moved the tile. Acoustic tile shavings were in my eyes and stuck to the damp skin on my face. I had to blink several times before I could look down and see him standing next to the cabinet. I presented him with Dickie Flynn's package.

"You guys always said the ceiling was the best place to hide things."

Chapter Thirty-nine

The TV powered up with its distinctive electronic snap, and a blast of full-volume static boomed from the set. The scratchy noise felt like sandpaper scraping across raw nerves.

"God Al*migh*ty." Dan scrambled for the volume control, punched the wrong button, and turned the static to blaring canned-sitcom laughter. Laughter, especially fake, felt obscene in the fragile silence and made our situation that much more surreal. He found the volume and turned it down as I fumbled with shaking hands to get the cassette out of the envelope.

"Where's the fucking remote?"

"Are you sure Delta's not going to mind us being in here?"

"I told you, we have a deal. I loan them a B767 towbar when they need it, and I get to use their VCR whenever I want."

I put the tape into the slot—tried to, anyway—cramming it in a few times before I realized one was already in there. Every step seemed to take forever as I found the button to eject, pulled the cassette out, and put ours in. Dan found the remote, killed the light, and moved in next to me in front of the screen.

His shoulder was warm against mine as we leaned back against the conference table, and I was glad that whatever we were about to see, I wasn't going to see it alone.

I took a few deep breaths, trying to stop shaking. It didn't work.

He aimed the remote at the screen. "Ready?" Without waiting for an answer, he hit Play.

Within seconds, the picture changed from the high, bright colors of situation comedy to the grainy black-and-white cast of a surveillance video. The date and time were marked in the lower right-hand corner, and the rest of the screen was filled with the image of a small aircraft parked in the rain on a concrete slab. It was a commuter, so there was no jetbridge, just a prop plane parked at a gate. I looked at the markings on the tail. A wave of recognition began as a tightening of my scalp when I realized that I also recognized the gate. The date— check the date again. The tight, tingling feeling spread from the top of my skull straight down my back and grabbed hold, like a fist around my backbone. It was March 15, 1995, at 19:12:20. The Ides of March.

Without taking his eyes from the screen, Dan found the Pause button. We stared, as frozen as the image before us, and I could hear in his breathing, I could feel in his stiffening posture, that he was thinking what I was, that it couldn't be, please don't let it be—

"The Beechcraft," he whispered.

The Beechcraft, he'd said, not *a* Beechcraft. I looked at him, grasping for reassurance, hoping not to see my worst fears in his face. But the odd TV glow turned his skin into gray parchment and made deep hollows of his eyes. Under a day's growth of dark stubble, he looked stunned.

"Are you sure? Is that . . ." I tried to swallow the lump in my throat. "Check the tail number."

He didn't check. He didn't have to check. We both knew what we were looking at. It was one of Dickie Flynn's surveillance tapes of the ramp, the one from March 15, 1995. That was the night that Flight 1704 crashed outside Baltimore. This was the Beechcraft that had gone down, and this was our ramp it was parked on. It was less than three hours before the fatal landing, and I had no doubt that when he raised the remote and hit Play, we were going to see things we weren't supposed to see. We were going to find out the things that Ellen knew, and maybe understand why she was dead.

I turned back to the screen, eyes wide, neck rigid, and stared straight ahead. A feeling of dread filled the room—Dan's or mine or both, I couldn't tell. It was growing, filling the small space and, like that heat in my office, pressing back on me and making it hard to draw a breath. I wondered if Dan could feel it, too, but I couldn't look at him. I was glued to the screen, afraid to keep looking, but afraid to look away.

He held up the remote, but before he restarted the tape, I felt him pull himself up, square his shoulders, and center his weight, like a soldier girding for battle. He hit Play and the rain began to fall again.

The rain was falling hard on the evening of March 15, 1995, hard enough that I could see the drops bouncing off the wet concrete. During the first minute or two of the tape, that's all we saw, the Beechcraft sitting in a downpour. Occasionally, a ramper would walk through the shot, or a tug would cut through the narrow passage between the airplane and the terminal, which they weren't supposed to do.

A fuel truck pulled into the frame. Dan had been still, but

when the truck stopped just behind the left wing, he started shifting his weight back and forth from one foot to the other.

"That's Billy Newman," he said as the driver climbed out and went to the back of his truck.

"Who's he?"

"A fueler."

"Does it mean something?"

"I don't know, boss. He's just another guy out there."

Not knowing exactly what we were looking for, everything meant something—or nothing. We had to watch every movement, every motion closely, and when Billy Newman disappeared behind his truck for an inordinately long period of time, we were both drawn a little closer to the screen. But when he reappeared, all he did was go about the business of fueling the aircraft. He hooked up on one side and stood in the rain with his hood pulled over his head. When the first tank was full, he went around and started on the other side.

"This is killing me." Dan pointed the remote and fired. "I'm going to fast-forward until something happens."

"Are you sure? We don't even know what we're looking for."

"If we miss something, we can start it over. Besides, I have a feeling we'll know it when we see it."

The tape whirred as the cockpit crew came out, stowed their gear, and boarded. Then the passengers appeared, most carrying umbrellas and forming a line to the boarding stairs. I tried to be dispassionate, to look with a coldly analytical eye for anything unusual in the high-speed procession. But in this moment captured on this tape, these people were about to die. I knew it and they didn't, and I thought maybe I should look away, lower my eyes and—who was I kidding? I was like any other wide-eyed, slack-jawed, rubber-necking ghoul. I felt ashamed and I felt dirty. At the faster speed, their movements were hyper and manic, almost comical, and I heard echoes of that canned sitcom laughter. We should slow this down, I thought. We're hurrying these people along when what they need at this moment is more time.

"*Wait,* stop it there."

"I see it." Dan was already pausing and reversing. "Goddammit." His gentle shifting from foot to foot accelerated to jittery rocking as he searched the tape, first going too far back. He hit the Rewind button, accidentally going still further back, then had to fast-forward again. I watched the seconds on the time stamp, each tick up and down winding the tension a little tighter.

Finally we were in normal speed. A tug towing a cart full of bags and cargo pulled into the frame. The vehicle, moving too fast for the conditions, skidded to a stop at the tail of the Beechcraft. I held my breath. The driver stepped out into the rain, stumbled, and nearly fell to the wet concrete. Dan saved him momentarily by stopping the tape.

"Oh, my God." I'd been staring at the screen so intently, my eyes were dried out and my vision was starting to blur. But there was no mistaking the identity of this man—his size, his build, the span of his wide shoulders. It was Little Pete, and Little Pete was drunk.

Dan was squeezing the remote with one hand. The other was on top of his head, as if to keep it from flying off. "That fucking moron," he said in a voice that was so quiet, it was scary.

"Did you know he worked this trip?"

"I didn't know he was in this kind of shape. No one did."

His hand slipped from the top of his head, brushing my forearm in the process. I almost didn't feel it. The pieces were beginning to fit together, each one falling into place with a dull, brutal thud that felt like a punch to the solar plexus. "Someone knew, Dan. Someone knew." A terrible feeling of panic began to take hold of me. But I had to stay focused. "Let's keep going."

He restarted the tape, and Little Pete continued his grotesque dance, reaching back for the steering wheel to keep from going down. He stayed that way for a few seconds, swaying as if the ground was a storm-tossed sea. And then, God help us, he began loading the aircraft.

My stomach tightened into a hard lump as I watched him lift a dog in its carrier out of the cart, stagger to the aircraft, and slide it through the aft cargo door, stopping to poke his fingers through the cage before pushing the carrier all the way in. I couldn't tell if he was teasing the animal or trying in some sloppy, sentimental, drunken way to give comfort.

In contrast to the passengers' movements, Little Pete's in normal speed were slow and dreary and indifferent, but knowing what had come later that night, every single thing he did was painfully riveting. Pete followed the dog with the bags, stopping occasionally to pull a scrap of paper from his pocket and make a notation.

Dan shook his head. "I can't believe he's actually keeping a load plan."

"It doesn't look to me like he's following any kind of a plan. He's stuffing the load wherever he can make it fit."

"You're right, but he is keeping track. See there." Little Pete pulled out the scrap again and made some adjustment with his pencil. He finished by trying to fit two boxes in the forward compartment. It didn't take long before he gave that up and shoved them in the back with the dog. "He didn't load anything forward," said Dan, "Did you see that? All the weight he put onboard is in the back."

"It was out of balance," I said, feeling the air go out of me as another piece thudded into place. Little Pete had been drunk the night of the fight with Terry McTavish and reversed the load on a jet, which is more or less what he'd done here. "Little Pete loaded it wrong, and the flight crew got blamed."

We watched him close the cargo compartments, almost slipping again at the rear door. He disappeared into the cab of his tug, then popped out with his glow-in-the-dark wands. Appearing remarkably composed, he stood in front of the aircraft, in front of the captain, and guided the airplane out of the frame.

Little Pete walked back into camera range and stowed his wands.

Dan and I stood for a long time staring at the screen after he'd driven away. Neither one of us made a move to turn off the tape, even though there was nothing left to see but rain falling on a bare concrete slab.

Eventually, I felt the insistent aching in the middle of my back and realized I'd been standing stiff enough to crack. Dan had started moving around. He looked as if he was in fast-forward mode himself, pacing around the table and talking to himself. "That son of a bitch. That cocksucking, mother-fucking, degenerate scumbag. He was drunk. He fucked up the load. He caused the crash. That's what this has all been about."

I found the light switch and flipped it on, but not having the energy to pace, I leaned back against the closed door as much for support as to ease my sore back. "How did the captain get the plane off the ground?"

"What do you mean?"

"If the load was out of balance enough to bring the plane down, how could he have gotten it off the ground? He would have been tail-heavy."

He answered without ever breaking stride. "It doesn't take that much on a Beechcraft to move the center of gravity. It's a small airplane. A couple hundred pounds in the wrong place would do it. He could have been able to take off but not land. That's possible."

"I can't believe it."

"Why not? They use flaps on landing but not takeoff. Plus, the fuel tanks are forward, so if the tanks were full, they could have compensated—"

"No. I'm saying I can't believe anyone would be that negligent, that stupid. How could they let him work like that? Even his father—especially his father."

"C'mon, Shanahan, you know these people. And how stupid are they if they covered it up and got away with it?"

"Yeah, how did they do that?" I dropped down into one of the chairs that ringed the conference table. Spread out in front of me was the stack of papers and documents that had spilled out of Dickie's envelope along with the tape. "The whole thing was caught on a surveillance video, Little Pete is clearly drunk, and yet the true story has never come out. The pilots took the fall for what he did. Obviously, the tape never came out, but still—"

"Lenny had to be part of it," he said. "He was the GM. There's no way this thing gets covered up and he doesn't know about it."

"No doubt. Little Pete Dwyer didn't fool anyone on his own." I traced the edge of the conference table, following the line with my thumb, avoiding eye contact. "And if Lenny was involved, Dan, I think we have to consider that Ellen was, too, at least in the cover-up. There's plenty of motive for murder here all the way around."

His response was instantaneous. "You will never, ever convince me that Ellen Shepard was part of this."

"Maybe she got sucked in. Once you've committed contract fraud, once you've gone that far, if something like this happens, you have to cover it up just to protect yourself. You keep getting in deeper even if you don't want to."

"Buying off a contract is one thing, but twenty-one people died here."

"And if the true cause had ever come out, there would have been no deal. You know that. You would have had investigations and lawsuits all over the place. Nor'easter would have been grounded, maybe even had their certificate yanked. What started out as contract fraud to make the deal happen ended up being a cover-up to make sure it didn't blow up."

He stood across the room from me on the other side of the table with his feet shoulder-width and his arms crossed. The look on his face was as closed as his stance. "Ellen didn't know about this."

He was so confident, so sure that even if he hadn't known everything about Ellen, he had known the important things. He simply refused to believe the worst about his friend. I rested my head against the high back of the chair and stared at the TV screen. The surveillance tape was still running. Neither one of us had made a move to turn it off. I envied Dan his certainty, and I wished so much that I had known Ellen. That I didn't have to draw my conclusions about her from what she hung on her walls, or what was left on her kitchen counter, or the look in her eyes in that dating video when she said she didn't want to be alone anymore. The rain continued to fall on the concrete on March 15, 1995. It was falling harder, and no matter what the facts said about Ellen, I wanted Dan to be right. I didn't want her to have known about this.

"Let's look at it from a different angle. Ellen knew nothing about the crash—the true cause of the crash—until she got to Boston. Dickie sent her this package, she saw the tape and realized that Lenny had used the money they'd stolen—"

He opened his mouth to object again, but I kept going. "Used the money for something besides the contract payoff. She got angry or scared, and that's why she took the evidence. When she figured out what he'd gotten her into, she panicked."

He stared at me for a long time, and I couldn't tell what he was thinking. But he must have been considering the theory, and he must have decided he could live with it. "She got to the evidence first," he said, picking up the thread, "she threatened to go public, and they killed her for it." He tapped his lips with the tip of his index finger. "Now all we have to do is prove it."

"That's not our job."

He turned away in frustration, then circled back and motioned to the TV screen. "Aren't you even curious about how they did this? That pisshead Dwyer kid took that Beechcraft down and is still out working the ramp loading airplanes. He's working tomorrow. What if, God forbid, something happened and we knew about this and didn't do anything?"

"We can take him out of service. Or assign him to the stock room."

"Boss, I don't want this guy anywhere near one of my airplanes."

Having seen what I'd just seen, it was hard to argue with that sentiment. With both palms flat on the surface, he leaned across the table. "Shanahan," he said, looking me directly in the eye, "I need to finish this tonight."

His tie had disappeared long ago, his shirttail was out, and I noticed for the first time how thin he'd become, too thin for his suit pants. His face was drawn, his forehead lined with every sleepless night he'd spent thinking about why Ellen had died and, more painful than that, what his role in her death might have been. I had a feeling that watching that videotape had taken more out of him than he could have admitted, and it occurred to me that he might have been leaning on that table because he was too worn out to stand up. No matter what I had promised Bill, there was no way Dan was going home tonight. With the answer right there in front of us on the table, he didn't have enough left to wait it out until tomorrow. It had to be finished tonight.

I checked my watch. Tom Gutekunst from Corporate Security would be in at six o'clock in the morning. We had almost eight hours. I reached out for a stack of papers.

"Sit down before you fall down," I said, handing him half, "and start with these."

Chapter Forty

Every once in a while I'd look up to see Dan's lips moving as he read through the papers in his lap.

I was still plowing through the first document I'd picked up. It was officially known as the National Transportation Safety Board Aircraft Accident Report for Nor'easter Airlines, Inc., Flight 1704, Beech Aircraft Corporation 1900C, Baltimore, Maryland, March 15, 1995. It looked like aircraft accident reports look—standard formats, factual, statistical—and I was having a hard time with it. I had just seen the people who had boarded that flight, human beings that were here reduced to tables and charts and codes. The loss of their lives and the loss of equipment were treated not dissimilarly with everything measured, weighed, counted, and set down on a page in black-and-white.

I flipped back to the beginning and started again, reading the same words I'd read twice already, looking for the highlights this time and trying to retain at least some of the information.

On March 15, 1995, a Beech 1900C which was operating as

NOR 1704 crashed on final approach to Baltimore. Nineteen passengers, the captain, and the first officer were all killed. The dog being transported in the kennel in the aft cargo compartment had survived.

In the section marked PERSONNEL INFORMATION, I found out that the captain had been forty-one years old. He'd flown with Nor'easter for seven years and worked as an instructor/check pilot for this type of aircraft. Fellow crew members described him as "diligent, well trained, and precise". The first officer was thirty-six. His position with Nor'easter was his first regional airline job, but he'd been flying for eight years. It was an experienced crew.

A few pages over and a couple of paragraphs down was the section marked HISTORY OF THE FLIGHT. On the day of the accident, the captain arrived at the airport in Baltimore at 1300 for a 1400 check-in. No one who saw him that afternoon reported anything unusual about his behavior. That day he and his first officer flew a round trip from Baltimore to Syracuse with a scheduled stopover in Boston each way. They flew two more round trips between Baltimore and Boston that afternoon and evening. Flight 1704 was the last scheduled for the day. They'd never made it home.

On that final leg, the flight was delayed in Boston due to bad weather, and didn't take off until 2015, ninety minutes after the scheduled departure time. Weather at the time of departure was heavy rain, low clouds, and poor visibility.

At 2149, the Baltimore tower cleared NOR 1704 to descend to and maintain 6,000 feet.

At 2156, NOR 1704 contacted the tower and requested the current Baltimore weather. It was thirty-seven degrees, low broken clouds, winds out of the northwest at ten knots.

At 2157, NOR 1704 was cleared for landing.

Ground witnesses who saw the aircraft on the short final approach to the runway said its wings began to rock back and forth. The aircraft went nose up, then into a steep bank and roll. The right wing contacted the ground first. Its forward momentum caused it to cartwheel, breaking into pieces and scattering wreckage over a quarter mile. The accident occurred during the hours of darkness. Part but not all of the fuselage burned. The aircraft was destroyed. No survivors.

I stared at the page until I thought I heard Dan say something, but when I looked up, he was still sitting exactly as I'd seen him before, with his feet on the table, one hand on the reports and the other on the armrest propping his head up. Behind him on the TV screen, the tape was still running. I found the remote control and turned it off.

"What's the matter?" he asked.

"Nothing." If I'd not said anything at all, I'm not sure he would have noticed. He was talking to me, but completely absorbed in what he was reading.

One of the appendices in my report was a map of the wreckage, a computer-generated diagram that showed the major pieces, of which there were many, and where they had landed relative to each other and the airport. I turned to the back and looked at it again, studying it more closely this time. I was trying to remember what this crash had looked like. I was searching for the image, that signature shot that is so visceral, so horrible, or so poignant that it gets burned into our collective consciousness and becomes shorthand for this and only this tragedy. Workers in hip waders and diving gear slogging through swamps with gas masks and long poles. A flotilla of boats out on gray seas with grim-faced men dragging parts of people and machinery out of the water. Scorched mountain-tops and flaming oceans and fields of snow fouled by oil and soot. Tail sections with logos intact, absurdly colorful amid the twisted, blackened ruins. I tried to remember 1704, but when I closed my eyes, all I could see was that patch of empty concrete. It was so quiet in the room I could almost hear the rain.

"Holy shit, boss." Dan's feet dropped to the floor, jarring me back to the present. "Holy *shit*."

His raised eyebrows and excited smile told me he'd hit pay dirt. "Tell me."

"You're not going to believe what this is. You've got the official version there of what happened that night"—he nodded to my report—"but I've got the real story." He held up a ratty pile of dog-eared, handwritten pages he'd been reading. It was stapled in the corner, but just barely. "This is Dickie Flynn's confession."

"Confession?" The word alone, freighted with all that Catholic significance, brought a shudder of anticipation. What sins were we about to hear?

"Everything that happened that night in order—bing, bing, bing. And see that? Dickie wrote it himself and signed it." He turned to the last page and held it up just long enough for me to see the scrawled signature of one Richard Walter Flynn. "According to this, Dickie was here that night and right in the middle of everything."

I set my report to the side. "How did they do it?"

"I'll show you. What did the investigators say was the official cause?"

"Pilot error. They say the pilot miscalculated the center of gravity, that it could have been as much as eleven inches aft of the aft limit, which significantly screwed up the weight and balance."

"In other words, he was tail heavy."

"Too much weight in the back," I said. "He lost control when the flaps were lowered for landing."

"Fucking Little Pete. Goddamn him." He was up now and searching for something. I assumed it was the remote and tossed it to him. Almost in one motion he caught it and started the tape rewinding. "Okay, let's walk through it. The captain is responsible for calculating the center of gravity, right?"

"Right."

"But he's got to have all the inputs to do the calculation. He needs passenger weight, fuel load, and the load plan for cargo—weights and positions."

"Yeah, yeah," I said, anxious for the punch line. "Standard stuff."

Dan raised one finger, signaling for patience, and I got the impression he was walking through it out loud to try to understand it himself. "In Boston, the Operations agent is responsible for collecting all the inputs on a worksheet. On this worksheet he converts gallons of fuel to pounds, applies average weights for passengers and carry-ons. Cargo weights are pretty much a pass-through from the ramper who loaded the plane. He radios the results to the crew and they do their thing. At the end of every day, the worksheets go into the station files."

A sharp click signaled the end of the rewind. He started the tape, and Billy Newman reappeared and fueled the Beechcraft again, this time in fast-motion. Dan switched to normal speed as the fueler walked toward the camera. "Here's Billy coming into Operations to turn in his numbers for the fuel load."

The next time he stopped the tape was after the last passenger had boarded. The ticket agent who had worked the flight closed up the airplane and approached the camera just as Billy had. "Here's the gate agent coming to turn in the passenger count."

Now we were back up to the point where Little Pete came flying into the picture, skidding recklessly up to the aircraft. He let it fast-forward through the loading. Before he stopped it again, I understood. "He never came into Operations."

"Bingo. He doesn't have a radio, and if he'd given them directly to the crew we would have seen."

"How do you know he didn't have a radio?"

"Dickie said."

"Okay, but he updated his own plan," I said. "We saw him."

Dan had his head down, checking the facts in Dickie's chronology. "Little Pete changed the load, updated his numbers, and never told anyone."

I tried to follow how this would have worked. We were supposed to have safeguards in place for this sort of screw-up. "First of all, Kevin Corrigan is a good operations agent. Without the ramp's input, he would have had a great big hole in his worksheet. He never would have let that happen, and even if he had, the crew couldn't have calculated the center of gravity without the cargo load. They wouldn't have even taken off."

"I agree with you. Kevin is a good ops man. It's too bad he wasn't working that night."

"Who was working?"

"Kevin was back in Ireland at his brother's wedding. It was Dickie."

I sat forward in my chair and concentrated hard. Between the heat and everything else that had gone on tonight, I was feeling addle-brained. "Are you saying that Dickie Flynn, *ramp manager* Dickie Flynn, was working as an operations agent the night of the crash?"

Dan was nodding. "Yes. He was a manager then, but he started out as an ops agent and he used to cover Kevin's shift now and then when he couldn't find anyone else to do it. That's what he was doing here that night"—he tapped the confession with two fingers—"and that's why he knew so much. He worked the trip, he and Little Pete."

"Dickie," I said, "was in a position to cover for Little Pete."

He nodded. "Now you're getting it."

"But Dickie still had to give the captain a number. Did he just make it up?"

"As near as I can tell, Little Pete called a preliminary load plan to Dickie over the phone before he ever left the ready room to work the trip. They're not supposed to do that, but sometimes they do because the loads never change on these little airplanes. Little Pete was drunk, which we just saw, and didn't load the airplane according to the plan. He put all the weight in the tail. He marked the changes on his own load sheet, probably intending to call it in. Then he disappeared."

"And no one ever got the updated numbers."

"According to Dickie, the storm was getting worse, the captain wanted to go, he couldn't find Little Pete, so he gave him the numbers he had, figuring Little Pete would have told him if he'd changed anything."

"Which meant the pilot's calculation didn't match the actual load, and it was enough of a difference to take the plane down. Jesus." I rested my forehead in the heels of my hands and considered the unusual confluence of events that had taken place that night. It's always that way with a plane crash. There are so many backups to the backups to the fail-safe systems and procedures that it always takes not just one but an unusual chain of strange events to bring one down. I looked up at Dan, who was sitting back in his chair as if it was a recliner. We were through with show-and-tell. Once again, the image left on the screen was that bare apron in the rain. "Why wouldn't the investigators figure this out?"

"No black boxes, for one thing. An aircraft either has to have been registered after October 1991, I think it is, or have more than twenty seats to require boxes. This one didn't qualify."

"I saw that in the NTSB report. No boxes and no surveillance tape because Dickie took it. The crew was dead. That means the only people left who knew what really happened were Dickie and Little Pete."

"They weren't the only ones who knew. When Dickie heard that the plane had gone down, he figured out what happened. He got scared and wanted to change the worksheet to cover his own ass. To make it look like the captain's mistake, he needed to know what the real load was. But nobody could find Little Pete or his plan. This is where our buddy Angie comes in."

"Angelo?"

"Big Pete called him at home that night after the accident and got him out to look for Little Pete. Angelo found him up in a bar in Chelsea and, get this, the knucklehead still had this right where he'd left the damn thing—in his pocket." He'd pulled a piece of paper from his stack and held it up. "This is Little Pete's load plan, that thing he kept pulling out of his pocket."

"Let me see that." It was a wrinkled, computer-generated load plan with one corner torn off, and it was a mess. Almost every position had been marked through or overwritten. "You've got to hand it to Dickie, he kept a thorough record."

Dan took the plan back. "Angelo stashed the kid somewhere and ran this copy back over to the airport. Dickie dummied up a second worksheet, gave a copy to Big Pete, who got it to Little Pete. Twelve hours later, the kid had sobered up, everyone was telling the same story to the investigators, and it looked like the fight crew made the mistake. Case closed."

"Until," I added, "Dickie decided he didn't want to go to his grave with the souls of twenty-one people on his conscience. No wonder he spent the rest of his life getting drunk. Does he talk about Lenny in there?"

"Oh, yeah." He smiled a killer smile. "Lenny was right there from the beginning. He came out that night, and according to Dickie, he and Angelo went on the Crescent Security payroll— at least for one big payday."

"That's what the pay stub in Ellen's file was all about. The ten grand, that was Dickie's portion of the hush money. Ten thousand bucks out of a total seven hundred thousand-dollar payoff. Not a very high price to sell your soul."

"Dickie always did get the short end of the stick."

We sat for a moment in silence with the papers and documents scattered all around us. All the pieces had come together in the worst possible way, and I felt the weight of all we had found out in that room. I felt crushed by the enormity of the thing—of all that had happened and all that was going to happen.

Finally, Dan roused himself to stand up and go over to the television. He was going to pop out the cassette, but I stopped him. "I want to watch it one more time."

He turned to look at me. "Why? Are you looking for something?"

"The passengers' faces." I needed to see them again, to see them as individuals—as men and women, children, mothers, fathers, husbands, wives. I didn't want them to be fused together into an entity that I knew only as "the twenty-one people killed in the crash of flight 1704."

Without a word, Dan sped through the tape and found the beginning of the boarding process. This time as we watched in normal speed, I made sure to look at each one as they passed by in the rain and climbed the boarding stairs.

Seeing their images on tape reminded me of Ellen's video, of how I had felt when I'd heard her voice, when I'd seen her smile, saw doubt on her face and frustration and determination—all the things that make us who we are. Seeing her that way had made real to me someone I'd never met. It had created a void in my life for someone I'd never even known.

As I stared at the screen, I thought about the surviving family and friends of these victims, what it was going to do to them to see the people they had loved, still loved, in their final moments, and the silent black-and-white image started to blur again.

Chapter Forty-one

Dan stared at my computer monitor. "Who's H. Jergensen?" he asked.

"I don't know." I was trying to wrangle the papers on the floor in my office into one pile so that Molly wouldn't have a heart attack when she arrived for work on Monday. The heat had finally stopped pouring in, and our offices were now merely sweltering as opposed to life-threatening. "Why?"

"Because you've got an e-mail message from him and it's urgent."

"What's in the subject line?"

"Matt Levesque."

Matt . . . H. Jergensen . . . H . . . *Hazel.* "Hazel. Is it Hazel Jergensen?" I raced over and almost lifted him bodily out of the way so that I could sit at the keyboard. "Move, move, move."

"All right. Jesus Christ. What is it?"

"It's the invoices to Crescent, finally. Or at least a reasonable facsimile." I sat down and clicked into the Majestic electronic mailroom to find the message. "Hazel Jergensen worked for Ellen on the task force and, according to Finance Guy, kept records of everything. He thought she might have a record of who signed the invoices to Crescent. Dammit." I was talking as fast as I could, typing as fast as I could, and missing keys. "We're going to find out once and for all if Ellen was in on this, at least the embezzlement part." After multiple tries I found the message, double-clicked, and waited for it to come up.

Dan hadn't responded, and when I turned to find him, he was as far away from the computer as he could be and still be in the office. "Don't you want to know?"

"To be honest," he said, "I've already found out more than I ever wanted to know."

"What if it wasn't her? We don't know for sure, Dan. This will tell us."

The CPU seemed to labor endlessly, whirring and clicking as I watched the blinking cursor on the screen. The wool fabric on my chair was making the hollows at the backs of my knees sweat right through my jeans. When the message finally appeared, it was in pieces. "Here it comes."

Half a note from Hazel appeared first, saying simply that Matt had asked her to . . . the rest of the message came up . . . forward the information. I punched up the attachment. The first section included titles and column headings—vendors, amounts paid, check numbers, and in the far right-hand column "Approved by:" I tried to stay calm, but it was tough. If it was all here, Hazel had sent us exactly what we needed.

"C'mon, c'mon, c'mon," Dan coaxed. I hadn't even noticed, but he was now leaning over my chair, breathing over my shoulder as the report began to appear.

The screen changed hues as the last of the data popped

up. The spreadsheet was so big, we could see only the first few columns.

I scrolled down through the A's. There were lots of B's. Lawyers, accountants, auditors, consultants—advisers of every stripe. At one point I got frustrated and went too fast, and we ended up in the H's. Finally I found it. My heart did a little tap dance from just seeing it there. Crescent Consulting—big as life.

I took a deep breath and heard Dan do the same. "Are you ready?" I asked him.

"As I'll ever be. Go ahead."

I shifted the view so that we could see the whole spreadsheet. When we saw the signature, we both sat back at the same time, me in my chair and Dan against the desk. I thought I heard him deflating back there. Or maybe that was me. I scrolled down until we'd seen all of the Crescent entries.

Ellen had signed every one.

I felt sad. That was the best way to say it. Disappointed and sad. Dan had drifted away again. "Dan, I'm sorry. But isn't it better to know than not to know?"

He turned around, started to say something, and his beeper went off. Before he could respond, mine went off and they beeped together, making for an eerie, syncopated stereo alarm.

"Operations," I said, silencing the tone on mine.

"Both of us," he said quietly. "It must be something big."

"Yeah, Kevin . . . uh-huh . . . in my office . . ." Dan held the phone to his ear. "No, I've had the phones rolled over . . . What? When?" He hesitated, glancing at me. "I'll get in touch with her. Okay, I'll be right down."

"We haven't dispatched an aircraft in over an hour," he said after he'd hung up. "We've got one on every gate, at least two on the ground trying to get in, more on the way, and visibility is for shit. Kevin says everything just stopped."

"Weather?"

"It's not the weather."

Even in the overheated, overcharged atmosphere I felt a deep, deep chill as he dashed into his office.

I followed him. "Then what is it?"

"All the rampers have disåppeared." He snatched a hand-held radio from the charger. "Kevin can't find anyone."

There was a current running through Dan. I could feel it. The high-voltage kind that's always marked dangerous. His engines were revving. I took a wild guess. "Are the Dwyers on shift?"

"Little Pete is. He must have swapped with someone."

I clamped onto his right elbow, afraid that he might be out the door and into the operation before I knew he was gone. "What are you planning to do?"

"I'm going to see if I can get some airplanes off the ground."

"Don't bullshit me. You're going down there to find Little Pete."

"I'm not going down there to find Little Pete, but if that cocksucker happens to be around, I won't walk away from him."

"There's something not right here, Dan. An entire shift doesn't just disappear. Someone's trying to get us down there. Don't be stupid."

"No one ever accused me of being smart."

He was standing still. He wasn't doing anything but looking at me, yet I could still feel his momentum pulling us both toward the door. I was panicked that if I let go, he was going to slip away, and this time I'd never see him again.

"Let me go, boss."

I looked at him closely. He was tired, disheveled, unshaven—and completely still. I'd never seen him so still, and I knew I had no chance of stopping him. I let go, but only to reach for the second radio still nested in the charger. Before I had it clipped in place, the door to the concourse opened and slammed shut. We stared at each other. "Dickie's package," I said.

"What did you do with it?" he whispered.

"Did I have it last?"

The footsteps were approaching, albeit slowly.

I bolted next door to my office and found the envelope on the desk, right where I'd left it. We'd never replaced the ceiling tile, and as Dan jumped onto the file cabinet, I handed the package up to him. The footsteps grew louder, but the pace was downright leisurely, out of place in an airport operation, especially in this one on this night. I thought I even heard . . . yes, he was whistling. Hurry, Dan, hurry *up*. As he maneuvered the tile back into place, he ducked and I flinched as something fell from the opening, bounced off the side of his shoe, and landed on the floor. I could see it back there between the wall and the cabinet. It was a small, plastic object, clear plastic.

Dan jumped down with a thud. "What the hell was that?"

"I don't know." It was just beyond my reach, and as I stretched for it, I had to turn my head flat to the wall and couldn't see what it was. I could almost reach it with my fingertips. It was so close . . . so close . . . *got it.*

"Yoo-hoo."

I didn't have time to look at it, but I could feel what it was by its shape, and I knew immediately that we had found the missing cassette tape from Ellen's answering machine. I didn't even have time to stuff it into my pocket. I closed my fist around it, put my hands behind my back, and turned around to see Lenny coming through the reception area straight toward us.

"Anybody home?"

He was looking sharp tonight in camel-colored slacks pleated at his narrow waist, an ivory shirt, and what appeared to be a very fine matching camel sweater. A pullover. He stood in the doorway leaning against the jamb, as calm as I was frazzled. "And what a stroke of good fortune to find the both of you together like this. I can't believe my luck."

We must have looked totally caught in the act. I was standing stiffly in front of my desk with both hands behind my back. Dan was behind the desk, and I hoped to hell he'd stay there. It was only a few hours ago he'd been talking about tearing Lenny's throat out with his bare hands. I swallowed hard, leaned back awkwardly against the desk edge, and reached for a calm voice. "It's kind of late in the day for you, isn't it, Lenny? Especially on a Friday."

He stared at us for a long time, looking from my face to Dan's and back again. He was sneaky enough to recognize sneaky when he saw it. "Is it?" He slipped a pack of gum out of his pocket and offered me a piece.

"No, thanks." He didn't offer any to Dan.

"In light of the disaster that is unfolding outside in your operation at this very moment, I would say if it's too late for anyone, that would be you. I must say, I've never seen passengers quite as angry as the ones out on your concourse at this very moment." The Louisiana drawl was extra-thick and creamy tonight, almost dripping. "What's keeping you all so busy in here tonight?"

"We were just on our way out," I said, casually stuffing my hands into the front pockets of my jeans, depositing the tiny cassette there.

"Good," he said, strolling into my office, taking his time, letting his gaze linger here and there. My heart sank when it lingered a little longer on the file cabinet, on the sprinkling of acoustic tile scrapings that were still there, probably because they still had Dan's footprints in them. He didn't go so far as to look up at the ceiling, but he knew. Dammit. He'd worked in Boston a long time. He knew.

I glanced back at Dan. "Maybe one of us should stay in here and monitor the phone," I said. That was a stretch, but the best I could come up with under the circumstances. I was mainly trying to get Dan's reaction, and I did.

"You can stay if you want," he said quickly, "but I'm going downstairs."

That was my choice. Stay with the tape and let Dan go take on Little Pete by himself, or go with him and leave the tape for Lenny to find.

Lenny was delighted. "Come on back in here when you all have got things under control."

"If it's as bad as you say out there," I said, "we could use your help."

"I was on my way to offer my assistance, but since you're both here, I'm very comfortable leaving things in your capable hands. Especially with Mr. Fallacaro here, one of the best operating men around. Isn't that right, Danny boy?"

I could almost taste the tension as something passed silently between them, something I could see but could not understand. What I knew was that these two men hated each other. It was for all kinds of reasons, but mostly for the secrets they knew about each other. I slipped around to the side of the desk so that I could be closer to Dan.

"I know what you did," Dan said to Lenny.

Lenny chewed his gum and smiled. "Don't know what you'd be referring to, Danny boy, but whatever it is, wouldn't you have to include yourself? In for a penny, in for a pound, my friend. And how is sweet Michelle? How is she going to like visiting her daddy in a federal penitentiary?"

Dan almost came over the desk. It took all my strength to stay in front of him as he screamed over my shoulder and jabbed his finger at Lenny. "You ever say my daughter's name again, cocksucker, I'm going to kill you. I'm going to rip your balls off and shove them down your lying throat, you filthy bastard."

Not surprisingly, Lenny was moving back and not forward. He stayed clear as I maneuvered Dan out the door and into the corridor. When he couldn't get past me to get to Lenny, he pounded the wall. "I *hate* that motherfucker."

"Stay out here, Dan."

"He's going to find it."

"Be quiet."

He lowered his already hoarse voice. "He's going to get the video and we won't have anything."

"There's nothing we can do. It's a surveillance video taped on company-owned surveillance equipment. It belongs to the company. Everything in there is company property. We'll think of something else. Don't come back in."

I went back to get our jackets. I also wanted my backpack, which still had my cell phone in it. Lenny, looking smug, was lounging in my doorway. "You all better skedaddle," he said, winking at me, "while you still have an operation left to save."

I was dripping wet again, but in the whole mêlée Lenny had never even broken a sweat. I guess reptiles don't sweat.

"And by the way," he said, easing into my desk chair, "when you get downstairs to the ramp, say hello to Angelo for me."

Chapter Forty-two

With the environmental-control system in the terminal gone haywire and all the moist, overheating bodies crammed together, the atmosphere was suffocating. The odor of sweating scalps and ripe underarms hung in the air like a damp mist. The angry determination on Dan's face made me nervous.

"We're looking for Angelo, right? Nobody else."

His distracted nod gave me no confidence. "I'll take the north end to the firehouse," he said, zipping his jacket, "and you take the south. And let me know what you find out in Operations."

He pulled on his gloves. Made for skiing, they were heavy-duty, but to me they looked like boxing gloves. He was so pumped up by the encounter with Lenny, I knew that no matter what I said, he was a heat-seeking missile headed straight for Little Pete. And there was no way he was going to win that fight.

"Stay in radio contact with me," I said into his ear, then pulled back so that I could see his eyes. "Please, Dan."

He could do no better than a grim-faced nod, and I watched him disappear into the crush of angry passengers. He'd been walking away from me like that since the day we'd met.

If the departing crowd that first night of my arrival had been hostile, these people were homicidal. My destination was Operations, but I couldn't take one step without someone stopping me to ask something I didn't know. Or to yell at me.

The quickest way to move was around the crowd. I worked my way over to the windows and what I saw there, rather what I couldn't see, stopped me cold. A DC-10, a very large aircraft, was parked just outside the window at the gate, but it was snowing and blowing so hard, it was barely visible. With my hands cupped around my eyes to block out the overhead light and my nose pushed up against the window, I could see more. Ground equipment was scattered everywhere, the bellies of the aircraft were open, and the cabin was lit, making for a ghostly line of blurry portholes that disappeared into the blowing snow. But as far as I could tell, the ramp was deserted. I couldn't find a single soul moving down there.

I felt a shove from behind and a sharp elbow to the kidney that flattened me up against the glass. I whipped around, but it was just a passenger who had himself been pushed. Someone else grabbed my arm and I jerked it back.

"Miss Shanahan." It was an agent, but it took a moment for me to register that it was JoAnn. She'd been working the night I'd arrived, and here she was again in the middle of another disaster, this one even worse. "I heard you were over here," she said, quickly. "I've got about a hundred people wanting to talk to the manager. Will you help us?"

The scene, I swore, was getting more chaotic as I stood there.

The noise level was rising with the tension, and her dark eyes pleaded for me to take charge again. And I wanted to. I wished more than anything that straightening out the operation was the biggest thing I had to worry about tonight. When I didn't respond immediately, the look on her face turned from desperate hope to cold cynicism. When I took off my Majestic badge and slipped it into the pocket of my jeans, she started to walk away.

"Wait a second." I put my hand on her shoulder. "Lenny Caseaux is in my office right now. Call him and ask him to come down. If he won't, start queuing up passengers to go see him in the administration offices. All right?"

As the idea sank in, she nodded with a sly smile. She could have fun with that one. More power to her.

The chaos upstairs had been almost unbearable, but the silence downstairs was worse. Somewhere at the far end of the long, deserted corridor, a door not properly latched slammed open and shut, and as I passed by open doorways and empty offices, I could hear the storm outside, the wind bellowing and the grit and debris raining against the windows.

Kevin was as beleaguered and overwhelmed as I'd ever seen him.

"Why did you send everyone home?" he asked without even looking up.

"What?"

His curly hair was limp from repeated comb-throughs with nervous fingers, and when he did make eye contact, he could barely focus on me. "Tell me what's going on, Kevin."

I waited as he answered a radio call from the irate captain on Gate forty-three who demanded to know the same thing.

Kevin calmed him down the best he could, telling him to sit tight.

"The assignment crew chief came in half an hour ago," he said, turning back to me, "to drop off his radio. He said he had authority from you to send everyone home immediately. He said you declared a weather emergency."

"I didn't do that, Kevin. It had to be Lenny." He answered the radio again, this time responding to JoAnn. I wanted to grab the mike from his hand and make him pay attention to me. Instead, I went to the closed-circuit TV monitors and checked every screen, but there was nothing to see in the near-whiteout conditions. By the time he'd finished his call, I'd projected all kinds of horrible scenes onto the white screens, and my temples were pounding with more possibilities.

"When's the last time you saw Little Pete?" I blurted.

"Little Pete was in here earlier," he said. "He was looking for Angelo, and that's another thing—"

"Angelo's still on the field?" He looked at me as if my eyes had popped out of my head, which they might have.

"He called about an hour ago from the mail dock. Why the devil did no one think to mention to me that Angelo was coming back?"

"Angelo has a radio, then."

"No. They were all out when he got here. He called on the phone, and I told him to go home. He said he'd just gotten here and he was staying. It's probably a good night for him to raid the freight house."

"Did you tell Little Pete where he was?"

"Of course I did. He's a crew chief. He was looking for a crew."

My hand went automatically to my radio. "Dan Fallacaro

from Alex Shanahan, do you read me? *Dan,* do you read?"

"He was looking for you, too."

"Who, Dan?"

"No, Danny called in about twenty-five minutes ago. Little Pete was looking for you."

I felt cold, frigid, as if the wall had disappeared and the storm had come inside, inside my body. "What—what did he say?"

"Danny? He said not to use the radios, that Little Pete has one, whatever the hell that means." The desk unit cackled with the angry voice of another captain. Kevin reached for the microphone to respond. Before he could, the captain spewed out a stream of expletives that would have made Dan blush. This time I did grab the microphone, told the captain to can it, then turned the radio off. Kevin stared at me, aghast.

"What did Little Pete say about me?"

"He said that he knew you were on the field and that he wanted to discuss his grievance with you. A few grievances, I think he said. And what do you think you're doing turning that radio down?"

I tried to stay calm by using the perspiration glinting off his high forehead as a focal point. "This is not going to make any sense, Kevin, but I need you to do something for me and it has to be right now and I don't have time for questions. Just listen."

His eyes drifted over to the now silent radio. "Are you sure you know what you're doing?"

"Get your phone book out. I need you to make some calls for me."

"Dan Fallacaro from Alex Shanahan, do you read me?" The ready room was abandoned, just as the locker room had been.

A desktop radio in the crew chiefs' office was on, blasting my calls, feeding back the heavy strain that was turning my voice hoarse. I knew Little Pete might be listening, but I needed to know how Dan knew that Little Pete had a radio.

"Dan, please respond. Over."

"This is McTavish to Shanahan. Do you read?"

"John McTavish? Is that you?" I suddenly felt a little better. John's solid presence had that effect on me, and I hoped that he was close by. "Where are you?"

"I just came up from Freight and I'm down at Gate Forty-five with my crew." I could barely hear him over the wind. "We're trying to get this 'ten out of here. What the hell is going on?"

"Have you seen Dan?"

"He's—"

The whine of an engine drowned him out

"Say again, John. I didn't hear you."

"My brother saw Danny heading toward the bag room."

"Inbound or outbound?"

"Outbound, I think. Terry says he was in a hurry. You want me to find him for you?"

I stood at the window looking out and trying to decide. "John, I need you to find Angelo."

I waited and got back nothing but static.

"Do you copy, John?"

"What about this airplane?"

"Forget about it. Take your crew and when you find him, don't let him out of your sight. Do you understand?"

"If that's what you want. McTavish out."

I went back through the locker room and swapped my light-weight jacket for a company-issued winter coat. Bulky and long, it enveloped me in the pungent odor of the owner's exertion. I put my cell phone and my beeper into the pockets, and my radio, too. I wasn't going to be able to hear it anyway. Then I zipped up, found the nearest door, and stepped outside.

All I could do for the first few seconds was huddle facing the building with my back to the wind. The cold went right through all my layers. I might as well have been standing there in a bathing suit. When I turned into the wind, a brutal blast blew my hood back, and I was sure that my hair had frozen in that instant. But I couldn't feel a thing because even though I was wearing gloves, my fingers were already numb. I could barely make them work to pull the hood back up, and then I had to keep one hand out to hold it in place. My eyes were watering. Ground equipment was everywhere. Vehicles were parked as if each driver had screeched to a halt and leapt out. Some of the bag carts sprouted wings when the wind lifted their plastic curtains out and up. It wouldn't have been surprising to see one of them take off.

I followed the most direct path to the bag room straight across the ramp and past the commuter gate, the same gate that Dan and I had seen on the videotape. When was that? I'd lost all sense of time. Another Beechcraft was parked there, and I wondered why no one had taxied it to a more sheltered spot. We'd be lucky if it was still in one piece tomorrow.

What was normally a two-minute walk seemed to take forever as I put my head down and trudged into wind. I stopped now and then to look around for Dan and to make sure I was still alone out there. Someone could have been right behind me and I wouldn't have heard him.

Stepping into the outbound bag room and out of the shrieking wind brought relative calm and deep silence. I stood inside the doorway, searching for my radio and trying to get some feeling back.

"Kevin, come in. Kevin Corrigan, come in please." It was hard to talk with frozen lips.

Bags were everywhere—on the piers, on the floor around the piers, and at the ends where they'd dumped off into huge, uneven piles that clogged the driveway all the way to the ramp-side wall. The bag belt had apparently run for a while before someone had figured out the crew had abandoned ship.

"This is Kevin. Go ahead."

"Do you have an update?"

"Partial."

"Call me on my cell phone."

"Roger."

It took seconds for him to call. "The troopers are busy," he said.

"*Busy?*"

"Everyone's occupied at the moment by an aircraft excursion."

"Whose?"

"TWA had one slide off the runway, so there's a bunch of them down there. Apparently the roads coming in and out of this place are a nightmare, so all the rest of them are on traffic control."

"*Traffic* control? Did you tell them what's going on?"

"I told them, but it's a pretty wild story, you have to admit."

I pushed a clump of half-frozen hair out of my eyes and would have gone to Plan B if I'd had one. I'd been counting on help from the troopers.

"They said they'd respond as soon as they could break a unit away. I'll keep calling them."

"What about Big Pete?"

"His wife doesn't know where he is, but she says he's got a beeper. She doesn't have the number, but Victor does, if you can believe that. I'm waiting for Vic to call me back."

"You haven't heard from anyone, have you?"

"Does Lenny count? He's upstairs hyperventilating. He sounds like he's going to have a heart attack."

"Good. Nothing from Dan?"

"No, but Johnny Mac called for you. Did you hear?"

"What did he say?"

"He talked to Terry and he says you should go to the other bag room—inbound."

"Goddammit." I was in the wrong bag room. I hung up, put up my hood, and went back out into the storm.

The door to the inbound bag room was a heavy steel slab, but it might as well have been balsa wood the way it whipsawed back and forth in the storm. I found the brick doorstop and used it. I wasn't sure that it would hold, but it was dark in there and dim light from the ramp was better than no light at all.

The heavy air trapped within the four concrete walls had smelled of plaster and paint and turpentine when I'd met Big Pete there. As I stepped through the doorway and around the drop cloth, the same one that had blocked my way last night, I couldn't smell anything. Hoping not to go any farther, I cleared away the anxiety that had lumped in my throat and called out, "Dan?"

The only response was the swishing of the tarps as the wind pushed in through the open door behind me.

To turn on the lights I had to find the fuse box, the one Big Pete had showed me. I wasn't sure I could remember where it was. I was sure that it was farther in than I wanted to go. I called again for Dan and listened. Nothing.

Damn.

I pushed the hood off my head—the better to sense someone coming at me from the side—then took a few edgy steps. I tried to feel left and right with my hands, but my fingers were numb from the cold. I used my palms to guide me, brushing them along the heavy drop cloths as I moved, trying to visualize the narrow corridor that they made. I could almost feel the darkness thickening around me as I moved deeper into the silence.

"*Dan,* are you *in* here?"

I leaned forward trying to hear, took a step, and landed on something slick. My heart thumped into my throat and stayed there as my foot skated out from under me. I made an awkward, spine-twisting grab for something, *anything* to keep me from going down, and for the longest moment I hung backward over the cement, clinging to a tarp that couldn't possibly hold my dead weight. Adrenaline kicked in as I pulled myself upright, driving my heartbeat into a wild, demented rhythm that made me dizzy. I leaned over, hands on my knees, and took a breath. Then I took another, and another, breathing deeply until the stars in front of my eyes had faded.

Even bent over with my head that much closer to the cement, it was too dark to see what I'd slipped on. But I had a sinking, sickening feeling that I already knew. I held on to the tarp as I slid my foot back and forth, trying to feel what it could be. I wanted to believe that it was oil or grease or some strange lubricant that only felt like blood, but the rational part of me wouldn't go for it.

I pushed aside the tarp I'd been squeezing, angling for some light. The second I moved it, it gave way from whatever had anchored it to the high ceiling. I slipped out of the way— barely—as it crashed into a heap. Everything in me said to bolt, but I was transfixed because without the tarp to block it, a slant of light had fallen across my feet. The light was dim, but enough to show that it wasn't a pool at all that I was standing in, but a thick stream that flowed along the floor under the drop cloths—a thick stream with a deep red hue.

This time my breath couldn't make it out of my chest. I kept sucking in air, fighting for oxygen, but nothing came out. I started creeping back, moving until I was backed up flat against a wall. There was so much blood. I stared at it, and all I could feel was a miserable, stinging pain in the tips of my fingers. They were starting to thaw out.

I reached down for my radio, held it close to my lips, and pressed the button, squeezing until I thought the housing would crack. "Dan Fallacaro, come in please." My tongue was too big and my mouth felt as if it were coated with chalk. "Dan, are you out there?"

Static.

I tipped my head back against the wall. This was the wall where Big Pete had found the fuse box, right? It *had* to be the same wall. If it wasn't, what else was I going to do? Slowly, I began to feel my way toward the place where I thought the box was. Once my knuckles scraped against the box's open door, it wasn't hard to find the heavy switches behind it. The first one I flipped turned on the overheads.

I closed my eyes, waited for them to adjust to the light, and opened them again. All around me were the blue tarps. I couldn't see farther than four feet in any direction. The dark stream at my feet had turned to vivid red. It was coming from the direction

of the bag belt. I turned myself that way, pushed aside the first
tarp, and made myself move as far as the next. The motion was
slow and forced, jerky and detached because I was afraid—terrified—to go forward.

"Dan, if you're out there, please respond." My breath vapor-
ized as I tried the radio again. The static seemed to go right
through me. I was coming apart inside. My eyes burned as I
pulled aside the next plastic curtain. I thought about Michelle.

"Please, Dan, *please.*"

I wondered what she looked like, if she had his green eyes.
I called again, I think I did, as I approached the last curtain,
and tears were coming because I knew he wasn't going to
answer. I lowered my head and squeezed my eyes shut. I hadn't
prayed to God in fifteen years, and I pictured him in his heaven
laughing at me as I tried to now.

*O my God, I am heartily sorry for having offended
Thee* . . .

I opened my eyes. My white running shoes were smeared
with blood. My head was pounding, about to explode. The
longer I stood there, the harder it was going to be.

*. . . and I detest all of my sins because of thy just punish-
ment* . . .

I put my hand on the edge of the drop cloth. It felt cold
and gritty.

*. . . but most of all because I have offended Thee, my
God* . . .

I moved it aside slowly. My eyes focused on the scene in
front of me and I had to turn away. And then I started to cry.

. . . who art all-good and deserving of all my love.

It wasn't Dan.

I covered my eyes with both hands and wept. It wasn't him.

Crying made my head hurt more and sobbing made it harder to breathe and I was boiling in that giant coat so I unzipped and let it slide down to the floor like the weight that had just slipped off my shoulders. The cool air that brushed against my damp skin felt like—*tasted* like—relief and I tried to pull it in in long, deep breaths. It wasn't him.

It was someone in a Majestic uniform. When the spasms stopped, I turned back to the gruesome sight. He was stomach down on the bag belt with his arms draped over either side. His left hand was in front of me, twisted back against the ground, palm up, and I felt some of the weight return because this man had long, slender fingers, fingers that I remembered from the coffee shop, ones that I had held in my own hand just a few hours ago. It was Angelo. I looked for his face, and when I saw it, bile came up the back of my throat, my stomach lurched in a dry heave, and I had to look away again. No wonder there was so much blood. His head was crushed, smashed between the belt and defective safety door that had dropped like a guillotine and cracked open his skull.

I felt it before I heard it. The pressure in the room shifted. The tarps snapped around me. The door slammed shut. By the time the hollow boom had finished caroming off the bare walls, I was on my knees, crouched, listening. The sound of the storm was gone. The tarps were still. It was perfectly quiet, and if I was really lucky, the door had slammed shut all by itself.

I crouched lower, trying to listen with my whole body. And then I heard him coming, not by the sound of his footsteps, but by the sound of his fingers sliding along the tarps. I tried not to panic even though I could barely move. Better to look around for a way out.

There was a door, the door to the terminal, and it wasn't

that far away. If I moved now, I could get there before he cleared the last drop cloth. But I had to go . . . *now.* I lunged out of the crouch, covering the distance to the door faster than I would have thought possible. I slammed my shoulder into the door—and it didn't move. It *had* to open. This door was not supposed to lock from this side. It was fire code. I pushed again and then again, but it was solid. I was trapped.

The sound of brushing fingers had stopped. He'd heard me. I imagined his head cocked just like mine, the two of us mirror images reacting to each other. Maybe I could make it to my radio and call for help. Maybe I should hide. Maybe—

"God*dammit,* who the hell is in here?"

If the door hadn't been there to catch me, I would have sunk all the way to the floor. My legs turned wobbly and all my bones seemed to dissolve as the tension flowed out. I closed my eyes and called out. "Dan?"

"Boss?"

I pushed toward him, and when I saw him I couldn't keep from wrapping my arms around his neck. Even though he was wet from the storm and ice covered his jacket, all I felt was his warm, living, breathing, completely intact body. He held me until I was ready to let go; then I stepped back so I could see his face. He looked so bewildered it made me laugh. "I thought you were dead."

"I'm not dead."

"Clearly. Where have you been?"

"Out looking for you. I found Angie and, Jesus, I nearly puked all over the place, and then I put my radio down somewhere and I couldn't remember where I'd left it—"

"We have to get out of here." I pushed him toward the door. "Why?"

"Because the door to the terminal is jammed and I think Little Pete did it and there's no other way out. Come on, come on, let's go."

He didn't budge. *"Dan . . ."*

"You can't go out there like that. Don't you have a coat?"

He was right. I went back for the coat, trying not to look at the body as I slipped it on. When we were both bundled up, we stood at the door preparing to go back out to the ramp and meet the storm's fury.

"Ready?" His voice was muted by the thick muffler twisted around his neck.

I pushed in close behind him and gave him a nudge. He leaned into the door, and the second it was open, the wind seemed to catch it and pull it out of his hands. The blast of air that hit me was so cold, it burned my eyes shut and I was blind. I heard a loud crack, my head snapped back, and I fell backward, landing hard on my tailbone. Something landed on my chest and stayed there, something heavy enough to crush the air out of my lungs. I couldn't breathe. I couldn't see. The bag room was spinning. I tried to throw off the weight.

"Jesus fucking Christ. Jesus Christ—"

The weight on my chest was Dan. He was on top of me trying to get up, and I was trying to get out from under him. My forehead was throbbing, the coat felt like a straitjacket, and I couldn't think straight. I couldn't think at all. The door slammed and it was quiet. Dan rolled off and I sat up. When my vision finally cleared, my brain unscrambled, and the fog lifted, I was staring up, way up, into the face of Little Pete Dwyer.

"You people," he said, shaking his head, "you goddamned people. You just couldn't leave it alone."

Chapter Forty-three

Dan made it to his feet before I did, then reached down and offered his hand to help me up. If he'd been a few inches shorter, he would have broken my nose when our heads collided. As it was, he'd cracked me pretty good in the forehead. I reached up and touched the throbbing, tender welt that was forming there.

Little Pete was like a mountain in front of the door. Dan was a foot and a half shorter and gave up at least fifty pounds to the guy, but that didn't faze him. "Get the fuck out of the way," he demanded.

The bigger man glanced down. "What are you gonna do if I don't? Write me up? Put a letter in my personnel file?"

He sounded calm, bemused even, but the scar above his eye was fresh and angry. He'd just come in from a raging storm, and I found it very disturbing that he wasn't wearing a coat. All he had on was his winter uniform over a T-shirt. The long sleeves were rolled up, the better to display those club-like forearms. He wasn't shivering. I didn't see any goose bumps. Whatever was burning inside him tonight seemed to be keeping him plenty warm—but it was making me shiver.

Dan made a sudden move toward the door. Little Pete raised one arm, putting his fingers on Dan's chest and stopping him cold. "Take a step back," he warned with a quiet resolve that I would have expected from his father but not from him. "Take a step back," he said, more slowly this time, "and give me your radio."

"Go fuck yourself, Junior."

I felt a warning tremor inside as Little Pete moved out of the doorway, pushing Dan in front of him. As he did, he turned slightly and my tremors escalated to a full-blown temblor. He had a gun. It was black and flat and stuffed down into the back of his pants. The handle was smooth, and though it looked very large to me, the weapon seemed like a toy against the broad expanse of his back.

"He doesn't have a radio," I said quickly, shifting to auto-rational. "Take mine." I fumbled the heavy unit from my pocket and offered it to him.

Little Pete was still staring at Dan. "I know he had a radio. I heard him using it."

"It's lost in here somewhere. We don't know where it is." I pushed my radio toward him again. "Here's mine."

When he turned to face me squarely, I saw the dark stains on the front of his shirt—dark and wet. While I was staring at the blood, Angelo's blood, he took the radio from my hand and, with what seemed like a casual flick of the wrist, sent it rocketing across the room where it exploded against the only cement wall that wasn't blocked by plastic. I stared at the ruined pieces on the ground, and then I was staring at the red stains on my own shoes. We both had Angelo's blood on us.

Dan's taunting broke the silence. "Big fucking man you are,

you jerkoff. You killed a *radio*. Old men, women, and radios. What's next? Puppies and kittens?"

I watched one of Little Pete's big hands curl into a fist and flex. Curl and flex. I'd heard all about this guy's towering temper, and I wondered how it showed itself. Did he do a long, slow boil and then explode? Or did it come in a blinding flash, an uncontrollable, indiscriminate blast that leveled everything in its path? I wished I knew what to expect from him.

"Cell phone," he said to me, still flexing and curling.

"What?"

He moved in close and leaned over me, close enough that I could smell his sweat, that I could feel his whispered breath like lighter fluid on my skin; it was worse than if he had touched me. "Don't make me say everything twice," he said, "I hate that."

I wanted to put both hands on his chest and shove him away. But I could feel something from him that was as strong as the stench of blood, tobacco, and alcohol. I looked again at the stains drying on his shirt. I looked into his eyes and saw the same dead-calm resolve that I had heard in his voice. This was a man who had nothing more to lose—and knew it.

I did what he asked.

"Good girl," he said as I handed over my flip phone. He admired the small device. "That's a nice one." Slipping it into his back pocket, he turned his attention to Dan. "Take off your jacket."

Dan, of course, didn't move, didn't even blink. Pete reached his hand up, and Dan slapped it away. I could feel drops of perspiration rolling down the underside of my arm as I watched the two men size each other up like a couple of junkyard dogs. Pete reached up again, quicker this time, and came away with one end of the muffler that was wrapped around Dan's neck.

It happened so fast.

"God, *don't*—" was all I could get out as I rushed toward Little Pete. He easily held me back with one arm as he used the other to jerk the muffler taut over Dan's head, lifting him almost completely off the ground. Dan's hands flew to his throat and he started to choke.

"Stay away," Pete barked at me, "or I'll break his neck."

I felt paralyzed. An image of Ellen flashed, Ellen hanging by the neck. It scared me so much, I stopped breathing, just as Dan must have. Little Pete was holding him up with one hand, flexing the long length of sinew and muscle that was his forearm. He was pumped up, turned on by his own physical dominance. But Dan looked as if he was dying. His face was blue, his eyes bulged, and he made a horrible, gasping sound.

"Let him down," I begged, "please, let him down."

He started to unwind the makeshift noose, one leisurely twist at a time. When Dan was free, he went to his knees, grabbing his throat with both hands.

Little Pete took the muffler and draped it around his own neck. "I can help you get that jacket off, too," he said, grinning, "but I might have to break your arms to do it."

I had no doubt that he would.

Dan was still bent and gasping, and I wondered if there was enough air in the room for both of us. I put my hand on his back. He looked up at me, his face red and eyes watering.

"Do what he says, Dan."

He struggled to his feet, and I helped him slip the jacket off. Little Pete stepped in, raised Dan's arms over his head, and gave him a thorough pat-down. Then he took the jacket from me.

"Where do you get one like that?" he asked as he searched the pockets. "You get it around here?"

"What?" I had no idea what he was asking about.

He shot me a warning glare. "I told you about making me ask twice about things."

"I'm sorry, I don't—"

"The phone. That little cell you got. Where'd you get it?"

"Denver," I said, struggling to stay in tune with whatever he was talking about. "I bought it in Denver before I came out here."

"What kind of range has it got?"

My jaw tightened. My legs were shaking so much, my knees were almost knocking. I didn't know the answer and I didn't know if that would upset him and I didn't know if I should make something up and—

"They don't let you have cell phones in prison, asshole." Dan had recovered his voice, just in time.

Having found nothing but a wallet, keys, and spare change in Dan's jacket, Little Pete dropped it on the floor, pulled a pack of cigarettes from his shirt pocket and, just as his father had last night, rolled a cigarette slowly between his thumb and forefinger before lighting up. He started to move as he smoked, brushing his shoulder along one of the tarps as he paced back and forth. I had a feeling he was trying to figure out what to do next. I wished Big Pete were here to tell him. God knows what he'd come up with on his own.

I unzipped my jacket. Had to. Even though it was cold in the bag room, I was so hot I was going to faint. Dan had both hands clamped against the back of his neck. With his head dropped back, I could see the long red striations beneath the collar of his shirt.

"Are you all right?" I asked him, keeping an eye on Little Pete.

He stared straight down at the floor, looking disgusted, ashamed even, and I remembered what his grandmother had drilled into him, that men were put on this earth to take care of women.

"Dan, he's bigger than both of us put together, he's been drinking, he has a gun, and I don't think he cares if he lives or dies tonight. Do you really think it's a good idea to provoke him?"

Still he didn't reply.

"The goal is to survive," I said. "If you don't care about yourself, do it for me. I don't want to be left alone with him." I looked into his eyes and didn't look away until he nodded.

Little Pete had his own radio clipped to his belt, and every once in a while it would report. He'd cock his ear and listen and check his watch. At one point I heard Kevin calling for me. We all did. It seemed to remind Little Pete that we weren't in a vacuum. After one last deep drag on the cigarette, he dropped it to the cement and stepped on it.

"You two quit your whispering over there," he said, checking his watch again. What was he waiting for?

"Go that way." He pointed toward the tarp-lined passageway, the one that led to the back where Angelo lay. I went first, then Dan. Pete followed. When I got to the opening around the bag belt, it was hard for me even to look at the corpse. Not Little Pete.

"Stand over there where I can watch the two of you, and don't do nothing stupid."

We moved to where he was pointing, to his left, and stood with our backs to the wall. We weren't far from the door to the terminal, the one he'd already blocked somehow.

He walked to the bag belt and bowed his head for a moment of reverential silence over the man he'd just murdered. "Fuckin' Angie," he said, his voice filled with moist emotion. Then he slipped one foot under Angelo's knee and, careful not to disturb anything, launched himself over the belt, over the body, and into the center of the racetrack. He went straight to the far side of the loop and came back with a box, one that rattled. He climbed back over and set the box on a painter's bucket. It was Myers's Rum, a whole case, probably up from the Caribbean duty free and most certainly swiped from some unsuspecting tourist. And it had already been opened. Just what this situation needed—booze.

"Compliments of Angie," he said as he uncorked one of the distinctive, flask-shaped bottles. Then he raised a toast to his victim. "Here's to you, old man." He tipped his head back, closed his eyes, and took a long pull. When he finished, he wiped the back of his hand across his mouth and addressed the corpse again. "You shoulda kept your big, rat-bastard mouth shut."

Dan could contain himself no longer. "What," he sneered, "it's *Angie's* fault you had to smash his skull in?"

"No, it ain't his fault." Little Pete whipped around and pointed the flask at Dan, and I cringed to think that it could just as easily be a gun as a bottle of rum. "It's your fault."

"*My* fault?"

"You're the one who called Theresa. You can't even handle the situation man to man. You gotta go and get his wife involved." Pete took another quick hit from the bottle. "He's laying there dead because of you."

"You are the biggest dumbfuck—"

"Hey," I said, mostly to Dan, "can we just calm down, please?"

Little Pete was smug. "He's just pissed off that I'm in charge tonight, that I'm the one calling the shots. Ain't that right, Danny boy?"

"The fact that you're still breathing pisses me off."

Little Pete laughed. "How about you?" he asked me. "Do you want to see me dead, too? Everybody else does."

"I don't want any of us to be dead, including you."

He nodded, smiling faintly. "She's smarter than you, Danny boy. She's smart enough to be scared of me. You should be scared of me, too."

"Why should I—"

"We're both scared of you," I said, cutting Dan off. "And you are in charge tonight. We both see that."

Little Pete narrowed his eyes, suspicious perhaps that someone actually agreed with him. "Let me ask you a question," he said, speaking to me now as if we were old friends. "Don't you think that a man's got a right to protect his name?"

"What name?" Dan snapped. "Dickhead?"

"I'm not talking to you." He turned back to me. "See, that's how I look at this whole thing. It's like self-defense. She knew what was going to happen if she didn't mind her own business. Once she was gonna do what she was gonna do, I didn't have any choice—but she did."

My jaw was trembling and my eyes were burning as I listened to him casually mention that he had killed Ellen. It was horrifying, and more so to hear his justification and to know that he believed it. This man was capable of anything.

"She made the choice herself," he said, "so she did kill herself. The bitch was warned."

It seemed important to him that I believe him, important that someone be on his side, and I'd decided that's what I would do. What I didn't count on was Dan's reaction. When he started toward Little Pete, I grabbed him. The muscle in his forearm was hard as bone.

"What do you think is going to happen here tonight, Pete?" I was talking just to talk, not saying anything, trying to stay in front of Dan and buy us some time.

"You think he even knows? Like this murdering bastard's got some kind of a plan. His pop's not around to do his thinking—"

"Shut the fuck up, asshole."

Yes, Dan, shut the fuck up. Little Pete was drinking more and thinking less. I could hear it in his loosening voice, see it in his dulled reactions, and every time he turned, the gun was there. Dan wasn't much better. His skin was drawn so tight, I thought I could see the muscles underneath, and he was literally vibrating with the effort to stand still. "You are such a worthless piece of crap," he yelled. "Nothing is ever your fault."

"Dan, *stop*." I was panicked because I knew he wouldn't. I knew exactly what was going to happen and I had no way to stop it.

"It's *my* fault you had to kill Angie. It's *Ellen's* fault you had to kill her. Let me ask you something. Whose fault was it that you killed those twenty-one people in the Beechcraft?"

I was almost afraid to look at Little Pete. He was standing perfectly still next to Angelo's body, about eight feet away from us. His long arms hung awkwardly at his sides. A quick lunge would have put him at Dan's throat in an instant. For a second I thought that's exactly what he would do, as he seemed to fight back the urge, squeezing the bottle in his hand instead. He squeezed it until it shook. I noticed that it was empty. When he noticed, he turned and walked to his rum stash, pretending he'd been headed over there anyway. He slipped the empty back in, pulled out another bottle, and uncorked it. "That was Dickie's fault," he said after slamming a third of the bottle back like Gatorade.

Dan threw up his arms. "Of *course*, it was Dickie's fault."

Little Pete turned. "The tape's going to show that. It's going to show that I didn't do it."

"How do you figure that?" I asked him, trying to keep him engaged.

"I gave Dickie the right load." Again he was trying hard to convince me—or himself. "He had the right numbers. He fucked it up when he gave them to the captain. It's all on the tape, which is why he had to hide it." Bottle in hand, he paced in a circle around his makeshift bar. "We never get what we need around here. Never enough manpower, equipment that's for shit, and then when something goes wrong, blame . . . blame the union." He was ticking off the points, but in a mechanical way, groping for something he used to know, was supposed to know. "Blame the union. I had . . . I had to try three tugs that night before I found one that worked. That's right. It took me an hour to find wands, I never did find a goddamn radio, and the tug that I did find was out of gas."

"Yeah, that's a good excuse. The simplest goddamn job in the world and you screw it up. You have to be the stupidest fucking moron on the face of the earth."

"I *gave* him the right numbers, and he never radioed them to the captain."

Dan pressed him. "How did you give him the numbers? You

just said you couldn't find a radio that night. And you never went into Operations."

Little Pete turned away and stood with his back to us, sucking down rum. The gun never looked more menacing. "You management fucks," he said quietly. "It was Dickie. It was Dickie, it was Dickie, it was fuckin' *Dickie Flynn*." He lowered his head and took a few deep breaths, and when he turned to face us, his eyes were dead. He seemed to have come to a decision. He never looked at Dan, and I had the terrifying feeling that Dan did not exist for him anymore. He touched the radio and checked his watch again. "Fuck this shit," he said as he reached around for the gun. "Let's go."

"Wait." I blurted it out, then just kept talking. "You never saw the tape, did you, Pete? You never would have. And you can't remember, right? All you know is what your father told you to say." I looked at him, at his face, and tried to understand what he was thinking. "You're waiting for Lenny. That's the plan. Lenny's supposed to find the tape and bring it to you. That's why you keep checking your watch, right?"

"It's all going to come out," he said, "after all these years."

"Listen to me. The tape will not vindicate you. And the other stuff that's with it will prove that Lenny was part of it. If he finds that package, he will destroy it."

He shook his head.

"He has to," I said. "Think this through, Pete. Lenny's not going to incriminate himself."

He rubbed his forehead with a hand that was shaking, the same hand that had reached for the gun and never made it.

"We can take you to it. The tape," I said. "We found it tonight and we hid it, and if you hurry up you can get to it before Lenny does."

He stared at me and I tried to look trustworthy, so sincere he couldn't question my motives. I felt that he wanted to believe me, that he wanted to believe that someone was telling him the truth. He began to nod, and for the moment I could breathe again. Barely. At least if we could get outside, we had a chance. We could lose him in the storm, maybe, or the troopers might show up. We had a chance.

Dan was behind me. I turned to look at him, and he looked back in a way that gave me a sliver of confidence that he would calm down, too.

"Do you drink?" Pete asked, rummaging through the box of rum.

Neither one of us responded until he turned to look at me.

"Do I *drink*?" I was stunned by the question, but more so by the fact that he was about to uncork his third bottle. I figured he was going to offer me some, which I took as a good sign. "Yes, I drink."

"I hate a woman who drinks. She was drunk that night," he said, bleary-eyed and talking almost to himself. "She smelled like alcohol. I hate a bitch who drinks." He took the bottle out and stuffed it into his pocket. When he looked at Dan, he was not so bleary-eyed, and when I saw the smile I knew before he said anything that it was all over. "How did she smell when you found her?"

Dan was past me before I had any chance of stopping him. I saw Little Pete's arm swing around toward the gun.

"Nooooo!" I lunged for his arm, but he whipped around and smashed me in the head with his elbow. Everything flashed white and the bag room tipped like a big, rolling ship. I went all the way to the floor. I saw Dan rush Little Pete—he seemed to be moving very slowly. He went for his knees and Little Pete

went down, they both did, falling backward into the open box of rum. The entire case crashed to the ground, rum spilled out onto the floor, and some of the bottles that didn't break shot across the concrete like hockey pucks.

I tried to get up. Everything was going too fast. The two men stayed down for what seemed like a matter of seconds. Dan had landed on top, but then he was on the ground on his back. Little Pete had tossed him aside like a newspaper. Dan came back. Little Pete shoved him again, and this time he bounced off the wall and cracked his shoulder.

Little Pete was reaching to his back, and the thought that any second the gun was going to come out broke through the cotton in my head. But then he fell to his hands and knees, crawling around on the floor. He'd lost it. He'd lost his gun.

My hand found one of the bottles on the floor and I grabbed it. Little Pete was still scrambling for the gun, not paying attention to me.

When he saw me coming, he ducked his head and put his shoulder down. It took both hands to hook him around the neck and keep from flipping over his back. I had to drop the bottle. He reared back like a grizzly bear trying to throw me off, but I held on and found the muffler that was still draped around his neck. I grabbed it, closed my eyes, and squeezed as tight as I could. He gripped my hands and tried to pry me loose. My face was pressed against the back of his head, and the smell of him was in my nose, in my mouth, my head—the sweat and the rum and whatever he put on his hair to make it spike. And blood. He smelled like the blood that was on his shirt. I held on. He tried to shake me off and couldn't. He reached back and tried to pull me forward over his head, and I felt his big, grubby hands groping my back, trying to grab hold. I wrapped my legs around his waist. Then he tried to stand up. I knew once he was up on those powerful legs, he would win.

I heard an ear-splitting yell, felt a brutal jolt, and then all three of us were tumbling through one of the tarps and into a wall. The tarp came down over us like some kind of a jungle trap. In the dark, arms and legs went flying everywhere, nobody landing any punches, nobody having any room.

The tarp came off and we broke apart.

I was on my butt, palms flat to the floor, my back against the wall. My jacket was gone and everything in my body felt broken or ripped. Dan was doubled over holding his gut, coughing up blood and trying to breathe. Little Pete was disappearing behind one of the tarps on his hands and knees, and I knew he would find the gun. I looked up at the wall over my head, then pushed myself up, crawling up by my shoulder blades. My legs didn't want to hold me, and when I made it to the fuse box I couldn't see the switches—something was in my eyes—but I could feel them. I flipped every one. If it was on, I turned it off; if it was off, I turned it on. The lights went out and the room went totally, blessedly dark. I wanted to sink back down to the floor and curl up into a ball on my side.

And then the alarm sounded—three long blasts like the dive signal on a submarine. Yellow-tinted warning lights in the ceiling flashed, making a weird strobe-like effect. A familiar rumble started, stopped, then started again as the bag belt tried to engage, then turned into a train wreck of calamitous noises—high-pitched whining and grinding gears and screeching metal. Angelo's body was mucking up the bag belt works.

I wiped my eyes and looked for Dan. When I got to where he'd been, he was gone.

Under the clanking and grinding, I heard them. The sound
of their scuffling was disorienting, suffocating under the flashing lights, and I felt as if something was about to fall on me
or into me and I'd never see it coming. I ripped down the tarp
that was in my way. As I stumbled toward the two men, I ripped
them all down, leaving a trail of plastic dunes in my wake.
When I pulled down the last one, I saw Little Pete straightening up and stepping back. It looked like an old black-and-
white movie, herky-jerky in the flickering light. Even the
grinding belt went silent as he raised his arm and pointed the
gun at Dan. But Dan was looking at me.

The shot was so loud, like an explosion. I drove into Little
Pete from behind, buckling his knees. He fell over backward
on top of me, and some part of me saw Dan go down.

Then I was moving, slipping, stumbling toward the ramp,
toward help. It was a straight shot to the door with the tarps
down. Just as my hand hit the knob, he was right there. He
grabbed my ankle and I fell through the door, onto the ramp
and into the storm. My chin hit the hardpacked ice and snow,
jarring every tooth in my head. The door had slammed open,
bounced against the wall, and slapped back against my elbow,
but I couldn't feel it. All I could feel was his grip, like an iron
manacle, as he tried to pull me back in. I clamped onto the
doorjamb with both hands as he gave my leg a vicious yank,
lifting me off the ground and nearly ripping both shoulders
from their sockets. It was harder and harder to hold on with
fingers that were cold and numb. I was slipping, gasping, the
door was flapping, and right in front of my nose was the brick
. . . *the brick*. The doorstop brick was *there*. Rough and hard
and heavy and within my reach. But I had to let go of the
doorjamb . . . only one chance to do it right . . . try to pull

myself forward . . . aching arms, then let go . . .

He pulled me inside, but when I rolled onto my back, I had
the brick in my hands. I aimed for the top of his skull, but it
was so heavy I couldn't wield it fast enough and he had time
to flinch. I got him on the side of the head, yet it was enough
that he let go and stumbled back and I was up and running.
Cold air and wet snow blasted me. I was slipping, barely staying on my feet, moving across the ramp. I turned to look and
he was coming, god*damn* him, he was coming with the gun in
his hand, mouth open, screaming. But I couldn't hear above
the roaring.

The Beechcraft was still there. When he raised the gun, I
ran to the far side, putting the aircraft between us. I stayed
behind the wing, well back of the engines because—*because
they were running.* This airplane was going to move. I leaned
down to peer under the belly, to find where he was. He was
crouched on the other side, one hand down on the ramp for
balance, staring back at me. For a split second we watched each
other. The wind was still blowing, the snow was coming down,
the noise was deafening, and he was just staring at me.

Then I saw a light, two headlamps and flashing lights coming
toward us. I broke forward toward the nose but slipped and
fell. From the ground, I saw that he was standing, saw his legs
as he circled toward the front of the aircraft. I tried to get up
and fell again—this time, I thought, for good because he was
rounding the nose cone, coming straight at me.

Behind me the engines revved. The aircraft was about to
roll. Every instinct pushed me away, out of its path, but I made
myself go backward, crawl on sore elbows, back toward the
engine and under the wing. Just as Little Pete cleared the nose
cone, the faint whine of a siren began to break through. He

heard it, too, because as he came toward me, he smiled and shook his head as if to say, "Too late." He stopped. He raised the gun. The aircraft began to move, and all I could think was that it was so loud I wasn't even going to hear the sound of the shot that would kill me.

I rolled into a ball on my side and covered my ears as the captain made a sharp right turn to taxi out. I saw Little Pete's boots as he tried to step aside. He had no time to scream. As the right wing passed over me, I closed my eyes, but even with my hands over my ears, I could still hear the sickening thump of a propeller interrupted.

And then it was quiet. Everything stopped except the falling snow. It had stopped blowing. The captain killed the engines, and the noise vacuum was filled by the sound of the sirens. For the longest time I didn't move. I just lay there listening. When I opened my eyes, they wouldn't focus. And they hurt. My elbows hurt, and my legs and my back and the side of my head.

I squinted down past my knees and saw a fireman leaning over something, reaching down to something toward the nose of the Beech. The second fireman to arrive looked down and turned away, gloved hand at his mouth. I turned on my back as someone arrived with a blanket and helped me sit up. The captain appeared, hatless in the snow. He bent over the body, looking where they were looking, put both hands on his head.

A fireman was asking me questions. Was I hurt? Could I walk? Did I need help? What happened? I watched his hand coming toward me and mumbled something that might not have been coherent. He helped me to my feet and wrapped the blanket around me. I was shivering and I couldn't stop. My chin stung, and blood was running down the outside of my throat and maybe the inside because I could taste it. I smelled like rum. He tried to help me over to his rig, but I pulled him instead toward the bag room, dragging him with me and yelling for someone to call the EMTs. The whole jagged scene began to replay in my mind, especially the part where the lights went out and the gun went off and I remembered, didn't want to remember, but I remembered seeing Dan fall. I put my hands over my eyes. I was trying to sort it out, and when I looked up, he was there. He was standing in the doorway, gripping the doorjamb, one arm limp at his side.

The fireman went for a stretcher. When I got close enough, Dan tilted his head back and looked at me through the blood running into his eyes. "Did you kill that cocksucker?"

"The Beechcraft killed him."

"Good."

I put his arm around my neck, but I wasn't too stable myself. "Did he shoot you?"

"I don't think so."

"Your shoulder is bleeding. Let's wait for a stretcher."

"Fuck no. I want to make sure that motherfucker is dead."

"He's very dead, Dan. Take my word for it."

The EMTs arrived and took us both to the truck. They were from the firehouse on the field, and Dan knew all of them, called them by name. He refused to go to the hospital, not unless they insisted, which they did.

Someone was pushing through the circle of firefighters and EMTs orbiting around the body. I heard the noise and looked out. They tried to block him, but nothing was going to stop Big Pete from getting to his son. He sank to his knees, leaned over, and tried to pull Little Pete into his arms. When they wouldn't let him, he dropped his head back, opened his mouth, and let out a long, terrible scream that in the snow and dying wind sounded otherworldly, not even human. He did it again. And again. Then he was silent, motionless, bent over the body. Someone put a hand on his shoulder. He reached down to touch his son one last time, then stood on shaky legs. He searched the crowd that had formed, searched and searched. When he found me, he didn't move and neither did I as we stared at each other. I didn't hear the people yelling, machinery moving, and sirens blasting. I felt the snow on my face as he wiped the tears from his. I pulled the blanket around me, trying to stop shaking and watched as they led him away. He looked small and old and not so scary anymore. Not at all in control.

I couldn't stop the shaking. I smelled like rum and I couldn't stop shaking.

The coarse blanket scratched the back of my neck as I adjusted it around my shoulders. I had passed the first hours of the morning in the company of Massachusetts state troopers—and this blanket, the one the firefighter had given me on the ramp. Without thinking, I'd walked out wearing it, which turned out to be a good thing since it was now covering the blood stains on my shirt.

Last night's events had thrown the operation out of whack, to say the least, and our concourse had the feel of leftovers, of all the ugly business left unfinished. It was still dark in the predawn hours, and the overhead fluorescents seemed to throw an unusually harsh light. Dunkin' Donuts napkins and pieces of the *Boston Herald* were everywhere. A few passengers with no place better to go were sacked out on the floor. Some were stuffed into the unyielding chairs in the departure lounges, chairs that weren't comfortable for sitting, never mind sleeping.

One of our gate agents must have taken pity on these poor souls. Some of them were draped with those deep purple swatches of polyester that passed for blankets onboard our aircraft.

I still had lingering shivers, violent aftershocks that came over me, mostly when I thought about how things could have turned out last night. And my nose wouldn't stop running. Reaching into my pocket for a tissue, I felt something flat and hard. The instant I touched it, I remembered what it was—the tiny cassette that had fallen from the ceiling of my office. I stood in the middle of the concourse cradling it in the palm of my hand, the missing tape from Ellen's answering machine. I stared at it. A clear plastic case with two miniature reels and a length of skinny black tape. That's all it was. It could wait. I started to stuff it back into my pocket. True, there would be no way to listen to it at my hotel—no answering machine— and if I left now it might have to wait for a while. Even if I wanted to listen to it, I'd have to go back to my office yet again, and I didn't want to do that. I didn't want to have to stare again at the gaping hole in the ceiling through which Lenny had apparently pulled Dickie Flynn's package of evidence. I looked at the tape. It was such a little tape. How important could it be? What more could we possibly need to know about the dirty business that Ellen had involved herself—and me— in? Could I even stand another revelation?

I closed my hand around the cassette and started walking, slowly at first, then faster, and the faster I walked the angrier I felt. Pretty soon I was fuming, cursing the name of everyone who had made my recent life such a hell on earth. As far as I was concerned, being sliced up by a propeller was too good a fate for Little Pete Dwyer. And Big Pete, he deserved to lose his son that way for being such a cold, arrogant prick. And goddamned Lenny, the sleazy bastard, I hoped he rotted in jail for everything he'd done and maybe some stuff he hadn't. Even the thought of Dan made me simmer, just the idea that he had almost gotten himself killed right in front of me. All I wanted was a hot shower, hot food, and cool sheets. Every last cell in my body was screaming for it. But no. I had to reach into my pocket and pull out the last detail. The world's biggest question mark. The mother of all loose ends. God damn Ellen, too, for making this mess to begin with, and for leaving it here for me to deal with. I stood in the doorway of my office and wondered why couldn't she just leave me alone.

Chapter Forty-four

The sun was coming up. It slanted through the venetian blinds in much the same way it had on the day I'd first walked into this office. The same bright ribbons of light lay across the old desk. Molly's answering machine sat atop the glass slab, in the center of the carved Nor'easter logo. The logo reminded me of what Molly had said that first day about why the desk had been hidden in Boston. "No one would ever look for anything good here," she'd said. I pressed the Play Message button and listened one more time to Ellen's final gift from beyond the grave. Molly was right. There was nothing good here.

I should go, I kept thinking. I should get up and take this tape to the proper authorities. But all I did was sit and stare and watch the sun come up. I couldn't seem to do much else.

The computer monitor flickered. Another report was up. I turned and looked, squinting at the bright screen to keep the characters from fuzzing together. When I saw what it said—same as the last one—the dull pain behind my right eye surged again, this time through the center of my skull. I pushed at it with the heel of my hand, but the throbbing wasn't going to stop unless my heart stopped beating. I punched Print Screen and slumped back in my chair.

"It's good to see you in one piece."

The voice, unmistakable, came from the doorway behind me. I hadn't heard him come in, but that's how Bill Scanlon always came into and out of my life—without warning and on his terms. I swiveled around to see him, too tired to be startled, too numb to have felt his presence.

He leaned against the doorjamb with his leather briefcase in one hand and that familiar blue cashmere coat in the other. His suit hung perfectly from his lean frame, a deep charcoal gray that brought out the fine strains of silver in this thick black hair. Impeccable, as always.

When I didn't answer, he stepped quietly into the office and put his coat and briefcase on the floor and closed the door. "Are you all right?"

I wasn't all right, might never be again. The look on my face must have told him as much because he started to come to me. More than anything I wanted him to. I wanted to put my face against his chest and feel the steady comfort of his breathing, to feel strong arms against my back, keeping me from flying to pieces. But before he could round the desk, I shook my head and nodded toward the windows. Someone might see. He stopped, but his eyes seemed to be asking, "Are you sure?" When I nodded again, he moved to the chair across from mine and sat down. "Tell me," he said, "I want every detail."

I couldn't find my voice. Instead, when he sat, I stood. Rising from my chair, my spine creaked and my muscles ached. Moving across the floor, I felt like a bent old woman that had lived too long. I felt him watching me as I stared out between the wide

slats of the blinds, and I knew that he would sit quietly and
wait for me, wait as long as I wanted.

The snow that had been so cruel last night was brilliant this
morning. Lit by the early morning sun, it was a glistening carpet
that rolled from the far side of the runways all the way down
to the bay. Beneath my window, rampers were filtering back
to start the first shift, and the scene was beginning to look
normal again. The only reminder of last night was the sweet,
sticky odor that kept drifting up from the dried rum stains on
my shirt. That and the answering machine on my desk.

"It would be easier if you tell me what you already know,"
I said finally, without turning around. If I didn't have to look
into his eyes, I could function at least marginally.

"Actually, I already know quite a lot. I was on the phone
all night from the airplane. I know that this Pete Dwyer person,
the son, he killed a man, the one you were trying to meet with.
Angelo, right?"

"Yes."

"Then he tried to kill you and Fallacaro. There was an alter-
cation of some kind and he ended up hanging from a propeller.
He's dead and you're a hero. Is that about the sum of it?"

It was hard to get the words out, hard to keep from crying.
"Keep going."

I heard him stirring behind me, pictured him crossing his
legs and leaning forward, elbows on the arms of the chair and
hands clasped in front of him. He would be uncomfortable not
asking all the questions, not directing the flow of the conversation. He didn't like not being in charge.

"Lenny is in custody," he went on, "for reasons I can't figure
out. There seems to be some indication that you were right,
that this Little Pete did kill Ellen, but there's still no evidence

to prove it and we don't know why he would do such a thing. As it turns out, with him gone, we might never know."

The tears started to come, flowing down the tracks worn into my face from a night filled with crying. I put my head down and covered my eyes with my hand. When I heard him stand, my breath caught in my throat. When I heard him move toward me, I told myself to step aside, to move away, to get out of reach before it was too late. But I felt so exposed. I felt as if my very skin had been stripped away and that even the air hurt where it touched me. I needed comfort so badly, and I knew that if I didn't turn from him *right now*, I might never turn away. Still, I didn't move. Couldn't. But I said the one thing I knew would make him stop. "The police have the package." Then I closed my eyes and waited.

My computer hummed quietly on my desk. A shout came up from the ramp, a man's voice muffled by the heavy glass window. Bill said nothing. I wiped my eyes and turned to face him. "Lenny tried to destroy the evidence," I said. "He had it. He took it down to the ramp last night and tried to burn it in a trash barrel."

His face was perfectly calm, placid even. When I tried to swallow, the front of my throat stuck to the back and it was hard to keep going. But I did. "The storm was so bad that he couldn't get it to burn. One of my crew chiefs caught him."

The thought of John McTavish with his big hand around Lenny's wrist while his brother Terry pried the envelope loose gave me one tiny moment of satisfaction in an ocean of pain.

"They saved the evidence, Bill. The confession, the video— the police have it all."

There was the slightest hesitation before a smile spread across his face. "That's great," he said. "So there *was* a package.

You were right about that, too." He probably would have fooled someone else. But I heard the forced enthusiasm, felt him straining under the veneer of graciousness. I knew with a certainty that was like a knife through my heart that the warm regard in his brown eyes, focused so intently on me right now, was false. He started moving casually away, tracing the edge of the desk with his index finger as he backed toward the window. "What was in this rescued package?"

"Don't make me tell you what you already know."

He smiled uncertainly. "I don't know what you mean."

I went to my credenza, where the schedules I had printed were lying in the tray. I lifted the first one out, laid it on the desk, and pushed it across the glass-top surface, a distance that seemed like miles. "That's your travel schedule for the past twelve months." He looked down and read it, then looked at me as if to say, "So what?"

I placed a second sheet next to the first, the list of Ellen's secret destinations, and tried to still the shuddering in my chest. "This is Ellen's. You were in the same city with her fifteen times out of a possible fifteen different occasions." I pulled the wrinkled page from my back pocket and smoothed it on the desk. Spots appeared like raindrops as my tears fell onto the page, bleeding into the paper, smearing the black ink as I read Ellen's note one more time.

> . . . I feel myself going under again, and the only thing that keeps my head above water is the motion of reaching up for him. And I can't let go. Because when I'm with him, I exist. Without him, I'm afraid I'll disappear. Disappear to a place where God can't save me and I can't save myself.

I laid it on the desk in front of him. "She wrote that about you."

He never looked at the second schedule. He never looked at Ellen's note. He looked at me. He fixed his gaze on me and wouldn't let go. "What are you trying to say, Alex?"

"I don't have to say anything, Bill." I reached across the desk to the answering machine and started the tape.

The voices had the hollow, tinny quality of a cheap answering machine, but there was no mistaking Ellen's voice with that light Southern accent, still so unexpected to me. The tape was queued up right where I'd left it, at the point where Ellen was talking, her words tumbling out in a torrent of anguish and pain.

"Crescent Consulting. I know you remember this. We paid them hundreds of thousands of dollars. I signed the invoices. Crescent Con—"

"Crescent Consulting. I get it." Bill's voice was a stark contrast—calm, rational, a little irritated underneath the clicking and popping of the static. He must have been in his car. *"What about it?"*

"It was a sham. Nothing more than a bank account that Lenny used for kickbacks. You knew about this, Bill. You had to have known."

"Let's not talk about this right now. I'm on a cell phone."

"We're talking about this now." She sounded panicked, almost hysterical. *"Don't you dare hang up on me."*

"All right, all right. Why would you say something like that?"

"Because of the special signature authority. All that garbage about how much you trusted me. You set me up. The only reason you had me request a higher limit was so that you

*wouldn't have to sign those invoices. Every single invoice from
Crescent you forwarded to me. Every one. You knew, Bill"*—
she was fighting back tears—*"and I can't believe you did this
to me."*

Finally, she couldn't hold on anymore, and her voice dissolved
into sobs, mighty, rolling sobs. As soon as one stopped, another
one started, and I knew that they had come from someplace deep
because when I had cried with her this morning the first time I'd
heard this tape, the pain had come out of my whole body, through
every part of me. It sounded like—felt like—a thousand years'
worth of holding in.

When she'd cried herself out, there was silence, and then
Bill's voice, gentle and soothing. *"I thought it was better if you
didn't know."*

*"Do you think anyone is going to believe that I didn't
know?"*

*"Ellen, you didn't do anything wrong. I'm the one who
screwed up, and I'll protect you."*

*"Tell me what you did. Tell me what you've gotten me
involved in."*

*"Back when we were working on the Nor'easter deal, Lenny
came to me with this idea that we wouldn't have to wait for
the vote . . . that he had some way of buying off the IBG—"*

*"He didn't just buy the contract vote, Bill. He used the
money to cover up this crash, this—the real cause of an aircraft
accident, for God's sake. We gave him that money, Majestic
did, you and me, and my name is all over—"* She stopped as
if she still couldn't believe the words that were coming out of
her mouth. *"That Nor'easter Beechcraft that went down in
1995 . . . I've got this surveillance tape, this . . . these documents that Dickie Flynn had put away in the ceiling. It wasn't*

the pilots. It wasn't their fault. It was Little Pete Dwyer, and Dickie Flynn, and Lenny— "

"*Do you have this package?*"

"It's right here in my hands, and I don't . . . I think I need to take it to someone. I can't—Oh, God, Bill, don't ask me—"

"*No, you're right, we need to get it to the right people. Let me just think for a minute.*"

"*Tell me . . . one thing,*" Ellen said, pleading. "*Tell me that you didn't know about this crash, that it was only this IBG contract business that you knew about.*"

He didn't hesitate. "*I knew absolutely nothing about it. I swear to you. And if Lenny did what you're saying he did, I'll have his ass.*"

"Thank God, Bill. Thank God."

"*We have to take this package forward. All I'm going to ask is that you hold off for a day or so until I can get out there. I want to sit down with you. I want . . . it's important to me that I get a chance to explain it to you. I want you to under-stand. And I want you to help me figure out what to do, Ellen. We can get through this together.*"

There was no response.

"*Ellen, listen to me. Don't think about what you're going to say to me next. Just listen. Are you listening?*"

I was listening, and my knees felt weak, knowing what was coming next.

"*I am in love with you, Ellen. I am hopelessly, desperately, pathetically in love with you, and I don't want to live my life without you in it. I'm not going to let anything happen to you, Ellen. Don't you know that?*"

I turned off the tape.

My hands started to shake and tears streamed down my

face. I had listened to that bit of tape over and over. There was nothing on that tape that I hadn't already heard. But listening to it with him, watching his face as he listened to himself deceiving Ellen, using the same line on her that he had used on me, was almost more than I could bear. Any expression, any reaction at all from him might have given me at least a seed of doubt, if that's what I'd wanted. But when he looked up at me, his face was stone. When he looked at me, I felt him measuring my resolve, wondering what it would take to get me to back down, and calculating his risk if I wouldn't. That was the moment when I knew that it was true—that it *could* be true. All of it.

"It was you," I said, backing away, taking one step, then another until I was up against the opposite wall, as far away from him as I could be in the cramped office. "You were Lenny's partner on the inside, not Ellen. You were the one who stole the money, and you used her to shield yourself, you bastard." The words came pouring out, searing the back of my throat and making my eyes burn. "You knew about the crash from the beginning. You knew that she would eventually figure it out, and you knew that she would take that evidence forward. You were the one who had Ellen killed, not Lenny. It was you."

His only reaction was to look down and touch Ellen's note, brushing his fingertips across her words, thinking, perhaps, that he could make them disappear. A tiny smile formed on his lips. "Ellen always did have a flair for the dramatic."

I felt my body begin to collapse in on itself, felt the four walls disappear and the world drop away until it was just the two of us standing in a barren wasteland, barren as far as I could see. And I knew that I was looking at the life that I'd made for myself, and when I looked again, I was alone, desperately alone.

He walked over to the window and stood with his hands deep in his pockets, rocking up and down on the balls of his feet. "That must have been some storm last night. It had mostly blown itself out by the time we landed."

I watched him, stared at the side of his face as he squinted into the bright sun.

"Have you seen the video?" he asked, in a tone that can only be described as jaunty.

"Last night," I whispered, leaning against the wall for support. "I saw it last night."

"I've never seen it. I imagine that it is quite extraordinary. I suppose I'll see it now. Everyone will, won't they?"

When he turned toward me, the light was coming from behind him and I couldn't see his face, but his manner was as smooth as ever and I knew that he was grinning. I could hear it in his voice. His tone wasn't flippant exactly, just light, and very, very confident.

It pissed me off.

"Why do you suppose she left it here that night?"

"Maybe she got smart and decided she didn't trust you after all."

"I have some ideas about that video," he said, "Would you like to hear them?"

"No." I pushed myself away from the wall and slowly made my way back to my desk. When I got there, I leaned over it, using both arms to support myself.

"What did you tell the authorities?" he asked quietly.

"I told them what I knew at the time."

"Which was what?"

"That on the night of March 15, 1995, Little Pete Dwyer worked Flight 1704 under the influence of alcohol, and his negligence caused that plane to go down. I told them that the incident had been recorded on a surveillance tape from beginning to end and that, as a part of a cover-up, Dickie Flynn, Big Pete Dwyer, and Lenny Caseaux stole that tape and altered official company documents. I told them that it was my belief that Dickie and another man, Angelo DiBiasi, were paid ten thousand dollars each to keep quiet about what they knew. I told them that Lenny Caseaux would have done anything to keep the sale of Nor'easter on track so that he could cash out his stock and become a rich man."

I stopped for a breath, but my lungs wouldn't fill. He was closer now and I could see his face, could almost see the wheels turning as he listened, sifting the facts, and pulling out what he needed.

"What else?"

"I told them that the money for these payoffs and others was embezzled from Majestic Airlines, that Lenny had an accomplice working inside, and that that person was Ellen Shepard."

I paused again as I remembered talking to the troopers just hours ago, how sure I had been about Ellen, how wrong I had been.

"She threatened Lenny with exposure," I said, my voice fading, "and he had her killed. Little Pete killed her." I sat down in my chair, suddenly exhausted. "That's what I told them."

"This is why Lenny is in custody."

"Lenny is in custody because his name is all over Dickie Flynn's package of evidence, along with both Dwyers, Dickie himself, and Angelo." The late Angelo. Another pang of guilt. The thought of him lying on that bag belt came back to me, and I knew that he was dead, too, because of Bill, that Bill had tipped Lenny off with information that I had given him, just as he must have told him about John McTavish. I'd told him enough that he'd figured out that John was the source. I'd blamed Dan, but I had been the leak.

"Did they believe you?"

"Why wouldn't they? I was very convincing."

"I'm sure you were. Is that all you're going to tell them?"

I plucked his travel schedule off the desk and held it up. "Are you asking me if I am going to tell them that it was not Lenny who arranged Ellen's murder? That you were the one she was expecting the night that she died? That you sent Little Pete in your place to murder her?"

His neck stiffened. "I never even met this Little Pete character."

"Of course not. That would be stupid, and we know that you're not stupid." I dropped the page back on the desk. "That's what Lenny was there for, to do all the dirty work. You gave him your key to Ellen's house. You gave him the security code, and you made sure that Ellen would be home that night waiting for you. Then you booked yourself on a flight to Europe and waited for news that she was dead."

"It sounds rather elegant," he mused, "when you put it all together like that, clearly thought out."

"You're saying it wasn't?"

He regarded me with a wistful smile, looking disappointed that I might think ill of him. "Do you know how much the stock price has appreciated since I started running this airline? Three hundred and fifty percent. Three *hundred* and fifty percent, and it was the Nor'easter deal that put us over the top. That deal was the last missing piece, and do you want to know the irony?"

He slipped onto the corner of the desk and rested there, half standing, half sitting. He picked up a dish of paper clips and seemed to find it fascinating. "All this business here in Boston, none of it made any difference. Looking back, the Nor'easter deal was going to happen anyway. Lenny takes credit for the contract failing, but it's my bet the thing would have sunk under its own weight anyway. It was all for nothing." He took one of the clips out and studied it, turning it over in his hand.

He dropped the clip into the bowl, put the bowl on the desk, and went back to the window, where he stood with his arms crossed. "A strange thing happens when you operate for any length of time at this level and particularly if you achieve any measure of success, which I have. You start to feel that you can't do anything wrong, that whatever you do is right just because you want to do it." He turned slightly. "Silly, isn't it? And extravagantly arrogant. But you need to be to get where I am." He waited a beat, then came back to the desk and stood across from me. "I convinced myself that I was the only one who could save this company. And Nor'easter. At one time it wasn't clear that the contract would fail, and I thought it best not to risk it. What was a couple of hundred thousand dollars against all the jobs I saved? The tremendous wealth I created?"

"What about Ellen?"

He sniffed, and with studied nonchalance glanced down and straightened the crease in his slacks. "You never plan for people to get hurt. That's one of the variables you can't predict. But things get . . . distorted. Once you're in, you're in. When a problem comes up, the only question that matters is, can you think your way around it? Are you smart enough?" He shrugged. "Ellen was a problem. She was going to be, anyway."

I stared at him. His tone was absolutely flat. We could have been analyzing a business deal gone bad.

"It's unfortunate," he said, "but Ellen was pulled into this whole affair by that drunken bastard Dickie Flynn, the self-serving son of a bitch." He looked at me and laughed as if he were relating a funny story that he was sure I would find amusing also. "Can you imagine saving that tape the way he did, then dumping it on poor Ellen? And Lenny, trying to cover up a damn plane crash with all those nitwits involved. The thing was flawed right from the beginning."

"You would have been smarter about it, no doubt."

"I never would have tried to cover up negligence. They told me after the fact, after it was too late, but in that situation you have to go public in a big way because there are too many people involved. And the risk if you're exposed is too great. You have to deal with it head-on, diffuse the risk, take away all the leverage. That's why this videocassette is so powerful for us. Do you see?"

"No."

"That video will be run over and over on every newscast, every news magazine, every cheap tabloid reality program. You can't buy that kind of exposure. So you ask yourself, how do you use that? You make an immediate disclosure, at which point you announce a very well-thought-out program of complete cooperation with the authorities, comprehensive safety reviews, and enhanced operating procedures. You prove to everyone that the people responsible have been dealt with, sternly, and—this is very important—you meet with the families of the victims face-to-face. In fact, you'd like to do that before you go public. And every time you open your mouth to talk about it, you tie the *crash* to Nor'easter and the *response* to Majestic. Pretty soon all people will remember is Majestic's great response." He smiled again. "Most people, Alex, are waiting to be told what to think."

"You already have a plan."

"I always have a plan."

"And where am I in this plan?"

"Don't you know?" He looked at me with those hotter-than-the-sun eyes beneath those long, lush eyelashes. Then he began to move around to my side of the desk. I stood up, backed away, and kept going until I felt the wall again against my shoulder blades.

"Don't I know what? That you are *hope*lessly, *des*perately, *pathe*tically in love with me?"

He seemed to be floating toward me, moving without walking, immune to the natural forces that tethered the rest of us to this earth. I could have moved away, but there was really no place to go. He was going to keep coming until he'd had a chance to play his final hand.

"I told you what I thought you needed to hear, that's all. I should have told you the truth."

The smell of rum surrounded me like a seedy cloud, but as he moved toward me, ever so slowly, his scent was stronger.

"What is the truth?"

"We're good together. That's the only truth there is, Alex, the only one that matters." He was very close now, and I could feel his whisper as much as I could hear it. "You wanted me the other night as much as I wanted you, and nothing that's

happened since has changed that. I want you right now. I want
you so bad I can taste it. And you want me, too."

I needed to be angry, and I was. I needed to hate him, and
I did. But I could also feel his breath in my hair. I could feel
the heat through his clean cotton shirt, feel the flush beneath
my own clothes. I could hear his breathing grow shallow, more
ragged as he got closer.

"As far as the police are concerned," he said, "what you told
them is exactly the way it happened. Lenny paid the kickbacks
on the contract with money he and Ellen stole, he took even
more money to cover up the crash, Ellen was so remorseful
that she killed herself, and I'm the guy who can make the whole
thing make sense. All you have to do is give me that little tape."

"What about Lenny? He knows everything."

"Lenny's not going to discuss his role or anyone else's in
an alleged murder. There's still no proof that she didn't kill
herself. Besides, he's going to need lawyers, and I can get him
the best. Lenny will be all right. But to really make this work,
I need you."

He leaned in closer, and now there wasn't much that separated us except for the smell of the rum. My back arched against
just the idea of his hands on me, his long, graceful fingers touching me in ways that no one ever had before or since. No matter
what else was happening, no matter what he had done or what
I might do, there was something between us and it was never
going away. And there was truth in that connection, if only in
that its existence could not be denied. Maybe he was right.
Maybe that was the only truth when you got right down to it,
and maybe it was foolish to try to fight it. Maybe that's what
Ellen had tried to say in her note, that life without that connection was no life at all.

*I think of how my life would be without him, and the thought
of letting go scares me to death.*

He bent his head down as if to nuzzle my neck. He didn't
touch me, but still I felt the rush of blood through my veins,
a powerful surge fueled by a heart beating so wildly, it threatened to lift me off the floor. I tried to breathe, but when I did,
I breathed him in. I closed my eyes, fighting for control, and
tried to remember the rest of the passage, hoping for some
kind of a message from Ellen, some kind of safety in her words.

When I think about life without him, she'd said . . . *my lungs
fill up with something cold and heavy, and I feel myself going
under and . . . and what? And the only thing that keeps my
head above water is the motion of reaching up for him . . .
without him I'll disappear to a place where God can't save me
and I . . . can't . . . save . . . myself.*

I opened my eyes and scanned the room, searching for the
note. I wanted to see it, to see that it was still there. It was on
the desk where I'd left it. I can't save myself is what she'd said.
"But she could."

"What?"

I hadn't even realized I'd said it out loud. "She could have
saved herself."

When I looked at him, he was wearing that smile, the one
that changed him, the one that changed me. "Ellen didn't need
you, she didn't need Dan, and she didn't need God to save her.
She could have saved herself. All she needed was to know that,
and she wouldn't have disappeared. You couldn't have made
her disappear if she'd known that, if she'd felt it. She couldn't
feel it."

He stared down into my face and I stared back.

"But I do."

He took a step away and then another, and I watched him back off, fascinated by what I was seeing—finally seeing. It was a reverse metamorphosis. The smile disappeared, and then the charm, the smooth self-confidence, the easy authority, all began to fall away. He was like a butterfly wrapping himself back into a cocoon, turning from awe-inspiring and breathtaking to small and tight and ugly. Ugly but, I knew, authentic.

By the time I'd completely exhaled, he was across the room, around the desk, and sitting in my chair. When he spoke again, even his voice sounded different. "You should give me the tape," he said, but with no inflection, conserving energy, saving the charade for some fool who would still buy it. He tapped the answering machine with one finger. "There's nothing on here to incriminate me beyond that silly contract business, and I can make even that questionable. Why put yourself through it?"

I was still catching my breath, but I was breathing. I was taking in buckets of air, filling my lungs, feeling the oxygen flowing through me. I felt lighter, almost buoyant. I felt as if I could fly. "Put *myself* through it?"

"I know you've thought about the consequences of making accusations against me, "The Man Who Saved the Airline Business." The hint of a smile appeared. "Who's going to believe you, a lonely woman with no life beyond her career who slept with the boss and couldn't take it when she got dumped? And, of course, one of the most effective defenses is to attack the accuser—that would be you—and the victim, Ellen." He was sitting up straight now, gears grinding, getting into it. "Ellen had plenty of secrets, some you don't even know about. My defense team will dig them up. My PR team will get them out there. What about you, Alex? Is there anything about you that you wouldn't like to see in the left-hand column of the *Wall Street Journal*? Because that's where this will all be played out. My team is going to set upon you like a pack of wild dogs. It won't be pleasant."

He looked at me expectantly, but I wasn't biting. I was too worn out and besides, there was nothing personal in this. He didn't really hate me, any more than he had loved me. The curveball I'd just thrown him was nothing more than a twist in the road, another detour, and he was having fun with it.

"The best opportunities come from disaster," I said.

"What?"

"That's what you told me once."

He smiled openly, genuinely. "That's right. That's exactly right. I think this just might qualify as a disaster. Certainly for you it does." He stood up, stretched, and meandered to the other side of the desk. "I'll have to resign, which is inconvenient. But there's always a demand for people like me. Hell"— he reached down for his coat and briefcase—"depending on how all this plays out, it might make me more marketable. It depends on how we spin it. Now that I think about it, you have more to lose than I do."

"You can't take anything else away from me, Bill."

"What about your job? I know you. You'd be lost without it. You love this business, this company—"

"No, I loved you. And I quit."

I'd said it so fast, I wasn't sure the words had actually come out, so I said it again, slowly this time, and tried to feel it. "I quit, Bill. I resign, effective immediately." It felt good. It felt right.

He stared at me as I rounded the desk and reclaimed my seat, the one he'd just vacated. It was still warm. I flipped open the trapdoor on the answering machine and made sure the tape was still in there. He laughed. "You thought I took it? Where's the challenge in that?"

"Just checking," I said.

He put one arm through his coat, then the other, then paused to straighten his tie as if he were about to go onstage. Maybe he was. To him, all the world was his stage. "So you'll be available to come and work for me again. That's nice to know. It's tough to find good people."

"No one's going to work for you. You're going to go to jail."

"I'm not going to jail. When you're dealing with the legal system, the smartest one wins. I'm smarter than they are, and I still think there's a possibility you won't turn in that tape. I'm not counting on it, of course, I'm just working the probability into the equation. I'm liking my chances better and better."

"I don't think you're getting out of this one, Bill. I don't care how smart you are, or how good your lawyers are. But if by chance you do, it won't be because of me."

He turned to go, opened the door and stopped. "It's good to hear you say that you loved me. I'm not sure that you ever did."

"Love you?"

"No, say it." He smiled. "I know that you loved me."

I leaned back in my chair and watched him walk away, through the reception area and out the door. Then I listened to his footsteps as he made his way down the corridor. Ellen's note was still on the desk. I pulled it in front of me and read it again.

. . . I think about my life before him, about the work that filled my days and the ghosts that walked the night with me,

and I feel myself going under and the only thing that keeps my head above water is the motion of reaching up for him. And I can't let go.

You should have let go, Ellen. I wish you had let go.

I put the note in one pocket and the tape in the other. Bill was wrong about me in one respect. I was going to turn this tape in. But he was right about me, too, as he had been so many times before. I had loved him.

But I had also let go.

Parts Unknown

Prologue

The sky might have looked like this in prehistoric times. Before cities, before streetlights, before electricity, there was only the pale moon and distant stars to illuminate the night. On a moonless night, there was nothing. Only darkness so thick you could reach out and lay the back of your hand against it.

But in prehistoric times there would have been nothing like the mammoth airliner that lies shattered across the side of the mountain. From a very great distance, the gleaming wreckage would look like a constellation of stars clustered around the ancient peak. Closer in, it would look more like a bright carpet spread across the rolling ridges and spilling down the steep incline to where the last piece of the aircraft, torn and gutted, had lurched to a stop.

After a while, the mountain regains its equilibrium, enfolding the wrecked airplane in a deep, gentle silence that is interrupted only by the crackling of the burning parts and the small, intermittent explosions muffled within the twisted remains. Every now and then a tree catches fire and ignites like a blowtorch.

A large section of fuselage teeters on a ridge. With the agonized shriek of metal on metal, it rolls and settles on its side. No one hears. All two hundred and three souls on board are gone, their corpses strewn across the rough terrain with the struts and panels, books and tray tables, wires, seats, and insulation.

1

Investigators will find the captain's watch still on his wrist, a Piaget given to him by his wife and four children to honor his twenty-five years as a pilot. It stopped at 2047, thirty-four seconds after the aircraft had dropped from the radar, fifteen seconds after one air traffic controller had turned to the other and said, "We lost them . . ."

At 2209, a distant sound from the valley below begins as a soft swishing, grows clearer, more clipped, then thunderous as helicopters explode from behind the ridge, bursting through the black smoke like two projectiles spit from a volcano. They swoop toward the wreckage with engines roaring, blades hacking—all identifying markings concealed. Anyone looking would not be able to see, behind the powerful floodlights, the heavy equipment, the special extraction tools, the masks that the men wear to work around the dead.

One helicopter passes quickly over the holocaust, flying as low as the heat and the flames allow. The second pilot steers his ship in search of level ground. The sooner he lands, the sooner he can get men and equipment to the scene.

Every second is critical. They have to be gone before the rescuers arrive.

Chapter One

The padded mailer was nine by twelve inches, barely adequate to hold its chunky contents. ALEX SHANAHAN was written across the front in blue ink, but the rest of my address was in black, as if the sender had filled it in at a later date. I stared at the handwriting for a long time because I knew I'd seen it before. I couldn't place it.

According to the postmark, the envelope had been mailed two weeks earlier from East Boston, Massachusetts. For a good portion of that time it had been sitting at the post office with postage due, which explained why it had taken almost two weeks to get from one end of town to the other. The idea of calling the police crossed my mind. Logan Airport was in East Boston, and anything mailed to me from Logan Airport should have been checked by the bomb squad. I decided against it. I hadn't worked there in a long time, and besides, whatever was in the package had the stiff outline and solid feel of a heavy book, not an incendiary device.

I went looking for a kitchen knife to use as a letter opener, forgetting that everything from my kitchen, indeed my entire apartment, was wrapped, packed, and stacked neatly against the wall in cardboard boxes. I found my keys and used one to slit open the end of the mystery package.

Whatever was in there was wedged in tightly, and I couldn't get a firm grip anyway because the contents came complete with a greasy film that rubbed off on

3

my fingers. I picked up the envelope and studied the problem. The only way I was getting it out was by performing surgery. Using the key again, I made rough incisions along two of the three remaining edges and created a flap, which, when I folded it back, provided a clear view of what was inside.

It was a stack of pages, torn and smudged, attached to a single thick cover that was smeared with the black grease and soot that had come off on my fingers. From the orientation of the pages, it appeared to be the back cover. That meant I had to flip it over if I had any hope of figuring out what I had.

There was no point in risking my security deposit two days before I moved out, so I found a section of the day's newspaper to spread across the countertop. I used the Money & Investing section of the *Wall Street Journal*—superfluous to someone who is completely broke. Using the envelope like a hot pad, I lifted the damaged book and nudged it over until it flipped onto the newspaper. I was right. The front cover was a victim of whatever trauma had befallen this book. The pages had drip-dried into stiff waves of pulp, some sticking together, and whatever had soaked them had bled the ink. Most of the pages were gone forever, but then there were some that displayed entries that were remarkably legible. The first one I could read was a captain's report of a seat in coach that wouldn't recline. Beside it was the mechanic's entry—the date he'd fixed the seat and his signature.

I knew what this was.

The second was a write-up on a fuel indicator light that refused to go off, and the one after that on a landing gear problem, each duly noted by the cockpit crew, and each duly repaired by the maintenance team on the ground.

Someone had sent me an aircraft logbook, or the remains of one, the kind I used to see routinely in the cockpits of Majestic airplanes when I worked at Logan. No front cover meant no logo or aircraft number, so I couldn't tell which airline it belonged to, but I knew what all airline people knew—logbooks are never supposed to be separated from their ships. The information they carry on their pages is irreplaceable. It's the entire history of an aircraft, recorded event by event by the pilots who have flown it and the mechanics who have fixed it.

Logbooks are as unique to an aircraft as fingerprints, as much a part of the plane as the flaps or the wings or the seats. Standing alone in an empty apartment staring at this one, I had to admit to feeling a chilly whisper of airline superstition. A logbook without an aircraft is like a wallet without a person. You just know the separation is not intentional. To know that an airplane was flying around without its logbook, to see the book in this condition, felt like bad luck.

When I picked up the envelope and turned it over, a wad of tissue paper dislodged from one corner and dropped to the counter. It was stained black on one side where it had been flattened under the weight of the logbook. But it wasn't completely flat, and something had to be inside to make tissue paper thud. After I'd unpeeled a few of the layers, I began to feel it, a nodule in the center that had some weight to it. I pulled back the last of the tissue to reveal a sight that was at least as stunning as it was bewildering.

5

It was a diamond ring, but in the same way the ceiling of the Sistine Chapel is a painting. It was thick and heavy—a complex latticework of gold studded with what must have been fifteen small diamonds. In the middle of the setting was a massive oval diamond that rested like a dazzling egg atop an intricate diamond-encrusted bird's nest.

I spread one of the tissue paper sheets flat on the counter. BURDINES was printed in light brown ink and repeated over and over in diagonal rows across the sheet. I knew Burdines. I remembered it from a trip my family had made to Miami when I was a kid. We'd arrived in the middle of a cold snap dressed for the beach. My mother had marched us all over to the nearest department store—Burdines—for sweat suits and heavy socks.

The ring felt heavy in my hand. There was no way this piece came from Burdines, or any other department store. It felt old and unique, as if it had been custom designed for the hand of a woman who was much loved and treasured, and I had the sense that it was real, even though it made no sense that it would be real. No one sends something that valuable via U.S. mail in a wad of tissue paper.

I checked inside the band for an inscription. The absence of one felt like karmic permission to do what I had been dying to do since I'd unwrapped it. I slipped it on my own finger. There was no wedding band to remove first, and no pesky engagement ring to get in the way. Jewelry wasn't something I bought for myself, so the coast was clear for it to slide right on. It was too baroque for my taste, and *so* big. I didn't know how anyone could wear it without feeling a constant,

6

unsettling imbalance, or without consistently smacking it into things. Wearing it gave me the same queasy sense of dislocation I had felt about the book—it belonged somewhere else.

I slipped the ring off and went back to the logbook. Toward the back was a place where the pages were less clumped together, almost as if there was a bookmark. I turned to the place. There was a bookmark, a single piece of white paper folded in half and stuck in between two soiled, damaged pages. My fingers were still black, so I went to the sink and washed my hands. Then I pulled up a dish pack to sit on and opened the note. When I read it, I felt myself growing cold from the inside out, starting with the marrow in my bones. A single line was written across the pristine page. This time I recognized the handwriting, but even if I hadn't, the note was signed.

I'll call you.
John

The logbook and the diamond ring had been sent to me by a dead man.

Chapter Two

The house was silent. Most houses are in the middle of the day. But the stillness in the McTavish home went beyond the quiet respite between the morning hours when a family disperses, and the evening hours when they drift back together again. There was a towering void in this house, a desperate emptiness made more achingly obvious by the raft of family photos that filled the walls and the shelves. I had felt it the week before when I'd been there for the wake, and I felt it now as I watched Mae stare at the diamond ring her husband . . . her late husband had sent me, holding it close to her face with a hand that trembled in short, subtle bursts.

"It can't be real," she said. "This isn't real." Her voice was solid, but her rhythms seemed speeded up and her speech pattern on fast-forward. She was talking about the ring, but she could just as easily have been talking about the sudden and horrible turn her life had just taken. "Is it real?"

"I took it to a jewelry store this morning," I said. "It's worth almost twenty-five thousand dollars."

"No. No, there's no way. This wasn't his. Where would John get something like this?"

"I was hoping you could tell me. You've never seen it before?"

She shook her head and handed the ring back. I set it back in the tissue paper nest on the low coffee table at our knees. Next to it was the lump of a logbook that

had proved at least as baffling to her. She started picking at the nubby upholstery of her durable plaid couch,
as if there were something encrusted there she had to
remove. "The police are saying it was drug related."

"Drug related?"

With an abruptness that startled me, she stood up
and, as if I wasn't even there, resumed the task I had
obviously interrupted by knocking on her door. With
brittle efficiency, she moved about the small den gathering her children's toys from the floor. A plastic dump
truck, odd-shaped wooden puzzle pieces, two Barbie
dolls—one without any Barbie clothes. She scooped
them all up with a jerky, kinetic intensity that made my
own springs tighten.

"I thought it was a mugging, Mae."

"Nothing was stolen from him."

"Okay, but where do they get drugs?"

"They said he was in Florida trying to pull off some
kind of a drug buy. Can you believe that? My John,
Saint John the Pure, in on a dope deal. If they knew
him, they could never think that."

I had to agree. If anyone had asked me—which they
hadn't—to list all possible motives for John's murder, no
matter how long that list, drugs would have been at the
bottom. His contempt for drug dealers and drug abusers
was well known. He had actually turned in one of his
union brothers at the airport for smuggling dope, an act
of conscience that had not endeared him to the other
union brothers. Even the ones that had no use for drugs
had less tolerance for rats.

"Is that it? It's not a mugging so it must be drugs?"

"I think they have more they're not telling us. And

he also called here early Tuesday morning and told Terry to lock all the doors and not to let us out of his sight until he got home on Tuesday."

"John did?" I didn't know if I was having trouble following her because she was moving and talking so fast, or because it was such astonishing information. As far as I had known, John's death had been a tragic and random murder in a city known for that sort of thing. "Did he tell him why he was so worried?"

"He said he would explain when he got back. The police say that's all part of the drug thing. That the people he was supposedly involved with have been known to threaten families."

She stood in the middle of the room. With all the toys put away, she looked anxious and panicky, desperate for something to do with her hands. Then a bright thought seemed to break through. "I'll make coffee." She took off, straightening the rug and scooping the remote control from the floor as she left the room.

Before I left the den, I took one last look at the gallery of photos—the living, loving chronicle of what had been this family's life in progress—and searched out John's face. In a few of the pictures, mostly the posed shots, he wore the serious expression I had known. Thick-necked and determined, he had always looked to me like an Irish laborer from the early nineteen hundreds who could have just as easily raised the steel towers for the Williamsburg Bridge as loaded cargo for Majestic Airlines.

But in most of the pictures, especially in the candid shots with his children, John was a different man. The weight of responsibility that had so often hardened his face was gone. The guarded expression he wore on the ramp was nowhere to be seen, and I saw in those photos, maybe for the first time, a man who was open and confident and comfortable in his role as husband, father, teacher, and protector. I saw the man he'd wanted his children to see.

I walked into the kitchen and the first thing I saw grabbed hold of my heart and squeezed. The kitchen table was set with three Scooby-Doo placemats. They still had toast crumbs and jelly stuck on them.

Mae was moving purposefully from cabinet to counter and back to the cabinet again, where she stopped long enough to take down two cups. "How do you take your coffee?"

"I'll take tea, if you have it. How are your kids doing?"

"Kids are strong. I look at them and I wish I could be that strong. I'm jealous sometimes because there are three of them. They have each other."

"What about Terry? Is he helping you?"

"Terry is not doing well. He was just getting over the accident. This I don't think he'll ever get over. He needs to get help, and he won't. He worries me."

Just what she needed. Three small children to worry about and John's kid brother, too.

I dropped my backpack on one of the kitchen chairs. The non-Scooby end of the table was stacked high with papers and folders and files. One of the piles had slipped over, and the top few pages were in imminent danger of jelly stains. My intention had not been to riffle through Mae's private papers, but the one on top caught my attention. It was a photocopy of a Majestic nonrevenue pass coupon, the kind employees use when they travel.

11

This one had the date and the destination filled in—March 5, flight 888, BOS to MIA. And it had John's signature. It was a copy of the coupon John had used to go on his doomed trip to Florida. The return trip information was blank.

Poking out beneath that was a receipt from a hotel in Miami called Harmony House Suites. It was also dated March 5. Then a pad of lined paper with a quarter of the pages wrapped over the top. The page left on top was filled with a task list. Some items were crossed out. Most weren't. The tasks still left to do included *Thank you notes for funeral, copies of death certificate to insurance co.s, change beneficiaries.* Everything related to the funeral was crossed off. There was a separate category titled MR AND MRS—REMOVE JOHN'S NAME. Underneath was listed *bank accounts, parish directory, safety deposit box, retirement accounts.* All the details and loose ends left over when one life that is inextricably entwined with so many others is abruptly ripped out by the roots. Toward the bottom was a shorter list. *Rental car. Cell phone. Harmony House Suites*, which was the name of the Florida hotel on the receipt.

I started to put the pad back on the pile when a couple of loose papers fell out.

One was a flight manifest for flight 887 from Miami to Boston for March 6, what I assumed would have been John's return flight home. It showed the names of all passengers on board, along with standbys and crew. John's name was there, but there was no seat assigned, which meant he had called reservations to put his name in the standby queue, but hadn't made the flight.

I looked for Mae. She was at the sink washing the

cups we hadn't used yet. "Mae, John was listed on a flight to come home?"

"Flight 887 on Tuesday morning," she said. "He called Monday night and said he'd be home on Tuesday, but we didn't hear from him. At first I wasn't worried because those flights out of Miami are so full you can get stranded for days waiting for a seat and I was sure he was going to walk through the door any minute and when he didn't I thought . . . I was sure he'd driven over to see if he could get one out of Fort Lauderdale. But he never called. Tuesday afternoon I was getting antsy. Tuesday night came and went and no John and I was really freaking out on Wednesday morning when still we hadn't heard and then Wednesday afternoon they called and told me he was dead."

The sound, sharp and sudden, cracked the quiet in the kitchen. Crockery against porcelain. It was loud and unexpected and made my heart shudder. I looked up to find Mae staring at me, and for a second I thought it was because I'd been prying, digging through her papers. But then I realized she was waiting for me to offer some adjustment, some correction to her recounting of events that would have changed the way it had all come out. When I couldn't, she turned back to the sink.

The cups hadn't broken. They rolled around and knocked against each other under the stream of running water. "He believed it was always on him to put things right," she said. "He shouldn't have even been down there. Some people just aren't worth the effort."

"Is that why he went down there? To put something right?"

"I am so angry with him." The muscles across her

13

back tensed. "I hate him for going down there. I hate that he left me here to raise these three babies all by myself." She dropped her head and reached up to touch her forehead with damp, shaking fingers. Her tears began to drop into the sink. "I hate him." I could barely hear her the last time she said it. She sounded as though she was afraid I would.

The steam began to billow up from the hot water that was still running. I turned it off, then reached down for the cups in the sink. For a moment we both held them. Her skin was red and warm from the hot water and I thought she might have actually burned herself. If she had, she showed no signs of feeling it.

Then she let go. "I don't really want any coffee," she said. "Do you?"

"No."

She walked to the table but could not bring herself to sit without stacking the placemats—crumbs and all— and taking them to the sink. When she returned, she started straightening the papers.

"This information about John's trip," I said, pulling out a chair, "is it for the police?"

"The cops don't want to know any more than they already know. No, it's for me." She sat, finally, with her hands in her lap and one leg pulled up underneath her in the chair. "I get these ideas. Just questions I want answered."

"Like what?"

"Like what was so important that he had to go see Bobby Avidor."

"Who's he?"

"He's an old . . . I won't call him a friend because

14

he's not. He's an acquaintance from the neighborhood. We all knew him. He's a maintenance supervisor at the airport in Miami. That's who John went to see."

"A maintenance supervisor for Majestic?"

She nodded as she reached for one of the stacks of papers. "I've got his phone number here somewhere. Not that it's doing me any good. He won't return my calls. Not Terry's either."

I watched her flip back through the used pages of the lined pad, searching for the number. "Do the police know about him?"

"They said they already talked to him. He wasn't any help."

"Why won't he call you back?"

"I don't know. Because he's one of those people who is just not worth it that John wouldn't give up on." After she'd flipped all the way back to the front of the pad with no luck, she pitched it onto the middle of the stack where it sat with its top pages curling from the bottom. She stared after it. "I'm not any good at this. I never have any time. I think I just want to know—"

We both heard the commotion at the same time. The back door opened and Terry McTavish was there, leaning on his cane, and trying to squeeze through without letting the family's big yellow Lab into the house.

"Turner, get back," he snapped. "You can't come in here."

Turner whined and pushed his big nose into the tight opening, maneuvering for leverage. He kept trying until Terry's cane fell through the door and onto the kitchen floor with a loud *thwack*. It startled the pooch for an instant, long enough for Terry to box him out with his

15

good knee and slip through. He slammed the door shut from the inside, then stood unsteadily, catching his breath, braced by one hand still on the doorknob.

The sight of him, of what he had become, still shocked and disturbed me. Before the motorcycle accident, Terry McTavish had been a smaller, more compact version of his older brother—sturdy, solid, and one of the few men who could match John's torrid pace on the ramp. Now, with one leg shortened and twisted like a dead branch, the most he could do was count stock at a local hardware store. It had been a stunning physical transformation. And when he turned toward me and I saw his face, I knew what Mae had said was also true. What the Harley hadn't crushed in him, his brother's murder had. His eyes looked dead.

The cane had fallen at my feet. I picked it up and offered it to him. "It's good to see you again, Terry."

He barely acknowledged me. Mae reached out for his hand as he wobbled into her radius. "I thought you were working."

"They didn't have enough gimp work today."

She reached her other hand up and held his in both of hers. "Stay here and talk to us. Miss Shanahan has something to show you."

He pulled away. "I'm going upstairs."

"It has to do with John," she said. "I think you'll want to see it."

"I don't want to see anything having to do with Johnny, Mae. I told you that." His tone seemed flat and lifeless, like the expression in his eyes. But there was something else. Hard to grasp, but there. A hard, thin thread of warning.

16

Mae either didn't hear it or chose to ignore it. "Sit down and talk with us for a few minutes."

He turned slowly around his cane. "Why can't you let him rest in peace?"

She blinked up at him. "Because I don't think John was in Florida doing a drug deal, Terry. And I know he won't rest in peace as long as anyone thinks he was. Especially his children."

Her purpose may not have been to provoke him, but that last thought acted on him like an electric cattle prod. His face flushed and the words spewed out as if shot from a fire hose. "It doesn't matter what we think. When are you going to figure that out? If the cops say he was selling dope, then that's what it's going to be because *they* are the ones in charge and *they* can say and do whatever they want and there's nothing we can do about it because I'm a gimp who can't even drive a car, and you've got three kids to take care of, and we don't have any *goddamned money*." He paused to take a couple of rasping breaths and his gaze landed on me. "That's what it means to be in charge, doesn't it, Miss Shanahan?"

It wasn't a question. It was an accusation—one that caught me totally off guard. I wouldn't have called Terry a company man when he'd worked for me, but he had valued his job, he had respected the work, and he had never been anything but polite and cordial to me.

"I don't know what you mean, Terry."

"Everything bad that's happened to this family started when Johnny decided to help you. Once he took your side, everything went to shit."

"Terry"—Mae's tone was sharp—"stop this."

"We're working people, Mae. All we've got is the

17

union. All we ever had was the union. She cost us their support, and after they turned on us, we never had a chance."

Mae let out a long impatient sigh, and I knew they were touching on a subject that was not new. "John was his own man and he made his own decisions. If you don't like what he did, blame him. And stop blaming me for not giving up."

"What does that mean?"

"It means you could be helping me, Terry. You could be making phone calls, talking to the detectives. There might be people up here in Boston you could talk to. You could be doing something besides sitting upstairs in the dark with the curtains closed."

"You are never going to figure out what happened in Florida from the kitchen table in Chelsea."

"I don't accept that." She swallowed hard. "And John never would have given up on you."

Terry paled. His face showed such a naked display of rage and betrayal and disappointment and grief that I felt like an intruder just looking at him. They were slashing deeper and deeper, and I knew these were two people who cared for each other and who had both cared for John. There was so much pain there, in both of them, but it was the fear that I felt more. The room was so full of it, it was hard to breathe. It made me scared. Scared that life could turn out like this for anyone. I wanted to do something. I wanted to fix it.

Terry's arm came up and the cane came up and I thought toward me so I scrambled out of the chair, almost knocking it backward. With one vicious slash, he swept everything that was on the table onto the floor.

18

Mae looked as if he'd just shattered her best wineglasses. On purpose. And then I thought she might take his cane from him and beat him over the head. But in the end, she slumped back in her chair and just looked tired.

"We will never know what happened to Johnny, Mae. We will *never* know. And all your little phone calls and notes and questions are not going to change it. We're fucked. Johnny's fucked. That's just the way it is."

Then he went upstairs, presumably to sit in the dark with the curtains closed. We heard every awkward step as he climbed the stairs. It took him a long time.

The papers were scattered all around me. I got down on my knees and started to gather them.

"Don't do that," she said, with a voice like lead. "I'll get them later."

I ignored her because that was what she was supposed to say, and kneeled down to gather the pages because that's what I wanted to do. Eventually, she crawled down next to me and started to help.

"I'm sorry," she said. "He's not himself."

"I know that." Not even close. People had always commented on how much alike the brothers had been. But what I had always enjoyed most about Terry were the differences. Terry had always had a sweeter disposition than John, a lighter hold on life, and a more spontaneous core. It was a contrast I had attributed to the difference between being the protector and the protected. And now Terry's protector was gone.

"He says he wouldn't have been laid off if the union had been looking out for him."

"Layoffs go by seniority. There's nothing the union could have done for him."

19

"He knows that. He's just looking for someone to blame for how he feels right now. In his mind, if he had never been laid off, he never would have lost his benefits, which means we wouldn't have had to pay all his medical bills, which means we would have the money to hire an investigator to go to Florida. And since he can't have what he wants, he doesn't want to do anything."

It may not have made sense, but it was a bitter, sulky kind of logic I understood. "Do you have any friends down there who could help you?"

She had reached far under the table to retrieve a scrap of paper and was now staring at the three discrete piles I'd been constructing.

"I'm organizing your notes," I said. "Force of habit. The first pile is all related to his trip. The second one is a list of contacts you've made. The third one is for everything else."

She dropped the scrap on the miscellaneous pile, then sat back against one of the low kitchen cabinets. "I don't know why I'm doing this. I say it's for John or for the kids, but I'm not so sure. The whole thing was so . . . too fast. He was here. He was gone. I think I need to know what was in between. Is that strange?"

"Not to me." If I understood anything about what she was going through it was the obsession, the compulsive need to fill in every blank and answer every question in the hopes that understanding how and why it had happened might help in accepting that it had happened. I wasn't sure it would, but I was sure I would be doing the same thing. In fact . . .

The phone rang. She stood up, excused herself, and

20

left me alone in the kitchen. I put the piles back on the table. And straightened them. I went over to the sink and looked out the back window at Turner the dog chasing squirrels. He was never going to catch them, but he had to chase them. Even though I knew it was a really bad idea, I tried to imagine a conversation where I told my new boss I needed time off before I ever arrived at a job it had taken me a year to find. It was inconceivable. I tried to work through the details of rescheduling a move that had been planned for a month. Impossible. I ran budget numbers through my head to figure how long I could really keep going without a paycheck. Not much longer. It was lunacy to even think about changing plans at this late date, and I could not afford to mess with this last best hope for salvaging my career.

That's what I had on the one hand.

On the other hand, if I took a week and tried to find out what happened to John, I risked losing a job. It was not a stretch to say John had once risked his life for me.

Mae was back. "I can't get used to my children calling me on their cell phones."

"Problem?"

"Erin doesn't feel like going to her dance class and wants me to pick her up. I have to go soon."

"Mae, I'd like to help you with your investigation."

"Really?"

"I'd like to take some time and go to Florida. I could take this logbook to the police and at least find out why—"

"You would do that?" She sounded calm, even

skeptical, but she couldn't completely hide the tiny fila-
ment of hope that had lit up in her eyes.

"Well, yes."

"Don't take this the wrong way or anything, but why
. . . I mean I would never ask you to do something like
that. How could you—"

"I owe John."

"He never looked at it that way."

"I can't look at it any other way." Her eyes were now
burning bright, not just with hope but with so much
anticipation and gratitude it scared me, and I found
myself backing off almost before I'd even fully committed. "I can't stay very long and I wouldn't want you to
expect too much. I'm an airline manager, not an investigator and—"

She came over and hugged me, which felt awkward
because I didn't know her very well and because I felt
as if someone had opened the starting gate before I was
ready. "There are some things I'll need, Mae."

She sprang back into hyper mode, digging around
the kitchen counter until she found a stubby pencil. She
retrieved her pad from the table and flipped to a clean
page.

"What do you need?"

"I need to know everything you know about John's
trip. You've got some of it here—where he stayed, if he
rented a car, restaurant bills, charge card receipts—"

"There won't be any." She had her head down, writing furiously. "John hated credit cards. He only carried
one because I made him, and he never used it. He didn't
even like carrying a mortgage. It killed him when we
had to take out a second."

"The card could have been stolen. It's worth checking."

"I didn't think of that."

"I need a list of anyone you've already talked to down there, including the cops. And I need you to call John's cell phone provider. I want to know who he called while he was in Florida." I hesitated on the next request, thinking about Mae's family room and the kind of photos that were there. "I'll need a picture of John to take with me."

After she left the room, I spotted one more stray piece of paper that had landed on the stove. At first I thought it didn't belong in our piles. It was a soccer schedule. But on the back was the name and phone number that explained clearly why it did.

When she came back, I held it up and showed it to her. "I need one more thing," I said. "I need to know who Bobby Avidor is and why he wasn't worth it."

Chapter Three

"Bobby Avidor is a worthless piece of crap. He's a prick. He's scum. He's a rat bastard, a two-faced, lying sack of shit—"

"Take a breath, Dan." His voice was the loudest in a small diner full of big voices.

He stopped, blinked, grabbed a couple of home fries from my plate, and slid back in his side of the booth. But he didn't relax. He never relaxed. In the year I had known him, I wasn't sure Dan Fallacaro had ever taken a breath. He seemed to run on adrenaline instead of oxygen.

"If you'd arrived on time," I said, "you could have had your very own breakfast."

"I don't have time to eat, Shanahan." He shot forward in his seat and began drumming the tabletop with his fingers, thumping out the chaotic beat that was his own personal rhythm. "I had two airplanes crap out on me before the sun came up this morning, both of them overbooked. I had a ramper who got thrown in jail last night for drunk driving and resisting arrest. I had my best lead agent at the ticket counter not show up for work because her twelve-year-old kid stole her car. To top it off, air traffic control had a radar tower blow over, which means we've been having ATC problems for three days."

"Welcome," I said, "to life as a general manager." Dan was thirty-six, two years older than I was, but I felt so much like his big sister I always had to resist reaching over and tousling his hair. And I knew for all his constant complaining he relished every moment of his life at the airport, which not too long ago had been my life.

"Life as a general manager sucks, Shanahan. Honest to God, I don't know how you did it all those years."

"Most of those years, I did it somewhere besides Logan Airport."

"Maybe so, but I've got a whole new respect for you, boss."

I hadn't been Dan's or anyone else's boss in over a year, and it felt good to hear him call me that. More than I wanted to think.

The waitress appeared, a solid block of a woman with a face sculpted from stone. She slipped a cup of steaming black coffee onto the table in front of Dan. "What can I get you, Danny?"

He smiled at her. "Just seeing your face is enough for me."

She beamed. Dan had lots of big sisters. "You gonna eat anything but her leftovers?"

"Nope." He reached over and took another deep-fried potato slug from my plate. I'd asked the waitress not to bring them with my egg white omelet, but here they were, a half-eaten testament to my crumbling willpower. Being unemployed had disrupted my routine, to say the least, and routine had always been the key to my discipline. I took one last forkful, wishing I'd never taken the first, and pushed the plate toward Dan. He applied a blanket of catsup and set upon the greasy pile.

"Bobby Avidor, Dan."

"Avidor used to work out at Logan throwing bags

25

years ago. He was before your time. He's a maintenance supervisor now down in Miami."

"Mae told me he saved Terry McTavish from drowning. She said—"

"And it's the best thing that ever happened to Avidor, that rat-fuck. He used to fill in on the McTavish fishing boat when they needed an extra hand. So one day, old man McTavish is home drunk off his ass, Johnny's trying to get the boat home in the middle of this big storm, and Terry's out on the deck doing whatever it is they do on fishing boats. All of a sudden, *boom*, this big fucking wave comes along and washes him over. Avidor happens to be standing right there. He looks down. He sees Terry dangling from this line. He does what any moron would do, which is reach down and haul him back in." He'd gone through the fries like a buzz saw and shoved the plate aside, leaving one uneaten cantaloupe ball to roll around in the greasy dish. "And by the way, I'm not convinced he didn't push him overboard to begin with just so he could save his butt."

"Don't you think Terry would have said something if he'd been pushed?"

"All I'm saying to you is Avidor's an operator and he knows a good thing when he sees it. Mae's right. He climbed aboard the Johnny McTavish gravy train that day, and he's been riding it ever since."

"How?"

"When Johnny started working for Majestic, he brought Terry in first, and right behind him comes Avidor. Avidor loaded bags for about two minutes before he got tired of freezing his ass off out on the ramp every winter. He decided he wanted to become an aircraft

26

mechanic. Work inside the hangar where it was warm. So Johnny loaned him the money to go to school. From what I hear, he never paid him back."

"Mae said he didn't."

"He's a piece of shit." Dan mumbled to himself as he dug around in the wad of suit jacket on the seat next to him. Somehow he found a toothpick. He started to stick it in his mouth, but something else occurred to him and he pointed it at me instead. "Avidor got caught stealing, too."

"Stealing what?"

"The union caught him stealing tools from some of his fellow mechanics down at the hangar. They went to Johnny and told him to take care of it, so he gave Avidor a choice—leave the station, or get turned in to management and get fired. Avidor did the smart thing and transferred out to the West Coast." He put the toothpick in his mouth. "Johnny should have cut him loose right then and there when he had the chance."

"Mae says John went to Florida to meet Bobby. She says she doesn't know why."

"She probably doesn't, but Terry does."

"He says he doesn't."

"He may not know the specifics, but he knows what everyone else around here knows."

"Which is what?"

He assumed his top secret, cone-of-silence pose, one I'd become familiar with during our time together. He leaned across the table and lowered his voice. "Ever since he got to Florida, Bobby Avidor has been sending wads of cash up here to his dear old mother. She still lives in one of those little towns up the north shore somewhere.

It's been one of life's great mysteries for the boys on the ramp, at least the ones who used to know him. First of all, why does anybody give up mechanic's pay to become a supervisor? Avidor was probably making more in overtime than his whole salary now. And second, making the salary he makes, how does he manage to buy his mother a nice SUV?"

"And what have they concluded?"

"Drugs. What else could it be?"

There were lots of things it could have been, but there was no point in arguing with Dan. He lived by the drumbeat of ramp rumors and, at least so far, it had served him well.

"He's running drugs on Majestic?"

"Not into Boston. No way. I've had the dogs in, the FBI, corporate security. No fucking way that shit's coming into my station. I can't speak for any other station. Listen, Shanahan"—he checked his watch. He'd been getting more and more twitchy by the second— "I'd love to sit here and shoot the shit with you, but I've got to talk to the asswipes in schedules. They're trying to cram in another six flights a day, and I don't have the gates. So if we're done here—"

"This drug thing and Avidor, is this a new rumor?"

"Hell, no."

"Why would John wake up one day and decide to get on an airplane and go confront a problem that's been hanging out there for a while?"

"How would I know that, Shanahan? Maybe he got fed up."

"Are you thinking Bobby killed John? Is that the rumor?"

28

"Ahhh, Bobby Avidor is a pussy. Whoever got over on Johnny had to have been bigger, tougher, and stronger than he was." He shrugged. "Or else it was five guys."

I wanted to probe further, but I was about to lose my audience. Dan's patience was dwindling fast.

"Dan, I need you to help me with something."

"I thought you already found a job."

"Not that kind of help."

I pulled the logbook from my backpack, but checked around the diner before slipping it onto the table. Maybe because of its condition, maybe because the man who had sent it was dead—for whatever reason, I couldn't shake the feeling I had something I wasn't supposed to have.

Dan had no such compunction. He grabbed the book, freed it from its careful wrapping, and turned it over in his hands. "Jesus Christ. What happened to this?"

"Be careful. You'll get that black stuff—"

Too late.

"What is this black shit, anyway?" Since he had no napkin of his own, he reached for mine and wiped his hands, and then used it to open the book and flip the damaged pages. He looked up at me. "What the hell are you doing with a logbook, Shanahan?"

I told him.

"Johnny McTavish sent this to you?"

"Before he left for Florida. This, too." I showed him the ring. When I told him how much it was worth he thrust it back at me, stiff-armed. "Take it back. It's making me nervous."

I wrapped it up and stuck it back into the pocket of my khakis, which may not have been the best place for

29

it, but I wasn't really set up to transport high-value cargo.

"Dan, do you think you can find out what airline this belongs to?"

"Probably. What for?"

"Because I have two places to start, the ring and the book, and I'm taking care of the ring."

"Whoa. Slow down. What are you starting on?"

"I'm going to Miami. I'm going to try to find out what happened."

"I thought you were supposed to be in Detroit on Monday. Hello? New job?"

"Temporary change in plans."

He stared at me. "Not for nothing," he said, "but you're the one who was talking about how your severance was expiring and how bad you had to get back to work and what a great opportunity this was—"

"They'll be there when I get back." I didn't want to talk about it. "I made you copies of all the pages I could read. There are several captains' signatures in there. Some entries have part numbers and mechanics' license numbers. I figured we could trace one of them back to the airline."

"We?" He reached over and snatched the file almost before I could get it out of my backpack. "Shanahan, how come I feel like I still work for you?" He was trying to sound annoyed, but had the file open and was paging through the copies.

"Be discreet. Whatever's going on, I don't want anything to get broadcast on the ramp before I get a chance to talk to Mae first."

He closed the file and looked down at the bag next to my booth. "What time is your flight?"

"I'm listed on the two o'clock. But if you give me a ride to the airport, I could probably make the ten-thirty."

He scanned the restaurant and caught the waitress's eye. "Are you going to see Ryczbicki while you're down there?"

"It would be hard to avoid him. He is the station manager."

He reached for the check when it came and pulled out his wallet to pay, which was the least he could do, given that he'd kept me waiting for almost an hour, then eaten all of my home fries.

"You tell him for me the next time he sends a damaged aircraft my way and blames it on Boston, I'm going to come down to his ramp with a fucking baseball bat and conduct my own investigation."

"Sure, Dan. That will be the first thing I bring up."

He glanced again at the check and threw down a twenty, which by my calculation represented more than a one hundred percent tip. Our stone-faced waitress would have another reason to smile today.

Chapter Four

The automatic sliding glass doors parted with a swish as I stepped from the warm, humid jetbridge into the terminal. The Miami International Airport was as I remembered it—an homage to marble, glass, and pink neon. Everything in it was canned, conditioned, and proudly artificial, especially the climate. Even the real potted plants looked plastic.

I hadn't spent much time in Miami, but what I always remembered was the slickness, the smooth and shiny surfaces that made me less surefooted, more aware that if I slipped and fell down here, I could get hurt.

I checked around and located the agent who had met the flight. "I'm Alex Shanahan. You paged me on board?"

She checked her clipboard. "Mr Ryczbicki asked that you meet him in the lounge at the Miami Airport Hotel."

I almost asked her, but then it occurred to me she probably wouldn't know how Bic had known I was coming. "Can you point me in the right direction?"

"It's on the concourse between E and F just on the other side of the security checkpoint. Look for the sushi bar in front. You can't miss it."

I went to the concourse between E and F, located the sushi bar, and there it was—a hotel inside the airport. It struck me as almost too convenient. At most airports, you had to step out to the curb to catch the shuttle to the hotel, which afforded at least a few seconds of fresh air and natural light. Not here. Here the lobby doubled as part of the concourse. I worked my way through and landed at the cocktail lounge.

It was roaring, not exactly what you'd expect at a bar at 2:20 in the afternoon, but then this was Miami International where people flew in and out from time zones all over the world. One man's dawn was another man's dusk. Phil Ryczbicki was perched on a tall stool at the bar, chatting with the bartender. He looked like a puffy frog on a tree stump. A frog sipping a martini. I set my backpack on the floor next to him.

"Are you keeping office hours here, Bic?"

The bartender looked at me as if I were the school principal and drifted away. "Heard you were flying in. Decided I could use a few belts." Bic turned and peeked at me over one of his soft, sloping shoulders. "What's it been . . . two years?"

"More like three. Dare I ask how you knew I was coming?"

"You don't want to know, and I've got enough problems of my own without you dropping in."

"It's nice to see you, too, Bic."

A few years and a few pounds hadn't made Bic any more congenial. He was still five foot four, and no doubt still bitter about it, which was one of the things that made him so darned affable. Round as an onion and balding on top, his distinguishing feature was a giant blonde mustache that made him look like a whisk broom with eyes. He was a kick-the-tires kind of guy who had never come to terms with the concept of women running airport operations, and never would come to terms with the idea that some of them did it better than he did. Dealing with him was not always pleasant, but he was consistent and I'd figured out the key to him a long time ago—give him a way to take all the credit and cover his ass, and you were welcome to whatever was left over.

"Dan Fallacaro sends his love," I said. "He claims you dropped a damaged aircraft on him. What's that all about?"

He snorted. "He thinks my boys creased a B757 with a Cochran loader, closed it up, and sent it damaged to Logan."

"Did they?"

"All I know is we both made our arguments and he got charged with the ding."

"You're a master, Bic."

"I don't make the rules, Alex. I learned to make them work for me. It's all in how you present it."

The couple to his left settled up their tab and left. Bic patted the newly vacated cushioned stool next to his. "We have to talk," he said.

I scanned the room. The Florida sun shone brilliantly outside, but only a sickly version of it made it through the wall of heavy Art Deco blocks, just enough to make visible the blue haze of dust and cigarette smoke that lingered over the cushy black leather seating pits and low cocktail tables.

"I'll catch up with you later." I reached down for my backpack and began to hoist it onto my shoulder. "I'm going down to claim my bag."

"Don't bother."

"Why not?"

"Because your bag is on its way to Honolulu."

"*What?*" My backpack hit the floor and I worried, belatedly, about my laptop.

34

"One of your pals in the Boston bag room misrouted it."

"That can't be. I personally handed my bag to Dan, and he personally loaded it into the belly. It never even went through the bag room."

"Then someone went to a lot of trouble to fish it out and retag it."

I sagged against the bar and started to feel that hopeless, helpless feeling I hated so much. The most deeply frustrating part of being harassed by a group, especially one as tight and organized as the International Brotherhood of Groundworkers, was that the act was always anonymous. There was never any way to find the one who had scrawled the filthy graffiti on the door to your office. Or the one who had made seventeen hangup calls to your home in the middle of the night. The person who had slashed your tires in the employee lot was never going to be identified. It was hit and run. It was guerrilla tactics. It was none of them and it was all of them and there was never anyone to stand in and engage the fight. The only real choice was to endure it. And after a time your skin thickened until you almost couldn't feel anything, and your resolve hardened into a clenched fist, and it changed you. And then you had that to be angry about, too.

A hint of a smile twitched the broom on Bic's upper lip. "Are you enjoying this, Bic?"

"I never enjoy a misrouted bag, not even yours. It means more work for me. I just can't believe you checked a bag out of Boston. What were you thinking?"

"Dan asked me to check it. It was a full flight and he wanted some overhead space for his paying customers.

35

And I was thinking sooner or later the boys in the Boston bag room were going to have to get tired of screwing me over."

"Now you see, there's your problem. They will never forget what you did. Not in Boston, not anywhere. You're on the shit list, and once you're on, there's no way off. My advice—never check another bag out of Logan. Maybe never check another bag on Majestic, period."

"How did you find out?"

"One of my rampers downstairs gave me a heads up. He's got a buddy up there who called to let the southeastern local in on the joke. I've already put out a tracer. If you're lucky we'll catch it before it leaves the mainland."

I immediately began trying to inventory what had been in my bag. All the unique, irreplaceable things—my oldest, softest pair of jeans that weren't ripped, my Walkman and all my best running music, that cool little toothbrush holder I'd found at Target one day when I'd been shopping for shampoo. And there were all the things that seem so mundane until they're gone—hair conditioner that I could find only at the shop in Boston where I got my hair cut. Face scrub. Underwear.

"In the meantime"—Bic sat back and rested his little hands on his thighs—"we have to talk."

"All right, let's talk. But not here. I make it a point never to breathe air I can see."

"Where do you want to go?"

"Have you considered your office as a place to conduct business?"

"That's the last place I want to be seen with you.

Why do you think I met you in the bar? Where are you staying?"

"Right here."

"How do you afford a place like this?"

"None of your business."

"Fallacaro got you a discount, didn't he?"

He was right, but no need to confirm that. He turned to find his buddy the bartender. "Raymond . . . Ray, we're going upstairs."

Glass in one hand, power spigot in the other, Raymond nodded in our direction. "You want a roadie, man? How about your friend?"

Bic shook his head. He threw back the last of his martini, set the glass on the bar, and hopped off his stool. "Put it on my tab."

The Top of the Port was a combination snack bar, lounge, and health club on the roof of the hotel. A turquoise swimming pool refracted the sunlight, and a green running track wound around the perimeter of the deck. It was a quarter mile at most, but it had a nice surface—easy on the knees.

I followed the track, walking around until I found the ramp-side view of the airport. We were high enough to see the entire ground operation, and the barely choreographed convergence of people, vehicles, and aircraft that made the whole thing go. That it worked as smoothly as it did never failed to amaze and enthrall me. A vast array of ground vehicles was on display—tugs, carts, push tractors, fuel pump trucks, catering and lav trucks, Bobcats, loaders, and buses. They flowed around the airplanes like tributaries around great, winged boulders.

37

At that moment, the lineup for takeoff included an Aeroflot B767 probably destined for Moscow, an airbus from Turkish Airlines that had to be headed for Istanbul, and an El Al B747 that was most certainly bound for Tel Aviv. Behind them, I could see the colors of Lan Peru, Iberia, Qantas, Sabena, and Surinam Airways.

Bic stood and watched with me. We had our differences, but we shared one thing in common. I knew he could stand there as long as I could—which was a long time—and never lose interest.

"Have you missed it?" he asked.

I used my hand as a visor to watch the British Airways B747 lumber down the long runway. Just when it looked as if it might run out of concrete, it lifted off with impossible grace and climbed until it faded into the late afternoon sky. You could have carved the heart out of my chest and I wouldn't have missed it more.

"Not really."

He surveyed the deck. "Let's go sit over there. Maybe if we sit out in plain sight someone will come up and serve us a drink."

We settled into a couple of molded plastic chairs beside a patio table. The breeze whispered across the deck. It ruffled the leaves of the potted plants and brought with it an odor so strong I could almost taste it. "What is that smell?"

"Smoke," he said. "Feels like the wind is starting to shift."

"Smoke from where?"

"Wildfires."

I sat up straight and checked out the view of downtown Miami on the opposite side of the hotel. Hanging over the city was a yellowish gray haze that dulled the outlines of the buildings.

"We came through that stuff on the way down, but I thought it was air pollution."

"We had to shut down the operation yesterday for over an hour," he said. "Diverted almost fifty flights."

"Because of smoke?"

"Our visibility was about two hundred yards."

"Where's the fire?"

"All around us," he said. "Up north fifty thousand acres of the Okefenokee Swamp is on fire. This smoke comes from a big fire in the Everglades." He sniffed the air. "This is not bad. Wait until the wind picks up."

There was something eerie about the acrid smell, the way it clung to your hair and made your skin feel grainy. There was something unsettling about the way the smoke flattened and diffused the light from the sun, making everything that had been bright dull and dirty. It made my eyes burn—not much of an improvement over the bar.

"What do you want, Bic?" I knew he would be blunt with me, so I figured I'd jump in first.

"I want you to turn around and go back to Boston. I'll forward your bag when it turns up." His tone was even, his expression hidden behind that mustache and a pair of trendy narrow sunglasses he'd produced from his suit jacket. Mine were on their way to Oahu—without me.

I settled back into my lounge chair and put my feet up. This was going to be one of those unpleasant conversations. "Do you even know why I'm here?"

"Don't know and don't care." That didn't sound right.

Bic had a reason for every ounce of energy he expended. He wouldn't have bothered with even seeing me if he hadn't had good reason. "People around you tend to have bad luck," he said. "I don't want to be one of them."

"Does Bobby Avidor work for you?"

"Why?"

"You know, that wouldn't be hard to verify, Bic. You could save us both a lot of energy by answering the easy ones, and fighting only on the hard ones."

"Yes, he works for me."

"And is he running drugs out of your station?"

"That would be a hard one, right?" He dropped his head back to let the sun fall on his face. "Who told you that?"

"Unidentified sources."

"Ramp rats in Boston."

"*Reliable* sources who relayed to me what appears to be common knowledge on the ramp in Boston."

"Let's say he was. Why would that be any business of yours?"

"Because a friend of mine came down here to meet him and went home in a box. I'd like to find out what Bobby knows about that."

"John McTavish was a friend of yours?"

"He was."

"I didn't think you had any friends on the ramp up there," he said.

"And you know more than you're saying."

"We shipped his body home last week. My station productivity has gone into the crapper ever since. No one around here can talk about anything else."

"Gee, what bad form for John to get himself murdered in your city. So what about Avidor?"

"He's not running coke out of here. Bob Avidor comes in, he does his job, and he never causes me any problems. And as far as any involvement with McTavish, the police have checked him out on that, and they've cleared him. So you've got nothing, except to say he's an asshole. As far as I know, there's no law against that."

"How can you be so sure about him?"

"You're not listening to me. If he was a bad guy, I would know, and I would take care of him myself. But I don't need you here, and I sure don't want you here."

The breeze came up again, stronger this time, and I thought I could feel the temperature dropping.

"You know, Bic, all this strenuous protesting is giving me the idea that you don't want me to look because you know there is something to be found."

He sat up as abruptly as his portly shape would allow and planted both feet on the cement. "Look, I've got nothing against you personally. From what I hear, that guy you killed up there was a piece of shit and he deserved to be dead."

"I didn't kill him. He got killed all by himself." I felt my voice flatten until it was all sharp edges. "And he was a murderer hell-bent on killing me, too."

"Whatever. He was a dues-paying member of the International Brotherhood of Groundworkers. He's dead, they blame you, and not just in Boston. They all hate you and they always will. There are assholes that aren't even been born yet who are going to join this union and hate you for what they think you did. That's how strongly they feel."

"What are you suggesting, that I crawl under a rock and hide?"

"I don't care what you do. I just want you to do it someplace besides Miami. I have a good relationship with my local. I'm on track for a promotion to VP, and I don't want you screwing it up. They've already been in to tell me if I do anything to help you, they're going to call a wildcat strike."

That was the motivation right there. Even the slightest hint of labor unrest would be enough to get Bic up off his ass and into my face. "Well"—I reached up and rubbed my temples. This was sounding all too familiar—"I hope you told them to go pound sand."

"What I told them was to get their butts back to work and never threaten me again. What I'm telling you is if you've got something on Bob besides ramp rat rumors, I'll nail his balls to the wall. But if you don't, keep your mouth shut because there's no way in hell I can defend myself against gossip and innuendo. You should know that better than anyone."

He stood up and shook out his pant legs so they weren't bunched up around his thighs. "You want to talk to Avidor, go ahead. Knock yourself out. He can take care of himself. But just Avidor. You want to talk to anyone else who works for me, you tell me first. And stay out of my operation. I'm not going to let you do to me what you did to yourself in Boston."

I watched him walk around the swimming pool and disappear into the hotel. After he'd been gone for a few minutes, I got up and watched a few more planes take off. This time they disappeared much faster after lifting off, swallowed up by the haze that had blown in, thickened the sky, and turned a beautiful sunny day to shit.

Chapter Five

C'mon, don't pick up. Keep ringing, phone, and roll me into voice mail.

Paul Gladstone's line was ringing at the other end and I was moving as best I could around my hotel room, which was basically a bed with four walls around it. The room did not benefit from the huge print on the bedspread—big, tropical flowers with blooms drawn in broad, looping strokes of pink and purple, yellow and lime green. At least it was a queen-sized bed. I chose to feel good about that.

By the third ring, I was thinking I was home free, mentally scripting the message I would leave for my future boss. "I tried to reach you," I'd say. "I hate leaving this message in voice mail, but since we're having so much trouble connecting—"

"Paul Gladstone."

Damn. I cleared the disappointment out of my throat. "Hello, Paul. This is Alex."

"Alex!" He sounded truly delighted to hear from me. "How are you?"

"You're working late tonight." I glanced at my watch, even though I didn't have to. I'd purposely waited until after nine o'clock in Detroit, hoping I would miss him. Again.

"I'm trying to keep my head above water. Where are you?"

"I'm in Miami."

"One last fling before the grind? Good for you."

"Not exactly. Listen, Paul—"

"Before I forget, we've got a couple of meetings on your calendar for next week. I should let you know . . . let me just find . . ." I heard the sound of keys clicking. "I thought . . ." More keys clacking. I stood up and started to pace. "I guess they're not on my calendar since you're going in my place." He chuckled. "That would make sense. How about this? I'll have my secretary give you a call when she gets in tomorrow morning."

"Paul, I'm not going to be able to make it in by Monday."

There was the tiniest pause, long enough for me to think about how long I had been without a paycheck. "That might not be a problem," he said. "I don't think the first meeting is until Wednesday afternoon. If you can get here by then—"

"I won't make it by Wednesday."

I could feel him going still at the other end of the line. He was listening more carefully now. The pause was longer and heavier. "How much time do you need?"

"I think a week will do it."

"Is everything all right?"

"Everything is fine. But I'm not in Miami on a vacation. Something has come up that's of . . . of a personal nature, and I have to take care of it before I start work." The words I had scripted for this conversation felt stilted. I felt evasive, and I felt him reacting to it.

"Is it something I can help you with? Because I'll be honest, if I can get you here on Monday, or even Wednesday, I would sure like to do it."

"I know. And I'm sorry to be dumping this on you

at the last minute. I know you're busy. If there was any other way—"

"Okay, okay. Let me think about this." I pictured him sitting at his desk with one hand around the phone and the other flat atop his head, the way he'd done a few times during the interviews. "I'll have to cancel my trip this week, but I'll . . . we'll be all right. Are you sure there's nothing I can do? I mean on a personal level."

I fell back on the flower print bedspread and draped my arm over my eyes. I felt guilty enough without his genuine personal concern. "No, really, everything's fine, Paul, but thank you for asking."

"Then I'll see you a week from Monday."

"Right. I'll stay in touch and let you know if it's going beyond that."

"If it does, Alex, then this becomes a more complicated problem." Now his voice was taking on more gravity, and I felt the weight of his concern like a stone hanging from my neck. "I have to ask you, Alex, are you having . . . you're not having second thoughts, are you?"

"No. I'm still fully committed to being there, Paul."

"Good. That's all I needed to hear." He sounded relieved, and I felt queasy and I wasn't sure why.

We chatted for a few more minutes. He told me about the freak snowstorm that had moved in the night before. I told him about how it was 78 degrees in Miami.

After I hung up, I stared at the phone for a long time. Eventually, I reached over and wiped my perspiration off the receiver.

An hour later I was still emptying out shopping bags. I'd picked up the basic replacement gear—running shorts, T-shirts, khakis, a couple of polo shirts. I'd spent

46

more time and money on my new pair of running shoes than I had on the marginally nice-for-the-price light-weight business suit. But then I knew I'd be spending more time in the shoes.

When the phone rang, I hoped it wasn't Paul Gladstone calling to be nice again.

"Hello?"

"I hear you're looking for me."

"Who is this?"

"Avidor. I have what you're looking for."

At first the whole scene struck me as surreal. When I stepped off the elevator and walked onto the concourse, I saw a woman in the beauty salon next to the hotel getting a manicure. A party of four was raising a toast in one of the restaurants, and next door to them, passengers shopped for that last minute bottle of duty-free Armagnac.

It was two-fifteen in the morning.

I blinked at colors that seemed too vibrant and lights that were too bright. Everyone moved as if they'd been dosed with caffeine. Then I realized I was the one out of sync. I was at Miami International Airport, where time had no meaning. It may have been the middle of the night for me, but the people who moved through this global way station came and went from time zones all over the world.

Bobby worked the night shift, mostly at the maintenance hangar, but he had agreed to take his dinner in the food court at Concourse F so we could rendezvous at the terminal. He was very clear he would be there no earlier than two-thirty and would stay no more than thirty minutes. But something told me not to be surprised when I rounded the corner and found him already settled in and halfway through his dinner when I arrived at two-twenty. He was at the Café Bacardi, a teeny restaurant with a massive bar long enough to warrant two television sets. They were both on and tuned to the same station, so we were treated in stereo to the hypnotic drone of a stock car race. Unless NASCAR ran at Darlington in the middle of the night, the few people scattered around the food court who were interested were watching a tape-delayed version of an earlier race.

"Are you Bobby?"

"The only people who still call me Bobby are from Boston."

"What do you want me to call you?"

"I don't care."

Bobby may have grown up with John and Terry McTavish, but he looked older. His hairline was receding and he had a thick, bottom-heavy shape that fit nicely into his plastic chair. He had buckled his belt one notch too far, bisecting a soft middle into two spare tires. His jittery eyes fixed on me briefly. It was long enough to see that his body may have been flaccid, but his eyes were diamond hard.

"May I sit?" I asked.

"Suit yourself."

I did. "What's up, Bobby?"

"I gotta set the record straight," he said, "on Johnny McTavish. I know that's why you're here."

"How did you know I was here at all?"

"We heard from Boston you were coming down. We

48

heard about the bag. And Bic called and told me I should get this thing cleared up."

"Bic told you where I was staying?"

"Is it a secret or something?"

"No." *In fact, I'm thinking of posting my schedule on the web.*

"Terry sent you," he said. "Am I right?"

I didn't know this man except by his lousy reputation among some good people. But even if I knew nothing about him, I didn't want to give him any information he didn't already have. "Who said anyone sent me?"

"It was Terry. I know it was Terry." He shook his head. "God bless him. He thinks I'm the devil himself. You'd never know I'd saved his life. You probably already heard that story, right?" He gave me another one of those quick-flick glances, and I knew he wouldn't need much encouragement to tell me his version of events on that fateful day.

"Someone may have mentioned it."

"I hear Terry's whacked out. Gone off the deep end. Is that true?"

I gave him a "beats me" shrug.

"How's Mae holding up?"

"Mae is fine."

"I hope you'll give her my regards. No matter what's happened between us over the years, I still got a soft spot in my heart for the McTavishes. All of them."

His grin was so greasy, and not from the sub he was eating, it almost had me reaching for a napkin to wipe down his face. "If you're so fond of them, why aren't you taking Mae's calls?"

He laid his sandwich down. All the planes of his face

flattened into somber concern. "Because I got nothing to say to her that will make her feel better."

"How about 'My condolences. I'm sorry you lost your husband'?"

"Believe me, anything I got to say about Johnny, she don't want to hear. Terry, neither."

"Tell me. I'd like to hear it."

He pondered that request as he looked left, then made a big show of looking right. No one was within ten feet. Still, he dropped his voice and spoke without moving his jaw much, which made it tough to hear him. "The truth is Terry McTavish knows what went down with his brother. He just don't want no one else to know. And if you're a friend of Johnny's, you won't neither."

"I'm listening."

"Johnny McTavish was down here because of a drug buy."

"A *drug* buy? John McTavish?" I almost laughed out loud. "That's an outrageous accusation, and you know it." And now I knew how the police came up with their theory.

"Listen to me. I didn't say he was down here to make a buy. I said he was here *because* of one."

"Could you elaborate on that distinction?"

"I said you wouldn't like it, and neither do I, but here it is. Monday before last, I'm down at the hangar working the end of my shift, when I get a call. It's Johnny."

"What time does your shift end?"

"0700 hours, but I worked over that morning, so it must have been around 0900 when he called."

"What did he say?"

50

"That he was getting on a flight and coming down to see me. I say what for? He says he'll tell me when he gets here, to just be at the gate to meet his flight. So that's what I did."

"You waited around at the airport for him? Until after two o'clock?"

"I didn't put in for no overtime, if that's what you're thinking. I don't even get paid overtime. I did some paperwork and other things I'd been needing to do. I haven't talked to the guy in years, right? I get a call out of the clear blue. I'm curious."

"How many years?"

"Since I went to LA, which was four and a half, maybe five years ago. Besides that he's done me a few good turns in my time. So he gets here and we go and have a cup of coffee. We're talking about this and about that and so on and so forth and then he starts saying why he's here. I'm listening to him and I can't believe what he's telling me, which is all about how his brother's surgeries and all the litigation had put him in a financial bind, him and Mae. They even tried to sell that business of theirs—you know about that business Johnny and Terry got going on the side?"

"The landscaping business."

"Only it turns out they owe more on it than it's worth. So Terry, who figures he caused the whole thing anyway, he decides he's gonna take matters into his own hands. He sets up a coke buy from a guy down here. Some connected guy. According to Johnny, it was a big shipment, a one-shot deal Terry was trying to do to get right, and get his family out of the hole he'd put them in. It's not like he can really work anymore."

I looked more closely at Bobby Avidor. Those light blue eyes, at least what I could see of them, did not seem at all connected to the things that came out of his mouth. His gaze kept jumping around, which made it hard to tell if he was lying. Dan had said it best—John would sooner cut off his arm than deal drugs, and anyone who knew him knew that. But I wasn't so sure about Terry. I thought about that display of anger back in Mae's kitchen, and I felt a little less comfortable because what I did know was if Terry had been in trouble, John would have done anything to get him out. Anything.

"If Terry doesn't have any money, how was he going to pay for a shipment of coke?"

"By providing the transportation. He was going to arrange to bring it up on one of our airplanes."

"How? He doesn't even work for Majestic anymore."

"He has friends that do."

If Bobby had concocted this story, he'd been shrewd enough to take into account both character and circumstances. "Let's say that was true," I said. "Why would John have flown down here and told you all of this?"

"Miami is a tough place if you don't know your way around. And Johnny was not a person who was plugged into the underbelly, if you know what I'm saying."

"And you are?"

He shrugged. "Being in Florida and working at the airport, he thought I might have heard some names I could pass along."

"Did you?"

"I don't know those kinds of people, and even if I did, I wouldn't have put Johnny in touch with them. He'd be a babe in the woods in that crowd."

52

"What did you tell him?"

"To go home and talk to Terry. And to tell Terry to talk to his priest."

I sat back, listened to the whining NASCAR engines, and tried to figure out what was wrong with this story, other than the fact that I didn't like its teller. "Let me make sure I understand this. You say John flew to Miami on Monday. The two of you spoke here at the terminal. He told you Terry was involved in a deal to smuggle cocaine on a Majestic aircraft, and he wanted you to help him stop it."

"Which I didn't do, because I didn't know how to."

"Did you see him after that meeting?"

"That was it. We shook hands, I went home, and I didn't hear from him again. I assumed he went back to Boston. I didn't even know he checked into a hotel."

He had an answer for everything, which meant either he was well rehearsed, or his story was true. "The police say you have an alibi for the night he disappeared."

"I was out with one of my buddies."

"I'm sure your buddy can verify your story."

"The cops already have, but you can talk to him if you want. I'll give you his number." He smoothed out a section of the butcher paper that had been wrapped around his sandwich. He took a pen out of the pocket of his short-sleeved shirt and wrote something on one corner. He ripped the corner off, folded it, and folded it again. Then he crumpled the rest of the paper into a tight ball that fit nicely into his fist. "By the way," he said, still fingering the note, "I hear your bag turned up."

From anyone else but him, that would have been good news. "Where?"

53

"Frisco." He squeezed the ball of paper and released it. "Don't quote me on this, but rumor has it it's coming in sometime later today. If it comes in before I leave, you want me to hold it for you? Maybe keep care of it for you?"

"I'm sure baggage service will take care of it."

"Okay. But I wouldn't want you being down here in Miami without the things you need." He put the note flat on the table in front of him and pushed it toward me. That same well-lubricated smile slithered across his face. Before it had been equal parts chummy and patronizing. This time I saw hints of a third element—menace—and I saw it in his eyes, too. They were dull and mean when he finally settled his gaze on me. Whether he was lying about Terry or not, we were on different sides of some very tall fences. He knew it, too. I just wondered how far he would go to keep me on my side.

"All's I'm saying is if you don't have everything you need to stay down here, it might be best for you to go back home."

"I appreciate your concern, but I can be very resourceful."

"That's your call."

He pulled back his finger, leaving the note in front of me. I picked it up and started to unfold it, but was jolted by a screech of metal on gritty linoleum that cut right through the sound of the speeding race cars and touched off a shiver down my spine. It was Bobby pushing his chair back from the table in the most ear-cringing manner possible. "I don't think," he said, rising slowly, "we have anything else to talk about."

"We might." I unfolded the scrap of paper and read the name he'd written.

When I looked up to find him, he was already gone, walking away with one hand in his pocket and the other wrapped around the balled-up butcher paper. From the way he was sauntering, it looked as if he might be whistling.

I almost went after him, but he wasn't the person I needed to be talking to. That would be the person who had been with Bobby the night John died, the person he said would vouch for his innocence. That would be Phil Ryczbicki.

Chapter Six

"What I'm asking you, Dan, is whether you believe Terry would do such a thing."

I had Dan on the phone and the early news on the TV, and neither one of them seemed to have good news for me. On the screen—huge clouds of black smoke boiling out of the flames and into the tropical jet stream as more and more of the drought-cracked Everglades turned into fuel for the raging monster. On the phone—a connection that was as balky as Dan as he did everything but answer my question.

"Where did you hear that?"

"Your friend Avidor," I said. "I saw him last night." I checked the clock radio next to my bed. "Actually, it was more like three hours ago. He said John was down here to undo a drug deal Terry had set up."

"That *cock*sucker. That shit-eating, crap-spewing son of a bitch. It's not enough he gets Johnny killed. Now he's smearing the whole family. Jesus Christ, Shanahan. Jesus *Christ.*"

"Then you don't think it's true. Thank God." I sank down on the edge of the bed and, for the first time since I'd left Bobby, let myself feel tired. When I'd gotten back to my room, I'd pulled back the covers and tried to sleep. But the air conditioner had been too loud and the bed too soft. The pillows had been too flat—still were—and my brain would not stop working. What if it was true? What if John had been murdered trying to protect Terry from committing a felony? What if Terry went to jail? What would Mae do then? If it was true, what would I do?

I realized we had lapsed into silence, unusual in a conversation with Mr Fallacaro, especially after he'd had his first cup of coffee of the day. "Dan?"

"I didn't say that."

"Didn't say what?"

"That Terry would never do something like that."

I was back on my feet. "What are you talking about? You just said—"

"Whether it's true or it's not, I don't like fucking Bobby Avidor talking about Terry that way. The McTavishes are good people. The kid's been through a lot. Tell me exactly what he said."

I found the remote control, which wasn't hard because it was bolted to the nightstand, and turned off the TV. I could only deal with one crisis at a time. I told Dan what Avidor had told me. "Just tell me objectively, if Terry felt desperate enough and guilty enough, do you think it's something he would do? I need to know what you really think. It's important."

"I've got to be honest with you, boss. Terry's different than he was before he cracked up on that motorcycle. I knew him pretty well when he worked out here, but since he got hurt, he's been hanging around with some of the hard-asses in the union and all they talk about is how the company owes him, how we screwed him out of his benefits. If he ever gets up in the morning one day and forgets to hate Majestic Airlines, they'll be right there to remind him. And the truth of the matter is Terry got screwed."

57

"Terry got a bad break, Dan. The worst, but—"

"Just stop right there if you're going to try to be rational, Shanahan, because Terry's not exactly in a rational mood right now."

I pictured Terry trying to maneuver around Mae's small kitchen with one good leg, one bad, and a cane. I remembered the look of bleak disappointment in his eyes, and the rage that had come off of him like a fever. "So what's your answer, Dan? Do you think he'd set up a coke deal?"

"The old Terry wouldn't have gotten involved in anything like that, but now . . ."

He let out a long sigh and for once I wanted Dan to talk faster. "But now you don't know?"

"What do you want me to say, Shanahan? Do I think Terry McTavish would decide to take from the company what he thought he was owed to begin with? No. Would it surprise me to hear that he did? Not that much."

After I hung up, I sat down on the bed again and tried to figure out what to do next. I had a full day scheduled, meetings with people who saw or might have seen John while he was in Miami. But I should call Terry, I thought, and quiz him. I should give Mae an update. What would I tell her?

My muscles twitched and ached from too little sleep. I was mighty annoyed at the turn events had taken, and deeply pissed off that I never saw it coming. The sun was beginning to show through the slats of the plantation shutters. I lay all the way back and closed my eyes against the bright intrusion. The next time I moved, it was to get up and answer the door. The maid wanted to know if she could clean my room before her shift ended. It was after eleven o'clock in the morning. I was already late for my first appointment. Probably not a good way to start off with the Miami-Dade Police Department.

Chapter Seven

Betty Boop stared down at the squad room from a high shelf. Her round button eyes and Kewpie doll lips gave her an expression of extreme surprise, not inappropriate given that she was staring down at a man handcuffed to a chair.

Detective Patricia Spain leaned against the desk where I was sitting. Her white silk blouse gleamed against her dark skin, and her peach-colored linen suit hung on a frame that was all corners and angles—long legs, plankstraight shoulders, and flat stomach. With her ultrashort hair and unlined face, she could have been anywhere from thirty to fifty years old.

"Spell your name, please."

She wrote down my name in her pad as I spelled it. She was a lefty, the kind that wrapped her arm around and pulled the pencil from the top—a difficult maneuver since she was leaning against a desk, trying to use her knee as a writing surface. Homicide detectives worked out of Miami-Dade Police Department headquarters. As such, she was a visitor herself to the Airport Station squad room. She had borrowed a desk, one of ten packed into a space as big as a small master bedroom, and given me the chair.

"Tell me again about your relationship with the victim."

I didn't like the word victim. I shifted in my chair and accidentally bumped a stack of manila file folders on the floor at my feet.

"Don't worry about those," she said before I had a chance to lean over and straighten them. "They go up in that chair you're sitting in. I'll put them back when we're done."

"John and I used to work together for Majestic Airlines in Boston. We became friends."

"Ummm-huh. And tell me again why you're here."

It seemed like a simple question. And I had lots of answers. I could have told her how when I had needed help at Logan, John McTavish had been there. How he had helped me uncover a deep, dark secret that just about everyone had wanted to stay buried. How he had chosen to stand with me against his union brothers—men he had grown up with and worked with side by side—when doing so probably meant risking his life. I could have told her that John was a good man who had worked for everything he'd had in life and did not deserve to be labeled a drug runner.

I looked at the detective. "Mae . . . John's wife wanted someone down here who could be closer to the investigation. I'm between jobs right now, so I told her I'd come."

"Are you an investigator of some kind? Do you have a license?"

"No."

Her eyes as she looked down at me were as dark as a couple of pitted black olives. It was hard to read them, but I felt as she stared down at me that she had decided something right then. "I've already told the family everything we know." She had decided not to talk to me. "I don't know what else we can do for you."

"With all due respect, Detective, they don't feel that

61

you've told them anything. Is that because you don't know, or because you don't want them to know what you know?".

She closed her notebook, crossed her arms, and leaned back against the desk. "When we have something to tell them, we will."

"Does that mean you won't tell me either?"

"There isn't much I could tell you that I haven't told them. Maybe a few unpleasant details."

"I'll take anything you've got."

She didn't sigh. She didn't roll her eyes. She just held eye contact for a moment longer than if she hadn't wanted me to go away. Then she reopened the notebook, flipped back a few pages, and began to read. Rapidly. "Mr McTavish was stabbed in the throat with a serrated blade, probably a knife, long enough to go in one side and out the other. He was killed somewhere other than where he was found, we don't know where yet, but it wasn't his hotel room. We haven't found the murder weapon. He didn't die right away. From the position of the body, it appeared he was trying to climb out. The ME says he bled to death."

"Climb out?"

"The body was found early Wednesday morning in a Dumpster by a homeless man looking for breakfast."

"Oh." That was a detail no one had shared with me, and I wasn't sure I was better off for having learned it. Bleeding to death on a pile of garbage was a graceless exit for an honorable man. I thought about Mae wanting the details, wanting to know everything John had done from the moment he'd left her to the moment he'd died, and I wondered if that was something she would want to know. I was glad I had just given her an update. I had a day or two to figure out how to tell her.

"When was he killed?"

"Sometime early Tuesday morning. We know he called home around one a.m., so it was after that. There's only one person down here we know for sure he made contact with, and he's got an alibi."

"Bobby Avidor?"

"Ummm-huh. Do you know him?"

"I met him for the first time last night. I've heard rumors that he's running dope out of the airport here."

The information did not bowl her over. She didn't even blink. "Where did you hear that?"

"His former colleagues on the ramp in Boston. They're usually right."

"Well"—she flipped her notebook closed for a second time—"I've talked to the detectives who work here at the airport and they've got nothing like that on him. *They're* usually right."

Touché, Detective. "Do you have a motive?"

"Nothing we're ready to talk about."

"John's wife told me you suspect he was involved in a drug deal gone bad."

"This is Miami. We assume everything is drug related until we can prove otherwise."

"John McTavish would not be involved in any trans-action related to drugs."

Detective Spain looked skeptical, and I didn't blame her. She probably heard the same thing about everyone's murdered friends and relatives. She responded with her own question. "Why do you think Mr McTavish was in Miami?"

63

"It's possible he heard the rumors about Avidor and he came down here to tell him to stop doing what he was doing."

"Why wouldn't he have called us? Or the FBI?"

"John didn't trust authority, and he was comfortable handling these kinds of problems on his own. He probably felt he had created it by bringing Bobby into the company. It would have been like him to try to solve it himself."

She'd asked the question, but seemed only half interested in the answer, and not at all interested in continuing the discussion. She tapped the end of her pencil on her pad. I sat in my allotted space and felt the weight of the log-book in my lap. It was inside my backpack, and the time had come for me to do what I'd come to do, what I'd told Mae I would do, which was turn over the book and the ring to the authorities.

Detective Spain was now sliding the pencil in and out of the little spiral at the top of her pad. When she got it stuck there, I stood up, which wasn't a good idea because wherever you stood in that squad room, you were standing in someone's way. Another detective almost tripped over me.

"Thank you for your time, Detective." I pulled one of the personal business cards I'd had printed out of my backpack, wrote the number for the hotel on it, and offered it to her. "I hope you won't mind if I stay in touch with you while I'm down here." She took the card and slipped it into her notebook.

I waited. She stared at me. "Detective, could I have one of yours?"

She offered a card and I took it, thankful that I had

64

gotten at least one thing I'd asked for from the good detective. I threw the backpack over my shoulder and walked out.

Chapter Eight

The Harmony House Suites was different from the place I had pictured when Mae had shown me the receipt. The lobby looked more like a sparsely visited shopping mall from the 1970s than the serene atrium it aspired to be. The indoor-outdoor carpet was too orange, the decorative goldfish pond in the middle of the lobby was too blue, and there was far too much glass, brass, and faux wood trim in evidence.

"Miss Shanahan?"

"Yes?"

"I'm Felix Melendez Jr. You asked to speak to me?"

He wore a beige and brown broad-striped tie and a tan polyester jacket with too wide sleeves. His Adam's apple was pointy, his spiky black hair had dyed-white tips that reminded me of cake frosting, and if he was a day over sixteen, I would have been shocked. "You're the manager?"

"I'm the acting general manager."

"What are you when you're not acting?"

"I'm one of the assistant managers. How can I help you?" His dark eyes conveyed a calm intelligence that was in high contrast to his eager, loose-hinged posture.

"I'd like to talk to you about one of your guests . . . a former guest. He stayed here a couple of weeks ago. His name is—"

"John McTavish."

"How do you know that?"

"Because the police have already been here. He's the dead guy, right?"

He stood with his hands behind him, head tilted attentively, waiting for confirmation or correction. He wasn't being a smart-ass. He wasn't even betraying a callous streak. He was just being young. "That's right," I said. "He's the dead guy. And I'm trying to find out what happened to him."

"Are you police?"

"I'm a friend of his." He continued to blink at me as if that explanation wasn't enough. "You don't have to talk to me," I said, "but if you can help me, I hope you will."

"That's no problem. I'll give you whatever you need. I was just wondering, is it true he worked for an airline?"

"Yes. In Boston."

"Cool."

"Is it?"

"Let's go back to my office."

The back offices of The Harmony House Suites were like back offices everywhere—drab and textureless, scuffed and cluttered with the accumulated detritus of an ongoing business. But Felix's office was a striking contrast. He slipped behind his desk, a veritable oasis of working space interrupted by only a monitor, a keyboard, and a mouse on a pad that said Limp Bizkit. He made up for the absence of windows with lots of framed posters—travel posters, including my all-time favorite from Majestic, Sacré Cœur at night—and his question about John's occupation made more sense. He must have noticed me looking.

"I'm trying to get into the travel business. An airport hotel is as close as I've come so far, but I'm thinking of going to school to become a travel agent."

"Why don't you apply to the airlines?"

"I have. Every one. They either rejected me or put my application on file."

He didn't seem dejected. He seemed cheerful about the whole thing, which made me think he was the kind of person who would not waste time worrying about the obstacles thrown up in his path. He'd find another way.

"I used to work for Majestic, too," I said.

He smiled and shook his head. "That is too cool. What do you need, Miss Shanahan?"

"When did you talk to the police?"

"I didn't. The other assistant manager talked to a detective the week it happened. But she told me about it."

"Did the detective leave a name?"

"She left a business card." In what seemed like a conditioned response, Felix's hand moved to the mouse and his index finger went to work. When he found the screen he was looking for, he turned the monitor and showed it to me. "I scanned it in. I had to put it in our activity report for the home office. Do you need a copy?"

I looked at the information on the screen. Detective Patricia Spain.

"I already have one of—"

Too late. He'd pointed and clicked and somewhere a page began to print. In keeping with the austere look of Felix's office, the printer was hidden from sight.

"Did you ever see John?"

"I never saw him. I worked nights that week, and he checked in during the afternoon before I got here. But one of our room service waiters took dinner up to him. The detective showed him a picture of Mr McTavish, and Emilio said that was him."

"Can I have Emilio's full name?" I started to go for a pen in my backpack.

"Sure. It's Emilio Serra. He'll be back in at"—Felix turned in his chair and with his eyes fixed on the monitor, clicked the mouse—"five this afternoon."

"And when is his shift over?"

"One o'clock in the morning. After the kitchen shuts down. You don't have to write any of this down. I can print it all out for you."

I found the pen anyway, and a piece of scratch paper, and put them on the desk in front of me on the off chance there was a bit of information floating about in the world he couldn't access with his mouse.

"When did John check out?"

"He checked in Monday afternoon and checked out on Tuesday." He was reading again from the monitor.

"And he left nothing in the room?"

"No. The police checked, but there have been four different guests in there since he was. If he'd left anything, we would have known by now. Or else it would be gone."

"How about phone records, a copy of his credit card receipt, or anything he may have signed at check-in?"

"The police took all of the originals. But I can print copies for you. I can tell you right now he had one phone call from his room, which the detective said was to his house in Boston."

"What time was that?"

"One in the morning on Tuesday." It was the call he'd made to Terry, the one warning him to watch the family. Had to be. I reached for the pen.

"I can print all of this out for you."

69

"Somehow it sticks in my head better if I write it down myself." I recorded the time of the phone call, which had been, as far as I knew, the last communication from John to anyone.

"Incoming calls?"

"We don't track those."

"Does the hotel have a voice mail system?"

"Yeah. It's called the front desk. No one there remembered taking any calls for him. If you want . . ." He paused, tapping his finger on the side of the keyboard. Right there on his face, I could see Felix's internal struggle playing out. His lips pursed and unpursed and his thick, dark eyebrows danced up and down as his expression teetered between cautious and excited. Excited won out. "I can give you his whole schedule while he was on our property."

"How can you do that?"

"When you check in, you get a unique card key, and every time you use it, the activity gets recorded. All that information goes into the system as a stream of data. I can tell you everything he did that required a card key. And what time he did it, too."

"Like coming and going from his room?"

He gave his head a quick shake. "Only coming. He wouldn't use it to go out. Do you want it?"

"Absolutely."

I took my scratch paper, walked around, and stood behind Felix's chair to watch him work. He was already clicking on a desktop icon that looked suspiciously like Felix the Cat. A menu came up, one that seemed navigable and well designed. He typed John's name into one of the blanks, hit enter, and leaned back. "We'll have to

70

wait. The hotel system sucks. It takes forever to compile the data. Oh, and you can't, like, tell anyone where you got it."

"Why not?"

"The data belongs to the hotel. I wrote my own program to access it."

"You hacked into your own company's system?"

"I had to. We have a lot of repeat business, and I like to know if a guest likes to use the health club, or always orders the same thing from room service. I tried to get our systems people to do it. My request has been sitting in some programmer's in-box for eighteen months. I'm like, 'Dude, it will take you an hour to write the code,' and he's like, 'Write it yourself. Just don't tell anyone.' So I did." He shrugged his narrow shoulders. "Why collect the data if you're not going to use it?"

The boy manager looked up at me as if I could explain why big corporations can be bureaucratic, territorial, insular, and at times downright prehistoric when it comes to embracing available technology. I couldn't.

"Felix . . . do you mind if I call you Felix?" "Mr Melendez" didn't seem to fit and he didn't object. "You'd be perfect in the airline business."

The remark drew a big grin, a loopy, high school marching band grin. I liked this kid. I liked how he was smart without being cynical or ironic. And I liked that he had a mass of perforations in his right ear, though sans earrings for the moment. He was, after all, at work.

"Here it is. Mr McTavish checked in at four o'clock in the afternoon on Monday." He glanced over as I wrote down that time. "He booked for one night, and . . . that's weird." His fingers flew over the keys. "He specifically stated when he checked in that he wanted to pay cash, but he ended up charging the stay to his card."

"MasterCard," I said.

"How did you know that?"

"His wife told me he hated credit cards. She had to remind him to carry one." I leaned in toward the screen to see what Felix was looking at. "Does that give you the name of the agent that checked him out at the front desk? I'd like to talk to that person."

"No one checked him out. He walked."

"What do you mean 'walked'? He didn't check out?"

He pointed to one of the fields on the screen. "His checkout time shows as noon on Tuesday. Noon is the default time the system uses for automatic checkout. That means he left without stopping at the desk. We must have used the credit card imprint he left when he checked in. That's what we do when people walk. See? It's not signed."

I wrote down "Tuesday, 3/6, noon—checkout."

"It wouldn't have been like John to walk out without paying," I said, "and he wouldn't have left the charge on his credit card."

"Then someone must have snatched him."

"What?"

"You know, abducted him. He wasn't killed in his room and you say he wouldn't have walked the bill, so either he left and never came back or someone came and took him. They gathered up all his stuff and let the system check him out. That way no one knew he was missing for a few days. In the meantime I've had two guests in there and the room has been cleaned up, wiped down, and vacuumed."

It made sense—I had no activity for John after the

phone call to Terry—but I couldn't get my head around the idea that anyone could have taken him someplace he didn't want to go.

"Here—" Felix started the printer and turned the monitor so I could see it. "I made this for you."

It was a timeline, his version of the one I had been trying to construct. "Felix, this is great. Is this what your program comes up with?"

"Basically, but I added a few things."

"Felix, I love this."

"Piece of cake, Miss Shanahan."

I looked over the list of activities, trying to picture John going through each one.

Day	Date	Time	Activity	Comments
Monday	March 5	3:47 P.M.	Check-in	
		3:55 P.M.	Arrived room	
		5:32 P.M.	Health club	
		6:45 P.M.	Gift shop	*Purchase*: 32 oz. Clear-Water— bottled water
		6:53 P.M.	Returned room	
		8:27 P.M.	Room service order	*Purchase*: Cuban sandwich (extra sauce); mashed potatoes; 2 Bud Lights
		10:11 P.M.	Room service order	*Purchase*: Pint Häagen-Dazs Vanilla

73

Tuesday	March 6	12:45 A.M.	Return room
		12:49 A.M.	Phone call to
			Boston
		Noon	Checkout

"Did your room service waiter see John to give him the ice cream?"

"Emilio saw him both times—to take him dinner and the ice cream."

"So John went out after ten o'clock, came back before one, walked in, picked up the phone immediately, and made the call. Where did he go?"

"He had a rental car, too. Did you know that?" Felix was on to another screen. "Red Ford Taurus, Florida license plate DK614V."

"I did. In fact . . ." I reached for my backpack again and fished out the receipt I'd taken from Mae's kitchen table. For its compact size, it had lots of information. "The car was dropped off at six o'clock Tuesday morning." I added the time to the list. "That narrows the window considerably. Now we're talking about a five hour time frame. If he was abducted, he probably didn't return his own car, which means . . ." I scanned the receipt. "Yep. The charge went to his MasterCard. I'll bet they hit his credit card the same way you did."

Felix had been paging through screens, and found one that warranted his close attention. "Hold on." His eyes scanned and his lips moved silently until he had his thoughts straight. "If someone took him from his room, it was probably closer to one a.m. than six."

I looked over his shoulder at the screen. Whatever he

was seeing was not obvious to me. "How do you know that?"

"See this entry?" He pointed to a small "NS" in a field next to John's name. "That means no service. Housekeeping puts it in the record when they don't have to make up the room, in case someone complains. That was my idea. They didn't change the sheets at all, which means he never slept in his bed."

"Felix, your talents would be wasted as a travel agent."

He beamed.

"Can you print this stuff out for me?"

"No sweat." He clicked his mouse, and the printer began to clatter again. This time, he turned, opened a door in the credenza behind him, and revealed the printer's nesting place.

"Is there anything else you can think of, Felix?" I almost hated to leave. This kid was a treasure trove of information.

He sat back in his chair and blinked up at the ceiling. "I might be able to get you a list of cars that were in the lot that night that weren't supposed to be there."

"Surveillance cameras?"

"Way more low-tech. We use a security company to make sure no one uses our lot for long-term airport parking. What they do is drive around the lot once an hour and write down the license plate numbers for any car that doesn't have one of our parking permits, which you get when you check in, so then if the car is there for more than two hours we can tell and we get it towed, only it usually takes forever to get a tow truck out here—"

"Felix, I would love to have that information."

"Okay. I'll have to make a few phone calls."

"Can I see the room John stayed in?"

"Oh, yeah. Sure. Absolutely. Let me just check . . ." He pulled up another screen. "Yeah, there's no one in there right now. I'll take you up."

He gathered the printouts and handed them to me. I followed him out to the front desk, where he made a room key. We stepped into the elevator and swooshed up to the sixth floor of a seven-story building.

This hotel had a totally different feel than mine. It was in Miami, but it could have been in Omaha for all the accommodations to the locale. I suppose if you're on the road for two hundred days a year, it's comforting to always see the same orange carpet and wide wooden doors with brass kickplates and doorknobs.

After a sharp knock, he slipped the flat key into its slot, opened the door, and flicked on the lights. He started to give me the grand tour when his radio crackled. He was urgently needed at the front desk. Something about a room mix-up. He clearly didn't want to go.

"Can I call you if I come up with anything?"

I gave him my card. "Please do. Use my cell phone number. It's the only number on the card that's still good."

"Cool." And he was gone, sprinting for the elevators, off to solve another problem.

That left me alone in the guest room, the last place anyone had seen John besides the Dumpster. As promised by the name on the bath soap, the room was a suite. The front room was made up as a sitting area with a couch, a console television, and a wide window that opened out onto a large center atrium. Heavy curtains covered the window in the bedroom. The room was spacious with two queen-size beds and a dresser. The air conditioner was going full blast, which I assumed signaled the expected arrival of another guest later in the day.

I didn't know what to look for—mainly I tried to get a feel for the place—but what I saw made me sad. Durable carpet, cheap phones with plastic overlays on the keypads, assembly line paintings on the walls. The place was spotless, antiseptic, and sterile—so different from John's house back in Chelsea where well-used toys littered the floor, and the most important use of walls and shelves was to display the family photos. What were you doing here, John, so far away from home?

Chapter Nine

It was dark by the time I made my way back to the airport. I'd stopped for dinner on the way, not because I was particularly hungry, but because it further delayed the assignment I'd given myself for the evening, which was to call Terry McTavish in Boston and ask him if he was doing a dope deal that got his brother killed. I made another pass around level six of the Dolphin Garage, which, with its light green signs, was not to be confused with the Flamingo Garage and its orangey pink signs. The sodium lamps that lit the vast concrete space made it seem even darker outside than the hour would suggest. It was a heavy traffic day. I ended up in a far corner of one of the higher levels and felt good about snagging that space. I felt even better when a kidney red sedan showed up just behind me and began circling. Good luck, buddy. Try the next level.

I dragged myself toward the elevator, slithering between the Mercedes coupés and Dodge Rams and Ford Explorers that were packed together well within door-dinging range. The sound of the airport hummed in the background, but in the top levels of the parking garage, it was quiet enough to hear the pings and ticks of recently extinguished car engines. I also heard the kidney car cruising around. If he was waiting for some-one to pull out and vacate a space for him, he was in the wrong place. There was zero foot traffic on this level besides me.

As he turned onto my row and approached from behind, I stepped to the left to let him pass. As he puttered slowly by, I caught a glimpse of his face in the rearview mirror. He was staring straight back at me. When our eyes met, his cut away and he immediately sped up. My heartbeat turned to an anxious flutter as he passed right by the turnoff that would have taken him up or down to another level. The flutter advanced to pounding as I watched him and realized he was not searching for a space. He was moving too fast.

I looked around to make sure there really was no one else within earshot. This was a public garage, for God's sake, at one of the busiest airports on earth. Where was the traveling public when I needed them?

He made the turn to my row and came around again. This time he didn't pass. He hung back, matching my pace, which felt far too slow. I slipped between a Jeep and a pickup truck, putting a row of parked cars between us.

Get the license number, I thought. Get a description, dammit. Do something besides acting like a scared rabbit. But when I tried to see inside the car, to put a face on the faceless pursuer, the overhead lights were too bright. All I could see was a black glare. And all I could hear was the quiet thrum of his engine. More like a vibration than a sound, it crawled up my back, up my neck, and laid its hand on the back of my skull. I was shaking.

What if he had a gun? What if he wasn't alone? I hadn't seen anyone else in the car, but that didn't mean they weren't there. That's what did it. The thought of being pulled into a strange man's car and driven somewhere. Somewhere dark and isolated. I turned and ran. His motor roared. His tires squealed on the slick cement. The acrid odor of burned rubber filled the air. He was in reverse, backing out of the row as fast as he could.

I made it to the elevator bank in seconds and without looking back shoved through a heavy metal door to the stairs. The echo of my footsteps bounced around the tall, narrow well of unfinished concrete and iron. My knees, stiffened by adrenaline, made each of the stairs feel awkward and narrow.

Halfway down. Stop. Listen for following footsteps. Hold my breath so I can hear. None. Take off again. Move fast.

At the crossover level, I stood behind the half-closed door, peeking through the crack. Other cars were circling, but no sign of the kidney car. And there were lots of people making their way on foot to the terminal. I took a deep breath, stepped out, and jogged the full length of the garage. I didn't stop until I arrived at the other end. I turned to scan behind me. If the red car was there, I couldn't see it.

Inside the terminal the moving sidewalk didn't move fast enough, so I motored along beside. I didn't slow down until I was standing in the blessedly crowded lobby of my hotel, with the elevator on the way. I bent over to catch my breath and ease the pain in my side. Perspiration ran down my nose and dropped onto the marble floor. When I felt a hand brush my shoulder, I bolted upright and almost took off again. If I had, I would have bowled over the man standing in front of me.

He took a look at my face. "Miss Shanahan, are you all right?"

"I'm fine."

It was the front desk agent who had checked me in. "I do apologize, but I called to you from the desk and I don't think you heard."

"No, I didn't. I'm sorry." The doors to the elevator I'd been waiting for were closing by the time I noticed. I reached for the call button, hoping to catch it. Too late. My heartbeat was coming into normal range, oxygen was flowing through my bloodstream, and the dizziness was fading when I looked at him again.

"I just wanted to make sure you got your message." He handed me a slip of paper. "The caller said it was important."

The message was from Mae, and it was information I'd been waiting for.

"Thank you," I said.

The elevator had come again. I stepped in and studied the list of phone numbers she'd left, calls John had made from his cell phone while he was in Florida. Two went to his house, one to what she described as a bar in Salem, Massachusetts. The last one was the most interesting. With a 305 area code, it was a local Miami number. When I got back to my room, I picked up the phone and dialed it. The call was answered in less than one ring by a woman with a crisp, authoritative voice.

"Good evening," she said. "Federal Bureau of Investigation."

Chapter Ten

There's a good reason not to go running in South Florida after the sun has been up for a while. The air outside turns sticky and thick and all the oxygen leaches out. If there's a fire raging nearby it also turns smudged and dirty, conjuring images of ash and soot darkening the tender, pink linings of your lungs. Your face throbs, your body loses copious amounts of fluids, and no matter what you wear on your head, you can still feel the sun baking your scalp.

But I had new shoes. New running shoes made everything right with the world. They made me faster and lighter because they came out of the box with Mercury's own wings. So despite Bobby Avidor and his dismal accusation, despite being chased around by an unknown pursuer, it had been a fast, hard run, and as I stood cooling down in the lobby of the hotel, I dared to feel good. It was the shoes.

"You just missed Mr Ryczbicki," I was told when I stopped at the desk for messages. "He was here looking for you not two minutes ago."

"Did he leave a message?"

"He said to tell you your bag was here."

I didn't like the scene as I came down the escalator and approached the Majestic Airlines baggage claim office. The ramp-side door was open, held that way by five or six baggage service agents clustered in the doorway. They stared out into the bag room, hands over their mouths as if they were telling secrets.

Baggage service agents are the most cynical of a cynical breed. By definition of their jobs, the only customers they ever see are the ones ready to unload with both barrels because their bags are missing, damaged, or pilfered. Eventually, even the best ones come to see the world through the warped prism of customer discontent. The unabashed curiosity of such a group on its own would have been cause for concern. But it was the smell from the bag room that really had me worried. As I got closer, I realized the agents weren't covering their mouths to whisper; they were blocking out the overpowering stench that hung like a putrid mist in the dense tropical heat.

My stomach started to churn.

I approached a petite agent with smooth olive skin and long black hair pulled into a thick ponytail. "I'm looking for Phil Ryczbicki. I'm supposed to meet him down here."

She asked for my name, and when I gave it, heads snapped around. The other agents stared at me with ominous recognition. Bic's voice boomed from inside the bag room. "All you people get back to work. Joe, go down to the freight house and get a forklift for this thing."

Forklift? My anxiety deepened. It was never a good sign when a forklift was summoned to the bag room.

The agents shuffled around so I could get through. They gave me a wide berth, careful not to get accidentally soiled by my sweaty running clothes. The gap closed behind me. . . and no one went back to work.

The odor inside the bag room was so rank the first whiff withered all my sinus membranes and forced tears from my eyes. Bic was there, standing over what was without question the source of the odor—my bag. "Close that door," he barked at the employees in the doorway. His voice ricocheted off the concrete walls like a bullet fired from a high-powered rifle. "Get back to work. *Now!*"

My bag was unzipped, splayed on the floor like a pig with its belly sliced open, and I wondered who had ventured close enough to unzip it. Everything that was pushing out was mine—except for all those dead fish. There was a big pile of them folded in among the underwear and T-shirts, the toothpaste and the blow-dryer, complete with heads, tails, scales, and rheumy dead eyes.

Bic had me fixed in a coldly furious blue-eyed stare. He didn't seem affected by the stench. Must have been the anger clogging up his sense of smell. "I told you I didn't want any of this crap starting here." He snapped the words off, leaving the sharp, ragged points. "This kind of garbage might be acceptable at Logan," he said, "but not here. Not in my station."

I was angry, too, and not just because all my stuff was marinating in fish guts. I was mad at myself for checking the bag in the first place and leaving myself open for a sucker punch. And that's what it felt like. A hard punch in the gut that had ripped a few internal organs loose.

"The boys in Boston may have misrouted my bag," I said, "but they're not the ones who added the fish of the day. That had to be your guys. This is an organized racket."

"I don't care."

"You don't care?"

"If you're not here, this—" He pointed to the bag. "This fucking *bull*shit doesn't happen. My operation is not in an uproar, and I'm not standing here getting stink all over my suit. That's on you and I am not taking the hit for it."

"Thank you for your concern."

"I don't deserve this shit you're bringing down on me."

"No one deserves this kind of shit." I wanted to kick the bag for emphasis but was afraid to get fish juice all over my new running shoes. "Including me, Bic. And if you had any balls you would find whoever did this and put the blame where it belongs."

"Where would I even begin to look? They hate you, Alex. They all hate you. That's what happens when you off one of the brothers."

That was it. I moved so close, I smelled his aftershave instead of the fish. "This is the last time I'm going to say this to you. The man got himself killed. All I did was get out of the way before he killed me, too. You were not there, Bic. You can't possibly know what happened, and I'm tired of your flip comments. I never want to hear another word about Boston from you. Do you understand?"

He didn't seem to know how to react. At heart, Bic was just another insecure, resentful, self-loathing short guy with an overcompensating ego who took out his miserable life on anyone who was smaller, weaker, and willing to put up with his crap. It was no coincidence three wives had dumped him.

We stared at each other for a long time. He didn't move and he didn't say anything, but in his eyes he backed down.

And not one second too soon. I held it together long enough to get out of his face and his bag room, far enough out on the broiling open ramp that if I broke down in tears, which is what I felt like doing, he wouldn't see me and no one would hear me.

He was right. A man was dead because of me, and lots of people hated me for it. I was right. I had been perfectly justified in what I'd done and the people who hated me for it were morons. And I could still see his bloody, mutilated body lying in a heap in the falling snow every time I closed my eyes. I felt responsible. I felt justified. I felt angry.

I felt responsible.

The pressure of the hot air felt good. It felt right, and as I stood in a sweat feeling sorry for myself, I took a moment to hate everyone back. I hated the weasel who had misdirected my bag. I hated whoever had put the fish in it. I hated Bobby Avidor for the things he had said about John and Terry. I hated him for lying, and if he wasn't lying, I hated him even more for telling me a truth I didn't want to hear. I hated Bic for not taking my side, for blaming me, the victim. I *hated* being the victim. And at the bottom of it all, I hated myself for being so confused and befuddled about what I had done in Boston, for constantly teetering on the fence between guilt and anger, anger and guilt. Pick a side and jump down, for God's sake. Handle it. But I couldn't. I couldn't jump down and stay down on one side or the other, and jumping back and forth was wearing me down.

And the sun was wearing me down. If I stood there long enough, I'd simply melt like a candle into a puddle of wax on the concrete. The forklift would roll over me on the way to dispose of my bag, leaving me imprinted with its tire treads.

"You're right." I wasn't sure if the voice had come from inside my head or from the real world. It was Bic. He had followed me out and was standing next to me, looking out of place on the ramp with his loafers and tie. "I'm going to launch an investigation to find out who did this."

"Good luck." I tried to sound more sardonic than hopeless and bitter. We had never caught a single soul in Boston for similar fun and games.

"Even if we don't catch him, it'll send a message."

He stared across the field. I looked where he was looking, which was probably at the forklift motoring our way. I looked down at the top of his head. "You know, Bic, you and I have had our differences over the years, but I never would have figured you for being the drinking buddy of someone like Bobby Avidor."

He whipped around and faced me. "Who told you that I was his buddy? Did he tell you that? Bob Avidor is a piece of crap. I would like nothing better than to kick his ass out of here. But he does his job, and if he's doing something wrong, I don't know what it is, and I can't catch him at it."

"And you don't want me to catch him, either?"

He turned and disappeared into the bag room behind the forklift, which had finally rumbled up. I took one last deep breath and followed him in. In the closed space, the diesel fumes mitigated the foul stench, but I still needed my hand as a filter. And I had to lean toward Bic to make sure he could hear me over the grinding of the engine. "Why didn't you tell me you were Bobby's alibi?"

"I told the police."

"Why would you keep that from me?"

"Why should I tell you anything?"

"Because," I said, "if he's running drugs out of here, I would think you'd want to know."

"He's not."

"Why are you so sure?"

"You're not the only one with sources on the ramp. And I am not his drinking buddy. I'd never been out with him before or since."

"But you do think he's up to something. I can tell."

His lips had tightened. He didn't look as soft as he usually did, and . . . Wait a second. "You've never been out with him before or since?"

"That's what I said, isn't it?"

For the first time I started thinking perhaps I wasn't the sole reason for his perpetually bad mood. Imagine that. It wasn't all about me. "It was Bobby who asked you to go out drinking with him that night, wasn't it?"

Bic's eyes narrowed to a squint even though we were in the deep, cool shade of the bag room, and I knew I was on the right track. He signaled to the driver to drop the fork assembly to the floor and scoop the bag from underneath. The bag was too light and the flat arms too far apart to gain purchase. The driver began a back and forth stuttering dance as he tried to hook some part of the bag on one of the tongs.

"Bobby set you up, didn't he? He needed an alibi for that night and what better alibi than his boss? He used you." Bic tried to peel away, but I followed him. The bag room wasn't that big. "And you don't want anyone to know. How's it going to look? The station manager out drinking with the potential suspect."

"He's not a suspect. If he was with me all night, then he's not your guy."

"No, but if he knew he needed an alibi, it was because he knew something was going to happen to John that night. He set John up and he made you his alibi."

He took a few steps away, as if he needed to watch the bag lift operation from a different angle. I tried to think about the situation the way Bic would—maximum credit for the least amount of personal risk.

"You've got a short list of bad options, Bic."

"How do you figure?"

"If I come out of here with something on Avidor, it looks as if you're not doing your job. And if I don't, I've managed to stir up enough shit for people to wonder. There's no way to defend yourself against rumors. Isn't that what you said? You should be working with me. That's the only way you're coming out of this whole." Another alternative occurred to me. "Unless you're involved in what's going on."

"I'm not involved."

"And I'm not going away. You help me, and I promise you I'll do everything I can to make you look like a star."

The driver had managed to work the tip of one of the tongs inside the bag and raise it. A large, greasy smudge was all that was left on the ground where it had been. A few of my shirts dropped out of the bag as it dangled, along with a couple of fish heads that thudded to the concrete and glared up at me through dead eyes.

The driver leaned out and yelled at Bic. "What do you want me to do with it, chief?"

"Burn it. And get Facilities up here to hose down the floor."

The sound of the airport, as always, hovered in the background, but when the forklift motored out, a relative peace descended over the bag room, and the air seemed to clear immediately. I could breathe again.

Bic turned and looked at me without a trace of emotion. "Why should I trust you?"

"There's nothing in it for me to cut you out, Bic."

I could almost hear the gears grinding in his head. "You keep me informed of everything you're doing."

"I will."

"But nothing that will get me into shit. I'll leave it to you to know the difference."

"Plausible deniability. I understand the concept."

He didn't offer to shake on the deal. He didn't even change expression. "What do you want?"

I told him I wanted to know everything he knew about Bobby, and everything he'd done to try to catch him. I wanted to know all about the night John died, and I wanted access to the ramp so Bobby couldn't hide from me on the field. I had more questions, particularly about anyone he knew who drove a kidney red sedan, but he was late for a meeting. We made plans to meet in a few hours, but I caught him with one more question before he turned to go.

"If you hate him so much, why did you go drinking with him?"

"It was the end of another shitty day with divorce attorneys, I wanted a drink, and he told me he might have information on some gambling that has been going on downstairs on the ramp."

"Did he?"

"Nope." He walked into the terminal and let the door slam behind him.

The last time I saw my bag, the forklift driver was scraping it off into the cart that would take it to the furnace to be incinerated.

Chapter Eleven

I couldn't get the smell off.

I'd showered. I'd showered again. I'd scrubbed my skin raw and rinsed all the essential oils out of my hair. I'd gone to the hotel laundry and washed my running clothes, but they seemed, like me, to be permanently tainted. Almost twelve hours after I'd inhaled the first whiff of dead-fish bouillabaisse, the stink was still with me, sitting like an unwanted guest in the passenger seat of my car.

Bic had come through with some interesting details about Bobby, but the only one that seemed actionable was the rumor that he liked to disappear from the field in the middle of his shift. Guys had disappeared from the midnight shift all the time in Boston, but Bic claimed it was unusual in his city, and I didn't have much else to go on. So there I sat in the middle of the night in my Lumina outside the maintenance hangar, with my adrenaline-hard stomach and my twitchy muscles, swinging between hoping for Bobby to come out to relieve the unrelenting boredom, and praying he wouldn't because I wasn't sure I could tail him without being spotted. I'd never followed anyone before.

He came out at a quarter to two. He wasn't hard to spot, driving out of the employee lot in the muscle car Bic had described, the black Trans Am with the big bird painted on the hood. I scrunched down in my seat, even though I was across the road parked in a lot with twenty other cars—a good place to hide, but not a good place to be when he took off like a rocket. By the time I'd turned onto the road, his taillights had turned into red pinpricks.

I caught him at a traffic light. Even then it wasn't easy keeping up. He turned onto LeJeune, a wide, chaotic, congested artery that was as bright as the Las Vegas strip, but sold burgers and gas instead of sex and gambling. Bobby was one of those people whose driving personality matched his car. He liked following closely, darting between lanes, and flashing his brights at anyone who displeased him. But I didn't have to worry that he would see me. He didn't seem to have much use for a rear view.

After a few hair-raising blocks on Chaos Street, he cut a woman off, sailed in front of her, and turned sharply. I checked my blind spot and found someone in it. Bobby had caught a green light and was moving away. I had to do a squeeze-in maneuver to stay with him, something I'd learned in Boston, which instantly set horns yowling. I risked the tail end of the yellow light, then had to floor it to keep him in range. Just as I did, a jet flew overhead on approach to the airport, gear down, roaring loudly enough to shake the plaque from my teeth. A few more screamers flew over before even that ear-splitting ruckus began to fade. The road signs began to stretch farther apart and the streetlights became more infrequent. We were on a highway that felt like the only lighted passage through an ocean of darkness.

We went a long way on that road. The bright half-moon and the stars became more prominent as we distanced ourselves from the city lights, and it occurred to me to pay closer attention when road signs did appear so I could find my way back. I didn't want to be lost out there. Ft Lauderdale. Orlando. Florida City. I couldn't feel the direction we were going. Key West. Tamiami Park.

After another fifteen minutes, we were in a deep, swampy darkness going deeper. The shoulders next to the roads had disappeared. Lit only by the beams of my headlights, the snarled vegetation that had replaced them looked as if it would reclaim the right of way completely if not beaten back with a machete on a regular schedule. The hairs on my arms stiffened, and I felt more and more relieved to be in the company of other cars when they appeared.

Then we were the last two out there, and I wasn't sure what to do. The only thing I could think of was to keep adjusting my intervals, letting him slide ahead until I could barely pick out his taillights. I would wait until I thought I was about to lose him, then reel him back, usually on the rare occasion when another car showed up and I could tuck in behind it.

Thirty-five minutes out. The thought of turning around came up more and more, but I kept pushing it away, kept thinking we had to be closing in on wherever he was going. But my body was having none of it. The back of my damp T-shirt stuck to the car seat because the instinctive part of me, the part that knew when to flee from danger, understood that I was taking a real risk, that Bobby could be fully aware of my presence and leading me to a place where no one would ever find me. The farther I went, the deeper we drove into the swamp and the less opportunity I had to change my mind.

Then he disappeared. One second he was there, then he was gone. I blinked in the darkness, hoping to see the taillights farther down the road. He wasn't on the road. I took my foot off the gas and coasted. Had he gone left? Had I seen it or imagined it? I took in a deep breath. I rolled the car forward slowly and scanned the brush and the trees for the place where he must have vanished.

It was there. A narrow gap to my left. Another road, this one the least roadlike of all. From the only light available, my headlights, it looked like a dirt path cut out of dense brush. It was the only place he could have gone. But no taillights. No sound of gravel under tires. Something was there, though, maybe a mile away. Lights in the trees.

I parked the car and got out. I climbed onto the hood, and when that wasn't high enough, onto the roof of the Lumina. From the higher perch, I could see a dim arc over the trees, a muddy center of light in an endless pool of darkness. Bobby was there. I didn't know what else was, but I knew that's where Bobby had gone. I felt it. Nothing else was stirring, at least not human, for as far as I could see.

I climbed down and stood staring at that dark road. I wanted to go down there, but my knees were shaking so much, just staying upright was draining all my energy. The rational me, the parental me was mortified by the idea, stunned by its recklessness, fighting for control and losing because I wanted to go down that road. Yes, I could come back in daylight when the whole situation would be, or at least would *feel*, less menacing. I didn't want to wait. I wanted . . . I didn't want to be scared. And if I went down that road, it would prove that I wasn't scared.

I got back in the car, started the engine, turned off the air conditioner, and opened the windows so I could listen as I went. The windshield instantly steamed up. I cleared it with the palm of my hand, put the car in gear, and nosed it into the narrow opening. Room enough for one car only. I thought of going in with the lights off. Impossible. It had looked like a dirt road but now seemed to be composed of nothing but gravel. I felt each ping as if it were bouncing off my rib cage instead of the undercarriage of the car. Then there were the ruts and bone-jarring potholes that snuck up in the dark. And the music. It sounded like . . . It was mostly the thrum of a bass, but as I kept going I started to hear the grinding of the electric guitars over the beat.

A violent bounce into a crater nearly ripped the steering wheel from my hands and left the car pointed at an odd slant. As I straightened the wheel my headlights fell across a silver mailbox marked JZ SALVAGE. Beneath was a big reflective arrow that pointed to a break in the tree line to my right. Beyond the break, I could see the lighted area I'd spotted from the road.

I killed the headlights and nudged the car forward, close enough to see that the arrow pointed to a long driveway blocked by a wide swinging gate—closed— the kind you'd expect to see on a large corral to keep the horses in. Attached to it was a handmade sign with bold, slashing letters that spelled PRIVATE PROPERTY. UNLESS YOU HAVE BUSINESS HERE KEEP OUT. Beyond the welcome sign, the drive ran across a swath of open field and down to what looked like a residence. It was a stucco cube with a crown of awnings and a perfectly flat roof. That's how they built them down here. No need for pitched roofs so the snow would slide off. It was also the source of the music, which was clearly audible now. Behind was a large warehouse, marked with a bigger JZ SALVAGE sign. Reclaiming the entire complex from the darkness was a couple of tall stadium lights with about half the bulbs lit. I couldn't see clearly what was behind the warehouse. It looked like a field of heavy equipment or even a used car lot. But I could see what was parked out front—a speedboat on a trailer, a couple of SUVs, a motorcycle, what looked like an airboat, a pickup truck, and toward the back Bobby's black Trans Am, which pleased me no end because it meant he wasn't lurking behind me.

I sat in the car with the lights off and the windows open, fighting off the urge to be sensible and bail out. There was no way I was going down the front path and through the front door, but if I could get across the entrance without being spotted, I could drive for a ways shielded by the brushy perimeter that seemed to surround the property. I tried to stop breathing so shallowly, wiped the sweat off the steering wheel with my shirttail, and pressed slowly on the gas pedal. I drifted out into the open as quietly as I could. It seemed to take forever to glide past that fifteen-foot opening. When I was safely across, I paused behind a cluster of trees and listened. Nothing but me, the night crawlers, and the sound of heavy metal thumping through the fern and fauna. I rolled on.

My fuzzy intention had been to follow the road around to the back, but the road looped and lapsed and didn't follow the property line. When I realized the light was behind me, I pulled to the side and killed the engine.

I had to get out. I knew I had to get out of the car and go on foot. I spent a minute gripping the steering wheel and releasing. Gripping and releasing. Gripping. Gripping. My muscles didn't want to release. I counted to ten. I opened the door. I got out.

The air smelled loamy and damp. It was thick and alive with sounds I hadn't noticed before. Clicking and twittering and rustling down in the bushes and overhead in the branches. I still heard the music, but from the new angle also heard loud banging—the sound of metal on metal, heavy objects coming together with force. Power tools, too, like drills.

It took four steps to cross the road, but I had to hike a long way through a dark, close thicket. I made my way by moonlight that came and went, wished I had thought to bring a flashlight, and kept an eye on the stadium lights ahead. I hiked as fast as I could, trying not to trip over the roots and vines and brittle, cracked branches that grabbed at my feet and slapped at my bare arms. My jeans protected my legs, but my shirt had no sleeves. I knew I had reached the property line when I found a chain link fence that cut straight through the thick collar of trees. I tried to see beyond it, but the growth was too heavy and extended too far.

Time to redefine my goals. More information would be instructive—like who was in that warehouse with Bobby and what they were doing. The banging or sawing or drilling or sanding was still going on. The sound of men's voices was now part of the soundtrack, drifting toward me on the night air whenever there was a pause.

What I really needed was to find a perch and it needed to be high enough to see over the fence and the trees. I began to move laterally. Every now and then the moon would appear as I came to a place where the brush thinned enough that I could see something of what was on the property. It looked like machines, and lots of them. Some kind of mechanical equipment. It was too far away to see what kind, and they were down in a depression. They didn't look like cars, but they were lined up that way, dim shapes in rows among the weeds, and I wondered what it was exactly that JZ Salvage salvaged.

As I moved, the mosquitoes and gnats that orbited my head came with me. I was breathing hard, but tried to remember to do so with my mouth closed. Eventually, I found my spot. It was a tree, a good one for climbing, with a thick and gnarly trunk, and tall enough that I could see what I needed to see. It had one serious drawback. It was inside the fence line about a hundred feet onto the property. I did another quick rationalization and decided it was far enough outside the range of the stadium lights that I would still be in the dark.

Scrambling under the chain link was an option—the fencing job was not that enthusiastic—but I didn't want to crawl through whatever felt slick and vegetal on the ground. I went over the top, came down on the other side, and waited at the bottom to see that all was still quiet. This time when I began to move, it was into the field and away from the fence and the only thing to hide in was the darkness. My skin tingled under my damp clothes.

I stayed low, moved fast, and when I got to the tree,

dried my palms on my pants, and started climbing. The coarse and peeling bark scored my palms and made them burn, especially with the profuse sweating I was doing. My foot slipped once and I dangled until I could latch back on. Running shoes are not ideal for tree climbing. I was already winded from the dash through the jungle, so I hoped the first branch that I came to that could hold my weight would be high enough for me to see what I wanted to see. I climbed up, threw my leg over, turned around, braced myself with my back against the trunk. I sat for a moment, looking out across the field, listening to myself breathe, and trying to comprehend the sight in front of me.

It looked like a giant garden of airplanes, a rich bounty of Cessnas, Bonanzas, Piper Cubs, Learjets, and Beeches. Most were small aircraft and most bone white, or at least looked that way under the glow of the moon. Every now and then a painted fuselage stood out. But the dusty light turned what probably had been bright reds and yellows and greens into dim shades of brown and beige and gray. On some that were closest to me, I could make out the corporate logos still on the tails.

JZ Salvage salvaged airplanes, which meant they had been pulled from trees, dredged from the bottoms of lakes, and scraped from gouges in the earth. Their wings had been detached, either from the force of the collision or after, and were stacked, mismatched and upright, in large racks at the ends of each long row. With missing or mangled landing gear, most rested on their bellies in the weeds. The rows and rows of upright tails looked like tombstones, which was fitting since all these airplanes were dead.

The men's voices continued to drift up from the warehouse and out over the field. It was easy to imagine them as the voices of ghosts that might linger in these hollowed-out echo chambers. It was easy to imagine the harsh, strident strains of the electric guitars as the cries of the people who had spent their last moments on earth hurtling toward it.

The first sign of movement from the warehouse caught me by surprise. I pulled my legs up under me and crouched on the branch, holding steady with my hands on the trunk behind me. The back doors were open, allowing brighter light to spill out from the interior work space. A man walked into the light. He was too far away for me to make out anything but a lanky build. I crouched lower in the tree as if that would help me see better. What I wouldn't have given for a pair of binoculars.

And then I saw something that made my stomach try to squeeze up through my throat. There was a dog. A big, guard-dog kind of dog with a dark, shorthaired coat, a thick square head, and a wide chest. He may not have been one, but he was certainly built like a rottweiler. The sign on the front gate had said nothing about a dog. BEWARE OF DOG would have given me pause. BEWARE OF ATTACK DOG would have turned me around for sure. And now I was thinking that this was not fair. And I was thinking it was too late.

The dog had shot out of the hangar behind the lanky one, and now pranced and spun as the man walked with him through the airplane graveyard . . . toward *me*. He hadn't . . . surely he hadn't seen me. I was much too far away. And besides, they weren't moving very fast. If that dog had sensed me, he would have shown it. So what were they doing?

They kept walking until they were a ways beyond the graveyard, but still on the other side of the field separating the airplanes from my tree and me. The dog danced and crooned until the man reared back and heaved something. It went high into the air, and into the field. The dog took off, kicking up grass and dirt and dust as he launched himself toward the object that fell just at the edge of the light. It was a tennis ball. I could tell by how far it went and the height of its bounce. The dog ran it down like a fuzz-seeking missile, snatched it out of the air, squeezed it in his pincer jaws of death—and did not run right back. He stopped. He dropped the ball. When he raised his great head to sniff the air, I pressed against the trunk of the tree so hard, the bark was going to leave an imprint on my back. I prayed the strong odor of rotten fish was in my head and not out in the air around me. The ball tosser yelled. After one last skeptical snuffle, the dog picked up his ball and hauled ass back to the hangar. I blew out a long breath and peeled my back off the tree trunk.

Jump down? Hang in? Wait for the game to be over? I bit off the sliver of thumbnail I'd been chewing. Go. *Now.*

I twisted down out of the tree, dropping at least six feet to the ground, and started to move, slowly at first. The ball was in the air again. With one eye on the charging animal, I moved faster, hoping my new running shoes still had Mercury's wings.

When I got to the fence, I stopped, leaned down to look through a couple of low branches at the progress of the game, and panicked. I couldn't see the dog. The man must have thrown the ball farther this time. I scanned the field, trying to will my eyes to see in the dark. Couldn't. *Jesus*, he could have been steaming for me right then. The man yelled. "Bull" was what he was calling out. I went down lower until my ear was almost flush against the moist ground, and strained to hear any sound at all that wasn't guitar strains or insects. Nothing.

I waited, so tense that if he had leapt upon me at that moment, I might have shattered into pieces. When Bull finally reappeared, ball in his mouth, I felt so much tension release I was afraid I wouldn't have enough energy left to stand up.

No problem. With Bull dashing in the opposite direction, I crawled up the fence, swung over, jumped down, and landed in a hole. My foot collapsed, my left ankle took all of my weight, and should have snapped in two. I had one numb moment to anticipate how much it was going to hurt. A charge of pain ripped up my leg, jumped to my spine, and would have come out of my mouth if I hadn't clamped my jaw. Instead it emerged through my eyes, which immediately sprouted tears. A wave of nausea rolled through.

I sank to the ground, sat in a heap among the dead palm fronds, and waited for my heart rate to stabilize. When it did—at about two hundred beats a minute— I got up and started moving again. The ankle was swollen and angry, but mechanically it worked. Every time I stepped on the foot, I got the sharp needles. Bad enough, but what if it gave out? Get back to the road and into the car. I hobbled along the fence, looking for the place to turn, the opening, the way I had come in, but . . . I didn't know where I'd come in. I couldn't figure out where I had come over the fence. Stupid, stupid, *stupid* to have wandered so far away. Insane not to have identified a landmark.

The cold blanket of panic started to descend. Which way? Couldn't decide. Searching for a familiar branch or leaf. A footprint. And then the air exploded. A metallic roar ripped through the humid night and sent me to the ground. I looked up in time to see Bull as he launched himself against the fence, a barrier that hadn't seemed substantial to begin with. It swayed out on impact and strained against the posts that were supposed to keep it upright.

He stopped and I saw him spot me. The sound that came out of his throat was like nothing I'd ever heard, vicious and guttural and wild.

I jerked to my feet, pushed off with the bad foot, fell down, scrambled up, and thrashed along the fence line. He was right there, step for step, on the other side. I could smell his frenzy.

The man was on the move now, his yelling getting closer. I veered into what looked like a solid wall of prickly, thorny trees and brush, and crashed a new trail.

Boom. The fence rattled and shook behind me. And then it was quiet. The sound of my own gasping filled my ears. Get to the road, was all I could think. Get to the road and into the car. Wrap that steel and glass around me.

And then he was coming again. I heard him. He'd crawled under or crashed through or chewed through the steel mesh, but he was on my side now and coming fast, choking on his own drool, announcing himself with a low, rumbling, murderous fury. I pushed ahead, tripped into plants and brush, scraped off of trees, ripped through leaves and hanging vines.

And then a surge of energy. I'd found the road. But which way? Which direction was the car? *Dammit.* I started right and heard Bull charging toward me. I turned and ran the other way. I could feel him on my ass. I could feel him closing the gap. And then I saw the car and I felt a stab of hope and I pushed toward it, arms pumping, heart thumping, feet barely touching the gravel. Almost there when . . . when . . .

A bright, cold light shot through my eyes and into my brain. I froze, caught in the high beams of my own car. Someone was in my car. I raised a hand to shield my eyes. Bobby? There was yelling. The dog was closing. I could hear his nails on the gravel road. There was more yelling from behind me, and now ahead of me.

"Keep moving. Hurry up." A voice from the car. "Get in. *Get in!*"

Jesus *Christ.* A split second to decide. Dog will shred me without a doubt. I sprinted toward the car.

"Other side, dammit. Other *side.*"

Too late. I was headed toward the driver's side. The dog was coming fast. The backseat window was coming down. Just as I pitched through, I heard a door open and a heavy thud, almost at once, and yelping. The driver's door had swung open and the dog . . . the dog must have . . . the driver had opened the door and the dog had run into it, and somewhere in the back of my brain I wondered how I was going to pay for the damage. I hadn't taken the optional insurance.

The car rocketed forward and slammed me against

the backseat. Dust billowed. Stones flew. There was bumping and fishtailing. The dog's hysterical frustration.

I lay facedown with my eyes closed and my nose
buried in the upholstery. My ankle screamed, every
painful throb a rebuke for having abused it so completely.

"Are you all right?"

It was a man's voice. I turned over on my back. I
wanted to sit up, but I couldn't will myself to do it. I
had to lie flat and breathe. From there I could see only
his hands on the wheel, hands in black gloves. He wore
a dark ball cap. He seemed tall in the seat.

"Hey!" He turned and I could see his profile. Roman
nose. Strong chin. I couldn't see his eyes. Understandably,
he kept them on the road. "What's going on back there?"

"I'm all right."

"Get up and see if there's anyone behind us." There
was urgency, but no panic.

The blood drained from my head when I sat up, but
I steadied myself long--enough to squint through the
back window, trying to see through the cloud of dust.
"It's too dark to see very far, but no one is there right
now."

He let out a long sigh that seemed to tighten the
tension, not relieve it. "That doesn't mean they won't
be coming."

106

Chapter Twelve

He looked like a commando. The black gloves had only been the beginning. His jeans were black, as were his socks and running shoes. Despite the heat, he wore a long-sleeved black pullover. Any skin that showed, including his face, was smeared with black camouflage paint. When he glanced over, what stood out most in a dark car on a dark road were the strands of silver laced through brown hair. His hair was long enough to poke out from under the black ball cap he wore pulled down low over his eyes.

And there was the gun. A pistol. It looked like an automatic, and it had been resting on the seat next to him until I'd crawled over to join him in the front, at which point he picked it up and tucked it back into a hip holster.

"Put your seat belt on," was the first thing he said.

I did, and then I looked at him again, but all I saw was that big gun. "Who are you?"

"I'm the one asking the questions," he said. His voice sounded like a well traveled back road—dusty, littered with rocks and stones, and pitted with potholes. "Who the hell are you?"

I hadn't totally calmed down and I wasn't thinking completely straight, but I was clear enough on a few facts. I had a sprained ankle, scratched and bloodied arms, sore ribs and pelvic bone where I'd slammed around going through the window, and a complete stranger behind the wheel of my car, which he had apparently hot-wired because the keys were still tucked in the pocket of my jeans. He was armed and I wasn't. He was bigger than I was, and if I'd had to guess, I would have said it wasn't the first time he'd been in a scrape like that.

The dynamics of the situation didn't favor me.

"I'm . . . my name is Alex Shanahan."

"That doesn't tell me what I need to know, Alex Shanahan. What were you doing back there?"

"I was following someone."

"Who?"

"Someone who went into that warehouse." I was stalling, trying to figure out what to reveal.

He was having none of it. "What is the guy's name?"

"Bobby Avidor."

He checked the rearview mirror, which he had done every thirty seconds since we'd turned back onto a real road. "What kind of car?"

"A black Trans Am."

"Yeah, I saw him." He nodded. "Why did you follow him?"

He looked at me sternly, and I suddenly felt that no answer I gave would be good enough. I wasn't sure there was a reason good enough to do what I had just done. No need to share that with him. "I'm not telling you any more," I said, "unless you tell me who you are."

He reacted as if I'd reached over and tapped him on the nose. His neck stiffened, which had the effect of pulling his chin toward his backbone.

"I'm the one who just saved your ass. Remember?" Obviously the dynamics of the situation weren't lost on him, either.

"You did, and I'm grateful. But I don't think it's a lot to ask for you to tell me who you are. I told you who I am."

"You told me your name. My name is Jack Dolan. What does that tell you?"

"Not much."

"How about this?" he asked. "Me first, and then you."

"Deal."

"The guy your buddy went in to see, the guy who owns the salvage yard, I'm watching him. And you walked right into the middle of my modest little stakeout."

"Oh." I felt mildly guilty, but mostly inept. "Are you a cop?"

"Private."

He must have finally felt that we were clear of the dog and whoever else was back there. He slowed down and took time to adjust the seat. He pushed it all the way back.

"Why are you watching him?" I asked.

"Someone paid me to do it. And the target is not someone you'd want to be introduced to under any circumstances, but especially not sneaking around his property. That was his dog, Bull."

The target. Annoying that he'd gotten me to reveal Bobby's name, yet was clever enough not to come across with the name of his guy. "Is 'the target' a drug runner?"

"That's not his business." He glanced over as he took a right turn. I was so glad to see that he knew where he was going. "Why?"

"Bobby Avidor is rumored to be running drugs out of Miami. He works for Majestic Airlines, and people who know him there—"

"This one works for an airline? This Avidor?"

"He's a maintenance supervisor."

He nodded as if that made perfect sense.

"What? Does that mean something to you?"

"Maybe." He took in a long breath, checked the mirror, took off his gloves, and relaxed a little more. He seemed to be coming down from high alert in stages. "Your turn. Why are you following Avidor?"

"He may be responsible for the murder of a friend of mine."

"And you were going to do what? Make a citizen's arrest?"

"I had no plan to approach him. All I wanted to do was follow him and see where he went."

"What were you going to do once you found out?"

"I was going to take that information and add it to what I already know and . . . process it."

From the side I thought I saw the beginning of a bemused smile. Apparently he found me more amusing than threatening. I didn't know if that was bad or good. He looked over and another part of him emerged from the black mask. He had a nice smile.

"You have no idea what you're doing, do you."

It pained me to agree, but it would have been difficult, absurd, even, to ignore the facts. "I'm new at this."

"Are you armed?"

"No."

"I can guarantee you the boys in that yard were armed tonight. Heavily. You have no idea how much danger you were in back there."

"I'm beginning to appreciate how much. But once you get to a certain level of danger . . . I would say to the point where your life is threatened as it probably was tonight—"

"Not probably."

"Then incrementally speaking, increasing amounts of danger on top of that don't make the situation worse. In other words, the risk does not increase proportionately with the recklessness of the act, once you pass the point where it's your life that is at risk, because that's the ultimate risk."

He gave me a sideways glance.

"You can only die once, is all I'm saying, no matter how stupid you are."

"Maybe so," he said. We drove for a few more miles before he spoke again. "Is that how you respond to being scared? Intellectualize? Analyze the thing that scares you?"

"No." I shifted in my seat. "That's how I respond to everything."

He chuckled. "Here's more input for your calculation. Bull was very close to chasing you down back there. If he had caught you, he would have pulled you to the ground so he could get to your throat, because that's how animals kill. They attack the most vulnerable spot. You would have tried to fight him off, and his teeth would have shredded your arms down to the bone, and you wouldn't have been able to push him off anyway because he's too heavy. He would have wrapped his jaws around that soft tissue"—he made his right hand into a vise and placed it on either side of his throat and for a second reminded me of how John had died—"sunk his teeth in, and ripped everything out. There would have been blood everywhere—your blood—because he would have torn the major arteries, and then—"

"What is your point?"

He left a long pause before he answered and when he looked at me, he wasn't smiling. "There are ways to die, and there are ways to die. Being mauled by a vicious animal is not one of the better ones."

I stared out my window at a drainage canal that paralleled our road. It was bone dry. I ran my fingers over the cuts and scratches on my arms. Superficial wounds from the bushes and branches. Mr Jack Dolan had done what I had failed to do for myself. He had scared me.

"Avidor is not running drugs," he said, changing the subject at just the right moment. "So if your murder victim—what was his name?"

"John McTavish."

"If John McTavish was killed over drugs, you've got the wrong man."

"No." I turned my attention back inside the car. "It's not the drug piece we're sure of; it's the other way around. We know John came down to Florida to see Bobby Avidor, and I'm reasonably sure Bobby set him up to be murdered. That it was about drugs is the speculation."

"By whom?"

"John's family. His friends. Coworkers."

"Which one are you?"

"Friend," I said. "John and I worked together at Majestic in Boston."

"Is Boston where you live?"

"For another week. If it's not drugs, then—"

"Here's why I'm asking. Wherever your home is, you should go there. You don't belong in places like we just came from."

Of course he was right. I just didn't like being told.

"How do you know I'm not FBI or DEA or ATF? I could be a private investigator. I never told you I wasn't."

He looked at me with raised eyebrows and half a grin that said he didn't take the comment any more seriously than I did.

"Just tell me what it is they do," I said. "What is Bobby into if it's not drugs?"

"Parts."

"Parts?"

"Aircraft parts," he said.

"Stealing aircraft parts?"

"At a minimum. My bad guy does the whole buffet—stolen parts, recycled, counterfeit, back door, strip-and-dip. You name it. If Avidor is hooked up with him, he's into parts. Bad parts."

"You won't tell me the name of this bad guy? This J.Z.?"

"Who said it was J.Z.? Where can I drop you?"

I hadn't even noticed that we had made our way back to civilization. The lights were on. Traffic was flowing. We were back in Miami. "You can drop me at the airport."

"Now you're talking. What airline?"

"No airline. I'm staying at a hotel there."

He checked his blind spot and changed lanes. "You're not going home?"

"Not right now. And you can't take my car. I need it."

"I wasn't planning on taking your car. Where do you want it parked?"

"The Dolphin Garage. Where is yours?"

"My truck is back at the salvage yard where I left it.

113

But it's parked far enough away that I can get to it without anyone seeing me." He enunciated clearly, just in case I didn't catch the instructive tone.

"I can drive you home," I said. "Where do you live?"

"No thanks. Plenty of cabs at the airport."

"How do you think a cabbie is going to respond to your camouflage?"

"This is Miami," he said. "The cabbies have seen worse."

We were at the airport now, approaching the parking garages. "Let me take you to get your car tomorrow. It's the least I can do."

"Did you say the Dolphin Garage?"

"We can talk more on the way out there. I have more stuff to tell you."

"No."

"Why not?"

"Because you don't know what you're doing."

"Which is exactly why I need help."

"I generally get paid for providing that kind of help."

"Okay, that's fair." He pulled the ticket at the garage and the gate went up. I had to think fast. "I could hire you. And I could pay you. Eventually."

"I already have a job. I just told you that."

"You could do both jobs at once. Obviously we're after the same players. Earn two fees for one job. It's synergistic. Economies of scale and all that."

"Economies of scale?" He was circling the garage looking for a space. "I'm going to try to get close to the elevator," he said. "So you don't have to walk far. These damn places are dangerous for women."

"I have something—" Something to show you, I

thought, if I trusted you. I'd been burned before. I took another look at him in the better light offered in the garage. Strong jaw. Hands resting easy on the steering wheel. Eyes that were always moving, but with the purpose of seeing, as opposed to Bobby's jittery eyes, which seemed to rove incessantly for the express purpose of not being seen. I decided to trust Jack Dolan.

"I have something that might be useful to you. My friend, John, before he died, he sent me an aircraft logbook and a diamond ring."

"Why?"

"I don't know. Maybe for safekeeping. I think his intention was to talk to me about it when he got back from Florida. But he never came back."

"Are you sure it's a logbook?"

"I used to work for an airline. I know what one looks like. And it's trashed. It's muddy and sooty and ripped up. I'm trying to track down which airline."

"You need to work through the homicide detectives," he said. "Whatever you have, give it to them."

"The police think it was a drug killing."

"Then it probably was." He pulled the car into a spot and killed the engine. "They're generally right about those things, which is because they do investigations for a living." There was that instructive tone again.

"They're not right about this," I said. "At least not completely."

"What does that mean?"

"They think John was setting up a drug deal. He wasn't. He might have been doing something for his brother, but—"

"His brother?"

115

"It's complicated. That's part of what I have to tell you."

The first thing he did when he got out of the car was check the damage to the door from Bull's head. I walked around to see for myself. My ankle had settled down during the long ride in, but now that the blood was flowing, it was really thick and sore.

Bull must have had a rock for a head. There was no way I was getting away with a dent like that on a rental car, which meant I was going to have to pay for it because I hadn't paid for the insurance, which reminded me of my financial crisis, which reminded me of my call to Paul Gladstone and the ticking clock. I had already used up two of the extra seven days he'd given me to get to Detroit. The thought made my head throb as much as my ankle.

"Just let me run you out tomorrow to pick up your car," I said. "Please?"

"You're trying to rope me in. You think if you have another couple of hours to work on me tomorrow, you'll talk me into it."

"Pretty much."

He smiled. "At least you're up front about it."

I followed him to the elevator, which wasn't far. It arrived with a clear *ding* that felt loud in the deserted space. He held the door so I could limp in.

"Do you know South Beach?" he asked.

"Not at all."

"I'll be at Big Pinks in South Beach tomorrow for breakfast. Meet me there. You can give it your best shot."

And then we walked, he in his black face and me with my limp, all the way across the garage, through the terminal, and to the elevator at the hotel.

Chapter Thirteen

The phone had probably been ringing for a while. The sound seeped into my awareness gradually, like a tune I was humming without knowing what it was. It took a long time for me to realize it was a phone ringing, and an equally long interval to remember what I was supposed to do about it.

"Hello?"

"What, you don't answer your phone down there anymore? What the hell's going on?"

I was lying on my stomach with my head on one of the flat pillows, which was like no pillow at all. I adjusted slightly so I could see the clock radio. "Dan, how can you call me at six o'clock in the morning?"

"Were you asleep?"

"I was in a coma." Every nerve ending in my body objected when I rolled onto my back, reminding me of what had happened last night. Actually, a few short hours ago. Parts of my body that weren't twitching, aching, or stiff were hard to identify. The makeshift ice pack I'd rigged around my ankle was now a soggy, gooshy, cold towel under the sheets at the foot of my bed.

"What do you want?"

"Your logbook belongs to Air Sentinel."

I sat up. Fast. "What?"

"I said your logbook—"

"No. I heard you." My head was swimming and it was hard to get my thoughts together. To top off everything else, I hadn't gotten enough sleep. And there was something bothering me. Something floating out there in the ether that I thought I was supposed to be paying attention to. "How did you figure it out?"

"I traced a couple of the mechanics' signatures by their license numbers. Turns out they worked at Sentinel. Then I took one of the part numbers that was in the book and called their maintenance manager here at Logan. He's an old buddy of mine. So I call him and I ask him to look up the part for me as a personal favor. I figured he could tell me what aircraft it belonged to and we'd know where the book came from. Ten minutes later he's standing in my office."

"It's at least a twenty-five-minute walk from Sentinel to your office."

"This is what I'm saying. The guy's sixty pounds over-weight and he's sucking wind when he gets here, all red in the face, asking me where I got that part number."

"What did you tell him?"

"Something about how Sentinel borrowed it from our inventory at O'Hare and I was trying to track it because we thought it had been stolen and . . . I don't even remember. It was a complete load of crap."

"What did he say?"

"Nothing. That's the weird part, Shanahan."

"Why is that weird, Dan?"

"This guy, my buddy, he's usually got diarrhea of the mouth; I can never get him to shut up. But this thing, he wouldn't say another word. I ask him, 'How come you blew a gasket hauling your ass over here? Is there something special about this particular part?' All he said was that I could stop looking for it, that he would make

118

sure Majestic got paid for it. And we should do lunch sometime."

"What do you think that means?"

"Beats the shit out of me. I thought you would have had it all figured out by now."

"I've got some pieces coming together. It's just that they're from an entirely different puzzle than the one we've been looking at." I told him what had happened the night before, about chasing Avidor out to the salvage yard and meeting Jack Dolan. I left out the parts that made me sound like a complete bonehead, which left only the marginally boneheaded moments. "Jack says this guy that Avidor went to meet is a known player in the bogus parts trade, which means Bobby is probably involved, too."

"No shit. Involved how?"

"Probably stealing them." I knew I sounded like more of an expert than I was. "And reselling them on the black market. Maybe worse."

"Stealing from Majestic?"

"Maybe."

"No wonder Johnny was so pissed at him."

"Yeah." I peeled the covers back to sneak a peek at my ankle. Ugly, as expected. As I stared down at it, an awareness started to emerge from my subconscious. I was supposed to be doing something. I had left something undone somewhere. I had no idea what. I swung my feet around to the floor, intending to get up and start the blood flowing. That was until the blood made it to my ankle and the throbbing commenced. I tossed a couple of pillows down to the foot of the bed, leaned back against the headboard, and propped up my injured

119

limb. There would be no running today. Walking was going to be a challenge.

"Doesn't it seem to you," I said, "that a logbook would have more to do with parts than drugs?"

"Like what?"

"I don't know. Maybe Avidor is stealing from Sentinel. Or selling to them. Maybe he sold them a bad part. Or he sold it to a broker who sold it to them. Dan, Sentinel had a crash not too long ago."

He was quiet for a microsecond. "Oh, shit yeah. A bad one down in Ecuador or Salvador or some fucking place. Took them forever just to get to the site."

A thought had popped into my head and tumbled into another couple of thoughts rattling around in there and pretty soon they were starting to stick together and form a critical mass and, damaged ankle or not, the momentum lifted me off the bed and pulled me across the room to dig around on the dresser where I'd dumped my keys and my money from the night before. "I have to find . . ."

"Find what?"

"Find my messages from last night." That's what it was. That's what was bothering me. "I had a message from the jeweler."

"What jeweler?"

"The one who appraised the ring, and I think the message was that he figured out who it belonged to, but it was this long, confusing message that went over to the back of the page and I was so out of it when I came in . . ."

The messages weren't on the dresser with my keys.

120

I looked around for my jeans, which turned out to be on the floor in the bathroom.

"How in the hell could he figure that out? There were no marks on that ring anywhere. I looked all over it."

"This Gemprint thing they do. They have this laser process where they can read the way a diamond is cut, which is never the same way twice, apparently. So it's like—"

"Snowflakes?"

"Yes, but more to the point, it's like fingerprints. People can have their diamonds identified and the information banked so that if the stone gets lost or stolen and turns up, it can find its way back. Only most people don't know about this process, so the jeweler said it was a real long shot but he took the reading anyway and I think . . ." I'd tried three pockets of the jeans. The messages were in the fourth, folded neatly, right where I'd stuffed them. One from Dan. One from Paul Gladstone in Detroit. One from the jeweler. And I was right. His message was that the diamond ring matched one in the Gemprint database belonging to a Belinda Culligan Fraley. Something else was written there that was trying to pull together all the other things I'd been thinking, but not comprehending. I was already moving toward my laptop.

"Hey!" Dan was still there, and he wasn't pleased to be left out. "What's up?"

"The woman who owned this ring is dead. I'll call you back, Dan."

"Shan—"

* * *

121

The image that filled my laptop screen was dim and blurry. The figures that moved through it looked like ghosts in hazard suits, stepping through a dark landscape, picking their way over dangerous terrain in the herky-jerky motion of an Internet video feed.

The first time I'd watched the short clip, my face had burned hot, almost as if the waves of searing heat from the fire had transcended time, distance, and the limits of technology and come through the screen. With my heightened sense of smell, I even thought I could detect the faint odor of jet fuel as it leached into the soil on a mountainside six thousand miles away.

The plane had crashed two months before—close enough in time that images of the catastrophe could still be easily retrieved from the memory bank, but distant enough that they had receded just out of reach of every-day consciousness. The stories and articles from the Internet had reminded me of the details.

An Air Sentinel B777, almost brand new and oper-ating as flight 634, had completed most of its journey from Miami to Quito, Ecuador, when it had dropped from the radar screen at 2046 local time. The next time it had been seen was several days later when rescuers finally made it to the crash site on the side of a moun-tain north of the city.

When the clip stopped, I restarted it and this time looked for the neon orange flags used to mark locations of human remains. They were hard to see, but they were there. I ran my finger over the rough diamond surface of the ring John had sent, and wondered which flag marked the spot where Belinda Culligan Fraley's remains had been found.

Chapter Fourteen

I almost hadn't recognized him without the combat gear, but Jack Dolan had been the only patron at Big Pinks who was not crowded under a big striped awning in a hubbub of eating, drinking, chatting, and smoking. Relaxing in the sun in a billowy, short-sleeved cotton shirt and baggy shorts, he had seemed younger than I had perceived him the night before, when his weathered voice, the glints of silver in his hair, and perhaps the whiff of paternal concern had put him in his late fifties. Maybe it was the huarache sandals, or the fact that he still had all his hair, which wasn't as long as I'd suspected, but neither was it meticulously tended, private investigation being one of those professions where tonsorial maintenance was optional.

He sat forward in his chair, took off his sunglasses, and studied the diamond ring. "How do you know," he asked, "that it came from the crash site?"

"I told you about the Gemprint thing where—"

"Gemprint I understand, and I believe you when you say the ring belongs . . . or belonged to this Fraley woman. What I don't understand is how you knew she was on the airplane."

"That part was easy. I went online and pulled up a list of the deceased. She and her husband, Frank, were both on Air Sentinel 634 when it went down. They died along with everyone else on board."

"Why would you think to do that?"

"Because the logbook is from Air Sentinel. Air Sentinel had a terrible crash a few months ago. The logbook is damaged in a way that is consistent with a crash. Bobby Avidor is involved in selling bad parts. This Fraley woman had died recently. It was a theory that seemed to make it all fit together."

"How do you know she was wearing this ring when she died?"

"I don't have *proof* that she was wearing the ring. I don't have *proof* of anything. But I believe the logbook came from the crash site, and if the logbook came from the crash site, wouldn't you have to think the ring did, too?"

It all came out too fast and with a higher acid content than I had intended, and I was immediately remorseful. Not smart to piss off the one guy I thought could help me, especially since he'd done nothing to deserve it. But my left ankle was bigger by half than my right, I was on the downside of a three-hour-old adrenaline rush, and I had really expected him to be more enthusiastic . . . okay, impressed by my discovery. I wasn't sure what to make of my own reaction. Maybe I was trying to compensate for screwing up the night before. Trying too hard.

He stared at me, and I couldn't read anything in his eyes except that they were brown. And intelligent. "I think you're right," he said.

"You do?"

"I'm testing your theory. Is that all right with you?"

"Ummm . . ."

"That's a technique we investigators use. Asking questions for understanding. An alternative approach would be for me to simply assume that you're right. Maybe you're always right, which means we don't have to investigate at all. I'll just wait for you to tell me the answer. That would be easier, of course. And quicker."

A grin was tugging at the corners of his mouth, but a gentle one, making it all right for me to smile at myself. When I did, he started to laugh. He was making his point without making me feel stupid, a technique that I thought I might need to brush up on. He held the ring out for me, and I took it.

"Okay," I said. "All right. I don't know that Mrs Fraley was wearing this ring, but I made that leap, perhaps an incautious one, but one that I think is logical given all the other circumstances. I suppose I could call the family and try to find out."

"There you go," he said. "Now tell me about the car that followed you."

I told him about the kidney red car that had chased me around the parking garage, and, from the tone of his inquiry, flunked the investigator lesson on being tailed. No license plate. No description.

"Kidney car," he said, putting the glasses back on.

"Not much to go on," I admitted.

"We're going to have to work on that. But in the meantime, what do you think all this means?"

"I think the crash might have been caused by a bad part, that Avidor was involved, maybe with the guy you're chasing, and that the logbook is some kind of proof."

"Of what?"

"Of the cause of the crash."

He sat back, stuck his legs straight out, crossed them

125

at the huaraches, and clasped his hands together on his belly. It looked like his thinking pose. "That could be one explanation," he said. "If your friend McTavish found out about it, that would be a motive for murder. Do they know the cause of the accident yet?"

"Officially, they're still investigating," I said. "It's only been a few months. But I'm wondering if they already suspect something, because of the way that Sentinel's maintenance manager reacted in Boston."

"Is it an NTSB investigation? Or the Ecuadorans?"

"Ecuador called in the NTSB."

"Good," he nodded. "That's good. Now I've got a question for you. You said you talked to Pat Spain over at Miami-Dade."

"I did."

"Why didn't you give her the logbook? For all you know, it's evidence. Why didn't you hand it over to the detective working the case? That's what most civilians would do."

"I almost did. I took it over there to give it to her. But then I got this feeling that it wouldn't have . . . not that she wouldn't have done the right thing, but that it wouldn't have helped John, or John's family, for her to have it. I feel responsible to them, and it seemed at the time that it was better for me to have it than for her to have it."

"You thought you could do more with it than she could?"

There was a delicate but unmistakable emphasis on "you." "I'm saying even if she *could* do more with it, I *would*."

"Subtle distinction."

126

"It didn't seem subtle at the time. Detective Spain had a theory and she seemed to be happy with it. She didn't seem interested in discussing alternative scenarios."

"Because something is obvious," he said, "doesn't mean it's not true."

"I know that. But I also knew John, and her theory doesn't make any sense."

"You said something about his brother last night. What's that all about?"

I told him.

"You know," he said, starting slowly, "one reason cops can do what they do is because they bring an objective point of view to proceedings. Sometimes people crack. Sometimes it's the people who've worked the hardest and the longest. I've seen it over and over. Sometimes you don't know people as well as you think you do."

"If you're saying I have a personal stake in this matter, you're right. And if you're saying you think the good detective should have the logbook, I'll take it to her. But I don't believe John was involved in a drug deal. Not for his brother. Not for any reason. He was a good man and he worked hard for everything he ever got."

He looked up into the awning, studying the under-carriage as if he wanted to see how it worked, what held it up. I couldn't see behind the shades but I felt a crack in his resistance. I saw it in the tilt of his head, in the way he pressed his fingers together. A bubble of antici-pation started way down deep, but I kept it in check.

"Let me talk to Patty on my own," he said. "I know her from when I worked at the Bureau. She might tell me things she wouldn't tell you."

127

The bubble turned to a rush. "You worked for the FBI? Where?"

"Mostly down here, but I spent time in the New York office. Why?"

"Because John made a call to the FBI from his cell phone while he was down here."

His interest level was rising steadily. "Was it the main number?"

"Yes. Is there a way to trace his call to a specific agent, or are we stuck with a call to the generic Feds?"

"Not traceable. The only way we could—" He stopped, smiled to himself, and shook his head.

"The only way we could find out who he called," I offered helpfully, "is for you to ask around at the FBI and see what you can come up with."

He let his sunglasses drop down his nose and peered at me over the rims. "I didn't say I'd do that." He paid the check and stood up. "Let's walk."

Walking slowly and at a distinct list to the left, I followed him down a small side street, past a pile of rebar that would turn a quaint old hotel into a featureless new condo development. We crossed another street and went through a park the size of a postage stamp where dogs inspected the grass, looking for their spot, and people with sand on their feet stood in line at public restrooms and changing booths. We went over a grassy swale, onto a wooden boardwalk, and there it was. I took in a deep breath and enjoyed my first real look at the ocean since I'd been there.

"Nice," I said, leaning against one of the plank railings.

It was more than nice. It was as if someone had lifted the lid off of the world, had opened it up to air it out, to make space for the uncoiling of the neighborhood, of the city, of the continent into the wide-open, endless repository known as the Atlantic Ocean.

He leaned next to me, and we stood side by side, looking out to sea. "It's nicer without the smoke."

It was true. The light from the sun was dulled by the haze of smoke, but the heat was full force, and it felt good on my arms and my face after the long winter in New England and the long night in a Florida swamp. I felt my own uncoiling inside. Jack must have felt it, too.

"The man your buddy went to meet," he said, "is named Jimmy Zacharias."

Jimmy Zacharias. J.Z. I squinted into the sun and smiled. "What is the case you're on?"

"Jimmy killed two men."

"He killed two men and he's still walking around in the world?"

"He's responsible for the helicopter accident that killed them."

"Oh."

The muscles in his forearms tensed. "Just because he killed them with shoddy maintenance instead of a hollow point bullet doesn't mean he's any less responsible. And it doesn't make it any less criminal."

"I agree with you. I just had a different image in my mind is all. Who's your client?"

"The insurance company for the manufacturer of the helicopter. Both widows are suing, but the manufacturer had nothing to do with this. This accident was caused by bad parts or bad maintenance or both."

"I assume Jimmy worked on the helicopter."

"One of his shops refurbished it and did some follow-up work. He has a financial interest in a handful of repair stations in the area. That's how he launders his dirty parts."

"Are you talking about FAA-certified repair stations?"

"No one would do business with one that wasn't certified. That's the whole point. He finds a business that seems perfectly legitimate, usually one that's in trouble and needs cash. Then he slowly starts to mix the bad parts in with the good. He dummies up the paperwork, and that shit flows right on through and into airline operations and inventories all over the world."

"Don't these stations get inspected on a regular basis?"

"Some of these repair shop guys know a lot more than their inspectors ever will. A lot of them were mechanics for Eastern and Pan Am. And when he does get into trouble, Jimmy just changes the name of the place and gets recertified. He ran one station under four different names that I counted."

"Where does he get the bad parts?"

"Wherever he can. From people like Avidor who steal for him. Jimmy was in the military, so he has access to a lot of military surplus. He has his own aircraft recovery and salvage business. That's what you saw last night. He also keeps an eye on the junkyards. He's not above doing a little strip-and-dip."

"Strip-and-dip? Do I even want to know?"

"He gets scrapped parts from the junkyard, cleans them up, paints over the corrosion, dummies up the paperwork, and sells them."

"Painting over the corrosion," I said, "that must be the dip part."

"You'd be amazed at how good they look with a new coat of paint."

"Jimmy sounds like a real peach."

"You don't know the half of it," he said.

"Why isn't he in jail?"

"He's smarter than your average swamp rat, and what he does, it's hard to prove."

"Do you think you'll be able to prove what Jimmy did on this helicopter accident?"

"I don't know. We've just identified the part that caused the crash. It's pretty badly damaged, but we've got metallurgists and mechanics and engineers looking at it. If we can demonstrate that it's bogus and tie it back to Jimmy, then we've got him."

"Tie it back how?"

"Maintenance records, purchase orders. The logbook. In this business there is always a paper trail. It's required. It's just that the paperwork is sometimes forged. But I have a feeling about this. I think we're going to get him this time."

"This time?"

"If there's no legitimate paper trail, I'll find someone to flip on Jimmy. That's why I've been watching him. I wanted to see who he's working with these days. The parts business tends to be a closed community. Jimmy and I, we know lots of the same people."

"And now you know Avidor. Maybe he'll turn out to be a talker."

"Maybe so."

We drifted into an easy silence. I watched a group of noisy volleyball players and realized for the first time I hadn't seen many children around. I looked as far as

I could see from one end of the beach to the other. There was not one small person in sight.

"Look, Jack, I really would like to work on this with you. I can scrape together ten thousand dollars from my retirement accounts. That's all I have to spend on the whole deal, including my expenses. So here's my pitch: You take my case and I'll give you all of the money that's left when we find John's murderer."

"We?"

"You and me."

"Together? That would be highly unusual."

"Do you really think I'm going to sit around the pool reading *Vanity Fair* and drinking Cuba Libres while you're out doing all the scut work?"

"Cuba Libres?"

"Isn't that what you people drink down here?"

"Not since 1954. Don't you have a job? Some place you have to be?"

"That's a long story, but what it comes down to is this is where I have to be, and that is my deal."

"Why are you so adamant about this?"

"Will knowing that make a difference in your decision?"

He gazed out over the turquoise waves and seemed to give the question serious thought, which I liked. "It might."

"John and I got involved in something together at Logan. The truth is I got involved and he decided to help me."

"What was it?"

"My predecessor there, the woman who was the general manager before me, had died. That's why the job was available for me. The police thought she'd committed suicide and that was the company line. The people who knew her couldn't accept that she had killed herself, and it turned out she didn't."

"Murdered?"

"By a ramper. One of her own employees."

He smiled lightly. "And you got involved?"

"He was my employee, too. I inherited him."

"Ah."

"I could have left it alone. Things in Boston had been left alone for a long time by a lot of different people. But there was something . . . I felt that I knew this woman—Ellen was her name—even though I'd never met her. We had a lot in common, and I couldn't let it go until I had figured out why she had died."

"Did you figure it out?"

"Yes."

"And John helped you?"

"He provided me with information from the ramp that I never could have gotten without him. Things I had to know to understand what had happened to Ellen and why. He warned me a few times. Even though I was a member of management, he took my side against his union brothers. These were people he'd worked with side by side for years. Some of them he'd known since they were kids. And they weren't happy about it. No one's ever stood up for me like that."

"That's important to you, is it? Having someone stand up for you?"

"Yes."

"What happened to the murderer?"

A cold wave passed through me, the same one I always

felt at this point in the story. "The man who murdered Ellen died."

"How?"

"He was chasing after me on the ramp. There was an accident and he died. Horribly."

He turned slightly, enough to see my face when he asked, "And you feel bad about this?"

It was my turn to stare at the shimmering ocean. "Sometimes."

He held out his hand. "Let me see that ring again." I gave it to him and he studied it, turning it slowly. "I'd like to see this piece get back to the family it belongs to. It looks as if it might be important to someone."

"And I'd like to find out who killed my friend. If it was Jimmy and we can prove it, maybe we both get something good out of the deal."

"Ten thousand dollars?"

"Whatever's left."

"I'll do it." I felt a quick flush of excitement, which he moved quickly to squash. "And I have a few conditions of my own. You have to do what I say when I say it."

"I will."

"You have to be available whenever I need you, day or night."

"I've given up sleeping, anyway."

"And you take the notes."

"Excuse me?"

"And drive."

"What?"

"All investigators take notes," he said, clearly seeing more and more merit in the idea. "And you said it.

134

I'm the professional. I know you don't want me slowed down by administrative duties. It wouldn't be cost effective."

"Are you making fun of me?"

"Yes." He laughed, but again in that comfortable way.

"It's been pointed out to me," I said, "that I can be a little structured at times."

"That's all right," he said. "I can use a little more structure in my life. Let's go get my truck. But first we have to stop at the office supply store around the corner."

"What for?"

"A notepad and pencil for you."

The route Bobby had taken me on the night before, as I had suspected, felt more benign by daylight. The masses of tangled trees and thatched brush lining the roadways were lush and full under blue sky and bright sun, not forbidding. The quiet that enveloped us as we moved farther and farther from the city was calming, not frightening. But then I wasn't alone this time. Jack was in the passenger seat.

I'd spent most of the drive out talking, filling him in on the details of what I knew so far. I'd given him the timeline Felix and I had made.

"What did you find out about the rental car?" he asked.

"Not much. Whoever turned it in left it in the rental car lot way off in a corner by a fence. This agent I spoke to found it and checked it in. It was the same deal as the hotel. John had wanted to pay cash—it was in their records—but they charged it to his credit card when he didn't show up in person to pay. Like the hotel room,

135

the car has been rented a half dozen times since the murder."

He set my timeline on the seat, leaned forward, and searched the trees. "Go up half a mile . . . right here, where it looks like there's no road, and make that corner up there. My truck should be back in the bush."

I pulled around the corner and stopped. We both got out. I didn't see any truck, but that was, I imagined, the whole point. Jack struck out on a nontrail into the undergrowth, and I wobbled after him as best I could, careful not to step in any more holes. I found him standing next to a gray low-slung truck that looked as if it had been in all the rough places Jack had been.

"An El Camino," I said. "I don't remember the last time I saw one of these."

His stance was odd—back rigid, arms straight at his sides, eyes turned skyward.

"It was two cops," he said.

"What was two cops?"

"The helicopter crash I told you about, the one I'm investigating. The two men who were killed were county cops up in the Florida panhandle. The county had purchased a helicopter for search and rescue. It was just this small county sheriff's department that was trying to do a better job. And what they bought was old, but it had been refurbished. They'd never even had it up before. A little girl went missing. Six years old. They weren't in the air fifteen minutes when it fell out of the sky—and crushed them both. They never had a chance." He started to go on, and didn't. The bundle of bone and muscle that hinged his jaw to his skull was working hard, clenching and unclenching. I'd known him for less than twenty-four hours, but I could feel the agitation churning beneath the calm exterior, and his struggle not to let it show.

"Did they find the girl?"

"They found her body."

I leaned back against the truck. It was dusty, but I felt the need to sag against something. "I'm sorry. Did you know any of these people?"

"I know Jimmy. I know he cut some corner or shaved a little something off here or there to put in his own pocket. And then he went home, went to bed, and slept like a baby."

He was very still as he stared up into the high afternoon sky.

The tight line of his shoulders under his lightweight shirt, the way he seemed to be searching the treetops, and especially the tilt of his head all reminded me of something I had seen the night before. The dog Bull had sniffed the air that way as he'd picked up my scent and had stood all aquiver with anticipation of the chase, and I suddenly felt as if I'd walked into a movie after it had started.

"Jack, is there something between you and Jimmy Zacharias?"

"Jimmy is just another scumbag in a long line of scumbags."

A little too much indifference, a slight turn away, and I wished all the way back to Miami that I had asked the question when I could have seen his face as he answered.

★ ★ ★

137

"Holy Christ, Shanahan. Are you sure about that?"

Dan and I were experiencing the usual techno-interruptus that comes along with mobile communications. But this time he was on a landline in his office and the problem was at my end. I was trying to get back to my hotel, but had to keep driving in a circle to keep my cell phone far enough away from the airport's electronic interference.

"Think about it, Dan. The impact and fire explains the damage to the logbook. The fact that the airplane crashed explains why no one's been looking for it. Everyone thought it was destroyed."

"And you're saying you think it was caused by a bad part?"

"Bad part or faulty maintenance. I think that's why your buddy over at Air Sentinel was in such a twist. He knew the part you asked him about came from the accident airplane."

"If that aircraft came down because of a bad part and the word gets out, Sentinel has got a big fucking problem."

"They're probably trying to figure out right now how to deal with the backlash."

A tollbooth loomed ahead. I had somehow gotten twisted around myself in my meandering route. I had to stop talking and pay attention to the road. That didn't mean Dan had to stop talking.

"This makes Avidor more of a scumbag than I gave him credit for. If Johnny knew about any of this—"

"John knew about it, Dan. He had the logbook. I don't know how he got it, but he must have known it had something to do with that crash. Proof of what caused it . . . maybe a record of a bad part that was used. I think that's what got him killed."

"That logbook is a mess, Shanahan. I don't see how it could prove anything."

"It's possible the killer didn't know that." I took the last exit before the tollbooth, turned back toward the airport, then found a quiet strip mall where I could park and finish my conversation. "I don't have it all figured out, Dan. All I know is it never made sense to me that John would wake up one day and decide to fly to Florida to confront Bobby on being a drug runner if he'd known about it all along. John would have roared into Miami if he'd heard Bobby was trading in bad parts."

Dan was silent, an event unusual enough for me to take note. "What's the matter?"

"I was just thinking . . . How many people went down on that ship?"

"Two hundred and three. No survivors."

"Jesus God."

He was thinking what I was. An airplane accident is bad enough when it's just that—an accident. A crash caused by a sleazy, back alley transaction between a couple of low-rent, self-dealing criminal entrepreneurs that may have netted each a couple of hundred dollars was so monstrous, so malevolent that trying to comprehend it just made your circuits melt down. It was mass murder.

"Listen, Dan, I don't think we should be talking about this to anyone. It's pretty volatile stuff."

"I don't even like talking to you about it."

"Good. And I need more help."

"That's a big fucking surprise."

"I have a theory on how John got the book. According

139

to his phone records, he called a bar in Salem from down here."

"So?"

"So Salem isn't far from Gloucester, and Gloucester is where Avidor and the McTavishes all grew up. Maybe Avidor still has friends back there, or he and John had a mutual acquaintance. So here's what I need you to do. I need you to drive up there—"

"Shanahan, do you know what kind of a week I'm having here? It's spring break. My loads are off the wall. Not to mention my own kid's out of school and she's up here with me . . ."

"A nice drive up the north shore will get you out of the airport and give you a little father-daughter bonding time with Michele. You can take her to lunch, have some chow-dah, and while you're there snoop around this bar and find the connection to Bobby."

He was quiet. I hated horning in on his time with Michele, limited as it was. But I couldn't fly up and do it. Given her circumstances, I wouldn't ask Mae to take time away from her children, and Terry couldn't even drive. "Dan, if it's true Bobby is selling bad parts to commercial airlines, or to anyone for that matter, wouldn't you do anything to make him stop?"

I heard a light thud and knew he had put the receiver down on the desk. I'd seen him do it when we'd worked together. It's what he did when he wanted a moment to think. I watched the rush hour traffic ebb and flow and waited. Dan had long ago surrendered himself— body, soul, and marriage—to the business of flying people from here to there. Like all good airline people, he preferred that the passengers who put their lives in his hands got *all* the way to where they were going safely. With their bags. Besides, he hated Bobby Avidor's guts. There was only one conclusion he could come to.

He picked up the phone and I heard him breathing. "Give me the name of this dive."

Chapter Fifteen

Jack's bungalow on South Beach was one in a long row of low-slung boxy structures that were painted peach and topped with terracotta tile roofs. The complex reminded me of pictures I'd seen of officers' quarters in the Pacific theater during World War II. I wouldn't have been surprised to see Douglas MacArthur, or at least Gregory Peck come striding out with a pipe in his mouth and an aide in tow. But the only one who came out was Jack carrying a cup with a lid. When he got in, the aroma of his coffee filled the car.

"Where to?" I asked him.

"Go back out the way you came and get on I-95."

"North or south?"

"North. We've got a very busy day ahead."

The landscape on I-95 north wasn't much to see. Thunder-boat factory outlets, truncated strip malls, and tire dealerships hunkered off to the sides. What there was could only be glimpsed intermittently through a solid wall of eighteen-wheelers, tour buses, and hulking SUVs with trailer hitches, all moving over twelve lanes of concrete at speeds that left no margin for error.

After he finished his coffee he settled back and got comfortable. "I thought," he said, "you spent fourteen years in the airline business. Why don't you know more about bogus parts?"

"I did. And what I knew about the maintenance function was all I needed to know—'How soon can you fix my airplane so I can get this angry throng out of my terminal?' What exit am I looking for?"

"I'll tell you when we're getting close."

Jack's navigation was making me rethink my commitment to being the designated driver. He was dribbling out the directions as we went, which I despised. I wanted to know in advance where we were going. I wanted to know how far it was and how long it would take to get there. I wanted to have in my mind a route of travel. But I quit arguing about it when I finally realized his brain didn't work that way. He went strictly by feel, and he liked the flexibility of keeping all his options open.

"I do know this—" I said, checking my blind spot for a lane change. "Majestic Airlines never had a problem with bogus parts."

"Dream on, kid. Majestic has a problem. All commercial carriers have the problem. They don't want you to know about it, and the FAA is helping them cover it up."

"That sounds vaguely paranoid, Jack. Slightly conspiracy theory-ish."

"The FAA won't even acknowledge the term 'bogus parts.' Their accepted term is 'Suspected Unapproved Parts.'" He laughed. "That doesn't sound as menacing as counterfeits. Or scrapped and sold as new. Or old and damaged military parts buffed up and sold 'like new.' Or new parts sold for unapproved purposes because they're cheaper than the right parts. Or hot stamped parts."

"What are those?"

"Parts with paperwork that says they were inspected when they weren't. The FAA has literally gone through their databases and reclassified accidents that the NTSB attributed to bad parts."

143

"There have been accidents attributed to bogus parts?"

"What do you think happens when an airplane is flying around with a car part in it?"

"Car parts? Could we be just a little less hyperbolic?" I adjusted my position in the seat. I'd been there for a long while, and my ankle was stiffening up.

"Lancer Cargo about five years ago," he said. "They got a couple of starters in that their mechanics didn't think looked right. They opened them up and found scrap and car parts inside. These were ten-thousand-dollar parts. But that's better than having a counterfeit or back door part slipped in on you because at least you have a chance of spotting a car part that's not supposed to be there."

"What's a back door part?"

"Say a foreman at a legitimately approved machine shop keeps the assembly line running after he's supposed to have shut it down. He makes an extra ten combustion liners that his boss doesn't know about, sells them out the back door to some dirty broker, and pockets whatever he gets. This is your exit."

I hit the brakes, sailed into the outside lane, and made the exit, barely. The black Mercedes following too closely on my tail honked his displeasure. If Jack noticed I couldn't tell. He was on a roll.

"A back door part doesn't get tested, which is bad enough, but at least it's been properly designed and is made out of the approved materials. You can't say that about counterfeit parts. These dinky little machine shop guys look at parts selling for ten or fifteen thousand bucks a pop and they say, 'Sheeeeeet, I can make me one of them.' And they do. Maybe they reverse engineer it and

144

make it out of whatever material happens to be lying around. As for accidents, there was a Norwegian charter flight a few years back, I think it was a Convair, that fell into the North Sea. Do you know why?"

"I'm sensing a problem with bogus parts."

"The fasteners—the bolts used to hold the tail on— were made from a lower grade of steel than the standard demands, and they hadn't been tested. When the airplane flew into turbulence, metal fatigue caused the bolts to snap. The tail fell off, and everyone died."

"If it wasn't reported, then how does anyone know?"

He reached over to adjust the air vent. I couldn't tell if he was too warm or too cold. I was feeling chilled myself. "Because the Norwegian version of the FAA wasn't afraid to say what happened. In this country, between the FAA and the airlines, they don't have the manpower, the resources, or the balls to solve this problem. Since they can't solve it, they have to hide it because if they didn't, no one would ever fly again."

Even with the windows closed, I could still feel the air taking on that familiar humid, swampy quality as we drove farther and farther from the interstate. We kept passing signs on the side of the road that promised tours of the Everglades, alligator shows, and airboat rides. I saw an official National Park visitors' station with a tall totem pole in the front yard.

Jack seemed to be searching for a specific street, staring at the infrequent signs until they were past.

"Jack, do you know the actual names of any of these streets?"

"No. What do you think would happen if John Q.

Traveler found out the fan blades in the jet engine on his airplane came from Rudy's Chop Shop?"

"*Came* from, or *might* have come from?"

"You would be amazed, Alex. You *will* be amazed."

"If it's such a big problem, how come we don't see more commercial airliners plunging from the sky?"

"It's more insidious than that and it's not at that stage yet. It's like termites that get into your house and start chomping away. You have no idea what's going on because the damage is underneath, and the truth is you're not looking all that carefully. What's even worse is when the guy you hire to inspect your house looks it over and tells you everything is copacetic."

"That would be the FAA?"

"Right. You think your house is stable and strong. You think it's going to last forever right up until the day it collapses around your ears. That's what's going to happen to the U.S. airline industry and its vaunted safety record one day."

"How do you know all this stuff?"

"Because it's one of the things I used to do at the Bureau."

"I think you're exaggerating."

"That's what you're supposed to think. It's the FAA's job to shill for the airline business—your business—and it's the job of the airlines to sell tickets. My job was to chase the termites, no matter where they went. I saw a lot of nasty bugs. Take your next right, go down and park in front of the first trailer in the third row."

"Am I about to meet one of your nasty bugs?"

"No. Ira was a good mechanic who never should

have tried to run a business. Unfortunately, those are the only ones who ever seem to get caught."

Ira Leemer looked like Rod Stewart without the benefit of your glasses. He had the elfin face, the sharp nose, and the tapering chin. He even had blonde highlights in his gray hair. But whereas Rod's features were still crisp and distinct, Ira's were puffy, droopy, and soft. And when he opened his mouth to speak, he sounded like what he was—a half-Cajun South Florida ex-con salvage dealer who lived in a trailer on the edge of a swampy marsh.

He was talking to me and he was on a roll, perched on the top step of his porch. The door was open and I could hear the sound of an oscillating fan inside. Ira was explaining himself and the unfortunate decisions that had sent him to prison.

"Well—" He twisted around to face me more fully. "Ever'body knows there's bad parts, and then there's bad parts. You take a B747. There's over six million parts on that sucker, and most of them don't make that airplane fly. If you know what's what"—when Ira said "what," it came out like "whuuut"—"which I do, you know never to muck around with nothing that's flight critical." He wet his lips with a sip of Fresca from a sweaty can. "The worst thing I did was fudge a little bit when I had to. I'd take parts from one unit that just come in to be fixed and use them in another one I had to get out the door. You weren't supposed to do that, swap parts around, but there ain't no real reason you can't do it other than they told you not to. And besides that anyways, these parts they call bogus, a lot of the times

147

they're just as good as the real ones. They don't have the paperwork behind 'em is all that is."

"Ira," Jack said, "you weren't working on crop dusters in the backyard." He was sitting across from Ira in a folding beach chair, the kind with the aluminum frame and the woven nylon strips. "You were an FAA-certified repair station doing work for major commercial airlines. You weren't allowed to run by the seat of your pants."

"I know that. All I'm saying is I paid attention to the things that mattered. Maybe I wasn't so good with the paperwork, all the manuals you got to keep on hand and updated and so on. I just never had the money to do it right. These fellows coming up in the business now, they just don't care if the engine runs or the airplane gets off the ground or even if it stays bolted together while it's up there."

Between declarations, Ira puffed the life out of a hand-rolled cigarette that was shaped like a knotty twig. Every time he exhaled, I felt my own lungs withering. I moved a few more inches upwind. "How did you get into the business?"

He shaded his eyes with one hand and pointed up at me with one of his yellowed fingers. "See now, that there was one of my main problems. You think of it as a business. To me it was just fixing airplanes like I'd always done. I was a mechanic for Eastern before that asshole Lorenzo showed up. Other buddies of mine, they'd started their own repair shops, so when I finally got laid off I figured what the hell, I'll give it a whirl. And so I did. Ended up doing twenty-one months. It don't sound like that much, but I'll tell you what, I

148

could'na done one more day. But I never went into it to be no crook. I really didn't. All I was trying to do was feed my children."

I reached up to rub the back of my neck. I'd worn my hair up because it had been so hot. It wasn't even nine in the morning and I could already feel the sunburn starting.

Ira nodded at Jack. "What about you, Bobo? I hear you retired from the FBI a few months back."

Bobo? Jack was busy ignoring me. Was this a nickname with meaning specific to Jack? Or was it Ira's catchall name for everyone? He hadn't yet called me Bobo.

"I left three years ago," Jack said.

"Whoooeeee! You sure do lose track of time when you're in the joint."

Jack stood up and stretched, pushing the arch in his back with both hands. "Ira, did you get anything on Avidor?" The catching-up-with-each-other phase of the interview was now apparently over.

"Well, I did. After you called I did me some checking around." Ira took a long drag of nicotine and checked back and forth with his eyes, as if he might catch someone sneaking around the side of his trailer to eavesdrop.

Jack glanced over at me. And he kept looking at me, eyebrows raised. I'd figured my role in this interview was to listen closely, learn what I could, and not disturb the flow. But after he stared for a while longer, it hit me that my role was to listen closely, learn what I could, not disturb the flow—and take notes. I reached into my pocket, pulled out my nifty notebook, and christened it with Ira's name and the date.

149

"What I hear—and I don't know nothing for sure 'cause I ain't never worked with this boy myself—is he's a good steady source. He works out there at the airport and he's in management, so he can get you what he says he'll get you, and he delivers on time. He'll get you papers, too, if you pay extra."

"What's he pushing?"

"Anything he can lay hands on, but mainly new parts. He's getting hisself a reputation, too. They're all still talking about a deal where he had this ol' boy stealing from out of his own airline's inventory and then selling them back to the same outfit. They was paying for the same gizmo twice and didn't even know it."

"Was it Majestic?" I asked the question, then braced for the answer. In spite of all that had happened, I still felt protective of Majestic Airlines. I'd left fourteen years of my life there.

"No. He don't shit in his own bed, apparently, which is the smart thing to do. I hear he uses these rent-a-mechanics a lot." He looked at Jack. "You know the ones I mean?"

Jack nodded. "Temps with mechanic's licenses."

"Thing is, they don't make much money, and they got access to everywhere because they go wherever they're needed." Something in the water caught his eye. He went over to a splintered deck that hung out over the mud and the water. "Look over there, Missy, in the sawgrass. See that? See 'em moving out there?"

I joined him and scanned the brown water where he pointed. And near as I could tell everything was moving. Everything was alive. Bugs crawled on the carpet of lily pads or swarmed across the surface in huge undulating clouds. Mysterious creatures pinched at the surface from underneath, leaving no trace except dissipating concentric circles. The drought had pulled the waterline down, exposing large expanses of black mud, tree roots and rocks that were slimy and encrusted, covered in black and green mold and algae. And then I did see what he was showing me and it gave me a shiver. It was a nest of small alligators—at least eight of them—knifing through the shallow water with only their snouts and bubble eyes visible.

"They're babies," he said. "The mother must be around here somewhere."

"What's Avidor doing for Jimmy, Ira?" Jack obviously wanted to get back on course. We went back to join him. He was still at the trailer, having shown no interest in checking out the indigenous wildlife.

"He's recruiting mechanics," Ira said, settling back in. "Dirty boys. You know the kind I mean. They got the feelers out. Somebody even asked me if I was interested."

"Recruiting them for what?"

"Don't know, Bobo." Ira's tone had turned cagey. "I try not to know stuff like that no more. And I told them no. I ain't going back to prison no way no how." He reached down and knocked on his wooden steps.

"Speculate," Jack said. "What is Jimmy up to these days?"

Ira took a last long drag and dropped the cigarette into the soda can at his side. The still burning butt hissed when it hit bottom. "I really can't, Bobo."

"Yes, you can."

Jack didn't move and Ira didn't move. All they did

151

was look at each other. But something had shifted between the two men. Jack's approach still felt casual and relaxed, perfectly in tune with the hot and still weather that slowed the world to an underwater pace. But there was an underlying firmness of tone that had crept in, a directness in his speech, a no-bullshit attitude that seemed perfectly pitched to Ira's frequency. And he responded.

"Far as I know, Jimmy's doing the same old shit. Pulling in parts from wherever he can get them cheap, and selling them for what the market will bear."

"Is he still pushing them out through the usual outlets?"

"Yeah, I guess. I don't know who specifically he's using these days, but it's got to be three or four of them little repair shops around town that got their FAA certificates and not much else. Probably the ones couldn't stay in business if it weren't for him propping them up." He reached into the slush-filled cooler by his side for another can of soda, and smiled as he popped it open. Then he reached into a deep pocket of his baggy pants for his tobacco pouch. "You after Jimmy, are you?"

"Maybe."

"What for?"

Jack looked as though he were considering how much to tell Ira. "The helicopter thing. The one that went down up in the panhandle."

"Those deputies, huh? I heard about that. You ain't never gonna get him on that, Bobo. Take my word. He's got hisself covered six ways from Sunday."

Jack paused before answering. "We'll see."

Ira sat shaking his head and staring down into his

lap, absorbed by the intricate process of rolling another tobacco twig. "Nobody ever used to get kilt in this business. But it's what it comes to when you get these drug people coming in."

Jack looked at him closely. "Drug people?"

"The business has changed since you and me were part of the landscape. It ain't the friendly, neighborly sort of confab it used to be. It's growing. New people are coming in, and some of them are crossing over from the dope trade. Not a good class of people, neither, if you want my opinion."

"Drugs and aircraft parts," I said. "That doesn't sound like a natural crossover to me."

"Why not? You can make almost as much money, the FAA is a hell of a lot easier to hide from than the DEA, and even if you do get caught like I did you don't do much time. I mean twenty-one months ain't nothing compared to a life sentence. Or the needle in the arm."

"Do you have the names of any of these drug people?" Jack asked him.

"No. You never know who these people are. They're used to keeping themselves hidden. They don't know nothing about fixing airplanes. That's the whole problem. The government grabs up the ones like me that don't mean no harm, really, and leaves the ones who are a menace to society out on the street. At least I always made sure anything I fixed would work."

"Ira"—Jack was still in that firm tone—"I need to know why Jimmy is putting together a crew of mechanics."

"Why don't you ask the Avidor fellow?"

"I plan to." Jack moved a step closer to Ira. The toes

of his shoes were almost touching the bottom step. "But I also need to know what you can find out. You said they contacted you. Call them back."

"All right. I'll do that for you, Bobo."

"I want to know something else, Ira. Air Sentinel 634."

Ira was busy firing up his cigarette. His eyes narrowed as he looked up at Jack. "What about it?"

"Do you know what I'm talking about?"

He studied the burning end of his cigarette. "I know about that airplane that flew into a mountain in Ecuador, if that's what you're asking me."

"What do you know about it?"

"Not a damn thing."

The answer came too fast. Ira knew it too—and didn't care. My inclination was to lean in because this was getting really interesting. But Jack stepped back and tilted his head to the sky. "You ever remember a fire season like this one, Ira?"

"No sir. Not in all my days. It's the drought is what it is." He nodded out to the swampy morass just beyond the deck. "Water levels are four or five feet low. It's so dry out here, you can see bottom in places. Yes sir. See things we ain't never meant to see."

Jack put one foot up on the step and moved his face closer to Ira's. "Tell me about the crash."

"I don't know nothing about that." Ira kept passing his free hand over his chest as if he were trying to wipe something off the palm of his hand. Then he started to rise, but Jack reached over and put one hand on the smaller man's shoulder, keeping him in his seat.

"Do you know something you're not sharing? Because

154

it feels to me as though you know something you're not sharing."

"No sir."

"I need you to get me something. A name. A place to start."

Ira's body began to list slightly in favor of his right shoulder where Jack's hand seemed to have gotten heavier. "That might be dangerous, Bobo. Might there be a little something in it for me if I get you what you want?"

"Get me something and we'll see."

Jack let go. Ira popped instantly back to center as if nothing had happened. "I'll scratch around a little for you," he said. "But I'll tell you right now, I ain't going too deep. I don't want no ex-drug runners on my ass."

We sat in the car with both doors swung open, waiting for the cabin to cool down. Jack was on the phone checking with his service for messages. He was having a hard time getting a signal. I was taking in the surroundings, things I had felt or heard but not seen when I'd been out Jimmy's way. Everything was green or brown, like plants and the water, or gray like the trunks of the ancient trees. Most of the flowers were purple. Purple seemed to be a big swamp color. There was an amazing variation of plant types, thousands of different textures and shapes and shades of green. Ferns that were six feet tall, bamboo stalks, twisted tree branches sprouting leaves as big as both my hands together.

"What do you think of Ira?" Jack had finished his call and was staring at the trailer. Ira had taken his cooler of Fresca and pouch of tobacco and trundled inside.

"If he turned down the work," I said, "he didn't do

it without finding out what it was. But if he didn't take the work, what other reason would he have to lie or withhold?"

"He's a snitch. He sells information. He could be playing both sides. The trick with someone like Ira is to get as much information as you can while revealing as little as you can. We'll wait and see what he comes up with." He closed his door and strapped in. "What do you think about this drug connection he mentioned?" He asked the question as though he knew I wouldn't like it.

I adjusted the vent on my side so the struggling air conditioner wouldn't blow hot air in my face, and tried to choose just the right word. "Interesting."

"Interesting?" He didn't seem satisfied with the one I'd chosen. "Did you tell Terry McTavish what Avidor said about his drug deal?"

"His alleged drug deal."

"What did he say?"

"He said it was more of Avidor's bullshit and he threatened to fly down here and beat the crap out of him with his cane. John's wife thinks it's a preposterous story. My friend Dan says no one on the ramp in Boston has heard anything about it. Terry hasn't been out of Boston since his accident and he's offered his phone records to demonstrate that he hasn't called any drug connections. No calls to Florida or South America."

"All right."

"I think it's a dead end, Jack."

"Okay."

"Aren't you going to argue with me?"

"I don't think it would be productive," he said.

The temperature of the air blasting out of the vents was approaching tolerable so I closed the door, put the car in gear, and pulled out of the trailer park. Dust flew and I was glad we had the windows up. Jack seemed content to stare out his window.

"What are we going to talk about all the way back to the city if you won't argue with me?"

"You can guess who we're going to talk with next."

"That doesn't sound productive."

"First clue—it's someone you already met."

Chapter Sixteen

Detective Patricia Spain had not offered her hand to me when we'd met at the police station. When she arrived at the restaurant and saw me sitting with Jack, she thrust it right out there and told me to call her Pat. It was a confident handshake. None of that stuff where you reach out and grab a dead jellyfish. I always admired that in another woman. I liked her better already.

As she settled in at our table, she reached over and touched Jack's arm, then did a double take on his face. "Baby, you look like hell."

He leaned over and kissed her cheek. "Thanks, Patty. You look great as always. I ordered for you. A large stack of banana pancakes with extra butter and extra syrup, a side of scrambled eggs and bacon—crisp—and a tall glass of orange juice. Is that going to be enough?"

She studied him critically, as if he were an oil painting at the museum. "You eat it, lover. You look like you could use the protein. And next time you want to meet with me, you make it someplace besides the airport. Could you have *picked* a more inconvenient place?"

"We're seeing someone here later. Besides, I thought you'd like a chance to get out of the office."

"Tell me what you need so I can get up out of here and go do some real work."

He sat back in his chair, looking marginally insulted. "Why do you always think—"

"I know you wouldn't be calling if you didn't need

something." She nailed him with her black eyes, but I could tell she was teasing him. Half teasing, maybe.

Jack's protest was interrupted when he had to push forward and let a family of six squeeze by our table, one at a time, each with their own large, clumsy rolling bag. Pat looked at me. "Why didn't you tell me you were running with this fool? I wouldn't have had my game face on."

"We hadn't even met at the time. I thought you weren't interested."

"That's not true. And I am sorry about your friend. I called the family after you left to see how they were getting along."

"Patty," Jack said, "you gave her the brush-off?"

"I wasn't even supposed to be talking to her. I've been instructed to refer all inquiries to the FBI. If I could save her from the experience of dealing with Agent Hollander, it's the least I could do." She spit out the agent's name as if it were a bug that had flown up her nose.

That was a name I hadn't heard. I dug out my notebook and wrote it down.

Jack pressed for details. "The Bureau took your case?"

"They did. And don't even ask me why. Ask Agent Damon Hollander. Maybe he'll tell you more than he told me, since all you Feebs come from the same DNA."

Jack shrugged. "Am I supposed to know him? I've never heard of him."

"He's too young for you, baby. He brought his tight little ass over to my office and snatched Mr John McTavish right out from under me. Didn't say this. Didn't say that. Didn't say boo."

159

"You let him do that? That doesn't sound like you, Patty."

"It's not like I don't have enough murders to fill up my idle hours. Besides that, the boss came in and told me in his quiet voice, which he only uses when he's serious, to let it drop. So I did. I let it go."

I looked at Jack. "Maybe that's who John called at the FBI."

"It would be a good place to start. When did he swipe your case, Patty?"

"Two days ago." She turned to me. "I'm surprised you didn't see steam shooting out of my ears when you came to see me because I was still hot about it."

"I thought you just didn't want to talk to me."

"But—" She sat back, straightened her shoulders, and let an exaggerated aura of calm and serenity come over her. "I've let it go now."

The waitress brought our breakfast. Pat pushed her pancakes toward Jack, ordered a side of toast, asked for extra cheese for her eggs, and proceeded to crumble the bacon strips into the scramble. This was a woman who liked to eat. My egg white omelet with fruit and dry English muffin seemed anemic by comparison. I picked at it while I turned the pages back and reviewed the notes I'd transcribed into it from our first meeting.

"Pat, you said you thought John's murder was a drug killing."

She nodded, but waited until after she'd swallowed to respond. "The MO, sugar. The whole thing with the knife, the serrated blade, the through and through in the throat, lots of blood—that's Ottavio's signature."

"Ottavio?" Jack knew enough to be surprised.

"Who is this person?" I asked him.

"Ottavio Quevedo. The DEA boys call him Ottavio. Or just O."

"Spell it."

"Octavio, only with a double *t* and no *c*." I wrote it in my book. "Colombian drug lord. One of the more vicious strains of the disease."

"He's been a busy boy, too." The waitress had brought Pat's extra cheese and she was busy sprinkling it on her eggs. "He's duking it out with a bunch of Mexicans who have been trying to move in on his East Coast market. Stiffs have been piling up in Dumpsters all over town, all linked in some way to O and his gang."

"I didn't even know there were Mexicans in the market," I said.

"Oh, sugar, two of the most powerful drug cartels in the world today are run out of Juarez and Tijuana. The Colombians are just not what they used to be. Medellín and Cali are shadows of their former selves."

"Correct me if I'm wrong on this, Patty, but the guerrilla armies run the drug trade in Columbia now—"

"They do."

"And Ottavio is lined up with them."

"That's right. He's got a whole damn drug army behind him, and they've got more firepower, more sophisticated equipment, and all around better toys than the official military." Pat had finished her eggs and was trying to get the top off a tiny container of grape jelly. It was a struggle. Her fingernails were too short. "So that's one big vote for a drug killing. The MO. And then there's the story Mr Bob Avidor gave us."

"He's lying. He's lying about everything." I hadn't meant to be quite so curt, but I was annoyed by this drug accusation, by the *persistence* of an accusation I knew in the deepest part of my heart to be false. "I can't explain the MO, but I can tell you that John McTavish's life couldn't have been any further away from some international drug lord smackdown."

Pat had managed to peel back the foil top and was digging out the deep purple spread with a knife. "I didn't say I believed him. We haven't found anything linking the vic—John McTavish or his brother to drug activity. At least we hadn't by the time I had to give up the case. But Avidor is not your man. His alibi is good."

Jack had eaten half the pancakes before putting his utensils down and concentrating on his coffee. "What's the alibi, Patty?"

"He was over at the Broken Arrow playing pool until almost two a.m. with his boss, Phil Ryczbicki. The bartender identified them both. Called them Mutt and Mutt. He remembered them because Avidor asked him to find him a hooker."

I didn't even look up, just wrote down *Avidor. Hooker. After two a.m.* The more I learned about Bobby Avidor, the less I understood John's loyalty to him, notwithstanding the rescue of his brother.

Jack took it in stride. "Did he find him a hooker?"

"Officially, no. Off the record, he gave me her name."

"So," Jack said, "Avidor stayed with Ryczbicki until the boss went home, then bought himself an alibi."

"Correct. Avidor was seen by quite a few people after he left the bar getting a blow job in his car in the parking lot. Then he took the young lady home. She was with him the rest of the night."

I amended my notes. *Avidor. Hooker. Blow job.*

"He couldn't have been much more conspicuous," Jack said. "Did you show McTavish's picture around the bar? He left his hotel room to meet someone between ten on Monday night and one the next morning. That's one place he could have gone."

Pat gave him an exasperated glance. "Baby, with you gone from law enforcement, I don't know how we manage to stay out of our own way."

"I'm just asking—"

"I may not be the FBI, but I did manage to establish that neither one of those boys saw McTavish that night, and neither one killed him. Avidor was doing his thing and Ryczbicki went back to the airport and slept on the couch in his office. He was seen by several members of his staff."

I stared down at Ottavio's name in my notebook as if it were a code or anagram that might rearrange itself and give me some answers. It didn't, but it gave me a question.

"Here's a thought. It makes no sense to me that John was moving into drugs, but does it make sense that Ottavio could be moving into parts?"

"Parts?" Pat looked across the table at Jack and seemed gently amused. "Are you still chasing aircraft parts?"

"Old habits die hard. We heard there's been some crossover between the drug and bogus parts industries."

"Where did you get that?"

"I tapped Ira Leemer on the back of the head and that's what rolled out."

"Good lordy, I hope that's all that rolled out." She looked at me with eyes wide. "You might want to consider getting a tetanus shot."

"Patty, let me float a theory here and see what you think. Air Sentinel 634."

"What's that?"

"It's a triple seven that crashed down in Ecuador not long ago. We have reason to believe the crash might have been caused by a bad part or bad maintenance. If that's true, the Bureau would be all over it."

"So?"

"If Avidor had something to do with the crash and McTavish found out about it and was murdered for it, it makes his death crash related, which could explain why Hollander showed up to take your case."

"I just told you Avidor was otherwise occupied."

"He could have set him up. I saw him out at Jimmy Zacharias's place the other night. Jimmy might not have an alibi, and he's perfectly capable of jamming a blade through a man's throat."

Pat crossed her arms over her chest. It made her seem broader and more formidable. "What were you doing out there?"

"It's another case I'm working on. Avidor walked into it."

Pat stared at Jack with what looked like concern. "You need to stay away from Jimmy Zacharias, sweetie."

"He's the target of my investigation."

With her arms still crossed she looked like a fortress. "Because he's a legitimate suspect, or because you can't stand his skinny ass?"

"I hate his skinny ass, and he's a legitimate suspect."

There was a moment where something was supposed to be said and wasn't, and all that was left was a silence that felt particularly awkward between two people who obviously liked each other. Jack was inscrutable. Pat was giving away nothing in her expression, but she seemed to want to say something. It was no doubt something I would have loved to hear, because there was clearly a history between Jack and Jimmy Zacharias, one that was beginning to feel more and more significant to what we were doing. I wanted to know what it was. But I wasn't going to hear it from Pat Spain.

"Your theory about the plane crash is nice, baby, except for one thing. Damon Hollander is a drug man. Came down from New York not too long ago. Brought with him some high-level sources in the drug trade from what I hear. And he's working on a case right now that's got everyone's attention."

"What is it?"

"It's not a what, baby. It's a who."

"All right. Who?"

"Ottavio Quevedo. That's why he took my case. Not because of parts or some crash." She looked at me. "I wouldn't have told you this was a drug murder unless I thought it was. Personally, I think it's Avidor that's involved and your friend ended up being in the wrong place at the wrong time. I'm sorry, baby."

The three of us sat quietly. I closed my notebook. I couldn't think of anything else to say. Jack broke the silence. "Patty, do me a favor and ask around a little. See if you can come up with anything about this crash or what Jimmy's up to these days."

165

"Ask around yourself. You've got a cell phone just like I do."

"The difference being you are still on the inside, and I am now on the outside."

"A distinction you'd best keep in mind, lover. I've been told in the quiet voice to stay away from this case. Why should I risk my job for you?"

"Because I bought you breakfast."

"These eggs weren't that good. And you ate my pancakes."

"Then do it because I never once treated you like Damon Hollander did."

"Let's take a walk," I said when we were out on the concourse. "I have some questions about what she said. Let's go check out Bic's operation."

We headed over to the Majestic concourse and cleared security. We found a spot near one of the gates where we could stand by the window and talk privately.

"I like your friend Pat," I said. "How did you get to know her?"

"We worked together on a task force once. She's good and she doesn't get the respect she deserves."

"She likes you."

"She's been a good friend."

"She seems worried about you."

He turned toward the window and ended up gazing into bright sunshine. Instead of turning back, he slipped on his sunglasses. "It's so clear today," he said. "You'd never know half the state was on fire."

"Jack, what is it between you and Jimmy Zacharias? And don't tell me he's just another scumbag."

He didn't even seem to have heard the question, but I decided to wait him out. "There are people in this world," he said finally, "who have no conscience, and he's one. He can do anything; he can do the worst things, and still get up in the morning and look himself in the mirror. That bothers me."

"I would venture to say that during your long career in law enforcement, you ran into more than one unrepentant criminal. What is it about *this* man?"

He left another long pause in the conversation. I figured he was trying to decide how much to tell me, and I was busy reacting to the idea that he would exclude me at all. I didn't want to be excluded. I liked him too much.

"What do you see," he asked, "when you look out there?"

"You mean on the ramp?"

"Yeah."

From where we stood we could see four, maybe five gates clearly, and there was an airplane being worked on each one. I scanned as I used to do in Boston, looking for any big problems. Saw none. I picked out one crew and watched as they loaded bags, boxes, parcels, and kennels from the cart to the belt loader to the belly.

"It's a tidy operation. The guidelines are all freshly painted. Everyone's in uniform, but that's easy. All they wear down here are short-sleeved shirts and pressed cotton shorts. It's hard to screw that up." I watched the crew working the flight. "They treat the oversized items with appropriate respect. Looks as if they have lots of golf clubs and surfboards down here. In Boston we had skis. Tractors, tugs, and carts are all painted, and parked where they should be. I don't see any rust or broken windshields. No debris lying around that could get sucked into engines. Everyone's wearing their ear protectors and their safety vests, and things seem to be moving smoothly. Bic runs a good operation. I have to give him that."

"You see things I would never see."

"That's my training. I've looked at a lot of ramps."

"And I've worked a lot of cases over a lot of years." He took his glasses off and turned to face me and I realized where he was going. He'd been a few steps ahead of me. "What's between Jimmy and me has nothing to do with you. It has nothing to do with this case." His voice caught. He cleared his throat and looked down at the glasses in his hand. "I'm asking you to trust me on that."

With his back to the sun, I had to squint to see what I wanted to see. "When you talk about Jimmy, Jack, your face changes. Your whole body reacts to the mention of his name. Something that powerful has to affect what you do and how you think, so I don't believe you when you say it won't affect this case." His forehead bunched and his chest rose and I could see the defensive response forming around his eyes, so I hurried to finish the thought. "But I trust you, Jack."

He shifted his weight to his other foot and looked harder at me. He seemed to be searching for signs of trickery. There were none. I wanted to know what was going on. I wanted to stand there and wheedle, coerce, or otherwise try to pry the story out of him, but it wouldn't have worked. He was a locked safe on this subject and I didn't have the combination. Not yet.

"Good," he said. "Let's go see Mr Avidor."

Chapter Seventeen

We found Bobby Avidor at the maintenance hangar. He stood with one balled fist on his soft hip as he stared up at the stabilizer of an MD-11, where two mechanics were working on a lift. When he saw us coming, he ignored me and spoke to Jack.

"Who are you?"

"Jack Dolan. I need to talk to you."

"What about?"

"John McTavish."

"Are you a cop?"

"Private." Jack had left his sunglasses on. He looked very cool when he said that.

Bobby looked at me. "Ryczbicki put me on the day shift."

"So I heard."

"What did you say to him?"

"Only that it was easier for us to find you on days. And he should keep an eye on you."

He didn't bother to conceal his contempt as he used his collar mike to radio the mechanics on the lift. He told them to let him know as soon as they'd found the problem.

We followed him into the hangar and up an exposed set of iron stairs to the admin areas on a second-floor landing. His office seemed like a palace compared to places I'd seen and worked in up on the line, but then hangar space wasn't quite as dear as airport terminal space.

His desk was tan metal with a laminated top. On top was a carved wooden slat that read R. A. AVIDOR that could have come from a souvenir shop at Niagara Falls. A couple of guest chairs faced the desk. The only other major piece of furniture was a bookcase crammed with all sorts of binders and manuals. Proudly displayed on his cork bulletin board, among other things, was a postcard photo of three exotic women posed elbow to elbow on a sunny, sandy beach. The caption below their bare breasts read: "Wet and Wild in Hawaii."

Avidor unclipped the radio from his belt, took off the collar mike, and rested his thick hips against the arm of one of his guest chairs. "What can I do for you?"

"You can't do anything for me except listen to what I have to say to you." Jack still had the shades on. "You claim that John McTavish was here to bust up his brother's drug deal, but you made that story up to cover your own ass."

Avidor's laugh was like the nervous twitter of a teenager. He crossed his arms, which made his stomach pooch out even more over his chronically too-tight belt. "I don't know what you're talking about."

"You're in the business of dirty parts. We know that. And you're in business with Jimmy Zacharias. We know that, too."

"I don't know any Jim—"

"I saw you with him, so shut the fuck up and listen." Bobby fell silent.

"You know something about the crash of Air Sentinel 634. Maybe you even caused it. We know this because John McTavish had in his possession the logbook from

170

that airplane, and a piece of jewelry that belonged to one of the victims."

"Where would Johnny get something like that?"

Jack sighed. Bobby didn't seem to be much of a challenge for him. "From you."

Bobby's normally active eyes looked like pinballs. "That's crap."

"You're the only connection that makes any sense," I said. "John found out what you did and came down to confront you. He probably threatened to turn you in."

Jack took a step closer to Bobby. "In my old line of work, we called that a motive."

"A motive for what?"

"For murder."

Bobby jerked up, walked around to his own side of the desk, and stood with his hands in his pockets. His big, high forehead was starting to flush. "I have an alibi."

"All that means is you weren't on the scene when it happened, but you did set him up. You called someone—my money's on Jimmy—and reported the situation. Then you got yourself an alibi, a good one, and proceeded to make up this ridiculous drug story. That's something I've always hated. Tarnishing the good name of a victim, a solid citizen who can't defend himself, just to save your own ass."

"That's not what I did."

Jack followed Bobby around to the other side of his desk and leaned against the inside edge. "There was no drug deal. There was a plane crash, and I think you had something to do with bringing it down. Sold a bad part . . . installed a bad part . . . the proof is in the logbook, isn't it?"

I watched Bobby closely. I figured Jack was throwing stuff at him to see what stuck. Bobby was lapsing into serious fidgeting—rubbing the ball of his thumb across his forehead, turning back and forth in the limited area behind his desk, trying not to trip over Jack's feet. "Last I saw Johnny McTavish, he was sitting up at the terminal drinking a cup of coffee. And I don't know anything about that plane crash, and I don't know anybody named Jimmy."

"Here's what I came to tell you, Bobby. You are way, way out of your league. You're a small-time dirty parts pusher who got mixed up with the big boys. Now you're in for a plane crash, a murder, and, if you're not careful, for the same thing that happened to McTavish. And I'll tell you why. John was only a threat to them because he knew you. And now that you have participated in his murder, you're an even bigger threat. In fact, I don't know why they didn't kill you instead of him. Maybe I'll ask Jimmy when I see him."

Bobby's expression froze. He wasn't even blinking.

"That's right," Jack said, "I know Jimmy better than you do. We go way back. I hate him and he hates me, and before this thing is over, you're going to find yourself squeezed between the two of us, and that's a bad place to be. You know what you should do, Bobby?"

If Bobby knew, he didn't say.

"Cut a deal while you still have the leverage, because depending on how much you know and when you knew it, you could be in line for the death penalty. We have that here in Florida, and we're not one of those pussy states that's afraid to use it."

Again, Bobby rubbed his thumb across his forehead. He adjusted his tie. He rocked back on his heels. And then he shook his head. "Any leverage I have I'll use where it counts and that's with the Feds, not you. You've got nothing to offer me."

Jack stood up and smiled down at him. "Call the cops. Call the Bureau. Call whoever you want. Just make your deal and don't take too long. And if you get stuck and you need help in trying to decide what to do, picture yourself bleeding to death in a Dumpster with a blade in your throat. See if that doesn't get you motivated to do the right thing."

Bic had provided a ride for us down to the maintenance hangar, but Bobby hadn't been so gracious as to provide return transportation. We were outside on foot, navigating the circuitous pedestrian route, since we weren't allowed to cut across the active ramp. We'd been walking a few minutes before Jack spoke again. "What did you get from that interview?"

"Besides the fact that Bobby Avidor is a loathsome pig?"

"Try to work around that."

"That would be tough."

"When you're talking to someone who may have done a murder, or committed any crime, you're going to get a lot of subterfuge. You have to make yourself look past it for what's important. And you can't let it be personal. When I look at Bobby Avidor, I don't see the worthless piece of crap I know him to be."

173

"What do you see?"

"I see a man on the other side of a business transaction. He's got a piece of this puzzle I have to solve. He's the connection between John and Jimmy, and if Jimmy did kill John, that's a key piece. We'd be doing well to get him to talk to us."

"Won't Jimmy know that, too?"

"Jimmy knows," he said. "If he did kill John and Bobby knows it, I don't understand why Bobby is still walking around. Jimmy doesn't leave loose ends."

"Maybe Jimmy still needs him for something."

He reached up and took his glasses off. "Maybe," he said, wiping the sweat from his eyes, "he just hasn't gotten around to this particular loose end."

Watching him sweat made me realize how hot I was. I lifted my hair off the back of my neck and held it up, waiting for a cool breeze. "So our job is to first help Bobby define his options, and then to help him see that we're the best one."

He smiled. "Exactly. And hope he's smart enough to make his choice before it's too late."

"How does Bobby know the FBI has this case? He didn't even mention the local police."

"Another good point," he said. "I plan to ask Patty if she told him. If she didn't, he might have been contacted by this Agent Hollander."

My cell phone rang. I flipped it open to answer, saw that the call was from Detroit. "What day is this?"

"Friday."

"Uh-oh." I flipped it closed without answering. My heart pounded out the classic I-overslept-for-the-exam panic.

"What's the matter?"

"I'm supposed to start my new job on Monday."

"Your new job?"

"Yeah. I sort of forgot about it, but I'm due in Detroit on Monday." I'd quickened the pace so much that even Jack, with his long legs, was having a hard time keeping up.

"Alex, you forgot you were supposed to start a new job?"

"I've been distracted. Can I catch up with you later, Jack? I have to go and take care of this thing."

When he didn't answer, I turned to find that he had stopped and was several paces behind me. Then I realized it was because I'd broken into a full-fledged trot. The good news was my ankle was feeling much better. I jogged back to him.

"How are you going to take care of it?"

"I'm not sure. I have to go make some calls. But you can use my car if you need it. You know where it is."

I started to reach for the keys, but he waved me off. "Call me later when you've got your life worked out. I can't wait to hear this story."

Chapter Eighteen

"Wow." I appraised the crowd. It spilled out the door and snaked halfway down the block. "I would like to eat sometime tonight."

"Don't worry." Jack put his hand on my back and led me past the line. The guy at the door—I wouldn't exactly call him a maitre d'. More like a bouncer—stuck out his hand the minute he saw Jack. "Hey, man," he yelled, "good to see you back."

Jack returned the gesture and leaned in so he could be heard. "Can you help me out tonight, Al?"

Al glanced at me. "Two?"

Jack nodded and we were in. I'm sure I felt more than one laser stare into the back of my head from the poor schmoes at the door who had to wait their turn.

Al took us through the small dining room, a bright, noisy place. Waiters and cooks were yelling over the serving bar. There was a lot of clanging—silverware on plates, plates going into the dishwasher, dishes shoved onto the counter. Several patrons in bibs worked on crab claws and lobsters. And there was lots of skin showing. This was the kind of place people came to in boats. Indeed, when we emerged onto the deck, I spotted a whole line of boats tied up in the boat parking lot, or whatever you call it.

"You sit over here." Jack held a chair for me, the one that faced the water. "That way you don't have to sit and stare at me all night."

The waiter came right over as we took our seats. He greeted Jack as if they were a couple of old pals and left two large plastic menus. When the waiter left, Jack was grinning.

"What are you smiling at?"

He shrugged as he unfolded his napkin. "I like this place."

"I guess so. I've never seen a red carpet rolled out so fast. How come they know you so well here?"

"I did one of the owners a favor once when I was on the job."

"Is Al the owner?"

"Al's his nephew. Ike and his brother Bernie own the place. It's been in their family for fifty years." He kicked at the splintering deck. "It hasn't changed much in all that time, either."

"What did you do for them?"

"Bernie likes to gamble. Ponies, dogs, football, basketball, jai alai—you name it. He got into some trouble once on some money he owed. He was about to have his liquor license yanked. I helped him work out a deal where he got to keep it if he paid off all his debts and entered a twelve-step program, which he did. It all worked out."

"That was a nice thing you did."

"Hey, I didn't want them going belly-up. They have the best stone crabs in town."

"It was still a nice thing you did."

He stared down at his plate, then rolled back in his chair and gazed out across the deck. Jack never seemed to know what to do with a compliment. "I hate these wildfires," he said. "But the smoke sure makes for some beautiful sunsets."

I opened the menu and checked out Bernie and Ike's offerings. A few items cooked simply. I liked it. "What is a stone crab anyway?"

He leaned forward and settled into a lecture pose. This was a subject he could obviously warm to. "It's a special kind of crab with huge claws. That's the only part you can eat. If you see one it looks like a couple of huge claws with this tiny crab body attached."

"What makes them so special?"

"Wait until you taste one."

"What makes them so expensive?" According to the menu, an eight-crab-leg dinner was almost twenty dollars.

"They're protected. It used to be you could walk out the back door and pick them up off the beach around here. Development pushed them south, so now you only find them in the Keys and along the Gulf Coast."

The waiter returned and we ordered. With a build up like that, I had no choice but to order the specialty of the house, the stone crab plate. I also ordered a beer, a compulsive move since I rarely drank beer. But it seemed like the only drink possible on a balmy early spring evening in Florida with stone crabs on the way.

Jack ordered club soda. When our drinks came, he took the straw out and settled back in his chair with it. "So, tell me about this job you forgot you had."

"I didn't forget I had a job. I lost track of what day it was."

"Airline job?"

"I'll be the Vice President of Operations for a startup in Detroit."

"That's impressive."

"We have two airplanes," I said. "Everyone but the president is a vice president."

"Will you be doing something you like?"

"I'll be working like a dog. My already limited social life will shrivel up and die. I'll be running the field operation, which is the part of the business I love, but I have to do it from headquarters, which is the part of the business I hate. I'll live in Detroit and I'm not sure how to feel about that." My entire body blanched at the very thought of one of those wicked winds skidding across the Great Lakes. "I've never been to the city, only the airport. It is a good sports town."

"Sounds like a great job," he said in a complete deadpan.

"But . . . ?"

"But nothing."

"This is the perfect job for me. I'll love it. Why are you saying I won't? Are you saying I shouldn't take this job?" I twisted in my chair and fortified with a sip of beer. It was cold and quenching and had definitely been the right call. "I've already accepted. They've turned off all their other candidates. I can't do that to them. Sure, they gave me another week, but only because I begged and pleaded and they didn't have any better alternative. I've probably already damaged their confidence in me, and I don't know when I'll be able to reschedule my move. I'm going to have to put everything in storage."

He set his drink on the table and crossed his hands in his lap.

"All right. The truth is, I've had a hard time being unemployed. It's been scary. I've always worked. I don't know what to do with myself when I don't work."

"You're doing something now."

"I'm not earning money. I need money. My severance is gone. I'm using the last of my savings to be down here. What if I get sick? I need health insurance and disability coverage and a retirement plan. I have to work. There's no one to take care of me."

"There's no one to take care of anyone. In the end we all take care of ourselves. Some do it better than others. Don't say you're taking this job because you need an income or benefits. There are lots of ways to earn money. You don't have to do what you've always done."

"I need structure." I used my finger to draw a line in the condensation on my beer glass. A straight line. "I like structure."

"I noticed. What I'm saying is to build your own structure. You're smart enough. You don't have to take the easy way out."

He smiled. I brooded, because he was on to something. I'd never been excited by the Detroit opportunity, and accepting the offer had felt like agreeing to move back home with my parents. There had to be something to the fact that I had forgotten about it. Completely.

"Look at it this way," he said. "If you really wanted that job in Detroit, why would you be sitting on a deck in Florida?"

I was left to ponder that question as the waiter served up our dinner. There was barely enough room on the table for the two big plates. The claws, as advertised, were huge. They were served cold with coleslaw on the side, a big basket of assorted rolls that smelled homemade, lots of drawn butter, and a metal pail for the refuse.

I waited until the waiter left to lean over and ask Jack, "Are they always served already cracked like this?"

He had already plowed in and was sucking a piece of meat from a tiny crevice in one of the big claws. "Unless you travel around with your own ball-peen hammer, I don't know how you'd get them open. Feel how hard the shell is."

The shell was indeed as hard as any I'd ever encountered, but not being a crustacean connoisseur, that didn't mean much to me. And it didn't matter anyway once I started to eat because he was right. Stone crabs were well worth the trouble. The meat was tender and sweet and firm—a rare and delightful experience, especially with all that drawn butter, and most especially when eaten on an open-air deck in good company and the presence of a violet sunset.

Jack tossed a shard of crab shell into the bucket. "Let's review the case," he said. "Start from the beginning."

"Me?"

"I want to see what you're writing down, what you're paying attention to."

A test. A challenge. That was all I needed to hear. I wiped off my fingers—eating stone crabs was a messy business; you had to peel off the shell with your fingers and dig out the meat. I pulled out my little notebook and flipped to the first page. "Okay. John flew down to Miami on Monday March fifth from Boston and arrived in the early afternoon. He met Bobby Avidor for a cup of coffee. Bobby says they talked about Terry's drug deal. I say John was here to confront him on parts. Whatever they talked about, John left for The Harmony House Suites and Bobby made sure he had a good alibi for the night. He asked Phil Ryczbicki out for a drink. They stayed out until after two. After that, Mr Avidor was observed in the parking lot enjoying a blow job in the front seat of his car.

"John checked in at The Harmony House Suites, did normal hotel things. Sometime after ten he left his room. He came back just before one in the morning. Wherever he went and whomever he saw, he heard something that worried him enough to call his brother in the middle of the night and assign him to look after his family. And he told them he was coming home. Sometime after that call and before six, he disappeared. Someone packed his things and returned his rental car so he wouldn't be reported missing." I flipped back to my notes from the first discussion with Pat Spain. "John's body was found on Wednesday in a Dumpster. He was killed someplace else and left there. None of his valuables were missing, and the murder weapon has not been recovered. Since then, we've established that Avidor is in the bogus parts business, probably with your pal Jimmy Zacharias, and that John was in possession of the logbook from an airplane that crashed in Ecuador. He had a diamond ring from the same crash. I think those are the high points . . ." I thumbed through the notes. "Oh, and the FBI has an interest in this case for reasons unknown."

"I think their interest has to do with the crash," he said.

"Why?"

Jack put down the claw he'd been working on to go for some bread. "I tried to reach Damon Hollander today. I was told he would be 'unavailable for several months and could someone else help me?'"

"That's no way to do business. What's that all about?"

"I suspect he doesn't want to talk to us, but the really strange thing was no matter who I spoke to over there, whenever I brought up the Sentinel crash, the conversation stopped dead. There is definitely something going on that no one wanted to tell me about."

"Can someone else help us? Don't you have any buddies over there like Pat who will give you the inside scoop?"

"No. Listen to this. Patty called me back. There's a group of detectives that work out of the airport station that specialize in crimes against the airlines. She asked around and found out they also had a case that was recently yanked out from under them by the Bureau. It's a repair station that they suspect is moving dirty parts. They think it's one of Jimmy's places. Guess who took the case?"

"Damon Hollander? He's supposed to be a drug guy. Why would he be interested in them? Unless it has something to do with John's murder."

"Exactly." He picked up the claw he'd been working on and resumed peeling.

"This is good," I said. "It feels like progress." I picked up my pencil. "What's the name of this repair station?"

"Speath Aviation."

"Speath?" I grabbed my notepad and felt that tingling thrill that meant something was about to fall together in a way that would make me warm all over. "I know that name."

"How?"

"Because Felix . . ." I couldn't find the page I needed.

"Who's Felix?"

"He's the kid I told you about who works at The Harmony House Suites. He's been trying to identify the cars in the hotel parking lot the night of the murder." I explained the low-tech security system and Felix's idea about finding cars that weren't supposed to be there.

"He found some?"

"Yeah, he called me back. I talked to him just before I came over here. Here it is." I'd written the notes on the back of a page. "He got two hits. A black Volvo registered to The Cray Fund, which is an investment firm here in town. And the second one was a green Subaru Forester. It belongs to a George Speath."

I looked over at Jack. He was leaning in, listening intently, holding his buttered fingers in the air like a surgeon. "That's him," he said. "He runs Speath Aviation. He was at the hotel the night of the murder?"

"He was there and not checked in or he would have had a placard in his windshield." I scanned my notes. I'd been writing so fast to keep up with Felix, they were almost illegible. I'd had to make him stop and take several deep breaths. But now I was starting to feel the same way. "Heavy aircraft maintenance facility. Been in business twenty-eight years. Started by a guy named Howard Speath and now operated by his son George—"

"Who was at the scene of the murder," Jack said, "and is being investigated by the FBI." He seemed more satisfied than excited, as if he knew we were running a marathon and I was trying to sprint. But I had a deadline.

"We have to talk to him," I said. "Tomorrow. This Speath sounds like the key to everything."

"Hold on. Slow down. Drink your beer and let's talk about this."

I sipped my beer, but hardly tasted it. My mind was going too fast and my sense of urgency had been heightened considerably by my discussion with Paul Gladstone. I had one week and one week only. There would be no more extensions on the Detroit job after that.

"From what Patty told me, it sounds as if George Speath is part of the business community and has never had any trouble with the FAA or the law. He's not the usual kind of partner who hooks up with Jimmy."

"So?"

"If he's not a pro, and the detectives don't think he is, then we might be able to turn him easier than we could Avidor. I want to find out a few things about him before we go blowing into his business."

"Like what?"

"This is the investigation part, Alex. We'll talk to some of the employees. Check out his inspection records. Talk to the FAA, vendors—"

"I don't have an unlimited amount of time down here, Jack. Or cash. The clock is ticking."

"It takes as long as it takes."

The motor on a boat kicked in behind me. I stared up into the palm trees. "Do you know if Speath does work for any of the major airlines?"

"Probably. Why?"

"I have a better idea." I pulled out my cell phone. "I have a guaranteed way to gain total access to his business."

"Without him knowing?"

"With his enthusiastic assistance. All I need is a little help from Bic."

★ ★ ★

185

The restaurant was even more crowded when we left. Jack put his hand on my shoulder to guide me through the ever-burgeoning group thronged around the door. It was one big party out on the sidewalk. Blonde women and tan men with big plastic cups of beer swirled around each other. It was later in the evening, so this was the crowd that had already drunk their way through happy hour and was out in search of something to eat. They were raucous. They were ribald. They were all having a good time.

After we'd made it through the gauntlet, Jack moved his hand to the small of my back, and kept it there as we crossed the street to my car. He'd touched me before, but this felt different. Purposeful. I liked the way it felt, and it started me thinking about how his hands would feel in other places.

He took my keys and opened the door for me. I turned and we stood for a moment and I looked at his face as if I had never seen it. I saw the curve of his mouth. How warm his brown eyes could be. And there was something else in his eyes. A connection. An attraction. That he was thinking what I was thinking, too. It was thrilling and unexpected and stimulating on so many levels and I wanted—

"I'm going to take a cab home," he said, stepping away.

"I'll . . ." I had to stop myself from stepping with him. "I'll drive you home."

"It's a long way out of your way. You should go home and take care of that ankle."

My ankle? I hadn't been thinking about my ankle. Is that what he'd been thinking? I looked into his face again. There was something there. There was a lot there. I was getting so I could read him, but there was too much for me to work out without a few clues from him. He didn't seem willing to offer them.

"I'll talk to you tomorrow, then?"

"Yeah." He turned and went back toward the restaurant, presumably to get Al to call him a cab. I looked for him as I drove by, but the crowd had swallowed him up.

Chapter Nineteen

Speath Aviation was expecting me. I could tell, not
because there was anyone in the small reception space
to greet me—there wasn't—but because of the letter
board sign standing just inside the door. It had WELCOME
and my name spelled out in magnetic white letters, only
they must have been short on *n*s because the last one
in SHANAHAN was a sideways *z*. But that was the only
thing that appeared to be improvised in the neat, carefully ordered offices. The rubber tile floors were scrubbed.
The bulletin boards on the pale yellow walls were hung
with directives and reminders and alerts that were carefully spaced and clearly visible. Lining one wall was a
row of twelve five-drawer file cabinets. All sixty drawers had typed labels.

That's what businesses look like when they're expecting an audit. It had taken one more day than I would
have liked, but due in large part to Bic's assistance, Speath
Aviation was expecting an auditor dispatched by Majestic
Airlines to check them out for possible overhaul work.
They had been encouraged to provide full access. To
everything. I was about to embark on my first undercover assignment.

Something caught my eye at the end of a short hallway. There was a door there that seemed to lead out to
the hangar. The door had a window about chin high,
the kind with safety glass. I wasn't sure, but I could have
sworn I'd seen a man looking through it at me. A man

wearing a cap. A baseball cap. It was one of those deals where the second I saw him—or thought I saw him—he vanished.

"Miss Shanahan?" I turned to find a large block of a man lunging toward me with his big, outstretched hand. His face was as wide as a stop sign, his features emphatically blunt, and shaking his hand was like trying to grip the wrong end of a Ping-Pong paddle. "I'm George Speath. I'm sorry to have kept you waiting."

"I just got here."

"Good. Did Margie take care of you?"

"Margie?"

I gazed about the empty office. A cup of hot coffee on a desk steamed in silent testimony to the fact that someone had been there recently, but not since I'd arrived. George looked around when I did and seemed to notice for the first time that we were alone.

"Shoot." He gave himself a verbal smack in the forehead. "Sorry. Margie must be in the back. Can I get you anything? Coffee? Tea? Cookies? We usually have these really good butter cookies. They don't look like much, but I can't stop eating them. I wish she wouldn't buy them, but she does."

"No, thank you. I'm fine for now."

"Okay. Well, then . . ." He started to lead the way out of the reception area to a long hallway, but then in a gesture that seemed both courtly and awkward, stepped aside and let me go first. As I passed, I felt again the presence of someone watching me. I took a quick look at that door with the window. Nothing.

George's office had the low-ceilinged feel of someone's basement family room. A Foosball table wouldn't have been out of place in the corner. Hung on the walls in inexpensive and mismatched frames were pictures of George and various people, and George and various airplanes. He looked happiest with the airplanes.

"Now," he said, standing in the middle of the durable, rust-colored carpet and rubbing those big hands together, "where would you like to begin?"

"First let me apologize for the extremely short notice, and I'm sorry to get you in here on a Sunday."

"That's no problem at all. We work seven days a week here."

"I assume you've talked to Mr Ryczbicki," I said.

"He called me yesterday. He's a nice fellow, isn't he?"

"Yes, he is." Bic must have really laid it on thick. "Maybe you could tell me what he's told you so we don't have to cover the same ground." When telling a lie, always best to see what has already been communicated by your coconspirator.

"Sure, sure. Whatever you want." He gestured for me to sit, then eschewed his big desk chair to settle across from me. The couch he sat on was too low for his frame, putting his knees almost up around his ears.

"Mr Ryczbicki said he was interested in asking us to bid on overhaul work for Majestic Airlines, mainly overflow situations. He's having trouble handling the volume, and he's hired you to do a pre-audit to make sure we're in compliance with FAA and Majestic standards."

"Just so there's no confusion," I said, "I'm not an employee of Majestic Airlines. I'm an independent auditor, and I'm not affiliated with the FAA, so you don't have to worry. Whatever I find here is between you and Mr Ryczbicki and me."

190

George put his hands up, palms out, and shook his head. "You're not going to find anything out of order. Needless to say, Miss Shanahan, this is very exciting news for us. We'd be so pleased to work with Majestic. We'd do a good job. I think I can convince you of that while you're here."

"Good." I pulled a pad and pen from my backpack. I was trying to look like an auditor, but I felt like an imposter, and the nicer he was to me, the more false my false persona felt. "I'd like to start by asking you a few questions."

He sat forward on the couch, ready to rumble. "Fire away."

"I understand your father started this business. Is that right?"

He smiled, revealing a crooked lower front tooth. "How did you know that?"

"I did my homework." Actually, Felix had done all the work. "When did you join him?"

"Seventeen months ago. After he'd already left. I was working at Honeywell when he began thinking about selling, so I talked him into letting me run it. He started five different businesses over the course of his career, and do you know he made successes out of every one? Five different industries, too." His expression was quizzical, as if he'd been studying this phenomenon for years and still hadn't cracked the code.

"Is he still involved here?"

"Oh, no. He's busy with a group of college kids that are starting up one of those dot-com companies. I'm not even sure what it is they do." He nudged his silver aviators farther up the bridge of his nose. "I always was more comfortable with a product I could touch and feel." He held up his big hands as if he were cradling a crankshaft between them. "I like standards. I like things I can measure."

"Is your father still involved in your business?"

"No." A rueful smile flashed and disappeared. "He doesn't have much time for aviation parts and repairs anymore."

Nor for his plodding son, I imagined. So far, it was hard not to like George.

I asked him questions from the list Bic and I had made up, things he and I had agreed we'd want to know about any business doing repair work on our airplanes. It was a long list. George answered every question thoroughly, but not succinctly, and a full hour had passed before I'd realized it.

"I'd like to see your operation now, George. Can we do that?"

"Sure. What do you need?"

"I'll need to take a look at all your certifications, all of your procedures for ordering, tracking, and receiving parts. I want to see your file of FAA directives. I'd like to take a look at your accounting system, your inventory system, and I want to talk to the person who receives your parts. I also need a list of customers."

"That's very thorough."

"Majestic has requested a full audit. They're selective about who works on their airplanes. And they only work from a list of approved vendors."

"I sure hope we can get on that list."

"Oh." I'd been scanning my list again. "How about

192

a business plan. Do you have something like that? Something recent?"

He was up and to his desk across the room in two long strides. "I've got exactly what you need. I made up a business plan for the bank. For a loan I needed." He rummaged around, looking first through a thick stack on top of the desk. Then he turned and thumbed through a pile at eye level on one of his built-in shelves. Finally, he punched a button on the phone.

"Margie, do you have my copy . . . *any* copy of the business plan?"

A voice came right back. "You have them all in there with you, George."

"Where? I can't find them." George was now down on his knees behind his desk. "Margie?" His voice grew muffled as he dipped down and his head disappeared behind the desk. "They're not in the drawer."

There was no response until the office door flew open and a woman—Margie, I presumed—stepped in. She stood for a moment with her hands on her hips, sizing up the situation. I could tell right away that she was a gold woman, although a younger version of this new species that I'd discovered in Florida.

Gold women usually had blonde hair, and however they chose to wear it, it always looked as if it had been painted over with clear fingernail polish. Their lipstick was lighter than their tanned faces, which were usually on the way to leathery, and they could never wear enough gold jewelry. The most evolved of the gold woman species, usually women in their late fifties or early sixties, had additional coordinating accessories such as gold handbags and shoes.

Margie had all the basics, including a pair of hose that made her long, tan legs a shade darker, but not too dark to dull her pedicure, which was shown to good advantage by the open toes of her high-heeled shoes. She walked on those very high heels across the office and straight for the credenza. "Move your feet, George."

He did as he was told. She opened a cabinet, pulled out a thick spiral-bound document, and handed it to him with a look that said, "Honestly, George." On her way back around the desk, she punched a button on his phone and hung up on herself.

George got to his feet—being a big man, none too gracefully—and started thumbing through his business plan. "Margie, did you meet Miss Shanahan?"

She looked at me with hazel eyes that shone brightly against nutmeg brown skin. "I must have been out in the hangar when you came in. You're the auditor?"

"Yes."

"I keep all the books, and I'm the only one around here who understands the filing system, so just ask me for anything you need. I'm usually out front, but if you can't find me, I'm back in the hangar with the boys. Just yell out there for me."

"Okay. Thanks."

She was as crisp, almost to the point of being brusque, and as direct as George was meandering. They probably made a good pair. She left me with George, who handed me the business plan. Then he stood, looking as if he were waiting for direction.

"Shall we go through your operation, George?"

"By all means."

He walked me through his operation. He had a

reasonably large facility, with seventy-five employees working three shifts. I did a quick scan for the baseball cap. Everyone I saw had one on. They appeared to be standard issue at Speath, so I assumed whoever had been staring at me from outside the door had been a curious employee.

The main part of his space was a huge hangar where he did engine, airframe, and structural work. George made an effort to introduce me to as many employees as he could as we walked around. Everyone seemed happy to see him, and the ones that were too far away made a point of waving or shouting a greeting.

"Is this your only facility?" I asked him.

"This is it. This is all I need. Watch out." His arm shot toward me in a move so quick I reacted without thinking. I jerked away from him, but not far enough. I felt his big hand on my back, nudging me forward a few steps.

"What?" I pulled farther away. "What are you doing?"

He pointed to a still wet, white grainy splat on the ground, perilously close to where I'd been standing. "Pigeons. That was a close one." He tilted his head back to search the rafters for the perpetrator of the poop bombing.

I looked up to where he'd been looking, intending to gaze sternly at the feathered offender, but what I saw was an entire squad perched overhead on the exposed steel struts. I had to settle for a blanket squinty-eyed condemnation.

George sighed. "We can't get rid of them."

I thought back to my own experience with hangars and pigeons. "Have you tried owls?"

"Look over there."

He put his hand on my back again and, as if he were turning a telescope, redirected my line of sight until I saw what he was pointing at. It was a fat, dark gray, in-your-face pigeon that had chosen the head of one of George's plastic owls as a perch.

"Tough birds," I said.

"It's a problem. Most of my guys make sure to keep their hats on when they're out on the floor. Would you like one? I recommend it if you're going to be out here."

"Sure."

George snapped the radio off his belt and raised Margie. She appeared almost immediately to deliver one of the heavy-duty black baseball caps with the Speath logo on the front and SPEATH AVIATION stitched in red across the back.

"What are you doing?" George stared at my hands as I rolled and shaped the bill of the cap, something I did without even thinking.

"I'm—" I started to say "making it less geeky-looking." Instead, I said, "I'm making it more comfortable. It's a great hat." I put it on and smiled at him. "Thank you, George."

He stepped back and regarded me with a bashful grin. The nicer he was to me, the worse I felt for lying. If George Speath was a bogus parts dealer, he had to be the kindest, most gentlemanly one ever. "It suits you," he said. "Come outside. I want to show you something."

I was glad for the hat as I followed him out onto the ramp. It kept the direct sunlight off my face, although it didn't help much with the sneaky rays that bounced off the concrete and ricocheted back up. But I forgot all about them when I got a glimpse of what he was so excited about.

It was an old twin-engine prop, with a polished aluminum skin that looked as fresh as if it had rolled out of the factory that morning. It had no logo or other markings, only an elegant maroon stripe that followed the classic lines of the fuselage, down both sides, and all the way to the tail. Powerful propellers fronted the engines, one each on elegant wings spread beneath the sun.

"Pretty impressive, isn't it?" George couldn't have been more excited if he had just given me my first glimpse of the Grand Canyon. And to be honest, for me it was almost as dazzling a sight.

"It sure is. Is it an Electra?"

He turned and looked at me with a new appreciation. "You know your airplanes. It's a Lockheed L. 12 Electra. They used one just like it in *Casablanca*. Or so the legend goes. I think they just used a cardboard version."

I made a complete circle, walking around the aircraft and taking in the grand sight. The aircraft sat on the tarmac with all the poise and presence of a movie star from the 1930s. Sleek and glamorous, it was definitely out of its time and place, but there was nothing about it that was faded. "This is . . . this is great, George. What are you doing with it?"

"I'm restoring it for an aviation museum out in Kansas City. I'd take you into the cabin, but it's a little dicey in there. We haven't even started the interior."

"What does it seat?"

"Six passengers and two crew. The engines are Pratt

197

& Whitney 985 Wasps. She was built in 1936, and do you know there are some still being used today? This one will fly when I'm through with it. I'm going to take her up myself."

"You're a pilot?"

"I've got my own plane," he said. "But it doesn't come close to this baby." He walked over and put his hand flat against the throat of the aircraft and held it there as if he were calming a wild horse. "Can you picture one of these Electras," he said, "propellers spinning, flying around the world in a trip that might take weeks and make a dozen stops? Those were the days, huh? They must have been, anyway." He gazed up at the airplane, squinting into the bright sun, and his smile was bitter-sweet. "Sometimes," he said, "I think I was born in the wrong time."

"How did it go?" Jack was at the other end of the line. I was in my car. We were cell phone to cell phone.

"George Speath is a very nice man," I said. "He gave me a nifty hat." I checked it out again in the rearview mirror. It really was a nice hat.

"Are you telling me," Jack said, "you've already been compromised as an undercover operative?"

"As far as I can tell, George Speath runs a good shop. His documentation is all in order. His inventory and his stockroom are well organized and properly secured. He deals with the same vendors over and over, only the ones he knows. His receiving procedures are layers thick with checks and double checks to make sure the part he's getting is the one he ordered. I talked to his FAA inspector, who loves him. Every employee I talked to loves him. His customers love him. Either he's too nice to be a crook, or he's too crafty for me to catch him."

"And he was at the murder scene and he's being looked at by the Bureau. There has to be something there."

"I wish we could find Agent Hollander and ask him what it is."

I searched the side of LeJeune Road for the Miami Sub Shop I'd designated for dinner.

"I've left several more messages for him," he said. "Patty has tried to reach him for me."

"Why don't we just go over to the FBI offices?"

"I told you he's not working out of the offices. He's set up off-site somewhere. If he doesn't want to be found, we're not going to find him. I know that better than anyone."

"You do? Did you use to hide when you were an agent?"

"I'm trying to tell you we shouldn't count on getting anything from Hollander, and I don't think we should give up on George. He's the best lead we've got so far."

"I'm not giving up. I'm on my way over to see Felix now." I found the sub shop. It was, of course, on the other side of the street and nowhere near a left turn lane. I was going to have to go down, turn around, and come back, which made me reevaluate whether it was worth it. There was always sushi at the hotel. Or the California Pizza Kitchen in the food court on Concourse F. I decided to skip it and went on to The Harmony House Suites, which was starting to feel like my home away from home away from home.

"Felix," he said. "Is that the hotel kid?"

199

"He's a hacker who happens to work at the hotel. I think he can help me with a little research I want to do. Where are you? Do you want to meet me here?"

"I've been out looking for Ira. He's gone AWOL. No one's seen him."

"That sounds bad." I pulled into a space and turned off the engine, which made it much easier to make out what he was saying.

"Maybe not. Ira can make himself scarce when he wants to. It could be he just doesn't want to talk to me."

"Are you going to keep looking?"

"No, I'm beat. I'm going home."

I felt a sinking disappointment that I was going to spend a whole day without seeing Jack. "Don't forget our appointment tomorrow," I said. "I'll come by and pick you up."

"What's tomorrow?"

"We have a ten o'clock appointment at The Cray Fund offices downtown."

"The financial people."

"Right. Their car was in the lot that night as well."

"Waste of time," he said. "Waste of time."

"You're the one who said we should keep all the possibilities open."

Chapter Twenty

It was dinnertime at The Harmony House Suites and the lobby was crowded with conference goers turned loose from their white tablecloths, cold Danish, and flip charts. Felix was easy to spot and not just because of his bleach-tipped hair. It was the way he moved, shambling through the crowd all floppy and loose-limbed like a young bird dog.

I fell in step behind him. "Felix Melendez Jr."

He spun around, ready to be of service to whoever needed him. "Yes, can I help—Miss *Shan*ahan." He took a step back and broke into that loopy grin. "What are you doing here?"

"I came to see you. Are you on your way somewhere?"

"It can wait." He stuffed his hands in his pockets and kept grinning, his head bobbing like a cork in mild seas.

"Felix, could we go somewhere where we can talk?"

"Oh. Oh, sure. Sorry." A hint of subversive curiosity stole into his eyes. "Somewhere private?"

"That would be good."

"There's someone using my office right now." He stood on his toes, craned his long neck, and searched every corner of the lobby. "Um, how about the health club? I can see it from here and it's empty."

"Lead the way."

The health club at The Harmony House Suites was like most hotel health clubs—a sorry collection of mismatched workout equipment picked out of catalogues by people who've never seen a sweat towel. The centerpiece was the obligatory Universal gym, the kind with myriad hooks and ropes and attachments that combined to give you four hundred different exercises. There was one old treadmill with a fraying belt, a couple of dumbbells in the corner, a slant bench, and two stair climbers.

Felix went straight to the thermostat—someone had left the air conditioner on full blast—mumbling about conservation and the destruction of the environment. I found the remote for the TV and muted the soap opera rerun. We came together at the Universal gym, where he draped his arms over a dangling straight bar.

"Would you like to do some work for me, Felix?"

His eyes widened and it's possible his spiky hair actually stood up a little straighter on his head. "Are you *serious?*"

"I can pay you a little, not much—"

"Wow!" He let go of the bar, causing it to swing perilously toward my head as he darted around. "I'd do it for free. *Wait!*" He stopped and patted himself down, searching his shirt pocket, suit jacket, and pants pockets, front and back. "I don't have anything to write with. We should go—"

I pulled out my pad, jotted down what he needed, ripped out the page, and handed it to him.

He read what I had written. "Speath Aviation." He nodded. "The dude whose car was in the lot the night Mr McTavish was killed." I could feel Felix's enthusiasm rising as his voice dropped inversely. "Is he a suspect in the murder of your friend?"

"Don't know yet. I want to take a close look at his

business from the inside out. You've also got the password there, which George says should provide full access to all of his systems."

"Cool. What are we looking for?"

"We think it's possible he's been laundering bogus parts through his business."

"*Way* cool." He stuck his thumbnail between his teeth, and I could see the wheels spinning. Fast. "Okay, okay." He started moving around the room, taking large steps in the small space, changing course every time he was about to smack into something. He rubbed his forehead. He took long, deep breaths. He talked to himself. "Parts, parts, parts."

Then he stopped. "What's a bogus part?"

I explained to Felix about how there were people in the world who made a living making, stealing, and selling used, damaged, counterfeit, and otherwise substandard parts to people and businesses—including commercial airlines—that unwittingly purchased them and installed them on their aircraft. He listened in rapt attention until I was finished, at which point he blinked and said, "That is harsh."

"Way harsh," I said. "I thought you could do that thing you do with your computer and see what you can come up with."

"That means inventory," he said. "And vendors. You're probably looking for who they buy from, who they sell to, background checks on the employees. I can roll through their inventories and figure out what they've purchased and sold in the past few months. Maybe get you copies of corporate ledgers, check registers, purchase orders, invoices, lists of accounts payable and accounts receivable, customer files. Is this a public company? No, private. I saw that when I looked him up. Okay, but someone does their books. I can find out who and possibly get in that way." He looked at me, face open and eager as if to ask, how am I doing?

Pretty darn well if you compared his list of specific ideas to my sketchy list of questions. Of course, I was limited by the fact that I didn't think like a hacker.

"Cut the data however you think it makes sense and see what you can come up with."

I looked up to see a man in track shorts, ratty shirt, and running shoes walking through the lobby and coming our way, clearly intending to work out. I remembered that John had worked out in this room. I looked around again at the equipment and wondered when I'd stopped thinking about him as a person, as a friend, and had started thinking about him as everyone else in Florida did—as McTavish, murder victim and case number. The thought of him, the feeling of his strong presence left in the room like sweat on the machines, caught me by surprise and pulled me into a sad place. I decided I needed to call Mae. I hadn't been talking enough to Mae.

"Miss Shanahan?" Felix was looking at me as if he had noticed something, but was too shy to comment. Or wouldn't know what to say. How old was this kid, anyway? Twenty? Twenty-two? I almost didn't want to know, didn't want to think how tender was the age at which I was introducing him to one of the more corrupt and sordid elements of a business he was trying to be excited about, and I was still trying to love.

"You still have my card with my phone number, don't you, Felix?"

"I scanned it in." Of course he had.

"Look specifically for any indication that Speath ever did work for Air Sentinel," I said. "He claims no, but I still want to check."

"Why?"

"There's a possibility, and I have nothing to prove this, that his shop could have installed a bad part or in some other way caused a plane crash."

"Oh." He thought about that, and seemed to come to terms with it rather quickly. "Okay. When do you need this stuff?"

"The sooner the better, but don't ignore your job."

That cracked him up. "My job mostly ignores me."

I started for the door. "Miss Shanahan?" He was standing still, feet together which seemed weird. "This is really cool. Thanks for asking me."

That may have been the first time I'd ever been thanked for asking someone to do me a favor.

The California Pizza Kitchen was sounding like a much better choice for dinner than sushi when I arrived back at the airport. On the other hand, I hadn't been running lately because of my ankle. Sushi would be less satisfying, but also less of a carbo load.

At some point, as I was resolving the dinner dilemma, I became aware that he was back there. Behind me. Moving as I moved. I stopped once abruptly to browse in the window of a bookstore. Out of the corner of my eye, I caught him trying to match my movements, but his reaction was a beat behind, enough that I could see him do it. He was definitely following me. Damn.

He wore a cap pulled low enough over his eyes that

205

his face was impossible to see, which meant I couldn't see when he was looking at me. He might have had a beard. He wore a black mesh T-shirt with the sleeves ripped out over jeans that bagged around his light-skinned, pointy-toed cowboy boots. A big, angry look-ing tattoo covered one upper arm. I was too far away to see what it was.

I stood at the window of the bookstore with one eye on him, trying to figure out what to do. Drift over to the Flamingo Garage and the airport police station. That's what made the most sense, but it was a long way away. A good ten-minute walk. He'd follow me until he figured out where I was going, peel off, and come back to haunt me another day. Frankly, I was tired of being followed around.

The airport was busy, and I kept getting buffeted and brushed aside by great moving tourist flows, clumps of people wearing loose, sunny smiles and big name tags. First it hit me that it was cruise ship day and I was in Miami, which meant the big air-to-water transfer and vice versa were underway. Then it hit me that I was in one of the greatest places in the world to get lost—a crowded airport—and I came up with a better idea.

I glanced over at my pursuer, who didn't seem to have moved a muscle the whole time he'd been stand-ing there. Then I picked out a particularly animated tourist clump, steadied myself, and dove in. I had to really clamp down on the adrenaline to match their pace, which felt excruciatingly slow. I had to if I wanted to stay nestled in their midst. I went a short way with them before I saw another group coming from the opposite direction, and moving more swiftly. I wanted to go the way they were going and needed to shift over, but couldn't find Mr Mesh Man. They were approaching fast when I picked him out. His back was to me. I waited as he turned, turned in my direction . . . waited . . . waited . . . there. He saw me. Go . . . *now*.

I crossed over, began flowing in the reverse current, hopefully pulling him behind me, and, if I'd done it right, without his knowing.

Always keeping him in sight, and letting him keep me in sight, I made a couple more shifty moves. He wasn't very big, and had to stop frequently to stand on his toes and scan. Every time he didn't spot me, he grew more agitated. I could see it in the set of his shoulders and the way his head swiveled. At one point he turned completely around and I wasn't sure he'd pick me up again. It was so crowded it was actually hard to keep him in sight.

By the time I landed in the snaky check-in queue for LOT Polish Airlines, my heart was hammering, but I was weirdly exhilarated by this game of cat and mouse. Perhaps it would have been better to be the cat . . . but still, I was exactly where I wanted to be—around the corner from the security checkpoint.

I did a radar sweep for Mesh Man and found him— staring straight at me. And approaching. Fast. I pushed through the line, past a skycap and his overloaded rolling cart. I went around a herd of flight attendants with rolling bags. I was moving fast, but when I looked back, Mesh Man was closing. When I looked ahead, I saw what I didn't want to see. A line at the security checkpoint.

If I hadn't been carrying my backpack, I could have

gone directly to the front of the line and sailed through the metal detector. If Mesh Man was armed, there was no way he was coming through behind me, and if he wasn't and followed me in, I'd simply turn around and ask him to state his business, right in front of all these people. But I had to get through, and fast. My Majestic ID had always been good for cutting the line. I wished I still had it. What I did have was the temporary one Bic had provided. I was almost running now and my hands were shaking. When I slung the pack forward, I almost dropped it. I had to try two zippered pockets before I found it. I was already standing at the front of the line, having cut in front of at least twelve people, when I finally extracted it. I flashed my ID. They made me throw my bag on the belt for x-ray, but let me pass through the metal detector. As I stood waiting for my backpack to come through, I tried to spot Mr Mesh Man. Couldn't. I was tingling all over and breathing hard. My ankle was sore and my legs were stiff when I finally saw him . . . the back of him, hauling ass away from the checkpoint. I stood there for a long time, cooling off and calming down, watching people come through, and wondering if he had just given up, or if I had been playing cat and mouse with an armed man. I didn't feel quite so exhilarated any more.

Chapter Twenty-One

The receptionist at The Cray Fund was a slim Latino man with long graceful fingers. His short dark hair and soulful brown eyes stood out against the overtly white walls, his white reception counter, and a white-and-gray marble floor that practically glowed in the bright light from the floor-to-ceiling windows. Once again I sorely missed my sunglasses, which had been incinerated along with everything else in my bag. Jack had his on.

"Cray Financial Services, how may I direct your call?" I thought he was talking to himself until I spotted the translucent earpiece and microphone sprouting from the side of his head. His fingers moved expertly across a console as he went back to a call on hold. "She's off the line now, I'll transfer you."

"May I help you?" he asked, glancing up crisply between calls.

"Alex Shanahan and Jack Dolan. We have a ten o'clock appointment."

"With whom?" He was exasperated with us.

"We're not sure," I said, courting even more derision. "I called yesterday afternoon and spoke to a gentleman, maybe you, who told us to come in this morning. We have questions about one of the firm's cars."

"Have a seat." His constantly moving fingers punched up another call.

Jack had already found a spot on the edge of the

white leather couch. He picked up a copy of the *Miami Herald*. I sank down next to him and picked up one of the company's prospectuses.

"Ten to one," he murmured, "the car in the lot in the middle of the night was this Cray out porking his secretary."

I gazed about at our well-appointed surroundings. The place reeked of money, in a tropical sort of way. "I doubt if he'd choose The Harmony House Suites for his romantic interlude, you're the one who says we have to be open to all possibilities, and *porking* his *secretary*?"

"I'm just going off years of experience running people and their dirty little secrets to ground." He set down his paper and took in the surroundings. "What do they do here, anyway?"

"They're investors. They run a hedge fund."

"Is that like a mutual fund?"

"Sort of, except a hedge fund is an investment pool for rich people. It's not regulated like a mutual fund is, so it allows much riskier investing, which can mean much higher returns. According to this"—I pointed at a summary page in one of the company's brochures— "their return last year was over seventy percent. Of course the converse is also true. The downside can be as big as the upside."

"You understand all that stuff?"

"I've had a few finance courses in my day."

A set of handsome double doors off the reception area opened and a man and a woman emerged. The man was large, muscled, and dressed like one of the Bee Gees. His polyester white slacks were tight across his thick thighs and flared below the knee. The rest of his outfit was all black—silk T-shirt, leather belt, and woven leather loafers. No socks. On his left wrist were a large gold watch *and* a thin gold bracelet, and on his right pinky, a thick gold ring in the shape of a cross. He was Hispanic, so the chest hairs that curled out above the rounded collar of his shirt were also dark. He walked past us without so much as a sideways glance.

Jack leaned over to whisper. "He wasn't the one following you last night, was he?"

I shook my head. Too big. Way too big.

The woman lingered in the double doorway, pausing—or posing—momentarily as she gave the two of us a good once-over. She was angular and elegant enough to have just stepped from a Richard Avedon photo—the long graceful neck and those high-fashion bones. What she didn't have was the proudly vacuous stare. In keeping with the blinding color scheme of the office, her silk suit was ivory and her hair shimmering blonde. I didn't think high heels were stylish at the moment, given all the chunky shoes that had been stepping on my toes lately. But she had that kind of style that made everything she wore look as fresh as if it had been designed for her the day before and whipped up that morning.

"I'm sorry to keep you waiting," she said, slinking my way first. "I'm Vanessa Cray."

And you're a girl, I thought, as I pushed myself up from the couch to greet her. "Alex Shanahan," I said. "This is Jack Dolan." I glanced at Jack, anxious to see how this unexpected development fit with his porking theory. Vanessa had turned her attention to him as well. She was tall enough in her heels to gaze directly into

Jack's eyes when she turned to greet him, which was enough for him to finally remove the sunglasses.

"Mr Dolan," she said, "it's a pleasure to meet you."

She had smiled at me with polite obligation. The way she smiled at him, the way she demanded eye contact and touched his arm with her left hand as she took his hand with her right made me think of how I'd had different résumés when I went looking for work, based on who the audience would be. Vanessa Cray was one of those women who had one personality for her own gender, and a very different one for the other.

Jack seemed very pleased to have caused such a response and was suddenly much more interested in taking the meeting. "The pleasure is mine."

"Won't you come in?" She detached from Jack and swept us through the double doors.

Two things hit me right off about Vanessa Cray's office. It was vast and it was cold. Really cold. This was in spite of her floor-to-ceiling windows that opened out to a gleaming South Florida day that was only slightly tarnished by today's serving of smoke and ash. The glass in her windows must have been heavily insulated because I couldn't feel any warmth from the sun. Seeing the brightness outside and feeling the cold inside made for a strange, disorienting sensory experience.

Another thing that was hard not to miss was the proliferation of flowers. One would think an office filled with flowers would have had a homey charm. But these flowers looked more like exotic specimens growing in petri dishes. The plant on her desk had neon orange blooms that were shaped like lobster claws and looked to be made out of rubber tubing. They were all like that, graceful little sculptures that practically shouted "hands off."

"May I get you a hot drink?" She addressed me from behind her desk, which was not much more than a piece of glass stretched across two fancy chrome sawhorses. She glanced up—but only for a second—from whatever had drawn her to her flat screen monitor. "You seem uncomfortable."

"Not really." It's just that my eyeballs were beginning to frost.

She continued to keep us waiting for what was turning into an uncomfortably long period as she tapped her keys and perused the screen. "Please excuse my obsessive-compulsive behavior," she said lightly, making it clear we had no choice. "I'm trying to keep my eye on things. We made some big trades today."

"How did you do?" I asked.

She smiled. "As it happens, extremely well."

Jack leaned over the dish of lobster claws on her desk. "You like orchids?" he asked.

Vanessa shifted her intense concentration instantly from the screen to Jack. It was like a heat-seeking missile acquiring a target. "Do you know orchids?"

"Not really, but my mother loved flowers. She had them all over the house when I was growing up. I couldn't help but pick up a few things from her, although I don't remember any that looked like this."

She swooped around her desk to stand next to him, and they both leaned over the dish while I stood to the side, feeling as if I hadn't been picked for the kickball team.

"It's unlikely your mother would have had these." She

213

ran a finger gently, lovingly along the outside of one of the blooms. "They're *Masdevallia velifera*. Their shape is quite unusual for an orchid. This one is called a Solar Flare because of the shape and the bright neon color. They grow mostly on trees in Andean cloud forests, where it's cool and shady and always bathed in mist. Their ideal temperature is fifty-five degrees."

That explained why she worked in a refrigerator. It was probably the least of the concessions she made to her passion. She was probably good at passion.

"They must be a challenge to grow in Florida," Jack said.

"That's why I grow them. And because they are so magnificent." She gazed down at the orchid in the same way a parent gazes upon her child—with endless wonder, as if it filled her with both pride and bewilderment to behold what she had made.

"Perhaps we could get started," I said. They both looked at me. "So we don't take up too much of your time."

"Certainly." She directed us to a cluster of chairs, small couches, and tables at the other end of the sparse office. I pulled my notebook from my backpack, opened it up, and noted the date and time and attendees.

"My assistant tells me you have a question about one of our cars. Of course I'll provide any information I can, but may I ask why you're interested?"

She was glancing over at my notebook, but addressing her questions to Jack, who sat forward on his chair with his elbows on his knees, and his hands clasped together in a posture that made him look both relaxed

214

and alert. I listened carefully to hear how much he would tell her, and how he would couch the information.

"The license number came up in a case we're working on."

"What kind of case?"

"We're looking into the murder of a man at The Harmony House Suites. A black Volvo 580 registered to your company was in the hotel parking lot that night."

"How," she asked, "do you know this?"

"Surveillance."

She tipped her head and gave him a teasing smile. "I'm sure my car wasn't the only one in the lot that night."

He countered with his own crooked grin. "We're eliminating possibilities."

"Then the car does belong to you," I said, climbing into the conversation.

"It belongs to my company. But you already knew that. That's why you're here." She glanced again at the notebook on my lap. "Are you Jack's assistant?"

If I had been a dog, all the hair on my neck would have stood up right then, although it was certainly her right to find out who she was talking to and why. And I *was* in a way acting as Jack's assistant, although I didn't understand why she felt the need to point that out, unless it was to make me feel as if I didn't belong there, as if I didn't know what I was doing, as if she and Jack were the real thing and I was an imposter, an interloper, a party crasher—

"Ms Cray," Jack said, "I—"

"Call me Vanessa."

"Ms Shanahan is my client. I work for her."

"I see." She had barely glanced in my direction and was now addressing Jack again. "I have a fleet of six Volvos registered to my company. All the same model. All the same year. All black."

"The license number is unique," I said, trying not to behave as if she'd just blown me off completely. It was tough.

"I'm afraid that won't tell you who was driving."

"The cars are not assigned?"

"Anyone who works here is welcome to use any car. I had intended them for business use only, but I must admit we've never kept careful track." She shrugged delicately, making it clear that keeping track of six forty-thousand–dollar vehicles just didn't make it onto her radar screen.

"How many em—"

"I have thirty-five employees."

"And no procedure for signing the cars in and out?"

"None."

"Does that mean your employees could hand the keys over to friends or family?"

"I don't see the need for stringent controls. I trust my employees."

Which meant we had to consider not only all thirty-five employees, but their friends, their families, and anyone else they may have felt like handing the keys off to. She couldn't have made the situation more complicated if she'd tried.

Jack picked up the ball. "Ms Cray—"

"I asked you to call me Vanessa." She gazed upon Jack as if he'd disappointed her. If he felt disappointing, he wasn't letting it show.

216

"Can you provide us a list of employees and contact numbers?"

"Of course." She reached over, picked up her phone, and asked whoever answered to bring a copy of the company's employee roster. A young woman wearing a serious suit and an expression to match appeared almost immediately with the file, and took the opportunity to say gently but firmly that Vanessa was late for her conference call with London. They'd started on time, she explained, and had gone as far as they could without her. I checked my watch. We had been with her less than twenty minutes and spent at least half that time watching her stare at her monitor.

"Tell them I'll be right with them." The assistant departed. Vanessa paged through the file quickly and handed it to me. "I think you'll find what you need in here." She took two business cards from a holder on the table next to her and gave us each one as well. "And if you'd care to look at the cars, I'll have my assistant call downstairs. Now I really must—"

"Your name is not on this list." My tone was more blunt than I'd intended, but then I wasn't trying too hard. This time when we locked eyes, I felt as though she were seeing me for the first time. I'd finally managed to get her attention.

"You asked for an employee list. I'm not an employee."

"I assume you have access to the Volvos."

"Yes, but I don't use the cars. I have a driver."

"I understand," I said. "What I'm asking you is if there is anyone else with access to the cars whose name is not on the list."

"Oh, I see. No, there's no one that I can think of

217

right now, but if you'll leave your information with my receptionist, I'll certainly call you if anything comes to mind."

She had walked behind her desk and settled in again to watch whatever it was she found so mesmerizing on her computer screen. If that wasn't enough of a signal, she punched up her assistant on the phone and requested to be hooked up to the London call.

We were dismissed. Actually, I had been dismissed even before we'd begun, but now she was apparently through with Jack as well.

We took the express elevator down from the Andean rain forest. The two of us stood, as people do in elevators, side by side facing forward. Jack stared up at the floor counter while I studied our images in the polished metal elevator doors.

I was studying Jack's image more than mine. He was an attractive man, especially spiffed up the way he was with his hair combed and a nice jacket on. I enjoyed that about him. Also his intelligence, his complexity, his sense of humor. His mysterious side. That sense that there were many more layers to him than he was showing. I didn't like that Vanessa Cray had just tried to crawl up his pant leg.

He noticed me looking. "What?"

"Do you think she did that to keep you off balance?"

"Did what?"

"Flirted with you?"

He brushed something off his jacket lapel. "Are you saying you don't think she finds me attractive?"

"I think she finds you attractive in the way a lion

finds zebra meat to be attractive."

He grinned. "I've been called a lot of things, but never zebra meat." He scraped the edge of her business card along his jaw, and I could hear the sound of stubble. "I've seen her somewhere before. I can't remember where, but I know I've seen her face."

"She's hiding something," I said.

"You just don't like her."

"I don't like her, and she's hiding something."

He turned his attention back to the floor counter overhead. "Did you ever consider that she was flirting with me to get to you?"

"Why would she do that?"

"She likes to play. And she recognizes you as the bigger threat."

"How am I a threat to her?"

"She's used to controlling men. That's obvious. But you're smart, and so is she. You like to be in control, and so does she. And you're a woman. You are more of a challenge for her."

We dropped a few more floors as I considered that. Better to be neutralized for being too much of a challenge, I supposed, than to be dismissed for not being enough of one. I decided to feel marginally better. Even so . . .

"I think she's hiding something."

"That's because you don't like her."

"Yeah."

We had to cross to another elevator to get to the garage, where we found the six black Volvos in reserved spots on the bottom level. They were all in, presumably because everyone was at work in the building. We identified the one we wanted by the license plate, and as promised, a parking attendant gave us the keys.

Jack piled into the driver's side and I slipped into the back seat. "What are we looking for?"

"Anything that might tell us who has driven the car lately."

I pulled an empty Snapple bottle off the floor and showed it to him. "All we're likely to prove is that someone drove the car at some point, not who drove the car to the hotel that night and for what reason."

He leaned over and opened the glove box. "Don't overanalyze. Keep looking."

"I'm not optimistic." I reached down into all the cracks between the leather cushions and felt around. All I came up with was a Tic Tac, a penny, some hairs, and a lot of really disguisting lint and grit that made me want to flee to the ladies' room and wash my hands.

"You know, Jack, they could have switched the plates."

"That's why we're going to search all six."

We did. It took two hours. The most interesting thing we found came from the first car we'd searched, the one with the license plate that had matched the surveillance. It was a credit card receipt for a gas purchase dated the Tuesday afternoon after John had been killed. The person who had signed was named Arturo. I held it up to the light and tried to read the last name. Impossible. It was nothing more than a long, illegible squiggle.

"I'm going to have to get someone to run that down," Jack said.

"I've got a better idea. There's someone I'd like you to meet."

Chapter Twenty-Two

All the rooms on this side of The Harmony House Suites had interior windows that looked out to the hotel's wide center atrium. In answer to my knock, room 484's curtains twitched. The deadbolt clicked, and the door opened, but only a crack. I could have fit through just fine if I was Gumby.

"Felix?"

"It's me, Miss Shanahan." Felix's voice was quiet, but not subdued. It was hard for Felix to restrain his innate enthusiasm for just about everything. The crack expanded to reveal the white-tipped hair, the dark eyes. "Are you alone, Miss Shanahan?"

"No. I brought someone to meet you." Jack stepped out so Felix could see him. "We have another assignment for you."

"Cool."

I waited. And waited. "Can we come in, Felix?"

"Oh. Oh, sure. Absolutely. Sorry. Come in."

He opened the door and let us slip through. Apparently, he'd taken over room 484 at The Suites and turned it into his command center. It looked like the one John had stayed in, only the floor plan was reversed. It also had a few additions. There were multiple electronic products around the room—a couple of printers, one of which seemed to be in many pieces on the floor, a scanner, what looked like some sort of external high-density drive, a CD player, and lots of hardware I couldn't identify. The center of all the gadgets was a laptop, which sat on the coffee table in front of the couch. With all the wires and cables running out of it, it looked like a post-op patient in the trauma ward.

"Felix, this is Jack Dolan. He's a private investigator."

"Hello, son." Jack extended his hand and Felix shook it. They were quite a contrast, these two. Jack with his calm, squinty-eyed, seen-it-all PI's stare, and Felix Melendez Jr with eyes that couldn't have gotten any bigger, so clearly delighted to meet a real live private investigator. I loved this kid's transparency. He moved to the seat on the couch in front of his laptop. The maestro preparing to work.

"What is a Limp Bizkit?" Jack was staring down at the mouse pad on the coffee table.

"It's a band," Felix said, waiting for the next question.

"We need to know whose signature this is." I handed him the credit card receipt. "Can you work with that?"

He snapped it out of my hand and checked it over. His face began to glow. He was like a kid at a spelling bee who had been given an easy word. "Just give me a couple of minutes, okay?"

"Can I watch?" I asked.

He was already deeply immersed. Jack settled into the armchair next to the couch, stuck his legs out, and crossed them at the ankles. I sat on the couch next to Felix and watched what he was doing. I didn't understand a lot of it, but eventually he got to some program that seemed to be doing a high-speed comparison between the credit card number we'd provided and a large database of other numbers.

"This is going to take a few minutes." He relaxed, but only slightly.

"Anything on Speath yet, Felix? Anything suspicious in the financials?" I asked.

"Nothing so far, Miss Shanahan, but I haven't had much time to work on it. We had a fire alarm yesterday and then there was a problem with a parrot that got loose and my restaurant manager called in sick—"

"It's okay," I said. "I told you not to ignore your day job. In fact, are you sure you should be using the hotel to do this work for us?"

"I'm not working on the hotel's time. They're getting, like, totally more coverage from me since I'm around here so much. I'm using my own computer and equipment. And I plan to bill you for the room and the phone calls. But," he hastened to add, "I get an awesome discount."

"You know, Felix, we haven't talked about this, but I should be paying you. What's the going rate for someone like you?"

"To do this kind of work, maybe $100 . . . $150 an hour."

"Oh."

"Don't worry, Miss Shanahan. I figure if you can help me get a job at the airport, it will be worth it." I was definitely getting the better end of that deal. "I'll have something to you on Mr Speath as soon as I crack the firewall. It shouldn't be much longer."

"Firewall?" Jack asked the question, but only because he beat me to it. "Speath has a firewall?"

"Oh, yeah. It's a good one, too. Most of his data is really accessible, but there's this one section he has walled off. I tried every way I know of to get past and I couldn't. But I will. I've been talking to some of my friends about it. We have ideas."

"It must be sophisticated," I said, "if *you* can't get in."

Felix's olive skin flushed, starting at his throat and rising all the way to his white tips. "Thank you, Miss Shanahan. And I will find a way in. I've just never seen one like this before. It's, like"—he stared up at the ceiling—"wicked tight, you know? It's a vault."

I looked at Jack. "Why would a little aviation repair company have a need for a data vault?"

"I don't know," he said, "but I'd like to know what's in there. I'd also like to know why he was here at the hotel that night."

"I have a theory on that," I said. "We're interested in Speath because the FBI is interested and because his car was in the lot the night of the murder."

"Yes," Jack said. "We hate coincidences."

"What if it's not a coincidence? What if the two things are not independent variables, but dependent?"

"What does that mean?"

"What if the FBI is interested in George *because* his car was in the lot, and his car was in the lot for totally innocent reasons?"

"Like what?"

"Why do people go to hotels in their own city? Maybe he got a room with Margie."

"Who's Margie?"

"She's his assistant, and she's an attractive blonde. A few too many ankle bracelets for my taste. But still, maybe we're looking at an appropriate application of your porking theory. Or maybe they were in the bar having a drink."

"I can check that." We both looked at Felix. "I mean I can try to see if they were here for other reasons, like . . . you know, like if they got a room together. We already know they didn't register their car with us, so they probably didn't, you know, use their real names. But they might be regulars. I can see who was registered that night and if they've been here before. I can check the registration cards for local addresses. After a while, you get so you can recognize certain things. I can also ask the bartender to go through credit card receipts. Sometimes people park out there who are just here for a drink."

"Do that," I said. "Maybe we can eliminate George from consideration altogether."

"Oh, hey. It's up." Felix checked his screen. "Here it is. Your data's up."

Jack came around to Felix's other side. "What are we looking at, son?"

Felix pointed out the highlights with his finger. "The credit card was issued against a Cray Fund corporate account, and here's the list of people who have cards." He ran his finger down the list. When he stopped, I leaned in to see who the winner was. "There's one Arturo," he said. "Arturo Polonia."

"I'll be damned." Jack shook his head. "This is supposed to be secure data. And you hacked in? Just like that?"

Felix puffed up his narrow chest. "One way or another, I can get in almost anywhere. And I'll crack Mr Speath's vault, too. I'll figure it out."

"How about an address or social security number on this Arturo character? I can get someone to run it and see if he has a record."

"Piece of cake, Mr Dolan."

While they looked for that, I found the file Vanessa had given me and searched the list of employees. I read over it twice.

"I think we just narrowed our search, Jack. There is no Arturo Polonia on the Cray employee list."

Chapter Twenty-Three

Jack paused between bites of his *chile relleno*. "Maybe she forgot," he said.

"Does Vanessa Cray strike you as a scatterbrain, Jack?"

"No. But she did strike me as someone who could get absorbed in what she was doing to the exclusion of everything else. She checked out on us before we ever left her office."

We were at the Texas Taco Factory for an early dinner, a storefront fajita bar in Jack's South Beach neighborhood. It had a neon Corona beer logo in the window and a hand-lettered sign that announced a senior citizens' discount, although the place didn't strike me as a seniors' kind of hangout. It was dark, with scarred heavy wooden tables and long benches to sit on. Next door was Pucci's Pizza and the Top Dog Gun Shop. Shorty and Fred's Ford Dealership was across the street.

"I still think having Felix do a background check on her is a good idea. He's dying to help us. All he would have to do is a quick search of the periodical databases at the library—magazines, newspapers, especially the business publications. I'd also like to know where she went to school, and if she worked anywhere before she started that fund of hers. That extremely successful fund of hers."

"You wouldn't be jealous, would you?"

"You mean because she turned out to be sexy and glamorous and beautiful and successful, probably rich, and undoubtedly more together in her life than I am in mine at the moment?" I threw back a mineral water chaser. "Heavens, no. I'm not jealous."

Jack crunched a few more taco chips. I took another bite of my fajita. I was trying to space them out, since I had to towel down after each bite. The salsa and other unidentified juices tended to leak out of the sides of the soft tortilla and run down my arm.

"What I want to know," I said, "is why you're dismissing her. Her car was at the hotel, she lied to us about this Arturo guy, and I still don't get why she would have screwed with us the way she did if she wasn't hiding something."

Jack was working on his main course—scrambled eggs, a choice for dinner I always found strange. But he said he'd had a taste for *huevos rancheros* all day. "She answered every question," he said. "She gave us what we asked for, and she volunteered her cars for inspection, so I don't see how she screwed with us. I'm not dismissing her. I'll get someone to run Arturo Polonia for me."

He took another long drink of ice water from a tall plastic glass. He was throwing down lots of water, no doubt to counteract the extra-hot salsa he'd ordered on the *huevos.*

"I'm just trying to get you to think about this critically," he said. "You don't see many women in the dirty parts trade, especially ones who wear silk. She's way, way out of Jimmy and Bobby's league, and if you're saying you think she killed John, I don't see how. He was stabbed, which means he was physically overwhelmed. And someone had to lift him into that Dumpster. You told me he was a big man."

"Maybe someone helped her. Maybe this Arturo person."

"Then let's talk about motive." More water. "You dismissed Ottavio because you couldn't conceive of a motive that made sense, and yet you think John might have come in contact with this woman? John was in no way involved in drugs, but he may have invested in a hedge fund. Is that your speculation?"

I had to smile. Jack's sarcasm was too gentle. Good sarcasm was supposed to be sharp enough to make you bleed. Yet he always managed to make his point.

"All right, that's fair." It was time to make another fajita, a process at least as treacherous as eating them. I pulled out a tortilla and started piling—meat and peppers and guac and salsa. "How about this? I get to consider the idea that Vanessa is involved if I open up to the possibility that Ottavio could also be involved. Be open to all the possibilities. That's what you said." Sour cream, rice, some refried beans. "I can do that. I would never want to be accused of being less than rigorous in my analytical approach."

"Now you're talking."

"I just feel something from her, Jack. I can't explain it."

"I understand. I don't feel it about her, but I do feel it about Jimmy. I think he's a much more promising suspect. I think George Speath is going to wind up being the key. He's a nice guy, right?"

"He seemed very nice to me. More than nice. Sweet."

"Nice guys are always suspect."

"Where do you get that? The only thing we've determined about George is he likes to keep hackers out of his data. He's an engineer. Maybe he just knows enough to protect himself. It would be hard to hack Felix, too, but that doesn't make him a bad guy."

Jack looked at me. I had become a tad more forceful in my defense of George than even I would have expected. "Why," he asked, "do you like him so much?"

"He loves airplanes. He can't be all bad."

"So it's a perspective you've gained through careful and diligent data gathering and analysis."

"Exactly. Similar to the approach you've taken with Jimmy."

"Jimmy is a bad guy. There is no question about that. And I submit that the man following you through the terminal the other day was one of Jimmy's people."

"Jimmy doesn't know I exist."

"Avidor does."

"True. Why would he be following me?"

"To scare you. To scare me. I'm going to find out." He scarfed down another handful of tortilla chips. Between the two of us, we were going through them pretty compulsively. "If you feel that strongly about Vanessa, you should pursue her."

"*I* should pursue her?"

"I'm going to track down Ira and see what news he has for me."

"Tonight?"

"I do my best work at night. So does he. And I have to follow up some leads on my helicopter case. I do have another client, remember?"

"Oh, yeah. I'll call Felix and ask him to do the background check. Maybe we'll come up with something that will help you remember where you know her from."

"Tell him to look at the orchid societies."

"That's a great idea. And what about this employee list?" I asked. "Am I going to have to interview thirty-five people and all their friends and family by myself?"

"You said you wanted to be an investigator." He said it with a twinkle in his eye.

"Actually, I think I said I wanted to watch you investigate."

"Give it to me." He took the list and folded it until it fit into the front pocket of his shirt. "I'll see if Patty would like to have something the Bureau doesn't have."

"Excellent." I finished off the last piece of skirt steak, wiped down, leaned back against the wall, and stretched my legs out on the long bench. My ankle was mostly fine, but it still throbbed at the end of a long day.

"You're not going to see Jimmy tonight, are you, Jack? By yourself?"

"Why do you ask?"

"I don't know. But it strikes me as not a good idea for you to do that."

"Why?"

"Because you keep telling me not to get emotionally involved. That it clouds my ability to get to the right answer. You have something going on with Jimmy that you choose not to share with me . . ."

I glanced over for a reaction, thinking I could guilt him into sharing with me. There was none. Nothing. His face had gone blank. I picked up my knife and concentrated on rolling it across the wooden table. Flat implements don't roll well. "Anyway, whatever it is, it seems intensely emotional to me."

231

"I'm not emotional about Jimmy." Now his voice was blank, too. Flat.

"I can see it in you right now." I had cleared a space and was twirling the knife, spinning it like a top. Harder and harder. Faster and faster. "You're so cool about everything else, so in command. But when you talk about him—just me talking about him now—your reactions are different."

"Different how?"

I shifted on the bench. It felt narrow. I hadn't meant to go so deep with this line of discussion. I looked again into his eyes and couldn't find anything to hold on to. It was as if a shroud had come down.

"Vulnerable, Jack. You seem very vulnerable around the subject of Jimmy. That's the only way to describe it. It's like he's a flat spot for you. A place you can't see and since you can't see it, you can't defend it. I don't know him. I don't know anything about him, but you said he's pretty smart and—"

"Where did you get your psychological training?"

I stared at him, hoping for the mild curves and rounded corners that usually accompanied his ribbing. It wasn't there. His eyes were hard. Mean, even.

"On the ramp in Boston," I said. "Crash course."

"And who's going to protect me? You?"

His tone had moved beyond flat to sharp, sharp enough to make me bleed. He was getting the hang of this sarcasm thing, trying to hurt me, or at least push me away. I'd poked around in something that was none of my business. The restaurant had turned festive since we'd been in there. A large group had come in, gathered around the bar, and started doing shots. Loudly. They

232

were just warming up while the temperature at our table had dropped below zero. For the first time, I felt uncomfortable with Jack Dolan.

"I'm sorry for digging around in your business and making assumptions I have no right to make. I do that, and I do it without permission." I swiveled around, put my feet on the floor, and sat up straight. "But don't ridicule my concern. I like you, and no, I can't protect you from Jimmy. From anything, probably. Surely you know someone who can? All I'm saying is I don't think . . . I would like for you not to go out and confront Jimmy on your own."

When I had faced forward, he had taken my pose, turning to lean his back against the wall and putting his feet up on the bench. He drank again from his big plastic cup of water, finishing off the slushy ice-water mix. He stared up at the ceiling fan, which was turning at a lethargic pace. "There's nothing you need to know about Jimmy and me," he said. "All you need to know about him is he killed your friend."

It was impossible not to feel the blunt finality of the statement. Nerves all through my body were twisting themselves into knots. It was as if the scenery I'd become familiar with had shifted and I was lost.

I took out a twenty and put it on the table. "Do you want me to drive you home?"

"I'm not going home." He made no move to get up.

I didn't want to leave, but I could feel everything in him pushing me out. I hated that he wanted me to leave. "You don't want me to go with you tonight?"

"I told you from the start I worked better on my own. I don't want you worrying about me." He turned

233

his face away to look through the window to the street. The beer signs cast a neon glow across his face that made him look like an Andy Warhol portrait. "I don't want anyone worrying about me."

I waited, but all he would show me was the side of his face. His jaw was set and his muscles tense. I gathered my things and left him sitting on his bench. In the parking lot, I checked to see if he might come through the restaurant door and perhaps look my way. I only looked once, but I looked for a long time.

Going back over the causeway to the city, it wasn't quite dark enough to need headlights. Downtown Miami looked calm and beautiful with the lights just starting to emerge against the gray dusk. In the sky over the ocean, the sun was sinking behind the flat horizon. It looked as if it were being lowered on a crane into the water. The sky above it was streaked in that stunning array of colors that get left behind when the sun departs—mostly pinks and oranges. It was so beautiful it made me cry.

Chapter Twenty-Four

I woke up all of a sudden, as if someone had reached out of the darkness and tapped me on the shoulder. I rolled over on my back, held still, and listened hard. All I heard was the laboring of the air conditioner. It was pumping fast, like my heart, but it was no match for the humidity that hovered over my bed like the sea of smoke that pressed down on the city outside. It was almost one in the morning.

It could have been the fajitas that had disturbed my deep sleep. More likely it was the specter of raging wildfires that had been planted in my consciousness by the evening news. Topping the headlines had been an eighteen-vehicle crash in central Florida, attributed to a nearby band of brushfires whose smoke had mingled with fog and drifted across the interstate. As I slept, a blaze was roaring north of I-75 near the Broward–Palm Beach county line, and had already consumed fifty thousand acres of tall saw grass. Yet another band of fires had threatened a warehouse in Miami-Dade County. The message seemed to be that we were surrounded by fires and they were moving closer.

I threw back the covers. I flipped my pillow, which was as soaked with perspiration as my hair. The sheets were also damp with the sweat that trickled down my face, under my arms, between my legs. It even seemed that the soles of my feet were sweating. I imagined an imprint of my body on the mattress that looked a lot like a chalk outline.

It was hard to breathe, harder when I thought about smoke and fumes and fog and fire, so I concentrated on inhaling and exhaling as deeply as I could, forcing air into my lungs and bad thoughts out of my head. But it was no use. When the phone rang, I was almost expecting it.

I sat in the Lumina, parked roughly where Jack had told me to park. I had followed his directions back to the swamp, driving almost forty-five minutes south and west from the city. It had been a nerve-wracking experience, driving dark and narrow roads, checking the rearview every few minutes along the way. If the kidney car, or any car, had been following me, I wanted to know before I'd gone too far from civilization. I had already worn myself out by the time I found Jack's rendezvous point.

According to him, if I was in the right place, I was half a mile from an old airfield and a large abandoned hangar. I was in the vicinity of the swamp I had visited while chasing Bobby, but supposedly a different section. It was hard to tell from the scenery. The roads had been just as black and forbidding with the same tunnel-of-horrors atmosphere that practically guaranteed something would leap out of the darkness at me when I least expected it. Jack had suggested killing my headlights at the final turn, but I had tempted fate, two eerie beams of light cutting through air that was as moist as a limp washrag and smelled like someone's basement after the flood.

When I'd reached the meeting place, exactly two

miles in, I was supposed to have pulled to the side. There were no sides. I stopped the car and killed the engine. Now I was waiting, listening through closed windows to a darkness that throbbed with the same otherworldly sounds I'd heard the other night. They came from everywhere—from the trees overhead, from the ground underneath, from great distances, and from very close by.

Jack had been all business on the phone. Nothing about our conversation earlier in the evening, which was probably best given what we were about to do. He'd told me to wear black. I hadn't purchased any replacement clothes that were black, so I used what I had. New jeans that were as dark as indigo ink and stiff as Styrofoam, and a dark blue T-shirt I'd bought for running. I'd solved the problem of the big, silver Dallas Cowboys logo on the front by turning it inside out, but I couldn't do anything about the short sleeves. My pale, bare arms felt incandescent in the dark.

With the windows up and the air conditioner off, it hadn't taken long for the windows of the Lumina command capsule to steam up, so the sharp, fast knock seemed to come out of nowhere. It ruptured the clammy silence and nearly sent me through the roof. My hand went instinctively to the ignition. Another knock. I saw a flash of light, and heard Jack's voice. "It's me. Open up."

He slipped in. "Here—" He placed a small flashlight in my hand. "Hold this. And keep it low."

The flashlight was damp with what I assumed was his perspiration.

"You got here fast," he said.

It hadn't felt fast, especially the last ten miles. "Where's your truck?"

237

"Not far. It's in another clearing."

Another clearing? Was this car-sized space in the trees considered a clearing? "I take it you found Ira?"

"Yeah. He was over on the Gulf Coast fishing."

"He doesn't sound conscientious about his snitching duties. Are you sure we can trust him? What is this place we're going to?"

"It's an old airfield that was used mostly for crop dusters years ago. The people who owned it got sued. I don't even know who officially has title. It's been in receivership for years."

"What's so suspicious about it?"

"There's an old aircraft hangar on the property. Ira told me there's been a lot of activity in and out of it recently. Heavy equipment. Flatbed trucks. He said they even had a helicopter land in there. Whatever Jimmy is doing, Ira says this is ground zero."

"Is anyone there now?"

"I've been out here for hours. Nothing's happened except a car comes around every two hours for a drive-by."

"Jimmy's security?"

"Must be. But they're not all that serious if it is. All the better for us."

Jack must have noticed my glow-in-the-dark arms. He reached into the garment he was wearing—it looked like a fishing vest with numerous pockets and flaps and openings—and pulled out a round, flat can. With benefit of the flashlight, I figured out it was camouflage paint and not chewing tobacco. "Put this on your arms," he said, "and your face."

While I did that, he took the flashlight back and laid

it on the seat so the beam caught his hands under the dashboard. And in his hands was a gun, the big automatic I'd seen before. A Glock, he'd told me. A 9 mm. With a few practiced strokes, he released the clip, checked it, and rammed it back in with a loud click. He slid the top back and pushed another small lever that I thought might be the safety. It all seemed terribly complex to me. I finished blackening my arms and started on my face.

He holstered the automatic, went back into the multi-faceted vest, and came out with another gun, this one smaller. "Can you shoot?" he asked.

This question made my temples pulse as I tightened the lid on the camouflage paint. "And hit anything?"

"Okay." He held the gun low so the light would catch it. "This is only a .22. It's not going to do much, but it's better than nothing." He checked the safety, then turned it around and offered it to me.

I hesitated. "I hate guns."

"You'd hate worse being dead."

"Are those the only two choices?"

"It would make me feel better if you had a firearm. If something happened to me, or if someone got past me—"

"Then I'd be in deep shit. Jack, I'd be just as likely to shoot you as anything else."

"No, you wouldn't."

He was right. I didn't really think I'd shoot him. But I didn't want the gun. It felt wrong. It felt as if I would be playing at something I wasn't. I was still an average citizen who in less than one week was going back to a life somewhere else. I needed to believe that.

"No," I said. "I don't want it."

He didn't respond, but I heard a protracted sigh, one with a hint of "You're more trouble to me than you're worth." It was a legitimate reaction. I felt bad about it, but I couldn't make myself carry a gun.

"Do you want me to stay back?"

"No." He put the gun back in his pocket. "Take the floor mats."

"What?"

He opened his door, leaned back in, and pulled out the front floor mat. Then he opened the back door and did the same. "We're going to need these. Roll them together so you can carry them."

I opened my door as wide as I could, given the close and steady presence of the surrounding brush. It felt good to unfold from the seat where I'd been crammed. As I labored in the small space to maneuver the floor mats into a manageable bundle, every sweat mechanism in my body proceeded to move into high gear.

"Let's go."

Jack was off down the road, which was more passable on foot, and I followed. He'd brought an extra flashlight, which I tried to keep pointed at my feet. I didn't want a replay of the twisted ankle fiasco. Even though the ground was dry, I couldn't shake the feeling that at any moment I would step into quicksand.

We ran for about five minutes. I didn't catch up with Jack until he stopped. It was hard to tell, but it felt as though we had emerged on the periphery of a flat, wideopen field. I could feel the openness, especially compared to the thick brush behind us. I crouched next to him.

"We're going across that field," he said, confirming the geography. "It goes right up to a fence that surrounds the hangar. Go as fast as you can, but watch the ground. There's a lot of junk lying around. Don't stop until you get to the fence. And don't lose the mats." He turned to look at me. All I could see were his eyes, but they were calm and steady enough to make me feel that way, too. "Ready?"

"Ready."

Without the thick cluster of trees around us, the bright moon cast enough light that I could see oilcans, car parts, parts of parts, and garbage bags with contents unknown. I moved quickly, trying to stay close as he ran ahead of me. I hadn't even noticed the large structure looming ahead until the fence appeared and we had to stop. Up close, the hangar was gigantic—tall enough to block out the moon and wide enough that I couldn't see either end of the building in the limited light.

The fence was chain link, topped with a generous twist of razor wire, and went around the outer perimeter of the hangar. We stayed low at the base for a full five minutes and listened. There were no city sounds to be heard, no cars or trains, factories or shopping centers. The sounds were from the swamp. There was no sign of any other humans.

I had assumed Jack would pull a set of wire cutters out of that hardware store of a vest he was wearing. Instead, he unfurled a car mat, stood back, and tossed it up and over the razor wire. Aha. He did the same with his second mat and with the two I was carrying. With all four spread out side by side, we were able to scramble up and over, although it wasn't easy. The Cyclone fence was tall and old and sagging. It was like climbing a thick, billowy curtain.

We dropped down on the other side and waited for the fence to stop shaking. I stared at the structure in front of us. From our location, I couldn't see any obvious points of entry. The hangar doors on this side were padlocked shut. The walk-in door was most certainly locked. The foundation was solid concrete, so there would be no tunneling in.

"This way," Jack whispered.

"Where?"

"There's a window on the other side."

Indeed there was. It was around the corner and halfway down the length of the building. The bottom of it was low enough for me to reach, I figured, if Jack lifted me up and I stretched my arms out.

"Give me a boost," I said.

He stuck his flashlight in his belt and offered his two hands as a step. I climbed up and, with my fingers on the sill, crept up enough to see that the window was open a crack. I uncoiled a little more to shine the flashlight and look in. I saw a toilet reflected in a mirror over a sink. I could also see the door was closed. I tried to lift the window with one hand. No dice. I shoved the flashlight into my waistband and tried it with two. It was stuck so tight I had to bang it with the heels of my hands. I did it once. An avalanche of dust, rust, and dried paint flecks fell down and stuck to my damp face and hair. I rubbed my eyes and listened for an answering sound. Nothing. I banged it again, this time with my head down and my eyes closed. It came loose and opened all the way to the top. Without even looking down at Jack, I braced my arms on the sill and climbed through. I knew if I'd waited to think about it I would have stiffened up.

The whole enclosure wasn't much more than a toilet surrounded by sheets of plywood paneling. The toilet didn't have any water in it, so it smelled like a Port-O-Let at Woodstock. The door had a hook-and-eye latch and opened out. I pushed it open a crack, just enough to see and hear that it was quiet in the hangar. And dark. Jack dropped in behind me just as I pushed it open. The hinges squeaked.

"Let me go first," he said, plowing ahead. "I *am* the one with the gun." He didn't waste time or a single motion as he slipped out. I tried to move in the same economical fashion, staying low and following the beam of his flashlight, which was woefully inadequate in the vast building. What dim light there was inside the hangar came from moonlight through a high bank of windows and large, intermittent holes in the roof. It came down unobstructed in places, especially from overhead, and created deep shadows in others. It was too diffused to be of much use, but I did have the sense of being closed in and surrounded, much like the swamp outside. It was a creepy sensation in such a big space. There was also a smell—strong and heavy and mostly gasoline or some other fuel. But that wasn't all. Underneath it was the odor of something dead or decaying.

"I can't see a damn thing," Jack said. "I think . . ." He held up his flashlight. "Those look like worktables a little closer to the front. Maybe there are some lamps or lights on them."

He headed in that direction with me on his tail. I tried to take small, cautious steps. Every time I got overly confident, I ran into a pile of something unidentified on the ground. Whatever it was grabbed at my feet. Cables? Wires?

And then there was light. Jack had found a lamp. When he turned it on, it made a small pool on a short section of a long workbench. Using his flashlight, he found a second lamp not far away, and I found a third.

"Okay," he said, picking up small items around the space and studying them under the flashlight. "Fuses . . . O-rings. . . bolts . . . switches . . . valves." He raked the light over the back of the bench and a neat line of cans and bottles. "What have we here?" He picked up a large brown bottle and read the label. Then he leaned down and read the other labels.

"What is it?"

"Spray paint, chemicals, soldering materials. All the things you need to cover over half-assed repairs, change serial numbers."

"Strip-and-dip?" We were talking quietly, but our voices seemed to echo anyway.

"Yep. Among other things. I think we've found Jimmy's bogus parts factory." He ran the light farther down and touched on a neat hutch of drawers, the kind my dad used in his garage to organize his screws and nuts and bolts. Jack opened one of the drawers, pulled something out, checked it, and handed it to me. I held it under the light. It was a small metal plate with a series of numbers engraved in it.

"It's a data plate," he said. "Probably stolen."

He moved down the table and found another light.

When I caught up, he was holding up a component. He turned it one way, then the other. "This is a rotor segment," he said. "Brakes." He rubbed over a rough section with his thumb. "This is where they've ground down the part number. They'll stamp a fake one on." He put it down and picked up another part. "This is the housing for a starter. If you look under the light"— he pointed to a thin, crooked line across the outer casing that looked like a healed scar—"you can see the solder marks. They'll clean it up, paint over it, throw on one of those data plates, and sell it as new. Or like new." He put the unit down. "I'll bet if we look around here, we'll find some fake packaging. And it will look as good as the real stuff. Also paperwork." He kept moving along the workbench until he found something and brought it back. "See these?" He showed me a stack of papers. "These are yellow tags."

They were single sheets of white paper—8½ by 11 inches. "They're not yellow. And they're not tags."

"They don't have yellow tags anymore. But they still use the term. This document, when attached to a part and signed by a licensed mechanic, means it's been repaired according to all the standards and specs and is ready to go back on the airplane or helicopter. That's what a yellow tag does. It's the mechanic's certification."

"So this is all that stands between me and an airplane flying with a car part?"

"This and the skill and integrity of the mechanic who hangs the part on the airplane."

I looked down at the stack. They were blank, and they were all signed. "This is like a stack of blank checks."

"Exactly. Jimmy fills them in for every part. He

probably paid a hundred dollars each for the signatures."

I took a step back, tripped over something, and almost went down.

"Be careful." Jack directed the light down to my feet. It was a box I'd stumbled over. He moved the beam back to the workbench, so I used my own light to see what it was. I picked up an in-flight magazine out of the box and held it under one of the lamps.

"Jack, look at this."

He turned, caught sight of the cover, and stared at it.

"Look at the date," I said.

He didn't say anything, but in the silence I heard his breathing slow down. He swung around and tried to use his flashlight to sweep the hangar behind us. It was useless. The beam was feeble against the overpowering space.

"I'm going to find a light switch for the overheads."

"Are you sure that's smart?"

"I'm sure it's not, but I can't think of what else to do." He used the flashlight to check his watch. "We should still have over an hour before that car comes around. I'm not leaving until we know what's going on in here, and we're not going to figure it out one lamp at a time. I'll flip it right off again."

As he moved away, I followed his progress in the dark by the light in his hand and listened to him carefully picking his way forward.

It took a long time. While I waited, I tried to make out the dark shapes that were all around, towering above me, and crowded into the back of the hangar. Some were as tall as the high windows along the ceiling. The longer I waited, the more my skin prickled. I rubbed my arms and felt the goose bumps forming. I came away with black paint on both my sweaty palms. I tried to wipe it off on my stiff jeans.

"Found it," Jack said. And the lights went on—overhead lights blazing so brightly and so suddenly, my eyes squeezed themselves shut.

But not before I'd seen it. Not before I'd seen enough to make me afraid to open them again.

I did it in degrees, looking first at the small space around me just to get oriented. Then I broadened my scope, looking up and out.

The first thing that registered was the tail because it was the least damaged and most recognizable piece of the thousands, perhaps tens of thousands, of airplane parts that lay spread on the concrete all around me. Except for the odd angle at which it was tipped, and the fact that there was no fuselage attached to it, the tail appeared as it must have the day the airplane had rolled out of the factory for the last time. That would have been the day Air Sentinel had taken delivery, because that's whose logo was emblazoned across the stabilizer. And that's whose in-flight magazine we'd found in the box. It was from January, the month of the accident in Ecuador.

I did a complete 360, and what I saw literally sucked the air out of my lungs. It was what looked like the entire aircraft in pieces. Broken pieces. Ripped and cracked and scorched and shredded pieces. Enormous structures and assemblies ripped apart with the force . . . well, with the force of a jet flying into a mountain.

I looked across the hangar at Jack. He didn't say anything, but the lights stayed on. He was probably, like me, too stunned to move. I started moving toward him.

Close to the front of the hangar where the two of us were standing, the parts were more or less organized into groups. Seats all together along one of the walls. A group of boxes that all had cables poking out. Sheet metal stacked on end in racks. One of the massive engines was mounted on a base of some kind. Pieces of it were scattered around it in boxes, on more workbenches, and on the ground.

Then there were the cosmetic pieces, some of which, like the tail and the in-flight magazines, looked eerily undisturbed. Carpeted bulkheads, first-class leather seats, tray tables, laminated safety cards. I could see them here and there, interspersed with severed cables and frayed insulation, smashed fuses and electronic components, valves, cylinders, and huge slabs of bent and twisted aluminum skin. It was like seeing a jumble of body parts—a face next to a ruptured kidney, or a couple of manicured hands lying next to a shattered spine and a broken fibula.

Toward the back, the parts were less organized. They were thrown together in a large jumble as if some massive force had lifted them off that mountain in Ecuador and flung them across the continents until they hit the back wall of this hangar and came to rest, piled at odd angles, almost to the ceiling.

There was also that strong smell. Aviation fuel and grease and something decaying and rotten, and I started thinking about the bodies and the blood and the tissue—the people who had been in this accident, and what such a catastrophic force had done to them. My mouth began to water, and fill with the taste of something sour coming up the back of my throat.

248

"This is the accident aircraft," I said, just to see what it sounded like out loud. "This is the wreckage from Ecuador."

"It's the Triple Seven that goes with your logbook," he said.

"What is it doing here?"

"I don't know how, but Jimmy must have stolen it."

I looked around, trying to process Jack's statement. Some of the parts were gigantic. Besides the tail and the engines, there was a large slab of wing, and what looked like the landing gear. "How do you figure he did that, Jack?" It seemed impossible to me.

"Maybe he stole it from the company that salvaged it. Maybe he bought it from them out the back door." He shrugged. "Maybe he took it off the side of the mountain himself."

"How does a private U.S. citizen get access to a crash site in South America? How would he get up the mountainside ahead of the authorities, whoever they may be, and cart off an entire airplane? Where does he get the equipment? How does he even know there's a crash?"

"I don't know the how." Jack nodded toward the worktable where we'd seen the soldering equipment. "But I know the why."

And that's the moment when it all came together for me. I took a step back, and then another, as if another few feet of space and distance might make it easier to comprehend the incomprehensible. What was even more overwhelming than the sheer volume of parts and the magnitude of whatever operation had to have been mounted to bring it all here was the notion that these parts, bent and broken and burned, were being readied to go back into the inventories of active commercial aircraft.

Jack stood shaking his head with an expression bordering on admiration. "Fucking Jimmy. He's got balls. I have to give him that."

The unmistakable sound of a slamming car door cut through the thick silence in the hangar. I looked at Jack just as the second slam sounded.

"Go. Go," he hissed. "*Go.*"

He pushed me back in the direction we had come and followed right behind me. The lights were on this time, which made it easier, but it was still dangerous to maneuver through the obstacle course of dense coils, sharp edges, hanging cables, and cardboard boxes.

The walls began to rattle and a dull rumble filled the hangar as the big doors opened. If there had been a warning—the sound of an engine or the tires rolling over cracked pavement—we had been too insulated, too stunned, or too far away to hear. And now it was too late. I looked up at the plywood bathroom door where we had come through. So close. We weren't going to make it. If we were going to use the noise of the rumbling door as cover, we had to do it fast.

My instinct was to drop to the floor. From there I saw Jack lunge toward a piece of the wing leaning up against the wall. It offered good cover if he could narrow himself enough to wedge in. The door was open and I could hear voices. I went all the way down, flattening myself to the ground, flashlight in hand. My jeans protected my legs, but I could feel on my bare arms that the cement floor was stained with grease, and thick with the dust and grit and God knows what else that had settled in it. It was also cold, probably because my skin felt feverishly hot.

I didn't dare lift my head. I turned it as far as it would go, which meant one ear was pinned to the ground. I was glad I hadn't worn earrings. I spotted a large piece of scorched sheet metal that had enough of a bow shape that I thought I could crawl under. I started toward it, inching on my stomach, stopping every few seconds to remind myself to breathe and to listen. Whoever was out there was loitering toward the front of the hangar. There were two different voices.

The edges of the sheet metal were as sharp as German kitchen knives. Once in, I didn't know if I could get out unscathed, but I had no time to go anywhere else. I stuck my head in and tried to angle my shoulders through. It was a very tight fit, and the sharp ragged edges kept catching my shirt.

They were coming toward the back, toward us, rummaging along the way. The voices were getting louder. I wriggled out and flipped over on my back. I used my hands to keep the jagged edge away and was able to squirm quietly into the hiding place. It was dark inside, and the air was close. I stuck the flashlight into my waistband. It was uncomfortable, pressing against my pelvic bone, but I didn't want it rolling away at the wrong time, and I wanted both hands free. I could see through a ten-inch hooded gap where the sheet metal didn't quite touch the ground. Hopefully, I was back far enough that no one could see my blackened face there.

It took a long time for the two of them to cross the distance from the front of the warehouse because they were picking their way through the parts field, stopping

251

every now and then to rummage around in the pieces of the aircraft.

I picked out the voices. One was deep and mellifluous. I pictured him as a big man with a barrel chest and a wide mouth. Like a bass. The second man's voice was thinner and grainier. He sounded like a tall, reedy smoker. They were getting close enough that I could begin to understand what they were saying.

". . . *shit*, man . . . *believe* this . . . what kind of . . ." That was Wide Mouth. His voice was louder and easier to hear. I couldn't understand everything he was saying, but from his excited and breathless delivery, my impression was he was seeing this stash for the first time.

I listened through every pore in my skin, trying to make out the words and put them together. "Take whatever you want . . . ," said Reedy Man. ". . . you got it."

"I might . . . some of them seats over there"—Wide Mouth was getting closer—"because I can sell them on the Internet. Put them up on one of them auction sites. I read an article the other day that told how some fool bought some B727 seats for six hundred dollars on eBay, some that weren't even in no crash."

"Whatever you take . . ." Reedy Man sounded exasperated. ". . . can't tell anyone where it's . . . fucking Feds . . ."

"Well, shit, Jimmy. That's what makes them worth anything at all."

Jimmy? A drop of sweat trickled off my forehead and ran back into my hair. It felt like an ant crawling across my scalp. That was Wide Mouth talking which meant Reedy Man was Jimmy Zacharias. Knowing that changed

252

the atmosphere, made the air more combustible. I wondered what Jack was thinking.

"Then pick something else, something you can sell straight up." Knowing it was Jimmy made him sound different, more menacing.

"You'll throw in all the paperwork?"

"Hurry up. They're going to be coming back soon. Fucking assholes left the lights on again."

One of them moved something that made my metal cover rattle. A jolt shimmered from the top of my head right on down my spine. They were that close? Of course they were close. If I could hear him that clearly, they were very close. There was more movement and someone's leather Timberland boot appeared next to my face. Close enough that I could smell the sweaty leather.

I stopped breathing and closed my eyes and concentrated every thought on being somewhere else. I pictured myself floating on a river in a tube on clear, cool water under a brazen blue sky. When someone started moving things around over my head, I tried to float along and relax my muscles and my brain and let the tension flow out.

Then it got worse.

The instant I heard the nails clicking across the concrete, I knew Bull was coming. He must have been out doing his business before, but he was there now. He didn't seem to be coming for us—his trot wasn't intent enough—but that didn't mean he wouldn't pick up the scent any second. I felt all the air go out of my hiding place. I imagined the grease on the ground as a pool of my blood, blood that would gush from my throat after Bull had ripped it out.

"I reckon I'd be better off with some of them smaller components up front." Wide Mouth was moving away. I heard him leaving, and then the boot—it must have been Jimmy's—started away as well. But the dog didn't. I heard him again. His gait was more purposeful. I imagined his nose to the greasy cement. I imagined him picking up the scent. I held my stomach muscles tight to keep from shaking.

"What's the matter with him?" Wide Mouth asked.

"He likes to scrape around in there for the rats. That pile is mostly cabin parts and it's crawling with them because of the dried blood and skin and shit. He's going to get hurt. Bull, get out of there."

No way. He came closer, his four paws dancing in primal anticipation. I couldn't see his head, but I heard his excited yelping.

"*BULL!*"

Bull was down on his stomach, his snout to the pavement, snuffling forward, trying to make himself flat enough to crawl under a piece of fuselage that was between him and me. It was me he smelled. It was my uninvited presence he sensed, and he looked as if he would chew through solid steel to get to me.

Jimmy jerked him back hard. The dog's squeal was pained and high pitched. "It's nothing but rats!" he yelled. "I told you that. You go in there you're going to get cut. Go on outside."

Bull was down on the floor heaving with all his strength against Jimmy's restraining hand. He did a frantic visual sweep, snout low to the ground. Just before Jimmy yanked him up by the neck, his eyes locked on mine. He went insane, and all I could think about was his powerful jaws closed around my throat.

Wide Mouth shouted. "Maybe there's something in there."

Bull bared his teeth and thrust his slobbering face toward mine. I could smell his breath. It took every ounce of concentration not to jerk away from him. Jimmy struggled for control, and I prayed he could find it. I could see Bull's hind legs as he leaped and yelped and tried to twist away. My arms were going to sleep at my side, the flashlight was pressed so far into my stomach I could feel it in my backbone, and I hadn't breathed in so long I was about to pass out. And if he found me, I didn't want to be lying there like a dead fish with arms that wouldn't work.

I used the cover of Bull's racket to bring one hand up from my side. That worked out okay. When I brought the other one up, my shoulder brushed my metal shelter, which caused something else to shift. Jimmy must have clamped his hand across Bull's snout and held his mouth shut. The dog held still and made the only noise he could, which was a sore, pinched whine. Jimmy kneeled down on one knee and started to lean over. But it took him a second because his big dog occupied both of his hands. I saw his knee come down. I wrapped my hand around the flashlight, the only weapon I had. I saw his hand touch the ground. I pictured him leaning down, but in that last second, something—a blur, a solid mass—skittered past my face. When it crossed my line of sight, a cold shot went straight through me.

It was a rat. A huge furry rat with tiny eyes, a long tail, and a pointy nose. It made a dash out from under my metal umbrella. It must have been mighty disoriented because that was also toward the crazed canine. It scampered right over Jimmy's hand. The thought of those rat claws crawling over bare skin made my shoulders shake and my jaw clamp and both my hands curl into fists without any conscious direction from my brain.

Jimmy wasn't taking it well, either. When he spotted the rodent coming straight toward his face, it startled him enough that he stumbled backwards and landed on his butt.

"Goddamn mother*fucker*," he yelled.

When Bull spotted the rat, he jerked away from Jimmy and took off, following the rodent to another part of the hangar.

I heard Wide Mouth rushing over. "Look at the size of that thing."

"What the fuck, Jimmy? What are you doing here?" That was . . . that wasn't the voice of either one of them. It was a new voice, a third voice coming through the door, and right behind it the sound of two more car doors slamming. "Get the fucking dog in the car, now."

Jimmy stood up. He and Wide Mouth moved away, talking the whole time. Jimmy was calling for Bull. I heard a lot of raised voices, but outside the hangar and too far away to hear what they were saying. Whoever had just arrived was very angry.

I heard all the sounds in reverse. The lights snapped off. The walls rattled again as someone pulled the big door shut and locked it. It sounded like a chain and a padlock. The voices faded out, and it was suddenly, blessedly quiet enough that I thought I could hear my own heart beating.

I wanted to cry from the release of the brain-boiling tension that had built up inside. A lot of good that would do. Instead, I took in many big breaths, unballed my fists, flexed my fingers, and kept my eyes peeled for more rats. It wouldn't be good to get startled again.

I don't know how much time passed before I heard Jack's voice somewhere close by. "Alex."

"Over here." I started to crawl out and snagged my shirt on the lip of the metal sheet. He reached down and carefully lifted my protective armor just enough that I could scramble out. The dimness felt comfortable, like an invisible force field.

"Are you all right?" he asked.

I didn't know, but I nodded yes. It was more for myself since he couldn't see it.

"Let's go," he said.

I followed him out the way we'd come, through the window and back over the fence, grabbing the floor mats as we went. This time as I crossed the field, I was less picky about where I put my feet as long as it was one in front of the other. I kept thinking about Bull, about the way he'd chased me before, and I kept looking back for him. As we moved into the trees, we had to slow down, but we still made enough of a disturbance to agitate the wildlife.

The return trip from the hangar seemed a lot faster than the trip in, but then we ran full speed all the way back. The car loomed ahead sooner than I expected. We were going to make it. We were going to crawl out of the swamp and back into civilization and take showers and wash the grease and the grit and the dog's slobber off and feel human again.

A cramp grabbed my side just as I reached the car and I had to stop and lean over to breathe. There didn't seem to be enough oxygen in the air. I set the mats down, stared at the car keys in my hand, and took a few more deep breaths. I straightened to put the key in the lock. A loud thump. The car shook. There was yelling and shouting. Men appeared from out of the brush and surrounded us. They all had guns. They were all shouting.

I looked for Jack. He was already pinned against his side of the car with his arms behind his head looking back at me. Someone pushed him toward the front and over the hood and pulled his arms behind him. I felt a hand on my shoulder and something cold and hard against my neck. My hands went straight over my head. I was so scared I didn't even realize until after I was handcuffed what they had been yelling.

Federal agents, they'd said. Step away from the car and put your hands behind your head.

Chapter Twenty-Five

Jack and I had been put into separate cars for the drive into the city. We hadn't had a chance to speak at all, but I had searched out his eyes as they had snapped the cuffs on. He had shaken his head and I had taken that to mean I shouldn't talk to these people. And I didn't. I didn't say one word to the two agents who drove me in. They didn't attempt to talk to me, and barely spoke to each other, which just made the ride seem longer. After about twenty minutes, a cell phone rang. Mine. I recognized the ring. The agent who was carrying it opened it and turned it off without a word.

Inside the hangar I hadn't had time to feel afraid. But now I couldn't stop thinking about a time when I had gone out hiking late in the day in an unfamiliar place and gotten turned around. I kept remembering the moment, the sinking, gut-stabbing moment when I realized I had taken a wrong turn or chosen the wrong fork in the path and no matter which way I looked, nothing was familiar. Nothing. I was lost. It was getting dark. I knew I was in trouble.

Sitting in the back of a car in handcuffs, staring at the taciturn profiles of two agents, and thinking about the events of the evening was like an extended, slow motion version of that moment. At least in the woods, I had been able to act, to do something. All I could do here was sit and feel the panic growing.

The sun was coming up when we arrived at our

destination, a nondescript office building in an area of town I didn't recognize. We took an elevator to the fourth floor. The best and worst moment came when they removed the cuffs and let me stop in the bathroom in the hallway. I was so relieved to have a moment alone. But when I stepped in front of the sink to wash my hands, I glanced in the mirror and wanted to cry. I had forgotten my face was smeared with greasepaint. Twigs and leaves stuck out of my hair at odd angles, and black-stained sweat had dribbled crooked trails down my neck and throat and pooled in my ears.

I put one hand on either side of the sink, closed my eyes, and tried to let my head drop forward. But the muscles in my neck were so tight, trying to stretch them touched off a sharp pain that knifed across my shoulders and all the way down my back. When I looked in the mirror again, my eyes were full and beginning to run over because I knew I was in over my head—way over my head. What about my new job? What if they found out about this in Detroit? Would I ever get another job? How was I ever going to find my way out of this mess?

I tried to stretch the muscles anyway, breathing through the pain, reminding myself that I had made it out of the woods when I'd been lost, mostly by being calm, backtracking, and reasoning through a logical way out. Jack had said that I should build the kind of life I wanted. Looking in the mirror at my fright mask of a face, I didn't know if this was a life I wanted, but it certainly was a long way from any life I'd ever lived. Maybe that was the point. Maybe Jack was right. If I truly was interested in the job in Detroit, I wouldn't have been drinking beer last night on an open-air deck in Florida, and I wouldn't be standing here right now.

Hot water and paper towels took care of most of the paint and grime. Then I went through the door to start searching for the way out of the woods.

The agents led me into a mostly deserted, generic suite of offices complete with cubicles and identical computers on every desk. Without a word, they left me in a cold, windowless conference room with the door closed. There was no telephone. There was no clock, and I had no sense of how long I spent pacing around the small table, shivering in my damp, sweaty clothes, wondering what had happened to Jack and what was going to happen to me. I concentrated on staying calm. Eventually, the door opened and I was taken to a larger meeting room. This one had a big conference table, a woman, three men—and Jack.

I was so wound up and happy to see him I almost started right in with my compulsive questioning. What happened? Who are these people? What is going to happen? Am I going to jail? Am I screwed for the rest of my life?

But the room had a bad vibe, and Jack didn't even look at me. I assumed everyone there was a federal agent, although no one had bothered to identify which agency, and it hadn't been written on the door. They were all dressed casually except the one who was standing. He was about my age, mid- to late-thirties, blonde, blue-eyed, and proportioned like an athlete in a well-cut suit. Not the football player kind with a neck as thick as his waist, but more like an extremely fit golfer, or a world-class tennis player. He must not have gotten the memo about casual dress day.

"Please sit down." He spoke in my general direction, but not exactly to me.

I had just been nose to snout with a crazed dog who had wanted to rip the flesh from my bones, so a guy in a suit in a conference room didn't seem all that intimidating.

"Who are you?"

"Damon Hollander. I'm a special agent with the FBI."

So this was the famous Agent Hollander, the one who had treated Pat Spain with so much respect. I checked out the others around the table. They all looked so damn smug in their clean polo shirts and neatly combed hair. "Can I see some identification?"

Agent Hollander reached into his inside suit pocket, whipped out a thin black wallet, and flashed his badge and ID. He did it with such cool, dramatic intensity I knew right away it was his favorite part of the job. The phrase Junior G-man sprang instantly to mind.

"Sit down, please."

I took the seat across from Jack, who finally glanced up. He had also washed the black from his face, so it was easy to read his expression, and it wasn't what I had expected. He was supposed to be angry. I was entitled to be scared and angry, but he was supposed to be bristling with uncomplicated outrage at this high-handed treatment we were receiving from his former employer. He wasn't. He was subdued.

Damon joined us at the table, pulling his chair out far enough that he could sit with his legs crossed. After he was settled in, he unbuttoned his suit jacket and smoothed it so that it dropped loosely at his sides and wouldn't wrinkle.

"We have a little problem here," he announced. "You people have stumbled into a federal investigation."

He was looking to Jack for a response. Everyone in the room was, including me. After an uncomfortably long silence, I spoke up. "What are you investigating?"

"I can't discuss that with you."

"Are you investigating the murder of John McTavish?"

"You'd be better off staying out of this discussion, Ms Shanahan. We're giving you the benefit of the doubt, so the less you say, the better off you will be. The less you know, the better off you'll be."

"It's good to hear you're so concerned for me, Agent."

He offered yet another smug expression, from what seemed like an endless assortment. He reminded me of all those young, strapping corporate officers that used to work at the airline. Young alpha males, every one, with the blessed-by-the-gods attitude. They had all come from the best schools, all dressed alike, all thought alike, and because of it had been given more responsibility than they had ever earned. Only this man carried a gun and had behind him the full force and authority of the federal government. Or did he?

I glanced around at the less-than-official-looking offices. "Agent Hollander, you followed me tonight. You stuck a gun in my ear, put me in handcuffs, and dragged me down here. You are now holding me against my will. By what authority have you done all of this?"

"He won't tell you." All eyes shifted to Jack. He was alive after all, and though his voice was thick and halting, it sounded wonderful to me. "And he won't answer your questions because he wasn't supposed to be out at that hangar tonight. Isn't that right, Damon?"

The young agent merely tipped his head in an attitude of patient benevolence. Jack sat forward in his chair and for the first time seemed to be present in the room. I started to review the events of the evening, trying to remember as much as I could, starting with the overheard conversation between Jimmy and Wide Mouth.

"You didn't follow her," Jack said, watching Damon for a reaction. "Or me. You were already out there." He nodded to the people sitting around the table. "You're the ones who are securing the hangar."

Damon had no reaction, but I remembered that Jimmy had referred more than once to the "fucking Feds." That didn't necessarily mean anything, but he had also said the assholes had left the lights on again. He'd said they had to get out before someone came back. If the two men in the car had been Jimmy's security, as we had assumed, why would Jimmy have been worried about them? On the other hand, why would the FBI be securing a hangar that housed a stolen aircraft?

"A secret hangar full of stolen aircraft parts," Jack said. "How does that fit into your investigation? And why doesn't anyone know about it?"

Damon's delicate hands stiffened just enough to convince me that Jack was right. I didn't know exactly what it meant that he was right, but he was. We weren't the only ones who had snuck into the hangar. Jimmy had, too, only he'd had a key.

"You're not with the Bureau anymore, Dolan. You don't get to ask the questions." Damon checked his watch and looked at me. "I'm requesting that you turn over the logbook that was stolen from the Air Sentinel crash site. And don't even bother asking how I know you have it. I won't tell you." He stared at me as if my complete predictability bored him.

"I'm not denying I have it." Who had told him that? Why wasn't he asking for the ring as well? I glanced over at Jack. A little help would have been nice.

Damon had followed my gaze. "Don't concern yourself with Mr Dolan. You're the one who hired him. Without you, he has no reason to be involved."

That's when it occurred to me that Jack must have already had discussions with Damon Hollander. Jack hadn't . . . surely Jack hadn't told him about the logbook? I looked at the other agents, the two men and the woman. They seemed to be following the conversation closely and contributing nothing. I wondered why they had to be here. The whole thing was making less and less sense.

"Agent Hollander, do you or any of your colleagues here drive a nondescript sedan? One that's the color of a kidney bean?"

"Why do you ask?"

"No reason. Maybe I should give the book to Air Sentinel. Or Barbara Walters."

"Stealing evidence from a crash site is a federal offense," he said. "I can subpoena the evidence if you refuse to cooperate."

"I didn't steal it from the crash site and you know it. I think you know who did."

"You're withholding it."

"Does it have something to do with your investigation of John McTavish's murder?"

"Go home, Ms Shanahan. Turn over the evidence and go home."

"Why?"

"Because I'm telling you to." Agent Hollander's pitch had changed ever so slightly. He was getting frustrated.

"Do you normally have good luck with this approach, Agent Hollander? 'Do as I say for reasons I won't tell you.'"

"Why are you protecting Jimmy Zacharias?" There was Jack again, dropping another bombshell out of nowhere. "Here's how I've got it figured, Damon. Jimmy stole the parts from the site in Ecuador with the intention of reselling them on the black market. He got them into Miami. I don't know how, but he did. The Bureau found out, because it's pretty damned difficult to hide an entire Triple Seven stolen from a high-profile crash, even from you. But instead of hauling Jimmy in, and Avidor, and everyone else who was involved in this thing, you're covering it up. You've got the lid on. You told Jimmy to stay away from the hangar, locked the door, and put two guys out front. Why would you do that?"

Jack was on to something. I could feel it. The other agents in the room had gone perfectly still.

"All I can figure is you want Jimmy out on the street, at least for a while longer, and maybe that's because he's one of these high-class confidential informants you're supposed to have. As if Jimmy could be a high-class anything. But that's neither here nor there. What's important is that it would be a pretty big coup for a kid like you at this point in your career."

"What would?"

"Nailing an international drug lord."

"Drug lord?" Damon seemed sad that anyone could be so misinformed, but he didn't deny it.

"Let's let our imaginations run wild. You're set up here off-site in some kind of ongoing operation. Let's say your target is a big fish from Colombia named Ottavio. It wouldn't hurt your career to be the one who reels him in, and you seem like the ambitious sort. Would it be fair to say you would do anything, or you would let your source do anything, to make that happen?"

All eyes shifted back to Damon. He was tightening up again, but in a controlled way. It was hard to see, but it was there in his voice and in the way he held his head. He seemed to communicate most directly through the angle of his head.

"I don't know what it was like in your day, Dolan, but even if that were true, we have specific policies and guidelines as to what sort of activities will be tolerated from a confidential informant. Even you can remember that."

"How about stealing an airplane? Would that be tolerated? What doesn't hang together for me, Damon, is that you're a drug guy. You're after Ottavio, and Jimmy is a parts man all the way. Parts and the occasional weapons deal. Even if Ottavio is in on this Sentinel parts scam, that wouldn't be enough for you. You want the big-time bust. Not some pissant, penny ante parts rap."

Damon crossed his soft hands over his knee. "That's a pretty complicated theory," he said, "coming from someone like you, Dolan. I'm amazed your brain can still handle complex thought." He turned to me. "I'm afraid Mr Dolan has misled you and put you at risk. He's wrong about this, among other things. But I suspect he can get confused."

"Why would he get confused?"

I had asked the question without thinking and was immediately sorry because I knew I had done exactly what he wanted. And I had an idea what the answer was going to be. I saw it in Jack's face, which was tense enough to make mine hurt. I saw it in the deep furrow that creased the bridge of his nose, and the way he stared straight down at the table. And I saw it in Damon's keen interest in my reaction to what he was about to say.

"Dolan here spent most of his time with the Bureau in a bottle. That's why he's no longer with us. He's an alcoholic. They called it early retirement"—his eyes slid over to Jack—"but he was fired. You knew that, didn't you? That he's a slobbering, falling-down, blacking-out drunk?"

I didn't look at Jack, but at the other agents around the table, the two men and the woman, and I understood why Damon had wanted them there. Only one of them, one of the men, had the decency not to stare.

Damon had asked me a question and was waiting for my response. I gave him the only one I could, the only one that made sense, given the circumstances. "Yes, I knew."

"I don't think so. If I were you, I'd think carefully about whether or not you want to trust your future, maybe even your life to someone like him. I wouldn't."

It was best, I thought, not to prolong this conversation, so I sat quietly and stared, as Jack did, at the table-top.

"Your cars," Damon said, smoothing his tie, "are in the back. Ms Shanahan, I'll send an agent over to your hotel to pick up the logbook and give you a receipt."

When Damon stood up, so did the others. When

Damon looked down at Jack as if he were a despicable waste of a human being, so did the others. Jack's hair was a mess and his eyes looked as if he'd been up all night, which he had. He still had a trace of camouflage paint on his chin and under one ear. He held himself perfectly still and endured the scrutiny, and I had the strong feeling it wasn't the first time he'd felt it. The fluorescents overhead threw light that was bright enough to catch the flecks of gray in the stubble on his chin, and harsh enough to show all the lines in his face. And I felt such a sense of loss from him. For him.

"You've been gone from the Bureau for three years," Damon said, "and you're still screwing up. Don't screw this up for me."

Chapter Twenty-Six

I found Jack just where he'd said he would be. He was the only patron at the Miramar Coin Op Laundry, a laundromat situated in a quiet enclave in the shadow of downtown Miami under a canopy of tall, leafy trees. The space was narrow and deep—what the real estate agents in Boston refer to as a floor-through. He was unloading a machine all the way in the back, taking out a load of whites and pushing them into a dryer. It was quiet enough that when he slotted his quarters, I heard them fall.

When he turned, I knew he hadn't slept since I left him early that morning. His face was almost gray, as if he'd been sketched in charcoal, and his eyes were as sad as the shabby surroundings. "I see you found me," he said.

"Only because you let me. This would not have been the first place I looked."

"Let's sit outside," he said.

We settled in the *al fresco* seating arrangement on the sidewalk. It was a lot like sitting outside on the Champs-Elysées in Paris, except the metal tables and chairs were rusted, the sidewalk was cracked, and there was no one to serve us. There was a restaurant at the end of the street, but in place of quaint little tobacco shops and hotels, we had a beauty parlor—closed for the evening—and a boarded-up bar across the street.

"Did you get any sleep?" he asked, folding the news-paper he'd been reading.

"I slept all day," I said. "I really like sleeping. What about you? How did you spend your day?"

"Looking for Ira. Trying to find Patty. I didn't find either one. All in all," he sighed, "not a successful day." I was glad to see a hint of irony in his smile, but I wasn't sure how to respond. We had said nothing about the morning's events when we'd parted, preferring, at least in my case, to defer until I'd had a chance to sleep and let things seep in. So it was all still there, everything Damon had laid on us, hanging in the air, as pervasive and hard to ignore as the sweet and heavy scent of the dryer sheets that kept wafting out of the laundromat. I decided to defer a little longer.

"When do you suppose someone at Air Sentinel is going to find out where their airplane is?"

"They might know. But it's better all the way around if no one else does for now. At least not until Damon gets done whatever it is he's doing."

"And you think what he's doing is hunting down Ottavio?"

"Without a doubt. And I'm pretty well convinced at this point that Jimmy is his snitch. I just don't know what he could tell Damon that would be useful to him."

"Jack, you didn't tell Damon about the logbook, did you?"

"Name, rank, and serial number was all he got from me. Why?"

"I was just wondering how he would have known about it. He knew about the book but not the ring. I think that means something."

"Maybe." From the sound of it, he didn't much care to think about it. A quiet breeze riffled the corners of the newspaper, and we lapsed into a silence that went on for a while. The predominant sound was that of the dryer drum rumbling around.

"If you live in South Beach, Jack, why do you come all the way over here to do your laundry?"

"It's not that far. It's just over the bridge. Besides, I like this neighborhood." He nodded to the boarded-up store-front across the street. "When that bar was open, I could throw the laundry in and sip a cold beer while I waited. They used to know me over there a little too well. I think they went out of business when I stopped drinking." He laughed, but with more bitterness than humor.

"Those things Damon said to you . . . about you this morning, the way he did it . . . He's a piece of shit."

"He is that. He's also right." He looked up at me, maybe trying, as Damon had, to gauge my reaction, and the thought flashed that I was glad it mattered to him. "That's the problem. Everyone has always been right about me. My ex-wife. People at work. You noticed, didn't you, that I don't have many friends left there. Patty Spain is one of the few who still takes my calls, and she's not even with the Bureau."

"Did something happen?"

"Nothing happened. It was all the little things that accumulate over time when you're a drunk. It's the way they pile up, eventually, into this big stinking heap that people can't ignore anymore." He shook his head. "I let everyone down. My wife. My son. My bosses . . . many bosses who kept giving me chances. Sooner or later, I let them all down." He was holding his reading glasses in his hand, opening one temple, then the other, clos-ing one, and then the other.

"You're sober now."

"Two years. I spent a lot longer than that drinking. I have many amends to make. Some I never can."

"Why not?"

He shrugged, and kept flipping those temples up and down. I thought if he did that enough, he was going to loosen the screws and the glasses would fall apart in his hands.

"Where is your wife?"

"She took my son a few years back and moved up to your neck of the woods. He's going to college at Dartmouth." He glanced over at me, I thought for a response or affirmation of some sort.

"That's a good school," I said, trying to give him what he needed.

He nodded, seemed satisfied, and dropped his glasses into the front pocket of his cotton shirt. Then he stretched his legs out under the wrought iron table, shooed a tiny winged visitor away from his face, and stared up with tired eyes into the trees overhead. He looked as if he might not ever get up. "Do you do that?" he asked, after a while.

"Do what?"

"Get used to certain places and keep going back to them?"

I'd tossed my keys on the table when I'd arrived. It was a mesh surface, and the longest key, the key from my rental car, had lodged itself in one of the openings. I set about dislodging it as I thought about that question. "The thing about the airline business is you're either unpacking from one move or packing for the next. There's enough time in between to find a dentist

273

and dry cleaners. Then it's time to go again. There's no time to get attached to a place."

"Or to people, huh?"

"That, too." The key came loose with a minor tug.

"Sometimes I think I should leave Miami," he said. "But I never do. No matter where I go, I always end up back here."

"What keeps you here?"

He lowered his gaze until he was staring across the street at the bar that had gone bust. "I like living in a place where I know I can always find my way home. It's useful to know the geography when you're a drunk."

I thought about all the places my airline career had taken me—airports and offices, ticket counters and freight houses, cities large and small. I'd lived in apartments, hotels, studios, condos, duplexes, and houses all over the country, and never once had felt that I had found my home. "There's a lot to be said for feeling at home," I said, "no matter who you are. Or how you define yourself."

He took in a deep breath and let it out slowly. It sounded almost as if it hurt him to draw breath, hurt somewhere deep down in his lungs. I had to keep myself from reaching out and touching his face and trying to make him stop hurting.

"I'm sorry," he said.

"For what?"

"For letting you hear those things about me from that little prick. I should have told you."

He was again staring up into the leaves, which were becoming less and less distinct as the evening wore on. I looked where he was looking, and wondered if we were seeing the same thing. I was pretty sure that even if we were, we were seeing it from different angles. "That would have been easier on both of us," I said.

"He's right about the trust thing."

"No. I trusted you immediately, Jack, and not just because you saved me from Bull and my own stupidity. I believe you know what you're doing, and I don't believe you'll let me down."

"One of the things I thought about today, all day, was about what could have happened to you in that hangar. All the different things that could have happened."

"I don't recall you forcing me to go in there with you. And you offered me a gun. I should have taken it. I should have listened to you. I will next time."

"You should go home, Alex."

"Is that what you want?"

He stared down into his lap and I tried so hard to see into his eyes, but it was too dark.

"You should go home and get moved and start your life and your job."

"Right now, this minute, Jack, I couldn't care less about that job. I'm asking you if you want me to leave. If my being here makes it harder for you in any way, personally, professionally, or otherwise, I'll go. But if you're saying I should leave because you think that's what's best for me, then I respectfully ask that you mind your own business."

His head was resting on the back of his chair. He turned it so he could see me, but didn't speak.

"I will not let that asshole Hollander step over John McTavish's body to get a promotion." My voice felt clear and strong and I knew it was because I was speaking the truth—my truth—saying what I wanted to say. "I hate what he did to you this morning, and I'm not wild about the way he treated me. If leaving here makes Damon's life easier, that's reason enough for me to stay. Beyond that, I want to finish the job I came down here to do. So sit up and look at me and tell me if you are asking me to leave."

He sat up slowly, and turned in his chair. He rested his arms in front of him on the table and seemed to sit stiffly. When all he did was stare past me, I figured he was searching for the words to tell me that I was making his life a mess and I should go home. Now, if not sooner. He didn't seem to want to look at me, so I braced for rejection and started thinking about how to tell Mae that I'd had to give up. She would be nice and maybe take my hand and—

"Stay."

"What?"

He was looking at me now, and giving me that crooked, endearing grin he'd used on Vanessa. I liked it better when he aimed it at me. "If you want to stay, I like having you here."

"Good." And it was good. I felt good. I felt the way I do after I've run six miles. Worn out, but exhilarated. "Now, tell me what is going on between you and Jimmy. I want to know everything."

Chapter Twenty-Seven

While Jack had moved his load of darks to the dryer, I had run down to the restaurant for a couple of sandwiches. It turned out the top floor of Perricones was a restaurant, but the bottom floor was a deli, and an excellent one. We both felt better for having a little protein in our systems—hot pastrami on rye with sauerkraut for him, and turkey on wheat with lettuce, tomato, and mustard for me. We were finished eating and I was still waiting to hear about Jimmy. By the time the streetlights came on, I wasn't sure I ever would.

A car rolled slowly by, the first in almost an hour. The driver found a place to park down the block on the street. A couple disembarked and headed into the restaurant. After they'd passed, Jack leaned over in his chair and kicked at a few stray pebbles on the sidewalk. "Did I tell you I served in Vietnam?"

I looked over at him. There seemed to be no end to the surprises he could come up with, and always in the most casual way. "No, Jack, you never mentioned that. What did you do in Vietnam?"

"I was a grunt. I got drafted and me and my low lottery number humped around the jungle like everyone else."

It never would have occurred to me that he had been a soldier, although it made perfect sense. He was the right age for it. But I was from a generation that didn't know war, at least not the low-tech version with ground troops, and without Scud missiles and CNN. I didn't know any soldiers. I never assumed anyone I ever met had been one.

"I thought . . . didn't you go to college?"

"I went after I came home. Uncle Sam paid for it, then I went to work for the Bureau. Everything I am I owe to the U.S. government." His laugh was bitter and I couldn't tell if the scorn was meant for his former employer or himself.

"How old were you?"

"I'd just turned twenty when I got there."

He sat back in his chair, turned his face to the dark sky, and went quiet again. I pulled my chair closer to the table. I sensed that everything he was about to say was something I wanted to hear.

"Thirty years ago." He shook his head. "Over thirty years. I can't believe it's been that long."

"Do you think about it much?"

"There are things that take me back there. The sound of a helicopter. Rotor blades always do it. Living down here, it can be the way the air feels when it has a certain weight to it. These fires out in the Everglades remind me a little of what it was like there."

"The smell?"

"Not the smell. The way the air presses against you. Vietnam had its own smell. I got it on me the first day I landed, and in some ways, it's never left. It's still so clear to me. You almost can't even describe it. Sweat. Jet fuel. Cordite. You always smelled cordite, no matter where you were."

"Cordite is—"

"It's gunpowder. Dust . . . fish . . . rain . . . chemicals.

278

Bombs leave a chemical smell in the air. You mix it all up together with the blood and the corpses. And then it gets hot."

"I imagine that's a smell that would stay with you."

"You see things in a war . . . in battle . . . things you never expect to see and can't forget. I carried wounded and dying men out of the bush to helicopters to be evacuated and I still see their faces. It does something to you to know that the ones who died, yours was the last face they saw."

He was looking at the sky and he was talking to me, but he was remembering for himself. I could see in his face that there was a lot he was seeing he could not, maybe would not describe. If he had tried, I wouldn't have understood. I couldn't imagine what it must be like to carry around, like cards in your wallet, the images of men who had died in your arms.

"Jimmy and I served in Vietnam together."

He said it using that same dry, matter-of-fact tone and I wasn't sure I'd heard right. "You and Jimmy knew each other in Vietnam?"

"We met there. He was from Everglades City and I was from Miami. We were in the same unit and we hooked up. Almost from day one."

I sat up straight and leaned across the table. The mesh surface hurt my elbows. "The Jimmy Zacharias who runs the salvage yard, you've known him for thirty years?"

"Off and on."

I drifted back again in my seat. I wasn't sure what to make of this news. It changed the way I thought about Jimmy, even though I'd never met him. And it changed what I thought about Jack because it changed what I knew about him. I was getting used to that phenomenon. "What was he like back then?"

"He loved being a soldier. He grew up out in the Everglades so he was at home in the jungle. He used to say he could smell the NVA. He always knew when they were around. He never got surprised and he saved my ass more than once. It was like he had a sixth sense for it. Jimmy was a good soldier."

"This is the same man you suspect of killing John?"

He drew in a deep breath that seemed to take a long time to come out. "You learn things about the people you serve with," he said. "A lot about yourself, too. Some things you'd rather not know. What I learned about Jimmy in Vietnam was how much he liked to kill. What I learned from watching him was how cheap human life can become under the right circumstances." He thought about that. "The wrong circumstances."

He sat up straighter and shifted his weight. The chair he'd been sitting in for hours seemed uncomfortable to him now. "I watched Jimmy shoot an old man in a rice paddy once from long range. This was someone's father or someone's husband or grandfather who took three bullets in the back of the head from a man he never saw for reasons that had nothing to do with him. His head exploded. He went"—he made a weak gesture with his hand—"he went right over, face forward in the mud. Jimmy killed that man and never looked back."

"Why?"

"He was lining up the sights on his rifle."

He'd been finding points in the distance to focus on as he'd talked, but now he was looking at me, hard. Waiting, I figured, for a reaction. I wasn't sure what to say. What he had described struck me as the act of a man who at best had lost his way, and at worst was a psychopath. But I didn't feel I had the right to judge, and I was very aware that whatever Jimmy had done, Jack had been there, too. "This old man, I assume he was a civilian?"

"Jimmy's philosophy was there were no civilians. You couldn't tell NVA from friendlies. You couldn't tell the children from the booby traps they sometimes carried. He killed everything and everyone that got in his way."

A cricket started chirping and I became aware of the deep silence we'd been sitting in. The dryer had stopped spinning. Jack was still watching me.

"When you're in a war," he said, "when you're actually in it and not thinking about it or wondering about it or training for it, you're in it up to your ass and you have to stay in it, it's like you've gone to a different planet. You're breathing different air than those people back in the civilized world. The rules are different, but you don't know that because everyone else around you is acting the same way. All your reference points shift and you can't get any perspective on it until you get back to the world. You can't wait to get back to the world, but once you're back, you start to realize what's happened to you. You begin to understand how completely and profoundly you are not the same person you were. And you never will be."

The light from the street lamp high overhead showed every line in his face, tiny threads that held him together and kept him from blowing apart. He looked as if he was in pain, and had been for a long time. "I don't know if Jimmy went over there that way, or if his time there made him that way. All I know is when I met him, I liked him."

He put his hands on his knees and started to get up. He paused for a beat, and then he did stand. I reached for his hand and held it because I wanted to touch him, and because I didn't want him to walk away. But I didn't know what to say. I could feel the barrier that stood between us, the one made up of all those things he had seen, and all the things I never would. It was an insurmountable barrier for me. Impossible for me to ever get to the other side. But Jimmy was on the other side with him. Impossible for him not to be.

He pulled his hand away, leaned down, and kissed the top of my head. Then he did walk away.

I followed him and watched him from the doorway of the Coin Op as he pulled the clothes out of the dryer and piled them on a folding table. His back was to me as I approached him. I laid my hand between his shoulder blades and felt how warm his skin was through his shirt. And I felt him responding. I moved my hand up, following the line of his backbone, reached over the collar of his shirt and touched the skin on his neck. It was lined and leathery and the muscles underneath were stiff and tight. He straightened and closed his eyes, leaning into the rhythm of my hand as I wove my fingers into his hair, across the curves and contours of his head. When he turned around, I held his face in my hands and ran my thumbs gently along the deepest lines in his face, the ones that made him look the saddest. I wanted to kiss him. I wanted him to kiss me. He put his hands around my waist and lifted me onto the table, onto the clothes still warm from the dryer. I wrapped my legs around him, pulled him to me close enough to feel the glasses in his front pocket between us. Our lips brushed. He opened his mouth and I tasted him. He tasted like Florida to me—sunny and tart, not sweet—and he smelled like clean clothes. I wrapped my arms around him and it felt so right to be holding him against my body, feeling his breath on my neck.

My arms fell away as he stepped back—I thought to kiss me again—but he kept moving back, out of my embrace. Out of my range. He caught my hands in his on the way back and kissed them, once in each palm. "Let's not . . . do this. This is not . . . it's not good . . ."

The expression in his eyes when he looked at me made me feel that I'd done something very wrong. "I'm sorry, Jack. I didn't mean—"

"It's not you. I'm not any good at this, especially now. For me it would be for all the wrong reasons. I like you and it's hard for me not to mess things up." He pushed a strand of hair that had fallen into my face and wrapped it behind my ear. "Do you understand?"

"Yeah. Okay." I let him go and we had this awkward moment where he didn't know what to do and I didn't know what to say and I was sitting in the middle of his laundry. When I jumped down from the table, I felt the pinch again in my ankle. It hurt.

I didn't stay long after that. Jack stood on the sidewalk in front of the Coin Op and reminded me not to park too far away from the elevator in the Dolphin Garage. I walked up the street toward the restaurant and my car, and knew that he was watching me all the way there. That felt good. Having him in my arms had felt better.

Perricones looked like a tree house the way it nestled under the leafy canopy. It was going full blast by then. Some of the tables were on the open-air deck, and dinner was being served to a lively New Orleans jazz accompaniment. The bawdy, brassy rhythm spilled out and rolled down the streets of the quiet neighborhood like coins tossed from the open doors and windows.

The smoke haze was not so bad, so I opened my windows to breathe unprocessed, non-air-conditioned air for a change. I could still hear the faint strains of the jazz band as I passed by the Miramar Coin Op and saw Jack, the only patron, sitting inside on one of the washing machines, hands on his knees, staring at the wall.

Chapter Twenty-Eight

Ira Leemer turned and greeted me with a yellow-toothed grin that was surprisingly engaging. "Hello, missy. Want a bag of peanuts?" He offered me a small red-and-white-striped paper bag lumpy with what must have been peanuts in the shell. It was a surreal moment. Ira cocked his head. "Fresh off the roaster and on the house."

I hesitated. I always liked those peanuts. But so much fat content. What the hell. "Thank you, Ira." I accepted his offering, which seemed to make him happy. The bag still felt warm.

This time Jack and I had gone to find Ira at his sometime place of work—Ft Lauderdale Stadium—where he was a peanut vendor and a spring training game was in progress. The Baltimore Orioles and the Mets. The three of us were in the cement-cooled shadows underneath the stands, but not too far from a ramp that led to the bleachers. I could see the bright square of sunshine at the top and hear the communal muttering of the crowd that always accompanies a game in progress.

"You work out here, Ira?"

"Since I been out. Yessirree. Only thing is they won't let me sell beer on account of I been in jail. That's where the real money is as far as the concession business goes. Anyhow"—he held up one of the bags—"these are the only parts I'm selling these days."

Jack was pacing, clearly not interested in peanuts.

"Why didn't you tell me what we were walking into out at that hangar, Ira?"

"Hold on a minute, Bobo. Just let's all calm down and let me get myself situated." He set his peanut tray on an unmanned snack bar counter, which freed his hands to dig out his cigarette paper and tobacco pouch. "I didn't know myself," he said as he started to roll one. "I just found out." He looked at me. "Saw them parts with your own eyes, did you?"

"Up close and personal."

"What was it like?"

Even if I could have described what I'd seen, what I'd felt, what I'd smelled and touched, I didn't get the chance. Jack was getting up close and personal with Ira, getting right into his face. "How did Jimmy get those parts? And don't give me any bullshit. I'm not in the mood."

Ira had to take a step back to look up into the taller man's face. "Went down and got 'em hisself, is what I heard."

"C'mon, Ira. How did he get them off the mountain? Where did he get the manpower and equipment? How did he get those huge units and assemblies into the country?" He articulated each question, as if his being clear might inspire from Ira a like response. "You know what I'm asking you."

"Hooked up with someone who was down there, I suspect, someone with some presence, who got in there, took what they wanted, and got out."

Jack looked as though he might take a swipe at Ira, so I gave it a try. "How did the bad guys get in there before the authorities? How did they even know there was a crash to go and scavenge?"

Something good happened on the field for the home team. A languid cheer drifted up from the crowd. It was, after all, spring training. By the time it petered out, Ira was rolled and ready. He fired up the cigarette and took a long pull. Then he spit out a piece of tobacco.

"I can't tell you what happened on account of I don't know, and that's the truth. I can tell you the story I've put together based on some of the things I've been hearing."

Jack took a step back and crossed his arms. It must have convinced Ira that he was in no imminent danger of being leveled, because he started to talk.

"As far as how they knew about it and the approximate location, they was monitoring radio frequencies. That was the easy part. Finding it and getting to it that fast, that was . . . that must have been the hard part. But once they got there . . . you know everybody's always talking about that airplane like it flew into the side of a mountain, but it didn't. It was a belly landing. Not much fire, so there was lots to take. But as far as getting there first, you are talking Ecuador here, missy."

"They have authorities in Ecuador."

"What they don't have is an NTSB Go-Team ready to show up on a remote mountaintop at the drop of a hat in the middle of the night. And who are the authorities down there anyway? You got your federals, your local authorities, your guerrilla armies—left and right wing. Who the hell is in charge? Probably whoever gets there first and whoever's got the biggest gun."

"Who got there first in this case?" Jack asked.

"Don't know, Bobo. That's what I keep on trying to tell you. But whoever it was had resources, because they

287

took it all. You saw that. Every last thing that wasn't burning or bleeding, and some"—he narrowed his eyes and looked left and right, just as he had done at his trailer—"some that was bleeding, is what I hear."

I hesitated, but went ahead with it anyway. "What does that mean?"

"They was in such a hurry, them boys didn't even bother to dump out all the body parts. Just lifted the whole kit and caboodle the way it was. Lock, stock, and barrel. Whatever fell out, fell out. That's what I heard. Looted the bodies, too. Got it all before the peasants climbed up there and picked over what was left. By the time the airline got up there, you could gather up what was left and carry it down in baskets."

More casual cheering from the crowd above, and though I was trying as hard as I could not to, all I could think of was climbing around in those parts, lying on the ground in the grease and other unknown matter. I remembered the smell—aviation fuel and something rotten. I thought I had imagined the something rotten. And the rats. Jimmy had said the place was crawling with rats. It all made me feel sick, and I wanted to give the peanuts back. Instead, I tried to focus on the task at hand.

"Ira, do you think it would be possible for someone to find a ring, a diamond ring, and the logbook in the wreckage that came up here?"

"Oh, sure, missy. You'd be surprised at the things that survive a plane crash. An aircraft goes nose down at full speed and turns into a burning hole in the ground. But around the crater, you might still find a pair of eyeglasses that ain't broke, or a fifty-dollar bill stuck in the mud.

I didn't hear about the logbook, but sure, someone could have pulled it out of that mess. No telling what you might have found tucked away in all the nooks and crannies."

"You wouldn't happen to have any firsthand knowledge of that?" Jack asked.

"Like what, Bobo? You mean was I down there in Ecuador? Hell, no. What do I keep trying to tell you? I'm telling you all that I know."

"I'm asking if you were one of the dirty mechanics working out at that hangar for Jimmy. Maybe doing a little strip-and-dip. You seem to know a lot about it."

"That's 'cause you told me to find out. No sir. I didn't want nothing to do with them parts. I ain't going back to jail. Besides, you know what they say. Even touching dead parts like that is bad luck. You remember that seven-two that went down around here back in the late seventies, don't you, Bobo? Went down in a bad storm."

"I remember. It went down in the Everglades."

"That's the one." He turned and directed his story at me. "The airline salvaged some of them parts and tried to reuse them, mostly galley parts. The company mechanics, of course, knew about all this and refused to even lay hands on equipment from a dead airplane, so they hired contractors. I tell you what"—there was that whuuuut again—"one of them contractors was electrocuted on the job. Another one's wife delivered a stillborn baby, and once them parts were in the air, the stews started seeing ghosts in the galley."

"What happened?"

"The company hired one of them exorcists, but that didn't work. Finally they ripped the parts all out, took

289

'em to the smelter, and destroyed them once and for all. That's when the ghosts left and not before. They went belly-up anyway, but not because of no ghosts."

It was a good thing Jack had plenty of room to roam because he'd started moving and couldn't seem to stop. "What's the point of your ghost story, Ira?"

"I'm just telling why I didn't want nothing to do with them parts out in that hangar. It's bad luck. That's all there is to that. Bad luck. Whoever did disturb that crash is going to pay the price. It's like grave robbing is what it is. I don't want no part of it."

I reached back and lifted my ponytail off my neck. It was making my sunburn itch. I remembered how the big diamond ring had felt on my finger, and how the logbook had felt in my hands. Bad luck. That was the best way to describe the uneasy feeling. I had taken the ring off and Damon Hollander now had the logbook. But the feeling had never gone away.

"How much would you figure Jimmy could get for what's in that hangar?" Jack asked. "He had the landing gear, both engines, which looked to be in decent shape, probably avionics—"

"The tail," I said, "intact and in good shape."

Ira leaned back against the snack counter and ran that one through his computer while he smoked. "New Triple Seven. Depending on whether they go domestic or overseas, piecemeal it, or find one buyer and move the whole load. Maybe three to four million."

"Plenty of motive for murder," Jack said.

"And a good way to tie Bobby to the whole operation," I said, "if we can tie him to the book."

Ira was staring up the ramp. "It's probably getting

toward the seventh-inning stretch. That's when I do some good business, Bobo. Let me get out there. I'll keep nosing around for you."

Jack didn't even seem to hear him. "The Bureau has taken down Jimmy's operation out there. He's locked out of his own hangar, but he's still on the street. What do your sources tell you about that?"

"Is that what happened? 'Cause they were going great guns when all of a sudden everything just stopped. I'll be damned. How did he get hisself out of that one? You know Jimmy always said he'd never done one day in jail and never would. That's a puzzle, yes sir, that is."

"Tell me what you think of this idea." Jack had stopped moving and now leaned against the snack counter next to his snitch. The two of them looked as if they could have been discussing gardening tips, or the game outside. "Jimmy is a confidential informant working for the Bureau in an operation targeting Ottavio Quevedo. Do you know who that is?"

"Everybody knows him, Bobo."

"Jimmy's got something on Ottavio the Bureau wants and they're protecting him."

"I don't know what that could be."

"Let's think about this logically. What I saw in that hangar, to get it down off a mountain, you said it yourself, Jimmy would have had to have had access to cranes, probably crane helicopters, trucks, extraction equipment, earthmoving equipment. Plenty of manpower. Right?"

Ira cackled. "It weren't no donkeys carried them jet engines down off that hill."

"Who would have resources like that sitting around? Or access to them?"

291

"Bobo, I couldn't say. It would have to be the military, I guess. Maybe it was an inside job. Is that what you're getting at? Maybe them Ecuadors did it themselves, the army or what have you, 'cause they're the ones that would have all that stuff."

"I was looking at a map. That airplane went down not too far from the Colombian border." Jack was talking to me as much as to Ira now, maybe even to himself, and it was getting very interesting. "What you were saying about whoever gets there first, I think you're right. Who got there first in this case could have been one of the guerrilla armies from Colombia. Or the militias. They're better armed and better equipped than the real thing, and that's because they're funded with drug money."

"Drug money. Drug armies from Colombia. I think I see where you might be going with this, Bobo. That might explain the C130, too."

"A C130? A U.S. military aircraft?"

"Yes sir, an old one, but it can still carry plenty. They loaded it up and flew the whole mess up here. Don't ask me how they got hold of one or how they got into the States because I don't know."

A Colombian drug army. A Colombian drug lord. We were right back where we always ended up. I looked at Jack. "Does Ottavio have a C130?"

He shrugged. "He shouldn't, but that doesn't mean much."

"You're saying . . . I get what you're saying now, Bobo, without really saying. Maybe this Ottavio fella is the one Jimmy hooked up with down there. Maybe that's what Jimmy is snitching about." His eyes lit up and burned almost as bright as the tip of his cigarette. "Whoooo*eeee!* Can you feature what would happen to old Jimbo if word got around that he's a stoolie for the Feds?"

Jack put his hand on Ira's shoulder, just the way he had on the porch of his trailer when he wanted to make a point. "That's exactly what I want to happen. I want to put Jimmy under pressure. Funny things happen to people when they're under pressure. All I want you to do is start floating the word that Jimmy is working for the government. Discreetly, Ira."

"That's all, huh?" Ira pooched his lips out and shook his head. He dropped his cigarette butt to the cement and stepped on it. "That's like saying you're gonna blow up his house, discreetly. That's like putting my head into the mouth of an alligator, discreetly. Are you sure you want to do that?"

"I'm sure."

I wasn't. "Why wouldn't we, Ira?"

"Because he's going to know right where it's coming from." He turned and looked at Jack. "He's going to know it's you, Bobo. He knows you're out here asking questions and making trouble for him. He's already put the word out for anyone who can to let you know to come ahead and come on. 'Get it over with' is what he says." He lifted his peanut cart off the counter, slung the strap around his neck, and shrugged. "Whatever's going to happen is going to happen I guess."

Ira the philosopher. He was obviously a determinist. I tended to come down more on the side of free will. I liked to think that we had input into how our lives turned out. That outcomes were shaped by the decisions we made rather than predetermined by the finger of fate. Jack was busy peeling twenties out of his wallet. I looked at him and wondered which philosophy he subscribed to. He handed Ira a few of the bills and nodded in the direction of the red-and-white-striped bag of peanuts that was still in my hand. "That's for the peanuts."

Ira took the money, leaned over, and stuffed it into his sock. The peanut tray bounced up and down as he adjusted it on his shoulders. "I'll see what I can do about putting the pressure on your old buddy Jimmy, if that's what you really want."

"That's what I want."

Ira made his way up the ramp and disappeared into the light. I couldn't be that close and not go up and take a look myself. Jack waited for me while I walked up the dim underground tunnel and into the sunshine. It was like walking out of a long dark winter devoid of box scores and *Baseball Tonight*, and into the bright spring of a brand new season. I loved baseball, and it hadn't occurred to me once since I'd been down here that spring training was in full swing.

The stadium was small—about eight thousand seats. It felt even smaller because of how close the seats crept to the field. The ballplayers seemed oversized at that distance, and even from several sections up I could hear sounds from the field I'd never heard before—the pop of the first baseman's bubble gum, and the scratching of the pitcher's spikes on the rubber. What truly struck me was the casual feeling in the stands. The people in this crowd hadn't paid sixty-five dollars for their seats. They lounged around with newspapers and suntan oil. They sipped beer and lemonade as they kept one eye on the game and chatted in the warm breeze. It was like going to a baseball game at the beach.

I caught sight of Ira making his way laterally across the stands. And I thought about Jimmy Zacharias and the showdown we were certainly building up to. Maybe Ira was right. Whatever was going to happen was going to happen, and there was nothing I could do to change it.

Chapter Twenty-Nine

Felix had called as we'd made our way back down I-95 to Miami, so we made a stop at his command post at The Suites. He was prepared for us. He had stacks of information—printouts, copies of news clippings, and what looked like SEC filings. They were laid out across one of the double beds in what he called the "Cray Room." He asked us to sit. I took a seat on the other bed. Jack pulled out the desk chair and turned it around so he could sit in it with his arms across the seat back and rest his chin. He looked exhausted and I wondered if he'd had any sleep since the night in the hangar.

Felix handed us each a neat packet that was stapled in the upper left hand corner and fronted with a cover page. It had a table of contents, an executive summary, appendices, and bullet points all presented in PowerPoint landscape orientation. It was as polished and professional a presentation as any you might find in the densely carpeted, mahogany-paneled boardrooms of old economy corporate America—and it was chock-full, I was sure, of stolen and pirated information. Gen-X meets General Motors.

Felix paced back and forth. I half expected him to whip out a slide projector and pointer, but all he did was continue to pace, head down, lips moving, and no sound coming out. It took me a second to realize he was rehearsing.

"Felix."

"What?"

"Go."

"Oh, sure. Sorry. Okay. Uh . . . Miss Cray graduated from the London School of Economics, where she took a degree in Economic History. If you turn to Appendix I you'll see her transcript."

Appendix I was an official-looking list of all the courses young Vanessa had taken in undergraduate school. They were heavy on economic history in places like Latin America and Europe. There was one called The Internationalisation of Economic Growth, and one I found particularly interesting called Gender Theories in the Modern World. Equally interesting was the fact that Vanessa's class grades covered the full range from A- to A+. Wow.

"How did you get this?" Jack wanted to know.

"I called the school and told them I was from Data Processing and that I was, like, upgrading the system and I needed the password."

"And they gave it to you?"

"No. So I put out an APB to some hackers at the school. I told them what I needed and they told me how to get it."

Jack and I looked at each other. "It's a whole new world," he said, and I resolved right then and there never to put my credit card number out on the Web again for any reason.

"She spent the year after graduation traveling abroad. She attended a gourmet cooking school in Paris, and took flying lessons in Germany. She speaks, like, six different languages—English, Spanish, Portuguese, French, Italian, and Farsi."

"That's not like six," Jack said. "It is six."

"Oh, she also speaks some Russian. I forgot to put that in. Sorry."

"Seven," I said, stretching across the bed and sinking down on one elbow.

"She came back to the States to attend business school at Stanford, graduating with an MBA, concentration in Finance. That's, um, Appendix II." I flipped to the back. Another 4.0. Perfection can be so monotonous. "After graduation, she was recruited by, like, every Wall Street and consulting firm in the world."

No kidding. "How do you know that?"

"It was in one of the articles about her. She went with a Wall Street brokerage house called Thierry Eckard & Dunn."

"Never heard of them." That's where the litany ended. I turned the page. "What happened then?"

He went over to his stacks on the bed, picked up another handout, and handed one to each of us. My heart rate elevated instantly when I saw the title— INDICTMENT. Now we were getting somewhere. I sat up straight, glanced over the executive summary, which seemed to be a chronology, and went straight to the detail pages. There were copies of articles from the *Financial Times*, *The New York Times*, *Barron's*, and *The Wall Street Journal*. They all described a joint 1992 undercover operation that involved U.S. Customs, the FBI, and the IRS. They were looking to find brokers with Wall Street firms who "willfully invested drug profits or otherwise engaged in transactions to conceal the source and ownership of dirty money." Felix had helpfully highlighted that passage.

"They were looking for money launderers," Jack said. He was perking up as well.

"And they found some." I was reading ahead.

It was an ugly scandal. Five brokers, all working out of the Panama office of Thierry Eckard & Dunn, were indicted in 1993 by a federal grand jury in Tampa on charges of money laundering. The next few articles detailed the slow, agonizing death of the firm as the case lurched slowly through the justice system. Still later articles profiled the brokers who'd been busted. Right there in the middle of a lineup of photos was Vanessa Cray.

"Our little Vanessa," Jack mused. "A money laundress."

"I can't believe it." I was up and pacing now. I had to be careful not to run into Felix, who never sat down unless he absolutely had to. "How can she run a hedge fund if she was indicted for money laundering?"

"They all got off," Felix said. "Some kind of technicality."

"What?"

"The indictments were thrown out," Jack said. "It doesn't say, but it sounds like a problem with the case." He turned to Felix. "This is good work, son."

Felix beamed. He was so pleased to be praised by Jack.

"Anything yet on George Speath, Felix?"

"Not yet, but there's more on Miss Cray. Did you notice her personal history began with college?"

I hadn't noticed. I'd been distracted by the juicier aspects of her story. But when he mentioned it . . . "Where is she from?"

"I don't know. There's, like, nothing, you know? No personal information anywhere that I could access about where she comes from, who her parents are. Brothers and sisters. I tried everything. Inoculation records, social security number, birth certificate—"

"What about the schools?" Jack asked. "She had to have filled out applications that included information about her parents. They would have had to sign them if she wasn't eighteen."

"Blanked out. No data in those fields. Nothing. It was like she was born at the age of eighteen. Weird."

I looked over at Jack. "Witness protection?"

"I thought of that," Felix said brightly. "I tried to hack into the federal marshals' database, but there was no way."

Jack blinked at him. "I think I'm glad to hear that, son. But if she went into witness protection at that age, chances are it would have been for something her parents did. Or saw."

"Maybe this has something to do with why you remember her," I said. "Or almost remember her."

"I don't know." Jack went back to the first package and flipped through the pages again. He ended up studying a page near the end. I looked over his shoulder. He'd ventured back to Appendix III, which was two sparse pages. The first was a list of three different associations with telephone numbers and addresses: the American Orchid Society, the Australasia Native Orchid Society, and the Associació Catalana d'Amics de les Orchídies. The second page was a copy of a newspaper clipping from the *Miami Herald*. It was an article with accompanying picture of a woman in full climbing gear hanging from the side of a rock. According to the caption, it was Vanessa. She'd scrambled up a sheer cliff face to see an orchid with a name I couldn't pronounce. Something quite rare, apparently, that not many people get to see.

"She doesn't do anything in half measures," I said. "You know what we never got from Vanessa, Jack?"

"Respect?"

"An alibi."

Chapter Thirty

Vanessa Cray was already forty-five minutes late. The ice in my glass was long melted. The water sparkled no more, and the slice of lemon I'd requested floated at the top like a dead goldfish. I was seated on the deck of the restaurant she had chosen, where I had been since I'd arrived, wilting in the humidity and watching the quiet street in front for a limousine, a Mercedes, or at least a black Volvo. But, as I was learning, Vanessa Cray did not always do the expected. She arrived by boat.

It was a sleek cruiser with a tall cabin, a powerful motor, and a wide deck to play on. The name of the boat, *The Crayfish*, was painted in fancy script across the back. As it approached the dock, one of the waiters hurried out to grab a line.

It would have been hard not to recognize the man that emerged first. It was the oversized Bee Gee, the same large, distinctive individual Jack and I had seen in Vanessa's office the day we had visited. Today he wore a gold chain, a diamond stud earring, and a dark, tight, V-necked sweater over black slacks. He stepped onto the deck in his soft leather loafers—not exactly deck shoes—and discreetly slipped the waiter a tip. He scanned the surroundings, turned, and offered his hand to the boat.

Vanessa stepped out of the cabin, took his hand, and practically floated onto the dock. They both started toward me, but the escort dropped off and settled three tables away. Vanessa approached my table and gazed over my head.

"Where is Jack?" she asked.

"He's busy."

She continued to stand, bag under her arm, hands clasped in front of her. Today must have been business casual for her. Her long black skirt hung low on her hips and flowed around her legs like crude oil. The matching top, which looked like a shrunken black T-shirt, came down only far enough to reveal a thin strip of her smooth, tight belly when she moved. Her ice blonde hair was up, hidden under a black straw hat with a very wide brim. Sunglasses—Sophia Loren ovals—and perfectly painted lips topped off the look. Simple, yet exotic.

I thought she might have been thinking about leaving, since there was no one here but "Jack's assistant" as she had referred to me. Turned out she was only waiting for someone—in this case the waiter—to hustle over and whisk her chair out for her. While he was there he offered a menu. She ignored it.

"I'll have the Salad Niçoise with no eggs and a glass of lemonade. Not too much ice." As she ordered she took off her hat and set it on the table. It was like lifting a serving plate off of her head. She never looked at the waiter once.

"And for you, ma'am?"

"Another—"

Vanessa's leather bag twittered. The waiter and I both stared as she reached in, extracted her cell phone, and flipped it open. She angled her body away, making clear the distinction between us and what was really important.

"Another bottled water," I said, handing over my menu. "With more ice this time, please."

Vanessa conducted the call in rapid French. I didn't need a translation to know she was not pleased with whatever news she was getting. When the call ended, she put the phone on the table. She sat back and crossed one narrow leg over the other, letting the billowy black skirt fall loosely around her.

"More questions?" she asked. "You seem to be the one with all the questions."

"I hate loose ends."

"And he was, after all, your friend, wasn't he? This murder victim?" She said it as if the mere act of discussing John's murder soiled her.

"His name was John McTavish. He had a wife and three small children. And yes, he was my friend."

"You knew him from your work at the airlines?"

I quickly replayed the interview we'd had in her office. If there had been any mention of my background in that conversation, I couldn't remember it. "How did you know that?"

She smiled. "I am an investor, Alex. I make very large bets every day with people's money. I have an excellent research staff."

"Did you find what you needed?"

"It wasn't hard. It seems your time in Boston was short but rather"—she pursed her lips, but delicately—"newsworthy."

She watched for a reaction. My reaction was how interesting it was that we were off in our respective corners researching each other. She had her staff. I had Felix.

304

"Given your background, this effort you're involved in, this quest to find a murderer seems a bit out of your realm. What on earth has drawn you to such a risky activity?"

"I wasn't drawn to it. I'm repaying a debt."

"You certainly could do that without involving yourself personally. Jack, for example, could handle this for you. Quite capably, I'm sure."

I hated when she called him Jack. She probably sensed that, which was why she kept doing it. The waiter stepped between us to deliver our beverages—cold drinks in sweating glasses on a couple of damp cocktail napkins.

"One could say the same thing about your ventures," I told her. "Making large high-risk bets with other people's money. Or climbing sheer rock faces to observe a rare orchid. I'm doing this because I have to. I'm not doing it for the thrills."

"Are you sure?" A thin smile spread across her flawless face. Behind it was enough ice to chill my mineral water without the extra cubes. Perspiration beaded on my forehead. I shifted in my chair. She'd kept me waiting for a long time, and I was tired of sitting.

"Perhaps," I said, "we could get to my questions now."

"Of course."

"We found a credit card receipt in one of your Volvos—"

"One of the company's Volvos."

"It was the one that was seen in the parking lot on the night we're looking at. Someone named Arturo Polonia signed that receipt. There's no Arturo Polonia on the employee list for The Cray Fund."

"Arturo would not be on the list. He's in my private

305

employ, and yes, I forgot to tell you about him. I hope you don't misinterpret that. It wasn't intentional. Tell me"—she leaned forward and removed her glasses, revealing intense green eyes, and I understood why she had been so successful. It was her ability to focus every ounce of her being on whatever it was she was trying to understand. Or control—"what was it like to kill that man?"

The world around us went still, as if we were the only ones moving in it, and I wasn't moving very much. I could not believe she had asked me that question. Even stranger was what I perceived as real curiosity, the first genuine human reaction I'd experienced from her. It burned in her eyes like the fever I was feeling, and I began to understand something about her. This woman was an insidious infection that got inside you in ways you didn't understand, and began to break you down before you knew what was going on. She was a virus. I knew it for sure because I wanted to answer her.

"Is there some reason," I asked, "you're so interested in me?"

"As you point out, I myself am drawn to dangerous activities. The bigger the risk, the personal risk, the more I like it. They say it's what makes me good at my job. I'm interested in others who are, as well. But it's all right if you don't want to talk about it." A comment that was, of course, a challenge in itself.

"What makes you think I would discuss something like that with you? I don't even know you."

"Don't you? I think we know each other quite well. Did it change you? Taking his life?"

"I didn't take his life. He was killed in an accident."

"While chasing you."

"Yes."

"Do you blame yourself? Do you think about him? Do you ask yourself every day if you could have done something differently to change the course of events? I understand he died rather brutally."

A quiet but insistent breeze brushed the white cotton tablecloth against my knee. It was stiff with starch. The same gentle gust billowed her skirt, which was far more fluid. It was a hot breeze, or it was a breeze that felt torrid against my burning skin, and I thought maybe my rising temperature was an attempt to fight her off.

"The receipt, Vanessa." I looked beyond her to her boat, but I could feel her holding me in that radioactive gaze, and I knew she knew she was very close. I took a drink of water because if I was drinking I couldn't be talking. Talking to her and playing a game she obviously played with a great amount of skill. "Arturo Polonia?"

"Very well . . . Alex." She slipped the sunglasses back on, making it safe to look at her again. "What would you like to know about Arturo?"

"What does he do?"

She looked over at her escort seated across the deck. "Is that him?"

"Yes. He's my driver."

"And he drives the company cars?"

"Arturo has carte blanche when it comes to all of my vehicles or the company's. He typically takes the Volvos to run errands."

"Are you aware—" I dropped my voice, realizing he could hear us. "Are you aware of his extensive criminal record?" I looked down at my notebook. "Assault, possession, possession with intent—"

307

"I told you I have a thorough research process. And I do background checks. I hired Arturo when he was on parole. It was a risk, but . . ." She let the thought run into a nonchalant shrug.

"You like taking risks."

"And as you can no doubt see, he has certain . . . attributes that compensate for any nastiness in his background. In fact, the nastiness in his background is precisely why he is so effective for what I need."

"He's your bodyguard."

"He is my security team."

The waiter arrived with her salad. He set it in front of her, and paused with the clear intent of asking if she needed anything else. She ignored him until he got the message and faded.

"Why do you need security?"

"I like to invest in emerging markets, which means I travel a great deal. My work takes me to Russia, Eastern Europe, Central and South America. It is not uncommon for someone with my net worth to seek protection in those countries. Domestically, Arturo is my driver. Globally, he is my security staff."

"A staff of one?"

"He's all I need."

"Has he been in any trouble since you hired him?"

"Absolutely not. It's a condition of his employment. And he is very well paid."

I looked over at Arturo. He was like a cat in a window watching everything that moved until he could no longer see it, and then picking up the next target. "May I speak with Arturo?"

"That would be difficult, unless you speak Spanish."

308

"I'm certain we can find an interpreter. Perhaps at the police station."

"You would like his alibi. Is that correct? For the night of the murder?"

"Yes, I would."

"I'll save you the time and me the trouble. We were both in the same place." She reached her hand out. Arturo pushed himself up, lumbered over, and handed her a business card. "Arturo was with me on the night of March fifth. We were on the island."

"The island?"

"A private island in the Caribbean. I have a small compound there." She offered me the card. "This is the telephone number of my caretaker. He can tell you what you need to know."

I took the card, but didn't feel good about it. The whole situation felt so handled. I felt handled by her. "How did you get to and from the island?"

"On my G-IV, of course."

Of course. Why wouldn't I have guessed she had her own Gulfstream to fly back and forth to her small compound on the private island? I handed back the business card. "Can I have the phone number of the pilot who flew you over there?"

She seemed to consider that question for a long time. Arturo had gone back to his table. Vanessa spoke to him, eventually, in Spanish with more than a little impatience. Whether her impatience was with me or with him, I wasn't sure, but one thing was clear. Whatever possibility there had been for a convivial mood between us, contrived or otherwise, was long gone. I could feel her defense shield almost as clearly as I could see her dark glasses.

Arturo pulled out a Palm Pilot and maneuvered around the small screen with his large fingers. He found what he was looking for and started to rise from his chair to rumble across the deck again. She cut him off and must have told him to simply read out the digits, which he did. I wrote them down.

"So you do understand Spanish," she said.

"I don't believe I said otherwise. When did you return from the island?"

"I was back in Miami for a meeting on Tuesday morning. And I'm afraid I'm late for a meeting right now." She started to reach for the big hat.

"I have a few more questions. Please, Vanessa. It won't take long."

She didn't respond, but she didn't leave. She picked up the glass of lemonade instead of the hat.

"Do you know a man named Jimmy Zacharias?"

"No."

"Bobby Avidor?"

"No."

"Ottavio Quevedo?"

"Of course. I know who he is and what he does. We're not personally acquainted, if that's what you're asking."

"Have you ever worked in Panama? For Thierry Eckard & Dunn?"

"Yes, I was assigned to that office. And if you know that, you must know that I was arrested, along with everyone else in the office, and indicted on a money laundering charge. Which means you also know the government dropped their case. Was that your question?"

She so enjoyed asking all my questions for me, and

then answering them. "I'm wondering how far your tolerance for risk extends."

"That, perhaps, is a conversation for another day." This time when she reached for her hat, she didn't stop. She picked it up and settled it on her coif.

"Vanessa, have you changed your name?"

"I beg your pardon?"

"Is Cray your married name? Or perhaps you've had a legal name change?"

She looked surprised, then burst into a musical, ringing laugh. "No. I have never changed my name. I rather like my name. And as long as my fund continues to do well, it is a valuable asset, indeed."

The waiter appeared with the check when she stood. He was not sure who to give it to. Arturo handled it.

"This was fun," she said brightly as she turned to go. With the glasses on and the hat pulled low, I couldn't tell if she was joking. "Perhaps we can chat again after you've found your murderer."

She boarded *The Crayfish* and disappeared below. Arturo followed. The waiter cast off the line. I stood on the deck, watching them go and hoping the sick, feverish feeling would leave with Vanessa. It didn't.

Chapter Thirty-One

Jack's office was an afterthought of a space, a geometric impossibility that must have been what was left over after all the surrounding spaces had been designed. It would have been eight by ten if there had been four straight walls, but there were more corners than feet of wall space. A large window above the desk was the only saving grace. The property manager must have slapped in a door, thrown down some carpet, and put it on the market just to see if anyone would bite.

We'd stopped by to check the mail. From the size of the stack and from the stuffy feeling in the office, he hadn't been to his office in a while. He opened a window, which helped immediately, and sat down with the pile at his desk. It was arranged so that he could look out the window as he worked, which left me staring at the back of his head. Or looking out the window and across the alley into the offices of the people who worked in the high-rise next door. They were doing what normal people did at work on Wednesdays, and I realized how relieved I was not to be one of them.

The only other thing in the office to stare at was a picture hanging on the wall in a dime store frame of a younger, happier looking Jack with a boy who looked to be six or seven years old. The boy was blonder than Jack, but they shared the same deep brown eyes and long lashes. With their faces side by side, the resemblance was strong.

"Is this your son?"

"Yeah. Better days."

"Are you in touch with him?"

"As much as I can be. I call him five times and he calls me once. That sort of thing. I keep trying to work the ratio down." His chair squealed as he leaned back in it and turned to look at the picture. The high-backed, dark blue leather chair looked, like most of the furniture in his office, as if it too had seen better days. "I thought you wanted to learn about money laundering."

"I do."

"Then come over here and sit down. I can't concentrate with you roaming around behind me." Given the size of the space, "roaming" was a generous term. I pulled a chair up next to the desk so he could go through the mail and talk to me at the same time.

"A good laundering scheme," he said, "is designed to be so complicated it makes your head explode, which is the reason it works."

"Do you understand the basic principles?" I asked.

"As much as I need to."

"Then explain them to me. I want to understand. I want to know what Vanessa was doing."

"What she was *accused* of doing. Pull that trash can over here, would you, please?"

I found the standard gray wastepaper basket and pulled it around so it was between us. "Whatever."

"All right. You're a successful Colombian drug dealer. You've sold a hundred million dollars' worth of drugs on the streets of the U.S. But you, señorita Shanahan, have a problem. The hundred million is in ten- and twenty-dollar bills in the suitcases of couriers all over the country. Your goal is to convert that money into a form that you can spend."

"I can spend cash."

"Only a little at a time." He handed me a stack of flyers, coupons, and credit card offers. "You're in charge of trash."

I dropped the stack. It fell into the bottom of the can with a soft thud.

"You don't want to be paying for your 360,000 dollar Rolls-Royce Corniche convertible with tens and twenties. And you can't take your boatload of cash down to the bank and open an account because there are banking laws designed to detect people like you doing things like that."

"This is the ten thousand dollar rule?"

He nodded. "Any cash deposit over ten thousand dollars is going to raise the red flag, and the banker is going to call me, law enforcement, who is going to start asking you a lot of pointed questions about where that money came from. Eventually, because I am a good agent, I'm going to track it back to the predicate act, which was the sale of illegal drugs, and then I'm going to bust you."

"Okay, so I have couriers sitting around with suitcases full of my dirty money. All dressed up and no place to go."

"But you do have a place to go. What you need is to disguise the true ownership of the proceeds and the source, and change the cash into travelers' checks, money orders, CDs, or a bank account that you can draw checks on so you're not carting around bricks of cash. All the while, you have to maintain control over your money.

314

The person who can do all that for you is the professional money launderer."

"Let's call her Vanessa," I said, receiving another pile of trash. "For lack of a better name."

"Okay. Vanessa the money laundress is going to take that money and legitimize it for you, and for her troubles, she's going to take anywhere from ten to twenty percent off the top."

"She's going to make ten to twenty *million* off this transaction?"

"She is, but you don't complain because this service is absolutely essential to your business. What good is the money if you can't spend it? Besides, you have plenty left."

"Okay, so she's rich, but I'm richer. I'm happy."

"You're especially happy if she's professional, never steals from you, accounts for every penny, and generally does a good job."

"How do I know how much money I'm starting with?"

"What do you mean?"

"Who counts the money in the suitcases before it gets laundered?"

He turned in his squeaking chair to smile at me. "Now you're starting to think like a crook. It gets counted and audited all the way up the ladder. Drug empires are like corporations. Their systems of checks and balances and controls would make IBM proud. However, the penalties for noncompliance are pretty severe."

"How do I get the money to Vanessa?"

"You have your couriers contact her. She gives them the name of a bank where they can take their suitcases

315

and deposit the money, as much as they need to, no questions asked. Someplace she's already scoped out. Paraguay works. Also Mexico—"

"We'll say Panama," I said.

"Panama's a good one. Getting the money into a bank is a big step because there are no laws governing bank-to-bank transfers. You can move as much as you want in transactions as large as you want without being questioned. That's how she gets the money out of the country and as far away from its source as possible, most typically to Europe."

"Why Europe?"

"Credibility. Banks in Europe are more tightly controlled than those in the southern hemisphere. She would open up a bunch of accounts in different banks in different countries with balances as small as she could reasonably make them. The goal is to take these massive chunks of cash and spread them around."

"These banks would take these deposits, knowing they came from Panama?"

"If she's been in the business for a while, Vanessa knows the banking laws in Europe. She knows, for instance, that Switzerland and Luxembourg are good places for her kind of business. Like any good business-woman, she's established relationships, so she knows which banks will take the money without probing too much."

"She's got her own banking network."

"Something like that."

"What's the next step?"

"Colombian surnames—Hispanic surnames—are a red flag all by themselves all around the world, so the safest thing to do would be to move the money again, this time to accounts with fake names, like Kornhauser, or Lautrec. Or she could deposit it into brokerage accounts. The point is to move the money all around to as many places as you can, to create so many layers of confusing transactions that it's impossible to trace it back to its origins, and yet still maintain control over the accounts, and the funds. That, of course, is key."

"All right. So now Vanessa has all of my hundred million dollars, less her cut, in far-flung places around the world. How do I get it back?"

"That's the last step. You set up corporations where Mr Kornhauser and Ms Lautrec can invest their money."

"Real companies?"

"Real ones or fronts. They provide a way to prove that the money was earned legally."

"Where are these businesses?"

"Colombia, Europe, the U.S. . . ."

"Miami?"

"Anywhere. By this point the money is washed so clean no one would ever know to look at it, and if they did, they wouldn't be able to trace it back to you. And that's how it works. Here you go."

He handed me the last of the junk mail, which left a thin stack of what looked like bills. The sun was starting to go down, so it wasn't quite so stuffy in the office. In the building across the street, people were packing up in their offices to go home.

"What kinds of businesses make for good laundering?"

"Any business that is cash intensive. You'll find a lot of restaurants and bars down here in South Florida that won't take credit cards for that very reason. I hear the video rental business is catching on as a sink."

"Sink?"

"That's the place where you wash the money."

Naturally. "What about a hedge fund. Would that work?"

"I don't know. I don't know enough about that business to understand how it could."

"Vanessa Cray travels all over the world with a body-guard. She speaks six or seven different languages. Doesn't that sound like the perfect profile for a launderer?"

"It sounds like a reasonable theory," he said. "But what if she is? What does that have to do with John's murder?"

"I don't know. But her car was in the hotel lot the night he died. And we know we have some kind of a drug connection going on here."

He stood up and stretched and let out an enthusiastic yawn. "Want to go to dinner?"

"Let me check my messages first and see if Felix has come up with anything."

I dialed the hotel first and found that no one had called except George Speath. When I dialed into my cell phone box, he had called there, too. Nothing from Felix, but there was something from Dan up in Boston.

The message came out in his rat-a-tat staccato rhythm. *"So I drove up to that bar you gave me and had a beer and I asked around and it turns out one of the waitresses is Avidor's mother only she had a different name because she got remarried and I ask her about Johnny's phone call to that bar and she admits she knows him. She says he and Bobby grew up together and I told her who I was and that Johnny used to*

318

work for me and that you're down there doing what you're doing and she starts crying, which I hate. I hate when women cry. But long story short, Shanahan, Avidor sent her the logbook and the ring. He wanted her to keep it for him. She gave it to Johnny because she didn't want it in her house. Something about evil spirits or some shit like that. Are you happy now? Don't ask for any more favors. And one more thing, Shanahan. That was a long fucking drive. You owe me."

Jack saw me smiling. I replayed the message and let him listen. It made him smile, too.

"Forget dinner," he said, looking rejuvenated. "It's time to go and see Mr Avidor."

Chapter Thirty-Two

Mr Avidor had not been home. He had not gone to work that day and, according to Bic, had been out sick for two days. I'd come back to the hotel to messages three and four from George, all inquiring in the most polite way after the results of my audit. When Bic woke me up early the next morning and suggested in the least polite way that I get Speath Aviation off his back, I decided I had to go and see George. The problem was, I didn't have anything to tell him.

The last I'd heard from Felix, he was still trying to scale the firewall George had erected. Scale it, bypass it, blow it up, go through it, under it, or around it. George's firewall had left Felix and his hacker friends alternately frustrated and in awe. It had left me with a problem. George claimed to have given me full access to his computer files. As far as he knew, I had no reason to suspect he hadn't. And we'd found nothing suspicious in the data he had made available. Nothing to even hint that he was buying or selling bogus parts. But why does someone build a data vault if he has nothing to put in it? I had to talk to Felix.

I tried him from my hotel room. I tried him from my cell phone on the way over to George's. I tried him as I sat in George's parking lot. I called him at home, at the office, and at his temporary headquarters in room 484 at The Suites. If I'd had his parents' number, I would have tried him there. I hung up, cursing the fact that he didn't have a cell phone. I was going to have to make something up. That was my plan, at least before I walked through the door at Speath Aviation and saw the welcome sign. This time the magnetic letters were arranged in a greeting to FELIX MELENDEZ, SOFTWARE SOLUTIONS.

Dammit, Felix. Apparently he had hit upon a new approach for getting around that wall.

Margie's desk was empty, as usual. A radio was playing somewhere. Salsa music. And I could hear the normal banging and whirring and grinding from the other side of the heavy door that led to the hangar. I went down the back hall to George's office. The door was open and the lights were on, but no one was home. I came back out and followed the sound of the music, checking rooms along the way. The break room was empty. The bathroom was silent. I found the source of the music when I went into the stockroom. It came from a cheap radio playing on a worktable. No George. No Margie. No Felix.

The stillness felt odd. Wrong. The musical accompaniment, small and tinny, made the walls feel close. The nervous beat of the Latin rhythm put my teeth on edge, so much so that I wanted to get out of that stuffy, windowless, inside space.

I turned to go, moving with some purpose, and crashed straight into a barrier, which turned out to be another warm body. Head-on collision. Full force. It knocked me back and was so sudden it took a few seconds for me to feel startled. When I did, a wave of adrenaline shivers erupted. He had come out of nowhere, this slight man with a goatee and thick, black eyebrows, approaching silently to stand behind me.

He was about my height. His hair, like his eyebrows, was wiry and dark and it stuck out from under a Speath Aviation cap, the same kind George had given me. I didn't know his name, but I'd seen him around the shop. He was one of the few employees who hadn't spoken to me—maybe the only one—which gave his wide-eyed, silent stare the weight of the unknown.

I asked him if he spoke English. He shook his head. Using my limited knowledge of Spanish, I asked him where George was. He pointed to the hangar, still completely silent. When I stepped toward the door, he moved aside, but his eyes moved with me. And I didn't turn my back on him. I got such a creepy feeling from him. From the room. From the whole situation. As I went down the hall, I heard the music go dead.

The door to the hangar opened from the other side before I reached it. My heart slipped out of my throat when I heard their voices—George and Felix—but it flew right back up when they walked through the door and into the narrow hallway and I saw them together. George was his normal, affable self, but next to him Felix looked small, vulnerable, and very young, and it hit me hard how much he didn't belong there, and how I was the one who had put him there.

For the first time since I'd met him, George felt dangerous. Not for any reason except that he was standing next to my kid friend, and I didn't know for sure that he wasn't.

"Alex . . . my word, what are you doing here? I didn't know you were coming. Did you get my messages?" He laughed at himself. "Of course you did. That's why you're here. Did you meet Felix? He's a software consultant.

Boy, this is my week for visitors, isn't it? Usually we can go for months in this place and only see each other."

I smiled at Felix and we exchanged what felt like obviously artificial, overly pleasant greetings. I had expected to see him, but he hadn't expected to see me— no one had—and he showed admirable restraint when I had popped up in front of him. He stood with his hands clasped in front of him, gazing directly but blankly into my face.

"We're going to lunch," George said. "Felix is trying to sell me a complete systems review. He's one of the few software people I've ever met who knows what he's talking about."

"Does he?" I asked. Felix couldn't suppress a grin that was equal parts bashfulness and bravado. I had to get him out of there.

George had a different thought. "Say, I've got an idea. Why don't you join us? We'll all go. Maybe you can share some of your insights with Felix about our capabilities and our needs. If we're going to do work for Majestic, we might want to upgrade our systems. What do you say?"

I checked my watch—two thirty eight. "It's a little late for lunch, isn't it, George? I was hoping to get some time with you."

"No, come with us, Miss Shanahan. That's a cool idea."

Felix's big eyes were on me, imploring me, giving me a preview of what it would be like spending an hour in front of George pretending I didn't know him.

"I'm sorry, George. I don't have time, and neither do you. We need to speak in private. Maybe Felix could come back another time."

If I hadn't known Felix, I might not have noticed how all the starch went out of him, how his head sank back into his shoulders. But I did know him and I did notice and it was all for his own good. He managed a smile anyway.

"Not a problem, Mr Speath. I'll go back to my office and work with what I already have. I'll see if I can scope out a plan for you."

"All right. I'll show you out. Alex, I'll be right with you." George put his big hand on Felix's back to guide him down the hall, much as he had done with me when steering me out of the path of the bomber pigeons. His hand covered almost the entire span of Felix's shoulders.

I fell in behind and followed them out. I was determined to see Felix walk out the front door, and was actually feeling a hint of relief until I glanced into the supply room on my way past. Mr Goatee was there. We locked eyes as he turned away from the door, and something in the way he looked gave me the feeling he'd been standing and listening to every word of our conversation. And that he understood. Maybe he did speak English after all.

Chapter Thirty-Three

Back at the hotel, I opened up my laptop and sent an e-mail message to Felix. It was similar to all the voice messages I'd left:

"Call me immediately."

"Get in touch with me ASAP."

"Do not go back to Speath's again."

"What were you thinking?"

I tried to reach Jack to tell him how Felix had popped up at George's, but he was off somewhere looking for Avidor. All I could do was wait. By the time I heard the knock on the door, I'd been swinging between worried and annoyed for several hours. I flew to the peephole and checked. When I saw who it was, I edged all the way over to angry.

I swung the door open. Felix looked at my face, and said, "Uh-oh."

"Get in here." I pulled him inside and closed the door.

"You can't see any of the airport from here. Wouldn't you want to be on the side where you could watch the planes taking off?" He was already at the window peering through my blinds.

"Felix, what were you doing at George's?"

"We tried again all last night to get past the wall. I decided to try another thing we sometimes do which is go in and pretend to be a software consultant or salesman. Sometimes if you offer a free upgrade to their system, they'll give you anything. Anyway, I started with the lady, Margie. She wouldn't give me anything. But then I met with Mr Speath and he was so cool. He showed me a bunch of stuff. I think I could have gotten in there if you . . . well, you know. If I'd had a little more time."

"Why would you do something like that? These are dangerous people we're dealing with. You have to appreciate that. We're—Jack Dolan is a professional. He does this for a living, and he has most of his life. You and I, we don't."

"I just did what you did, Miss Shanahan. You went in as someone else to get information. That's what I was trying to do. I was trying to help."

"I know you were. I'm not a professional, but I've got good reasons to be taking risks like that. Felix, you don't. You have no stake in this at all. You have no reason to risk anything for me or for Jack or for John McTavish. I want you to be safe."

He started to respond and stopped short.

It was a soft brushing against the door, a sound that felt like cold fingers across my skin. He had heard it, too.

It was quiet, and then the brushing sound again.

Signalling Felix to stay back, I crept forward as quietly as I could. I moved in front of the door and latched my right eye onto the peephole.

There was no one out there.

I angled to scan left and right. The emergency exit was across from my room and half a door-length down, so it wasn't easy to see it, but when it happened, I saw it. The door moved. I fixed on the dark crack where the door was slightly open and saw four fingers, the four fingers of the person who was standing on the other side, holding it ajar. An icy tingle crept up the back of my neck because there was no way past him. There was no way out.

I turned around and stood with my back to the door. I thought about Mesh Man. I thought about the kidney car. I thought about Vanessa and Arturo and Jimmy and George and Damon and God knows who else who might have a reason to want to do me harm. Reasons I didn't even know about. And then I thought about a scene from an old Burt Reynolds movie where a woman was cut almost in half by a shotgun blast—right through the closed door of her apartment. She'd been looking through the peephole.

Quickly, I fled inside toward the bed and the telephone.

"What's going on?" Even when he stood still Felix looked hyper. It was the way his face constantly changed expression based on whatever he was feeling at that moment.

"Someone is out there," I said. "Across the hall in the stairwell. I saw him."

"Really?" He headed for the door at warp speed.

"*Felix*, don't go over there." I was trying to punch the buttons on the phone and pay attention to him. "Stay inside here."

Too late. He was looking through the peephole. "Hey, there is. It's—"

I hung up, followed him over, and pulled him into the bathroom with me. The two of us cocked our heads and listened. "*Señorita, por favor.*" The voice was barely audible.

"Miss Shanahan, it's just this little dude with a baseball cap and a goatee and—"

"He has a goatee? What else did you see?"

"He's got black hair and he's not that tall. That's about what I saw."

"Stay here, Felix. I mean it."

I crept back over to the door, and back to the peephole. The black cap filled the line of sight at first. But then he tipped his head up and I saw his face. It was the man from George's stockroom. Only this time he didn't look menacing. He seemed more fearful than furtive. Behind his heavy eyebrows and neatly trimmed whiskers, he was more frightened than I was.

"Who are you?" I called, trying to air out my throat.

"Julio Martín Fuentes."

"What do you want?"

He responded by ripping into an impassioned and seemingly profound explanation of himself and his presence in my hotel—in Spanish. I motioned Felix to join me. He listened as Julio rambled. Whatever Julio Martín Fuentes was saying went well beyond my high school español vocabulary. I did, however, comprehend a number of references to señor George sprinkled throughout the hyperactive monologue.

"What did he say?"

"He works for George, and he wants to talk to you."

"Why?"

"He thinks you're an auditor and he wants to come in right now. He's scared to be standing out there in front of your door."

"What do you think?"

Felix asked a question and Julio responded. Then Felix nodded for me to open the door.

"What did you ask him?"

"I asked him if he was here to hurt us and he said no."

Great. I felt better.

"Ask him," I said, "to step back against the wall."

While Felix did that, I watched through the peep-hole. Julio had taken off his cap and was glancing and blinking in the direction of the elevator. He still looked as though he wanted to melt into the carpet. When he stepped back, I didn't see any firearms, at least not any obvious ones, so I turned the knob and opened the door.

Julio came as far as the doorway and stopped. That's when I saw the tattoo. He had sleeves on his shirt, but they were short, and I saw it poking out below the hem. It was a cross of some kind. Julio was Mesh Man. He stood working the black cap with nervous fingers until I realized he was waiting to be invited in.

"Come in, please, *señor*."

Felix ushered him into the room. The two of them sat in the chairs at my tiny table. I closed and locked the door and joined them, settling in on the bed with my feet up. They were already deep in conversation. Words were flowing swiftly and they talked over each other a lot. What I could tell from Julio's animated and emphatic gestures was that whatever they were talking about, it mattered a great deal to him. He ended the conversation with multiple repetitions of "*muchas gracias*."

"He works at Speath Aviation," Felix said. "He's a bookkeeper there. He's seen you around with George and he knows you're an auditor."

"What's his story?"

"First of all, he wants you to know how much he

329

respects his boss. He's in awe of him. Julio used to be a mechanic, but when Mr Speath found out he was trying to become an accountant, he took him off the line and gave him a chance to go to school." Felix leaned in and lowered his voice. "I think it's sort of a father-son deal there."

Julio had clean fingernails—the hands of a number cruncher, not a mechanic.

"This is the best job Julio has ever had, and he doesn't want to get Mr Speath in trouble. He's good to his people, and he tries hard to run a good business. Every Christmas he—"

"Felix, the more good things you say about George, the more worried I'm getting. Is George laundering dirty parts? Is that what he came to tell me?"

"No." Felix's voice became quiet enough that I could hear a thread of tension running through his usual irrepressible enthusiasm. "Mr Speath is using his business to launder drug money."

I sat up and edged to the side of the bed. I didn't want to make any quick moves. Julio offered a polite smile, but his forehead gleamed with perspiration, and both knees bounced as if he were trying to run somewhere sitting down. I knew the feeling. I wanted to call Jack, but I didn't know where he was, and looking at Julio, he wasn't going to want to hang around after he'd told his story. I found my notebook and opened it up.

"Drug money, Felix? Is that exactly what he said?"

The two of them nodded in stereo. Julio obviously knew a little English. Probably about as much as I knew Spanish.

"Does he sound as if he knows what he's talking about?"

"For sure. And he's way depressed about it. At first, he wasn't certain since he's new at this, but he's been paying attention and keeping good notes. Now he's sure."

"How is George doing it?"

Felix turned to Julio and they were off and running again in another high-speed dialogue.

Julio seemed excited that we were so interested. Felix was beyond excited.

"Mr Speath plays with the inventory accounts and makes it look as if he's bought more than he really has. They make up the difference with laundered cash, and because parts are so expensive, Julio says they can wash a lot of cash with only a few fake transactions."

He paused, and I thought he was going to check with Julio again, but the pause turned into a full stop. "Felix?"

"I was just thinking, no wonder we're locked out of his system. This is what Mr Speath is protecting behind his firewalls. I wonder how I can get around them."

Julio's knees were still churning, and I thought soon he might start rattling the lamps with his nervous fidgeting. He could hardly keep himself in his seat.

"Felix, ask him why he's so scared."

Julio responded to Felix with another blast of accents and tildes, and somewhere in there, I heard the secret password, maybe the word that would unlock the whole case, answer all the questions, and bring all the loose ends into a tight bow.

"Get this, Miss Shanahan." Felix was on his feet now. "It's money that belongs to this dude Ottavio, who's a big drug lord down in Colombia, which is where Julio is from, which is why he's so scared because he has family there and he's afraid if the word gets out that he's informing, his relatives will be wiped out. This Ottavio is some vicious dude who has all kinds of corrupt officials looking out for him. Wow! This is . . . this is unbelievable."

"Ask him if he'd be willing to talk to the authorities."

I didn't need a translation to understand Julio's response. His face turned so pale I could see all the individual wiry whiskers of his goatee. He had gone as far as he would go—I could see that—and told Felix that if asked to repeat the accusations, he would deny them.

"Ask him why George would do such a thing."

He did.

"He says he doesn't know, but he thinks Mr Speath is under financial pressure. He has a whole stack of unpaid bills and they've been having cash flow problems."

No wonder George was so anxious for the Majestic business. "Felix, did he tell you who George is working for? Who represents Ottavio here in Florida?"

Julio didn't know, but I thought I might. I'd only met one money launderer while in Florida on my great adventure.

"They did change outside accountants about six months ago," Felix said. "He thinks that's when it started. He gave me the name. In fact—" I could see Felix slipping into his hacker's trance. He stopped in front of Julio and asked him a few questions, to which Julio responded.

"I am so psyched, Miss Shanahan. He just told me enough that I might be able to get into Mr Speath's vault. I can't wait. Can I go?"

"No, you can't go and if there's any chance they can find out you've been in there and trace it back to you, I don't want you screwing around with it. We're talking about drug traffickers here. In fact, ask Julio if they have a way of tracking back to you if you try something like that."

"I don't think he'd know if they did."

"Ask him anyway."

Julio responded with a shrug and a blank stare. "He doesn't know, but I think I can figure that out once I get in. Anything else?"

I looked up at the sprinkler head in the ceiling of my room. It was a good place to focus.

"Speath Aviation is a repair station that we now find out is being used to launder—but drug money, not parts. Right, Felix?"

"Right."

"Who's the drug launderer in this little scheme we've got going here? It's not Jimmy. Jimmy is parts. It's Vanessa. Ask Julio if he knows that name. Vanessa Cray."

He didn't.

"Ask him if he's ever heard of Jimmy Zacharias."

Never.

"Does he know if George is also laundering dirty parts?"

No again, which blew up the elegant theory I was concocting in my head. Too bad; it made a lot of things make sense that didn't seem to make sense. But then Julio kept talking and something came out about the

333

"effay-bee-ee." The FBI.

"What did he say, Felix?"

"Hold on."

I strained to try to understand, but it was all too fast for me. I had to be patient and wait. Finally, Felix turned my way. He was shaking his head.

"What? What, Felix? What?"

"He said that a bunch of parts had come through recently that Mr Speath had suspected were bad. Bad paperwork. No traceability. They looked used and were supposed to be new."

"Yeah. What did he do?"

"He gave them to the FBI."

"The FBI? George is a money launderer and he called in the FBI?"

"Julio said that Mr Speath couldn't stand the idea of someone trying to sell substandard parts." It made no sense, but in a way, it did. I thought back on George's face as he'd gazed up at that beautiful Electra out on the tarmac. He was capable of money laundering, apparently, but drew the line at washing dirty parts. George loved airplanes too much.

"Ask him . . . Felix, ask him if he knows who at the FBI George has been working with."

Julio listened to the question, hesitated, then pulled out his wallet, a red nylon fold-over with a Velcro closing, and dug deep to find a business card, which he held in his palm, hidden like a playing card.

Felix translated. "He said he and Margie and Mr Speath are the only ones who know about the bad parts, and that Mr Speath had asked him not to say anything to anyone because he was afraid if you found out, you

334

would give them a bad audit and they wouldn't get the business from Majestic."

Julio handed me the card. I read it, handed it back, and thanked him very much. I didn't need to keep it. I already had one from Agent Damon Hollander.

Chapter Thirty-Four

Jack put his glasses on and sat down on the couch, deftly avoiding the empty pizza box that had been lying fallow for several hours. Felix and I had been through many meals in room 484 as we'd tried and finally succeeded in using Julio's information to crack George's data vault. Actually, Felix had done all the cracking. I'd done the analysis of what was in there.

"How am I supposed to read all those tiny numbers?" Jack held the page I'd handed him under the lamp.

He was right. Felix had reduced the large spreadsheets so much the numbers looked like black pepper sprinkled across a white tablecloth. He took off his glasses and held it at arm's length. "What would I be looking at if I could see?"

"I'll summarize for you," I said. "I told you about how Julio the Whistle-blower came to see me and told us that George has been using his business to launder money."

"Right."

"For Ottavio Quevedo, famous drug lord."

"I got that part, too."

"That's what was in the data vault. George keeps records in there of how much money he's laundered and through what accounts. We spent all night going through it and we think we understand how he's doing it. And Felix found a pretty handy link in there, too."

"What kind of link?"

"It was a way for me to get into the accountant's mainframe computer, Mr D. I didn't think I could at first." Felix was starting to rev up. "But then I found some code I could use and I—"

Jack smiled and gently cut him off. "George's accountant?"

"When George started laundering," I said, "he picked up a new outside accountant. It turns out this accountant has a bunch of other aviation repair stations as clients."

"Maybe that's his specialty. He has a particular expertise. It's not that unusual. Word of mouth . . . that sort of thing. These aviation people all talk to one another."

"That's not this accountant's particular expertise. Give me the list, Felix."

Felix dug around in the pile around his computer until he found the page I wanted and gave it to me. I passed it over to Jack. "This is the list of the stations, all using the same accountant, remember. Do any of them ring a bell?"

Jack put on his glasses and glanced over the names. "Dirty parts. These are Jimmy's places. Many of them anyway. They're all suspected of moving bogus parts."

I pointed to the list. "Every one of those stations has cash coming in on a regular basis in some form or another from Panamanian registered corporations that do their banking in the Cayman Islands."

He looked again at the list. "Money laundering? These rinky-dink places?"

"Yep. Jimmy's stations are multipurpose laundering-facilities. You can get your dirty parts washed there, or your drug money. Take your pick." Felix started to giggle. We were both a little bit loopy.

337

"Hold on." Jack wasn't loopy. "Are you saying Jimmy is a money launderer? That can't be. Jimmy is a compulsive gambler. He'd be dead within a week if he had access to that kind of money."

"No. I don't think he's the launderer and maybe he doesn't have access to the money. But he might have access to the records. Incriminating records, such as the ones we found tonight in George's vault. It's good stuff. Any up and coming FBI agent would die to get his hands on what we found."

Jack set the page of names on the coffee table at his knees and stared at it. He let his head tip back and forth, as if to look at the idea from all sides. Then he looked up at me with that deep crevice over the bridge of his nose and started nodding, and I knew he was putting the information together the same way we had.

"What you two found," he said, "is what Damon has been after."

"Yes. This is Ottavio's drug money, Jack. The same repair stations Jimmy uses to wash parts are also used by Ottavio to launder his drug proceeds. It's the only scenario that makes everything work. And it explains all the connections."

"How?"

I looked around for my notepad. I'd been writing down bits and pieces all night. "Felix, where is my notebook?"

"I think I saw it in the bathroom."

It was there, next to the sink. I retrieved it, sat down on the couch next to Jack, and turned to the page labeled "Jimmy and Ottavio."

"You were wondering, Jack, about how Jimmy and

338

Ottavio were linked in this Sentinel parts deal. I think Jimmy knew Ottavio to begin with, because he was letting Ottavio use his stations to launder money. It was a preexisting relationship. When the crash happened, Jimmy had someone to call down there."

"Someone with a lot of juice," he said. "Someone with access to a C130 transport."

"Exactly. Ottavio used his ties to whatever guerrilla or paramilitary group he's aligned with on the drug side of his business." I turned over to Vanessa's page. "As for Vanessa, being the only one with laundering experience on her résumé and a stint in Panama, I nominate her for Ottavio's launderer. Although we still don't know who she really is."

"That makes her Jimmy's partner."

"That's right," I said. "And she claimed she'd never heard of him."

Jack stood up and started moving around. It wasn't easy. The suite was covered over almost completely in spreadsheets and hamburger bags and printouts, but he made a path. He went to the window and opened the curtains. Felix and I both cowered like a couple of bats. It was light out there in the central atrium. The sun was up. What time was it, anyway?

Jack stared through the window. "Jimmy loans his repair stations out to Ottavio," he said, "for money laundering, probably for a fee, knowing him. Damon finds out. The next time Jimmy gets hauled in and charged with something, Damon is there waiting to offer him a stay-out-of-jail pass. All he has to do is sneak Ottavio's laundering information out the back door. Documentation of a money laundering operation.

339

Damon would definitely be interested in that." He turned to me, grinning. "One sink, two laundering operations. Very synergistic. Isn't that what you would say?"

I smiled back. I liked when he teased me. "Synergistic indeed. I'll bet that was Vanessa's idea, being the 4.0 Stanford Business School grad that she is. But synergy works the other way, too. Jimmy, Ottavio and Vanessa, even Damon—they're all connected through the stations so that if Jimmy goes down, say for the Ecuador parts deal, he takes the stations down with him. And if the stations go down, the money laundering operation folds, Vanessa is out of business or in jail, and—"

"Ottavio loses his laundering operation, and a large pile of his drug profits gets confiscated." Jack finished the thought for me and added his own. "And Damon Hollander loses his big bust."

"That," I said, "makes a lot of people interested in maintaining the status quo." I shoved the pizza box onto the floor so I could spread out more on the couch. It had been a long way and taken a long time, but we were finally at the bottom line. "Which is why John is dead. When he came down and threatened Bobby, he threatened to knock down the house of cards. Someone killed him for it."

Everyone was quiet for a few minutes. I lounged on the couch with my head back and my eyes closed. They burned from hours of staring at the computer screen in the dark and a sea of tiny numbers. Jack was back at the window studying The Harmony House Suites atrium. Felix was busy disassembling a balky printer that had given us trouble all night. He was on the floor with the parts spread out around him in a sunburst pattern.

I heard Jack take a deep breath. I opened my eyes and he had turned back into the room. "Okay," he said. "Part two. Everyone in this twisted scheme has something to lose, which gives everyone a motive for murder. The only person we know who didn't commit the crime, at least not that crime, is Bobby Avidor because he has a solid alibi."

"You didn't find him?"

"He's nowhere."

I sat up and looked at my wrist. No watch. I'd taken it off at the same time we'd unplugged the electric clock radios in the suite. Looking at the time had proved a distraction we didn't need. "What time is it, anyway?"

"It's one-thirty in the afternoon."

"Felix, it's one-thirty in the afternoon. Have we been . . . we must have—"

"We were here all day yesterday," he said, "all night, and all of this morning. Yes, ma'am."

"Don't you have to go to work or something?"

"I took a comp day." He felt around on the carpet for a screwdriver. "I've got about three weeks' worth in the bank."

Felix looked the same as he always did—ready to go out and run a sack race at the company picnic. I felt like crap. My legs ached. The throbbing in my ankle, which had almost gone away, was back with a vengeance and had dispatched companion aches to all my other limbs along with my neck, my back, and my shoulders. We had to get this over with before my brain shut down.

"I'm going to give Damon the benefit of the doubt," I said, "and assume he's not a murderer."

"That's a good assumption," Jack said. "Damon would

341

have plenty of options short of murder to move John out of the way if he had to. What about your friend Vanessa?"

That was a trickier and more complex thought process. I had to rub my head some more. "Vanessa might have had a motive, but only if she knew that John was in town and that he posed a risk to her operation. How would she find out? I doubt seriously that Bobby has any lines of communication open to Vanessa Cray."

"No," Jack said. "Avidor would have told Jimmy. If he's not already dead, he can verify that."

I filed that away, the idea that Bobby was dead, for later processing. Right now I was still on Vanessa. "I don't think Jimmy would have told her."

Felix piped up. "Why not?"

"Why bring her in? If he's got a good deal going, why tell her something that might encourage her to take her business elsewhere? If he is working with the Feds to build a case against Ottavio, then he needs her to be in business with him. What do you think, Jack? Do you see Jimmy bringing her in?"

"Jimmy doesn't take unnecessary risks. Vanessa also has an alibi. Didn't you check that, Alex?"

"I did. She and Arturo both, although I still think it's suspect. The people who provided the alibi work for her." I stared down at my notebook. I really wanted some orange juice. I found the phone and dialed room service. "Is any of this making any sense?"

"It makes a lot of sense," Jack said, "and it brings us to the last man standing."

"Jimmy." I was on hold. "He didn't want to lose his stay-out-of-jail card. Would that be motive enough, Jack?"

342

"Jimmy would kill himself before he went to jail. And he'd kill John McTavish before he killed himself."

The room service operator came on and I ordered a large, fresh-squeezed orange juice. I was, after all, in Florida.

"There's still a piece of this thing that doesn't really fit," I said, after I'd hung up, "and that's the Sentinel parts. Felix and I have been trying to figure that out and we can't."

"What about them?"

"If Jimmy was interested enough in the status quo to kill John, why would he risk everything by stealing that airplane?"

"Yeah," Felix said. "It's, like, a way bigger chance to take." He thought about that. "I mean, it sort of is. Killing someone is worse than stealing an airplane, but . . . I don't know how to say it—"

"It's the magnitude," I said. "Jimmy could have killed John all by himself, although it would have been quite a fight. But stealing a jet from the side of a mountain, schlepping it to Florida, and hiring a bunch of mechanics to break it down . . . how many people must have been involved in an operation like that? I would classify that as an unnecessary risk."

"Not for Jimmy. For him it's a calculated risk. Jimmy's a gambler. And he's an old soldier. He loved everything about the military. This would have been a chance for him to throw on his cammies and his war paint and go play Delta Force. For him, it would have been worth the risk just to see if he could pull it off. Killing a man is easy. Stealing an airplane, that's a risk worth going to jail for. That's the way he thinks."

343

"I'm guessing he didn't confer with his FBI handlers before he went down there."

Jack smiled. "Damon must have been pissed as hell."

I leaned back against the couch and rested my eyes again. "I think we've got it. The question is what do we do with it?"

"That's easy," he said. "We're going to take inventory and see how much leverage we have. Are you up for it, Felix?"

Felix sprang straight up off the floor. "What do you need, Mr D.?"

"I want to find out everything we can about Vanessa Cray. If she's going down with Ottavio, then she has just as good a reason as we do to get Jimmy. I want to know who she really is."

Felix was already at work, booting up the computer and cracking his knuckles.

Jack looked at me. "As for you, I think it's time we had a talk with our prime suspect. Do you think you can stay awake long enough to take a ride out and see Jimmy?"

Chapter Thirty-Five

I had been chased by his dog. I had heard his voice. At long last, I was about to lay eyes on the man himself.

From a distance, Jimmy Zacharias looked tall and lanky, but as we came down the drive to his house, I saw that he was the whittled-away kind of skinny, the kind that suggested there had been more to him at some point, and needed to be more now. His lips were so thin they seemed to have been drawn on his narrow face with a sharp pencil. His eyes were dark behind the squint, and his face desperately pockmarked. He wore his hair parted straight down the middle of his scalp. He looked like an Indian warrior who had been doing heroin, lounging in the doorway of his house, shirtless, forearm braced against the jamb above his head.

The sight of Jack induced in him a dark laugh that turned into a deep wet cough. "What do you want, asshole?" He managed to spit the words out between sticky, sucking eruptions. "I thought they kicked you out of the FBI."

"You were misinformed." Jack climbed the steps to the porch and stood alarmingly close to Jimmy, close enough to get coughed on. "I'm retired."

"Then what the fuck are you doing here?"

"I think you know."

Jimmy was only slightly taller than Jack, which meant when they stood nose to nose, they were staring directly into each other's eyes. They seemed comfortable doing it.

"Where's Bull?"

Jimmy smiled. "*Hey, Bull!*"

I heard him, snorting and growling. The adrenaline spread through my body like grasping tentacles, twisted around my heart and squeezed. I prepared for the sight of that big ball of muscle with teeth to come flying toward me, but he never showed up. The sound of his barking never got any closer.

Jimmy enjoyed my anxiety. "He's in the back. Should I get him for you?" He stepped into the shadows. The next thing I saw was the front door wheeling toward us, which must have been the very reason Jack had pushed in so close. He caught the door before it slammed. "Thanks for asking us in," he said.

The feeling inside the house was dim and cramped. Thin mustard-colored draperies that looked like big dish towels hung on the windows. Helped by the aluminum awnings that hung outside, they kept out the direct sunlight. But that didn't mean it was cool. The air was hot and stale and smelled of cigarettes, garlic, and something like Lysol. I was glad for the floor fan and the open door.

"Stay here," Jack said. "I'm going to see about that dog." He disappeared into what looked like the kitchen. Jimmy had disappeared, too, and I soon heard where he had gone. The bathroom must have been nearby.

Alone in Jimmy's lair, I took a look around. Besides an ugly brown couch shoved up against the wall, the major piece of furniture in the front room was a console stereo, the kind with the lid that opens to reveal the

346

turntable. My parents used to have one. On top was a small trophy, the cheap kind that gets handed out every summer by the tens of thousands to little league and high school teams all over the country. The inscription read *Jimmy Zacharias—Winning Pitcher—1969 City Champs—Everglades .City, FL.* Next to it was a picture of him in army fatigues, down on one knee and leaning on a rifle. His hair was dark and chopped short, but the shape of his face and the warrior squint were undeniably his. I looked at it and wondered what Jack had looked like back then. Next to the stereo on the floor were a bunch of magazines piled into a fire hazard. I reached down to flip through the stack. *Aviation Daily*, *Aviation Week & Space Technology*, a big fat pile of yellow newsprint called *Trade-A-Plane*, and something that looked like a military weapons digest. Mixed in were copies of *Hustler*, *Screw* magazine, and a local *TV Guide* from three months ago.

"Who are you? And what the fuck are you doing in my stuff?"

Jimmy had emerged from the bathroom under cover of the flushing toilet. I hadn't heard him until he was practically standing on top of me. He had donned a grayish T-shirt that probably used to be white. "Superbowl XXVIII" was emblazoned in blue letters across the front of a big faded Georgia peach that covered his entire chest.

"I was just . . . I'm sorry. I didn't mean to—I remember that game." I pointed to the shirt. "The Cowboys won. Their second in a row, I think. It was one of those big blowouts, the kind you could turn off in the first quarter if you didn't care about seeing the commercials."

347

I couldn't seem to find the appropriate point to stop talking. This man made me very nervous, even without his dog. "Were you there?" I asked him. "In Atlanta?"

His face tightened into what could have been a smile. "Who *are* you?"

"She's with me." Jack had returned, and his hasty response only served to arouse more interest from Jimmy, which made me very uncomfortable.

Jimmy's eyes never left me. "You don't have a name?"

"I do have a name." I wasn't sure what the best response would be to a murder suspect. "But it doesn't seem to be relevant to what we're doing here."

"Come over here and sit down, Jimmy. Let's have a talk."

"A mystery woman. I like it." Jimmy actually did smile then, in a way that made me think he could read the dynamics in the room as well as anyone. That may have been the scariest thing about him. He walked the three steps over to the narrow brown sofa and eased down on the flat cushions. He leaned back and put his feet up on the coffee table. His toenails could have used a good clipping.

Jack remained standing, so I did, too, although he looked more comfortable doing it. "That was some job, brother, you pulled off in Ecuador. My compliments."

Jimmy held eye contact and allowed a ghost of a smile. "I don't know what the fuck you're talking about, Ace."

Ace? Everyone seemed to call Jack something different, but Jimmy's name for him did not strike me as a term of endearment. He had let it roll off his tongue with a measure of contempt that seemed to instantly

348

elevate the tension in the room a few anxious notches.

"Air Sentinel up on the mountain. The Triple Seven. That would be right up your alley. Mobilizing in the dead of night. Swooping in on helicopters. A tight military operation, well timed and perfectly executed. Lots of dead bodies. It's just the kind of thing to get your heart pumping."

"You and me both, Ace. You and me both." Jimmy waited for a response. When Jack gave him nothing, he moved on. "Air Sentinel. Now that was a tragedy. But all I know is what I see on CNN. Just like you."

"Did you make it down in time, Jimmy? Did you get to see the blood? Smell the bodies?" Jack glanced at me. "Jimmy developed an appetite for blood in the jungle and now he's got to feed it. It's hard to do back in the world."

"Everybody finds their own way back to the world. I adjusted to the world as well as you did." Jimmy cocked his head back and stared up at Jack. "You want a beer, Ace? We could raise a toast to old times."

Jack's jaw tightened. Now it was Jimmy glancing in my direction. I tried not to look as nervous as I was. "How about your friend? Maybe she'd like one. How much does she know about you, anyway?"

The air in the house was starting to feel explosive, and I could almost hear the sound of the two men brushing against each other like two sheets of sandpaper, raw and ready to throw off an igniting spark. The second Jack took a step toward the couch, I spoke up.

"I think I will have a beer. Can I get you one, Jimmy?"

I made a point of stepping between them instead of

walking around behind Jack to get to the kitchen. He had to take a step back to let me through. As I did, I gave him a little shove in the chest to move him back farther. The tension didn't dissipate, but it did seem to stabilize.

Jimmy's kitchen was only slightly larger than a galley on a wide-body aircraft, and at least as organized and efficient. Dishes were stacked neatly to drip-dry on the counter next to the sink. A matched set of pots and pans hung from a rack in the corner. Bottles of exotic looking oils in various shades lined a shelf over the stove. Jimmy Zacharias may have been a no-account scum in every other part of his life, but his kitchen would have done Martha Stewart proud. Go figure.

"Beer's in the refrigerator, Mystery Lady."

"Coming up." I found the Tecate and took a bottle out for Jimmy. I thought it best not to join him. My brain was already mush and I was so sleep deprived I was only retaining about every fifth word anyone said to me, which made it difficult to keep up under the best of circumstances, which these most certainly were not.

I was looking for the bottle opener when I saw Bull. Actually, he saw me first. When I heard him snarling, I looked out the back kitchen window. It reminded me of standing in Mae's kitchen back home what seemed like a hundred years ago. I had watched Mae's dog Turner chasing after squirrels in his goofy not-quite-a-puppy loping gait. This dog was chained to a stake in the ground, which in my opinion was not nearly substantial enough. His eyes were like two shiny black marbles as he pulled against his restraints and watched me through the window. Mostly I saw his teeth. Long, white, and sharp, and covered with the foam that came frothing out of his mouth every time he threw another canine invective my way.

I brought the bottle out to Jimmy and handed it to him. Jack was at the front window, peeking out through the yellow curtains. He spoke without turning.

"Did you ever see the logbook from the Air Sentinel crash, Jimmy?"

"Did they show it on CNN?"

Jack turned his attention back inside the house. "Here's the way I've got it figured. Bobby Avidor was working for you, helping you salvage the wreckage that you stole, when he came upon the logbook. That's got to be worth something, right? The logbook from a fatal crash. So he stashes it. Sends it home to his mother. That wouldn't be a big deal except his mother found the whole thing ghoulish. She gave the book to an old family friend whose name was John McTavish. John figured out what was going on and came down here, looking for Bobby and loaded for bear. Bobby called you and had to explain the whole problem and that he caused it because he took this logbook without telling you. Because he did, you could have heat coming down on you. So you killed McTavish. What do you think?"

"You always could spin a good tale, Ace, but nobody gets killed over airplane parts. You're talking about the death penalty. It's not worth it."

"You haven't heard the best part. The book wasn't all Bobby stole from you. Somewhere in all that mess, he found a finger or a jewelry box or something and with it a diamond ring, and that diamond ring was worth twenty-five grand."

One of Jimmy's eyebrows twitched.

"Bobby didn't share that with you, did he? Somewhere in his pea brain he thought that little detail would get lost and he would never have to answer to you."

"How would you know any of this?"

"That's what I'm leading up to. I had a discussion with Agent Damon Hollander of the Federal Bureau of Investigation. Your handler."

"What the fuck, handler? What are you talking about?"

"Shut up, Jimmy, and listen. Damon knew about the book, but not the ring. That tells me his information came from you, and your information had to come from Bobby. Why would you be talking to the Bureau unless you were working for them?"

"You're the one with all the answers." Broad sweat bands were growing on Jimmy's shirt under his arms. "You tell me."

Jack took a step forward and squared himself so he was facing Jimmy head on. "Damon's got you by the balls, and he's got your little Ecuador operation out there in the swamp shut down, and he's got agents keeping the hangar secure. The way I see it, you scavenged a crash site, stole the parts, committed a whole list of federal offenses, and got caught. And yet here you sit in your crummy little shack, free as a bird. It just gets curiouser and curiouser, Jimmy. How far would you go to stay out of jail?"

Jimmy sipped his beer.

"The only thing I couldn't figure was what information you had that would be worth anything to Damon. And now I have that piece, too. What do you think Ottavio would do to you if he knew you were selling him out to the U.S. government?"

"First of all, I am no fucking snitch and I never will be. Even you should know that. I would never be a snitch for anyone." Jimmy threw an arm up and let it rest along the back of the couch. "And second of all, we're pretty isolated out here. I don't know any of these people you're talking about."

"Do you have an alibi for that Monday night? Because Bobby does."

"I don't have to account for my time to you, Ace."

Jack moved even closer to Jimmy. "You would have been better off taking out Avidor than a civilian."

"That's right. You've got a thing for civilians." Jimmy kept his head low as he looked up at Jack. "Are you sure you don't want a taste of something? Tequila is your drink, if I'm remembering right. A shot of tequila with a Tecate chaser sounds good to me. I might even have some lime out there. And if you're lucky, maybe the Mystery Lady will serve you, too."

A hot breeze wafted through the screen on the front door, bringing with it the smell of stale brown water and moss covered trees. The only sound in the room was the spinning of the fan on the floor, and before anything at all had happened, I knew it was already too late.

I stepped forward. "Jack, maybe we should—"

Jimmy was up. All in one motion, he had put his feet on the floor, dropped the bottle of beer, and started for Jack. His other hand, the one that had been dangling behind the back of the couch, came forward. He was holding something. A gun. Jack was over the coffee table and driving into the Georgia peach on Jimmy's chest. They landed in a heap on the couch. The couch shoved into an end table. The lamp on the table crashed to the floor. The bulb exploded. As loud as a gunshot, the pop reverberated through the steaming house and out to the backyard, where Bull heard it and went crazy.

They rolled off the couch to the floor. The coffee table shot across the room as if it had been on wheels. I had to jump out of the way or take it in the shins. Jimmy was on top of Jack. They were grunting, scratching, yelling at each other. They were a pile of swinging elbows. Their legs whipped at each other. Jack was larger and more powerful. He gripped Jimmy's right wrist, just below the hand that held the gun. I knew there was something I could have been doing, but it was happening so fast . . . I had no instinct for it. I stayed where I was, next to the kitchen counter, and somewhere at the edge of my concentration, I heard Bull. His deep chested, big dog bark was getting louder. I saw him through the front door. He was dragging the iron spike behind him at the end of a long chain, and he was almost to the steps. I made a dive to close the door, tripped over someone's foot, and fell flat, rattling my teeth and knocking all the air from my lungs. All I saw was Bull's broad chest as he launched himself up the steps and against the screen door.

I put my hands over my head. He was going to land right on top of me. I heard the crash against the screen door, which inexplicably held fast. I raised my eyes to see him there, still on the other side, his big paws braced on the collapsing screen. He was close enough that I could feel his hot breath and see the black stains on his pink gums.

I crawled toward the door, reached for it with my

fingertips, and sent it sailing shut. It bounced hard against the dog's snout and came wheeling back. Now he was really pissed off. With one strong jump, his whole head and chest would be through the flimsy screen—and he'd be bringing his teeth. I stood up, swung the door as closed as it would go, and threw my weight against Bull's. He was powerful, and close enough to tear off my ear. I dug my feet in and gave it one more push. The door closed and latched tight.

When I turned around, the room was in complete disarray, with furniture and tables thrown around and knocked to the side. Jack was sitting on the floor, propped against the couch with Jimmy's raggedy body draped over his like a blanket. His arm went easily across the slimmer man's chest to where he'd grabbed hold in the opposite armpit. With his other hand, he held a gun, his .22, to Jimmy's ear. Jimmy's gun was on the floor next to them. I went over and picked it up carefully and laid it on the console stereo.

"Do you remember how heads used to fly apart in 'Nam? Did you ever wonder what that felt like, Jimmy, when you did that to people?" Jack's voice was loud enough to be heard over the dog, and as harsh and cutting as it had been in the bar when he'd been mad at me, but it came from someplace deeper, some toxic pit that was filled with more rage and hate than he could ever have for me, that was perhaps reserved just for Jimmy. "A .22 is not an M-16, but it will have to do."

His tone was odd, dead. It was like a trickle of icy water running through that sweltering place. I moved over to the window. Bull was on the porch. He had destroyed the screen barrier. He was now trying to tunnel through, scraping frantically with his sharp nails, working hard at it. The thought of being out there with him was terrifying. But it scared me less than the scene playing out inside the house.

"You know what, Ace? I never think about that shit anymore." Jimmy's voice was a tight rasp. "You're talking about your own nightmares, not mine."

"Don't fucking call me Ace," Jack lifted his elbow and jammed the barrel of the gun against Jimmy's ear.

"Jack." The dog threw himself against the door again. *"Jack, damn it, we have to get out of here."*

"You need to taste some blood, Ace?" Jimmy was yelling, too, now. We were all yelling over the yowling animal. "All good soldiers like the taste of blood. And so did you. You're no different than me, and you never were." Jimmy's face was sunburn red against his silver hair. "The job was to kill—kill as many of them as we could as fast as we could. And it didn't matter if you blew them up or cut off their heads or shot them fifty times. Dead is dead. And you did all the same things I did."

I could see every muscle and every vein in the forearm Jack had lashed across Jimmy's heaving chest. His face was almost completely hidden except for his right eye, which stared out at nothing, maybe into that same place he was looking the other night at the laundromat.

"I know you, Dolan. I've always known guys like you. You tell yourself you didn't like the killing. You know what I think? I think you liked it a little more than you want to admit to yourself. I think—"

"Shut up, Jimmy." It took a second for me to realize the words had come out of my mouth.

"You liked it, Dolan, and you know it."

I had to make him stop talking. I grabbed the gun off the stereo. It was heavy. A revolver. I knew a revolver didn't have a safety. I raised it and pointed it toward the door.

"That's why you're a drunk. That's why—"

"Stop talking right now, Jimmy, or I'm going to shoot your dog."

With both hands holding the gun steady, I prayed Jimmy wouldn't open his mouth again, because I didn't know if I could pull the trigger. And if I did, what happened then? Five seconds went by. Bull was still agitating, the iron spike clanging against the front steps. Ten. If it was possible for me to hold even more still, I did, willing my internal organs—heart, lungs, stomach, kidneys, liver—to pause their orderly function while I waited. Twenty seconds and he still hadn't spoken.

I walked over and crouched next to Jack. "If you're going to kill him, tell me now because I don't want to watch. If you're not, we're leaving here."

The two men breathed in unison, as if they shared the same set of lungs. I had no idea if Jack was capable of shooting this man in cold blood. He shifted his weight and drove the barrel into Jimmy's ear. I shrank back, believing he was going to do it. Instead, he twisted the gun until a stream of bright red blood appeared. It trickled down, met up with a river of sweat, and spread down Jimmy's throat. Jack put his mouth close to Jimmy's other ear. "Yours is the only blood I want to see." Then he dumped Jimmy onto the floor and staggered to his feet.

Jimmy crawled to the edge of the couch and pulled himself up. Several strands of hair that had come loose

357

from his ponytail stuck to the sweaty, bloody stream that covered the side of his face and throat. He touched his ear with his fingers, saw the blood, then pulled off his shirt, wiped his face with it, and balled it into a compress for his wound.

Jack shook himself out. His head and shirt were soaked. I thought I saw his hands tremble as he switched the gun from one to the other. Jimmy was bloody, but still sharp-eyed and alert. If there had been a tremor, he had seen it, too. We had to get out of that house.

As I moved toward the window to look out, I realized I still had the gun and didn't know what to do with it. I wasn't going to leave it for Jimmy to take a few shots as we pulled out.

"Keep it," Jack said, guessing what I was thinking, "until we get out of here."

"Tell Bull to sit down, Jimmy," I said, still watching out the window.

"Fuck you."

"He's either going to sit down," Jack said, "or I'm going to shoot him. One way or another we're walking past him."

Jimmy stood up on shaky legs, walked over to the door, and called through the door. "Back off, Bull."

"Don't tell him to go away," I said. "Tell him to sit there."

Bull seemed skeptical when he heard his orders, but he was also well trained. He went down to the bottom of the steps and sat, waiting eagerly for Jimmy to emerge.

"Jack, I think we should lock the dog in the house and take Jimmy with us as far as the car."

Jack grabbed Jimmy's ponytail, wrapped it twice

around his hand, and pointed the gun to the back of his head. "I'm not with the Bureau anymore, asshole. I don't have to play by their rules. And when I get enough to prove you killed McTavish, I'm coming back for you."

"Here's a bulletin for you, Dolan. I didn't kill anyone. And I'm not a fucking snitch. Stop telling people that I am."

"Alex, get behind me." I did. "Open the door," he said to Jimmy, "wait until we're off the porch, then order the dog into the house. I've got no problem putting him down. It's up to you."

Jimmy let his hand rest on the knob. When he opened the door, he let in a blast of humidity that seemed to have been leaning against the door, eavesdropping. I stood behind Jack with my hand on his back as Jimmy moved out first, opening the screen door. All that was left was the frame.

Bull watched intently as the three of us moved in unison down the steps and past him. Jimmy talked to him all the way, trying to keep him calm. He looked like a torpedo in the tube as he trembled against every canine instinct in his body.

Once we were past, Jack told Jimmy to order him into the house. After he'd done it, I crept up the steps to close the door. Bull stared at me from inside with vicious intent. The most perilous moment was when I had to lean inside to reach the doorknob. Bull looked at me in the grim light of that house and I figured I had one chance. I took a deep breath, focused on the knob, thrust my arm forward and grabbed it. The instant the door was closed, he was there, scraping from the other side, and it wasn't clear to me he wouldn't try to come through one of the windows.

"Jack, let's go."

Jack had Jimmy lie flat on his stomach in the yard and put his hands behind his head. He took Jimmy's gun from me, opened the chamber with a quick flick of his wrist, and emptied the bullets out in his hand. He threw them down the long driveway, then heaved the gun in the opposite direction.

It was my turn to have shaky hands, and I could barely fit the key into the ignition. Jack climbed in the passenger side and shut the door, sealing us in with the sour odor of sweat and fear.

"Go. *Go!*" he yelled, twisting around to see what I was seeing in the rearview mirror. Jimmy was up and heading for the front door of his house, and I wished I'd thought to lock it.

I finally got the key in, turned the engine over. I felt Jack's reaction a split second before I heard the thud. As loud as a gunshot, it reverberated, filling the inside of the sweltering car and making me feel as though the big dog had leapt with full force and fury right into my arms. In fact, he had thrown himself against the passenger side door—Jack's door—and stood there now, his big paws braced on the glass, his chain and his spike rattling, his big teeth banging on the glass as he tried to chew through it.

Jack had pulled away from the window to my side of the car; his shoulder bumped my elbow as I put the car in gear. As I hit the gas and pulled away, I caught a glimpse of Jimmy, watching from the doorway, lounging casually, shirtless. He was laughing. We left him exactly where we'd found him.

★ ★ ★

"Pull over." Jack's tone left no room to question.

I checked my mirrors and started to pull to the shoulder. Before we rolled to a stop, his door was open. He leaned out as far as he could, straining against the seat belt, and threw up.

I stared at my hands on the steering wheel and listened to him gasping and choking and spilling his guts out all over the side of the road.

When he was done, he pulled inside the car and fell back against the headrest. He left the door open.

I looked at his face, damp and pale in the midday heat. He raised his arm to wipe it with the sleeve of his shirt. This time his hand was clearly trembling.

"What happened back there?"

He turned his eyes toward me and did not appear to have the energy to respond. But he did. "You were there. You saw the whole thing. I did what I went to do."

"Put us both in the most absurdly risky position you could think of?"

His head rolled back to center and he closed his eyes.

"Did you know going in that he might pull a gun on us?"

The mention of a gun reminded him that his was still stuck in the waistband of his pants. He pulled it out and leaned down to re-holster it at his ankle.

"I asked you a question, Jack. Did you plan that?"

"It was a calculated risk, but you were safe."

I wanted to lay into him like a pile driver, but my tongue was thick with the fear that had started in that shithole house and, now that we were safe, was turning more to rage with every word he stammered. There was

361

only one thing I could get out. "Fuck you, Jack. Fuck you."

The smell of sweat and vomit, the humidity, the reheated adrenaline—it was all beginning to get to me, and my own stomach felt ready to blow. I opened the window on my side and took in a few deep breaths. The air was tinged with smoke. "What's between the two of you?"

"I told you what's between us."

"There's more. There's something you're not telling me."

"You said you wanted to tag along. This is how it goes sometimes."

"No." I turned in my seat to face him. "He knows things about you. He knows things I don't know, which puts me at a disadvantage if I choose to stand next to you, especially, Jack, if you might murder him one of these days when I'm with you."

He turned and looked at me with that same dead calm I'd seen in his eyes back at the house, only now it just looked dead.

"Take me back to the Beach. Or anywhere close. I'll find my way home."

I turned and faced forward, hands on the wheel. "Would you have killed him?"

"Every time I see him I want to put a bullet through his head. I haven't done it yet."

"He's not afraid of you, Jack."

"I need to get out of this car, Alex. If you don't want to drop me somewhere, I'll get out and walk."

I completely forgot that his door was still open. But that was all right because I pulled out so fast it slammed shut all by itself.

Chapter Thirty-Six

I lay on the bed in my hotel room staring at my favorite sprinkler head in the ceiling. I'd been watching it for a few hours and it hadn't moved, so I could have broken off surveillance, if only I could have closed my eyes. The sun was going down. I could tell by the way the shadows played across the wall. I'd been trying to sleep ever since I'd dropped Jack off and driven, in a complete trance, back to the hotel. I was thinking of going up to the track on the roof for a short run. That would have been stupid. My ankle was basically healed, but I hadn't slept in thirty-six hours. It was early evening, not too hot, clouds had moved in and turned the sky gray, and it felt like months since I'd been out. I thought if I didn't get up and move around, I might just fall into a permanent stupor from which I'd never return. Yep, running was a dumb idea, and I was lacing up my shoes when the phone rang. I answered, hoping it was Jack.

"Do you know who this is?"

It would have been hard not to recognize that blend of youthful arrogance and smug vitality. "Yes, Damon, I know it's you."

"We need to talk. Tonight."

I walked the long line of batting cages at the Miami Tides recreation center, peering into each one as I passed. Special Agent Damon Hollander was taking his swings in the very last cage. He was decked out in gray cotton jersey shorts, clean white socks, and cleats. His shirt-sleeves were three-quarter length, the kind baseball players wear under their uniforms. He looked as professional and crisp as anyone I'd ever seen in sweat clothes.

As I approached, he adjusted the shiny batting helmet on his head, assumed his stance, and waited for the next ball to come out of the chute and hurtle toward him.

"I'm here," I said. "What do you want?"

He hit the ball foul. He didn't look at me, just pushed up his sleeves, as if it was the extra weight on his forearms that had thrown off his swing. He then proceeded to pound four straight against the back netting—every one on the nose—leaving the perfect aluminum ping vibrating in the air. He turned and looked past me, back the way I had come.

"Is Dolan with you?"

"You told me to come by myself. Why is that, Damon?"

He dropped in the last of the quarters he had sitting on the machine and swapped his aluminum bat for a wooden one.

"Because Jack Dolan is a drunk"—*Thwack*. A low liner in the direction of left field—"and I don't trust him."

Crack. A hard opposite field arc that would have surely cleared the wall at Jacob's Field, or at least the short porch at Yankee Stadium. I envied his swing—so graceful, fluid, and consistent.

"You trust me?"

"I trust you not to be stupid and emotional."

"You might be giving me too much credit, Damon."

He hit the rest of the pitches, fastballs every one, right

on the nose, and I was willing to bet anything he couldn't hit a curve. I wanted to see him try, but I was also willing to bet that Damon never did anything unless it was a sure thing. He came out of the cage and we walked over to a wooden bench where he had his gear. A light sheen of moisture had appeared on his forehead, which made him seem to glisten. He pulled a towel from his gym bag and wiped his face.

"What do you want, Damon?"

"I asked you to come so I could deliver a message. The message is for you. You can give it to him, too, if you want. Or not. I don't care."

"What's the message?"

"Go home."

He dug around in the gear bag until he came up with a water bottle. He tipped his head back and squeezed a long, slow stream into his mouth.

"You delivered that message already."

"And you're still here."

I sat down next to him. I was tired. "I might consider going home if I had some assurance the FBI was looking into my friend's murder."

"I'll do that. I'll see that your friend's murder is properly and thoroughly investigated."

The sound of ball bashing was all around us—tight pings as balls hit aluminum, the sharp cracks of wooden bats on horsehide. I looked up into the sky, black behind the high lights. I knew what was out there. Dark clouds heavy with rain, ready to open up and pour down, and not a moment too soon if you were a firefighter. I couldn't figure Damon's angle. There were lots of options. Easier to just ask. "Why would you do that?"

"It's my job."

"And . . . ?"

"People are always telling me I'm young to be in the position I'm in, to have achieved all that I've achieved."

"You must be very proud."

"My success comes from a simple approach. I anticipate all possibilities and eliminate the ones that don't get me what I want."

"And I'm one of those rogue possibilities."

"If it takes making that commitment to you, that John McTavish's death—"

"His murder."

"That his murder is investigated, if that's what it takes to get you to leave Florida, then I'm willing to do it."

"And if the investigation leads to Jimmy Zacharias?"

He shrugged. "I can't predict the outcome. The investigation will lead where it leads. All I can tell you is we'll do a thorough and professional job."

A few cages away, a dad was showing his son how to hold a bat. It was a big bat and a little boy, but they were having fun. It made me think of John's sons, Matthew and Sean. Sean would never know his father. "He must have wandered into something really big."

"McTavish? He did. And he paid a price. If you continue to pursue this matter, you could easily be killed, which would be a shame. I assume Dolan has at least tried to impress that on you. If he hasn't, shame on him. There's no question if you stay here, you will compromise my operation."

"And you're unwilling to tell me what that is."

"It's better for you if you don't know."

He tipped his head back again and took in a long

stream of refreshment. He was making me realize how dry my mouth was. All the time. I'd been dehydrated ever since I'd set foot in Florida. The rain was going to feel good. "I won't leave because you tell me to go. You're going to have to give me something."

"What would you need to be convinced?"

"Give me information so I can understand. Is Jimmy your informant?"

"I won't tell you that."

I stood to leave.

"What I will say"—he waited, and I decided not to walk away—"is I work with a number of confidential informants. I have one that is highly placed and in a highly sensitive position right now, and you doing what you're doing can compromise that person's safety."

I sat back down on the bench. "This hypothetical informant, why would he be cooperating with you?"

"Informants cooperate for all different reasons. They don't want to go to jail, they want revenge, they're scared. Sometimes they want a competitor out of the way."

"Would this informant give you access to multiple targets?"

"Why would you ask that?"

"Because I have more information now. I know, for instance, that you've been over to see George Speath. I suspect it was to clean up after Jimmy and pick up the dirty parts he loosed upon the town. I give you credit for at least that much."

"I can't discuss the details of my investigation with you."

I pushed out farther on the bench and angled so that

I could watch his eyes. "I know that George Speath is using his station to launder dirty money." If Damon had a reaction, he didn't show it to me. He seemed marvelously calm and unconcerned. "And I know that Ottavio uses a bunch of Jimmy's stations to launder his drug proceeds, which might give you what you need to nail the drug lord and get the big bust."

One nostril twitched negligibly, but he could have been sniffing for rain. And I could have been quoting Dr Seuss to him for all the tension in his face. He retained a pleasant, unbothered expression. "Let's just say it's a big investigation and leave it at that."

"Does Vanessa know that Jimmy is a snitch?"

"Who's Vanessa?"

"That's what I thought. So she would be very interested if I told her about Jimmy. That if Jimmy brings down Ottavio, she goes down right beside him."

"Why would you even think of doing something like that?"

"I'm checking to see how much my chips are worth."

"Your chips aren't worth anything if you're dead. The stakes in this game are too high for you." He had such a patronizing way of speaking to me, I knew I was in danger of doing something stupid just because he'd told me not to.

"Let me ask you something else, Damon. How does a confidential informant, a guy working for the government, end up with the wreckage of a Triple Seven in his garage?"

"Again, I don't know what you're referring to, but as a rule, you can't control a CI all the time, and sometimes they do stupid things. They are criminals."

368

"Would Jimmy have been stupid enough to kill John? If John were going to screw up whatever deal you made with Jimmy and it looked as though he were going to jail, would he have killed John?"

"I don't know who killed him. That's why we investigate. To find out."

I sat on the wooden bench and listened to the subtle rumbling in the distance. The thunder sounded far away, but the air was starting to feel electric with the coming storm.

"There's one thing I don't know, Damon, and I don't know how to find out except to just ask you. If Jimmy did kill John, would you let him get away with it to bust Ottavio? Is it that important to you?"

Another rumble in the sky, this one louder and closer, drove the father and his son out of the cage and toward the exit. The little kid wanted to stay.

"I'll tell you this much," Damon said. "I would never risk blowing my informant's cover for stolen aircraft parts."

"That much is clear, and it's not what I asked you."

He pulled a windbreaker out of his bag and pulled it on. "This operation you're threatening to screw up, I've been working on it for almost two years. A number of people have been working on it for a long time, and we're *that* close. I believe as much as I believe anything that taking down my target is the most important thing I'll ever do. He's that bad. What he does reaches farther and does more damage than a single murder."

He tossed the plastic bottle into the bag and stood up. "And this is not a perfect world. But you know that."

He zipped his bag with a loud rip and slung it over

his shoulder. The aluminum bat jangled against the wooden one as he propped one foot on the bench next to me. "If you go away now, Dolan disappears back into his stupor or the woodwork or wherever it is he lives. If you stay here and keep pressing, there will be consequences—for both of you. It's up to you. That's the real message. It's your call."

Chapter Thirty-Seven

When I got out to the dirt parking lot the air was thick with the twin menaces of smoke and the impending thunderstorm. The wind had shifted and picked up, but it felt as if the night was getting hotter. I almost wondered if the fires were coming closer and raising the temperature.

Inside the car it was quiet enough to hear my own breathing, so when I got on the road, I tried the radio. The first station featured a Spanish-slinging DJ rattling off something in a deep baritone. It was the verbal equivalent of a bullet train. The next two stations had music playing, loud, peppy salsa tunes that were too boisterous for my dark mood. I stopped surfing when I found an English speaker. It was a talk show where people from all over the South called in to praise Jesus.

I turned it off when I realized with a creeping sense of alarm that I didn't recognize any of the scenery. Had I . . . ? Did I miss . . . ? I strained to find a landmark, something to convince myself that I wasn't totally lost. But when I looked out, it was into a darkness that seemed to extend from the edge of my high beams to forever. Somewhere along the way, I must have missed my turn back to the highway. Back to the *lighted* highway—that wide road with street lamps and big green direction signs. I didn't even know if I was going in the right direction. I decided to turn around and try going back the way I'd come. Maybe something would look familiar from the reverse angle.

I stiffened in my seat and clamped my hands to the steering wheel in the ten o'clock and two o'clock positions, just as they'd taught me in driver's ed, and pretty soon my face was damp and my chest was tightening because mile after mile went by without a place to turn around. No exits. No U-turns. Just a wide median of grass that sloped into a deep trough, probably to discourage people like me from creating their own turnarounds.

I was straining just to see through the darkness when I heard the first dull thud on the windshield. Then another. And another, and the rain was no longer coming. It was here, and it was coming down hard. It pummeled the windshield. I looked in all the obvious places for the wiper controls—God knows I hadn't had to use them so far—and when I finally hit the magic button, I discovered that even though my rental car was equipped with windshield wipers, sadly, they were not the kind that actually functioned.

My choice was to try to see around the wide, cloudy streaks they left with each creaky pass, or turn them off and try to see through the pounding rain unaided. Some wipers were better than no wipers, I decided, but then I had to scrunch down in my seat to see through the one clear line of sight they provided. I forgot about finding the way back. I had all I could handle keeping my vehicle on the road.

When I first saw the truck in the rearview, it was a couple of bright, runny specks in my lane, but far behind me. I stayed the course, puttering along at a stately fifty-five miles an hour. When I looked again, the truck was closing fast. He must have been pushing ninety, and he wasn't changing lanes. I tapped the brakes lightly to

make sure he could see me. His headlights got bigger—
huge. Over the sound of the rain, I could hear him
rattling over the wet road—that and the sound of my
own thick breathing. I looked to the right for a place
to bail out. If he hit me from behind, I didn't want to
be launched over whatever was out there that I couldn't
see. I made a move to the left lane, the inside lane, thinking I'd rather be down in the median trough than down
with the alligators. But no sooner had I committed than
he did, too, and there was no way he was going to
change course again at that speed. His horn blared into
the night as I jerked the wheel hard and skidded back
to the right. I went onto the shoulder and ricocheted
back, barely holding it in my lane.

He threw a serious backwash over my windshield, so
I couldn't see him, but I could feel him thundering by
my driver's side door, his wheels inches away from my
left shoulder. And I could hear him. They probably could
have heard him back in Boston as he laid on the horn,
letting it blast out angrily into the night until he was
well past me, still going ninety, his red taillights blurring
together in my cloudy windshield.

My insides untwisted, and then shuddered with a dose
of adrenaline that I could taste in my mouth. I wanted
to stop moving. I wanted to be still for a moment and
ponder what had certainly been a near death experience, and savor the fact that I was still breathing, but
the rain was still coming down and I was getting farther
and farther away from where I wanted to be. Now there
was another car behind me, and what the hell did he
want because he was almost on top of me. Must have
been behind the truck.

I tapped the brakes. He sped up. I moved to the other lane, making a slow, gradual transition. He stayed right on my tail. I tried to see who was driving. Saw nothing. His lights were up in my eyes. It was a pickup or an SUV, something bigger and more powerful than my Chevy. Probably four-wheel drive. The wipers kept slashing at the rain with a terrible scraping sound, reminding me that I was in a driving rainstorm with limited visibility. There was no way I was going to outrun them, and there was no way I was going to outdrive them. I let the car slow down gradually as I felt around blindly for my backpack. My phone. My phone was inside the pack. *There*. It's there. He was honking now and I was pulling out my phone and wrapping my hands around it and flipping it open. No signal. I felt like smashing it against the dashboard.

I rolled to a stop but left the engine running and kept the car in gear. The truck pulled in behind me. The driver killed the headlights, and I saw them—two silhouettes, dark shapes visible from the shoulders up. As they sat and talked, I listened to my engine running and to the sound of the rain, which was tapering off to a slow, steady patter. I was breathing, but just barely, in a rhythm that was shallow and quick.

The driver's door opened. There was no mistaking the tall, skinny build of the man who stepped out, and I almost did stop breathing. It was Jimmy.

I bit my lower lip to keep from going numb. I could see that he was about to slam his door shut, and the loud pop still made me jump. He was wearing jeans, a cowboy hat, and a tank top with armholes that reached to his waist. As he approached, I saw that his shirt was oddly bunched on one side, held there by the gun stuck in his belt. I lifted an unsteady foot. He put his hand on the door latch. I jammed the gas pedal to the floor. The car hesitated, lurched, and blasted off the shoulder. The wheels spun on the wet roadway for an agonizing interval. Then the four tires caught hold, slung the car forward like a rocket, and slammed me back against the seat.

In the rearview, I saw Jimmy scramble back to the truck. I hadn't planned anything beyond the swift take-off. All I knew to do was to keep going until something else happened.

It did. They caught up.

Jimmy pulled up close and rammed my bumper. My head snapped back. They were next to me. Then they were in front of me, and I had nowhere to go. I had to stop when they did.

In the seconds it took Jimmy to cover the space between our cars, I searched my car's interior, the glove box, the floor, for anything to use as a weapon. Jack's .22 caliber automatic was sounding like a good idea to me right then. Jimmy rattled the handle on my door. When he started to go for the gun I unlocked it. The dome light came on. I felt a hand on the back of my head, then fingers twisting into my hair. I tried to pull away toward the passenger side, but he yanked my head straight back. The rest of my body followed and I spilled out of the car backwards and cracked my head on the pavement.

It took a few seconds for my vision to clear and my brain to regain focus. This time, both men were out of the car. The passenger stayed in the shadows. I couldn't see anything but his thick neck and bulky shape. Jimmy stood over me.

"It's the Mystery Lady." He reached down, grabbed me under my armpits, and leaned me up against the car. When I could stand by myself and didn't feel dizzy, I pushed his hands away. I heard a low rumble, which was not thunder. Jimmy's pickup truck was parked directly in front of my Lumina, and standing in the back was Bull. His fur was slick from the rain. His glassy eyes were on me. He was hot and panting and when he saw me staring, another vicious rattle worked its way up from his broad, muscled chest. I blinked the rain out of my eyes.

Jimmy leaned in so his face was close to mine. A stray hair from his ponytail brushed my cheek, and his powerful scent drifted into my sinuses and stayed. It was oily skin and tobacco and dirty clothes and wet dog, and I wondered if he meant to kill me.

I tried to turn away, but he clamped a viselike hand on my jaw and held it. "I want you to give Dolan a message for me, and I want you to tell it to him exactly as I say it."

When he took his hand from my face, my skin burned where he had touched me. He grabbed my wrist, pulled it chest high, and stuffed something into my palm. It felt like a plastic bag filled with warm milk. He wrapped his fingers over mine and squeezed. Something leaked down my forearm. Bull sniffed the air, twitched, and went into a yelping frenzy. Jimmy told his dog to shut the fuck up. The other man didn't seem to want to go near the beast.

"Tell Dolan I am no fucking snitch, and tell him if

he doesn't back off, I'm not going to kill him"—he gave my hand a sharp twist and whatever was trickling went all the way down my arm and dripped off my elbow— "I'm going to kill you, Mystery Lady. Tell him to remember what happens to civilians who get in the way. In my way."

Even in the dark I could see how he looked at me, how he wanted me to be scared of him. It was almost as if he needed for me to be scared of him, and I was. But I also had a dim, throbbing thought that if I had something Jimmy needed, I sure as hell shouldn't give it up. My lungs felt as useful as a couple of big rocks and I could barely stand up, but I locked my jaw tight, forced myself to breathe deeply through my nose, and wondered if that was blood splattering out of my nostrils. I grabbed on to every vicious, angry moment that had ever burned inside me, wrapped them all into one laser stare, and channeled it directly from my eyes into his. Then I snapped my wrist and twisted my hand out of his bony grasp.

He didn't seem to know what to make of it.

"Keep your hands off of me."

A couple of cars went by on the other side of the median. The second man, who until then hadn't said a word, called to Jimmy in Spanish from the far side of the truck. Jimmy didn't move.

"Why—" I had to clear the dryness from my throat. "Why don't you deliver your own messages?"

"I like this way better."

"Maybe it's because you're afraid of Jack."

His smile was quick. "He's afraid of me. He's always been afraid of me. You can tell him I said that, too."

The lookout called again and must have pointed, because Jimmy's head turned. I looked to see where he was looking, at two headlights approaching on our side of the road. As they came closer, the car decelerated as if the driver might be interested in the show. Please, God, please make him interested enough to stop.

Jimmy leaned down and pretended to be looking at my tire. Bull stared from the truck. He'd caught a scent and was sniffing the air, whining miserably. Jimmy straightened and gave the passing car a friendly wave. They moved on.

"Deliver the message," he said. "Tell Dolan to fuck off, you go back to where you came from, and if you're real lucky you'll never see me again."

He opened his door, slid behind the wheel, and roared out even as his door was closing. Bull slipped against the tailgate, then found his balance and stood in the back of the truck, head raised to the rain, barking.

I stood for a long time feeling as if I were suspended there in the dark, hanging by the slimmest of threads to something above that held fast and kept me from total collapse. I couldn't swallow. My muscles wouldn't respond. I forced myself to breathe. Oxygen began to flow. I began to feel my body again.

Jimmy had torn out a handful of my hair, but my whole scalp burned from it. Something was trying to bang its way out of my skull, hammering from the inside, mostly in the back where I'd hit the pavement. I closed my eyes. It helped, but neither bending over nor arching my back relieved the sharp pain that followed the path of my spine. My shoulder throbbed. Something was wrenched out of place. I rolled it up, back, and around, trying to work out the soreness. I reached down to my elbow to pull it into a stretch and felt the damp streaks on my arm. Whatever Jimmy had folded into my hand was still there, soft and mushy.

Like an idiot, or someone who'd been hit on the head recently, I tried to see in the bag, to figure out what it was in the near total darkness by the side of the road. Eventually, it occurred to me to get in the car and use the cabin light.

I opened the door. The incessant bonging began, a reminder to either close the door or take the keys from the ignition. My automatic response was to reach around the steering column to get them. When I did I saw the bright red streaks, like ribbons flowing across and around the pale skin of my other arm. I opened my hand.

It was red, it was in a plastic bag, and it was misshapen enough that at first I didn't recognize what I was holding. My stomach heaved. I tasted bile in my mouth. I was holding *a human ear*.

I dropped it as if it were a live scorpion. It fell on my leg. I twitched and convulsed in the car like a bird caught in a trap. I swatted it away so that no part of it would touch any part of me. It landed in one of the cup holders inches from my thigh. I had to get out, to get air, and I was on my feet, walking quickly away from the car, up the shoulder of the road, shaking out both my hands. The car was still bonging. My head, God my head ached. I turned and walked the other way, toward the car, passing it on the other side and continuing down the shoulder. My hair and the back of my shirt were damp from the rain and sweat and I was shivering. Either that or I was rock steady and the whole world was trembling around me. When I was far enough away, I stood staring at the Lumina from behind. I didn't see the car. I saw a detached human ear surrounded by a vehicle.

What in *hell* was I doing out here in the middle of *Florida* with a severed human *ear* in my car? This was so far away from my real life. I felt like crying. I almost laughed. *What* was I *doing*?

I paced the width of the car back and forth a few times. I decided that on my tenth round-trip I would continue walking to the open door. I stood outside looking at the smeary red Baggie. I reached across, opened the glove box, and found the free map that comes with all rental cars. I laid it out on the passenger seat. Then with two fingers, I lifted the dripping bag of horror by one corner, laid it on the paper, and folded it up. I put the whole package on the floorboard on the passenger side. Only then did I feel comfortable enough to get back in the car and close the door.

I started the car and drove directly across the road, down into the grassy trough of a median. The car rattled and bounced, the tires spun in the mud, and it was a struggle to get up the other side. But I made it, and I found my way and I drove all the way back into town with the dome light on.

Chapter Thirty-Eight

Jack opened the door and all I could think was thank God he was home. He was there and I was safe and I didn't want to but I couldn't help it and I cried. He reached out for me and I walked into him and held on and wept into his shoulder. The darkness and the rain and being lost and the way Jimmy had touched me and the way he had smelled; the way my own fear smelled; the ear in my hand—that small flap of cartilage and tissue through a warm, slick Baggie membrane. And then the thought of being in the hangar in the swamp with the corpse of a dead airplane and all the ghosts inside; the dog and the rat and the petrifying panic and the tension and the smell of blood and bones and bodies. A ring . . . a diamond ring torn from a dead woman's finger and slipped onto mine. It all came up and out with so much force—it was like a catapult that had been loaded up and loaded up and loaded up and finally launched and, once loosed, could not be called back.

I cried and cried and it was very possible I would never have let go if Jack hadn't disengaged to close the door. When he turned around I grabbed him again and he held on to me until I stopped shaking. I was still damp down to my bone marrow and I was getting him wet, too. I don't know how long it was before he gently took my arms and pushed me out far enough that he could check me over.

"Are you hurt?"

"No."

He took my left wrist and turned my hand palm up. "You have blood all over you."

"It's not my blood."

"Whose is it?"

"I don't know."

He looked at me, waiting for an explanation that I didn't think I could blubber out in any comprehensible manner. Instead, I handed over my car keys. "Go look on the floorboard on the passenger side of the car."

He took the keys. "Is it a surprise?"

I wiped my eyes. "It was for me."

Jack came over to the kitchen table and handed me my tea. I wrapped both hands around the cup, lifted it up, and felt the steam condensing on my face, which was still hot and thick from my crying. But at least I wasn't damp and cold anymore. I had taken a long, long, long hot shower and Jack had given me a sweat suit to put on. I sat at his kitchen table with my feet pulled up under me and a blanket wrapped around my shoulders.

The ear was there. Sitting on his kitchen table in the middle of the map-wrapping, it looked like some exotic specialty that had come straight from the butcher. Every time I looked at it I cringed. Jack reached over and pulled the blanket tighter around me.

"Tell me again," he said, "exactly what Jimmy said."

"That civilians sometimes die when they get in the way, in . . . no, in *his* way. Especially when they get in his way. That you should remember what happens then." I wasn't being terribly articulate, but it was coming out the way it had lodged in my head. "He said he's no

382

fucking snitch and if you don't stop saying so, he's not going to kill you, he's going to kill me. And he said you're afraid of him, that you've always been afraid of him."

He nodded, then leaned down and poked at the bag until the severed appendage was lying flat.

"He said to give you that ear."

"Yeah."

"Why? Do you know whose it is?"

"No, but that's not the point. It's part of the message. There were guys in Vietnam who liked to cut off ears to show how many people they'd killed. Jimmy liked to do that. We had a few discussions about it." He went back to the sink and twisted a couple of ice trays and dumped the frozen contents into an aluminum mixing bowl. I heard the cubes sliding around on the bottom. "He used to string them together and keep them in a little pouch."

"Why does he call you Ace?"

"The Ace of Spades is the death card," he said. "The Vietnamese thought it was bad luck. Grunts would wear them on their helmets. Sometimes they'd leave one sticking out of a corpse's mouth. They did it to scare the enemy, and sometimes as a warning."

I sneaked a glance at the ear. "Do you think this means Jimmy's killed someone else?"

"I don't know, Alex. Why did you go out there by yourself?"

"Damon said he wouldn't talk to me if you came. I tried to call you, Jack. Check with your service. I left a message."

"I went to meet Bobby," he said, "and I tried to call

383

you. We must have missed each other. Bobby called and asked to meet. He said he was ready to talk."

I searched my memory for the last thing I remembered about Bobby Avidor. "He's not dead?"

"He wasn't earlier this afternoon," he said. "Although he might be lighter by one ear. He could be dead *and* missing an ear."

"You didn't see him?"

"He never showed. Didn't call. I went to his house. No sign of him." He slipped the bowl of ice onto the table and set the ear gently on top. Most of what blood there had been in the bag had already seeped out when Jimmy had squeezed it into my hand. But there was still enough to dribble down and stain the ice cubes pink. He put the whole thing in the refrigerator, leaned back against the counter, and crossed his arms.

"Jack, do you think Damon set me up?"

"That's what it feels like to me."

"He didn't even give me a chance."

"A chance for what?"

"To go home. To . . . he said . . ."

I realized I hadn't shared with Jack any of the pre-storm, pre-ear conversation I'd had with Damon. "I need to tell you what he said."

"Tomorrow. You don't look too good. I want you to sleep."

"Can I stay here?" The words flew out of my mouth. The important parts of me were functioning on some back-up power system, because the primary source, my brain, had shut down.

"I wouldn't give you any other choice."

My eyes started to burn again. I pulled the blanket

384

around me, but no matter how tight I made it, it didn't feel like enough protection. If I was going to sleep, I needed the protection of his arms around me. "Jack, will you stay with me?"

He tilted his head and looked as if I was handing him a monumental responsibility that he took very seriously.

"Until I fall asleep. I feel safe with you." I was afraid he would say no. Instead he came over to me and reached for my hand. When I gave it to him, he pulled me up, put his hands on my shoulders, and steered me into his bedroom. He pulled back the covers and tucked me in, then he lay down and pulled sweatshirt, sheets, blankets, covers, and me all into a sheltering embrace. I closed my eyes and the world disappeared and I fell asleep.

The sun was trying to get in through the blinds when I opened my eyes again. Sounds from the unit next door floated in from somewhere, through the walls or the windows or the vents. Kids getting ready for school, so it must not have been too late.

I felt the weight of Jack's arm across my waist. I felt the solid comfort of his body curved around mine. He was still asleep, his breathing steady against my neck. I kept still and enjoyed the feeling. It had been a long time since I'd opened my eyes in a man's arms.

My mobility was limited if I didn't want to wake him up, so I let my eyes wander around his bedroom and saw what I could in the alternating light and shadows. It was neat, but not in a finicky way. More utilitarian. There wasn't much—a bed with a headboard, a tall four-drawer dresser, a closet with the door closed. But everything that was there had a place. All the books were on the bookshelves. The hardback titles, which were the only ones I could read, tended toward biographies and war books, many on Vietnam. *Hell in a Very Small Place*, *Vietnam: A History*, *The Things They Carried* by Tim O'Brien. There were several books by O'Brien. Books on World War II and some on law enforcement, and rows and rows of what looked like paperback mysteries. A compact and not very complicated stereo system fit on top of the dresser and I wondered where the CDs were. Sharing the space on the dresser with the stereo were three framed photos. I couldn't see what they were, but one looked like a graduation day, maybe his son graduating from high school. Along the floor leaning against the wall were a few citations from his days at the FBI and I wondered if they were going up or coming down.

I reached up as quietly as I could to the headboard, remembering that I had put my watch there the night before. My fingers brushed across a row of plastic jewel boxes. The CDs. I tried to crane my neck without moving too much to read the titles.

Classical, jazz guitar, rock—not much after 1975, a big blues collection with B. B. King, Keb Mo', and John Lee Hooker, what looked to be everything Leonard Cohen had ever recorded. At the far end was an entire section of artists I'd never heard of. I slipped one out but had to reach across Jack to do it and, in the process, woke him up. I could feel the shift in his breathing, followed by the slow turning and testing and stretching that signaled the return to consciousness.

He lifted the arm that had been wrapped around me, and left a cold swath where it had been. And when he untangled from me and rolled over on his back, I felt the chill of sudden and unwanted exposure.

I turned toward him but got twisted up in all the covers. His weight on top of the sheets and blankets held them taut and pinned me to the mattress. I had to pull some slack from the other side of the bed so I could roll up on my elbows and see his face.

His eyes were only half open when he looked at me from the cushy middle of one of his big pillows. "Feeling better?"

"Like a new person." I showed him the CD. "Jack, gospel music?"

He lifted his head enough to see what I was looking at. It was a small move that seemed like a big effort in the lazy glow of a good night's sleep. "What about it?"

"Do you like gospel music?"

"I do."

Huh. I'd never actually met anyone who liked gospel music. Or at least that I knew of. "What do you like about it?"

He let his head sink back on the pillow, rubbed his eyes, and yawned. "The singers are glorious. Their voices are amazing, and it's the most uncynical music there is. You don't have to figure anything out. Just listen. Simple. I like that."

"Quite a contrast to Leonard Cohen."

"I like them both." He smiled with his eyes closed. "I guess that makes me complex."

He drew in a deep breath and let it seep out slowly

387

through his nose. He did it a few more times and almost seemed to be breathing in the energy he needed to get up and start the day.

"Thank you for staying with me last night."

"You slept well," he said. "I woke up a few times and you never moved."

I had to reach over him to slip the CD back in its slot. Everything in its place. I felt him under me—solid, substantial, real. When I pulled back, he was looking at me, searching my face. "Your eyes are gray," he said.

"Ever since I was born."

"They're pretty." His hand was close enough that I could feel the warmth from it, and I knew he wanted to touch me and I was desperate for him to do it, but all he did was barely brush close enough to touch my hair.

"Jack . . ."

He took my left hand, the one that had held the severed ear, and pushed up the sleeve of my sweatshirt. He inspected the palm, the fingertips, the fingernails. Every part of my hand with his hands. He was in no hurry, and he was driving me crazy.

"Are you sure you're not hurt?"

"My head hurts."

He rolled up on his side and reached around and felt the tender place on the back of my skull. He ran his fingertip along the bare ridge where Jimmy had pulled out a handful of hair. "Here?"

"Yes." My face was very close to him now, to his chest. We were both wearing his sweatshirts, and I could smell the scent of his laundry, the sweet fragrance of the dryer sheets that had filled the Miramar Coin Op the night I'd sat on a pile of his laundry and put my arms around him. This time I decided to hold still and be quiet, go at his pace and hope he went where I wanted to go. "Jimmy pulled me out of the car," I said. "I hit my head on the cement."

"I'm sorry." He pulled me closer and kissed the top of my head. Then he lifted my chin and kissed my forehead. And then he rolled back and looked at me. "Why did you kiss me the other night?"

"Because . . . I was . . ." His hand had moved from my head to my shoulder, and his fingertips were exploring along the edge of the collar and underneath. "I kissed you because I was attracted to you. I am attracted to you."

His fingers kept moving back up to my head, then slowly down again, lower each time, finding their own path along the folds and crevices of the sweatshirt, like a stream following a dry creek bed. I was getting lost in his eyes, brown eyes that looked at me with the gentleness I had seen there from the beginning, and the desire he was letting show for the first time.

"Why didn't you kiss me back?" I whispered.

"I wanted to." He pulled me closer so he could reach all the way down my back. "It took all that I had not to."

"Why?"

"What I said. I'm not good with people." His hand had made its way under my shirt. The stream was more like a river now, pushing where it wanted to go, making its own way across my topography. "I get tired of disappointing people." He brushed his lips across mine.

"I'm not disappointed." I moved with the rhythm of

389

his hand floating over my skin. I reached for his leg and pulled it across my body. I wanted to feel him, too, but layers of bedding and clothing separated us and he seemed content to work through it all in his own time.

"I don't know why you want to be with me." His voice was getting ragged, and I could feel him against me, responding to me even through all the layers. I moved in closer and began to explore on my own, feeling along the vertebrae that ran down the middle of his back, climbing the steps one by one along the graceful slope up to his shoulders, and all the way down to the back of his legs, where I found thick, sturdy muscles. He shivered against me as I followed their line down and around and back up until I found the drawstring to his sweatpants.

"I don't think I'm good for you," he said, but not with much conviction.

"You don't get to decide that for me."

"I'm too old, I'm a drunk, I'm—"

I shut him up with a deep lingering kiss as I pulled the drawstring on his sweatpants. He'd already found mine and loosened it, and it didn't take long after that for me to crawl out from under the covers and for him to crawl out of his sweats and for both of us to kick all of it—covers and blankets and clothes and everything else that separated us—off of the bed and onto the floor until there was just the two of us making love.

We had pulled the pillows off the floor and the sheets over us as we lay on the bed together. Jack had gotten up to open the window, so the sounds of the wakening neighborhood were coming through along with a slight, cooling breeze. A gospel singer was on the stereo, someone I'd never heard of, but someone he liked. I liked her, too.

"Jack."

"What?"

"You're not like Jimmy."

He shifted, so my head rolled a little to the side and I had to readjust to fit again into the crook of his right arm and against his chest. He didn't answer.

"Jack."

"I heard you."

"That's what scares you, isn't it? You're not scared of him. You're afraid you're like him. You're not."

"How do you know?"

I raised my head and crawled up to look into his eyes. I turned his face to make sure he was looking at me. "The only thing you have in common with Jimmy Zacharias is you were both from Florida, and you both served in Vietnam, which put the two of you in the same place at the same time with the same set of crappy options." I curled into him and put my head down again. "It's not in you to be like him."

I listened to the music and tried not to think about the moment, coming soon, when we would have to get up and take showers—or maybe one together—and put our clothes back on and go back to the world. He was quiet, stroking my hair.

"Where did you grow up?" he asked.

"All over."

"Where were you the longest? Where do you think of as home?"

"Seattle."

"What neighborhood?"

"Ballard."

"Try to picture a company of North Vietnamese soldiers coming out of the trees one night in Ballard. It's foggy and it's hard to see. They look like ghosts carrying machine guns and hand grenades and rocket launchers. But they're not ghosts and they woke up in the morning pissed off and they walk in pissed off. They walk up and down the streets of the neighborhood rousting people out of bed, out of their homes. They bust into bedrooms and kitchens and living rooms and basements. They're looking for the husbands and the sons because this is supposed to be an enemy stronghold. They think they're there. They've been told they're there, and they find weapons, but mostly what they find are mothers and sisters and grandmothers and daughters." The slightest tremble crept into his voice. "They find babies."

I felt him stiffening. When I tried to put my arm around him, he turned so that it was hard to be close to him at all. I moved away and wrapped myself in the sheets.

"Now they're really pissed off, these soldiers. So they go up and down the streets of Ballard from house to house, killing the family pets—shooting the dogs and running the cats through with their bayonets, just for the hell of it. Just because they can. Now they're not sure what to do because if they leave all these people there alive, one of them could steal off and alert the enemy and they could end up in an ambush and all die."

"What do they do?"

392

"After a lot of arguing, they set all the houses on fire and they leave. They're walking out. They're almost out of there, when someone fires a shot. A shot is fired and all hell breaks loose. The soldiers become convinced they're under attack. They turn around and start shooting and they empty their weapons into this little neighborhood. They keep firing until there's nothing moving. Nothing."

The song on the CD changed, and he seemed to be listening. "It was so easy to kill people over there because after you'd been there for a while"—he made a flourish in the air with his hand, a magician's wave intended to make something disappear—"they weren't people anymore. You got so that you didn't even feel it. There never seemed to be any consequences."

"Is that story about you? Was it some village in Vietnam?"

"We killed them all."

"How many?"

"Seventeen."

"Were you under attack?"

"That's what the report said."

"What do you think?"

"I think"—he pressed the heel of his hand into his forehead just over his eye—"unless you've seen it, you can't imagine what the percussive force of an M-16 does to the human body. Bones shatter, organs and limbs explode, bits of skin and blood spray everywhere." He stared straight up at the ceiling. "I think . . . it didn't matter to us at all if we were under attack."

"Jimmy was there?"

"It was a good day for Jimmy."

I found his hand among the covers and held it and listened to the gospel singer. Jack was right about her voice. It was glorious—strong with the fervor of what she believed, pure in the simplicity of her convictions, and irresistible in the strong current of hope that pulled you along to be saved with her.

"Do you ever talk to anyone about this? Have you ever gotten help?"

"I've talked to shrinks. Bureau shrinks. I go to A.A. meetings."

"Do you share this stuff at your meetings?"

"What they tell you at those meetings is to put your faith in the higher power. The higher power. What is that? That's taking the weight off your own shoulders and putting it somewhere else. We all have to carry our own weight. In the end there's no getting away from the things you did."

I put my hand on his cheek and felt the hard cheekbone beneath his rough skin. I felt his whiskers against my palm. I felt the edge of his hairline with the tips of my fingers—all things that made him a human being.

"You said it yourself in the laundromat, Jack. The rules are different in war. You were twenty years old. It was dark. You were scared. You thought you were under attack. Whatever you did, you did. What happened there is part of you. It's part of what you've become just as it's part of what Jimmy has become. But in a different way."

"Different how?"

"You think about the people who died. You think about them as fathers and mothers and sons and daughters, people who could just as easily have been living in

394

Ballard, Washington as some province in Vietnam. You grieve for them. You understand that part of you was lost over there. Jimmy probably thinks . . . I can't say what he thinks. Maybe that's what makes him so mean."

"What?"

"He sees you, and there is so much about you that is good and honorable, and so much about him that is twisted and dead. He knows what happened to him. He knows what he is, and it really pisses him off."

He smiled. "You give him too much credit."

"Probably."

"You give me too much credit."

"You don't give yourself enough."

He pressed his cheek against my hand and closed his eyes. I looked at him and couldn't stop thinking about something I'd seen once on the Discovery Channel. It was about a climber who had fallen eighty feet down an icy cliff and was stranded where he lay for two days. When the rescuers came to get him, you couldn't tell by looking at him what his injuries were. He looked perfectly fine. But when they pulled off his boots, they were filled with blood, and when they cut away his pants, his injuries were almost too gruesome to look at. The misshapen forms below his knees were unrecognizable as part of the human leg. The sharp points of broken bones poked out through bloody gashes, and his toes were black, frostbitten stumps. Over thirty years later, Jack was still bleeding into his boots, getting up every day and trying to stand on broken and bloody stumps. I put my arm around him and pulled him close and wondered what, if anything, would ever help him heal.

Chapter Thirty-Nine

We were both hungry when we finally got upright, and didn't like the thought of cooking with an extra ear in the house, so Jack took me to breakfast at his favorite Cuban restaurant. Once again, the man behind the lunch counter knew Jack and greeted him warmly and offered to seat us at the best seat in the house, which was like all the other seats in the house—vinyl chairs at tables with laminated tops under baskets of fake ferns. After we ordered, the waiter brought some plain old tea for me and a strange brew for Jack—Cuban coffee.

"Too bad you don't drink coffee," he said. "This is great stuff."

It was a coffee cup full of milk with the blackest coffee I'd ever seen served on the side in a creamer.

"Alex."

"What?"

He checked around and leaned in so only I could hear him. "Do you always carry condoms in your bag?"

That made me laugh. I hadn't been with a man in so long I'd almost forgotten how to use them. "No. I bought them the other day. After the laundromat." I shrugged. "In case you changed your mind."

"Ah." He stared down into his cup and concentrated hard on his Cuban coffee ministrations. Either it was a highly complex procedure that took great concentration, or he was anxious for a change in the subject.

"I never told you what Damon said."

"Tell me now."

I did. I recounted the warnings and the veiled threats. I told him Damon had confirmed without ever saying so that Jimmy was his informant.

"I knew it," was his response. And then, "So?"

"So, what?"

"Are you going to take his advice, and Jimmy's, and go back to Boston?"

"I told you the other day I was staying."

"Things are different now. Jimmy threatened you."

"Yeah, it seems really dumb to stay here. The problem is, I don't feel driven by rational impulses. I don't feel the danger. Even when I think back on what happened last night, Jimmy scared me, but I still thought . . ." I stopped and searched for the words, trying to articulate something I didn't understand myself. "I don't know how to say it except I should have been more scared of him. I was more pissed that he would do that to me."

"Jimmy is dangerous. Killing is no problem for him. It would be dangerous for you to stay. That's not complicated."

"I know that. I know it would be stupid to stay. But the 'being stupid' argument is not persuasive. Apparently I'm willing to be stupid. So then I look at the other side of the equation. What are the right reasons to stay? That's even more problematic."

He was grinning at me. "This is great," he said. "You're such an analyst."

"You're making fun of me again."

"Yeah."

"This is the way I think."

"I know. It's fascinating. Keep going."

"I keep picturing myself checking out of the hotel, getting on a plane, and flying back to Boston. I envision the scene where I tell Mae I've given up. I'll say something like, 'I did everything I could, but now the authorities have to do the rest.' She'll thank me for all I've done. She thanks me every time I talk to her just for coming down."

I stared over Jack's shoulder at the warped wood paneling on the wall and the hand painted mural of Cuba in better days. "The truth is I couldn't care less about a job I signed up for in a city I've never been to. I can't see myself sitting at a desk anymore in my hose and my heels and my earrings, filling out head count reports and apologizing to some overwrought passenger because there are only fourteen seats in first class and he's number fifteen."

"Why is that a bad thing?"

"Because I feel as if I'm using him . . . using John's death as an excuse to keep me from doing what I should be doing. That's my dirty little secret. I'm not brave and honorable. I'm just less scared to stay here and face a homicidal killer than I am to go home and face my real life."

"That's bullshit."

"Excuse me?"

"First of all, what John did for you at Logan, I'm sure it was something you needed and no doubt he did stand up for you, and I know that's important to you, but no one's motives are ever as pure as you're trying to make his out to be. He got something out of it, too. Maybe he had to be the hero. Maybe that's why he's dead."

I thought about Mae standing in her kitchen, telling

me what I already knew, that John always wanted to save the world, and how she had wanted him to stop trying to save the world.

"And second, it sounds to me as if your old life is not enough for you anymore. You've found a life you like better."

"What life?"

"The life of an investigator."

"What?"

"You're good at this. You're a good investigator. You're smart. You ask the right questions. You can read people. You're tough enough, especially if Jimmy doesn't scare you, although that might fit in the category of recklessness. Or lunacy. I think you were born to do this work."

"I don't have any training. I don't even know how to shoot a gun. I wouldn't even know where to start. I need money."

"You can learn. And you can earn money as an investigator. I'm not a good example, but take my word for it."

"It would never work."

"Why not?"

"It's not a real job. I already told you I'm a single woman. I live alone."

"You're making this far too complicated. Here's the real dirty little secret. Doing this work excites you. It gives you a thrill like a nine-to-five job never could. It gives you a rush. It makes you feel alive. I know because I get the same juice. You've found something you really want to do, and you won't let yourself do it. You've got some kind of repressed self-punishment thing going on. Are you Catholic?"

"Sort of."

"That would do it."

"You're saying there are no Catholic investigators?"

"I'm saying you should do what you want, not what you think you should, and see what happens."

That was a wicked thought. Do what I want? I tried to think only about where I wanted to be right then and what I wanted to be doing, and I started to get a thrill, a power surge, just thinking about directing my life that way. "I want to stay here and see this to the end. Jimmy killed John, and I want to see that he's punished for it."

"Do you care how?"

"Are you asking if I want to kill him?"

"No. I'm not suggesting that. Maybe something that's not your traditional approach to law enforcement is all." He smiled. "If the cops can't help us, and the Feds won't, we have to find someone who will, and give them a reason to do it."

"I vote for Vanessa," I said. "I think she's the key."

A cell phone rang. We both reached, but it wasn't my ring. It was Jack's. He answered and did a lot of listening. I heard a lot of uh-huhs. He started looking around for something to write with. I pulled a pen from my backpack and handed it over. He used it to write an address on his napkin.

"How about a phone number?" He paused to listen. "Are you going to show up this time?" Another pause, shorter. "Okay"—he checked his watch—"half an hour."

He hung up and smiled at me. "Guess who just resurfaced?"

Chapter Forty

The address Bobby Avidor had given us turned out to be in a warehouse district along one of the seedier sections of the Miami River. We took a downtown exit off the interstate, turned away from the gleaming chrome and glass towers, and drove down into an industrial enclave of dead end roads and concrete docks, where bars covered the windows and air conditioners dripped on asphalt sidewalks. There were no tourists here.

We parked underneath a drawbridge, and before we got within a hundred yards of the building, we ran right into a stench that was overwhelming. And overwhelmingly familiar. The place turned out to be a small fish-processing plant, and I had last inhaled that odor while standing over my bag on the floor of Bic's inbound bag room.

"Is Bobby taking up a second career?" I asked.

"He said it's his cousin's place."

Inside the building I flagged down a small old man wearing nothing but shorts and unlaced track shoes. His brown skin hung on his chest like soft suede as he struggled to roll a metal barrel on its edge across the crusty floor. He didn't speak English. Jack asked him in Spanish to find Bobby and tell him we were there.

We waited on the dock behind the warehouse where the smell of dead fish was cut by the industrial aroma of the river. Every once in a while a boat would motor by. They tended to be working boats—trawlers and tugboats—rather than the pleasure craft that jammed other venues.

We heard Bobby before we saw him. "What the fuck . . . do you think I'm coming out there to stand next to you in plain sight?"

We turned toward the voice. It was so bright outside that looking back into the warehouse was like staring into the mouth of a black cave. "Where would you feel comfortable?" Jack asked him.

"Nowhere, goddammit. But if you want to talk to me, you come inside."

And so we had to wade back into an odor so thick you could lean on it, and stand on a cement floor caked with dried fish guts. When my eyes adjusted again to the dim interior, I took one look at Bobby and turned to Jack. "Another mystery solved."

Bobby looked as if he were wearing a cockeyed turban when in fact it was a thick gauze bandage wrapped around his head, with special consideration for the place where his left ear had once been. He reached up reflexively to touch that side of his head.

"Too bad." Jack stuck his hands in his pockets. "If we'd known sooner, maybe they could have reattached it."

"What are you talking about, reattaching? How do you know what happened?"

"I was the lucky recipient of your detached ear," I said. "It came to me in a Baggie full of blood. But it took me a while to figure out what it was, and I certainly didn't know it belonged to you."

Bobby turned, and the light from outside fell across his face. The sight of dried brown blood and yellow pus caked along the edge of his bandage was bad enough, but the thought of what it must have looked like under the bandage made my stomach lurch.

"Why did Jimmy take your ear?" I asked.

"He thought I told you he was a snitch."

Jack turned to me. "Where would he get that idea?"

"Beats me."

Bobby's jittery eyes shifted from one of us to the other. He appeared to be struggling for just the right word. Instead, he put on a spiteful smirk and walked over to a bucket a few yards away. It was filled with the same vile stew that had defiled my allegedly lost bag. "Too bad about that bag of yours." He looked as smug as anyone with one ear can look.

"Bobby, I can get a new bag."

The smirk faded and his hand drifted up once again to tug nervously at the bandage. "I need protection."

"Apparently." I marveled again at how flat the left side of his head was.

"You said you could do that, right? Keep that crazy-ass Jimmy away from me?"

Jack took a step closer to Bobby. "How do you expect us to do that?"

"Get him the fuck in jail."

I took a step toward Bobby. "How do you expect us to do that?"

"I'll give you what you need. You make sure it gets where it needs to to lock his ass away."

"No deal," I said, "unless you tell us what happened to John."

"I don't know what happened to him."

"Let's go, Jack."

"Honest to God," he whined. "I don't know who killed him. But I know who he went to see the night he died."

That was good enough.

"Bobby," Jack said, draping his arm around his neck, "let's go next door and have a chat. I'll protect you while you have a beer."

Next door was the deck of a run-down bar, where the rats had the decency not to strut about in the open. It had a silver disco ball, a stuffed parrot, and a chain-link fence that kept patrons from pitching over the side into the river. It also served tuna fish on Ritz crackers. They weren't appetizing, but they looked better than the other free condiment—a bowl of pickles swimming in sour juice. I reached for a cracker.

Bobby drank beer and held forth while I took notes and Jack drank strong, black coffee, which seemed a cruel and unusual refreshment on such a humid day.

"It happened," Bobby said, "the way I said. Johnny showed up here out of the blue. He called me that morning and told me to meet him for a cup of coffee when he got in."

Jack seemed content to sit back and let me ask most of the questions. "What did he say to you?"

"All the things I would expect him to say, being the self-righteous bastard that he is . . . was." He lifted his chin into a defensive pose. "He said he was ashamed he'd ever known me, and he was sorry to say it on account of me saving his brother the way I did. He gave me two choices—go to the cops myself, or sit and wait to be arrested. One way or the other, I was out of business."

"And your mother gave him the logbook and the ring?"

"Fucking bitch. '*I don't want the ring from a dead woman's finger in my house.*'" He'd pitched his voice into a high, unkind imitation of a woman and made the sign of the cross. "'*May God have mercy on her soul.*' Ignorant fishwife. That's all she is and all she ever was. I shouldn't have even told her what was in the package."

"Why did you?" Jack squinted at him. He wasn't wearing his sunglasses.

Bobby turned toward him. "Because I thought it was so frigging cool, and I couldn't tell anyone about it. I couldn't show it to anyone. My mistake believing she would ever think anything I did was as good as anything the great Johnny McTavish would do."

Jack chortled over on his side of the round table. "Bobby, I don't think you're cut out for a life of crime."

"What else happened with John?" I asked.

"He told me I had twenty-four hours to think about it, that he would be at The Harmony House Suites, and at the end of twenty-four hours, he was going to walk into the police station."

"When would that have been?"

"Three o'clock the next afternoon. And I knew if he said three p.m., that's when he'd be there."

I reviewed my notes. John had checked into The Suites around four o'clock on Monday afternoon, so that would have made sense. "What did you do next?"

"I tried all the stuff that usually worked on him before." He set the beer bottle on the table so he could press his hands together in a prayer pose. "'I'm sorry,' I said. 'I fucked up. I know I did, but I can fix it.'" His

405

wheedling voice matched the exaggerated gesture of contrition. "'Johnny,' I says, 'I would never want you to be ashamed of me, and I want to do my best for you. Give me another chance . . .' I could always get to him before, but not this time. He said I'd gone too far. He said stealing tools is one thing, or even selling drugs, which on my mother's eyes I never did, by the way. He said at least people make a choice to take drugs. But no one makes a choice to be on an airplane with a bad part. Pretty screwed up logic, if you ask me."

John was not the one who'd been screwed up and Bobby knew it. He tipped back and finished off the rest of his beer. Then he looked for the waitress to bring him another.

"After he left for the hotel what did you do?"

"I was on the phone first thing to Jimmy. I said we got a problem here. This guy Johnny McTavish, I know him from back home and he will do what he says he will do which is to turn us in. Jimmy says, 'He don't even know me.' He's testing me, right? I say, 'If I get picked up, everyone's going to know everything I know. I just tell you that up front so there won't be a misunderstanding. I'll flip on you in a second if it will help me.'"

Jack thought that was pretty funny, too. "Were you on drugs, Bobby?" The tone suggested he must have been.

Bobby's shoulders stiffened. "I wanted him to see that my problem was his problem, is all that was."

"You're an idiot. Not only did you turn yourself into a huge liability for Jimmy, you also involved yourself in a conspiracy to commit murder."

"There was never any discussion about killing him."

Jack pushed forward and stretched his arms across the table. "What did you think Jimmy was going to do? You gave him no choice. He either had to kill John, or kill you. He'd have been better off killing you."

"Jimmy wanted to scare him is all."

"What are you saying?" I set down my notebook. "Jimmy was just trying to scare John with a knife and things got out of hand?"

"No. Nothing like that. Jimmy asked me for personal stuff I knew about Johnny's family. Like where his kids went to school. I didn't know that. I didn't even know about the baby, but I told him what I knew, about his neighborhood, his address, and what the house looked like. He needed it to make Johnny think they were watching his family." He caught sight of the two of us staring at him. "I figured it was better than him ending up dead."

Jack sat back and crossed his arms. "You're a pitiful bastard." That pretty much summed up how I felt, too.

"I didn't ask him to come down here. If he'd have just stayed home and minded his own business, he wouldn't have got killed and I would still have both my fucking ears."

I looked hard at Bobby. "Don't say it that way."

"Say what?"

"'He *got* killed,' as if some nameless, faceless force beyond anyone's control reached down from the heavens and for reasons none of us will ever understand snatched his life away."

He stared at me. He didn't get it. The fact that he never would just served to get me more cranked up.

"People who get struck by lightning, Bobby, are killed. People who drown in rivers or have houses fall on them in tornadoes are killed. But that's not what happened here. John was murdered. Jimmy Zacharias took a knife that was nine inches long and stuck it into his throat. He just about cut his head off, and when he thought John was dead, he tossed him into a Dumpster. But he wasn't dead. When they found him, his arm was hanging over one side. He'd tried to climb out, Bobby. He was fighting for his life right up to the end. He wanted to live." People a few tables over were beginning to take notice of our conversation. I lowered my voice. "Don't ever say again that John McTavish was killed. Don't even think it. When you think about John, think about the fact that you're the reason he was down here. You're the reason he's dead."

He stared down at his beer, and then he found something out on the brown river to stare at. Nothing I had said was going to change anything, but it made me feel better. It helped purge some of the emotional toxins that had been building up in my heart like plaque. I wanted to be finished with Bobby before I felt the need to purge again. I picked up my notebook and looked at the timeline. "What happened after Jimmy made his threats? Why did he kill him if John was going home?"

"I didn't say Jimmy threatened him."

"You just did."

"I said I gave Jimmy the information. It was his idea, but I never said he was the one who did it. He got that little FBI prick to do it."

Jack put down his coffee cup. "Who, Bobby? Give me a name."

408

"Damon Hollander."

Neither one of us had an immediate response. At least not a verbal one. Bobby looked at our faces. "You didn't know about him? Why do you think I'm talking to you, and not the Feds? Jimmy's got that little prick in his pocket."

Everything about Bobby seemed to come into sharper focus. It was as if I had adjusted my zoom lens and I could see the tiniest details—the little scar on his jaw where his beard stubble didn't grow, a few nose hairs poking out, the way the perspiration pooled in the cleft of his upper lip. I tried to see inside his head, to figure out if he was lying and if he was, if he was smart enough to have a good reason for it. I thought no on both counts.

"Jimmy sent Damon Hollander to meet with McTavish the night of the murder." I said it just to see how it sounded. "Is that what you're telling us?"

"That's the only way it would work. I knew it would never work to just threaten him flat out. Jimmy thought if Hollander looked him up at the hotel, flashed his badge, and suggested he go home for his own good, he would. So that's what he did. Hollander picked up Johnny at the hotel and took him for a ride. He told him he had me under surveillance and some shit about a wiretap and how he'd heard me giving all this personal information to some bad guys. Like maybe we were planning to get to him through Mae and the kids. He told him all the personal stuff and said he'd got it from the wiretap."

"What does Jimmy have on Damon?" Jack asked.

"What do you mean?"

"Jimmy is a criminal. Damon Hollander is a federal agent." Jack was speaking slowly in short, simple sentences, presumably so Bobby could follow along. "Why would Damon do something that Jimmy asked him to do?"

"I don't know. I never knew. Jimmy just is always saying how he can do whatever he wants, that he has protection. No one is going to touch him. Then when you two came around and said he was a rat for the government, I thought that had to be it. This prick Hollander was protecting his source. I figured if a little of that protection rubbed off on me, so be it. Good for me."

I looked at Jack. "Damon tries to warn John off. He picks him up and takes him on the ride. But Jimmy has second thoughts about the plan. He decides no risk is better than low risk. So he swings by the hotel after Damon has dropped him off. He grabs John, takes him out and kills him."

"It could have happened that way," Bobby said, "but I don't think it did."

"Why not?"

"Because Jimmy called me the next day and asked me if Johnny had gone back to Boston."

I could never remember to crack the windows open when I parked in the sun. When we got back to the car, it must have been pushing one hundred and fifty degrees inside. The seat belt tongue was so hot it singed my fingers. But I couldn't wait to get away from the curb, and out of the odor radius of the fish factory. I closed the door and took off.

All my thoughts and ideas were beginning to fuse together into a hardened, impenetrable lump. I couldn't pull the threads out anymore and follow them.

"If Jimmy didn't do it," I said, "who did?"

"I'm not convinced he didn't. He could have been covering his ass with that phone call." Jack had dropped his head back and squeezed his eyes closed. I didn't, since I was driving. "But if he didn't kill him, I bet he knows who did."

I'd already made two passes trying to figure out on my own how to get back up to the interstate, but I had somehow gotten caught up in an endless loop of oneway streets. It felt the way this case was going. "A little help here, Jack?"

He sat up straight and checked our position. "I thought maybe driving around in circles was one of your concentration techniques. Turn left up there. We have to go out of our way a couple of blocks to get back on the other side."

I made the left as he'd instructed, and was immediately buoyed by the fact that we were no longer trapped in the shadows beneath the interstate.

Jack pulled out his phone. "Let's check in with Felix," he said. "That kid always cheers me up. We'll see if he's figured out yet who Vanessa is."

411

Chapter Forty-One

Felix must have been standing at the check-in desk watching for us because when we walked into the lobby at The Suites, he was there, wearing his wide-armed polyester suit and brown striped tie. Something about seeing him back on duty, back in his normal job, gave me comfort.

"Wait until you see what I found on Miss Cray," he said. "You are going to be so psyched."

Jack leaned against the front desk. "Did you figure out who she is?"

"No. Better. Well maybe not better because that would be good to know too but what I found is awesome. It is so cool. I think you're going to really like it."

As we walked to the elevator, he called to someone at the counter to say he was taking a short break. They could reach him in 484. All the way up in the elevator, he was bobbing up and down, rocking back on his heels and forward on his toes. He was like a little kid that had to go to the bathroom.

He had straightened up the room since our marathon session had ended, and I wondered when or if this kid ever laid his head down to sleep.

He went to the place he was most comfortable, to the seat on the couch in front of his laptop. "So, like, when you asked me, Mr Dolan, to find out about Miss Cray, I thought and thought and I finally decided to try something totally off the wall and I did and it worked and I got in."

I sat down next to him. "What did you get into?"

"Miss Cray's private files."

"How did you do that, son?"

"It wasn't easy because there are no references or links or anything in the accountant's files. But then I remembered all those orchid societies she belongs to and I called them up and asked them how I could buy their membership lists, how that would work technically for me to get that data, file formats and all that, and they told me enough that I figured out how to bust in and grab all the enrollment data myself and what I got was all kinds of information about what orchids she likes and . . . and anyway, I got her e-mail address. I got Miss Cray's private e-mail address, and then I just sent her a message from one of the societies. It wasn't about anything, but that's how I got in. Through her e-mail. I did a Trojan horse and accessed her hard drive from there."

"You got in because she loves orchids?" I found a certain amount of satisfaction in that.

"It took me a long time and I got lots of help, but we found this little quirk in her system and I was able to slide through. All you need is to find a portal and I did. And I went in and looked around and found what I needed. What you need."

Jack pulled one of the desk chairs over, turned it around, and sat in it backwards. "What did you find?"

"First of all, she is definitely in the money laundering business. And she makes a lot of money doing it. I couldn't believe it. She's got seventeen different clients." He started tapping the keys and I heard his external CD drive start to whir on the table at my knee. A

413

spreadsheet appeared with seventeen rows and a bunch of columns.

"See?"

I did see, but it didn't mean much. They were in some kind of code, identified only by a series of numbers, maybe account numbers. "Can you tell who they are?"

"No. But she has one that's really, really big, a lot bigger than the others, and it's the one that channels cash to Mr Speath's place." He paged down and zoomed in on one of the accounts. As he moved across the screen, I could see it was bigger than the others by at least a factor of ten.

"That's Ottavio," Jack said. "He's the biggest fish in whatever sea he's in."

"Okay," Felix said. "Here's the good part. So I'm in there and I'm cruising around and looking at the entries and seeing how she does it and all and I find this second set of numbers for Ottavio's account."

I leaned in to see the screen. "Two sets of books?"

"Yeah." He went down and clicked on another tab that brought up a separate analysis. "It turns out," he said, "she's stealing from him."

"Vanessa is skimming?" I leaned in closer. "From Ottavio Quevedo?"

"She's either very smart," Jack said, "or very stupid. Either way, she's got nerves of steel."

I pointed to one of the totals. "What's this number? Is that . . ." I counted the zeroes. "Is that fifty million dollars?"

"That's what she stole from him. She's got it stashed away in offshore accounts. I couldn't believe it, but I added it up and that's what it is and I wondered how someone doesn't figure out they had fifty million dollars swiped from them but then I looked at how much money she moves around just for Ottavio and it's a drop in the bucket and she's been doing it for a couple of years and—"

"Felix." He was getting more and more wound up, and I thought if I didn't step in he might twist himself into the couch. I was beginning to see what sleep deprivation did to Felix. "This is important. You need to calm down and think about this. Are you sure Vanessa can't tell you've been in her files?"

He was almost insulted. "No way, Miss Shan—"

"Think about it," Jack said. "Just sit there with that question for a few minutes and think it through."

That was asking a lot from the kid. He might have exploded if Jack hadn't given him the nod. "What I'm saying, I'm saying she had two different burglar alarms on and I found them both and disarmed them. They were pretty good, too. I learned a few things from her."

The CD drive whirred again. "Where are you keeping this data, Felix?"

"I burned two CDs."

"Take this one out," I said, nodding to the one he was using, "and give them both to us."

He did. He had already selected the jewel boxes for transport, one that used to hold a CD by Rage Against the Machine, and another by Matchbox 20. He handed them over to me and I turned them over to Jack.

"I put them in there to disguise them. A CD, you know, can hold up to 650 megabytes of data and—"

"Did you leave anything on your hard drive?" I asked him.

415

"No."

"Okay." Jack returned the chair to the desk. "Do you live with someone?"

"I have a roommate but he's in school and he's never home."

"Stay here at the hotel, then. Stay around people. Don't go out. Order room service. I'm very serious about this. You stay holed up in here until I give you the high sign. Is that clear?"

Felix looked at him with a mixture of excitement and concern and nodded. I knew he understood what Jack was saying. I did, too, and it scared me.

"Let's go, Alex." Jack held up the CDs. "We just found our leverage."

Chapter Forty-Two

It was hot in Jack's truck, which inexplicably had no air conditioner. It wasn't that the AC was broken. He had purchased a truck to drive around in Florida with no cooling device whatsoever beyond the open windows.

"That's the place," he said. We were on Collins Avenue in front of the Delano, one of the old Art Deco hotels in South Beach that had been gutted and redone. It had a big circle drive in front filled with exotic cars, but the entrance was mostly hidden by tall shrubs. We made two passes and I managed to get a glimpse behind the green barrier. It had a spacious, covered porch, which was a good plan because their patio furniture seemed to be covered with chintz and silk. Not your standard deck chairs.

"We have half an hour." Jack turned to make the block again. "You should go in and look around. I want to find a place, too, where I can keep an eye on you."

We'd decided I would meet Vanessa, since she and I seemed to have a rapport, of sorts. We also thought it best if she didn't have us both in her line of sight at the same time.

"Tell her what we want," he reminded me, not for the first time.

"I will."

"Give her one disc and tell her we have the other one."

"What if she says no?"

"We'll think about that when the time comes. But she's smart. She'll do what she needs to do, but she probably won't say yes right away. She'll tell you she wants to think about it so she can come up with her own plan. Give her the deadline, and try to set up the next contact in advance. Two hours. That's it. That's what I told Jimmy."

"What else did you tell him?"

"I didn't give him too many details. I told him generally what we were up to. He said he didn't kill anyone and to go fuck myself."

"What did you say?"

"I told him he's killed too many people, but if he didn't kill John McTavish, he should lay low for a couple of days. He said to go fuck myself."

He'd pulled into a pay lot and parked, so now we didn't even have the breeze from the open windows to keep us cool. It was two o'clock in the afternoon and sticky. I was sticking to everything—the car seat, my clothes, my leather backpack. Jack was low on quarters, but between the two of us, we managed to scrape up enough silver to buy two hours on the meter.

We found a spot in the shade and stood there long enough for him to go over everything again. He seemed to be getting more and more anxious, pushing his hands into the pockets of his chinos, pulling them out again. It was starting to make me jumpy, too.

"Jack, I've got it. It will be fine."

"Maybe this is not such a good idea," he said. "Maybe I should go. Maybe—"

I pulled him down and shut him up with a long, deep, soul-scraping kiss. "Are you ready?" I asked.

418

"I'm ready."

"Then let's go."

Judging from the lobby, when they'd gutted the Delano, they had dragged out a whole lot more than they had brought in. To call it sparsely furnished would have been generous.

I had entered through the front door into a vast open space with planetarium-height ceilings. Instead of walls, they had huge columns to separate the check-in desk, sushi bar, lounge, lobby, and pool table, and long, delicate white curtains that tended to drift back and forth with the breeze every time a door opened. It was a capsule of cool on a broiling strip of Florida oceanfront, and I was glad for Jack's suggestion to come early and check it out. Otherwise I would have been too distracted to pay attention when Vanessa arrived.

Of the furniture that was there, every single piece was different from the next. Leather and velvet and fur were a predominant theme. The floors were wide cherry or mahogany planks, covered here and there with pieces that looked like Mark Rothko paintings that had been dragged down off the wall and turned into area rugs. There were tall vases filled with even taller stems of exotic flowers, and lots of candles, including floor candelabras. They needed candlelight because the electric version was either so indirect or so high up in the ceiling as to have not been there at all.

My very favorite feature was the unusually narrow interior doorways along the perimeter walls, including those that led to the bathrooms. They reminded me of the templates we used at the airport to catch oversized carry-on bags. "If your bag doesn't fit in here, it's too big. You have to check it." Only the message here was "If you're not thin enough to fit through this narrow door, you don't belong here. Turn around and check out."

It felt forbidding, but that was the whole point. It was an Ian Schrager hotel, designed with the in-your-face, you-don't-belong-here-no-matter-who-you-are veneer that he had helped create at Studio 54. He had somehow managed to import the attitude intact to his hotels, and I was surprised there hadn't been a bouncer out front to usher in Bianca Jagger and Liza Minnelli, or at least their new millennium successors, and keep out riffraff, like me.

Vanessa was not riffraff. When she slipped through the front door, she fit right into the airy atmosphere. She had on bright green linen Capri pants, a black sleeveless top with a high collar, and little black sandals. Her blonde hair was plaited and wrapped on top of her head. She could have been wearing cutoffs and a bra top and still have looked right at home in this place. It was all in the attitude.

"I'm early," she said. "And you're even earlier. Isn't that interesting?"

"Shall we find a place and sit?" I asked.

"Down to business. I like that."

I let her lead the way into the lobby/lounge, as if I had any choice. She chose a corner with a leopard-skin loveseat and a chair that looked like a big, high-heeled shoe. It was metal and didn't seem to have been designed for sitting, but she went straight for it. Maybe she liked pain.

"How is your investigation coming? Have you found your murderer?"

"My investigation is going well," I said.

"Did you check my alibi?"

"Of course."

"And did it check out to your satisfaction?" Her tone was slightly mocking.

"It checked out."

"But not to your satisfaction." Her skin seemed particularly translucent in the early afternoon light that came in through the patio doors. She was so pale, like a soapstone statue.

"An independent sighting would have been more satisfying," I said. "The people who claim to have seen you all work for you."

"And here I thought you invited me out to tell me I was off the hook."

A slim man with long sideburns who had been wandering about stopped by. Turned out he was a waiter. Vanessa ordered a Metropolitan. I asked for my customary sparkling water and couldn't wait to see what kind of bottle came out. I knew it wouldn't be Poland Spring.

We settled back into our quiet conversation. "I've found out some new things about you, Vanessa. About your clients."

She sat back in that horrible chair, crossed her legs, rested her elbows on the armrests, and made a steeple with her fingers. She pointed it straight up under her chin, and I could tell by the way she waggled her leg that she knew where I was going. And she was ready. "I have many clients. I manage their money. Where they get their money is of no concern to me."

"I'm talking about your other business. You launder drug money for a living, your biggest client is Ottavio Quevedo, you use Jimmy Zacharias's repair stations as sinks, and I believe you know who killed John McTavish."

Her sedate, satisfied smile made me think she was not surprised, but pleased, at last, to be given full credit for what she was and what she did.

She raised her eyebrows. "And . . . ?"

"And I'm here to ask for your help in catching the person who murdered John."

"You want to bring him to justice?"

"Call me an idealist."

"Very well. Let's take these items one at a time, shall we?" She glanced around the general vicinity. The closest patrons were two knife-thin boys shooting pool in the corner. One of them had a lizard tattooed on his shoulder blade.

"You are correct," she said. "I do provide a service to individuals with a specific kind of problem related to their cash flow, and Ottavio is a particularly active user of my services. I know of Jimmy Zacharias through Ottavio." She leaned forward. "And why on earth would I help you do anything?"

"You skipped a point, the one about how you know who killed John."

"Jimmy killed your friend."

I had expected her to say that, whether it was true or not, but not so quickly and not without encouragement. "What did you say?"

"I said Jimmy killed your friend. That's what you wanted to know, isn't it? But I find that point to be irrelevant, unless you can convince me that it's not."

The waiter slinked by and set down two drinks, including my bottle of water, which was a tall, frosted glass cylinder. I'd never seen one like it. I waited for him to clear out.

"How do you know Jimmy killed John?"

"Arturo saw him at the hotel that night."

"You said Arturo was with you on the island."

She blinked at me over the martini glass and I knew if she hadn't been sipping, she would have been smiling.

"Did Arturo see the murder?"

"No."

"What was he doing there?"

"That's a long and complicated story."

"I have a big bottle of water to drink," I said. "At least thirty-two ounces."

She sighed and I wondered if I was going to have to whip out the discs to encourage her. Somehow I thought not. "Will you stop bothering me if I tell you?"

"I'll stop bothering you when I get what I need from you."

She turned her head to watch the boys playing pool. Like all pool tables, this one was covered in green felt, but not billiard green. Olive green. She let her top leg bounce a few times and didn't seem anxious to leave. When she turned back, she looked as if she was ready to gossip. "Several weeks before that night, I was contacted by Ottavio and told to use his funds to make a loan to Jimmy. A rather substantial loan."

"A loan for what?"

"Something to do with parts. I don't know. I hate that business. It's filthy and the people in it are filthy scum, Jimmy chief among them. I pay him and I pay him well not to use those businesses that way and he does it anyway. It's not worth the risk."

"Was the money for the Sentinel parts?"

"Was that the unfortunate incident in Ecuador?"

"It was."

"Then the answer is yes. As I understood it, Jimmy was to use the money to get an organization in place to refurbish and sell a large quantity of parts. A highly speculative venture if you ask me, especially for someone who claims to be so risk averse. Ottavio never invests in my funds. But he didn't ask me."

"Why would a drug lord get in bed with Jimmy on a parts deal?"

"Jimmy talked him into it. He kept telling him what a great business these parts were. Ottavio was on the fence, but he was intrigued, and then an airplane dropped out of the sky practically on his head. He took it as a sign." She shrugged. "What would you expect from an ignorant drug dealer?"

"Was he thinking of making a career change?"

"He was thinking of diversifying." She had already downed over half of her Metropolitan. The elixir seemed to loosen her tongue, although it was also possible she'd been dying to share this story with someone. "And, as I understand it, Jimmy also promised him several hundred cases of AK-47s if he would provide the backing on this job. Jimmy has access to those sorts of things."

"Tell me about the murder."

"All I know is this. Jimmy's been paying the loan back to me in installments. The night your friend died happened to be a night Jimmy owed us a payment. I sent Arturo to pick it up. Jimmy wanted to meet him at The Harmony House Suites."

"Why there?"

"He said it was convenient for him because he had other business there that night."

I felt a tug in my stomach, picturing what the other business had been.

Vanessa continued. "That's why my Volvo was seen in the parking lot. It was Arturo meeting Jimmy to pick up that week's payment. Nothing more than that."

"We haven't been able to put Jimmy at The Suites that night."

"I know he was there because Arturo came home with the money."

She had answered all my questions so quickly and logically, I had to regroup and find more loose ends. "Did Arturo have any business that night with George Speath?"

"George Speath?"

"Speath Aviation," I said. "One of your sinks."

"No. We normally don't do business that way. Only with Jimmy."

"Why would Jimmy have used Ottavio's MO for the murder?"

"Because he's a very clever boy. Maybe too clever for his own good." She'd drained her glass and ordered another drink before I'd finished half a glass of water.

"We'll need a statement from Arturo," I said.

"You're joking."

"I'm not. According to you he can put Jimmy at the crime scene."

"Please, I would expect better than that from you. Arturo is too valuable to me. It's out of the question.

425

And obviously his activities can be traced back to me. I can't help you beyond what I've already told you, and I've already told you too much."

"Wouldn't it be better for you if Jimmy goes to jail?"

"Why?"

"Because he's a confidential informant for the FBI."

Her eyes brightened. "On whom would he be informing? Those scummy brokers he works with, or those—what does he call them . . . 'parts-pickers?' The U.S. government must be desperate."

"We think he's working with the FBI on an operation to take down Ottavio, and not for stolen parts."

"That would be a profoundly unintelligent plan, and Jimmy knows it. He generally has a keener sense of survival than that."

"Maybe he doesn't have any choice. Maybe he got nailed and this is his best alternative."

"Crossing Ottavio is never the best alternative. There is nothing the FBI can do to Jimmy that would be worse than what Ottavio will do to him."

"Isn't it true that if Ottavio goes down, you go down with him? You are, after all, his launderer."

"Jimmy has no access to anything important. I am quite well insulated, which is a necessary precaution when doing business with Jimmy and people like him. I'm afraid you'll have to find another way to get him. I can't help you."

Someone opened the patio door, causing the air pressure in the room to shift. All the white curtains billowed out like parachutes, and I knew this was the moment. "What would Ottavio do to you if he knew you were stealing from him?"

She managed to control every part of her reaction, except that her already pale face turned white. I had her.

"Of your seventeen different clients, Vanessa, Ottavio's are the only accounts that are light. So we know it's not because you can't count. You've been stealing from him, systematically siphoning off funds that go straight into your own secret accounts. Fifty million dollars at last count." I pulled the jewel box out of my bag. "We have copies of your files, the whole road map, in a convenient CD format."

She had regained her equilibrium and even managed to pump some blood back into her face. "It's a mistake to threaten me."

"I'm simply laying out alternatives and hoping you'll choose the one that benefits me. Personally, I'd rather not meet Ottavio. But then I can always FedEx these files. Or . . . does he have an e-mail address?"

"What do you want?"

"I told you what I want. I'm tired of chasing Jimmy around. I want to nail him, and the best way I can think of to do that is for you to help me."

"If I help you, you will give me that disc?"

"You can have this one." I passed it over to her. I'd chosen Rage Against the Machine for her copy. It seemed to suit her.

"How many are there?" she asked calmly.

"Only one more. Jack has it. We'll turn it over when you give me something I can use. I'm not interested in your operation. If Ottavio had nothing to do with killing John, I'm not interested in him either."

"How do I know you won't keep copies?"

"There is nothing else I want or need from you, Vanessa. You hand me Jimmy, I hand you the disc, and our business is over."

She considered that. "I will not give up Arturo. If I help you, it will be some other way."

"What other way?"

"I have other ideas, but I will have to do research and get back to you."

"You have two hours before we start looking for a way to contact your biggest client. I'd much prefer to work with you on this than Ottavio, Vanessa. But one way or the other, I'm getting what I came down here for."

Her eyes were burning. Glimmering green emeralds in a geisha-white mask. And I knew what she was feeling. She wasn't used to being pushed around and she didn't like it. I wouldn't have wanted to be in her position, either.

Jack wasn't at the truck when I got back. I started toward the beach to see if I could spot him when he sauntered over from the street side.

"Where were you?"

"Keeping an eye on Arturo." He unlocked the truck and we got in.

"Where was he?"

"Outside on the patio sitting where he could see her. He just drove her out. She was on her cell phone the second you left her."

"She said Jimmy did it. She told a convincing story, too." I relayed what she'd said, including as many details as I could remember.

428

"Maybe he did do it," he said. "We'll wait and see what she comes up with."

"We've got two hours." I was relieved to have the meeting behind me, but still juiced by the experience. I reached over and traced the curve of his ear. "Want to wait together at your place?"

He smiled and started the engine.

We had all the phones lined up on Jack's headboard—my cell, his cell, and his cordless. Vanessa was supposed to call me, but she had all the numbers. At one hour and forty-five minutes after the Delano meeting, it was my phone that twittered out my distinctive tone. I reached up to answer, and it was Vanessa.

She didn't even offer a cordial greeting. "Go to Jimmy's house and look for a box with all his Vietnam souvenirs. It's there. Check the fingerprints and you'll have all the evidence you need."

"What am I looking for?"

"The murder weapon."

Chapter Forty-Three

Even as we made the turn and started down the long driveway, we heard Bull crying—sending forth long, high-pitched, wailing laments from somewhere in the back of Jimmy's house, from somewhere in the depths of his canine soul.

Jack had already reached under the seat and pulled out the Glock. "You should stay out here," he said.

I turned again to study Jimmy's stucco cube. It looked exactly as it had the last time we'd come to visit, except all the curtains were closed. I didn't see any windows open, at least not from the front. It would have been sweltering inside.

"What are you going to do?"

"I'm going to go see what's wrong with that damn dog."

My heartbeat started to drag, not accelerate. Everything seemed to slow down, and I wanted to ask if we shouldn't call the police.

"I want to go with you," I said, though that's not exactly what I meant. What I meant was "I'd rather do almost anything else at this moment than go in that house, but if you insist, I believe I should go with you so you won't be by yourself and since I'm the one who basically got you into this in the first place."

His answer was to reach down for the second gun, the one he carried in his ankle holster. It was the .22, the one he'd tried to give me the night in the swamp.

Seeing it reminded me of how much I didn't want to carry it, then or now. But I also remembered that I had promised to take it the next time it was offered.

"That's an automatic," I said. "You have to tell me how to use it."

"Here's the safety." He pointed to a small red switch. "It's off now, ready to fire. It's a double action, so if you do this"—he pulled back the piece on top—"it's ready to fire. All you have to do is point and pull the trigger. Aim lower than where you want to hit. You've got a full clip, which is eight rounds. When you're not pointing it, hold it up in the air like this, away from your body and your head. You don't want to shoot your ear off. Don't shoot first. Don't sweep across me."

"What do you mean?"

"You'll be behind me. If a target moves across the front of me, don't follow him and shoot me instead."

"Good point."

He turned the gun and offered it to me. When it was my turn to hold it, I had a sudden, desperate urge to embrace my old life, the one where I sat at a desk and reached for a calculator, not a gun, and the most dangerous thing I did was go running along the Charles River after dark. That all seemed very far away.

I took the gun.

It was a Smith & Wesson. It said so right there on the barrel. It had a crosshatch design etched into the grip that I could feel when I wrapped my hand around it. I touched the trigger. It felt tight. He was right about there not being much to a .22. It certainly wasn't going to weigh me down with its heft, but it had its own gravity that had nothing to do with its mass. It made me

431

nervous, holding-a-bottle-of-plutonium nervous, but I also couldn't deny that behind the anxiousness, and not too far, was a surge of something—power, exhilaration. I didn't want to admit to feeling it, but it was there.

We climbed out of the car. I kept my eyes nailed to the front door as we moved toward the house. He hadn't yet fixed his screen door.

Short rapid bursts of barking and slow stretches of inconsolable whimpering embroidered Bull's long, mournful howls. He seemed inexhaustible, and I wondered how long he'd been at it.

When we got to the door, Jack motioned me to one side and stood on the other. He started to reach for the bell, then pulled out a handkerchief and used it to press the button. Bull reacted instantly, pushing his howls to the next level, an almost unimaginable hysterical keening that made my spleen hurt. Something was definitely keeping him in the back of the house.

"Jimmy. *Jimmy*," Jack called out as he tried the knob. Locked.

Sweat ran into my eyes and made them burn. I wiped them with the sleeve of my shirt.

"Let's go to the back." Jack moved in that direction. "We'll see what that damn dog is so excited about. Either that or I can shoot him. Stay behind me."

"Don't worry." I had no plans to blaze any new trails.

Bull heard us invading his sanctuary as we approached the back door. He tried to tunnel out, frantically scratching the wall or door—whatever was holding him in. It was apparently an old habit of his; the outside of the back door was a scarred landscape of deep furrows and rough gouges.

432

"It sounds like he's trapped in an inside room some-where," Jack said. "You were in this kitchen the other day. Do you remember if there was a closet or pantry? Any kind of inside room?"

I closed my eyes and tried to picture the kitchen from the inside. "Yes . . . there is a laundry room or pantry. If we walk in through that door, it will be to our right."

"Good. Let's hope he can't get out."

Jack held his gun in his left hand. I held mine in my right and tried to do exactly what I saw him do. As he reached toward the tarnished doorknob with the hand-kerchief, I flattened against the wall and breathed, but the air seemed to go somewhere else besides my lungs. He twisted the knob. The lightweight door opened with a pop. It sounded like a starter's pistol, and my heart began the race.

"Take the safety off." His voice was quiet and close. "Don't touch anything." He disappeared through the open doorway. Just like that. No deep breath. No moment of contemplation or anticipation.

My fingers felt too thick, but I reached around and managed to flick the safety off. It made the gun feel different. Hotter. I had to take a contemplative moment to test and make sure all my limbs were working. When I was convinced they would respond when called upon, I started into the kitchen. Then stopped. Confused.

Ringing. Cell phone ringing. Panic. *My* cell phone ringing. Clipped to my waistband. Hard to get it open with one gun and two anxious hands. Ringing again, goddammit. Bull out of his mind. Open it. Hit the power button and turn it off. Wait. Sweat. Listen.

433

Nothing. Not even Jack coming back to see. Saved by Bull's raucous din.

Stale and humid air wrapped around me the second I stepped into the kitchen. And I smelled . . . I thought I smelled . . . it had to be. Blood smells like nothing else on earth. Once you smell it you never forget. The rich odor came in though my nostrils, permeated my sinuses, then raced throughout my body, crackling along every nerve ending until I felt the odor more than I smelled it.

"Stay close to me." As soon as Jack saw I was with him, he moved forward, through the front room, and toward a hallway where welcome sunlight spilled through the first door we came to. The room was what I think is called a Florida room, complete with full plantation shutters that had been left open. It must have been Jimmy's junk room because that's what was in there. Jimmy's junk looked the same as everyone else's—cardboard boxes, an old floor lamp bent in the middle, a pile of wadded-up beach towels, and an old toaster.

The next door led to the bedroom. The only piece of furniture there was the bed. It was made. One room left. If Jimmy was in the house, he was in the bathroom.

I watched Jack move toward that door and I concentrated on simply reacting to whatever he did. He motioned for me to stay back, then raised the gun and pointed it straight up toward the ceiling, keeping it away from his head. He called out for Jimmy. The only response came from Bull.

This time he did pause to gather himself, taking a breath as I had done on the back porch, and I wondered what he was contemplating. The scene I was imagining made my insides want to rupture. A gunshot blast. Jack thrown back against the far wall. Down on the floor. Eyes open and unseeing. It was the worst possible image I could think of, conjured up from the fact that I cared about him and I didn't want to lose him.

I kept my eyes open, maybe couldn't have closed them if I'd tried. He swung into the doorway. His face turned pale. He rose from his firing stance and let the gun drop to his side. He leaned his shoulder against the jamb and all the energy drained out until he looked like a coat hanging on a hook.

I made myself step in beside him, and looked at what he was looking at.

"Jesus. Jesus Christ, Jack."

Jimmy had been taking a bath. His arms, head, and most of his torso hung over the side, but his long legs were still in the tub, mostly submerged. His two kneecaps stuck out like white ice floes in dull red water that was as flat as the mirror over the sink, and now certainly cold.

Much blood and brain matter had sprayed across the back wall of the tub. More was on the floor, having gushed across the tiles from a large hole in the back of his head. The pool of blood on the tiles was thick with his long, silver hair. Whoever had killed him had probably shot him through the forehead, blowing most of the back of his head off.

But that wasn't his only wound.

His hair was pulled to the side to show the knife, a long knife with a thick, black handle buried to the hilt in his throat. The murderer had plunged it in below his left ear. The bloody tip stuck out the other side, and had lodged against the tub in a way that kept Jimmy's head twisted at an unnatural angle that left his dead eyes glaring up at us.

I put my hand over my nose and breathed through my mouth. Jack still hadn't moved. His hands were trembling, and when I looked into his eyes, I saw pain. I reached out and touched the sleeve of his shirt.

"He was a soldier." He pressed his lips together hard. "I hated him. I hated the things he did, but he was a soldier once." He blinked up at the ceiling, and maybe he was back there in the jungle seeing the sights and hearing the sounds only he could hear, and when he looked at Jimmy again, maybe he was thinking there was one less person in the world who had been there with him. No matter what he had done later, no matter what he had become, Jimmy was one of the men . . . the boys who had stood next to Jack in a place where no man should ever have to stand.

He turned and walked down the hall.

I wanted to be with him but he had walked away from me, so instead I counted nails. Jimmy's was an old house and all the nails in the floor in his hallway were not flush with the hardwood. Some of them were coming up, making little booby traps, the kind that snagged your hose when you walked around in the morning with no shoes, trying to get ready for work. Or provided something good to stare at when you didn't want to stare at a bloody corpse. I counted twenty-seven of them. I counted them again. And then I went out to find Jack.

He was in the front room with his gun in his holster and his hands in his pockets, staring at the trophy for the State Champs of Everglades City, Florida, 1969.

Bull seemed to finally be running out of steam. His cries were more intermittent now, more mournful and desperate than angry.

"Are you all right?"

"He didn't deserve that. I thought I knew what he deserved, but it wasn't that."

"We should call the cops, huh?" I pulled out my phone and turned it back on.

He nodded. "Call Patty. Tell her we found the McTavish murder weapon."

The screen on my phone was flashing, telling me I had a text message marked urgent. I hadn't even known I could get those. It had to be from Felix. I had no other friends who were that technologically capable. I futzed around with the buttons until I figured out how to pull it up and scroll through it.

"Oh, my God, Jack."

Chapter Forty-Four

Jack had looked bad at Jimmy's house. He looked worse as he put my phone to his ear and listened again to the voice mail message Felix had left for me. I tried to concentrate on the road. On my hands on the steering wheel. On getting us to The Harmony House Suites as fast as the Lumina would take us. Anything but what had been in that message. And anything but the fact that Felix had been the one calling when I had turned off my phone.

He had wanted to tell me that Vanessa knew he had been in her system. He'd been "busted," as he put it, by a superior alarm that he had overlooked—a "hacker trap" that he had never seen coming. He was sure they knew who he was, and was calling to find out what to do.

Jack was dialing again, as fast as the little cell phone buttons would allow. I knew he was calling the room at The Suites again. He'd been doing that compulsively since we'd walked out of Jimmy's house. If he hadn't been doing it, I would have. He pressed the phone to his ear and we both waited. And waited.

"C'mon, son," he kept saying. "Be there, kid."

The waiting was excruciating. Finally, someone answered, and it wasn't Felix. It was the hotel operator wanting to know again if Jack wanted to leave a message for room 484. Apparently, no one was home.

$$\star \quad \star \quad \star$$

We had no way to get into the suite when no one was there to answer our knock. Jack kept knocking anyway. Banging, really, taking out on the intractable door all the same fears that were pinballing around inside me.

"Felix," he yelled. "Felix. *Son* . . ."

The curtains in the room next door moved—someone wondering about all the commotion, no doubt. But nothing from 484.

"I'm going down for a key," I said.

The see-through elevator showed that both cars were on the ground floor. I went for the stairs and flew down four floors. By the time I hit the lobby, I was sweating, every breath had a catch in it, and my mouth tasted as if I'd been swilling milk of magnesia.

There were three agents at the front desk working a queue. According to one of the bellmen, the small-ish, youngish, roundish woman in the middle was in charge. She was the other assistant manager besides Felix.

"Excuse me," I said, stepping in front of her.

"Hey." A guy with a salesman's gut and a suit that didn't fit because of it was fuming behind me.

"I need your help," I said quietly to the woman. "It's an emergency."

She seemed stunned and stood blinking at me. "What?"

"We have an emergency upstairs. I need to get into one of your rooms immediately."

"Oh."

Still with the staring, and I understood completely why Felix had been named acting general manager of the place.

439

"Room 484," I said, more urgently. "Can you make a key and let me in?"

She responded by looking down at her keyboard and typing. "That's Felix's room."

"Yes. We need a key. We need to get in."

She turned to the agent working next to her. "Sherrie, I need to help this lady—"

"*Now*," I said.

She turned and looked at me with stern eyes and a locked jaw.

"I'm sorry. Please. This is important. Can you just make a key and give it to me?"

Of course not. After she had made the key, we stood at the elevator and waited because I thought it would be faster than encouraging her up four flights of stairs.

Jack was on his cell phone when we arrived. It felt as if I'd been gone for an hour. "I called Patty to let her know what was happening. She's sending some units over."

We both stood back and waited as the assistant manager gave the door a dainty rap. "Felix?"

"Open the damn door now." Jack must have startled her. She fumbled the key. Almost dropped it. Recovered. Had a tough time sliding it into the slot. It didn't work the first time. The second time the lock clicked. She pushed the handle down and the door opened.

"Stay back," Jack said to her. "Don't come in here." He pulled out his gun and I thought she would faint. He walked in first. I went behind him sans weapon because in my haste I'd left mine behind in the car.

It was dark. Cold. The air conditioner was pumping and the chilled air made me shiver. The sound was faint because the bedroom door was closed. Felix was not in the front room. Most of his stuff was still there.

"Jack." He angled slightly to see where I was pointing. "His laptop is gone."

"Shit." He approached the closed bedroom door, checking the bathroom quickly as we passed it. Empty. He pushed back against the wall, put his hand flat on the door, and paused to look down and take a quiet breath. He wrapped his hand around the knob and turned it. I heard the latch release, felt the pop in my chest. A wedge of light slipped through, fell across the durable carpet in the bedroom, and widened as Jack pushed the door slowly open. The sound of the air conditioner seemed deafening.

The darkness inside the room scared me, not because I thought someone was going to jump us. If Felix had been in there and able, he would have answered. He hadn't.

Jack reached in to turn on the light.

"There's no wall switch."

We both jerked at the sound of the little girl voice behind us. The assistant manager had crept within a few feet without either of us hearing her. The trepidation had gone from her eyes, and now they were burning with a weird light that was beyond innocent curiosity, but not all the way to lurid.

"Step back," I said. "Get out of the room."

"You have to turn on the lamp that's on the dresser."

"Thank you. Please go out and make sure no one comes in here."

While she trundled out, I looked for and found the switch for the light in the ceiling over our heads. When

441

I flipped it on, it threw enough light that we could see the bed where Felix had laid out his notes on Vanessa. They were gone. Jack was inside the bedroom now, and I was just outside the door. He found the lamp. Turned it on. I quickly scanned the room. Nothing. Jack looked on the other side of the far bed. He shook his head.

One more place to look. He moved to the closet and signaled for me to stand behind him. He rubbed the palm of his right hand against his jeans, and I felt my own palms dripping. He swung the door open, stepped around it, and stood with his gun pointed inside. I couldn't see around the door. The muscles in his forearms twitched and his face went blank and I felt the temperature in the room drop a few degrees. I pulled the door all the way open.

The closet was empty.

Jack seemed to want to lean on something. He used the wall. He holstered his gun, leaned over with his hands on his knees, and took a few deep breaths. I put my hand on his back and leaned on him. His shirt was soaked through, and I could feel his heart working hard.

"They took him," he said. "Him, his laptop, and all his notes. They've got him. *Damn* it all to hell." He straightened up and covered his face with his hands, then let them slide down, as if he could wipe away the ache. I felt it, too.

"My God," he whispered. "What did we do?"

Chapter Forty-Five

The woman in the next room over, the one who had been peeking through her curtains, told us Felix had left with two men and a tall blonde woman about half an hour before we showed up. It was now an hour and a half after that and still no one had called. No ransom demand. No contact of any kind. The working theory, the only one we could stomach, was that Vanessa had snatched Felix and would trade him for the account information. I kept reminding myself that getting rid of Felix while we still had it didn't make much sense. But it was hard to ignore the next conclusion in that logical sequence—that getting rid of all three of us after she had what she needed made a whole lot of sense.

Jack and I were in the Lumina, out in the city, trying to stay in motion. Our first stop had been at Jack's bungalow to pick up more weapons. He was now heavily armed. Next we'd gone to Vanessa's office. She wasn't there. We'd checked the garage. All Volvos were in.

The police had been to her house. Someone had gone to the airfield and checked her Gulfstream. *The Crayfish* had been found, boarded, and eliminated as a possible refuge. It was hard to eliminate all the possibilities—to even think of all the possibilities for a woman with so many resources.

In place of conversation, we had the radio. It wasn't much of a distraction. Constant emergency reports interrupted whatever program we chose to listen to. I couldn't scan fast enough to avoid them. The wind was due to shift, and the smoke from the largest of the fires nearby would turn by afternoon and blanket the more heavily populated areas to the south and east, which meant Miami and Miami Beach. Small children, asthmatics, and the elderly were warned to stay indoors.

"Where would she go?" I asked. Again. "Where would she take him?"

"She has to leave town," he said, finishing the routine we'd been working over and over. He had his cell phone to his ear, checking his service and my hotel again for messages.

"I think she has to leave the country," he said. "When Ottavio finds out Jimmy is an informant, he will have to assume she was in it with him, especially if he finds out she's been skimming. The smart move is to take the money and go hide. Although, if Ottavio believes she was working for the government, there is no place for her to hide."

"But why take Felix? I would have given her the disc."

"Insurance. We fucked up. We underestimated her."

I drove around for another ten minutes or so, retracing parts of the town I had come to know in the past two weeks. Eventually, I was headed back toward the airport.

"Where are we going?"

"To George Speath's place," I said. "We know he had a connection to Vanessa. He was working for her, in a sense." He didn't answer and I wasn't thrilled about the idea. But it was all I could think of besides the fact that we had to be running out of time.

* * *

444

They may as well have had a "Going Out of Business" sign posted in the window. Speath Aviation was locked up tight. The hangar door was shut and padlocked. My car was the only one in the dusty, crushed gravel parking lot.

I peered into the front window of the dark offices. The only movement was from a screen saver on one of the computer monitors. It was a little antique biplane that did acrobatic aerial stunts across the screen. It always pulled up just as it was about to crash.

"I don't think anyone's home, Jack." I looked around and realized I was talking to myself. From around the corner I heard the sound of glass shattering and plinking to the ground. Jack had found another door around the side—this one with a window—and he had his entire arm inside when I arrived.

"Doesn't seem like much security," I said, "for a place that has parts lying around." I had begun to grow much more security conscious as I'd learned about bogus parts.

"Didn't you tell me this is usually a twenty-four/seven operation?" The door opened. He slipped in and I went after him and closed the door behind us.

"You're right. They probably always have someone around." Which made it particularly strange that no one was there now. "What should we look for?"

"Let's start with the files." He stared at the twelve file cabinets that lined the wall.

"He's got files in his office," I said. "Anything that would be of interest to us is probably in there."

I led him back to George's office. The door was open. Jack went behind the desk. I started with the credenza where a picture of a smiling George and one of his airplanes was proudly displayed. "It's still hard for me to believe George is a money launderer. I can't believe I was so far off on him."

"Sometimes good people do bad things."

Something banged against the wall from the other side. I stopped and listened. The other side of the wall was the hangar. More sounds—clattering and scraping. Someone was in the hangar.

Jack listened, too, head cocked toward the sounds. "Did you hear voices?"

I hadn't. He pulled his gun, and then he was out the door, feeling his way in the gray light along the hall toward the front of the offices and the noise we'd heard. This time I'd remembered to bring the .22, so as he approached the first corner, I fell in behind him, back flat against the wall. It occurred to me that I knew the way and he didn't.

"There's a short hallway around that corner," I whispered. "There are two doors on the wall closest to us. One is to the stockroom. The other is to the break room. There's one door on the far wall and it goes to the bathroom. There's an extra-wide door at the end of the hallway. It goes out to the hangar, which is where the noise is coming from. They had a DC-8 in there."

He nodded. "The door to the hangar, which way does it swing?"

I closed my eyes and pictured George holding the door for me. "In. It opens into the hallway. Toward us."

We crossed over to the far wall. We'd move a couple of inches. Stop. Listen. Move. We were halfway when we heard keys jingling. He was in the hangar, he was close, and he was coming in. Staring down the long

446

hallway reminded me of the distorted view through the peephole, but it was only the sweat in my eyes. I took the safety off.

The deadbolt slipped. The knob twisted. I raised my gun and squeezed it in both hands. Jack rushed the door just as it opened. A flash of yellow. A loud, hollow boom as the door slammed shut. A man's high-pitched cry as Jack grabbed him and shoved him face first into the wall. Keys dropped to the ground. The man cried out again, a long, plaintive wail. I saw his face. It was white, a frozen twist of terror that pinned the heavy eyebrows to his forehead. Heavy eyebrows and a neatly trimmed goatee. A goatee?

"Do you have him?" Jack shoved his knee in the small man's back. "*Alex*, do you *have* him?"

I leveled my gun at Julio Martín Fuentes. "Yes. And I know who he is."

I must have subconsciously expected to see George, because I was surprised when it turned out to be a small Hispanic man in a yellow T-shirt. Julio's hands were uncomfortably high over his head. His eyes were squeezed shut, and if I understood his *muy rápido español*, he was praying.

"Jack, that's Julio. He's okay." I started to shove the .22 into my jeans, remembered the safety. "He's the one who told me George was laundering. We're scaring him to death. He probably thinks Ottavio sent you to kill him."

Jack let his hand slip from Julio's back, but not before frisking him first.

"Julio." I touched his shoulder. "Julio Fuentes." I wouldn't call what he was doing shaking. It was more violent than shaking. "*Está bien, Julio. Lo siento, señor.* We're sorry to have scared you."

He opened his eyes. First into slits, then wider. I didn't know how to tell him in Spanish, so I signaled for him to turn around. "*Está bien, Julio.*" He stared at me until recognition replaced panic, then lowered his arms and turned to face us. His cheek where he'd been mashed to the wall was imprinted with the texture of the concrete blocks.

"*Señorita?*" His voice was weak and wavering.

Jack picked up the keys from the floor and handed them to him. I picked up his baseball cap, which had fallen to the ground, and gave it to him. He accepted each offering with a small bow and a "*muchas gracias.*"

Jack also apologized. He spoke more Spanish than I did. I caught about every other word. One that kept coming up was *policía.* Julio asked to go to the men's room, then darted across the hall and shut the door behind him. Jack and I went to the break room.

"He thinks I'm a cop," Jack said, pulling out a chair to sit. "I didn't disabuse him of that notion."

"That's probably how the cops behave where he's from."

"Where's that?"

"Colombia," I said. "Can you understand him?"

"If he speaks slowly," he said.

We waited for Julio to come back. I was still hyped up and dying to pace, but Jack thought Julio would relax more if we all sat with our hands on the lunch table. I asked Julio if he wanted something to drink before we settled in. He wanted a Coke from the refrigerator. I set the can on the table in front of his chair, but he didn't sit. He stood holding his black cap in both hands, working it with nervous fingers the way he'd done at my hotel, and I realized he was waiting for me to sit down. I did, and put both hands on the table. Only then did he pull out a chair and sit. Stiffly.

The three of us communicated as well as we could. Jack knew some words I didn't and I had some on him. Julio knew almost no English, so it was a slow, painstaking process. Julio's Coke can was empty by the time we had ascertained that George had shut down the business indefinitely, but he'd asked Julio to come in and do the payroll. He wanted to make sure his people were paid all the way through the end of the pay period. When Jack asked him why George had shut down, he ripped into another of his energetic monologues that went beyond what Jack and I could figure out together.

I tried to tell him that we were looking for Felix, the kid who had been at the hotel with us. I thought he might have gotten it, but couldn't understand his response. I kept asking about Vanessa Cray in every way I could think of in my stilted second language. I could not help but be reminded of how Vanessa spoke seven languages. She must have found it very easy to move through the world. I tried to ask if he knew her name. Didn't seem to. I asked if he had seen George with a blonde woman. Margie, he wondered. No, I said. Vanessa.

"Jack, I have an idea." I pulled up my backpack and dug out a file. "I have visual aids."

Inside the file were pictures I'd accumulated of our suspects—mug shots for Arturo and Jimmy, and the newspaper shot of Vanessa hunting orchids. I asked Julio if he had seen señor George with either Arturo or Vanessa. I threw Jimmy's picture out there just because I had it.

Julio looked at the pictures and shook his head.

It had been worth the thirty seconds to try. I started to collect the pictures, but Julio reached down and stopped me. He stared at each face, first Vanessa's, which was a copy of a copy of grainy newsprint. He picked up Arturo's picture, squinting first, then holding it out at arm's length until he seemed to have satisfied himself. Then he looked at Jimmy's. He put the pictures down, put both palms flat on the table, and said something in Spanish that I thought I understood, but wasn't sure I believed.

Jack leaned forward and asked him to repeat his statement more slowly.

I listened again. I had understood exactly what he'd said, and it was still hard for me to grasp. I turned to Jack. "I gather from the look on your face that he just said what I thought he said."

"He says the woman in the picture, the woman we know as Vanessa Cray, is Valentina Quevedo. Ottavio is her father."

"And Arturo," I said, "is her brother."

Chapter Forty-Six

When we stepped outside of George's offices the air had thickened considerably. The sun was going down, and when I pointed the car to the north and west, I saw the eerie orange glow that made the horizon look like a throbbing wound.

Three and a half hours since Felix had disappeared and still no contact.

We had one more idea we had gotten from Julio. He'd told us about an old abandoned airfield where it was rumored that Ottavio used to bring in his drug shipments. On a C130. It was the same old airfield where Jimmy had stashed the Sentinel parts.

"It makes sense," Jack had reasoned. "If Ottavio brought the parts in for Jimmy, he would have used a place he knew."

Vanessa's regular pilot had been accounted for and her plane confiscated, so she might have asked Daddy to send someone to bring her home. It was a ridiculously long shot, but we had no place else to go.

"I can't believe it," I said. "I can't believe she's his daughter." I'd been running everything I knew about Vanessa over in my mind, filtering it through the lens of Julio's bombshell. "No wonder she changed her name."

"She changed her name after she was kidnapped."

"Who was kidnapped?"

"Vanessa."

"Vanessa Cray was kidnapped? Recently?"

He shook his head. "This was maybe twelve or fourteen years ago when I was working up in New York. She was taken from her private boarding school in Pennsylvania. She must have been about seventeen years old. It got interesting when Ottavio refused to pay the ransom."

"Refused to pay?"

"Like I said before, he's one of the more vicious strains of the disease. I should have remembered her. You don't run across too many fathers who refuse to pay, especially if they have the means. Granted, he probably wasn't doing as well back then, but even so, all they were asking was a million."

"What did Vanessa's mother think about withholding the ransom?"

"She was dead by then. Died of cancer, I think. Natural causes, anyway. She was an American."

Which probably explained where Vanessa got the blonde hair and green eyes. "Who kidnapped her? Was it for money, or was it some enterprising competitor?"

"Definitely money. A couple of crack heads."

"You'd have to be to grab a Colombian kingpin's daughter. Did Ottavio want her back?"

"Put yourself in his shoes. If he submits to a ransom demand from a couple of punks, he would have told the world, at least his world, that to get to him all you had to do was snatch a member of his family."

"I can see how some of his lifestyle choices put him between a rock and a hard place. At least it put Vanessa there. How is it that she's alive today if he didn't pay?"

"She killed her kidnappers."

"Both of them?"

452

"Shot dead at close range. One twice in the head. The other four times in the chest. She got free and used one of their own guns."

Close range. She had asked me what it had felt like to kill a man. She herself had two kills from a range close enough to have their blood spatter on her. "I guess she didn't like being a victim."

"But she was. They raped her. This damn thing dragged on and on. The more unhinged these idiots got, the more they took it out on her. They kept her chained in a closet and only took her out to rape her and beat her."

"I'm guessing things were never the same between Vanessa and Daddy."

"Can you blame her?" I had been changing lanes as I could, trying to pick the one that was moving. Every once in a while I had to turn on the wipers. They weren't much help in the rain, but they were great for flicking ashes. We were close enough to one of the bigger fires that the traffic had slowed considerably. We passed some cars that were parked along the side of the road. Some people sat sealed inside with the windows rolled up. Some held handkerchiefs and towels to their noses and mouths. Some stood on the hoods gazing in the direction of the blaze, even though all anyone could see was smoke. All along the side of the highway, home owners patrolled their rooftops, moving like ghosts through the haze with garden hoses, the only protection they had available. Eventually, I was all the way over on the outside shoulder, moving faster than I should have past traffic that was mostly standing still. But just because I had an unobstructed lane didn't mean the view was clear.

"Jack, I can't see anything. I don't know how much farther we can go."

Just as I said it, a Florida highway patrolman materialized in front of the car with his hand up. I hit the brakes. Before the trooper had even raised a knuckle to knock on the glass, Jack's door was open and he had one foot out on the road. "Stay in the car," he said.

I lowered the window and smiled at the trooper. "I can't let you go any farther," he said. He had to raise his voice to be heard over the chop of rotor blades overhead. "The road up ahead is closed. And," he added with a weary sigh, "you shouldn't be driving on the shoulder like that, ma'am."

"Officer." Jack approached the trooper, wallet in hand. "I'm retired from the Miami office of the Bureau . . ." And that's all I heard as Jack skillfully moved the officer away from the car and out of earshot. I saw him open his wallet and hand it over. When the trooper took off his glasses to read whatever it was, presumably Jack's license, I could see even from a distance how the air had soiled his face and given him raccoon eyes.

I sat in the car and thought about Vanessa, about how she must have felt locked in a closet waiting for her father to come through for her. Finally realizing he never would. I thought about how much she must hate him, and what kind of profit motive there must be to get her to go to work for him. How powerful her lust for money must be.

And then I thought . . .

I thought back over the conversation I'd had with Damon, the one at the batting cages. I pictured myself there, in the hot, humid night under the lights, listen-

454

ing to the sky rumble and watching Damon's face. I tried to replay every word, and then I played it over again, looking at the whole conversation, the whole case from a different angle.

Jack opened his door and slipped back into the car.

"She's the source, Jack."

"What?"

"Vanessa is Damon's informant. It wasn't Jimmy. It was never Jimmy."

"I thought you said Damon told you it was."

"He never said Jimmy was his informant. I assumed he was. I had it in my mind that it was Jimmy from the start, and Damon gave me just enough facts to let me convince myself. Then Vanessa fed me the story that Jimmy murdered John. She was absolutely convincing. But you said it right from the start. Jimmy never had what Damon needed to put Ottavio away. All he knew about was parts. It's Vanessa. She's got the records. She's got his money. And she has the motive."

"Which is?"

"Revenge."

Jack had his head back against the headrest. He was staring straight ahead into the smoke, running the facts through his brain, looking for holes. He must not have found any, because he was smiling. "Work for him, steal from him, stab him in the back, and send him to jail for the rest of his life. Take his fifty million dollars and move to the South of France." He turned to me, still smiling. "Revenge is a beautiful thing."

"And powerful. It's a brilliant plan," I said. "So diabolical. So . . . Shakespearean. It's almost a shame to screw it up."

455

"I bet she thought so, too."

"Yeah." The pieces were almost pulling themselves together now. "She killed John, Jack. Or more likely had that thuggy brother of hers do it and make it look like one of Ottavio's drug hits."

A couple of helicopters flew overhead. They sounded low enough to scrape their skids across the top of my car. "What's going on up there? What's causing this?"

"A real mess. It's not the fire that's closed the road. There are five tractor trailers piled up on each other about three miles down. They have fatalities and injuries. Those are medevac flights overhead. Along with news choppers, and Broward Fire and Rescue and the Division of Forestry bringing in more firefighters. They're trying to keep the fire from jumping I-75 and moving south."

It sounded like a disaster area, someplace I shouldn't want to go, but I was completely in my head trying to work through the details. To make it all make sense.

"Here's what I think happened. John flew down here, met with Bobby and gave him the ultimatum."

"Turn yourself in," Jack said, "or I'll do it for you."

"John went over to the hotel to wait for Bobby to do the right thing. Bobby didn't want to kill John, but he wanted John to be gone. So he called Jimmy and put the problem on him. 'If I go down, you go down. And by the way, here's the hotel where John is staying.'"

"Jimmy's sitting in his house. What is he thinking?" Jack was getting into the spirit. "He's thinking 'I stole an airplane and got caught and the only reason I'm not sitting on my ass in jail right now is because of this Damon Hollander.'"

456

"Do you think he knew why? Do you think Damon told him why he was keeping him out on the street?"

He thought about that. "I think that's why Jimmy was out. Whether Damon told him or he figured it out for himself, I think he worked a deal. Something like 'I know what you're up to and I'll keep my mouth shut until you bust Ottavio. But you've got to . . .' Fill in the blank. Keep me out of jail. Get me a reduced sentence. Whatever. So when Bobby comes along with the news that John's going to turn them all in, Jimmy calls Damon and gives him the problem. Now Damon's thinking 'Goddammit, who is this asshole who's come to town and is threatening to screw up my operation right at the last minute?' He goes over to the hotel, flips his badge out, and tells him to go home before the bad guys do something to his family."

"I don't know what happened next," I said. "Jimmy called Vanessa. Or Damon called Vanessa. Someone alerted Vanessa, maybe just to tell her to lie low until they figured out what to do."

"Or," Jack said, "Damon called and told her what was happening, knowing exactly what she'd do."

"Whichever it was, Vanessa was not into waiting and she was not trusting her fate to the Junior G-man. She took matters into her own hands, and John ended up dead in the Dumpster. And as a bonus, one last dig at Daddy, she made it look as if he did the murder. It was her," I said. "All the motives we attributed to Jimmy still work, but it's Vanessa who did it. She had the most to lose. Think about how long she must have been working on this scheme. How long it took her to set the trap. She wasn't going to let John screw it up. John had

457

no idea what he was walking into. He never had a chance."

"She's tying up loose ends," Jack said. "Like Jimmy."

He didn't say it, but I knew he was thinking what I was. To Vanessa, Felix was one big loose end.

"Start the car," he said.

"What?" I looked up and the trooper was waving at me. I rolled down the window and he told me to drive over the service road, go half a mile to the shopping center, drive under the police tape and park there. "Jack, what are we doing?"

"I got us a ride." Just as he said it, I looked up and saw a sheriff's helicopter dropping down to land on said parking lot.

"How did you do that?"

"I still have a few well-placed friends around town. Let's go."

The pilot told us he would have to fly out over the Everglades and come back to the old airfield in order to go around the smoke. He flew low, skimming over the thousands of small islands of grass and mud that made up the vast network of waterways and inlets. It was amazingly intricate, as complex and impenetrable as the network of arteries and capillaries that carry blood to and from the human heart.

We approached the airfield in a swooping roller coaster arc that disrupted the workings of my inner ear and left my stomach in a free fall. With all the holes in the roof, the hangar looked from above as if it had been bombed. The lights were on. Parked in the front were two flatbed trucks, one with a crane attached. Next to them, a silver

Mercedes with a dark blue drop top, and a dark red four-door sedan—kidney bean red.

"Jack." I pointed, but he had seen it, too.

The sheriff's deputy wanted to make sure we really wanted to land there. Jack assured him we did, then gave him his card after writing Pat Spain's phone number on the back. He asked the pilot to get in touch with her and tell her where he'd left us.

He put us down out in a perimeter field, as far away from the hangar as possible. After he left, it took a few minutes for me to adjust to being still, and to the quiet. Between the visual pandemonium of the smoke and ash and haze, the incessant thumping of the rotor blades, and the chaos going on inside my head, standing on the ground in the stark quiet of the abandoned airfield felt like an altered state of being.

Jack was all business. Besides his Glock and what I was coming to think of as my .22, he'd brought a bag of extra goodies. It was a good thing we hadn't had to clear a security checkpoint before we'd gone up. He pulled out a pump action shotgun, and boxes and boxes of extra rounds, which he stuffed into the pockets of his hunting vest, the same one he'd worn the last time we were here. He gave me an extra clip for my gun and showed me how to load it.

We watched the hangar as we worked. The air was not very clear and we were far away. There could have been movement and we wouldn't have seen it. "Do you think they heard us?"

"It would have been hard not to. But between the news people, the fire departments, and the forestry service, a lot of helicopters have been flying around here the past few days. If we're lucky, they heard us and didn't pay any attention. We're lucky Jimmy's not with them. He would have heard us."

"Do you think Felix is in there?"

"If he's alive."

"Why didn't they contact us?"

He didn't answer. I wasn't sure I wanted to hear the answer.

"Did you check your weapon?"

"Yeah."

"Are you scared?"

"Yeah."

He put his hand on my shoulder. His solid touch and level gaze made me feel steadier, made me want to be steadier. "Follow my lead. Follow the plan. You can do this. And remember, we got lucky. We found them before they got out of here. One way or another, we're going to find that kid. If they hurt him, I will personally blow their fucking heads off. Ready?"

My eyes started burning and watering the instant we began to move. The air felt as if it was filled with tiny, searing particles that embedded themselves in my corneas. I could feel the soot and ash building up on my skin.

Jack carried the shotgun in his right hand away from his body. My .22 kept working its way out of the waist-band of my jeans, so I took it out and carried it in my hand.

It was faster and easier getting into the hangar this time because it was familiar and I knew what to expect, and because of the intermittent noise overhead that served as cover for our movements. After scrambling through the window, the two of us stood in the bathroom and peeked out into the lighted interior of the hangar. It was my second time seeing the dead aircraft splayed out in pieces large and small across the floor and the workbenches. But it wasn't any easier. We heard voices toward the front, which was the part of the building with which we were least familiar. I recognized Vanessa's voice. She might have been talking to Arturo, but the man's voice was hard to hear, and I couldn't remember if I'd ever even heard Arturo speak.

"What about those FBI guys?" I whispered. "Shouldn't they be patrolling around here somewhere?"

"This area has been evacuated. I don't even know how these two got in unless they've been out here for a while."

A helicopter flew over and we used the opportunity to push through the door and move out into the wreckage. The smells were all still there, strong and acrid, blended into an aroma I was sure I would never smell again. Jack had said Vietnam had its own smell. So did this place.

We moved up slowly, taking our time, slipping from a pile here to a massive assembly there. It was easier to move through the wreckage if I thought of the pieces as my protection rather than what they really were. At one point, I caught sight of the two of them.

Vanessa, who I would have expected to be the cool one, was pacing and jittery. She wore a bright red pantsuit that made her look like the only flame of color in an otherwise black-and-white landscape. Arturo stood a few feet off to the side, his big arms folded over his chest. He wore his traditional black garb and even had on dark sunglasses. No sign of Felix.

461

When we were close enough to hear both sides of the conversation, we stopped and listened. My body, as I rested against a larger piece of the aircraft, was so tense my muscles felt as if they'd been wrung out and twisted dry. Their voices were hollow in the large warehouse, and they spoke to each other in Spanish. I had to strain just to hear the words. All I could really get were the tones—Vanessa's, as usual, arch and superior as she prattled on at her brother in clipped and forceful sentences. She may have been anxious, but she hadn't lost her abusive spirit.

Jack looked as if he might be getting most of it.

"What's she saying?"

"She's talking about Jimmy. About what a horrible place this is. Something about how disgusting this whole affair has been and all for nothing. A pile of junk. Tons of crap. That sort of thing. She's really pissed off. She called this place a monument to Jimmy's stupidity."

"Can you hear Arturo?"

"He basically agrees with whatever she says."

"Anything about Felix?"

"No. I think they're waiting for someone or something to happen, but she hasn't said what."

"Do you think it's just the two of them?"

"So far." He poked his head up. "I can't see anyone else, and she hasn't spoken to anyone else. But if someone else is coming, we need to do something fast."

I looked out and spied Vanessa pacing and Arturo standing. They were in an open area next to an enclosed office. "They're not expecting us," Jack said. "We can take these two. You and me. Let's figure out how."

I looked around to see if I could find where Vanessa

had left her bag, and hoped it wasn't in the car. I spotted it, sitting on one of the workbenches with her keys on top. It was the same flat, black clutch she'd carried every time I'd seen her. Must have been a favorite. It wasn't an ideal placement for what I had in mind, but it would have to do. I pulled out my cell phone and looked at Jack. "I have an idea."

A few minutes later, Jack was working his way around to a particular spot in the wreckage he liked. It was close to one of the engines where the pieces were piled into something like a box canyon. A long piece of wing laid on its edge ran almost the length of the hangar on the side closest to Vanessa's bag. I found a place to squeeze in behind it and moved along to the end, which actually put me past them, closer to the front hangar doors than they were. From the looks of it, it was as close as I was going to get and stay hidden.

Vanessa and Arturo continued to talk to each other, mostly Vanessa rattling on in what was beginning to sound like compulsive dialogue. It was good that I couldn't understand her. It made it easier to tune her out.

When Jack's signal came, it was loud. Louder than I had expected. The hollow, warped sound of a flat piece of sheet metal hitting the ground, followed by the crashing and banging of things, multiple heavy things falling on top of it.

I pushed the speed dial on my phone. Vanessa spun toward me and her chirping bag. Arturo pulled his gun, snapped at her, and headed for Jack's position. He must have told her to silence the phone. She was ten feet away from me, her back turned, her long red nails on

463

the bag as she unsnapped it. I heard something over in Jack's quadrant. A shout. Couldn't tell whose. Vanessa's hand was in her bag. The phone was still twittering. Do it, I thought. *Do* it. *Now*. I pushed forward and up, raising the .22, and yelled at her.

She turned, twisted in my direction, and shot at me.

She *shot* at me. The gun must have been in her bag. It was small, smaller than mine, but just the same it made a hole in the wing inches from my shoulder. I ducked behind one of the workbenches. It didn't work as cover unless ... It was solid and heavy and piled high with heavy tools and crap. The bullets were dancing around me, splintering wood, bouncing off metal, shattering plastic. I could feel them whizzing by in the air. How many damn bullets did she have? I put my back against the bench, found something to brace my feet and pushed with both my legs. It tipped. It teetered. It went. It crashed over into the next bench, and the two of them went over in her direction like dominoes, dumping all those heavy tools and stolen parts at her feet. The firing stopped. She tried to turn and run, twisted out of one of her high heels, tripped, and fell flat on her stomach. The little gun banged the cement and went scuttling across the floor. Before she had a chance to even turn over, I was on her. I grabbed the collar of her jacket, put my knee into her back, and jammed the gun against her head. I was so pumped up, it was hard to hold still, but that's what I did. I stayed on her until I started to breathe again.

She turned her head. Her pale face was a sharp contrast to the dark floor. "Kill me," she said. Her tone matched the contemptuous sneer that turned her beautiful features ugly. "Can you do it?"

She had emptied her gun at me. She might have killed Felix. She was probably responsible for John's murder. I didn't know if I could pull the trigger and put one of those small, stubby .22 caliber bullets through her blonde head. But if there was anyone I could have killed, it would have been her.

I heard the sound of a helicopter outside. This one seemed closer and louder than usual. It masked the sound of Arturo coming toward me. I caught the motion out of the corner of my eye. His hands were cuffed.

Jack was behind, pushing him along. He smiled as he came upon the two of us and waited for the sound of the chopper to pass. "Good job," he said. "Any sign of Felix?"

"We've just gotten started." I backed off and pulled Vanessa to her feet by the collar of her jacket. She stood up, kicked off her orphan shoe, and smoothed the wrinkles in her suit. "Put your hands behind your head . . . Valentina."

She ignored me and beamed at Jack as she assumed the pose. "It's nice to see you again," she said. "Although I would have preferred different circumstances. Did you recognize me the day you came to my office? I was certain you knew my secret."

Jack's response was to raise his gun and point it under Arturo's chin. "Where's the boy?"

Her forehead crinkled. "What boy?"

He nudged the gun high enough to tip Arturo's head back. "What did you do with Felix?"

She looked genuinely perplexed and she stared first at Jack, then me. Then she asked Arturo in Spanish, "Who is Felix?"

Chapter Forty-Seven

Either they were very convincing liars, which was entirely possible, or Vanessa and Arturo had never heard of Felix Melendez Jr. After another few minutes of tense, frustrating, and fruitless Q&A, Jack decided to take Arturo out and check the cars. That left Vanessa and me alone in the hangar. We had found a length of rope among the ruins and used it to tie her hands behind her. I had her sit in an old kitchen chair that came from the office, and I dragged over a stool from one of the workbenches. I liked towering over her. And I liked having the gun.

"You never told me," she said.

"Told you what?"

"You never told me what it was like to kill that man."

"You already know. You killed two men. At least."

"I know what it was like for me." Her smile grew more intimate, sultry even. She blinked at me coolly, and settled back in her chair. "A rush like I'd never felt before or since. I can't get it from money. Not from my orchids. Not from climbing mountains. Sex doesn't even come close. Revenge. Only revenge. I love the word. I love the way it sounds. I love the way it feels in my mouth. It's the best drug. The only drug. It fills you. It fills you in places you didn't even know were empty."

"Like the revenge you've planned for your father?"

"He is not my father. A father does not leave his child to die with the wolves. Not even wolves. Scavengers. Curs. Mongrels who take their pleasure . . . A father does not leave his daughter to die alone in a closet. To be . . ." Her face seemed to grow harder and softer at the same time, as if her shell was stiffening, but also turning transparent so that I could see what was beneath the surface—see it but perhaps never touch it. Probably even she couldn't touch that part of herself. She looked at me with stone cold killer eyes. "They raped me. They took turns."

"Ottavio deserves everything he's got coming to him. But John had nothing to do with it. John didn't deserve what you did to him."

"Necessary losses." She tried to cross her legs. It was awkward with her hands behind her back and God knows she didn't like looking awkward. She gave up. "Losses are sometimes unavoidable."

The hangar door slid open. I looked up for Jack, hoping to see an extra silhouette, a slight one with spiky hair, against the darkness. Felix wasn't there. I slipped off the stool and circled around to put Vanessa in front of me. There were five silhouettes, five men coming toward me. Arturo was no longer handcuffed. Jack walked with his hands on top of his head. Behind them were three new guests at the party, two of whom carried automatic rifles.

The last man to enter the hangar was not armed. He had dark olive skin, almost black eyes, a dark mustache that rivaled Bic's for thickness and camouflage. His hair was on the bushy side, black with signs of graying at the temples. His looks were wholly unremarkable, but he carried himself like a general leading an invading army, even if in this case it was only an army of three. When Vanessa jerked up from her chair as if I wasn't even there holding a pistol at her head, I knew exactly who had just walked in. I just didn't know what to do about it.

"Poppy," she said, in almost a whisper. "Poppy, what are you doing here?"

"My dear Valentina. As beautiful as ever. Every time I see you, I am startled by how much you resemble your mother."

Ottavio's English was as flawless as his daughter's. He turned his attention to me. "Lower your weapon."

"Poppy—"

He raised a languid hand that shut Vanessa down instantly. "Put your weapon on the ground and put your hands over your head. If you do not do that, I will instruct my associates to shoot this man"—he nodded casually to Jack—"and then to shoot you."

In the time it took me to find Jack's face, to understand that there was only one choice here and he knew that, too, Ottavio had gone back to stand between Arturo and his thugs. "Do it now." I knew it was the last time he would say it. I put the gun down and raised my hands.

"Excellent. Arturo . . ." He gave him an order in Spanish, which must have been to free his sister's hands. Arturo whipped out a jackknife and cut through the thick rope around Vanessa's wrists with one deft stroke.

Vanessa stood in her elegant red silk suit with pant legs that pooled around her feet because she no longer stood on high heels. "Poppy," she said again, "why have you come?"

"You said you wanted to be rescued."

"I said . . . I asked that you send a plane for my use."

468

"And where were you planning to take my airplane?"

"To Colombia. Back home."

"You haven't been home in seventeen years, *hijita*." He walked over and touched her face as tenderly as any father would touch his daughter. She let him, but looked as though it was all she could do to endure it. "Who are you?" he asked, facing me. "What is your business here?"

If it's true that whatever does not kill you makes you stronger, this man looked very strong, indeed. It was in his eyes. He was a man who had not just survived but prospered in the world's most dangerous profession, by his wits and his willingness to do harm. I wasn't about to lie. I wasn't about to test the instincts of a drug lord.

"Can I lower my hands?"

"You may both lower your hands."

I let my arms swing to my side. My hands tingled and my fingertips hurt as the blood rushed back. I swallowed to loosen my throat and took a breath that was meant to give me momentum, but only made me shudder.

"My name is Alex Shanahan and this is Jack Dolan. I came down from Boston to find information regarding a friend of mine who was murdered. The cops think you did it because of the way he died."

"How did he die?"

"Someone shoved a serrated blade into his throat and left him in a Dumpster."

He considered that. "What was his name?"

"John McTavish."

He couldn't exactly dismiss the idea that this murder would have been related to his business. He must have been sifting through recent events to see if John's name rang a bell. Perhaps one of his captains had turned in an activity report to HQ to that effect. "I had no business with a John McTavish. I have no business in Boston. I did not kill him."

"He had no business with you either." I pointed to Vanessa. "She did it and blamed it on you."

Vanessa didn't even wait to be asked. "I killed no one, Poppy. Jimmy killed him. I warned you not to do business with him. It was a disagreement over parts. I have nothing to do with airplane parts, as you know. It is a filthy business."

Ottavio nodded to Arturo. The big man walked over and I thought my legs might give out right there because he placed the barrel of his large caliber automatic weapon against my right temple. The air that was in my lungs got stuck there. I couldn't get it out. I couldn't blink. I felt the cold barrel against my head and I couldn't move anything.

"Hold on," Jack said. "Wait."

"No one speaks unless I ask you." Ottavio moved in very close to me. My head began to pound and my eyes to throb in rhythm with the blood hammering in my ears. The closer he came, the harder everything throbbed. "Are you lying to me?"

Jack tried to take a step toward us. One of the thugs raised his weapon and the other yanked him back.

I made myself maintain eye contact, hoping to convince Ottavio with the power of the truth. "I'm not lying. John was killed because he threatened to expose Jimmy's parts operation. Vanessa couldn't have that, so she killed him. Or she had him killed."

470

"*Es verdad*, Valentina?"

"Losing the stations would have been inconvenient, Poppy, but of little consequence to me. I have many other options." I could hear the calculations running in Vanessa's voice as she went through her high-speed emergency damage control. "And she's lying about this man from Boston. He found out Jimmy was stealing from us, Poppy. That's why Jimmy killed him. Jimmy killed him, and brought unwelcome scrutiny as a result. It brought these two. And he *was* stealing from us. *He* was our problem, Poppy. And I solved it."

Ottavio had no problem maintaining eye contact. "There is your answer."

"My friend had nothing to do with bad parts or drugs or anything else. He was a man with a family who came down here to try to put something right. He threatened to upset her plan to take revenge on you. That's why she had to kill him."

"Poppy, she would say anything right now to save herself."

Ottavio kept his eyes on me. "Tell me about this plan."

"Please remove this gun. I can't . . . I can't talk . . . I can't even think with it pointed at my head."

He glanced at Arturo and I felt the gun pressing harder against my temple, closer to my brain. I squeezed my eyes shut. "Your daughter," I said, and stopped. No air. I couldn't make the words come out. I knew what to say and couldn't make them come out. "Your daughter . . . is a government informant. She's . . ." There was only one thought in my head now. No room for any others. A tear squeezed out of the corner of my eye and ran down my cheek. Every muscle contracted and at

471

the moment when I thought I was going to die . . . I wondered who was going to call the movers.

The gun fell away. I opened my eyes to find that Arturo had stepped back. A flood of delayed . . . something . . . rolled through me. Delayed stress. The room started to spin. I found Jack's eyes, looked at him looking at me, and I saw something there to hold on to. I centered my breathing and tried to get the world back in focus.

Ottavio's eyes had narrowed ever so slightly. His head was canted toward Vanessa, but he was still looking at me. "What did you say?"

"I said your daughter is an informant for the government."

"What agency?"

"The FBI. She's been helping them build a case against you. She couldn't let John turn Jimmy in. If he went, the stations went. If the stations went, so did she, and the federal case against you would have blown up. She couldn't let that happen. She wants to see you in jail."

"Vanessa's the one who has been stealing from you," Jack said. "We can prove it."

The disc. I'd forgotten about the *disc* and Jack was reminding me and thank God for his presence of mind. "We have documentation of all of your accounts," I said. "How much was taken from where and where she's got it all stashed. I came here today to trade it for Felix. I'll give it to you. It will prove what we're saying."

"Who is Felix?"

"He's . . . he's just a kid who was trying to help us out. She took him, too."

Ottavio walked over to his daughter and reached out to her. She shrank from his touch, and it occurred to me she had just failed a test. "Valentina, do you still hate me so much?"

"Poppy, I will open up my accounts to you and let you see that I have never taken a cent." She started moving back, stumbling over one of the many items left strewn about by the crashing workbenches. "I have done a good job for you. I would never steal from you. I have all the money I need." She kept moving until she was blocked from behind by one of the heavier pieces of the aircraft. She pressed back against it, thinking perhaps she could move the obstacle through the sheer force of her will. It was how she had moved every other obstacle in her life—all but the one standing in front of her.

"Tell him," she commanded, glaring in her brother's direction. Arturo was a sphinx. "I said *tell* him, Arturo."

Ottavio approached her slowly. "He did tell me. He told me everything." This time when he reached for her she had no place to go. He drew in a deep breath as he let his fingertips stroke her hair. His voice was quiet. "I sent him to watch over you, Valentina. And he has been watching."

She clenched both arms across her stomach and bent at the waist. "You were supposed to take care of *me*, Arturo. You were sent to protect *me*." When she straightened, Vanessa Cray was no longer svelte and elegant. She was skinny and drawn. Her clothes seemed to hang on her in a different way. It wasn't just her facial expression that had changed. Her facial *features* seemed different. The shape of her eyes when she looked at her father, the fullness of her lips, the way the muscles in her face moved—they transformed her, or perhaps returned her to what I could now see was her natural state. With her father, she was still the terrified, brutalized teenager he had abandoned to a horrible fate.

"Did you think I could forgive you, Poppy?" Mascara stained tears streamed down her face. "Did you think I could *ever* forgive you?"

Ottavio was unmoved. "I never asked your forgiveness. Only your loyalty and respect."

"Loyalty?" She heaved back against the fuselage, perhaps trying to move out of his reach. When it didn't move, she turned that force on her father. "You arrogant, selfish bastard. I was chained in a closet for *six days*. Where was your loyalty to me? Where was your respect *for me*?" She banged her chest so hard it must have hurt.

"I have explained all of this to you. If you could not accept my decision, then you should never have come to work for me. You made a choice."

"You *ruined* me, Poppy. You wrecked me. You destroyed my life. I died in that closet. I was seventeen years old and I was already dead and the only thing that gave me reason to live was the thought of hurting you. Of making you pay for all that you took from me." She was moving, stalking back and forth. If her nails could have grown a couple of inches, I was sure they would have, the better to tear into his flesh. "I thought about having you killed. I could have done it. I know the ways to get to you. But you wouldn't have suffered enough. I wanted you in prison. I wanted you to be raped, Poppy. To be held down by someone stronger than you and forced to submit to his will."

Dressed in that red suit, she seemed like one big force

474

of pure hatred. She launched herself at her father. Ottavio's bodyguards, including Arturo, started to go to his aid, but he stopped them with a loud, barking command. He grabbed Vanessa's upper arms as she struggled against him. When she couldn't use her fists, she tried to kick him. She wrenched and pulled and twisted for a long time. He let her fight. When she was spent, she sank to her knees on the ground in front of him and cried like a child with her head bowed. "Why didn't you come for me?" She reached out for her father's hand, took it in the two of hers, and laid her cheek against it. "Poppy, why did you not want me back?"

He bent down and pulled her up to her feet and into his arms. "Everything is all right," he whispered. He took her face in both of his hands and kissed her fully on the lips. It was a long, lingering, tender, creepy kiss.

Ottavio took a step back. Vanessa straightened. She was a wreck. As she wiped her tears and brushed the damp hair from her face, Arturo raised his gun hand and placed the barrel against her head.

If her father gave a signal, I didn't see it. What I saw in her last moment of life was that she closed her eyes, and then opened them. She was looking at me. I thought she started to smile. The gun exploded. The shock of the blast snapped my head back. I saw the bullet erupt from the other side of her head, and with it a fountain of blood. Her body dropped as if her bones had turned to lead. She fell on her back with her eyes to the ceiling. They were open.

The warehouse was completely still. Ottavio, Arturo, Jack, the two goons, and I made six people, but I couldn't hear a sound. I smelled the gun, the cordite stench. I was aware that Ottavio was looking at us, maybe even talking to us. I was aware of the sound of a helicopter overhead again. But I was staring at Vanessa, at her startled eyes, her interrupted skull, and the growing circle of blood on the floor. It looked like an extension of her bright red suit, as if her body were melting into a pool of blood. Ashes to ashes. Dust to dust. Blood to blood.

The noise from the helicopter grew louder, the loudest one yet, and I didn't even hear the big garage doors rolling open behind us. All I saw was a phalanx of men surging through the door. They were dressed in black with helmets and masks and carrying big weapons, screaming.

"Down . . . *down* . . . DOWN—"

". . . weapons *down* . . ."

"On the ground . . . *now*."

My hands flew straight over my head without any conscious direction from me. Someone came up from behind. I felt the rough force of the heel of his hand between my shoulder blades, shoving me to the ground.

"*Spread your legs. Hands behind your head.*"

I did as I was told and lay there frozen with one cheek mashed into the concrete, looking over at Jack, who was in the same position. Whatever panic I had managed to subdue until that moment came rushing over me in wave after wave of violent shivers. I was convinced that the slightest unexpected move would cause a chain reaction, that I might have survived the Colombian drug lord only to be killed by the good guys. I assumed they were good guys.

The commandos swarmed around us, guns drawn, shouting to be heard over the oppressive racket of the

476

still hovering helicopter. I caught sight of a second group coming through the door, six people dressed in blue jeans, windbreakers, and baseball caps. Some had holsters strapped to their legs. This group seemed alert, but not on testosterone overload, and I started to feel that maybe I wouldn't be accidentally annihilated for sneezing.

The sound of the helicopter began to dissipate as it must have moved off from a position directly overhead. I started to pick out individual voices again.

"She's all right." It was a woman's voice, and it was familiar. "Let her up."

Someone reached down and helped me to my feet. I had to take a few seconds to reorient to an upright view of the world. The warehouse that had seemed so massive before was now teeming.

"Alex."

It was that voice again. I turned around. A woman approached. She wore the dark windbreaker and the jeans and a long blonde ponytail that came out of the back of her cap. I stared. She laughed. It was . . . it was . . . *Margie?* George Speath's *secretary?*

"I'm Agent Laubert."

"You're who?"

"Susan Laubert. George is over there."

She pointed toward Vanessa's body. His back was to me, but it was impossible not to recognize George's bulky shape, and for the first time I noticed the big yellow letters stenciled across the back of the windbreakers. DEA. George was DEA. George and Margie. DEA.

Jack was getting to his feet. He was bleeding from a small cut over his right eye but otherwise seemed fine.

I walked over and put my arms around his waist and tried to disappear in his arms. I wanted to cry, but my eyes were too wide. They wouldn't close. I felt dried up.

George was cheery when he saw me. "Hi, Alex. You seem to be in one piece."

"Felix," I said. I was unable to get any of the thoughts out of my head in a coherent manner save that one. "We have to find Felix."

"Felix is fine," George said. "We had to pick him up earlier this afternoon. It was for his own good. We've got him back at the office debriefing."

"*You* picked him up?" The woman in the room next door had seen Felix picked up by two men and a tall blonde. I looked across the hangar at Margie. Tall and blonde.

"Smart kid," George said. "And boy can he talk. We might have to hire him just to keep control of him."

"Who are you?"

"I'm Agent George Weir." He held out his big hand to me and smiled. "It's nice to finally meet you."

Chapter Forty-Eight

George stood on the tarmac around the back of Speath Aviation. I stood next to him admiring the old Electra. "What about that whole story you told me about your father running the company?"

"This company was run by a man named Howard Speath. He got into some trouble with us, of the money laundering nature. As a way of staying out of prison, he offered the use of his business as a cover. We'd heard about the inroads Ottavio was making down here in his laundering activities, so we decided to set up the operation."

"You've been running his business for two years?"

He couldn't suppress a satisfied smile. "I made more money in that time than Howard did in the five years before that. I got them back in the black, strengthened their balance sheet."

"That shot of Ottavio's dirty cash must have helped a lot."

He shrugged. "I could have done it even without the dirty cash. I could have gotten a bank loan."

He probably could have, too. George had turned out to be quite an impressive guy. "And Marg—Susan was part of the whole thing?"

"She's my backup. We had to teach her to type."

"Did you set up the operation to get Vanessa?"

"Ottavio by way of Vanessa. We'd tried to get her before in New York, and she always managed to wriggle out. It was Damon Hollander tipping her off. After we shifted our investigation down here, this Damon kid popped up again and we figured out what was going on. We decided not to bring the FBI in. Actually, I insisted. I wasn't about to have my cover blown by some snot-nosed kid bucking for a promotion."

"What happened with Damon?"

"As near as we can tell, he was working on the task force in New York that was investigating a money laundering ring down in Panama. He started watching Vanessa. One thing led to another and she came up with this scheme to get Ottavio. He was more than happy to oblige. He worked it—it's more accurate to say that she worked it out so that she got off the hook on that deal. They all got off the hook. Damon set up a formal relationship where she was his informant and he was her handler. She refused to work with anyone but him. Not too many people knew about it, even within the Bureau."

"Did Damon know she had John killed?"

"No, I don't think so."

"What's going to happen to him?"

"The FBI's Office of Professional Responsibility is very interested in talking to him."

"I don't understand why they killed John if he was going home."

"He was a good guy, your friend. He thought it over. He talked to his brother, and he came back to Damon and told him he wanted to stay and help."

"He wasn't going home?"

"He knew these boys were dealing in dirty parts and wanted to stop them. He trusted his brother to watch over his family. He told Damon he would stay, wear a wire. Whatever they needed."

That sounded like John. All the strength—and the weakness—that had made him who he had been. Mae would understand what happened. She wouldn't like it or agree with his decision, but at least she would now understand. She could make sense of it. And Terry would be happy to know that John had trusted him with the most precious thing in his life. His family.

"Did Vanessa provide any confidential information to Damon, or did it all go the other way?"

"She provided a lot of information to Damon, always in favor of Ottavio and against his competitors. He made some big busts up in New York. Down here too, from what I understand."

"And then she turned on Ottavio?"

"I think that was her plan right from the start. She was a good girl long enough to build up her bank account and his trust. Once she was set, she got Damon to start working on a plan to reel him in. But things started spinning out of control pretty fast. First Jimmy went and stole the airplane. Damon had that more or less handled until John showed up. And then you. She never counted on all that."

"And she never counted on her brother being a spy, I bet."

"Arturo was her half-brother. She thought Ottavio had sent him up here after the kidnapping to watch over her. What he was really doing all these years was watching the money. Arturo figured out that Vanessa was skimming. He told Colombia, and Ottavio came up so he could kill her himself. This is what we're hearing, anyway.

481

He figured if he made an example out of his own daughter, no one would ever try to steal from him again."

"Did you get Ottavio?"

"We got him. We got Arturo, too. Like I said, he's no dummy. He's talking up a storm. The thing about being the head guy, the top dog, is you've got no bargaining power. You've got no one above you. The buck stopped with the big O. He's going away for a long time."

"So in the end, she got what she wanted. Vanessa sent her father to prison." I remembered the look on Vanessa's face just before she died. I remembered her looking at me, and the beginnings of the smile that died with her.

"What about you, George? Are you out of the parts business now?"

"Yeah. I'm going to miss it a little. I meant what I told you. I love airplanes. I've got a pilot's license and I do restorations when I have the time. This old bird"— he nodded to the Electra—"is a real job we were doing. I hate to let her go."

He turned and looked at me. "What about you? Can I buy you lunch?"

"I'm leaving today. I just stopped by on my way to the airport."

"Back to Boston?"

"For now. I'm not sure where I'm going to be living." I looked up at the Electra. "The only place I know I won't be is Detroit."

My flight had already been called when Jack finally showed up. I spotted him working his way through what must have been a cruise group moving slowly through the concourse. He was easy to spot. He was the tallest,

482

the youngest, and the only one in the bunch who didn't have gray hair.

"I thought you were going to stand me up one last time."

"I had to stop for these." He handed me a box, the kind they use at Logan to ship fresh lobsters. "Something to remember me by."

It could only be one thing. "Stone crabs?"

"The best crabs in the world."

"Is the shell already broken, or will I have to unpack my ball-peen hammer?"

"If you want it bad enough, you'll figure out how to get it."

I set the box down, reached into the pocket of my backpack, and pulled out a few things. First the ring.

"This is the address of Belinda Culligan Fraley. She lived in Coconut Grove. Would you make sure it gets back to her family?"

"It would be my honor," he said.

Next, the check I'd written that morning after a long chat with my bank. I offered it to him. "I'm pretty sure this won't bounce, but you might want to wait a day or two to cash it. When I get back to Boston, I'm cashing in a retirement account and I can send you the rest."

He opened the check and looked at it. I couldn't tell from his face if it was more than he expected, or if he was disappointed. "I know it may not be enough, but—"

"Why don't you wait and pay me after you've started the job?"

"I'm not taking the job. I called this morning and we had an amicable parting."

He smiled. "Was that hard?"

"Really hard. But more because of the position I put them in. But they were nice about it. And I gave them someone else to look at."

"Who?"

"Phil Ryczbicki. I told Bic if he'd give Felix a job, I'd pass his name along. Felix starts at Majestic next month."

He folded the check and ran one finger along the crease. "Do you know what you're going to do?"

"I'm going to do what I want to do. I just have to figure out what that is."

"In that case"—he opened the check and tore it in half—"take this and invest it in yourself. I can't think of any better use for the money." He handed me the two pieces.

"Are you sure?"

"I don't have room for a washer and dryer in my place, anyway. Just promise to come back and see me." I felt like crying. Maybe it was because we knew without even saying it that we didn't fit into each other's futures. Maybe because, for the first time in my life, my future was so uncertain. And exciting. Instead, I opened my arms for a hug. He walked into it, wrapped his arms around me, and squeezed tight.

"Take care of yourself, Jack Dolan."

"Ladies and gentlemen, this is the cockpit. We're next in line for takeoff."

I finished my drink and put my seat-back all the way up.

"It's a beautiful day for flying. As of last night, it looks as

though the wildfires you might have heard about down here are mostly under control, so you should have a good clear view out your window as we leave Miami today. So sit back, relax, and enjoy your flight to Boston . . . or wherever your final destination may be."